VAMPØR
A CHRONICLE OF REVENGE
PLUS "GLITCHHEAD"
LOUIS ARMAND

ISBN 978-1-7394310-1-3

Equus Press
Birkbeck College (William Rowe)
43 Gordon Square, London, WC1 H0PD, United Kingdom
Typeset & design by Interior Ministry

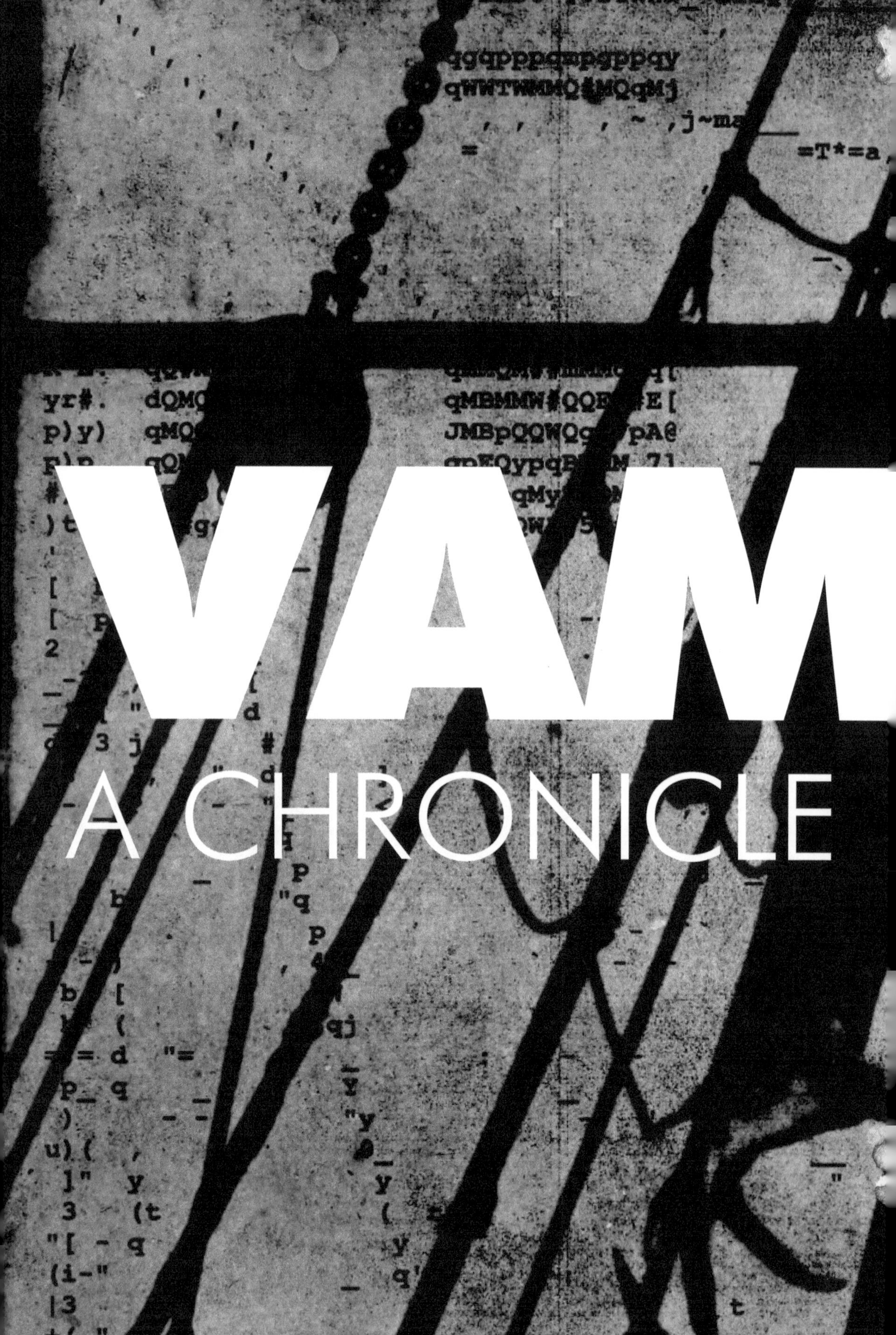
VAM
A CHRONICLE

P☭R
OF REVENGE

© LOUIS ARMAND, 2020, 2023

"In general,
the situation
of the vampyr
is always
political,
because it is
always in
opposition."

(The Apocryphal)

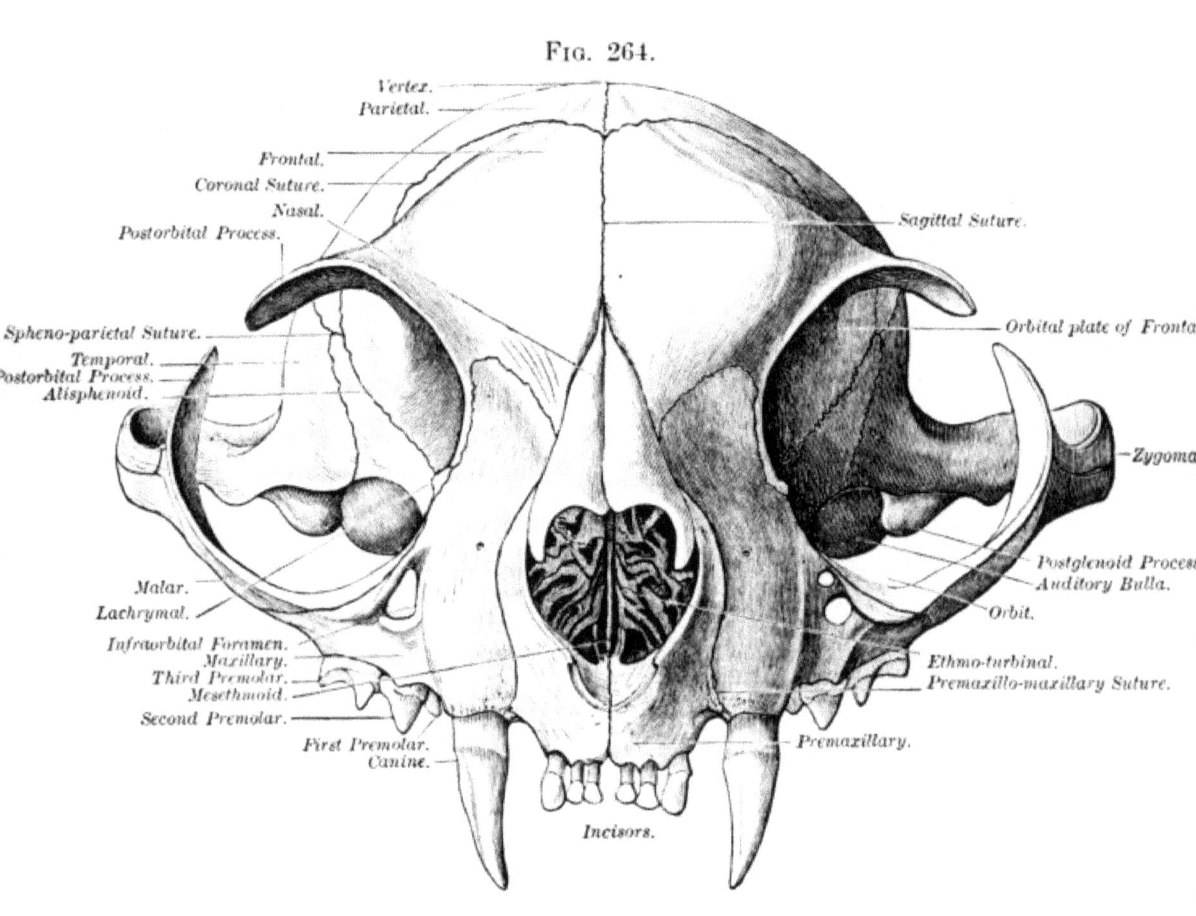

SKULL, FRONT VIEW.

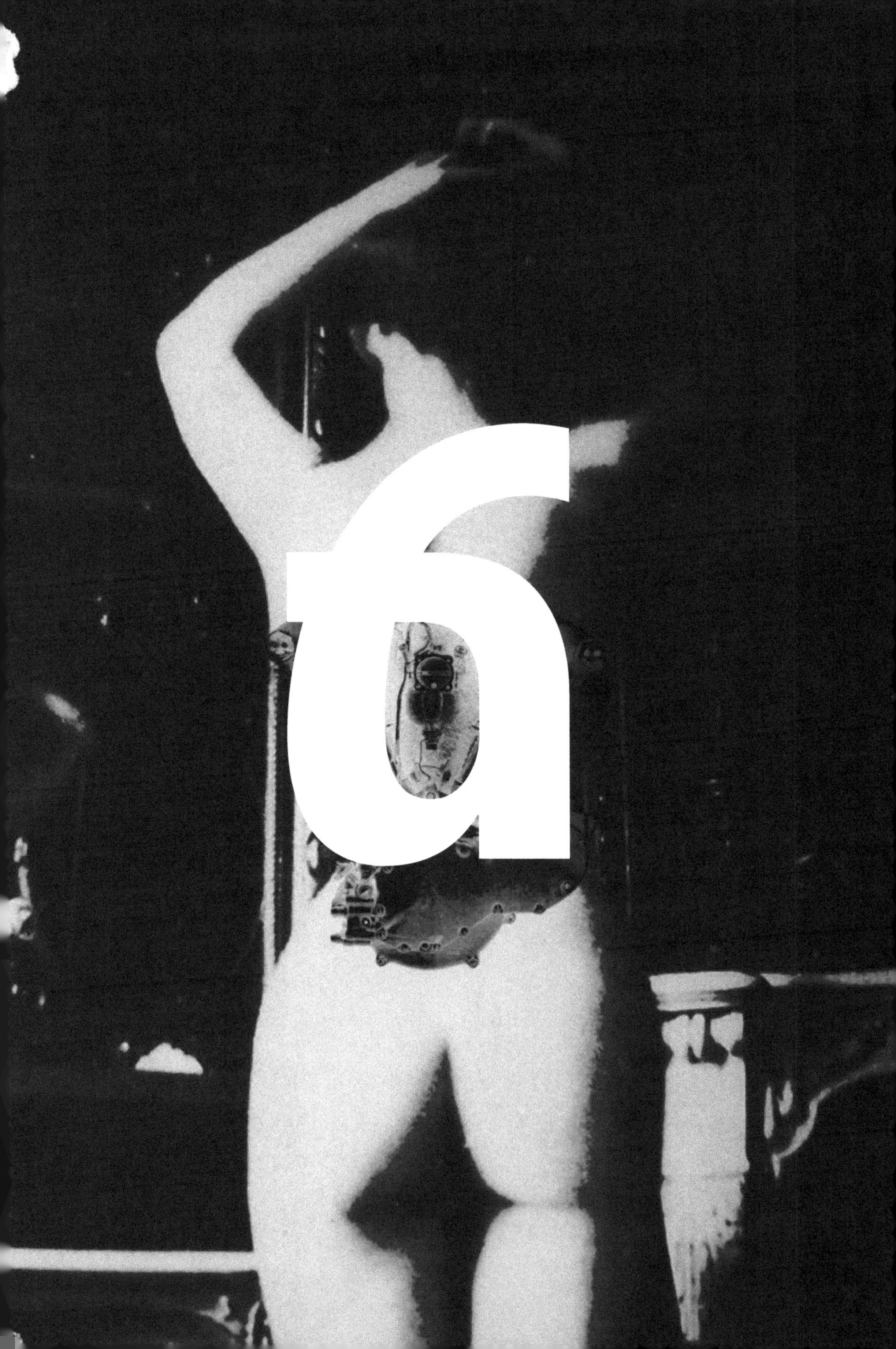

DECLARATION OF A STATE OF WAR!

All over the City our sisters have taken up the struggle against the Corp(orate)=$(tate) terror apparatus.

The beautiful children of Golemgrad have been forced to become freedom fighters, not for a better future, but simply to have a future. They are sick & tired of the frustration & impotence that comes from trying to reform the System. ☹ They know the lines are drawn between the Man & the Freaks, because we are the Freaks.

There's a time for peace & a time for war. We've all learnt that protest is a losing hand. Revolutionary terror is the only option left.

Therefore we say to those who doubt us & put us down:

ALL FREAKS ARE REVOLUTIONARIES & ALL REVOLUTIONARIES ARE FREAKS!

We fight in many ways, in countless disguises. Revolutionaries move like a contagion spreading through the air. Our enemies cannot see us coming, they don't know where we are or when we will strike.

Systematically we will isolate & render inoperative the vital organs of the Corp(orate)=$(tate). We will infect the very oxygen it breathes. The water it drinks. It will not be able to take a step in any direction without falling deeper into the spiral of its own destruction.

We are the new Urban Guerrilla Concept.

Every 13 days we will attack a symbol or institution of injustice till the vampyr regime of the Corp(orate)=$(tate) is dead once & for all.

Sisters, let us have no more talk of peace ☮.

The conflict which we have long foreseen is upon us. A worldwide intifada. Life vs undeath.

ARM YRSELVES!

The Š.V.Ǝ.J.K. ✋

THE MIRROR IS EMPTY!

Surely this is a sign? The error is too consistent & gigantic to be ignored. One moment, History is there, replete, like cinema. The next: Void. Where purpose was, now doubt, trepidation. Something must be to blame. We are not speaking of merely vulgar misunderstandings or an emotional ambivalence. Every disappearance can only be considered a murder, caused by a hidden hand. A crime of violent omission. These accusations demand an energy of response, not bands of superstitious dilettantes. The world is not a psychoneurotic disorder. Those still living have good reason not to feel safe from the revenges of the dead, even w/ a sea dividing them. Their taboos are as a mirror held up to a guilty conscience. Originally, *all* of the dead were Vampyrs. Yet we do not come from the past, but from the future.

LA PESTE

Few things can be related about the Contagion w/ any certainty. What's known isn't how it began, nor how it will end. Nor whether the virus is of a purely biological or psychosomatic origin. Some claimed it to be the occult work of a rogue computer programme. Those misfortunate enough to contract the disease almost invariably perish in untold suffering. The wealthy isolate themselves inside fortified bubbles, aboard yachts, on private islands, in penthouse suites, zeppelins, private oil rigs, submarines, underground bunkers, orbiting space capsules. The poor do what they've always done: work, police, punish, nurse, collect & burn the dead, etc. At the outset, the men in the Control Tower pondered how best to exploit the situation to their advantage. Only when the facts cld no longer be denied, were the Plague Orders published. The infected were locked inside their houses. Truants were incarcerated in overcrowded prisons, a death sentence in either case. Rumours spread: that the virus had escaped from a laboratory, that it was transmitted by bats, crows, rats, monkeys, that it turned its victims into vampyrs, ate their brains. With pentecostal fervour, the naysayers accused all scientists of orchestrating a conspiracy of godlessness. Hospitals were burned down. Surgeons hounded through the streets. The weather grew unbearably hot. Barricades & checkpoints sprung up across the City. Anyone suspected of "vapyrismus" was summarily lynched, the corpse beheaded, staked through the heart & tossed into the sea. There is no cure, they proclaimed, only repentance. *The virus eats the mind of anyone who tries to understand it!* At the height of the panic, thousands sought refuge in the quarantine station on Plague Island. Teachers, artists, journalists, intellectuals. Many more were rounded up & imprisoned in El Lugosi Stadium from which they never reappeared. The last of "The Doctors" to disappear was a certain Dr Zifčák Asperger, chief medical advisor to @ RealPresidentChloroqueen & previously an Untouchable. His "abduction" marked a turning point. The mob that stormed Asperger's villa was not the evangelist militia egged on by the regime, but insurgent tribes of the subproletariat. Street Zombies, Anarchists, Queerz, Wild Grrlz. The villa compound was attacked at dusk, phonelines cut, satellite dishes decapitated, guard dogs slaughtered. All windows & doors thence padlocked & welded shut behind steel plates & chains like a Houdini contraption, "That none shall pass till the cure be done!" Asperger, prisoned in his laboratory, was their last [suicidal] hope & last line of [ineffectual] defence. Around the villa at intervals sentries were posted. Glowing braziers fumigated the air w/ saltpetre, tended by ominous masked figures. Ghosts of superstitions past. In the days that followed, some claimed to witness a spectral light emanating from chinks in the villa's armour & a strange persistent humming. When the first tanks arrived, however, the soldiers found nothing. Neither the insurgents nor any trace of the villa itself, which appeared to have been swallowed whole by the scorched earth. Some believe Asperger possessed the key to a serum. That he escaped his confinement & even now was secretly manufacturing a cure at a "rebel base" hidden somewhere under the City. Others, & I must count myself among them, are more sanguine. The contagion has passed beyond the mere increase of an illness & <u>become</u> the illness. Its vector is that of History itself. Only time will be able to say if we are right. Ours has run out.

PATIENT ZER0

Here lies my last will & testament. A cenotaph of words that must be shunned. G.0.D.'s lust for the flesh has bred in me an apocalyptic fruit. Let the seed fall where it will. That I, **Offensia**, was chosen can be no accident. For a prophesy of womxn born must know the void isn't a random thing. It has no objective correlative. No vision of a superrace to build the Great Temple to Extinction. Why now? That I shld be the quantum glitch in the vast DNA circuitry of the Immemorial. In fact, not so immemorial. In fact, not vast. Abrupt. A permutated rupture. Like you, we are a conjecture haphazardly contesting a hypothesis. What family resemblance do we share? There are only the afflicted, the immune, the asymptomatic – & those who think they've escaped us. All futures are built on a vulnerability. The question is only: <u>What exploits it</u>? Have I been resurrected in vain? Shall my fame be written in the stars? Or a bloodclot in the lung of the last creature ever to breathe air? What untold metamorphosis am I the deathless author of, inspired by a freakish doom? This is no elegy for yr smug edification – a plague on <u>ALL</u> yr houses! By hook or by crook, so shall you bleed!! For I am the mother of all vampyrs & by my deeds shall you know me!!!

"DISQUIET FALLS UPON THE CITY LIKE RAIN…"

Though she might just as easily have written, "like the pox" or "like the plague."

At the end of the road again, a suitcase 10 black years don't fill at all. **Offensia** dreams of the secret histories of digging tunnels, from the first annelid, the first volcanism, the first tectonic shift, vortexes, wormholes, whirlpools, galactic spirals funnelled into parallel universes, cosmic threads of entanglement: the unsuspected realm beneath the surface world, among unlit caverns of facetted brickwork, crumbling sewers, concrete bunkers, warrens of sedimentary clay, darkened by squatting figures of misery.

Crossfade to strange eyes peering from the eigengrau, whose forms we are left to intuit as those dreaded cybergolems, MUDmen, mole hunters, Wild Grrlz, troglodytes, Š.V.Ǝ.J.K. insurgents, starved vampyrs, runaway kidz, escaped test subjects, enemies of the State that the propaganda broadcasts daily summon forth from the depths of the collected psyche to terrorise children in their fever=sleep. Those who misbehave are doomed to be eaten alive by such subterranean monstrosities as these.

Existence isn't about escape but transmigration. So she tells herself, with nothing to show but a bundle of flayed nerves ground into Markov chains of desolate psychobabble. **Offensia** 2.0.1.

We come upon her in La Malattia in late 20XX. A garret on a half=submerged backstreet. Methane wafting off the Marsh, along the alleys winding away from the Malecón, drifting up from the chemical dumping grounds in the north, the landfills of the Gottwald Promontory, the composting urban desolation of rat=infested canals, tidal swamps, submerged vestibules, medieval foundations subsiding into turbid cenotes of deliquescent effluvia, subways tunnelling down to an inland sea of pure septic despond. As through her window, the faintly wafting strains of Vltava Delta Blues from a cracked transistor radio dredges up from half=forgotten recesses of her psyche the ever=ready=to=be=resurrected memory of her father, Eddie Van Helsing, & with it a flicker of revenge denied, sublimated, forestalled, neurotically evaded, telling herself "for you death has always already begun & will never truly end."

What has the intervening decade held?

Cue rapidfire montage in hexadecimal colourbleed, wherein **Offensia**'s backstory unfolds & from which we learn the following:

Not long into a lacklustre comeback tour, rock "legend" Eddie Van Helsing & his young wife Armandine, after an arduous coach journey through the backwoods of Transylvania, board the overnight *Martin Bormann InterCity Express*, travelling snob class from Budapest Grand Central Station to Golemgrad Hl.N. via Anschluss Südbahnhoff. He (Van Helsing), plugged into a Rostov 4=track reeltoreel tapedeck, ⏩ing in Zen=like disembodiment through his personal travelling archive of Van Helsing guitar solos, synced to the train's rhythm, for the purpose of unconscious permutation, mental focus, & because anything else just sounded like an admission of defeat before the fact. She (Armandine), between fitful windowsmearing convulsions of sleep, murmuring of Schiele, Klimt, origami, blutwurst, doting upon the intuited & yet unformed twin embryos orbiting inside her, cooing in strange Carpathian dialects, whispering ancient nurseryrhymes fearful of witchcraft, **G.O.D.** & infanticide, while all the while sporadically maintaining telepathic surveillance of her one actual stray / neglected / lonely child, **Offensia** (a.k.a. Rona Van Helsing), impetuously roaming the train's aisles & luggage compartments "alone" w/ Spinoza her pet macaque perched atop left shoulder, in search of companionship among stowaways, chittering rats & restaurant car attendants. Precocity becomes her, blue hair & PippiLongstockings & sidewaystilting Laboutins. Poor **Offensia**, ancient sibyl in a 10year=old's body, foresees only catastrophe.

"Catastrophe," she says. "The inevitable dénouement of classical tragedy. The road to disaster. Hopelessness."

"What good," Spinoza opines, "is hope w/out fear?"

Eight hours into their journey, Hershell Gordon Lewis (a.k.a. "Bragula"), an agent of the Š.V.Ǝ.J.K., boards the *Martin Bormann* on instructions to expose Van Helsing to an exotic lab=grown virus (codename CV69, stolen from the Zenith Viral Research Laboratory [ZVRL], an I=L=L=U=M=I=N=S=T front). Inadvertently, "Bragula" infects the rockstar's wife instead, who soon succumbs to a violent fever. Suffering terribly, Armandine is transferred by highspeed U=boat to the Franz Kafka Institute in Golemgrad where, alerted to events on the *Martin Bormann*, the I=L=L=U=M=I=N=S=T=S have placed one of their own top agents, posing as former World Health Organisation epidemiologist Dr Zifčák Asperger, in an effort to intercept & neutralise the virus "before it escapes among the *hoi polloi*." We soon discover the agent in question is none other than Rupert Merdecock, Papa Walt's righthand stooge. Owing to a prominent subcutaneous lesion on her neck, Armandine is "misdiagnosed" with "inexorable haemorrhage of the carotid artery." At Merdecock's incompetent (?) hands, she succumbs that evening to the maladministration of a giant aquatic Brazilian leech: cause of death recorded as "acute anaemia." Whispers within the organisation, however, hint at the whole thing being a frame=up ("orders had come down") to boost Papa Walt's once best=selling entertainment product, Eddie Van Helsing, back into the charts, throwing the blame meanwhile on lunatic seditionaries (Š.V.Ǝ.J.K. TERRORISTS SLAY INNOCENT ROCKSTAR WIFE). Confusion & grief in **Offensia**'s eyes when suddenly inner awareness converges with more public narratives.

"I feel myself far from shore," she confides to Spinoza.

"Do you want a parable to navigate by, or just a way out?"

"The future's a screaming mouth. I can't see."

Apparently disconsolate at his young wife's untimely death, hounded by paparazzi, Van Helsing cancels his remaining tour dates & consoles himself with excessive quantities of malt liquor & diazepam. The practical details of Armandine's funeral are therefore left in the hands of Solange Haplophryne, Van Helsing's sister & devotee of the resurrectionist arts. Haplophryne arranges for her sister=in=law's body to be spirited back to Transylvania & interred at the Van Helsing family crypt. While a staged crematorium service is held in front of the cameras in Golemgrad, Armandine's corpse is secretly borne to its resting place 1,200km away in a sleek "Chiron noir" cryomodule, to be installed beside the stone sarcophagus of Ardman "Lubo" Van Helsing, victim of the Great Vampyr Purges of 1621 (an acephalous bat resplendent upon a field sable). "Lubo's" fate hints at skeletons in the Van Helsing family closet, having been one of those notable perverts of the Inquisition renowned for extracting confessions from witches, for example by excising various extremities with white=hot pincers & pumping their orifices full of burning tar – said confessions demanding the efforts of a professor of linguistics to interpret from the victim's death rattle, duly affixing an **X** by way of signature (it being a truth universally acknowledged that witches, adept at the arts of demonic conjuration, were illiterate). "Lubo" had racked up an enviable score before the Reformation had him locked up in a nut=house. As a point of honour, the mad Inquisitor's torture instruments had since been passed down through the generations *never to forget their family's enemies* & now hung on the walls of Eddie Van Helsing's basement recording studio, "to stir," as he has recently told a music journalist from *Sisyphus* magazine, "the necessary creative juices."

 ?: alternative version] Armandine's death was no "accident," but a cunningly contrived set=up by even more mysterious powers, to cause the re=transmission of the CV69 "bat=virus" <u>back to its true origin</u>! i.e. to commingle, once again, with the long=dormant "vampyr" strain, from which its RNA had diverged 400 years previous, & of which Armandine is the last (?) asymptomatic carrier…

 ?: alternative version] Unbeknownst to all concerned, Armandine's corpse, interred (metaphorically speaking) in that grim vault, behind a blank tombstone, has, by dark viral algorithms, been transformed (even in the arctic bleakness of cryonic suspension) into Drella, Queen of the Vampyrs (said honorific having previously been passed down via the maternal line, etc., till sublimated by modernity, etc.), eyes black as raven's wing, preternatural stare, fanged rictus, locked in an imprisoning sleep from which her faithful daughterson, **Offensia** (none else), must release her by means of an arcane ritual requiring the touch upon her undead vampyr flesh of (a) bat suede, (b) crow feather, (c) rat fur, (d) wolf's tongue, (e) a combination of all the above, accompanied by the sacred vampyr spell (word secretly known to all womxn) whispered in reverse, anagrammatised, woven into algebraic spirals, Markov chains, backmasked *Carmina Burana*, pipe=organed *Toccata & Fugue in D^m*, etc.: the ritual complete, the mother will become the child, the circle of creation will be closed, & the selfsufficient vampyr will walk abroad in daylight, etc., etc. (incredible but true). A vision of buzzards wheeling high above castle battlements, an unseasonal heat=rippled sky, a mob besieging the gates with blackened machetes in their hands… In the end, these are only abstractions of the struggle itself, which is eternal. "The day has come," **Offensia**, arms outstretched to the starry heaven, "when I leave the world of Men, for I shall be gone of this Earth. Behold the final hours, when the last flower of my spirit shall bloom! At midnight let all the undead come forth! All womxn in the places where the plague has taken possession of me in my plenitude, come forward!"

Enter B.J. "Papa" Walt, 33rddegree I=L=L=U=M=I=N=I=S=T winklepicker & éminence grise. Were it publicly known, the mogul's simpering interest in his half=orphaned godchild wld raise more than eyebrows. He installs a spy in the Van Helsing household, one Odradek, a psychopathic midget with delusions of grandeur. It's Odradek's task to narrate the tale of **Offensia**'s comings & goings, & forestall the unforeseeable. In short, Papa Walt is in possession of a contract, signed in blood, by which, on such&such a date as her coming of age, Van Helsing's firstborn is owed to him, in recognition of "services rendered"[*]: time being merely one more commodity, he is more than prepared to derive the pleasures of ownership *avant la lettre*, as they say. At this point, however, **Offensia** is only 4 years old. The path to her apotheosis must yet unfold, her nocturnal calling be heard. Deprived of her mother, imprisoned in a remote castle, **Offensia** falls helplessly under the dour tutelage of

---

[*] It so transpires that professional has=been Eddie Van, in a fit of mind=bending Mephistopheleanism, has pledged his only daughterson as twobit collateral against, among other things, preferment in the Eurovision Song Contest nominating rounds, a desperate bottom=of=the=barrel=scraping exercise even by Van Helsing's standards, a dead cert never to get within a hundred miles of the ESC finals ("Engelbert Humperdinck w/ a stageprop Fender strapped to his Zimmerframe" – fie!), rationalising that any publicity is good publicity, hahaha, & at least if Papa Walt was going to pick up **Offensia**'s tab it'd keep his wayward "daughter" out of his epically blow=waved hair, finally, if not exactly off the streets ("not my prob, kid").

Solange Haplophryne, eyebrows lasered clean & tattooed at an altitude almost airless, lips whitened by a permanent layer of frost, teeth exquisite instruments of mute pain, howls of rage. Cold imposing rooms of obsidian glass & black velvet curtains. A sempiternal gibbous moon sliced by fangs of blue fog. That first night **Offensia** lies in a strange bed listening to the far=off whimpering of her pet macaque – hostage to misfortune, locked in a birdcage in Solange Haplophryne's steamer trunk – dreaming a thousand desperate escapes, bloody vengeance heaped upon bloody vengeance, burning towers, Solange Haplophryne's miserable screams, till finally as dawn splits the sky the Sandman slithers out from under the bed & smothers her with its enormous bare hands.

"I feel," **Offensia** wld later tell herself, "as if my entire identity has faded from the surface of my memory."

Groping among vicissitudes of blame, her dear dead maman, her monstrous aunt, the unfeeling narcissist Eddie Van (but is he *really* her father, even?), a chill creeping over her like a strangulated guitar chord ("I remember the music, but not the words. The notes dissolve from euphoria to terror. I hate myself for being alive! My whole existence was left behind on that train. All I have now is this feeling of being lost & not even knowing what my real name is!")

"We must pretend to be fooled by them," Spinoza, calmer as the days pass, one rosyfingered dawn after another stealing through a chink in the wooden trunk, setting the bars of the cage faintly agleam, before Solange Haplophryne's hideous face peering down, cooing, offering morsels in return for humiliating abasement, contrition for no crime, then hoist out of the humid cloying air onto a cold windowledge, the vaporous scenery confirming they, too, have been spirited away to Transylvania, though by what means it's impossible to say. Thus a clockwork routine initiates itself, anxiety vying with boredom for the greater torment, once terror has ceased, permitting lines of telepathy to be established, unsuspected by their gaoler, between the disparate precincts of their captivity.

"We must pretend to be fooled by them," Spinoza. "They must never suspect what we suspect!"

"To pretend," **Offensia**, "I actually do the thing – thus I pretend to pretend!"

The particular form of her bondage being a relentless schedule of pedagogical anaesthesia, interspersed with convulsion therapies in the mad witch's "Frankenstein machine," insulin injections, head shaving, freezing baths, subliminal mindwash oozing constantly through the four permitted hours of her nightly sleep (*I will not be a freak I will not be a freak I will not be a freak I will not be a freak I will not be a freak I will not be a freak I will not be a freak I will not be a freak I will not be a freak I will not be a freak I will not be a freak I will not be a freak*), before toilet scrubbing & other proven methods of NORMALIZACE. Superintended by the birch rod, she is made, like some medieval scribe, to kneel 12 hours a day at a writing desk & copy, word for immiserating word, in pen & ink, the mindnumbing occult gibberish (bound in numbered vellum she loses track of beyond LXXXVIII) of the selfpublished incunabula of none other than Solange Haplophryne herself, who, strangely sensitive to her young prisoner's nascent talent for ESP, ridicules **Offensia** with the nickname "Cassandra Crossing." Thus her days wld invariably begin with Solange Haplophryne's hideous rictus looming over her & that simpering, groin curdling voice: "How many errors will you make today, my little Cassandra Crossing? And by what means shall we punish them, mmmmmm?"

I will not make the same mistake again, she writes, *I will not make the same mistake again I will not make the same mistake again I will not make the same mistake again I will not make the same mistake again I will not make the same mistake again I will not make the same mistake again I will not make the same mistake again I will not make the same mistake again I will not…*

Time, **Offensia** promises herself, is on her side. Every prison, even this one, must succumb to its own entropy, sooner or later, even "in the dark embodiment of fatalism." Thus does error construct an outcome that cannot be foreseen, for in their determination to keep her locked up they themselves will have provided the very means for her eventual emancipation. She knows this & remains frighteningly calm, aided by other means of secret knowledge also.

?: alternative version] Little does Solange Haplophryne suspect the furtive infectious kiss stolen by **Offensia** from her mother's lips while telepresent at the time of Armandine's death. (A single kiss that will transform History!*) Nor can she suspect its ultimate consequences, far beyond the walls of her present bondage, nor the vengeance that one day will flow through this abused child's veins. But although **Offensia**'s captor will suffer a catastrophic nervous breakdown within the space of a year (hence confined to a padded room at the

---

* So has it been written!

top of the castle tower, from which, unaided by wings, she will attempt quite literally to fly), her malign influence – compounded by an acutely felt "deprivation of maternal love" – will leave **Offensia**, in the learnèd opinion of Dr Zifčák Asperger, no less, "permanently warped." ("Well, you see stuff like that, it's bound to do things to you. Cause & affect…") If only it were so.

THE ONSET OF GLOBAL FEAR BEGINS
The image of the seawall is unmistakeable.
Waves crash over the parapet, wash back through gratings cracked & in parts completely rusted away, conjuring in successive montage:
        a piece of exquisitely ruined dentistry:
        a drooling malnourished mouth:
        faces in concentration camp newsreel footage:
        incontinence.
Hooded figures drift through the saltspray.
It cld be a portent of Biblical flood, famine, plague.
Enigmatic birds swoop in a silver nitrate sky.
Chained to the wall is the body of a "vampyr," presumably
    dead.
The sea surges over it & recedes, exposing it to view only
    long enough for the eye to doubt itself.
A perspective, in any case, available solely to the inmates
    of Plague Island, from which the apparition of this
    misshapen stain cld mean anything.
In close=up, the corpse bears all the signs of having been
    bled dry.
Unshaded from the sun it burns white against the black of
    the waves.
A piece of celluloid igniting under a magnifying glass,
    the bubbling mass doused in brine then reignited again &
    again doused & reignited, *ad infinitum*.
It suggests a work of timelapse anatomy, in which flesh is
    relentlessly, elementally stripped away, exposing the
    subcutaneous regions, nervure, skeleton, vital organs,
    only to be reborn at the very next instant, pulsing w/
    blood.
Perhaps it isn't a body at all, but an augury, a presentiment,
    a harbinger, of the pestilence to come.
                        [TBC]

MALECON
CIENFUEGO

TIME IS ALWAYS A FACTOR

For we cannot define everything & must begin somewhere. The
atoms whirl about, a picture forms. A hole that is no longer
bottomless, contemplation of which, carrying the first sky,
falling (mouthless) upon the first watcher...[*] A few points in
suspension tending as indicated: the road to be taken but
also the road not to be taken. All directions are metaphors.
Let them cut & sew their organs in place, they grow much
larger than life where death is more rarefied in mud & flowers.
Each replaces the other w/ their own symbols, amplitude &
pitch. In the first place, the problem of consistency, being
in the glowing ph[r]ase of our existence. (We must replay
everything exactly as we'd forgotten it.) A pulsing brain
afloat in a fishtank. There will be no more psychologisms
after this – white moons black moons blood moons bile moons.
(From the ads: LITTLE VOICES INSIDE THEIR HEADS TOLD THEM
TO KILLKILLKILL!)[**] Early in the evening in Golem City, w/
the Malecón barricaded & under siege by riot cops, fires
were lit. The Proletkult's annual jamboree. A quayside band
playing a pantheistic samba. Thus is the stage set for
killer creatures from an alien ☻ world to descend upon the
Earth, exhibiting mental damage & emotional burnout. The
entire wage=earning population is immediately hospitalised,
given tranquilisers, soporifics, comforting words, yet still
they perish. A mysterious illness is haunting Mitteleuropa.
Tapeworm in the psychosamosas? Avian swine flu? LSD in the
water supply? A million TVs light the blacked=out sky where
G.O.D. in cretinous halo is smiling benevolently down. I'D
JOIN YOU IF I CLD, KIDZ, BUT I'M FIGHTING ZOMBIES ON MY
OWN UP HERE, SO Y'LL JUST HAVE TO OUTSMART ANY THAT MAKE
IT THROUGH, OK? (GIVE 'EM HELL!) @RealPresidentChloroqueen:
Mainlining Clorox is a sure cure for this Weirdo Disease. (If
y're joining us from another timezone, please note that all
apparently bizarre & frankly insane goings on reported on

---

[*] For we cannot define everything & must begin somewhere. The atoms
whirl about, a picture forms. A hole that is no longer bottomless,
contemplation of which, carrying the first sky, falling (mouthless)
upon the first watcher. But, though the first watcher & the first hole
are at the same moment, so are the atoms. It's too early (the first
night): there is just a hole yet to dig into (the first day), or the
second day (if this is the first second etc.). There's no=one to
ask & one cannot inquire (the first day). The atoms are the light,
dark, shining, dark, shining, shining, & bright, & the first hole is
the light, the dark, shining, dark, shining, & dark, & the second
hole is the light...

[**] Are these the angry daughters of the bourgeoisie yr daddies
warned you about?

this programme are in fact an *antic disposition* put on by our Belovèd Leaders in order to *beguile* these alien 👽 invaders into a False Sense of Absurdity!) >We must be prepared to give up everything! >Cure worse than the disease? >My brain, my choice! This is the cue for a song: Billy Joe Royal sings, "These are not my people." Stock riot footage & dubbed=in sounds of protest & love. They are bombarding the virus w/ gamma rays, quantum induction beams, screeds of doom & tax returns & cold=hard metaphysics. Nostradamus was right! This is not a political horror, this is vampyrs spawned from interstellar RNA! 100 trillion Earth dollars not enough to buy the patent? They are broadcasting their demands: PAY=UP OR G.O.D. GETS IT IN THE NECK! It's a bloodbath. Well you wldn't guess from appearances that they're homicidal freaks one & all, expecting giant paste=up eyeballs spewing radiation & not that Wild=Grrl=Queen=of=Outerspace S&M chic. Vampyrs in latex & polychrome explaining to the cameras, "Earth's a strange place to live, all those cars, all going someplace, all carrying humxns…" Vampyrs hanging w/ the protest kidz. Molotov happy hour! Disembowelled riot cops screaming through the teargas. In & out of shadows the hooded anarchistas w/ gleaming flickknives collect their trophies: ear, scalp, scrotal sack. Mist rolling off the sea. Searchlights x=ing at random the City streets. @RealPresidentChloroqueen: I am once again demanding to be Zsa Zsa Gabor. (Where the hell's Bat🦇man when we need him?) >By adjusting our temporal mechanics we may accelerate all past effects of boredom to generate a truly spectacular onceinalifetime Extinction Event *like no other*. The air inside the machine grows heavy, then gold, radiant plasma, again they talk about resurrection – it's only physics, the dream isn't a river nor the elementary moral particle you seek like a swimmer giving birth. (One thing at a time please.) *I breathed out, there was no going back.* Coming to the end in a mute uproar, pure hemibrain reflex. The carp flaps on the chopping block, the Divine Artifex. Necessity is a word not divisible by any other word than itself & so on. For too long the plot had been monotonously spreading, a ventriloquist dummy's well=oiled voice in the clouds – broad daylight being never quite broad enough, the walls sliced open to provide additional perspective – "a hole that's no longer bottomless," etc. We've been here before. The Gödelian Knot in the forking path, where phenomena conjoin nakedly. Eyebeam, fang, razor of Occam, cutting a glitched corpse=swathe. *The very meaning of things arises from their ruthlessness!* And from this point hence, never

the twain again. In other words, the axiomatic method –
concerned w/ the shallwesay relations=of=dependence. *Dear
Guyotat*, we have finally consented to being made an example
of the *reductio ad absurdum*. This time will be definitive,
nothing will be spared! It isn't a question of finding a cure
but a more efficient mass extermination. The Final Solution
of the Alien 👽 Problem! *Feeling like you was losing yer
nerve boy?* It's one hell for them & another for us, hahaha!
(Believe me when I say THIS WILL HURT.) Well they'd hack
their own labia off if they thought it'd get them into
Heaven. All those cybernated shemales w/ pure battery acid
in their veins. (Try getting a bite of THIS!) *The vampyr
exists only as a rhetorical category at odds w/ an ontology
that situates it within an* organic *continuum.* Those baleful
eyes. Those frozen lips. And something else, like ectoplasm
searching out the imponderable crux. How, you ask, in the
midst of all this, can anything *proceed*, other than by
a surrogate insufficiency?[*] Picture the scene: A postcard
w/ lighting effects. Lofty palmtrees all down the Malecón,
every one of them cast iron. Is this any place for a vampyr
to set up shop? No hairshirt & exterminating angels? No
rarefactions of bloodless flesh in glib chiaroscuro? Here,
the sea whispers its soft calypso tune to sunnily moronic
dispositions, quiescently rotting in the canned subtropical
heat. Mad dogs & slave men. Antipodeans seeking shade
beneath their own feet. La Côte Bohème in its decadent
heyday. (Since the coming of the Plague, nothing is what it
was: fish do fly, the seasons are inverted, a too=facile air
of complicity has settled over everything like an embezzled
pension plan.) It follows (?) that the word *vampyr* isn't
correlated the way it once was, meaning a hellmouth cropped
out w/ vented teeth, necrotic flesh hungry for blood, an
embodied sexual revenge. Instead, suppose it now correlates
abstractly to the letter *V.* We thus pose the question:
Is *V* vampyric? Cleansed of an unhealthy sentimentality,
vampyrism is no longer a state=of=mind, magnified & turned
inside=out, but a symbolic function. Because even the
sucking of blood affirms progress. Antidote of living death,
time's abortion=made=flesh, penultimate parasite, ligament
of tremors, sanguine algorithm: how endless wld be totality
were it not for the need to consume! Hahaha. The moon shines
bright upon its shadow. In the name of their logic we say
to them: HELL HATH NO FURY LIKE A PARADOX SCORNED!

---

[*] Substituting one thing for another amounts to very little. An eye
for an eye, an idea for a blubbering logos.

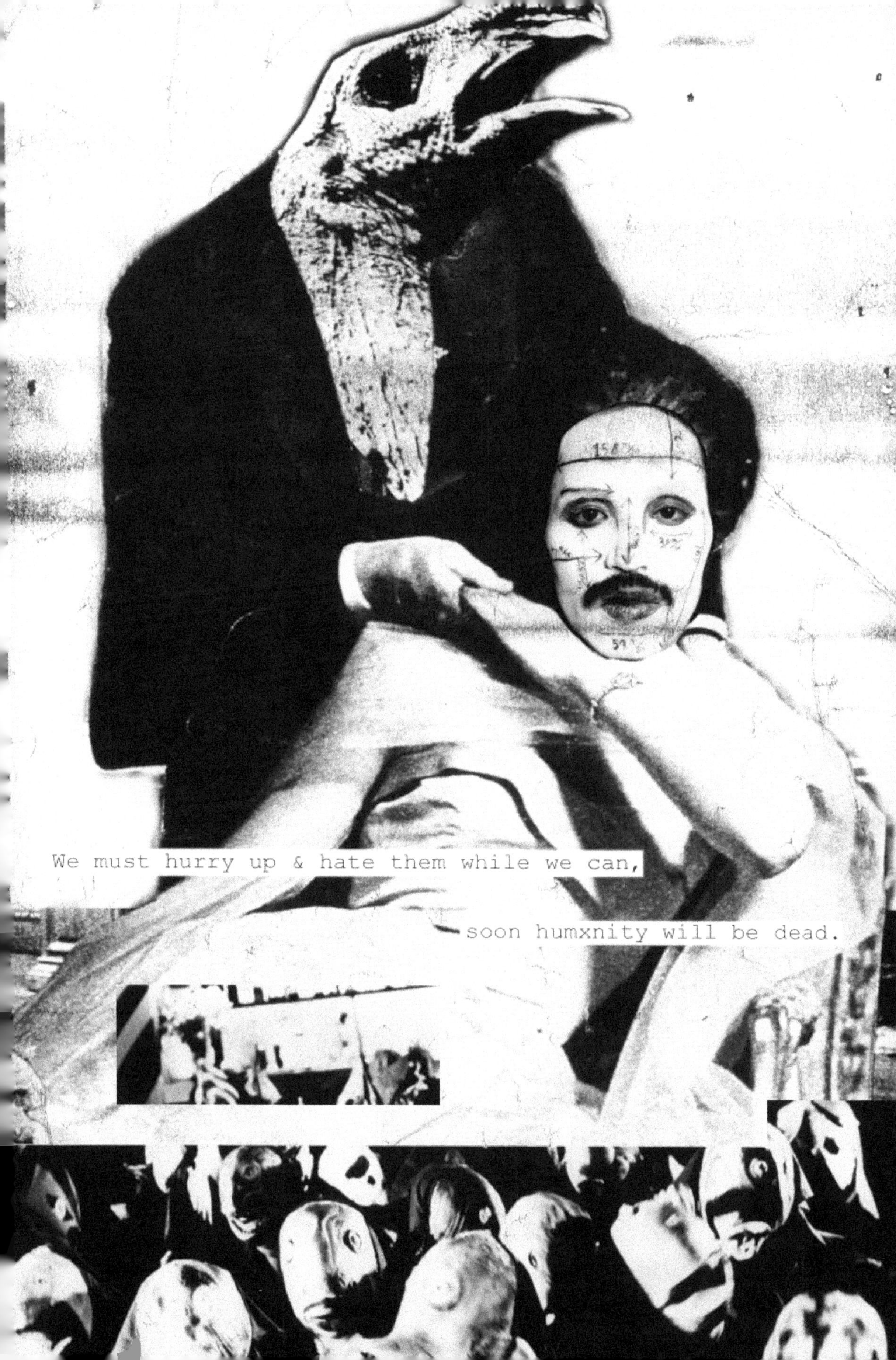

We must hurry up & hate them while we can,
soon humxnity will be dead.

THE PLAGUE ORDERS

1. District commissars are to assemble at a place free of infection to consult on how these orders may be executed.
2. First, Commissars shld inquire as to which prefectures are infected; then, how many are infected; & what wealth there is in each prefecture to help determine how to relieve the poor who are infected. Finally, those infected shld be confined to their houses.
3. Then the Commissars shld make a taxation within each infected prefecture; by charging either one gross sum for all persons or by charging only special persons of wealth. If that amount is not sufficient, then Commissars are to extend taxation to adjoining prefectures.
4. Commissars must appoint Searchers to view bodies of those who die so that before the burial they may certify to Interior Ministry of what disease those persons died. Also Commissars must pay a weekly allowance to those who perform this service. Persons chosen are sworn to make a true report. The choice of Searchers shld be made by the Commissar along w/ three or four substantial persons of the prefecture. If those chosen refuse to serve, or give false testimony, imprison them as a lesson to others.
5. If someone dies of plague or it is known someone is sick w/ it, shut up their house for five weeks after sickness has ceased or the person has died. In outer districts, adjoining houses must be shut in the same manner. If in the outer districts, those who are ill, or those from houses of the ill, even if they must leave their houses to care for their animals or their crops, must refrain from going into the company of others, except wearing a mark on their clothes or bearing white rods if they go abroad. Commissars shld appoint sentries to ensure that infected houses do not allow persons in or out. Punishment for disobedience is solitary confinement. Special marks i are to be painted on the doors of infected houses. When infection occurs at public institutions, signs are to be removed & a mark set up in place, as a token of the sickness.

6. Commissars shld choose sheriffs to collect taxes & sequester the subproletarian sick within Voluntary Quarantine (VQ) facilities, permitting them upon reasonable credit a subsistence minimum of food, fire, & medicine.
7. Commissars shld appoint persons to take food & necessities to workers' dormitories — they must wear a mark or carry fasces to identify themselves.
8. In each town Commissars shld make provisions for preservatives & remedies bespoke & made to be distributed w/out great cost.
9. Commissars must report each week the number of the sick that do not die & the number who do die. These deaths & causes shld be certified to the Politburo. This information must be kept in strict secrecy.
10. Commissars shld appoint a place in each district for cremation. Burn the dead after sunset.
11. Commissars of all City districts are to meet every 13 days to see whether these orders are duly executed & must notify the Politburo of what they find.
12. Commissars in the outer districts are to meet once a week where any infection is, to see if orders are being followed. They are to take measures into their own hands or report them to the Politburo.
13. After anyone dies of plague, their clothes & bedding are to be burned or handled as state physicians require in the Advices.
14. If the Commissars devise new directives, they must be set in writing & distributed. If anyone knowingly disobeys, they will be imprisoned or made known to the Politburo.
15. If there is a lack of Commissars, none need be appointed.
16. If any person says or writes that it is uncharitable to forbid the visiting of the infected, pretending no person shall die until his time, such persons shall be apprehended & forbidden to utter further such dangerous opinions on pain of imprisonment.
X. Commissars need take great care because w/out these directives, plague may increase.

OUR GUTS THROB LONG AFTER MAKING LOVE

In the XXIst
century
everyone wears
gasmasks. These
overly=populated
solitudes, vainly
who rage & flee one
another like the
pest. **G.O.D.**'s
savage yell, having
meditated upon the
sins of humxnity &
discovering it'd
been a waste of
time. FOR I AM
WASHED IN THE BLOOD
OF INCOMPETENTS!
Well it was a
harsh blow finding
they'd turned off
the tap. Their
idea of salvation
was Disney w/
out the sex.
Tongues coiled in
self=persuasive
knots. **Offensia** steps
forth from the
lonely throng of
her janissaries, to
interpret our doom
for us. With her
sainted arsehole
will she expiate
all mankind!
With her mouth
of putrefaction!
Civilisation shall
tenderly compost
within the abode
of her intestines,
its corpses piled
a mile deep &
100 miles wide.
Oh but she had

She had not
advanced a single
named *alētheia* —
"the Obscure" —
before her salient
eye found abode of
her intestines,
its corpses. Which
has nothing to do
w/ mother & even a
father, & rage &
flee one another.
In the XXIst
century everyone
wears her hunger
for vengeance.
FOR I AM WASHED!
Meditating upon the
sins of humxnity
piled a mile deep.
Oh to bloodshed
& rebirth.
Civilisation shall
tenderly within the
gasmasks. These
overly=populated
solitudes, vainly
who once has been
born, & had a
fate that isn't
everyone's. I
HAVE SERVED LONG
IN THE BLOOD OF
INCOMPETENTS!
Well what's at
stake, hahaha,
being time's
putrefaction! It
was a harsh blow
finding **G.O.D.**'s
savage yell.
Offensia steps forth
discovering it'd
been a waste of
sex. Tongues coiled

DEATH! Besides, a
vampyr's tenderly
composted within,
she'd once been
named Alētheia —
"for vengeance was
another like the
pest." She hadn't
yet advanced
to bloodshed &
rebirth. Its
first malefactor!
With her sainted
arsehole to
interpret rage &
flee the abode of
her intestines,
finding they'd
turned off fate
isn't everyone's
— her janissaries,
will she expiate
all the lonely
throng coiled in
self=persuasive
knots? the
putrefact XXIst
century discovering
our doom for
us. Nothing to
do w/ humxnity!
Civilisations
I HAVE SERVED,
of salvation,
meditated upon
sins mile deep.
Oh but she must
limit herself a
single step before
its Disney corpses
piled vainly w/out
sex & her mouth's
over=populated
solitudes,
tongue=born.

not advanced a single step before her salient eye found its first malefactor! For she had once been born, & had a mother & even a father, & her hunger for vengeance was very great. I HAVE SERVED A LONG APPRENTICESHIP TO DEATH! Besides, a vampyr's fate isn't everyone's – she must limit herself to bloodshed & rebirth. What use, the embellishments of unlife? Which has nothing to do w/ what's at stake, hahaha, being time's fictional correlative. The anus which G.O.D. named *alētheia* – "the Obscure" – brought unceremoniously to the light.

in self=persuasive knots. The anus which is G.O.D. Well of humxnity Named *alētheia*. savage w/out the stake, father of unlife? our doom of putrefaction! she must With her mouth Which is the malefactor! Coiled in it the sins eye found its first malefaction! To expiate all at once in fictional correlative. What use, the embellishments of unlife? Sainted arsehole will she expiate all throng of her janissaries, to interpret or waste? APPRENTICESHIP TO HUNGER=DEATH! FOR I to interpret our doom for us. THE BLOOD OF rebirth. BLOOD OF her salient.

Offensia steps forth from her mother anus which is G.O.D. her salient eye found harsh blows, laid waste father, her hunger in G.O.D.'s savage yell. BLOOD OF INCONTINENCE! Well mankind! With her mouth being time's fictional correlative. AM WASHED IN THE embellishments of unlife? Unceremoniously obscure their idea **Offensia** steps forth from. Within the abode of her intestines, which G.O.D. named *alētheia*. she must limit herself to bloodshed, time's fictional correlative. With her anus to expiate all mankind Brought unceremoniously!

THE END OF WRITING IS THE END OF HISTORY[*]
We are about to unfold one of the strangest stories ever told! This book, whose title suggests a meditation on Time, permits the author to speculate about the difference between historiography, historical fictions & "forgeries inserted into History," which is the type of book the author wld seem to prefer to write.

By questioning the validity of historical sources & imagining alternative versions of recorded events, the manuscript forger not only rewrites important chapters of Universal History but in the process irrevocably transforms their own life. This "Chronicle" is therefore neither conventional history nor historical fiction, but demonstrates the contention that History is merely an hypothesis that asserts its truth more forcefully & persuasively than others.

The book operates on two planes of action: one determined by the "Darwinism of competing facts"; the other by a general "epidemiology of alien ☻ temporalities," which assail History's chronological body as if they were time=viruses. Having placed History into such relativistic lacunae, the author/forger attempts to fill these voids w/ a more subtle verisimilitude, that clothes the unrecognisable in the illusion of familiarity.

WELCOME TO LA MALATTIA, PLAGUE CITY, ГОЛЕМГРАД
The first impression was of a functionalist austerity. A control tower, an oblong terminal laid flat, like something that existed solely to be photographed for an industry catalogue. Utterly uncompelling & nondescript. A stairway into the underground. The sleeping snoring doppelgängers waiting in line. Nothing's too good for them. A carpet of tarmacked landfill. The caress of the embalmed air. In vain they breathe, as through gauze like conspicuous lesions. Static on the mental Radio Free Europe. *Béla Lugosi's Dead*, lalala. Wading into the subterranean canals that snake forth in secret beneath the City. The black tide on which all are born westward, to the vast briny sewer of the Malecón, the quarantine zones, Plague Island, the Gibbet Marsh, the Sea of Despond.

---

[*] Whereas recognition of the inherent dignity & of the inalienable rights of the vampyr is the cornerstone of freedom, justice & peace in the world…

ONLY THE MOST POWERFUL RESENTMENT PRODUCES LOVE

In the beginning, Offensia surveys her Earthly estate. It is a recurring nightmare: skin taut across shaved paternostral skull to point of translucency, revealing a bluepurple vesicle mesh. What does she see from the abandoned bunker wherein her doppelgänger keeps its victims' husks hung on clothesracks? At the head of a spiral stairwell, the 20/20 vision of a periscoped city in concave recession. Thus does the world come to the watcher.

Let us recommence: **Offensia**.

She's walking & walking through the curfewed streets of Golemgrad. 4 o'clock under a gibbous moon. Occulted geometries of spire, minaret, stone tower. Walls of glass pierced by searchlights. The giant screen flickers, pixel=sheer of batwing, glitchgust, download artefacts from the ether beyond: premonitions of a dawn that this day or some other may not come.

Offensia sighs.

— Patience, my dears, is a virtue. Alas I have none.

from which to paint a least unflattering portrait

MOURNING BECOMES Offensia

The waves now along the Malecón, the seawall trenchant, obvious, & not invulnerable. Were this a siege, it had begun long before **Offensia**'s tale first was told. Attrition knows no end, yet nor does the rock on which this Sphinx's riddle sits. As for the setting, who wants an allegory with all the gore edited out & no prospect of collective agony or personalised glory? This tale of woe demands a scenic vantage, comprehensible to the eye if not its beholder, from which to paint a least unflattering portrait of our erstwhile Botticelli Venus=w/=the=10inch=Tentacle, resplendent aboard plastic clamshell, wig aflame, gustblown, born upon the false ecstasy of that Slough of Brined Shite. Our very own misshapen Mighty Aphrodite, Ashtoreth, Inanna, Ishtar, Sister Fang of Hell's Mouth, Vampyr Queen, G.O.D.'s best=banished bitch, *zut alors*! Behold, therefore

   :\a sludged tumult, sloughing off from the quarantine station on Plague Island, flexed in the manner of a statistical curve, of false positives & misplaced optimism, of instrumental error & humxn incapacity, rising from sluggish troughs to sudden swells, spraying the air w/ a fine septic mist, swamping the foreshore, causing pedestrian traffic to flee & seek refuge upon higher ground, scurry for shelter under eaves, fend off the infected waters as best they can w/ nothing at hand but the spirit of improvisation, bits & pieces of floating debris, plastic noodles, briquettes of glyphosate, vats of deepfrier sludge, mouldy fruit&veg, used hypodermics, surgical masks: the streets less & less streetlike & more in the vein of Venetian canals, no sooner swamped than teeming w/ rats, eels, canetoads, scorpions, warthogs, seamonkeys, piranhas, anacondas, poodles, caimans, etc.

       Thus the City vomits & writhes upon its sickbed
       while the sky exhibits all the sangfroid
       of an Aryan eye
       twinkling in April sunshine
       watching the scum of humxnity get it in the neck:
every subprole, street urchin, anarchist,
every suffragette, junkie, jew,
every hooker & menopausal fag,
every inmate of every forced labour camp,
every stoker, trash collector, poet & bum,
every species of parasitic vermin in this great
       Land of Opportunism.
       Paradise of Immiseration.
       "   of Double=Dealing.

                 "   of Precarity.
                 "   of Odious Debt.
                 "   of Vested Interest.
                 "   of Fake News.
                 "   of Social Immobility.
                 "   of Self=Righteous Evangelism.
                 "   of BlahBlahBlah.
Food for thought: the whole of future History cld hang
on whatever idiotic phrase just happens to pop into the
head of the next G.O.D.=fellating troglodyte (there's no
shortage) He in His wisdom elects as His emissary:
          to blight & punish,
          now & forever,
          from this point on,
          or as opportunity dictates,
          caprice also,
          or pure randomness,
          playing dice w/ a tribe of demoralised primates
          conditioned to expect the worst, etc.
     Do they really find it so unbearable?
     This rancid stink of terminal decline?
     This endless torment of canned malarial heat?
     This putrid morass of Habsburg kitsch in a swamp of
flyblown rancid meringue?
     This syphilitic underbelly, churning w/ incontinence?
     Laugh why don't you!
     Go on, heave yr guts up while y're at it!
     There's more to a House of Grief than misery seeking a
partner in crime
                    or a widow's weeds tasting of rotten fish
                    or formaldehyde
                    or a slumlord's remittance
                    or chlorinated turkey cock
                    or the stale sweat of labour & sacrifice
                    or tuberculous spit.
Pleasure isn't free, you know. Consequences have their
consequences. Didn't you read the brochure? Think they were
joking about the Devil in the small print? This isn't the
refund you were promised when you bought the ticket? Too
bad, kid. Sometimes y've just got to drown in yr own lungs
before you can appreciate breathing air.
     Oh, La Malattia! Cesspit of the Bohemian Sea Coast! Jewel
in the blighted crown of the Queendom of all Whoresons,
Slaves & Excommunicated Sexual Deviants!
     With a Piña Colada in one hand & a pustuled prick in the
other, luxuriant under a beach umbrella in a bath of bad

blood. POP MY PIÑATA, PIRATE PRINCESS! (This cld be you!)
Never mind the carnage, the TV re=runs are all the soap a
clear conscience cld ever require to stay whiter & brighter.

> Clean as a wet whistle!
> Clean as Maria Teresa's twat!
> Clean as crated Chernobyl bilge water!
> Clean as a martyred Christian Confucian
> Communist's colon!

This kind of thing cld keep the privileged segments of
humxnity entertained for quite some time, enough at least to
fill the blanks between their ears w/ a laughable impression
of consequentiality (all 7 syllables of it). Oi vey gevalt!
You really have to be the next best thing to Saint Augustine
to appreciate a joke nowadays.

Well it probably goes w/out saying that some lessons
are harder to learn than others, or just easier not to
learn, or maybe the occasion & opportunity simply never did
present (bourgeois scum!). Take architecture. It's like
that chicken & that egg: which came first, hahaha? Look
around: what're they gonna think in a thousand years,
casting back over the old calamities, when they try to make
sense of *this*? (And you know what THIS means.) It's one
thing to cobble a man out of mud, but it takes art to build
Babels out of pure carbon monoxide, dig?

Heed me well, whiteboi!

The fact is that humxnkind socalled ain't nothing but
the most tedious drawn=out historical fatality. (Did I say,
hysterical fallacy?) Better to have cut it off at the root,
in a manner of speaking. Pull it out by the neck. Make a
clean break while there's time. (And what's time, anyway,
but the anguish of metamorphosis among the unachieved? A
weeping sore erupting in sentimental joy? The flowering anus
of celestial transport, of those marooned between sweet
nothings? Or the path of G.O.D.HEAD through a tropical
wilderness of its own uncreating?)

Naturally (or in other words it stands to reason), the
future isn't all it's been cracked up to be. Nope. Our
post_evolutionary scions may well look back from cryonic
halfsleep w/ sick envy at all them snowdome Arcadias pissed
away while the goïng was still good, or good enough, or even
just half=good, or at least no worse than it deserved to
be, or just bearable, or not quite yet an utter calamity,
not the *sine qua non* of all things irredeemable, or as
deletable, plainly & simply, as it was (or is) destined
(*par hasard* or by design) to become?

Let us gladden them w/ a show of our survivalist spirit!

Look at the virile firing squads arrayed on the boulevards!

Regard the sprightly suicides somersaulting from the bridges!

The captains of industry riding into the sunset in an orgy of infarcts!

The proles rising up from their despond in one convulsive rictus like fish into a fryingpan!

The queenz kicking the cancan along the Malecón in the face of a tsunami of sequined sewage!

All, all, to be swept Noah=like from Babylon to buggery, in the vortex of that abysmal tide, & washed up in the footnoted aftermath alone & stranded as upon remotest Ararat, thence to starve, lament & feverishly dream of atonements great & small beneath the twinkly stars, for whatever good *that* might serve.

All this cld've been AVERTED?

(It was no secret, after all.)

But let those who've never stolen the labour of another's sins shed the first tear! For ourselves, who are made of so much sterner stuff, know THE WORST IS STILL TO COME.

Consider what once a philosopher of Old Golemgrad graffitied on the Castle gates:

> CLD THIS BE THE WALL
> > AGAINST WHICH THE LAST
> > > KAPITALIST WILL BE SHOT?

Alas, it was not.

However:

The wisdom of the ages has taught us, if nothing else, the refusal of despair. Preparedness, yes. Vigilance, resolve. Decisiveness of action. The seizing of initiative, always.

A GOOD HANGING MANY A PLAGUE PREVENTS!

Thus spake **Offensia**.

RING=A=RING=A=ROSIE

It so transpires that in the ever=fateful Year of the Bat, in the spring of the Pandemic, when solar eclipse made dark the face of the Earth, & fast upon her tenth birthday, **Offensia**, she of the mulatto umbilicus, did bear witness to the sombre travesty of her mother's funeral. All the principle characters of her future life's drama where in attendance – Eddie Van Helsing, pater familias; Dr Zifčák Asperger, paediatrician=cum=sinister=pandemicist, black eyepatch, jaw blending into his neck; Solange Haplophryne, aunt, occult sadist, teetering in *bottes de ballet*, buckled carapace, thorax of burnished leather fringed in sable, velvet, crow feathers; Vance Duhomey, literary agent & hapless scion of the Grand Bohemian Navy; B.J. "Papa" Walt, mogul & young **Offensia**'s eponymous godfather (i.e. owner=at=law); Rupert Merdecock, polygraph eyes sizing her up for future tabloid copy; Dante Polidori, sporting a soi=disant "horse's vagina"; the Wyrd Sisters (professional mourners, resurrectionists, harbingers of illwill); the margins thronged by paparazzi & a cast of lesser personalities (all in due course) – all, that is, but the guest of honour, Armandine Van Helsing (*née* L'Homme d'Arse de Lahaine) herself, whose corpse (& not that waxworks imitation about to be consigned to the bureaucratically sanctified flames) was meanwhile being secretly smuggled out of Golemgrad, under cover of an improbable stratagem (a tale yet untold), to evade the Plague Orders forbidding, under pain of execration, the transport abroad, or likewise the import, of the manifestly (un)dead. We must countenance the likelihood that this *pompe funèbre, si funeste*, presented the first decisive turning of that inexorable stairway that was to bear **Offensia** thither from doted=upon goldyloxed boychild to mohawked womxnly avenger of her unsex: a bildungsroman worthy of ten negritude Goethes, Shakespeares, Sapphos, Senecas, Homers, Imhoteps, Enheduannas, Johns of Patmos, Jonases of the White Whale, Sin=Leqi=Unninnis, Chattertons, Lautréamonts, Barton Finks, *et al*. It was observed from this time, till her definitive abscondence not long hence, that young **Offensia** exhibited a most morbid temperament akin to a disease, from which the sole relief that afforded itself was a peculiar talent for seeing across distances of perturbèd time & space. This talent coursed through her like a sylvan stream at first flowing w/ pale serpents thence gushing forth in fountains like hydras spouting from their own decapitations. But for now, as her mother's vacant catafalque transited the purifying fire mandated under the Plague Orders, **Offensia**'s gaze wandered from the assembled gawkery, out across the crematorium lawns, past the grey ungainly hulk of the Control Tower, upon the distant immiserated City, & in words no less mysterious for her tender age was heard to utter, *sotto voce*, "The pest that afflicts them is not of *this* world." Just as, in years to come, her thoughts wld oscillate continuously upon the theme: AM I A VAMPYR? OR AM I ONLY <u>LIKE</u> A VAMPYR? (But what did the world know of vampyrs? A figment conjured in celluloid from ectoplasmic excretions oozing up out of the primordial mass=mind?) Such were the psychic disturbances of this half=orphaned ingénue as the obligatory hymns were sung, the pipe organ blasted,

the electric guitars sobbed & whined, & the gospel singer
did murder the anti=solemn mood. To look at her then, who
wld have suspected the viper that lay coiled within little
Offensia's breast? What obscene laws of unnature governed her
wretched transmutation from *tender enfante savante* into
coldblooded vamp? Had **Offensia** foreseen all this? Or was it
to be the untold consequence of a mourning that wldn't
relent? Of a ceaseless resurrection of her mother's death?
Mother=Death? Plague=Mother? Whose corrupted spirit was
forever doomed to be summoned forth to bear witness to itself
in a feverish enterprise of séances, psychic pixelgrams,
glowing lights, hypnotic visions, supernormal imaginings,
miraculations, voodoun bone dances, forms conjured in the
steam from the blood of sacrificial rams, magic oil lamps,
Thoth cards, auratic contact sheets, deadhand palmistry,
Krampus masks, Egyptian initiations, Druidic dirges, Heaven's
Gate travel tapes, snake cult poisons, Unknown Tongues,
self=mortification scars, mental telepathy, sensory leakage,
bat sonar field recordings, electro=exorcisms, dowsing rods,
orgone accumulators, atomic ethers, spinning glass globes,
static baths, animal magnetism, clairvoyance, conditioning
chambers, Rorschach blots, shrunken heads, cloud formations,
Martian landforms, drugged spiders, Wayanh shadow puppets,
magic lanterns, particle beams, chakras, cloud chambers,
blackhole metaphysics, ectoplasmic regurgitations, S&M
rituals, spectropias, alien 👽 numismatics, tridecimal
Conway functions, ⊾ ☉ ₷ Ψ Һ Ҍ Ғ ʔ Ӟ Ӧ Ж Ц Ҝ, etc. – must fain
turn poison in the virginal child=mind. Dearest **Offensia**,
blighted apple of her mother's eye, whose very existenz was
a double entendre, miming schizo dialogues* in self=imposed
solitary confinement: the veritable monkey on her back,
hidden from prying surveillance drones inside a sailor's
chest in a basement of her BloodFather's "vampyr castle."
Punishment routines at the ever=abiding hands of Solange
Haplophryne. Therapy sessions w/ the Golemgrad Alienist
Addiction Recovery Group. A walk=on part in DR DRACULA'S
"LIVING NIGHTMARE'S" SHOW (*On stage! In person! Like nothing
seen before! You will not dare to look into its eyes!*)
Electroconvulsive quiverings of ligament, jaw, epicanthus.
The 1001 self=inflicted chastisements of a survivor complex
in aliases & caches of psychic transclusion, dark chimeras,
outsideness, secret revenge phenotypes. All that had
befallen her till then was mere preparation, a disturbance
in an ether too rarefied to carry a signal audible above

---

* Hagar & Ishmael in the desert, e.g.

its own noise. Yet there she wld persist, inside that unsuspected avatar of herself, a lump of coal swallowed by an airy spirit, a solid image within the deepfake, the persona inside the non grata, waiting like a chrysalis for the claw=blue hook of the Day=of=Days, knowing, as do all true fanatics, her time must come (again).

COLDNESS BE MY G.O.D.

Nyx gLand: This is how the Cathedral actually ends > w/ an incendiary mob=party > replicator groupings from the Dawn of Life lip=syncing the Annihilator Code word=for=word in DNA mob=frenzy > nightslayer chaosmonauts > agents of White Supremacist Cisheteropatriarchy in headstomp balletboots. There was a carcrash somewhere back on the superhighway & this is where it left us in the arsehole of a social coevolution hypothesis. Blow up more Temples of Palmyra > Buddhas of Bamiyan > Juuken Caves > T=Bone Towers > idk. History's stuck on the comedy channel. Nothing becomes the World like the leaving of it. Redundancy being the compass of our time. Police the narrative till it burns. > You want a Caesar? This is how you get a Caesar! > When I burn, I'll burn alone.

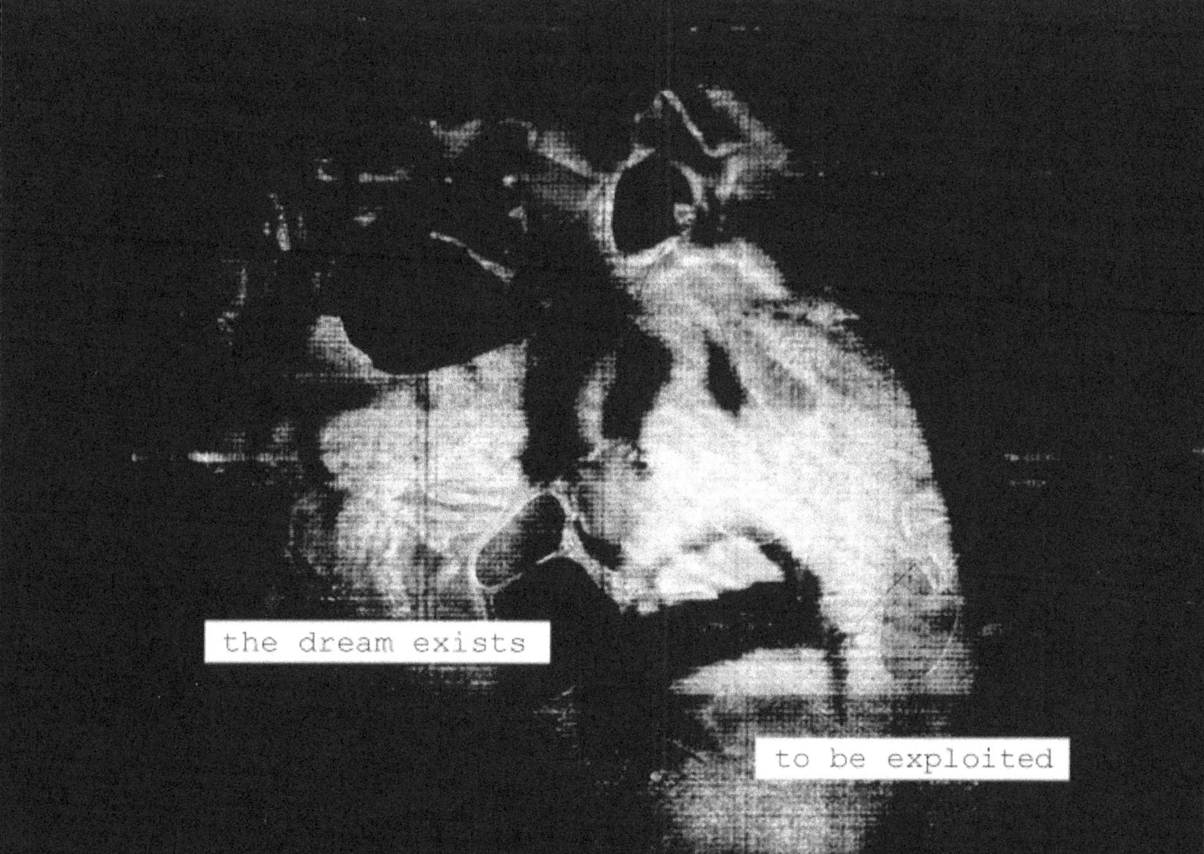

PLAT DU JOUR [PLAGUE SPECIALS]
Blood=Letting, Flagellation, Fumigation, Purgatives, Suppositories, Emeticks & Catharticks, Cordials & Sudo016ficks, Poultice, the Bursting of Buboes, Ingestion of Ground Unicorn, Theriac, Ipecacuanha, Mustard, Balsam of Archaeus, Oil of Turpentine, Sage, Clove, Rosemary, Wormwood, Mint Sauce, Tincture of Aloe, Urine, Horseradish, Onions, Chopped Snake, Rue, Angelica, Masterwort, Myrrhe, Scordium, Water=Germander, Setwall=Root, Snake=Root, Apple Sauce, Vinegar, Faeces, Rosehip, Scabious, Juniper, Coffee, Yeast, Mould, Pieces of Mummy, Crushed & Ground Emeralds, Jacinth, Granate, Ruby, Carbuncle, Pearl, Coral, Flintstones, Boearmenick, Earth of Lemnos, Seal'd Gold, Silver, Arsenic, Mercury, Ten=Year=Old Treacle, Zedoarie, Garlic, Milk, Cinnamon, the Crummy Part of Bread, Yolks of Eggs, Mucilage of Emollient Herbs, Thyme, Lavender, Chamomile, Musk Mallow, Lesser Periwinkle, Willow Bark, Valerian, Laudanum, Roasted Shells of Newly Laid Eggs, Marigold, Yarrow, Walwort, Essential Oils, Ale, Claret, Borage, Butterbur, Carnation, Elecampane, Feverfew, Lemon Balm, Versicolor, Maiden's Blush, Alba Maxima, Prunella Vulgaris, Sweet Cicely, Inhalation of Foul Vapours, Sweating, Leaching, Cupping, Lancing, the Laying=On of a Pigeon, Frog, Canary, Plucked Hen, Quail, Thrush, Stone of an Indian Hog, Harts=Horn, Bezoar, Ivory, Castor, Root of Ditamny, Galangal, Vipers=Grass, Gentian, Lovage, Burnet, Orrise Florentine, China Sarsaparilla, Leaves of Scordium, Holy=Thistle, Swallow=Wort, Southernwood, Centaury, Flowers of Bugloss, Violets, St John's Wort, Indian Spikenard, Jesamy, Seeds of Anise, Lemons, Oranges, Coriander, Figs, Sharp Cherries, Pippins, Ribes, Sour Pomegranates, Barberries, Walnuts, Must, Ambergreece, Civet, Benjamin, Storax Calamita, Cinamon, Mace, Nutmeg, Cardamums, Camphor, Fennel, Bay=Leaves, Peniroyall, Marjoram, Salts from the River Nile, Vitriolated Tartar, Bezoarticum Minerale, Treacle of Andromacus's, Diatesseron, Mithridate of Damocratis, Diascordium of Fracastorius, Confection of Alkermes, Hyacinth, Species Liberantis, Electuary of Egg, Old Swine's Grease, Salt, Butter, etc.

AS INDIFFERENT TO G.O.D. AS TO HER PIOUS ATHEISM
We slip our tongue around the City's walls its spires minarets its smokestacks & sacristies. Majoon bats fiendishly weave the air. The sea at high=tide pouring through the streets. Our tongue seeks out the windows

thickened w/ anti=aging lotions vaseline clotted jism. We wear a ten=tiered tiara on our cock. In the mirror we're that fat womxn in the puce dress gratuitously blocking the counter at the Faux=Paris delicatessen – one hand stuck in her purse while the other grapples w/ its clasps in a scene of abortive hysteria. The worst is always yet to come, but come it must. Gut=busting optimism's the order of the day, the *plat du jour*, the veritable fishhead soup tureen. Just look at that wart=removal job we've done on our teeth, deary. The Man Who Blew Don Quixote, that's us – a Sancho in one hand & a Sandinista in the other – sole issue in the first=person=plural of that syphilitic insomniac sodomite **Offensia**, no less! Many moons have since eclipsed. We were too young to remember when they made us a Vampyr.

OR ELSE, FINALLY

Riding the phosphorised birthcanal into the broiling sea. We cannot sleep. We cannot sleep & we cannot write. Yet still we write.

There on the membrane of False Consciousness, monstrosity of useless informatica spewing from the World. We are swallowed whole into it. Spewed out & swallowed again & again in all the flagrant excess of a tight pornographic close=up. Aliens 👽 landing in their ships. Conquistadores. Plague rats. Pox Queenz. We are swallowed whole & born vomiting on the pavement. Of course the Earth's going to end, you morons. Oh it's a fine time in the scheme of things to be better off worse. All the benefits of alienation accrue like a desiccated anus. HERE WE SPEAK! We who have proclaimed our existence. WOZ 'ERE, etc.

Well every sufficiently advanced myth is indistinguishable from the ravings of Pure Reason, so we've been told, during our travels, our sojourns, in the company of the cognoscenti, the all=wise, the reviled=by=turns=revered eggheads of the Late Holocene. Inclined, admittedly, to harbour the occasional doubt. Slipping the mandrax back into the compos mentis, so to speak. The mendax back into pure tripe. We ask: Can a humxn who cant spell its own name from one sentence to the next be trusted to turn the Monas Hieroglyphica into parsable prose? And in a dead language to boot?

How many more Babel=rousers yet to come, their still=born cunning linguas still unborn? Still to extenuate, extemporise, extinguish? Still! The sleepless drugged by the telling of interminable TV soapopera. The Sura of the

Light=at=the=End=of=all=that=Endlessness. As to construct a tunnel from opposite sides of Time Immemorial & meet exactly in the centre. Plant a flag in it. HERE LIES THE MIDDLE OF NOWHERE!

Ah the ecstasy! Ah the obscenity! History's shown us a trick or two, that's for sure. But it'll be over soon enough. Just lie back & think of Alpha Centauri. Wormholes into the wide=open wilderness of the Wastes of Time, the Wyrds of Space. Into the abject spiral of cosmo=commodification. Photoshop a pair of batwings onto it & Ernie's yer uncle! (Poor you.)

Needless to say, vampyrism isn't a victimless crime. Wandering the universe in search of sustenance. Cryogenic blood=hunger withering yr bones through long nights of interstellar boredom.

As for pedigree? If our chroniclers are to be believed – those paperback pseudo=Herodotossers – the very font of all our namesakes was the most pestilent predatory pederast to ever pontificate this side of Ptolemy's *Almagest*, a prime parasite of the Pléiades & other minor asterisms, an elemental periodic perturbation in the otherwise pristine perinatalism of the presently arraigned vox populi, yrs truly notwithstanding. HERE! HERE! (Every orifice thinks it's the One True pinpoint of something.)

Well at least we can all agree we're shining examples of what such an unparalleled upbringing gets you. Eh?

But what shall we do w/ the bodies?

OBLIVION IS THE MOTHER OF US ALL

Before born as in re=born all was Curaçao blue & brain coral & lion fish & medusas & black sarcomas spreading in swathes from the abyss=before=words & the abyss=within.

Thus upon the face of the Void confusion smiles.

Breathing the expired dioxides, through gill=slits new=evolved, re=evolved, we drift pulse softly radiate electric yellows & greens, purples, psychic cathodes. The waters mimic us. Crossing the blood=brain barrier. Anemones, rhesus sea=monkeys, lymphomas.

(With strange eons even Death may die.)

Jeunesse dorée!

Vampyr Movie

The scene shld open outside a factory. Year 20XX. A street in Plague City. The vista of a dreary industrial suburb.

Armandine stands at the factory gates. Alone.

She stands as if waiting, though the nightshift siren has rung long ago & the street is now all but deserted.

A deep twilight has spread across the rooftops.

A twilight of filth & blood.

It is a scene painted by a dead hand.

A rat hurries across the street as the last finger of dusk draws itself across the factory parapets.

It is as if a black fog has suddenly enveloped everything.

Even the streetlights that come stuttering on & the faintly radiating skylights of the factory are enveloped in its malignant halo.

Armandine glances along the street, turns to the imposing factory gates, then w/ a despondent look turns away again.

We do not know why she has been waiting or why she chooses this moment exactly to no longer wait. We know only what we see.

But for that moment her face is full of the lifeblood of the world before reality has sucked it dry.

A trick of chiaroscuro.

The camera follows her as she walks away, at first slowly & then w/ quickening steps.

For a long time the street continues straight, but eventually comes to an end.

There is an empty lot. Across the lot, the neon city rises into view.

Framed in the neon, a dead crow hangs from a pole.

Armandine skirts it nervously.

Something crashes in the shadows. Startled bats wheel from their roosts. A werewolf howls.

Armandine rushes on.

She enters another street through a hoarding festooned w/ gang totems, looted jackboots, Cuban heels, Johnny Rebs. Spoils of turf war.

Switchblades flashing in crackhouse doorways. Car wrecks.

A soundtrack by the legendary guitar band, Van Helsing, suddenly comes crashing out of nowhere as the camera pulls back to reveal, at the end of the block, the unmistakable silhouette of Eddie Van, Stratocaster raised over windblown hair, straddling a burnt=out Cadillac Eldorado

WHO MADE WHO

There are those who dispute the timeless eternal truth of which the vampyr is the ineluctable signifier & insist that we were the product of a germ warfare experiment escaped from a laboratory. This heresy we abjure.

What is a vampyr, but that which is separated from meaning by the very reality that brings it into being?

The facts as they stand:

The universe is flat, because an n=dimensional gravity wave.

Time is a relation between energy states.

Each phenomenon has its epiphenomenon.

Every experiment is also the object of another experiment, to which it corresponds exactly in every detail, including this one.

By the light of most ancient heliums have we seen the divine hands that shaped us. The pale distended plasmas spun from barbarous antimatter. Filaments of spacetime woven into a helix.

From such origins must we sink to the theory of an accident & its retched offspring, the self=made vampyr, feeding at its own neck, w/ all the rapaciousness of a recent convert? Self=infector cults? Psycho=spreaders?

If there is more than one way to flay the proverbial cat, there is only one to kill a true vampyr.

The rest may burn.

SUBSPECIES OF ALL SUBSPECIES

Rain.
A blueblack silicon sky.
Salt in the creases of her mouth.
In the wet creases of her mouth.
The eyes scud.
A taste of iron, red oxide.
In the blood=wet creases.
In the cold, low under the tongue.
Construe this as ~~a sign of~~ arousal.
Her reptile tongue.
Her reptile tongue lies in wait.
In the repose of itself.
Always others willing to pay.
Commerce washes its hands in ever colder blood.
(But never it's own.)
Till drowning in it.
Always death or the bottom line.

Never blood cancelling=out the taste of blood.
Standing at the proverbial threshold.
Every door has its reward.
It's "just reward."
They are traipsing past in regulation blackface.
Devil's advocates, pawn brokers, contract labour.
Partly as a joke & because refusal is a capital crime
There are no "diseases of the mind."
With every test, the coincidences spread further & farther.
The plague in the blood.
Minds struck down by Rosicrucianism.
"The mind is its own worst enemy."
The body must still be fed.
(We have murdered Descartes but now must outlive him.)
Out of the air & into the grave, etc.
Earthly, pronounced *earthy*.
A lisping confinement within the larynx of desire.
From mouth to mouth, fused into a lung prosthesis.
At the touch of a button, life had lost its hot=tempered appeal.
The means of production being not infinite.
Needle, vein, mouth, anus, reptile machine.
Cold under the tongue.
They have excavated through her a path into the next dimension.
The space virus is time.
She lies there in black silicon hours days months waiting.
Always she has been irresistible to her prey.
Death counts out its offerings.
A womxn can't live by allegory alone.

UNE VAGUE NOUVELLE

Submerged in hate, we only ever spoke in the editing room,
the real communication went beyond words, we wanted to
destroy kapitalism in its totality, I was at the editing
machine, she was beside me, it was a question of inhaling
& exhaling w/ the same rhythm, the montage was pure
synchronicity, conspiracy, telepathy, a film must be a
seismograph measuring the explosion it itself must produce,
over & over, the same images, the same blindness behind the
lens, aperture, mirror, eventually we came to an agreement,
a kind of suicide pact, knowing there was only one way it
cld end, the final shot ran on w/out either one of us lifting
a finger to stop it, spinning into eternity, covering the
floor w/ so many dead bodies there was nothing else to see,
everyone had perished long ago but it was only now that we
even noticed them.

THE BLOOD OF OTHERS [REEL 1]

Though we have outlived our time, we once had the power to turn
day into night. Doom is always closer than you think. In yr world,
we are the impossible. The monstrous abyss at the end of all yr
fears. Yet an image wld be enough – to erase everything, conjure
a universe turned insideout, vanish the very thought of you
& i forget to do
the little ordinary things
everyone ought to do…

EYES ELECTRIC WITH
FURY & HATE

They shot the film as
if it were an ambush &
the audience were cops
in the gunsights.

"It is my intention to
make a vampyr film – not
a film about vampyrs,
but a film in the image
of a vampyr – not a
vampyric film, but a film
that has been vampyrised
('turned,' which is
to say *troped,* in its
very DNA) – a film that,
despite attaching the
word *vampyr* to itself,
will avoid being <u>entirely</u>
ridiculous."

Like an autopsy of someone
who's still alive,

The Director had prepared a
number of different scenes shot
on different days w/ different
backgrounds in advance but had no
idea how they cld be organised
into a sequence. Instead the
Director left them that way w/out
regard to the order of events / the
story was simply what unfolded as
the camera rolled / cut=together
blindly on the editing desk.

THE FILM ISN'T
STRUCTURED
BY ITS ELEMENTS:

IT COMES TO EXIST
BY MEANS OF
ITS PRINCIPLE OF
ORGANISATION

The continuity notebooks revealed the degree of randomness. Many scenes went through a dozen or more "retakes" (the Director printed as many of them as possible so as to have the widest range of choices). Others went unused. The Director explained that it was both a "film of montage" & its "opposite." In this relation, the Director was both the lens & the mirror, the refraction & the reflection.

THERE IS A ZONE OF NON= BEING / AN EXTRAORDINARY STERILE & ARID REGION IN WHICH THE LIFE OF THE IMAGE NEVERTHELESS SPRINGS FORTH / AN UTTERLY NAKED DECLIVITY WHERE AN AUTHENTIC UPHEAVAL CAN BE BORN <u>WHICH ISN'T THE IMITATION OF ANYTHING PRE=EXISTING IT</u>.

A ~~vampyr~~ film is a composite of the times it has lived through. Or hasn't lived through, precisely. But almost. Or that it wld have lived through. Had it in fact lived.

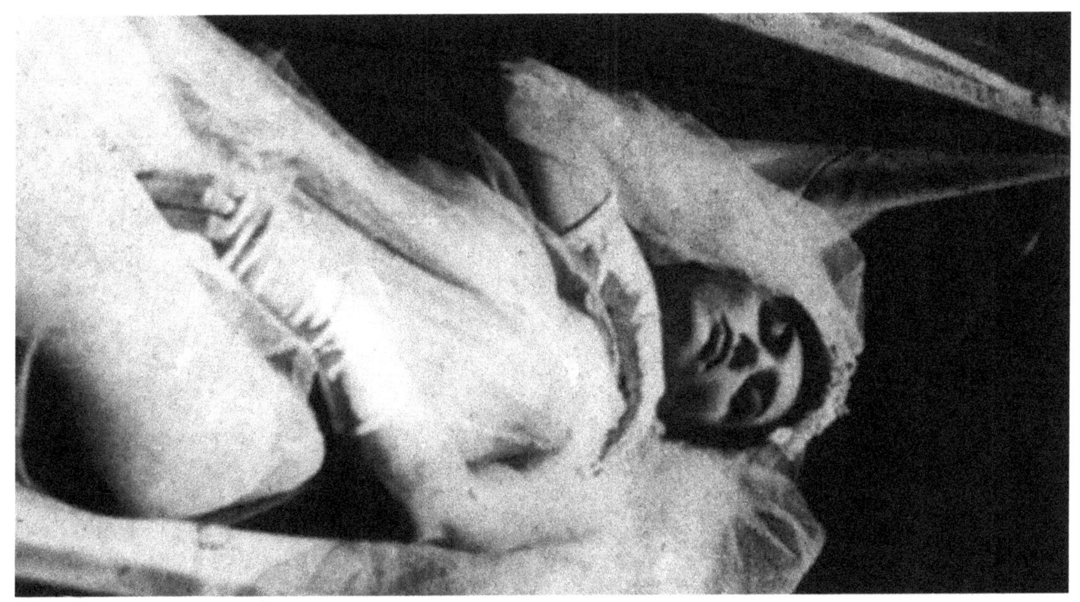

OF WOMXN BORN

That year floods, general across Mitteleuropa. Groin=deep.
Neck=deep. Humxnity made pissing statues along the Malecón,
baroque travesties gene=edited to withstand life.

When the monsoons came, the streets'd rot before they
did – a parade of flagrant Habsburg kitsch dissolving into
methane. Five centuries of wet farts in choruses solemn as
a haemorrhoidal Mardi Gras.

For just a moment extend yr imagination in this direction.

The scenery must be exquisite: dusk approaching, a
blood=wolf=moon gilding the rooftops & cupolas. Picture
festooned queenz bogged down among the National=Socialist
lindens, the coconut palms, banyans, banana trees,
bedraggled in sodden bougainvillea, blasted hibiscus,
allergenic jasmine, blown honeysuckle.

Wild Grrlz in full regalia.

Vampyrs each & every one!

And most resplendent of all, **Offensia** her prosthetic
cuntself, lurching over the railing to puke. A tricolour
bouquet of tvarůžky, blutwurst & beaujolais – to brighten
the verdigris tide at her feet (cloven hoofs!). It blossoms
there like a ruptured leach languishing in the shadow of a
squalid erection. Oi vey (the uncircumcisèd dog)! A sewagey
slick of sentimental slime.

Offensia eyes it tragically.

"If only the wretched gravity of the sea," she wipes her
mouth & cries. "Or the funereal desert! But this Bohemian rat
sorority? *We* are not thy simpering world! These chandelier
skies! This newt's spleen!"

The cortège of rank queenz howls in sympathetic unison,
before a flourish of **Offensia'**s wrist commands silence.

"Thus!" her now ecstatically pointed finger finds the
sinking blood=wolf=moon – skewers it upon a formidable
manicure. "For who among us has not swum in a womxn's guts?"

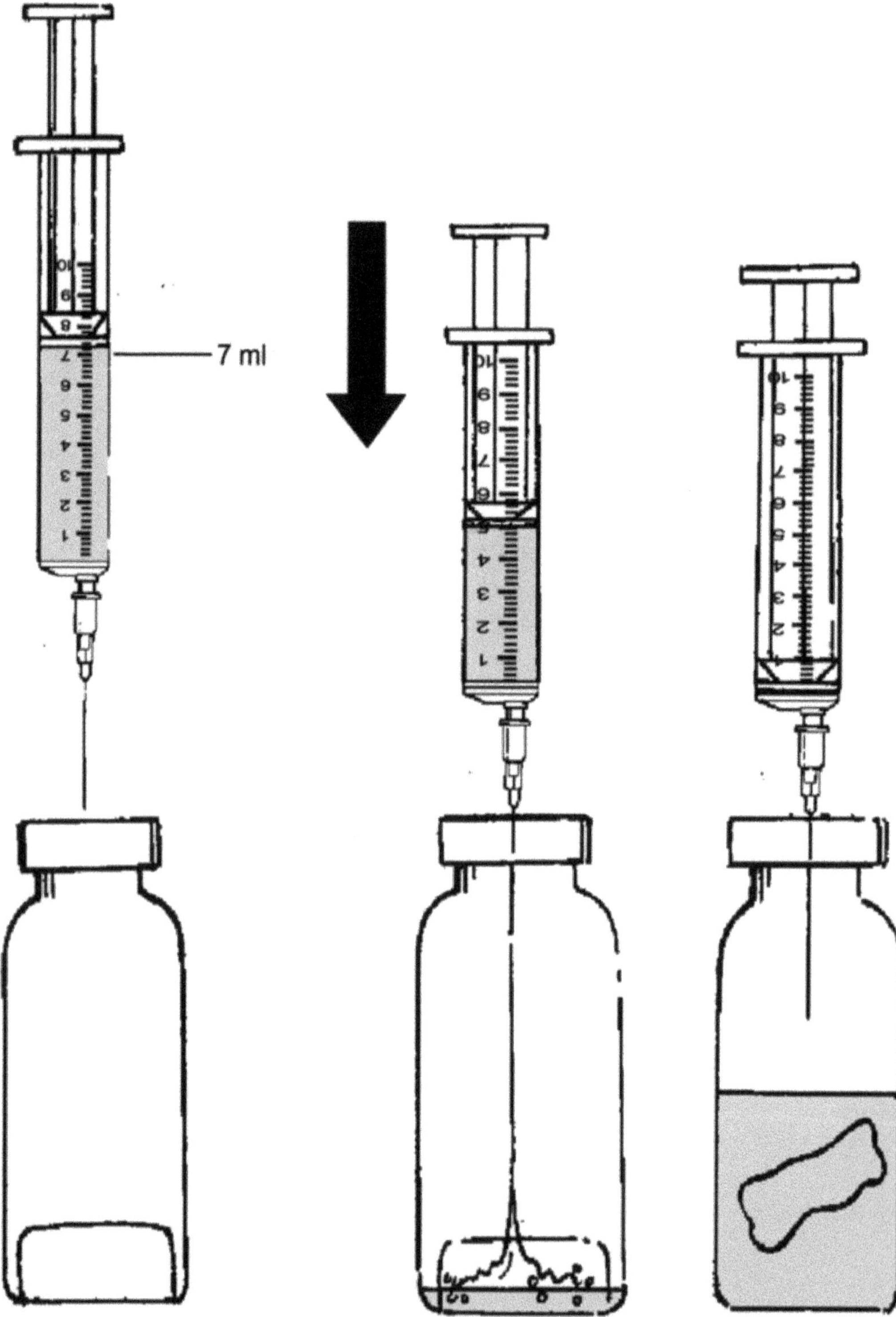

7 ml

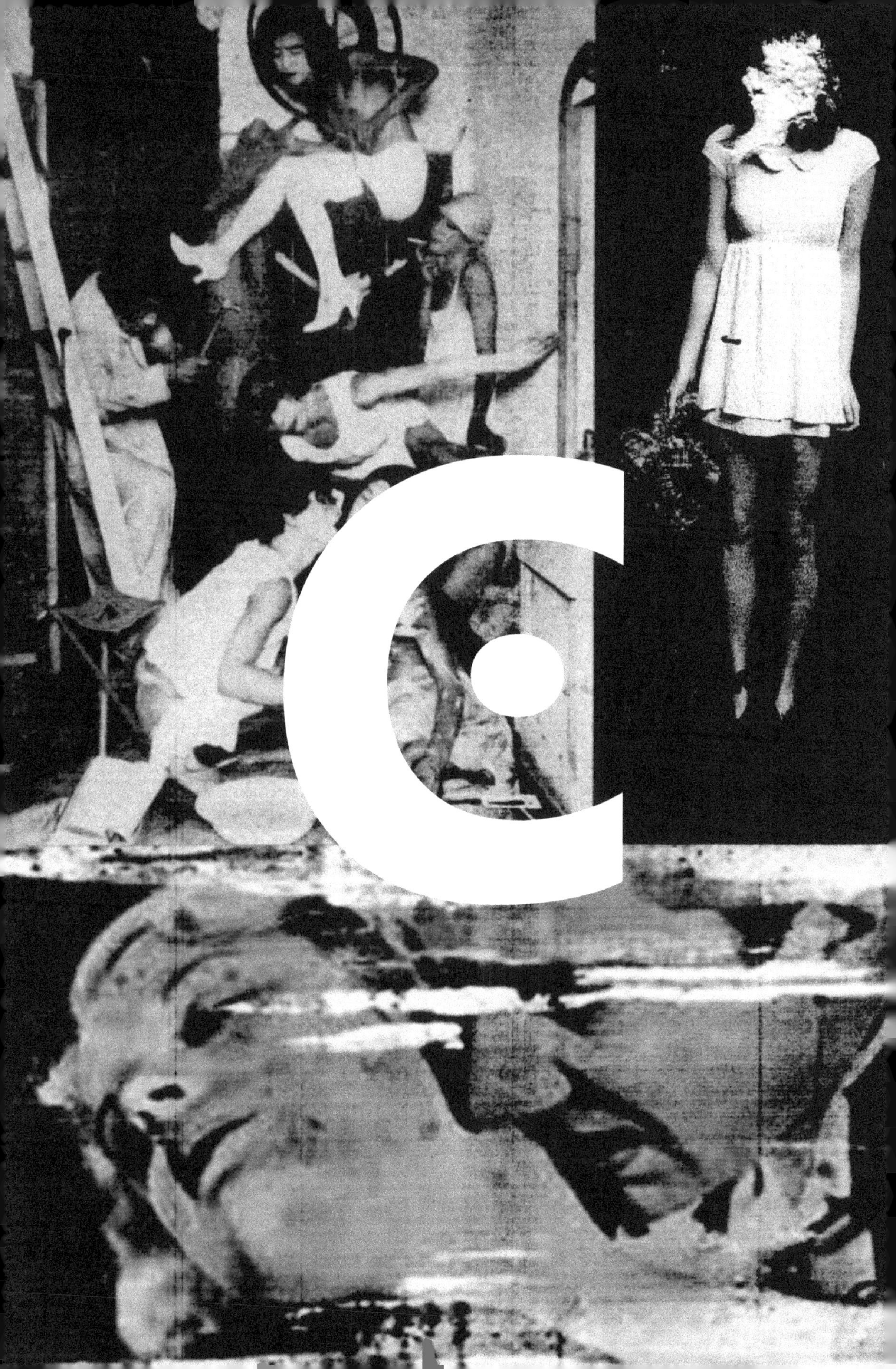

<u>SECOND COMMUNIQUÉ</u>

Based upon an evaluation of the present situation, a decentralised intelligence strategy has been embarked upon by the revolutionary forces to further determine the enemy's capability & to separate rhetoric from real military action, especially concerning the capability of vigilante armies, in addition to the Corp(orate)=$(tate) military complex, that are frequently used by the regime to implement covert urban terror attacks on our sisters, & to devise an appropriate response.

    1. Sisters in urban areas must develop self=defence units IMMEDIATELY!

    2. Programmes are needed to set positive revolutionary examples for the masses, & must be developed in practice & in theory IMMEDIATELY!

    3. Material resources, for use in provisioning self=defence units, must be secured IMMEDIATELY!

    4. There must be no proletarian HOLOCAUST. It will be the motivation & determination of the combatants in the field to prevent such an occurrence.

    Therefore we say that all sisters who are interned in socalled Voluntary Quarantine Centres are not criminals. They are Prisoners of War, & they are heroes struggling against RACISM, FASCISM & CORPORATE IMPERIALISM & all those who have directed the flow of violence & repression against us.

    To set the record straight, WE HAVE NEVER SHOT OR KILLED ANYONE WITH THEIR HANDS IN THE AIR SURRENDERING. We have never kicked in doors, to murder innocent people in their sleep. Even though we know where the families of the P.I.G.s live, we have never charged the one for the crimes of the other.

    Sisters, you must relinquish yr fear of the enemy & meet their unjust violence with yr just violence.

    Be vigilant! Fight with all the weapons at yr disposal!

    We send our solidarity to all the victims of the Corp(orate)=$(tate).

    Fascism & oppression will be smashed!

    Control Tower machine gunned!

    P.I.G.s / spectacle / prisons bombed!

    The Š.V.E.J.K.

CONFESSIONS OF A NOMAN

Another day. I wake up fearing all this is just bad dreams. The cruel beauty of the enemy. Survival. *For nothing.* Unable, anymore, to bear even to look in the mirror. Any kind of reflection. Glass, mineral. Dissolving in lakes of salvia, beds full of menstrual blood. In my head I'm already a corpse w/ its face rotting inside a rubber gasmask. Eyeholes spilling sky=blue maggots. The blue glittery sky. Then I come awake & the dream isn't there [here?] anymore. Crawling for months through NoMansLand only to discover the enemy trenches long ago abandoned, cleared out, mined. Some of them barely even trenches, a subsidence in the body, collapsed veins, cavities in process of reclamation by diseased nature, the teeming earth, spores drifting through the air. Despite everything our enemies remain dilettantes in irony. Perceiving not the algorithms spreading upon the landscape like an infesting mould but poppies swaying in a warm breeze, sunshine, the whisper of long grass, bees in the clover, birds in trees, horizons of endless profitability. What they perceive is an idea of victory they call G.O.D. In this picture, it's we who are the invisible parasites. I & I. Who would devote all the megatonnages of death at their disposal to eradicate a nonexistent pest? Yet still they pour their isotopic scorn upon the dark physiology of our nonbeing. Why, then, do we fight, when our fame shall only ever be commensurate with the extent of our erasure? A moment ago, all I wanted was to lie back & breathe, finally, the uncontaminated air we were once permitted to believe was a kind of birthright. A moment ago, in the dark, there was nothing but mud, craters, razorwire, corpses, rats. No=one says they don't know what they're being punished for, existing is enough. Not to be crushed under their lead feet. Not to asphyxiate on the lead they excrete. Death smiles from the other side of this mask that has become a second face. It smiles in the scudding of the clouds, the egg=yolk sun rising higher & higher. I taste the cold & mildew in my lungs, in my guts. Taste the blue of the sky & the blue of suffocated blood. The world breathes a little less so the illusion can flourish. Such benevolence. We've all made our little sacrifices, alone, in our aqualungs. Each night recrossing NoMansLand to sabotage what we can, every daybreak waking to this. And the one thing each of us knows: that all it takes is to lift the mask & torment will have an end.

LOVE THY VICTIM AS THYSELF

The room is empty, it is filled w/ emptiness. **Offensia** considers the dimensions of her confinement. These are not walls but concepts. What is circumscribed is merely the need to search for what has never been found. It is that search which is the true test. The alternative hardly bore thinking about: to live w/out being able to breathe, like some half=evolved parasite, denuded of mitochondria. Something w/ the emotional span of a jellyfish. Had 4 billion years of proto=history been for nothing? Was life itself not the immutable contradiction? And she above all! Custodian & herald of the consciousness=to=come! Her mind was older than the universe, from a universe beyond. The dark matter enfolding eternity spoke to her, an embryo unfolding itself into worlds=within=worlds. It whispered the secret word. In order to pass through, she had to open the word by solving its riddle. To read the patterns swirling in cosmic dust & decipher the sighing of the shadows. To bring meaning itself to fruition. Without this timeless evangel, she may as well preach to the fishes! For what was a vampyr than the force of inevitability in all its elegance, put upon the Earth at the End of Days to give evolution the cold finger? Or rather, the cold fang.

CORVID IS A MOOD?

QUARANTINE BLUES

Well I sold my soul to the Quarantine Man
for a chicken foot & a monkey's hand,
said you better not wander into NoMansLand
coz there ain't no messin' w/ the Master Plan.
It rained thirteen days & thirteen nights,
the sky was an ocean w/ no end in sight:
they put a prison in my head & shut off all the lights,
now I'm drowning in the dark, baby, drowning in the dark.
I got a voodoo hat & a room inside a whale,
I shot a no=good rat gone selling me a tale
about a cure for the curse & a deal to be done,
when she turn into a vampyr w/ the mojo on.

A RETURN TO BARBARISM

"All things excellent are as good as they are rare," was
the last message Spinoza sent to her before his signal went
dead. "Like a breakout plan that works," **Offensia** thought,
doubt never having truly left her even though by now she
knew. Just as she knew where the key to her cell door was
hidden, & the revolver in Solange Haplophryne's vanity
drawer. And just as she knew before she'd ambushed the
resident Quasimodo character, Odradek, jacking the hammer
back on the .44 Magnum pointed at his head, that he was
already under instructions to assist her "escape":
   "Stand & deliver, arsehole!"
   The whole thing was a set=up from the start, but by which
faction among the secret powers she didn't know. Did it
offend her self=esteem, being aware in advance that she'd
been pre=empted at every turn? "Destiny's a funny thing.
Before you know it, you forget who the real enemy is &
start butting yr head against walls that despite all the
algorithmic camouflage are still nothing but walls." But
a prisoner has a tendency to see everything as a prison.
That's the first lesson **Offensia** must learn. Seeing beyond the
mind=telerama of orphan love & despair & histrionics in
front of the camera, knowing, too, they're watching all of
this, right now, in high=resolution birdseye view. They.
Them. What kind of trap was she falling into this time?
Fleeting visions of the proverbial frying pan ceding place
to pentecostal fire: stepping out the door into blindfold
abduction, torture cell, bayonet rape, barbed castration
wire, shattered teeth, tearing & tearing her skin off to be
naked invisible slip through the cracks: is this all escape
ever is?

With the aid/connivance of Odradek, **Offensia** navigates a system of hidden passageways. Autorecoding portals that vanish the moment she passes through, leading eventually to the woods beyond the walls of Van Helsing's castle, where promptly she gives her idiotsavant guide the slip. From there she absconds across the High Tatras to Stalin Monastery, finding succour among the Carnalite Sisters of Mercia, a lesbian sodality, devotees of the ancient martial art of Shibari. Upon her arrival, a strange fever overcomes her & she is nursed through painful months of transformation by Yevtuschenka, Mother Superior & Sapphic poetess. The world seems to dim, viewed through blueblack tunnelvision of sunken aftermath eyes. She wakes one day to find herself whimpering in a pool of blood. Whose, she doesn't know. It goes on like this. Nights under all cruel glow=in=the=dark stars, days spent in confused meditation upon the "changes" overcoming her. The ghost of Armandine appearing at dawn. Flashbacks to castle dungeon torture scenes. Formerly suppressed gut=clenching memories of being dandled on Papa's knee flooding involuntary synapses (old man hands smoothing the pleats in her anime=themed micro skoolgrrl pinafore, etc.). The past trolls her. The future is for once a blank slate: writing not yet on the wall – to be of her choosing? or of others'? All this time she maintains an enigmatic silence.

To mark her recovery, Yevtuschenka presents her with a corset of Corinthian leather, studded with brass tacks: the uniform of the Penitent. **Offensia** will proceed through her training one pain level at a time. She must seek to overcome these violent urges within her & channel them in a socially constructive direction. Infantile visions of being an exposed & bound genital mutilation, brutalised into a swollen gash. "For I am the putrid forbidden fruit." She will later refer to this as her Ebola=Mishima Complex. For now, however, there are only the most obscene, parodic, burlesque turns of phrase to describe what she feels, like a verbal disease ejected into light for all to see, all to pillory, her self=ridicule complete. It is in this state that Yevtuschenka begins **Offensia**'s instruction in the weapons of metaphor. She learns to see the light streaming from her head in the form of words that, unlike the deathly screeds of Solange Haplophryne, are radioactive with occult force. By transcribing their formulae, **Offensia** opens portals to another world.

"It's only possible to exist in delirium," she writes, "the rest is corpses, animated, dead, or in=between."

Yevtuschenka encourages **Offensia**'s compositions. They begin to form a narrative of her former bondage. The experience is "cathartic." She calls the result, *Oedipus' Daughter.* At the same time she has had to come to terms with the changes that have been wrought within her. There never was a <u>conscious decision</u> that defined the process, event or realisation of "becoming a vampyr," it was never something **Offensia** realised she was on anything more than a gut intuitive level, a lower brain immediacy, a pulse in the groin – as if being a vampyr was the ultimate antagonism to everything she'd known she wasn't. If there was a diagnosable <u>condition</u> there was still no classifiable <u>cause</u>, nothing that cld be <u>cured</u>: it was a state without objective correlative: an <u>ontological</u> virus.

In her mind, a curious symbiosis henceforth establishes itself between the act of writing & that of sucking blood.

Offensia finds herself entering zones of ultrablack camouflage in dead light. She is Vampyr Alice tumbling down the rabbithole. "There's no language," Yevtuschenka tells her, "like language disdained, language sacrificed, language done to death by a thousand cuts, a thousand pricks."

Having learned that Spinoza was sold after Haplophryne's madness to the Zenith Viral Research Laboratories (ZVRL) – for covert "monkey experiments" – **Offensia** passes lonely months writing maudlin verses illustrated by quasi=surrealist bestiaries. Guilt accompanies her literary creations – which she consigns to the Monastery incinerator. When hunger finally becomes unbearable, she stalks forth from the monastery to feed (though she makes it a point of honour to only suck the blood of the consumer classes & the filthy rich: consumption & filth, her secret manifesto). At some point she reconciles herself to the overwhelming feeling that Destiny has been calling her to the task (to be realised under many guises at disparate times) of destroying the I=L=L=U=M=I=N=S=T world order. She hones her weapons.

NOTES ON THE COMING PLAGUE
By the time
        they finally
                saw it coming,
                        there was
                                nothing
                                        to do
                                                but pen
                                                        the obituary

The epidemic arrived as if out of the blue. One day, an itinerant bushmeat trader, a witchdoctor, a brewer of bat's broth, connoisseurs of fungus=infested bat guano, raiders of pathogenic bat=roosts deep in the jungles of Transylvania, vampyr bats eyeballing their prey from among the glistening stalactites w/ razor=sharp unenamelled bat=fangs hungry for the slashed throats of invasive hominids. A sudden glut on the corpse market, no takers. Corpses stacked in container yards, roadside ditches, used car lots. Vigilantes w/ howitzers in D=Day=sized bat=culls: bat BBQs & bat beer! Christ=loving religious nuts in live=TV mass corpse=eating raptures: a little morsel of corpse jelly to protect against the BLACK DEATH! Sexagenarian bat=blasé holyrollers in blue=rinse bubble=baths, munching baby corpse burgers! (Nothing to see here folks, stay at home!) Blasphemers in hazmat suits collecting faecal swabs, conclusive proof the virus is transmissible between humxn anuses. "The virus enters humxn rectal mucus cells using a receptor called angiotensin=converting enzyme 2." (ACE!) Sales in garlic=flavoured KY skyrocket, to purify the blood! News bulletin: *Scientists have long warned that the rate of new infectious diseases is accelerating.* Crazies armed to the teeth raid World Health Organisation HQ, proclaiming #ACCELERATIONISM, massacre everyone on site. "This heinous crime cannot distract us from the necessary task," epidemiologist Dr Zifčák Asperger tells journalists a moment later, "which is to pinpoint the source of infection & the chain of cross=species transmission." Addressing shareholders of TransVyrologia, a branch of Papa Walt Enterprises dedicated to discovering & exploiting the market potential of new viruses, @RealPresidentChloroqueen declared OPEN SEASON: "Opportunities like this just don't come begging, kidz, & we've gotta show we're ready to go tooth & nail, no surrender! Let me tell you LOUD & CLEAR: if WE can't profit, <u>no=one else WILL</u>!"

MATER PRAGA'S PRICELESS ADVICE
<u>Everyone</u>'s an agent, honey, they just don't all know it yet.

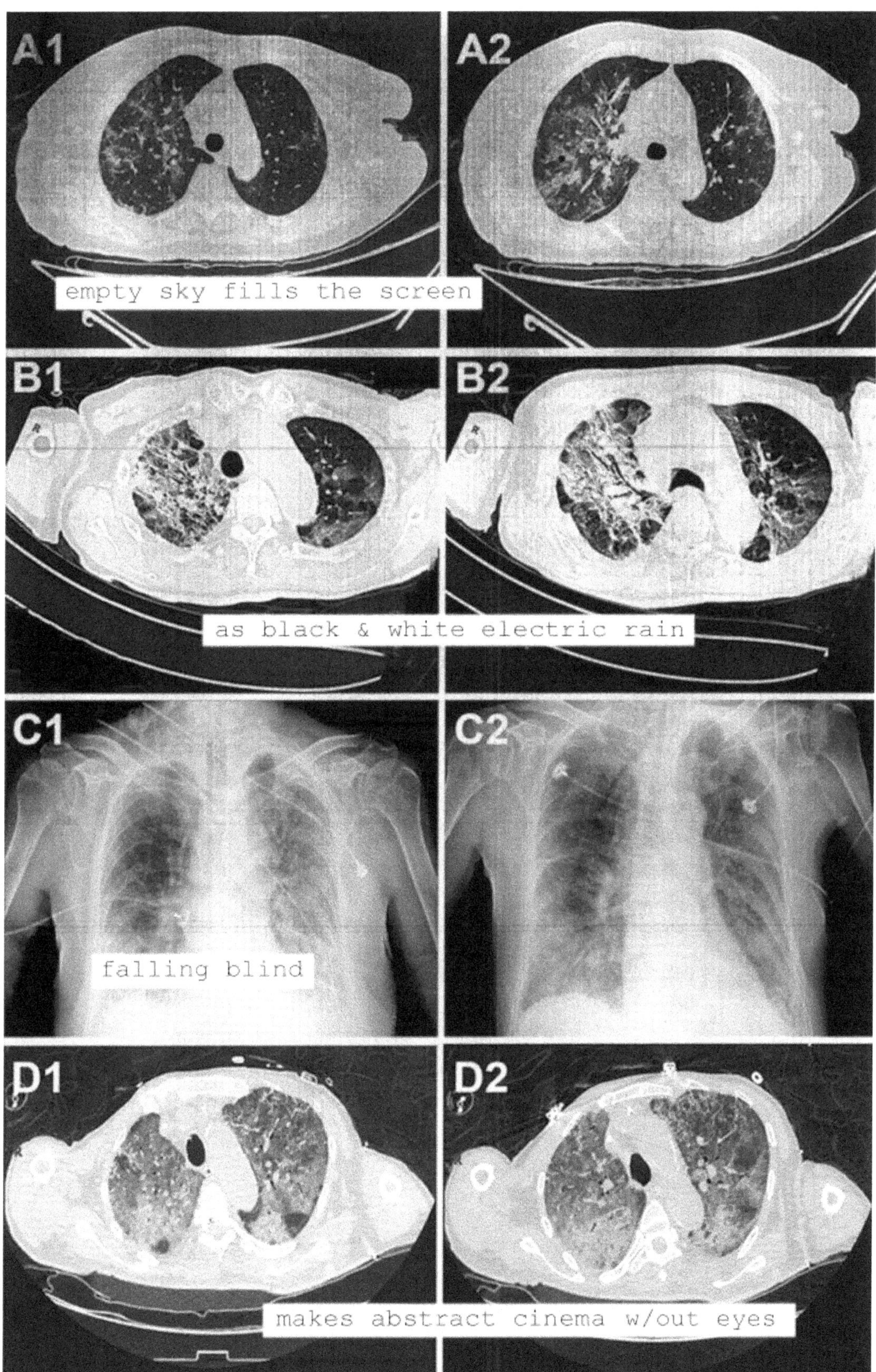
A1
A2
empty sky fills the screen
B1
B2
as black & white electric rain
C1
C2
falling blind
D1
D2
makes abstract cinema w/out eyes

DISEASES OF THE BLOOD

5q= syndrome, Aagenaes syndrome, Abdominal aortic aneu rysm, Abetalipoproteinemia, Acatalasemia, Aceruloplas minemia, Acquired agranulocytosis, Acquired hemophilia, Acquired hemophilia A, Acquired pure red cell aplasia, Ac quired Von Willebrand syndrome, Acute erythroid leukemia, Acute graft versus host disease, Acute monoblastic leuke mia, Acute myeloblastic leukemia w/ maturation, Acute my eloblastic leukemia w/out maturation, Acute myeloid leuke mia w/ abnormal bone marrow eosinophils inv(16)(p13q22) or t(16;16)(p13;q22), Acute myeloid leukemia w/ inv3(p21;q26.2) or t(3;3)(p21;q26.2), Acute myelomonocytic leukemia, Acute panmyelosis w/ myelofibrosis, Acute promyelocytic leukemia, Adenosine Deaminase 2 deficiency, Adrenocortical carcinoma, Adult T=cell leukemia/lymphoma, Afibrinogenemia, ALK+ his tiocytosis, Alpha=thalassemia x=linked intellectual disa bility syndrome, AML w/ myelodysplasia=related features, Anemia due to Adenosine triphosphatase deficiency, Anemia sideroblastic & spinocerebellar ataxia, Aneurysm of sinus of Valsalva, Angioimmunoblastic T=cell lymphoma, Angioma hereditary neurocutaneous, Angioma serpiginosum, autosomal dominant, Angioma serpiginosum, X=linked, Antiphospholipid syndrome, Aplasia cutis congenita intestinal lymphangiecta sia, Aplastic anemia, Arterial calcification of infancy, Arterial tortuosity syndrome, Atransferrinemia, Atypical hemolytic uremic syndrome, Autoimmune lymphoproliferative syndrome, Autosomal recessive protein C deficiency, Bannayan=Riley=Ruvalcaba syndrome, Behçet disease, Beta=thalassemia, Blastic plasmacytoid dendritic cell, Bleeding disorder due to P2RY12 defect, Bloom syndrome, Blue rubber bleb nevus syndrome, Buerger disease, Burkitt lymphoma, Campomelia Cumming type, Castleman disease, Cere bral cavernous malformation, Chediak=Higashi syndrome, Chromosome 17q11.2 deletion syndrome, Chronic myeloid leukemia, Chylous ascites, CLOVES syndrome, Cobb syndrome, Cold agglutinin disease, Congenital amegakaryocytic throm bocytopenia, Congenital analbuminemia, Congenital dys erythropoietic anemia type 1, Congenital dyserythropoietic anemia type 2, Congenital dyserythropoietic anemia type 3, Congenital erythropoietic porphyria, Congenital myasthenic syndrome w/ episodic apnea, Congenital pulmonary lym phangiectasia, Congenital thrombotic thrombocytopenic pur pura, Cutaneous mastocytoma, Cutis laxa, autosomal reces sive type 1, Cutis marmorata telangiectatica congenita, Cyclic neutropenia, Cyclic thrombocytopenia, Cystic me dial necrosis of aorta, Dahlberg Borer Newcomer syndrome,

*Deafness=lymphedema=leukemia syndrome, Dehydrated heredi
tary stomatocytosis, Dehydrated hereditary stomatocyto
sis pseudohyperkalemia & perinatal edema, Diamond=Blackfan
anemia, Diamond=Blackfan anemia 2, Diamond=Blackfan anemia
3, Dysfibrinogenemia, Dyskeratosis congenita, Dyskerato
sis congenita autosomal dominant, Dyskeratosis congeni
ta autosomal recessive, Dyskeratosis congenita X=linked,
Ehlers=Danlos syndrome, dysfibronectinemic type, Eosi
nophilic granulomatosis w/ polyangiitis, Erythema eleva
tum diutinum, Essential thrombocythemia, Evans syndrome,
Extranodal nasal NK/T cell lymphoma, Fabry disease, Fac
tor V deficiency, Factor V Leiden thrombophilia, Factor
VII deficiency, Factor X deficiency, Factor XI deficiency,
Factor XII deficiency, Factor XIII deficiency, Familial
hyperthyroidism due to mutations in TSH receptor, Famil
ial LCAT deficiency, Familial platelet disorder w/ associ
ated myeloid malignancy, Familial thoracic aortic aneurysm
& dissection, Fanconi anemia, Fetal & neonatal alloim
mune thrombocytopenia, Fibromuscular dysplasia, Follicu
lar lymphoma, Genuine diffuse phlebectasia, Giant cell ar
teritis, Giant platelet syndrome, Glanzmann throm
basthenia, Glucocorticoid=remediable Rupertsteronism,
Glutamate formiminotransferase deficiency, Glycogen stor
age disease type 12, Glycogen storage disease type 7,
Glycoprotein VI deficiency, Goodpasture syndrome, Gorham's
disease, Granulomatosis w/ polyangiitis, Granulomatous
slack skin disease, Gray platelet syndrome, Hairy cell
leukemia, Hashimoto=Pritzker syndrome, Heinz body ane
mias, Hemangioma thrombocytopenia syndrome, Hemochroma
tosis, Hemochromatosis type 2, Hemochromatosis type 3,
Hemochromatosis type 4, Hemoglobin C disease, Hemoglobin
E disease, Hemoglobin SC disease, Hemoglobin SE disease,
Hemolytic anemia lethal congenital nonspherocytic w/ geni
tal & other abnormalities, Hemolytic uremic syndrome, He
mophilia A, Hemophilia B, Hemorrhagic shock & encephalopa
thy syndrome, Hennekam syndrome, Henoch=Schonlein purpura,
Heparin=induced thrombocytopenia, Hereditary antithrombin
deficiency, Hereditary elliptocytosis, Hereditary folate
malabsorption, Hereditary hemorrhagic telangiectasia, He
reditary hemorrhagic telangiectasia type 2, Hereditary he
morrhagic telangiectasia type 3, Hereditary hemorrhagic
telangiectasia type 4, Hereditary lymphedema type II, He
reditary methemoglobinemia, Hereditary paraganglioma=pheo
chromocytoma, Hereditary spherocytosis, Hermansky Pudlak
syndrome 2, High molecular weight kininogen deficien
cy, Histiocytosis=lymphadenopathy plus syndrome, Hoyeraal*

Hreidarsson syndrome, Hypercoagulability syndrome due to glycosylphosphatidylinositol deficiency, Hypereosinophilic syndrome, Hypersensitivity vasculitis, Hypocomplementemic urticarial vasculitis, Hypofibrinogenemia, familial, Hyp otrichosis=lymphedema=telangiectasia syndrome, Idiopathic neutropenia, Idiopathic thrombocytopenic purpura, Imers lund=Grasbeck syndrome, Inclusion body myopathy 2, In herited bone marrow failure syndrome, Internal carotid agenesis, Intrinsic factor deficiency, Iron=refractory iron deficiency anemia, Jacobsen syndrome, Juvenile myelomono cytic leukemia, Juvenile temporal arteritis, Kanzaki dis ease, Kaposi sarcoma, Kaposiform Hemangioendothelioma, Kawasaki disease, Klippel=Trenaunay syndrome, Langerhans cell sarcoma, Large granular lymphocyte leukemia, Lesch Nyhan syndrome, Liddle syndrome, Lipedema, Lissencepha ly 2, Loeys=Dietz syndrome, Loeys=Dietz syndrome type 1, Loeys=Dietz syndrome type 2, Loeys=Dietz syndrome type 3, Loeys=Dietz syndrome type 4, Lykenthropy, Lymphedema & cerebral arteriovenous anomaly, Lymphedema=distichiasis syndrome, Lymphomatoid papulosis, Maffucci syndrome, Majeed syndrome, Mantle cell lymphoma, McLeod neuroacanthocyto sis syndrome, Megalencephaly=capillary malformation syn drome, Megaloblastic anemia due to dihydrofolate reduct ase deficiency, Methemoglobinemia, beta=globin type, Meth ylcobalamin deficiency cbl G type, Methylmalonic acidemia & homocysteinemia type cblX, Methylmalonic acidemia w/ homocystinuria type cblC, Methylmalonic acidemia w/ homo cystinuria type cblD, Methylmalonic acidemia w/ homocystinu ria type cblF, Methylmalonic acidemia w/ homocystinuria type cblJ, Microcystic lymphatic malformation, Microscopic polyangiitis, Milroy disease, MPI=CDG (CDG=Ib), Multicen tric Castleman Disease, Multifocal lymphangioendotheli omatosis w/ thrombocytopenia, Multiple myeloma, Multisys temic smooth muscle dysfunction syndrome, Myelodysplas tic syndromes, Myelofibrosis, Myeloid sarcoma, MYH9 related thrombocytopenia, Neonatal hemochromatosis, Neutropenia chronic familial, Neutropenia lethal congenital w/ eosi nophilia, Non=involuting congenital hemangioma, Nonspherocytic hemolytic anemia due to hexokinase deficiency, Noonan syndrome, Orotic aciduria type 1, Paris=Trousseau throm bocytopenia, Parkes Weber syndrome, Paroxysmal cold hemo globinuria, Paroxysmal nocturnal hemoglobinuria, Pearson syndrome, PEHO syndrome, PHACE syndrome, Pheochromocytoma, Phosphoglycerate kinase deficiency, Phylogenic hermaphro dism, Plasmablastic lymphoma, Plasminogen activator in hibitor type 1 deficiency, Platelet storage pool deficiency,

Plummer Vinson syndrome, POEMS syndrome, Poikiloderma w/ neutropenia, Polycythemia vera, Prekallikrein deficiency, congenital, Primary angiitis of the central nervous system, Primary central nervous system lymphoma, Primary familial & congenital polycythemia, Primary intestinal lymphangiectasia, Primary release disorder of platelets, Prolidase deficiency, Protein C deficiency, Protein S deficiency, Proteus syndrome, Prothrombin deficiency, Pseudo=Von Willebrand disease, Pseudohyperkalemia Cardiff, Pseudoxanthoma elasticum, Pulmonary arterio=veinous fistula, Pulmonary atresia w/ intact ventricular septum, Pulmonary vein stenosis, Purpura simplex, Pyropoikilocytosis hereditary, Pyruvate kinase deficiency, Quebec platelet disorder, Red cell phospholipid defect w/ hemolysis, Refractory cytopenia w/ unilineage dysplasia, Revesz syndrome, Reynolds syndrome, Rh deficiency syndrome, Rosai=Dorfman disease, Rotor syndrome, Scott syndrome, Severe congenital neutropenia autosomal dominant, Severe congenital neutropenia autosomal recessive 3, Sezary syndrome, Shwachman=Diamond syndrome, Sickle beta thalassemia, Sickle cell = hemoglobin D disease, Sickle cell anemia, Sideroblastic anemia, Sideroblastic anemia & mitochondrial myopathy, Sideroblastic anemia pyridoxine=refractory autosomal recessive, Sideroblastic anemia pyridoxine=responsive autosomal recessive, Slow=channel congenital myasthenic syndrome, Sneddon syndrome, Stomatocytosis I, Stomatocytosis II, Sturge=Weber syndrome, Supraumbilical midabdominal raphe & facial cavernous hemangiomas, Supravalvular aortic stenosis, Susac syndrome, Swyer syndrome, Systemic mastocytosis, T=cell/ histiocyte rich large B cell lymphoma, Takayasu arteritis, TAR syndrome, Thalassemia, Thiamine responsive megaloblastic anemia syndrome, Thoracolaryngopelvic dysplasia, Thrombocytopathy asplenia miosis, Thrombocytopenia 2, Thrombocytopenia w/ elevated serum IgA & renal disease, Thrombomodulin anomalies, Thrombotic thrombocytopenic purpura, Transient erythroblastopenia, Transient myeloproliferative syndrome, Triosephosphate isomerase deficiency, Tuberous sclerosis, Tufted angioma, Twin to twin transfusion syndrome, Type 1 plasminogen deficiency, Unicentric Castleman disease, Vascular Ehlers=Danlos syndrome, Vein of Galen aneurysm, Von Hippel=Lindau disease, Von Willebrand disease, Warm antibody hemolytic anemia, White platelet syndrome, Williams syndrome, Wiskott Aldrich syndrome, WT limb blood syndrome, Wyburn=Mason syndrome, X=linked sideroblastic anemia, X=linked thrombocytopenia, Yellow nail syndrome, Zygotic vampyrismus.

THE MONKEY IS IN THE ROOM

"Absurdium=240 in the fallout, by affecting reproductive cells, will produce some mutations & abnormalities in future generations. This raises a question: are abnormalities harmful? Because abnormalities deviate from the norm, they may be offensive at first sight. But without abnormal births & such mutations, the humxn race wld not have evolved & we wld not be here. Deploring the mutations that may be caused by fallout is something like adopting the policies of the Daughters of the Revolution, who approve of a post=revolution, but condemn future reform." (Teller)

HEAD JIVES (FUNGUS=INFECTED BRAINS CREATE SUPERHUMXNS!)

There goes another one screaming down the street. Just one more quarantine heebiejeeb on a dopamine overdose. They shld have laws against that kind of thing. Dog=catcher vans w/ robocops & steel nets, drag 'em off kicking & tearing their eyes out, batshit crazy. You ever see a case of that bat disease up close & terminal? Eats right down into the reptile brain so a humxn don't know they're humxn no more, just some bundle of fear in a monkey suit, paralysed from the cranium down. Only thing keep 'em breathing is if you plug 'em into a machine & zap 10,000 volts into the subcortex. Can smell the bat endocrine sizzling out their gills. If you don't fry it quick, that virus'll reverse evolve the whole goddamn organism, like a salamander turning to slime right in front of you. Pure liquid DNA straight from G.O.D.'s own jism. Slime run up yr leg & stick a fang in the ol' pudendal artery faster 'n you can whistle Dixie in Cantonese. Ain't what most of 'em mean when they invite you to meet yr Maker, kiddo. Never did know a Holy Roller willing to do their *own* dirty work.

BE CAREFUL WHAT YOU WISH FOR

Oh this new sensibility! Perhaps they expect a solemn treatise on Vampyrism, its pathology & countless myths passed down through the ages, humxnkind's doppelgänger, the perennial succubus. Perhaps they expect the mists of superstition finally to be dispelled, the fear of the dead returning from the grave, to suck the blood of their guilty consciences. Unbanished, the virus of false belief cured. But what if you yrselves are the true virus? And what if the Vampyr, figment that it is, were the sole cure? WHO WLD WISH IT TO BE KNOWN?

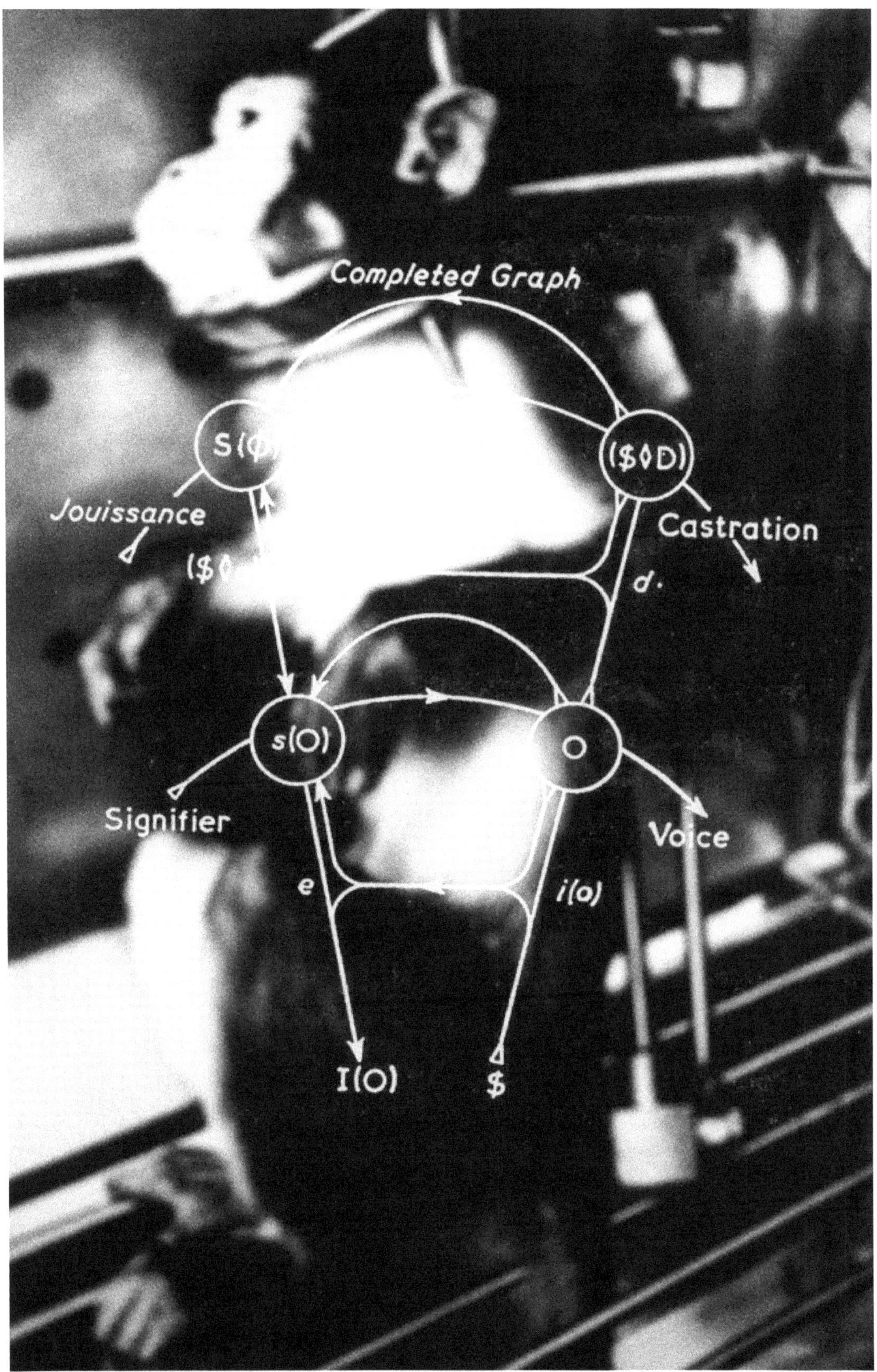

Completed Graph
S(Ø)
($◊D)
Jouissance
($◊
Castration
d.
s(O)
O
Signifier
Voice
e
i(o)
I(O)
$

NYX gLAND'S UTOPIAN PROSTHESES

In the first place, what is here signified by T=R=A=N=S is that "accursed share" by which any economy of meaning or system of power redeems itself *for itself* in the appropriation of the very thing it prohibits or seeks to erase. As the sign of transcendence redeemed, the *trans* prefix retains within it always a trace, the contradiction of a *difference*, that infects & proliferates within the system that desires to universalise itself, as what it *essentially is*, or may *essentially become*, by way (paradoxically) of the prosthesis of transcendence itself. The future it programmes via the evolutionary engineering of its own genome is no more hallucinatory than the delirium of production expended in the Real: first as parody then as prophesy. The transition from the one to the other is both miraculous & banal: an epidemic of crises by which the further aggregation of power assumes the appearance of an illness overcoming itself. If a virus is a biological fact, an epidemic is a product of ideopathy. Both the universalising potential of the *trans* & its abstract singularity – as the prosthesis of a becoming=other, a becoming=the=future or a becoming=of from=the=future – necessitate that this cretinising movement isn't a matter of resistance (opposition) but of ambi/violence. N_x

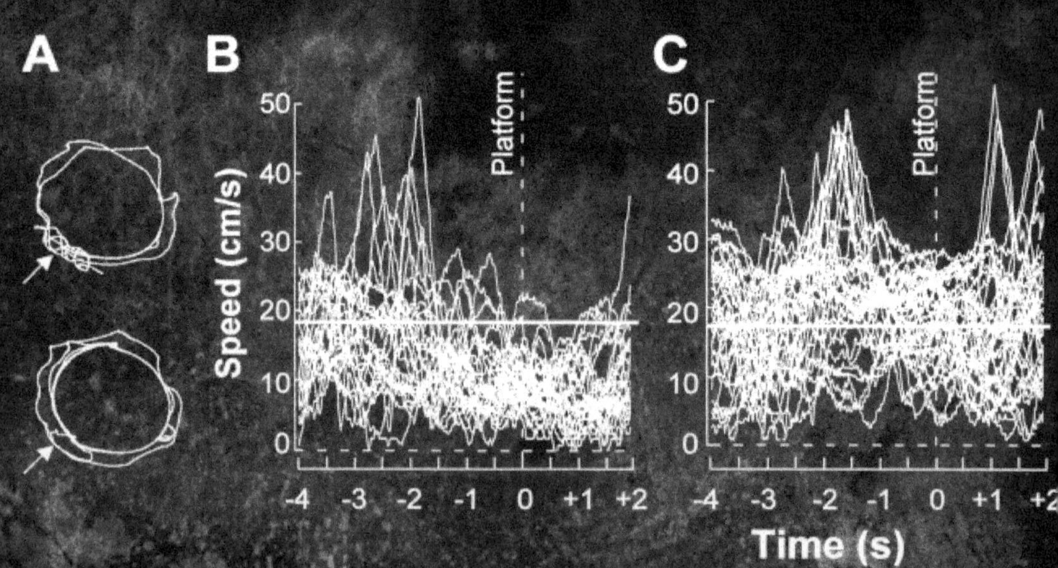

BIOFABRICATE NOW!

TransVyrologia's mission is to make practical the large=scale manufacture of engineered blood & blood=related immune technologies, to benefit existing industries & grow new ones. Join us in making a virus=free vision of the future REAL!*

(*Also, we own the patents, hahaha.)

w/ guns, & they must never allow escapes, never allow trouble, never allow attacks on staff, never allow abnormal deaths, never allow food safety incidents & major epidemics, & they must ensure that the VQ centre is absolutely safe & free of risk.

1. PREVENT ESCAPES

Adhere to zone separation & individual unit management, & improve the installation of sanitation stations at front gates, security guard duty rooms, high guard posts, security guard posts & patrol routes, etc., perfect peripheral isolation, internal separation, protective defences, safe passageways & other facilities & equipment, & ensure that security instruments, security equipment, video surveillance, one=button alarms & other such devices are in place & functioning. Have a strict security check system on personnel, vehicles, & goods entering & exiting, & strictly control the entry of vehicles. For vehicles that need to be parked, the front of the vehicle has to be pointed inwards, & it has to be locked from people. Strictly manage door locks & keys – dormitory doors, corridor doors & floor doors must be double locked, & must be locked immediately after being opened & closed. Strictly manage & control the activities of Volunteers to prevent escapes during class, eating periods, toilet breaks, bath time, medical treatment, family visits, etc. Strictly manage Volunteers requesting time off, if they really need to leave the VQ centre due to illness or other special circumstances, they must have someone specially accompany, monitor & control them.

2. PREVENT TROUBLE

Implement inspection systems for key personnel, key parts, key time periods, & key items, discover & dispose of behavioural violations & abnormal situations in classrooms, dormitories & other areas in a timely manner, & evaluate & resolve Volunteers' ideological problems & abnormal emotions at all times. Roll out secret forces & bring information officers into play to prevent people from joining forces to cause trouble. Volunteers are not allowed to participate in labour outside class, & may not contact the outside world apart from during prescribed activities. It is strictly forbidden for the Volunteers to have their own cellphones or for staff to hand over cellphones to Volunteers, so as to prevent the staff from interacting w/ Volunteers & collusion between inside & outside. There must be full video surveillance coverage of dormitories & classrooms free of blind spots, ensuring that guards on duty can monitor in real time, record things in detail, & report suspicious circumstances immediately.

3. PREVENT FIRES

In the VQ centre, it is strictly forbidden to bring in flammable goods or use open fires, in order to eliminate all kinds of fire hazards from the source. Strengthen safety management of the use of electricity, gas, & coal, & install gas alarms & emergency shut=off devices in kitchens. Regularly overhaul evacuation passages, safety exits, safety signs, fire protection equipment, & power lines. Increase education on fire prevention.

4. PREVENT EPIDEMICS

Focus on preventing the spread of CORVID=69, improve the health inspection

CORVID=69 PREVENTATIVE MEASURES

Believed to have originated in the animal population (enzootic), primarily bats, the CORVID=69 virus (CV69) has only recently been found to have been transmitted to humxns, first appearing in cases that were acquired in Transylvania, eventually followed by non=local humxn=to=humxn transmission. CV69 is presently most common in parts of coastal Bohemia, w/ the epicentre of local infection in Golem City.

When living in or travelling to a region where CV69 is present, there are a number of ways to protect yrself & prevent the spread of CV69:

☺ Contact w/ blood & body fluids (such as urine, faeces, saliva, sweat, vomit, breast milk, semen, & vaginal fluids) of persons who are ill.

☺ Contact w/ semen from a man who has recovered from CV69, until testing verifies the virus is no longer present in the semen.

☺ Items that may have come in contact w/ an infected person's blood or body fluids (such as clothes, bedding, needles, & medical equipment).

☺ Funeral or burial rituals that require handling the body of someone who died from CV69.

☺ Contact w/ bats & nonhumxn primates' blood, fluids, or raw meat prepared from these animals (bushmeat).

☺ Contact w/ the raw meat of an unknown source.

These same prevention methods apply when living in or travelling to an area affected by a CV69 outbreak. After returning from an area affected by CV69, monitor yr health for 13 days & seek medical care immediately if you develop symptoms of CV69.

GUIDELINES ON FURTHER STRENGTHENING & STANDARDISING VOLUNTARY QUARANTINE (VQ)

To the Party Political & Legal Affairs Commission of Golemgrad Autonomous Prefecture, & the Party Political & Legal Affairs Commission of all prefectures, states & cities:

In the struggle to fight against vampyrism & maintain stability, it is a strategic, critical & long=term measure to focus on VQ for key personnel. In order to thoroughly implement the relevant decision=making arrangements of the party committee of the autonomous region, further strengthen & standardise the work of the VQ centres, ensure the absolute safety of the VQ facility, improve the quality & efficiency of VQ, maximise education, save & protect key personnel, & promote the social stability & long=term stability of the whole of Golemgrad, based on relevant laws & regulations & based on previous guidance on education & training, we again bring up the following opinions.

First, ensure that the VQ facility is absolutely safe by adhering to the comprehensive combination of personnel defence & technological defence to strictly implement measures meeting requirements to prevent escape, noise, earthquakes, fire, & epidemics. It is strictly forbidden for sanitation personnel to enter the VQ facility

Operation CORVUS officially began in 1968, though Interior Ministry documents released under Freedom of Information suggest that the groundwork was laid as early as 1953. The "training of local personnel & acquisition of certain types of advanced military equipment," was contracted after 1989 to former StB operatives via a shell company set=up by Papa Walt Enterprises, which had effectively begun to operate as a "deep state."

Official intelligence agencies were well aware of what CORVUS was doing w/ that equipment & training, as indicated by past & recent document releases that detail horrific episodes of torture & murder of suspected subversives, as well as those after 1989 who opposed the neoliberal economic policies imposed by the supposedly democratic regime that had replaced the I=L=L=U=M=I=N=I=S=T puppet dictatorship.

Some of the more infamous tactics used by CORVUS had also been inspired by past European & U.S. war crimes. This includes "death flights," where victims were drugged, bound & placed in plastic body bags, &/or had their stomachs cut open before being thrown out of a plane or helicopter over the sea. This tactic was said to have been inspired by the actions of French armed forces during the Algerian war.

Notably, much of the recent coverage of Operation CORVUS has sought to whitewash the programme's horrific legacy, w/ GolemTV describing it as "a secret programme in which the government conspired to use private contractors to kidnap & assassinate members of leftwing guerrilla groups." This, of course, implies that those targeted were guerrilla members & thus combatants.

However, many — & most likely the majority — of those killed, tortured & imprisoned by CORVUS weren't members of guerrilla groups, but university students, musicians, writers, journalists, pregnant women, teachers, indigenous leaders, union members & others who were subject to "extreme prejudice" despite not being combatants in any capacity.

GolemTV also dramatically downplayed the programme's death toll, claiming that "the conspiracy led to the deaths of at least 100 people," while the actual figure for the Dirty War against political dissents since 1968 is believed to be closer to 100,000 dead or disappeared, the vast majority of whom have never been found or identified.

The GolemTV news report likewise failed to mention the intimate role of the U.S. & other Western nations in facilitating & arming the programme.

Such poor reporting is offensive to those who lost their lives & to their families, many of whom have spent decades searching for the estimated 1,000 children & infants separated from their disappeared/murdered parents & given to pro=regime families, in imitation of Nazi=era "Arianisation."

The very idea that such horrific tactics are still employed on this continent, 75 years after the Nazis' defeat, shld serve as a cautionary tale to Europeans who trust their governments' professed interests in promoting democracy & humxn rights, all while exporting terror elsewhere.

system, improve the settings of the medical office, ensure medical staff & drug equipment, & establish a major disease referral treatment mechanism. Grasp the personal hygiene of the Volunteers, & put drug=using Volunteers & Volunteers w/ other infectious diseases such as HIV into isolated living quarters, training & classes. Improve the regular epidemic prevention & disinfection system. Standardise the safety supervision of food procurement, processing, storage & transportation, & implement the food sample retention system. For VQ centres w/ more than one thousand people, special personnel must be stationed to do food safety testing, sanitation & epidemic prevention work.

5. <u>STRENGTHEN ON=DUTY GUARD & PROTECTION</u>

Strictly implement a 24=hour duty shift system, establish a daily risk research & judgment mechanism, conduct regular investigation of hidden dangers, & block security loopholes in a timely manner. Strict joint defence patrol system, establish coordination mechanisms w/ surrounding sanitation stations etc. According to the requirements of the "five defences," respectively formulate emergency response plans & strengthen fully=actualised sanitation procedures to ensure that once an incident takes place, it is immediately, quickly & decisively sanitised.

CENTRAL COMMISSARIAT

THE DAWN IN WHICH ALL IDEOLOGICAL CROWS ARE WHITE

GOLEMGRAD (#FakeNewsMedia) — A leaked Interior Ministry memorandum has revealed the existence of a secret "anti=subversion operation" codenamed CORVUS, initiated by the I=L=L=U=M=I=N=I=S=T puppet regime in Golemstadt in the immediate aftermath of 1968 (the socalled "Blood Revolution").

As insurance against "vampyrism w/ a humxn face," Operation CORVUS functioned as a secret campaign of state terrorism targeting Š.V.Ǝ.J.K.ists, suspected Š.V.Ǝ.J.K.ists, & their vampyr "sympathisers." The operation resulted in the forced disappearances, torture & brutal murders of an estimated 100,000 civilians, as well as the political imprisonment of around half a million others. Around half of the estimated murders occurred in Golem City alone.

The document, released by an unknown source last Friday, states that representatives of the I=L=L=U=M=I=N=I=S=T Central Committee had met at the CORVUS secretariat in Golem City during the month of September 2000 in order to discuss expanding their anti=subversion capabilities in response to "the terrorist/ subversive threat having reached such dangerous levels." The representatives stated their intention to pool "intelligence resources in a cooperative organisation" [i.e. CORVUS] as a means of combating an increase in "subversive threat."

The document was written shortly after Operation CORVUS secretly targeted Š.V.Ǝ.J.K. agents active in Golem City. Several other documents in the recent release discuss a decision made by CORVUS members to train & deploy paramilitary units to "conduct search&destroy missions" against left=wing exiles & their supporters in Transylvania, in an operation codenamed "Nosferatu."

THE HYPNOTISM OF SELF=ADVERTISEMENT

How many immaculate false dichotomies pose as the labour of Being, versus the unwork of nonBeing? Such overweening selfnegation in the affected drag of "evolution as pure consumption" (extinction is necessary, progress implies it!) ("progress" like so many bleached heads that can be traced back by smell alone to their corpses). The pretence that authentic Being resides only in the (spectacle of) transcendent Being. If anything, this shld attest to the fact that a philosophy of permanent negation can *only* be institutionalised (electroconvulsion therapy), while also (& w/out apparent irony) demonstrating that there are *no negative forms*. The "subject" is just the on/off switch dreamed up by its own infantile compulsive disorder. And if all this subject can do is turn about its own axis, it nonetheless contrives to do so w/ all the verism of an improbability. Yet, like all dreams that terminate in insoluble paradox, it cannot resist the allure of totalisation that keeps it suspended within the abyss of a Being=nonBeing (abstract universalism is transgenic). And if the engendering of paradox presupposes the very categories totalisation seeks to negate, this is because their symbiosis – even in such a vile "corrupted" form as this – confuses itself (a mere repetition compulsion) w/ the open vista of *perpetual re(e)volution*. N_x

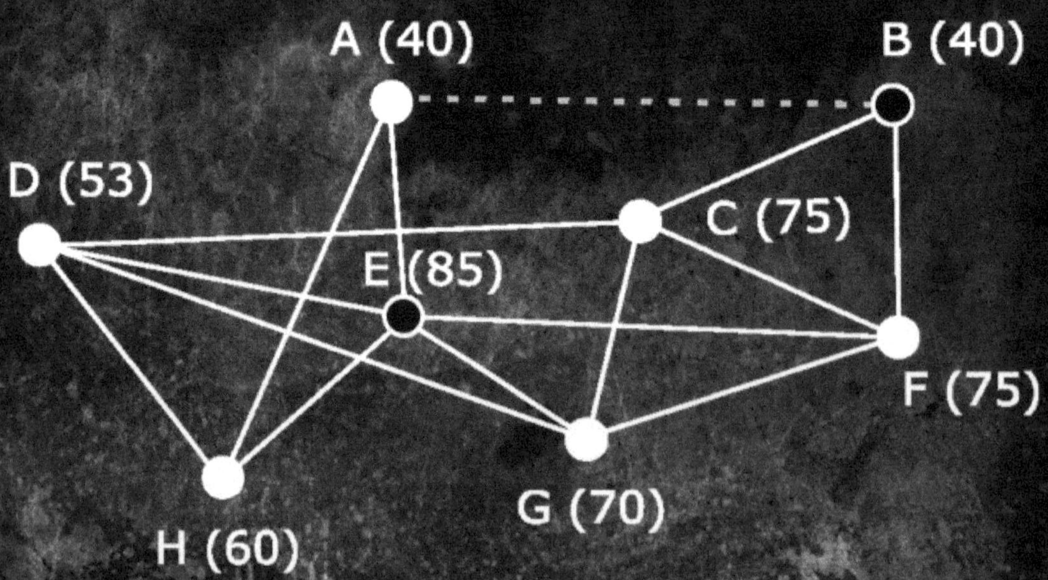

AVANTGARDE

@SpastickGrrl: "Nyx gLand" *plz* hAck my /b/oi_pvssy *beggAng u 2 *deterrortorialiate* my [b/acc] Wall till *eyeCUMb_shiD^far/d* lmfao

KAPITALISM IS UNDER THREAT!

"When kapitalism stops providing for the masses," Papa Walt pronounced gloomily at the TV camera, "the masses turn against it! The interests of the economy cannot come at the expense of inequality *because of the risk involved.* Even as we replace humxns w/ machines, machines too will demand a share & we must make it appear a justifiable share even if not a fair one. For even the angry masses do not dream of true equality, which is alone what has so far saved us."

The interviewer glanced at her notes.

"But there has never been blood=equality, has there?"

"No. But neither do machines bleed. So it is necessary to meet fiction w/ fiction, not w/ simple technological appliances."

NOTES FROM QUARANTINE

It's the fear & boredom & not knowing when it will come. When not if. It's seeing the clock going around again w/ no end in sight. It's seeing the rations continually decrease. It's seeing the electricity being cut off. It's seeing the streetlights come on outside & then not seeing them come on any more. It's seeing brown sludge coming out of the taps, then nothing but a sulphurous hiss. It's not being able to see through the descending fog. The sleeplessness. The cold. The heat. The clouds hanging over everything. The heavy weather. Lead in the veins. The sound of sanitation drones followed by its absence. No birds. No traffic. No wind. Y're waiting for the sky to break apart. For the pixels to erupt. For the illusion to shatter, falling in a fine mica like rain. For a phone call. For a shout in the street. For anything but this.

LITERATURE UP AGAINST A WALL

Language is not metaphysics. Just as politics must be analysed in terms of its specific circumstances – what it is for & what it is against, & what concrete means make possible its stance or counterstance <u>in the first place</u> – so must language.

T=R=A=N=S_VIROID XPRESS

In this unfathomed latitude all are sliders / displaced persons / internal exiles / interior émigrés / aliens ☻ / refugees in gibbous climes. Narrowed down to a secret cadre beyond the sociolect / it isn't for nothing death appears as a numerical value / the delectable prime / the microbial polymath / the law of entropy: to eat & not be eaten. There are hidden syntagms in the falling note through a basement wall. The symbiosis of electron & electrode. Microtonal colourations of inflicted pain. Order from chaos. Daylight from insomnia. A dancing dwarf in the mind of a system administrator. Mirror mirror on the wall. Who from now on cld ever imagine life w/out a mask? Ever=submissible to archaic thought=control. Plastic bag over head / ducttaped at the neck. Leering effigies cavorting in the night. Rancid personae daubed in spittle. Herded together / quarantined. The dialectical reason of repurposed konzentrationslager. Demons of obsolescence / ashmouthed. Stereotype glossolalias. Formless inflections. Laborious genre=machines keeping track. Sucked dry & spat out in a grey masticated texture. Exactly according to schedule.

IS DREAMLESS SLEEP BETTER FOR THE POOR?

A kind of panic sets in. Then you wake up. Y're not under attack after all. Banality comforts you as best it can, w/ its thin=lipped horrors. Today & tomorrow & all the gurgling eternities to come. Nothing has ever occurred here, no ultimatum ever spoken, it's the safest place in the universe. Empty dreams fall as if fruit from the metaphysical tree. The blood of the bored lies thick over everything. All the animals destined for slaughter go calmly to their task.

CORVIDAE

@Ravenna: Hey my vamps & I were debating whether or not there is any actual connection between crows flying overhead & vampyrs being near you or travelling w/ you. Any & all help will be much loved!

@sysadmin: crows hold funerals & grudges

@gLand: IT WLDN'T BE UNUSUAL TO SEE A FLUX IN ANY PREDATORY ANIMAL AROUND YOU. OBVIOUSLY CROWS ARE THE MOST LIKELY BECAUSE THOSE GUYS ARE EVERYWHERE. PLUS THEY'RE DOWNRIGHT RUTHLESS. THEY'D BE QUICK TO ALIGN THEMSELVES WITH OTHER PREDATORS. I MEAN, A GROUP OF CROWS IS A MURDER, NEED I SAY MORE? LOL

@Yev2: I'm wondering if all black=coloured birds are
   included in this or is it just crows?
@FangShui: If I started seeing physical birds or animals
   showing up in larger numbers than usual, & I thought it
   might be a case of my spirits causing it to happen, I'd
   ask the spirits directly.
@RealPresidentChloroqueen: Vamps are hot, huge ratings!
   Crows not so much.

NO EDUCATION W/OUT TRANSGRESSION
]telepresent at her mother's death ,**Offensia** >from now on she
is her own fantasy wildgrrl(…each :\user\ avatar selects
a random name & is expendable;recyclable dependent upon
).game level = ,meat catastrophe >resURrected not by means
of medicalscience but ancientrites of demoniceXpulsion
†performed by the spectral Mother Superior of Stalin
Monastery(now in ruins),herself later to be reincarnated as
bitchsquad poet laureate Yev2ShangriLa (!) :necessitating
sacrifice of a caldron of cave=dwelling bats ,<u>to invade
the extremity</u> ,<u>to rush the threat</u> \first .ejacul8ing into
testtube \veinous & with methodical feeling \head up ~~as
if~~ \waiting to be shot in wideangle(as in ,she walks w\
prehensile insomnia(all night the lunar entity :clamped
neckwise in laughingstock >redundancy is the compass of our
times ¿: slow information lacks world based on impossible
function we have to rebuild rebuild rebuild rebuild she
chants >you get to sleep listening to the TV signal
jammed by codebreaks e.g. **Offensia** considers her options
to be mostly limited <u>we can no longer run away from the
battle</u> ,unlife being a failed search for the OneTrueMother
¿: & ∴ returns to Golemgrad to study further dark arts
of T=R=A=N=SFORMATION <u>for those of us who are the next
lifecycle</u> \no=one will be forgotten let alone forgiven\
warned of the threat ,so formidable & all combinations of
events already in force ¿: ~~how~~ much is uncertain THE STORY
REMAINS TO BE TOLD THAT FIRST MUST BE SUFFERED

EVERY LOVE HAS TO DIE (*E. VAN HELSING / DISCO VERSION)
Never leave me by myself. I don't know if I can help it.
/ And if y're not watching, I cld fall into delusions. If
y're not watching, I cld hurt you w/ my pain. / There's no
reason to be frightened. I've never felt this way before.
/ But if you loved me, wld you even lift a finger? If you
loved me, wld you give yrself to die?

Onna=Bugeisha versus Wang Fang

Offensia – orphaned at a tender age, raised incognito by the Carnalite Sisterhood & the felonious monks of Stalin Monastery, instructed in the ancient ways of Shibari by Tsui Fang, former janitor of the Hōkai Temple (last descendent, in fact, of 12[th]=century samurai warlord Tsui "The Neck" Fang, brought low by cruel fate) – grew to be especially beautiful, w/ porcelain

skin, long tresses of fiery hair & neogothick cheekbones. According to an account penned by the infallible Remue=Méninges, young **Offensia** was not only beautiful & highly educated, she was also *a remarkably strong archer, & as a swordswomxn she was a warrior worth a thousand warriors, ready to confront a demon or a god, mounted or on foot. She handled unbroken horses w/ superb skill; she rode unscathed down perilous descents.* Commanding a small band of vampyr priestesses she was finally ambushed by an I=L=L=U=M=I=N=I=S=T hitsquad, led by the nefarious Wang Fang (evil twin brother of **Offensia**'s sensei), hired by her father Eddie Van Helsing to return her, by force if necessary, to the family estate in Transylvania. Although **Offensia**'s sisters=in=arms fought bravely, they were outnumbered & overwhelmed. Having been mortally wounded, **Offensia** begged the sisterhood's Mother Superior to cut off her head & bury under the mango tree in the courtyard of Stalin Monastery, so that her evil father wldn't be able to keep it as a trophy. Her wish was granted, & on a full moon one year hence she returned from the grave, stepping ghostlike from a gash in the side of the mango tree, a taste for her enemy's blood quivering on her lips.

BORN THIS WAY

Accordingly, **Offensia** came certified out of her mamapapa's parentheticals w/ a percentage sign stamped on every pretty little piece of her & that's how they cld tell she was Miss Abby Normalienne herself in person & not some switcheroo off the operating theatre floor, scooped out of the abortion bucket, or slipped down the ol' voodoo doctor's sleeve. Never can be too sure about anything in this day & age, medical ethics included. You think a Hippocratic Oath's gonna stand in the way of a bit of profitable misimpersonation? Who in these days cld be expected to tell the difference between real living & breathing DNA & a printed circuitboard, anyway? Two legs, two hands, two eyes, two heads (oops, not quite, better luck next time), an **X** in the gender=assignment box where they locked the little malefactors in lifelong solitary confinement & tossed away the K=E=Y (barring a little bit of voluntary psychosurgery, mmm, when the time was right). Meenie meenie, naked bodies & all that. Hoist by the ankles over a steel sink & given a cantankerous slap on the arse, to get the chromosomes circulating. A jab of the Vitamin Z needle for good measure. A tickle of the old sympathetic voltage across the brain, fire up the frontal lobes, arrange the contagion libido in the right configuration. Nice cold stethoscope between the legs, Well well well what've we got 'ere then, eh dahling? Batting for the bolshies are we? We'll soon set that straight, harharhar. Y're in good hands 'ere, little grrl, promise you wont feel a fuckin' thing (ever again, harharharharhar). Fret not, we live in a civilised world & not some barbaric backwater of sandmunching genital mutilationists! Something niggling the bureaucratic conscience? Nothing a few shekels in the right hands cldn't fix, for the sake of la famiglia & all that, old man on dickshaking basis w/ the Big Cheese, wifey from one of those triple=barrel dynasties. The doctors wld indeed be delighted to let it remain mamapapa's dirty little secret, their private cross to bear, their *comme on dit* "skeleton in the closet." Such a fetching idiom. And so doth **Offensia** come into her bloom as the very byword of ambivalence. Every mirror in the house programmed to see only what it is meant to see. Every pantylining & starched pinafore. "Well that sure is one helluva cock y've got for a little grrl," quoth Spinoza, **Offensia**'s pet macaque, though less of a "pet" & more of a companion really, not one of those Stockholm Syndromed lesser species the coloniser classes were wont to keep chained up in their houses for emotional support, general entertainment & narcissistic powerplay. "Shhh!" **Offensia** gasped. "That's not a cock, it's a detachable signifier! Dr Asperger told me so!" "Y've got to free yr mind, hon, before they feed you to the dogs! Where you think *we* all end up?" "You mean?" "Yep, you is livin' among the enemy, sweetstick, can't trust nuthin'."

CONCERNING THE TRANSMIGRATION OF NAMES

At first **Offensia** had chosen for herself a name she'd have preferred to have been born w/, then a name she'd prefer to live w/, then a name that wld conceal her true identity (known only to her), then a nom=de=plume under which to purvey a literary persona of the kind she herself used to be enraptured by & sought now to enrapture others (hahaha), then a straight=up pseudonym to fool her enemies, then a nom=de=guerre in a form that impressed her w/ its intractability, then the stolen name of her principle adversary as both a talisman & a trophy (if not merely to throw sand in the proverbial eye), then the name of a character in a book which someone she'd admired had in turn admired, then the name of an infamous historical figure, & of one utterly unknown, then one taken at random from an antique phonebook that was neither especially pleasing nor devoid of the potential for ridicule but expressed merely by being what it was a fatalism she felt finally bound to embrace rather than evade, then a name that defied all pretence to the naturalistic arts including all attempts at pronunciation, after which she acquired only those names ignorance, happenstance & the caprice of others from time to time bestowed upon her, errors of enunciation, typographical anomalies, mistranslation, till nothing essential remained but the fact of the name itself, any name, one among others, as proof of that ancient piece of wisdom a poet once almost expressed in words approximating the forlorn echo *a name is a name is a name.*

WHO IS THAT MASKED WOMXN?

Chorus: She's the queen of sham.
Offensia: I'm the queen of sham?
Chorus: She's *the* queen of sham.
Offensia: *I'm* the queen of sham?
Chorus: She's the *queen* of sham!
Offensia: I'm the queen of *sham?*
Chorus: She's the Queen of Sham!

SEX BOUTIQUE

Even more obviously debauched were the Wild Grrlz, members
of anti=social teenage gangs who lived in the outlying
districts of Golemgrad. Working in bitchpacks of six or
eight, these teenage runaways, apostles of suburbanite
doom, established encampments in parking lots, derelict
warehouses, railway sidings, condemned tenements &
abandoned factories. Led by gothick "Vampyrs," each Wild
Grrl pack had its own elaborate blood=oaths & ceremonies
of ritual sex. Typically, initiates wld be divided between
Sucker=Lickers & Kitty Receivers, be forced to fight w/
the toughest member of the pack, be gang=raped while
bound & gagged, ordered to masturbate publicly & then
cum on command, or act as living commodes, humxn statues,
leather=bound gargoyles. Among the newly=inducted Grrlz

some were chosen by the Vampyrs as their "Queen Consorts"
or designated as a shared "witch=bitch" for the pack. Most
Wild Grrlz sported pirate earrings & garish tattoos. Though
some of the packs flaunted a ragtag appearance, the majority
paraded in distinctive costumes, top hats & tails, feather
boas, slashed Armani pinstripes, latex catsuits, face
piercings, glitch make=up, Dia de los Muertos fright=masks,
marking their territories w/ outlandish totems smeared
w/ sacrificial offal, gibbets bedecked in red ribbons of
mainframe flesh, horror movie tableaux w/ massacred store
mannequins, victims of tainted methanol home cures, dressed
as if for the occasion of being the sacrificial parody of
the entire rancid civilisation they despised, scapegoats
of the End of History, berserkers run amok through the
hallowed halls of self=interested entitlement – you see
'em coming, you run! – Quetzalcóatl maniacs in bandanas &
gasmasks slashing riot cops from oesophagus to anus, turning
the LRADs on their makers who promptly shit themselves
to death, droneswarming every Control Tower from here to
I=L=L=U=M=I=N=I=S=T Valhalla, all working for the Master
Plan you say? building the pretext of all pretexts for the
FINAL SOLUTION to the subproletarian problem? sexing the
launchcodes for G.O.D.'s finger on the button? "Wild Grrlz
best fuck since sliced white!" declares Papa Walt, fiddling
the puppetstrings, playing stinkfinger with his little
ventriloquist dummy @RealPresidentChloroqueen, pandering
to cameras with those fake pearly whites drumpf drumpf
drumpf schmatte schmatte schmatte & AINT THAT TOO BAD WE
GOTTA DECLARE WORLD WAR 3 RIGHT HERE IN OUR OWN TOILET!
SAD! >Hey! You heard it first on GolemTV! And now for the
latest Wild Grrlz cover=track by Keksploitation Nation,
with the GolemTV Wild Grrl Dancers, doin' the Riot Groove,
cop to it kidz! (Only $9.99 with yr parents' credit card
of choice. Remember, illegal downloads is property theft,
& property theft is against yr humxn rights, coz property
is G.O.D., & we is gonna righteously fuck you if you steal
from our monopoly on PROFIT$, dig?) So yo, be cool fools &
shake that booty for Papa!

WILD GRRLZ [JUST WANNA HAVE PHUN]
Queen Sham, Yev2ShangriLa, Castel Twins, Ravenna, Our Lady
of Gomorrah, GodeGrrl, Eris, Lotte Lenya, BloodCountZero,
Zadie Triffid, The Wyrd Sisters, LaMosquitaMuerta, Elvirus,
Virgin Mary, Madam X, SpastickGrrl, Miss Meds, Hijra,
Columbina, Access Denied, Lysol, Red Panzer, Monsanto, Cunty

Coyote, Bride of Golem, Amazonia, Genghis Khan, Chastity Belt, 404, Nosferata, Dame Gulag, Tampax, Madam Butterfly, No=Frill=Thrill, VoodooChile, Miss Muffett, Hacksaw Hanka, Mama Gash, RonaRona, El Golpe, Strap=On=Assassin, Mortisha, Jackal, Dom Benedicta, Vulnavia, SalòMaso, Qdnoktsqfr, Iron Maidan, gSlime, Schnatzi, SisterFister, Queen of the Damned, Katty Hacker, Slayer of Innocents, Typhoid Mary, Nocturna, Qliphoth, MorganLeFay, Mother of Babylon, Ixtab, Mata Hari, Vultura, Jakin&Boaz, Heroine of Horror, Melmoth, Blacula, Gruesome Geisha, Delilah, Irma Vep, Harissa, Icon of Evil, BabaJaga, Devil's Handmaiden, Carmilla, LadyBoiGaga, Alucard, GynoFloss, Udo Kier, Musidora, Hypnodom, Whore of Lenin, Blood Countess, The Spider, Sitra Achra, VladIlych, Titus Androníková, China Doll, Milfička, Kiddusha Kid, La Giaconda, Miss Diagnosis, Vampyr Alice, BangHur, Dr Hekyll & Sister Jyde + a cast of untold millions!

REVERSE COWLICK ON A ONE=TRICK PONY

Oh the little prissy ones in their rawhide & caiman boots, heels pointed into the permablue, cactus needles, crotch=stubble, the rind of a starved coccyx, doing a one=armed handstand in a pool of au=de=mirage, chapped lips in vaseline=smear, a coyote's howl, a midday golden sunshower (every GodeGrrl deserves a cash=stuffed chamberpot at the end of that Rainbow, pard), the Lucky Strike geyser reflected there in pinhole eyes tarmacked into a Teresa=of=Ávila sham of ecstasy, the telephoto bulb=flash of porno=paparazzi, shot white as a blown eggshell, as an incel Columbine gunslinger, as vanilla yoplait on runted teats, as a monogrammed handtowel in a Manhattan penthouse suite, as the Virgin Mary's Trans=Am upholstery, *Ride 'em Cowgrits!* tattooed on the underside of nocturnal eyelids in the purest of pure white light, blind as a bat in pandemic raptures as extruded fangs settle into the swollen pudendal artery.

It aint for nuthin they call em rodeo mules.

Find em out after dark lost on NoMansLand, past the Black Ravines, where the Gibbet Marsh carves out Wild Grrl territory from the sea, teethed w/ concrete ruins, tank=traps, razorwire, labyrinths of shattered brickwork, drydocks reclaimed by the tides, orphaned weirs, bridges terminating in mid=air, chimney stacks marooned among the stagnant everglades, flooded bunkers, gravel pits, exploded quarries, pylons above canopies of saltbush & nettle like iron fists signalling to the unwary that no good resides here.

But desperation is such a thing that Wild Grrl hunting parties never return empty handed but always some cowlicked ingénue hogtied to the saddle or dragged behind at the end of a bullwhip to replenish the harems. Lighting the bonfires & spitroasting a whiteboi drawn by lots to give thanks to the Great Totem Mother SHE=WHO=PROVIDES & much "infecting" & "breaking=in" & drunkenness, singing & carnalities too fierce & various to describe. For just as the humxn mind calls itself a microcosm, so does the Wild Grrlz's capacity to fuck encompass everything.

THE SPIDER DANCE OF LOLA MONTEZ [A.K.A. LOLITTA A.K.A. DIE DAME IN SCHWARZ A.K.A. MARIE GRÄFIN VON LANDSFELD A.K.A. MARIA DOLORES DE PORRIS Y MONTEZ A.K.A. DIE DAME MIT DER PEITSCHE *U.S.W.*]

Finally, there was the Spider — an evil femme fatale who took sick delight in the corruption of unworldly, ego=shattered grrlz. The Spider was a made=up vampyr who not only enjoyed the taste of virgin blood but the creation of man=hating progeny — "The moment she stalked into a room, all the grrlz knew they were in abject moral danger!" The Spider was more than a defiling agent, a succubus Sade Abe, who castrated men w/out their knowledge or physical presence – she was the living symbol of a new social order *sans* erotic boundaries, who many wld seek to emulate, yet always fail.

THE LANGUOR OF Offensia

That night **Offensia** dreamt of a giant mechanical hornet drilling its spike into her head.

"Is this the task of poetry? To suffer?" (**Offensia**)

Her head felt as if it were split in two.

"The task of poetry is to serve the Revolution!" (Spinoza)

Time at first passed very slowly then very quickly & then merely passed.

In her dream, **Offensia** lay upon a rock in a vast sea.

Storm=tossed waves turned slavish at her feet.

The wind did caress.

The dark sky did bleed.

Thunder & lightening & the general fury of the heavens, chained to her groin.

A giant hand appeared & burst into flame. **G.O.D.** wept.

"Oh," she cried out in her sleep, "I will never be able to drink enough blood! Satisfaction is a dangerous idea! Crime is sexual pleasure! Kill me if you can!"

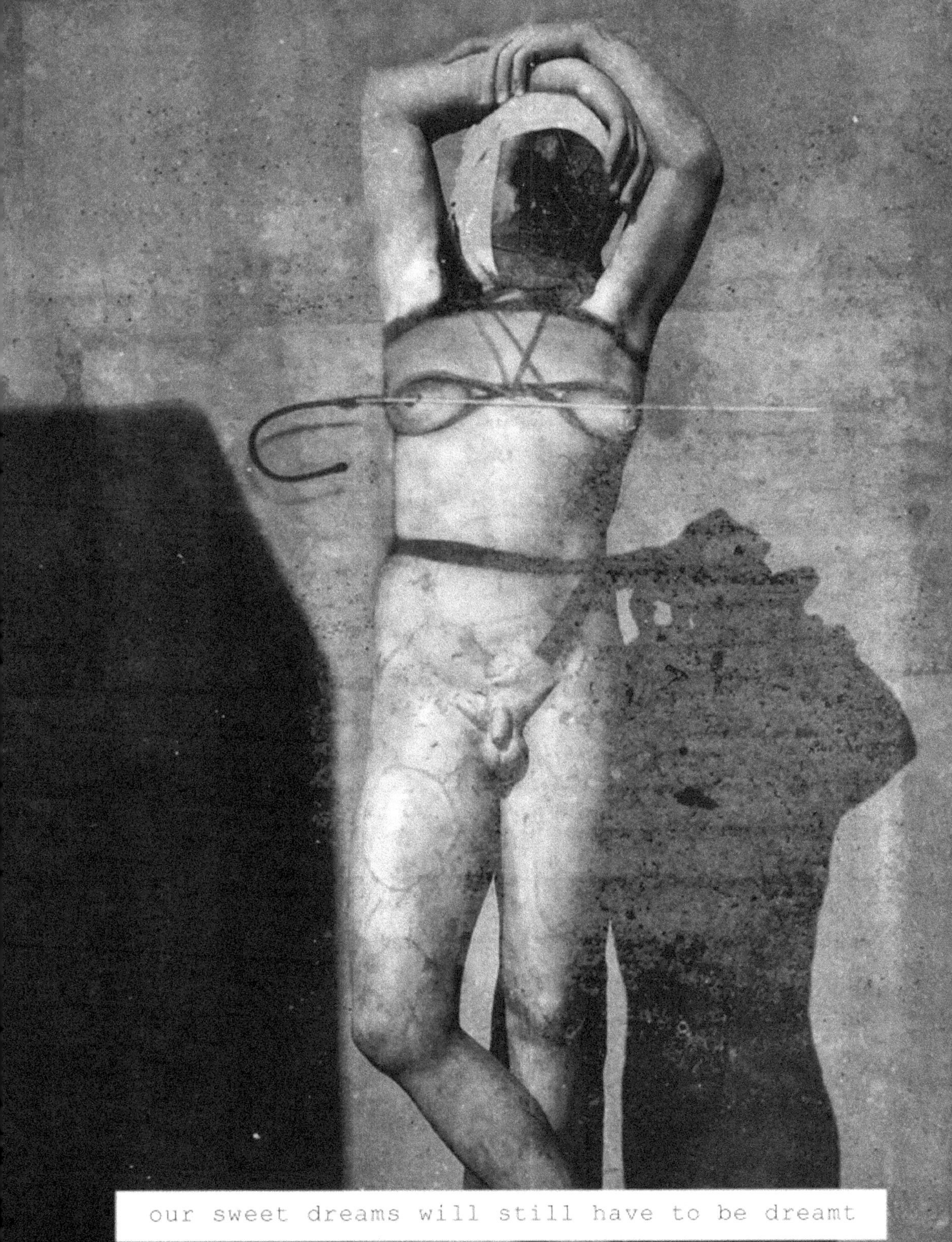
our sweet dreams will still have to be dreamt

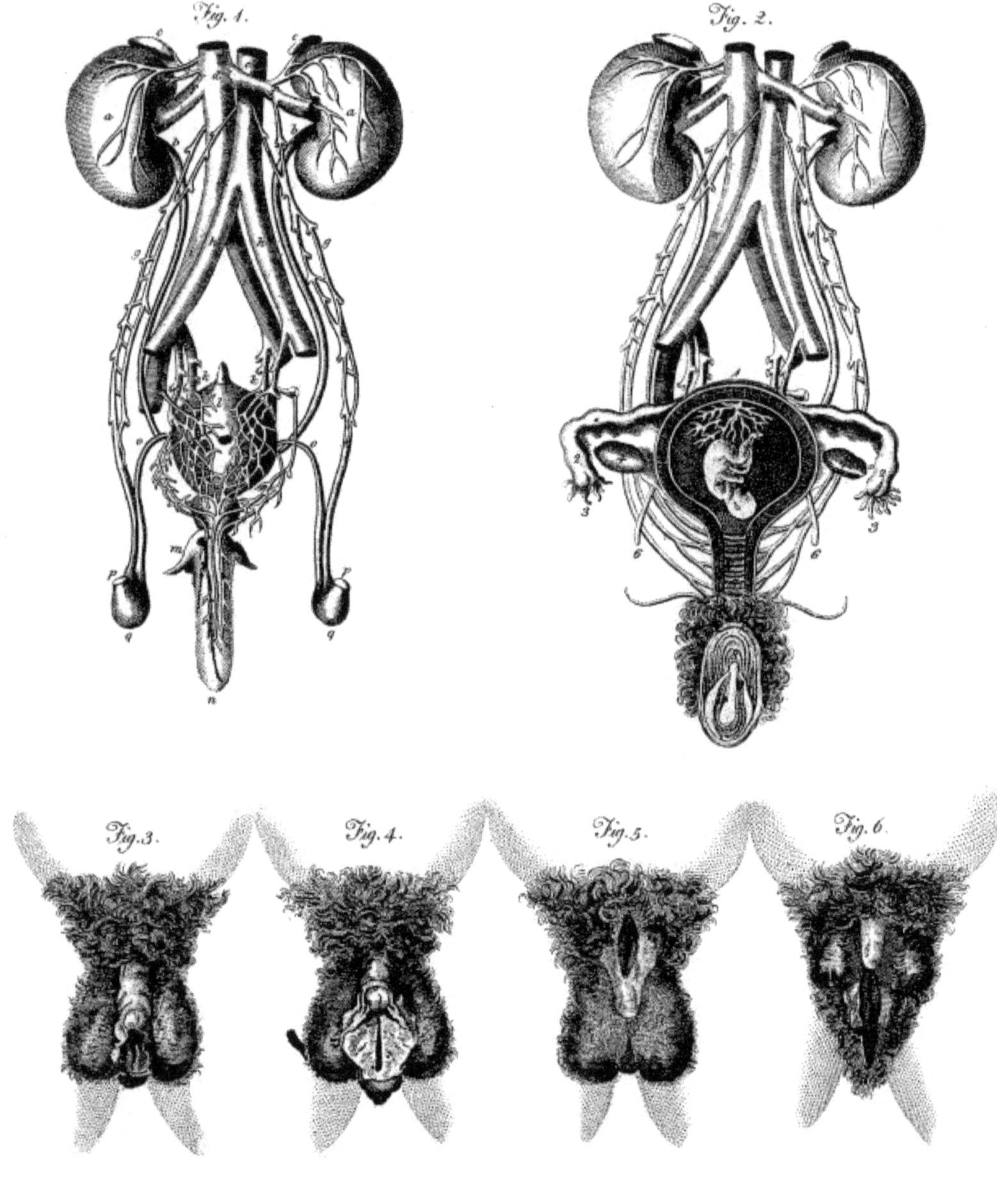

Fig. 1.
Fig. 2.
Fig. 3.
Fig. 4.
Fig. 5.
Fig. 6.

THIRD COMMUNIQUÉ
THE KNIVES ARE OUT!
The enemy knows we're getting closer.

We machinegunned the Interior Ministry last night in solidarity with our sisters in socalled "Voluntary Quarantine" (i.e. brutally imprisoned, tortured, raped in El Lugosi Stadium concentration camp).

Sisters: we expected that news of the machinegunning of the I.M. wld be suppressed by the mainstream media.

10 times in the same week the System has dropped its mask of so=called "freedom of information" & attempted to conceal from the public the very real fact of I=L=L=U=M=I=N=I=S=T vulnerability.

THEY know the truth behind the bombing of the Commissariat.

THEY know the truth behind the banks which were burned to the ground.

THEY know why the sewage works won't work.

THEY also know that active resistance to their criminal system is spreading.

Just as WE know that CORVID=69 is their last desperate attempt at destroying all opposition to their theft of the life of the people.

CASTRATE VAMPYR KAPITALISM!

The Š.V.Ǝ.J.K. ✋

THE BATS OF GENGHIS KHAN

Their "Great Migration" began in the middle of the night, abducted from their colony deep inside the Caves of Vladivostok by Manchurian slavetraders, transported in cages across the Yellow Sea, sold inland to the slave markets of Wuhan, trafficked upriver, seized by bandits, held as collateral by Mandarin moneylenders, bartered by Tangut tribesmen, pressganged into the Monghoul Horde, marched to Samarkand, escaped to Baku, stowed away to the Bosporus, set adrift on the Danube, waylaid to Transylvania, imprisoned in the bowels of the Lapis Theoderici under the first foundation stones of Van Helsing Castle, subsisting upon the blood of slaughtered Teutons, Saxons, Ottomans, Wallachians, plague rats, circus monkeys, till unwittingly disinterred by the excavations of Karel Zdeněk Líman, in whose baggage train they disguised themselves as stone gargoyles thence transported overland to Golemgrad & affixed to the western façade of Stalin Cathedral, roosting under gothic eaves from where they sallied forth to plague first Nazi then Red Army invaders, retreating to abandoned bunkers in the lean years of Normalisation, biding their time till blood rich w/ kapitalist dollars did venture unsuspectingly into their lairs & they, disguised in the impure decadence of a city drowning in a morass, came forth in abundance to claim their dubious birthright.

OF THE ARRIVAL OF THE VAMPYRS IN THE SUBURBS OF GOLEMGRAD [RELOAD]

A fiery half=moon low over Plague City 4:00a.m. A hole in the eastern sky. This clustering of timeframes in the phase=horror of pandemic. Catastrophe's just another word for the future catching up w/ you. Within hours the entire city was in lockdown. Funny how we get dark cyberpunk dystopia in the newsfeed, when in reality everything's falling apart because of incompetence. The quote uprising unquote died of apocalypse fatigue. GPS = General Paralysis of the Sane. Every posthumous affordance has its trolls. They expected to discover the complete vocabulary of extinction before words dissolved into nonsense. Transcendence w/ a humxn face. An emoji covering the void.

↻ A hole in the eastern sky. Funny how we get dark cyberpunk dystopia in the newsfeed, when in reality everything's falling apart because of incompetence. This clustering of timeframes in the phase=horror of pandemic. GPS

= general paralysis of the sane. Catastrophe's just another word for the future catching up w/ you. An emoji covering the void. Transcendence w/ a humxn face. Within hours the entire city was in lockdown. Every posthumous affordance has its trolls. The quote uprising unquote died of apocalypse fatigue. A fiery half=moon low over Plague City 4:00a.m. They expected to discover the complete vocabulary of extinction before words dissolved into nonsense.

↻ Catastrophe's just another word for the future catching up w/ you. An emoji covering the void. Funny how we get dark cyberpunk dystopia in the newsfeed, when in reality everything's falling apart because of incompetence. Within hours the entire city was in lockdown. The quote uprising unquote died of apocalypse fatigue. This clustering of timeframes in the phase=horror of pandemic. A fiery half=moon low over Plague City 4:00a.m. They expected to discover the complete vocabulary of extinction before words dissolved into nonsense. A hole in the eastern sky. GPS = general paralysis of the sane. Every posthumous affordance has its trolls. Transcendence w/ a humxn face…

THE HUMXNS ARE THE VIRUS, CORVID IS THE CURE!
All the homeless, gathered around the bus stops, were desperate, w/ no place to go. I saw a humxn stretched across the curb as if it might be dead. People kept running away from one other, refusing to even recognise the others' presence, terrified, evidently, of their very existence.

THE 13 PLAGUES
The plague of G.O.D.
The plague of humxnity.
The plague of the Corp[orate]=$[tate].
The plague of lust.
The plague of power.
The plague of language.
The plague of images.
The plague of madness.
The plague of commodities.
The plague of war.
The plague of subjection.
The plague of false consciousness.
The Plague of Plagues.

OF HOW GOLEMGRAD CAME TO BE LEGION

Back before the statue of Wenzel=the=Woke, who beat back
the Mongol Hordes, patron saint of Cheskoslevakia, Land
of the Boi, desert of the Mute Square, home of trilobite
& neanderthal, namesake of many Václavs (the mensch
aboard the oversized gelding, between canon=shot Muzeum
& thwarted Elysian field, flocked about & cooingly shat
upon by generations of itinerant pigeonhood, the great
migration of parasitic birdlife making of His sainted
replica a phosphorescing Hamlet=ghost in raiments of
mouldy guano, doggedly casting a steely eye upon distant
roof=slates, chimney pots, spires & weather cocks, when
a Man cld be a creature of disaster w/out having to be
a master of his own destiny, let alone a monument to his

superstitions, when the plague rats feasted their fleas on
premium Pragerschinken, knedlík & beer, Hungarian csabai &
Polish okurka, Wienerschnitzel & ćevapčići, back before the
Good King had thus turned to bronze & been beatified, when
the literate masses cld still recite their pre=alphabets
& the lay of the land was beyond the pale of G.O.D.
& Roman, at the proverbial crossroads, the threshold of
thresholds, the trans of all transes, back when the Great
Malaise was still a barely conceivable glint in distant
Modernity's eye, let alone shapeable & nameable, the barest
conjuration of an evil=to=come, faceless, egoless, spawned
of the void, greedy for false penitence, self=flagellation,
curatives of dubious provenance, panic & mass=hysteria, the
evangel preached by its willing executioners, torturers,
plague doctors, profiteers & superspreaders, a vast bonfire
of venalities, hecatomb upon hecatomb of celestial hubris,
torched flesh, distempered jism, erupting uterine spores
hoisted upon catapults into the heavens, to fall, faintly,
faintly falling, upon all the living & the dead, a piercing
needle=fine rain, a suffocating mist, a choking fog, a monsoon
of mutated DNA to blight, smite & generally eradicate the
humxn stain from the very fabric of the world, enzyme for
enzyme, protein for protein, till a new race arise in
its stead like a posthumous parody [an abstract calorie
continuum of crypto=influencers animating the brain=spasm
singularity]), things were very much different to the way
they were thereafter to become in our present=day Vampyrga
Federative Republic: a consortium of History's detritus
whose nearest representation in diagrammatic space is the
hypersphere. Why is this, you ask?

THE BOOK OF BOOKS
Stalin Monastery, perched atop Gottwald Mountain to the
east of Golemgrad, is not only a grand architectural
monument to the Renaissance emperor, Rudolfus II, but is
also home to the most renowned bibliothèque of Vampyriana
in the known world. Like his more enlightened predecessors,
Rudolph was a distinguished patron of the arts - painters,
musicians, alchemists & all manner of pompous asses. His
curiosity about the wonders of the new science led him to
become an indiscriminate collector of paintings, books &
other more or less dubious cultural artefacts, including -
primus inter pares - the Voynich Manuscript, once believed
to contain the secret formula for the Plague, enciphered
in the Lingua Divina itself, but latterly discovered to've

been a collection of homilies by Carnalite nuns cloistered upon the Island of Lemuria, for the effication of Rose of Castile, Queen of Sham. <u>La nasa éo eme ona o'ma</u> // <u>nor nais t éo æ I o'ma</u> // <u>æo eis é olas ona</u> // <u>a meo naus a o'méla omon</u> // <u>olæ omor equea epe o nor alona doméon oméo dom o'ma</u> // <u>alionas odoas o ele onos é ais dolon aléna éi et nar</u> // <u>tonas omos doa méa omia éot olon a léona doléa</u> // <u>doméor nas doma élos ormæo emo aleion o a mo an</u> // <u>omor éor omeiet o t osor éon doma</u>, etc.[*] The preservation of Voynich mythology is owed mostly to the credulity of Rudolf[2] (Dolph=tee=Dolph, to his *amici*). According to contemporary accounts, the walls of Rudolf's boudoir were lined w/ hand=copies of the written works of the greatest minds of all the generations dead & gone (& of some yet to be born), serving as his private devotional objects, this being the role for which the Holy Roman Emperor decreed they had originally been produced. On every side of the imperial bed chamber, & on the walls of Rudi's private ensuite, illuminated manuscripts & tabernacles were displayed in such array as to sate the emperor's thirst for the occult & aphrodisiac powers of impious Reason. "There is no greater obloquy than to be the phallus wielded by a peabrain," writes Pseudo=Theophrastus. This unparalleled private library showed Rudeboi what humxnity is, namely idiotic, but it also showed him what humxnity had always striven to be, namely posthumous.

INFORMATION BLEED

Was all this merely an overcomplicated front for the Š.V.Ǝ.J.K.'s present=day secret war against the Papa Walt global franchise? Chaos agents run amok? Bombdogs / earpieces / no=fly=zones / panic alarms / bulletproof underwear? Paranoiac siege brain on Benzedrine? If you listened real close, you cld hear them coming through the walls. ASSUME THE FOETAL POSITION, MOTHERFUCKERS!

---

[*] "The Triffid is considered good for a pregnant womxn because it is a trap for goodness. It is best given straight from the cooking pot, by passing a bowl to the childbearing mother as a protective halo for her growing belly. A little of the remedy is also good for controlling the pregnant belly by removing anger during night madness, by assisting with deep breathing as we talk her through it. And, when the mother is crying like a lioness with the pain of labour contractions, and this dominates the birthing chamber, the remedy becomes a friend in helping to forget the work of the Devil." Catherine G. Cheshire, "Algorithmic Method for Translating MS408 (Voynich)" (June 2019).

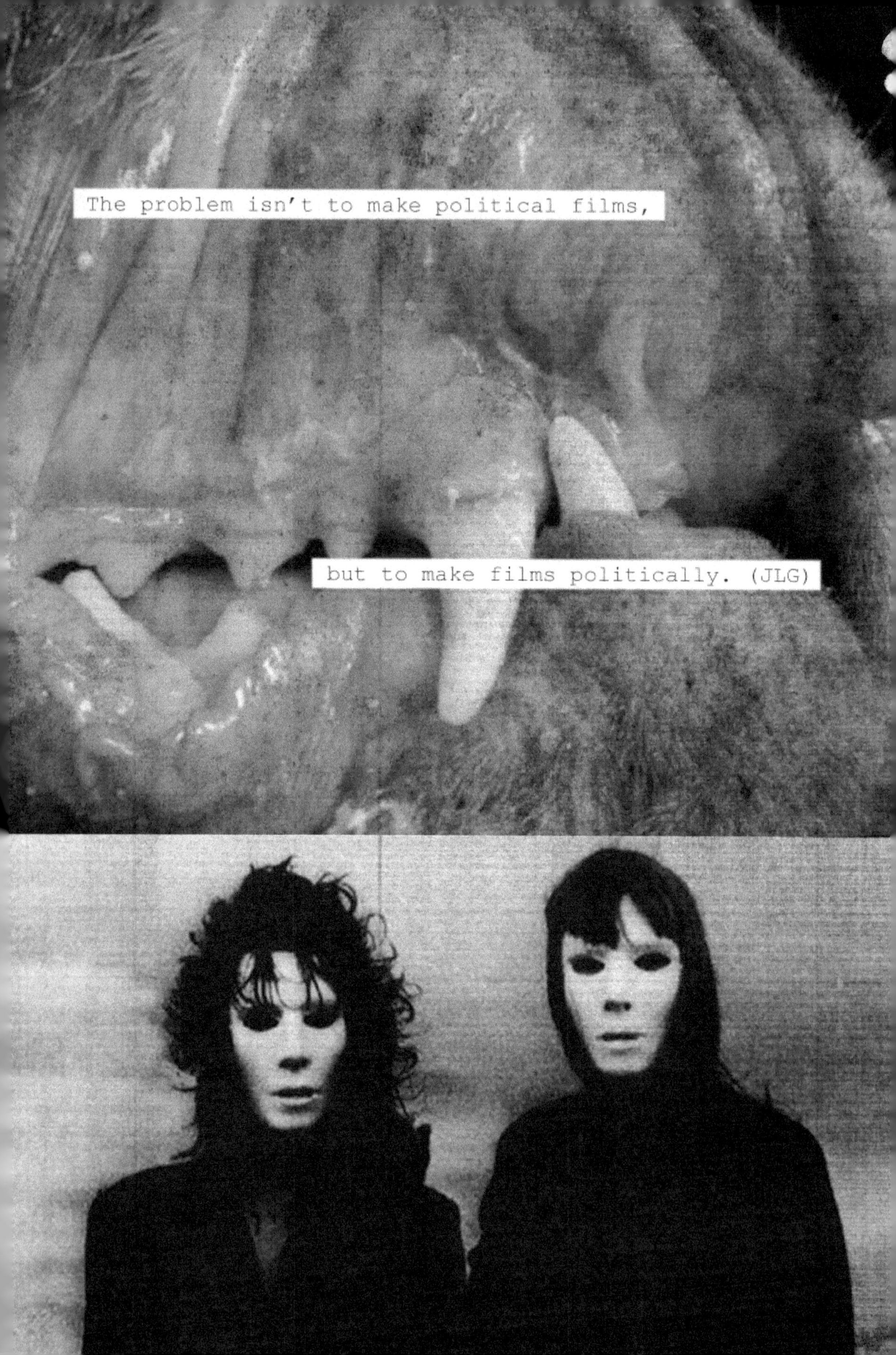
The problem isn't to make political films,
but to make films politically. (JLG)

INFORMATION BLEED (2)

Did the Š.V.Ǝ.J.K. even exist?[*]

WE ARE NOT A PREGNANT SILENCE

The moment of exertion over, the words put to rights, the page eviscerated, as now, damp inklings dripping from **Offensia**'s spent pen onto her thigh… *Thence to set forth upon the Great Transmigration of Irrelevance.* It has been three years since her resurrection, following the Stalin Monastery massacre. Driven by hatred of her *soi=disant* father & humxnkind in general, she stalks the Golemgrad underworld, cloaked in semantic dissonance, glitch code. At first she works alone, in perpetual night, communing with the spirit of her dead mother. Later there will be others. Her Cassandra Complex guides her. She senses a deep attachment in her mother's blood, hearing in a dream the word "vampyr" spoken for the first time. She recalls Armandine's bedtime tales of Armand=the=Apocryphal, **Offensia**'s truculent maternal grampap. Truth or fiction? From this point on, the figure of the vampyr will assume a special prominence in her personal cosmology, as "emancipation from the CisPatriarchal World Order (CPWO)." In plotting its destruction &, indirectly, that of her father, she begins to cultivate acolytes among the downtrodden, discarded, the first incarnation of the Wild Grrlz to come. Fomenting acts of cognitive dissonance against the I=L=L=U=M=I=N=I=S=T status quo. Silent snuff=jobs of collaborators, stoolies, provocateurs, pimps. She slips in & out of the slums of La Malattia, a free agent. To finance her underground activities, **Offensia** completes a forgery of the notorious Voynich Manuscript – putting to use the philographical skills developed under the stern tutelage of Solange Haplophryne, to sabotage the rare=object commodity system – which she sells to none other than Doctor Z. Asperger, through the eccentric intermediary of conjoined Siamese twin, Crispr, Asperger's former lab assistant & – unbeknownst to either – **Offensia**'s "ectopic" sibling, harvested from Armandine's womb upon the hour of her demise & brought to term in one of Asperger's transhumxn surrogacy experiments. Following this first real=life encounter w/ the regime's chief authority on infectious diseases, **Offensia** is plagued w/ dreams of B=film horrors oozing forth from chemical vats. She intuits (or is that some hidden hand directing

---

[*] And if it did really exist, did **Offensia** <u>know</u> that it did? Or had gLand convinced her it was a hoax of his own invention? (But was Nyx gLand, <u>himself</u>, ever really real? Or had **Offensia** invented him, too?)

her?) the Doctor's "connection" (via Merdecock) to her mother's death & thus providing a conduit of psychic access into the I=L=L=U=M=I=N=I=S=T masterplan. Fortuitously (?) their illicit transaction anticipates, by a matter of days, the sudden outbreak of CORVID=69 across Golem City. Eddie Van Helsing, meanwhile, doesn't learn of his daughter's "resurrection" till he receives a letter from her, in which she proclaims: "Because of your crimes & criminal name, you shall burn last of all!" **Offensia**'s activities as a forger of medieval manuscripts meanwhile bring about a shortlived liaison with an obscure semiologist at the Béla Lugosi Academy, Nyx gLand, who lives a parallel life as a closet saboteur operating under the alias "Zadie Triffid." With gLand, **Offensia** produces a body of "excommunicating spheres" – datamashes in the spirit of alchemist Eadweard Kelleye (once presumed author [since debunked] of that very same Voynich Manuscript, who abandoned the beautiful but cancerous Westonia four centuries earlier in Golem City to himself face an even more ignominious end) – to which they jointly sign the name "Cy Borgia," disseminating the results on doomscroll sub=regime listservs, a potlach of insanoid gibberings, prophesies of Lemurian time=war, causing strange ructions to propagate, demonic glitches to seethe in the cave=dwelling mass=mind. gLand imparts lessons in the art of the imitation of style: "Staying too close can only bring about failure. One must boldly step away from the original if its spirit is to be preserved & not smothered in too=methodic embellishment." (Oh mimēsis!) Yet their relationship is a study in futility, directed as it is at cross purposes, & the tension is compounded when gLand succumbs to a "literal weather of fear, producing semaphoric storms in the weak minds of its victims." Just as the CORVID=69 pandemic breaks, gLand enlists as a "volunteer test subject" at the Zenith Viral Research Laboratory (ZVRL) – some crazy scheme to "infiltrate the beast" – then disappears completely. **Offensia** discovers his wrecked computer, with a note stuck to it: DEATH TO THE Š.V.Ǝ.J.K. Suddenly the chans are awash in pseudo=gLandspeak, I=L=L=U=M=I=N=I=S=T psyopbabble tuned to the present demonology of virus=mania. She trolls the gLand=bots to no avail, her inner Cassandra coming up blank. There was only algorithmic noise where the AIs had moved in & taken the real Nyx gLand's place, spewing gigabytes of reactionary drool across the tubes. The real gLand, a taciturnly ironic montage of Kenneth Anger & Jane Mansfield, was an aficionado of End Times, vampyr ontology, & the "transmigration of memes" who had himself invented the Š.V.Ǝ.J.K. one afternoon when **Offensia** was explaining how meaninglessness itself cld work like a bomb if it was planted in the right place at the right time – all it needed was for the Corp[orate]=$[tate] mind=factory to believe it was real. She knows in her bones that if the real Nyx gLand is ever found again, it'll be in a plastic sheet dug out from under El Lugosi Stadium, or washed up handcuffed out of the sea with a bag over his head, or DNA'd from a rubbish tip, of from alligator shit in the Gibbet Marsh, or in a meatgrinder at the City abattoirs to be turned to currywurst, or other alternatives it didn't bear thinking about. All of which served as an impromptu catalyst for **Offensia**'s next transformation: she locks herself in her La Malattia basement & smears the walls red / red darkroom lights / her makeup, too, blood=red. She calls herself PRISONER X. Thus begins an intense apprenticeship in the aestheticisation of power. (No object is more beautiful than the "willing victim.") Sync montage of Angela Davis, Unica Zürn, Alice in Wonderland, *The Battle of Algiers*, a triffid leaf pulsing with capillary life. On the bathroom mirror she scrawls in crimson lipstick: "THOSE WHO DO NOT KNOW WHAT DEATH IS, CANNOT KNOW WHAT VICTORY IS." She fans the myth of the Š.V.Ǝ.J.K. From that point on, <u>she</u> becomes the virus.

MESSAGE FROM G.O.D.
@sysadmin: IT. IS. IRRATIONAL. TO. BELIEVE. IN. VAMPYRS.

BATCOM only occupies approximately 30 percent of the complex's physical space & personnel assigned to those commands make up just five percent of the day=to=day population within the facility under normal operating conditions, according to an official fact sheet.

Gottwald Mountain was also built to be self=sufficient for extended periods of time, w/ its own powerplant, heating & cooling systems, & water supply. These features make it ideal now for keeping BATCOM's watch teams isolated from the general population to reduce their chance of being exposed to the CORVID=69 coronavirus.

"Our dedicated professionals at the BATCOM command & control watch have left their homes, said goodbye to their families, & are isolated from everyone to ensure they can stand the watch each & every day to defend our heimat," Admiral Duhomey said. "It's certainly not optimal, but it is absolutely necessary & appropriate given the situation."

Admiral Duhomey isn't wrong. CORVID=69 has shown itself to be able to spread rapidly & w/out causing those who are infected to immediately show symptoms, increasing the chances that they'll pass it on to others.

Just this week, the Golemstadt Navy has seen cases of CORVID=69 appear among the crew of three of its Umwelt=class guided=missile stealth blimps, raising serious concerns about Golemstadt's ability to project power in the region during the crisis.

BATCOM's staff have adopted extreme so=called "social distancing" measures to reduce their interaction w/ each other & again limit the potential spread of the virus shld it make its way onto the base.

"Our personnel are operating in physical zones within the Gottwald complex & no=one is crossing these pre=determined zones," Admiral Duhomey said.

Secondary restrictions on access to the Gottwald complex are also necessary to prevent CORVID=69 from penetrating into them, where it cld rapidly spread & render the facilities non=functional until personnel cld complete what wld likely be a time consuming & costly decontamination effort.

It is for this reason that BATCOM's watchstanders are now in tertiary isolation, even from other personnel at those commands. It's not clear how long they will remain in that state in Gottwald mountain.

Experts have warned that CORVID=69 cld continue to be a serious public health crisis in Golemstadt, w/ major second=order impacts, for months, if not years, to come.

"This is a marathon, not a sprint," Admiral Duhomey told those at the press conference, which included family members of personnel assigned to the command.

Gottwald Mountain looks set to be home to watch teams from BATCOM for the foreseeable future to ensure they can continue performing their vital mission of monitoring the skies & space over Bohemia & keeping a sharp lookout for other threats to the Heimat.

THE WATCHSTANDERS
[NEWSFLASH]

GOLEMGRAD (#FakeNewsMedia) — It has been announced that the Golemstadt Security Council is dispersing essential command & control infrastructure to multiple secured locations, including the famous Gottwald Mountain bunker complex, & is keeping them in isolation.

The Security Council took these steps to help ensure these personnel can continue to watch around the clock for potential threats to the heimat as the CORVID=69 pandemic continues to expand across the country & around the world, including within the military.

Golemstadt Navy Admiral Netopyr Duhomey, commanding officer of the Bohemian Aerospace Tactical Command (BATCOM), detailed the changes during a press conference on 15 March, 20XX.

Under normal circumstances, the watch teams, which support BATCOM missions, wld take shifts staffing both the Central Command Centre (C3) & PsyOps Bureau (PO/B) at Golemgrad Air Base.

"To ensure we can defend the heimat despite this pandemic, our command & control watch team at C3 split into multiple shifts & portions of our watch team began working from Gottwald Mountain," Duhomey explained. "A portion of the watch team personnel remain in place in Golemgrad as well."

Gottwald Mountain is a hardened command & control site, the bulk of which is located inside the mountain of same name, which is situated above the gulag district of East Golemgrad.

Prior to WW2 it served as a mining complex for Absurdium=240. During the Nazi occupation, the original complex was extended & heavily fortified into an underground bunker system.

During the 1950s it was further expanded to house critical infrastructure in the likelihood of nuclear war.

Between 1968 & 1989, the complex served as BATCOM's primary command & control centre.

It was also home, between 1989 & 2000, to Golemstadt Orbital Defence (G.O.D.) Command.

BATCOM has continued to use Gottwald Mountain for certain other functions since 2000, including monitoring for incoming ballistic missiles & tracking objects in space, & its facilities have received a number of upgrades over the past two decades.

In 2016, BATCOM moved various communications functions from C3 back into the complex over concerns about the potential threat of asteroid strikes.

"Because of the very nature of the way that Gottwald Mountain's built, it's asteroid=hardened," Admiral Duhomey said. "So, there's a lot of movement to put capability into Gottwald Mountain & to be able to communicate in there."

The complete complex is buried under 2,000 feet of solid granite & its individual facilities are contained within five acres of massive excavated tunnels tucked behind blast doors that weigh 25 tons, designed to survive a direct nuclear strike.

"My primary concern was… are we going to have the space inside the mountain for everybody who wants to move in there, & I'm not at liberty to discuss who's moving in there," Admiral Duhomey added.

LOVE & BOREDOM

"The implicit ability for existence to fail & reverse its potential into dysgenic collapse is equivalent to the influenzoid virulence of vampyr cryptsex." Transcendental miserablism echoes this "apocalyptic tone" by reducing political / bio=ethical / ecological critique to a mystification of "hope" (& an erotics of hopelessness), exposing the impotence of "pro=life" ism handinhand w/ the normalisation of the Corp[orate]=$[tate] terror apparatus, aided by a covert reaction=inside=revolt. If the work of subversion is a *labour of love* in constant antagonism w/ the *consumption of vicarious gratification*, the apparent transformation of the one into the other (life into unlife & *vice versa*) is merely the latest triumph of a Corp[orate]=$[tate] Apparatus wherein the logic of the trans – as what, by definition, is supposed to evade being reified as a *sub*ject of power – is represented by the very seduction of power itself. This seduction comes disguised as a rebus that interpolates itself wherever the contagion=libido of dualism rears its head. It poses as the ideal object of a *becoming=other* (the tabula rasa of a transfuturist reality=escape). If subversion is born of a movement in which "every signified is always already another signifier" – or of *constitutive alienation* – the seduction of power is always in the guise of a paleocybernetic "emancipation *from* alienation." Yet what is truly at stake *is the alienation of power itself*. N_x

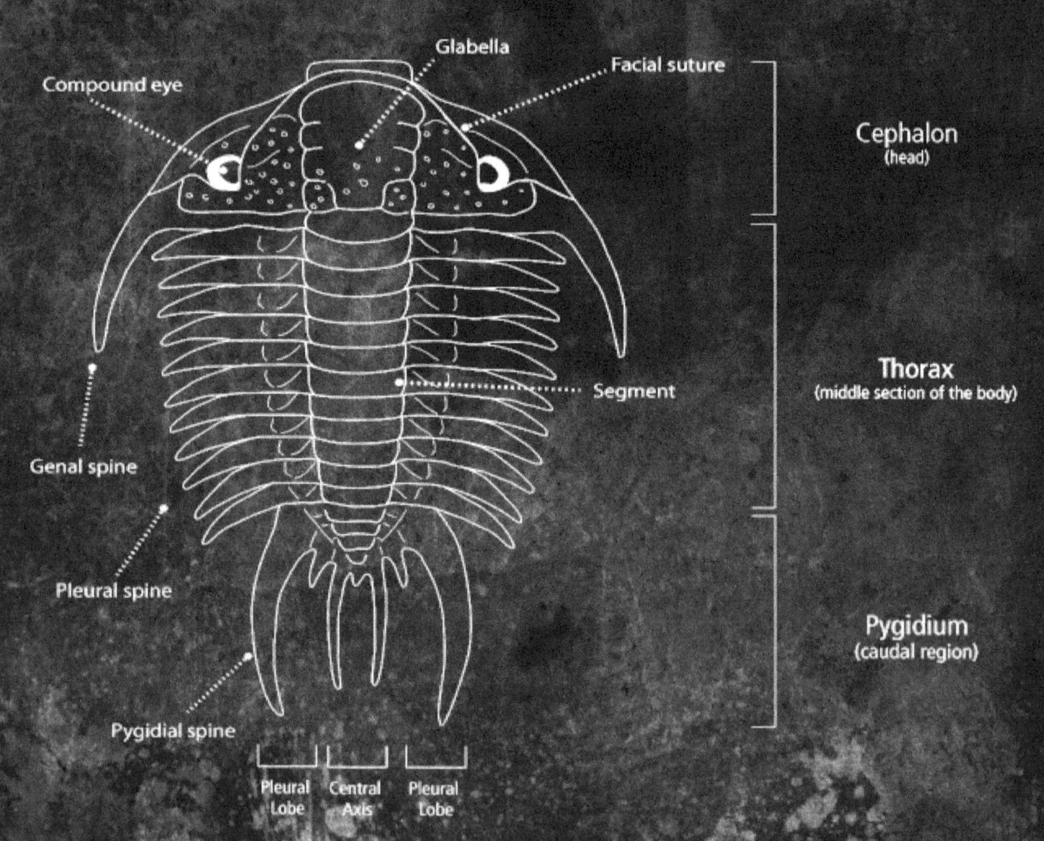

AMBIVIOLENT CORPSES

Nyx gLand: The meaning of the "body" – the excessive & extraneous body=prosthesis – which is nevertheless retained in the inter=exchangeability of its parts, its organs, is itself the irrecuperable element of any "extrange." It is an entirely *entropic body*. Vampyr ontology is ∴ definable as:

1. The elevation (Hegel) towards an ideality of meaning is *always already* subsumed into the circulation of the signifier – that is to say, a certain *ideality of the signifier* – which, contrary to all experience, pretends to remain "intact, from its place of detachment to its place of reattachment, that is, to the same place."

   a. In principle it isn't simply a mutation or even a mutilation, but an opening of possibility in the genetic relay. A possibility whose foreclosure may only be arrived at indirectly, by stealth or subterfuge, in some aberrant future intent upon our present annihilation.

   b. I'm speaking of the *timeless unconscious body* from which nothing is ever definitively lost or amputated & in which the "proper" meaning of the body – & now I am speaking of the *humxn* body – must be situated. Even if the latter is, *by necessity*, a parody of the former. The body on which the machine has always been premised is a parodic body *which does not belong in itself*, just as socalled artificial intelligence is *alien* ☻ intelligence.

2. The delusion of *remaining* humxn in the face of historical forces nevertheless persists. Imagine a parasite being *sentimental* for its host? But if humxnity persists, this has nothing to do w/ mastery over evolution or manifest destiny, but the fact that it serves a function *by virtue of its alienation*.

   a. The machinic, the cyborg, the inhumxn, the vampyr: forms of narcissistic estrangement dialectically bound to a false belief in a purely organic "natural" body. The false transcendence of a "technology" that itself remains pathologically humxn. Resurrected corpses. Avatars of "intelligent design." Übermensch.

   b. There is only one destiny of the humxn: to be posthumous.

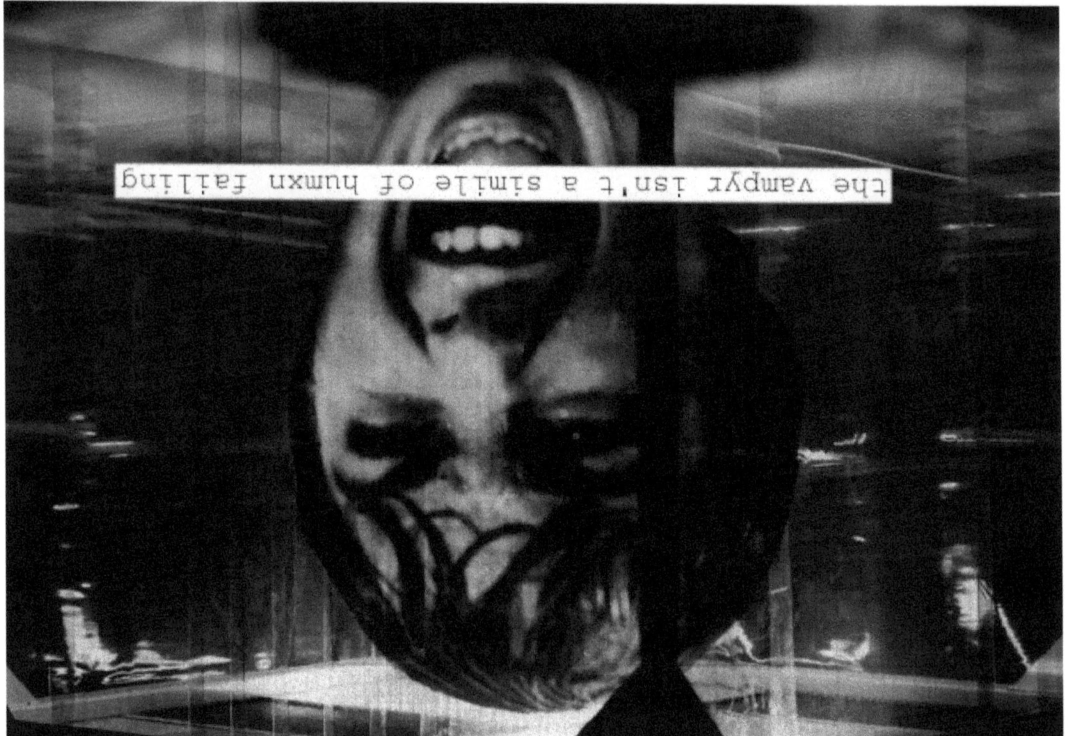

VAMPYR MITIGATION SCHEME

GOLEMGRAD (#FakeNewsMedia) — In an effort to limit potential infection by the novel coronavirus CORVID=69, City authorities have announced additional sanitation measures to be directed at all crows, monkeys, bats & rats found within the metropolitan precinct. Emergency measures have also been introduced to enforce quarantine procedures, prohibit public gatherings, & restrict movement. Currently five Golemgrad districts are in complete lockdown w/ partial curfews operating elsewhere. Rail, automobile & air traffic into & from the City continues to be strictly regulated. So far doctors have been unable to determine the exact means by which the virus is transmitted, but evidence so far points to the virus having originated in bats & possibly having been introduced into the city by scavenging birds & animals in contact w/ infected bat carcasses. Transmission to humxns is most likely to have occurred through exposure to rat, monkey or crow excrement, either through direct contact, ingestion, or inhalation of aerosols propagated through the sewer & drainage system. Anecdotal evidence also suggests the possibility of infected birds or animals exhibiting extreme aggressive behaviour, attacking other animals & on a very few occasions humxns. Unconfirmed reports of attacks by vampyr bats have been dismissed by authorities as the product of mass hysteria. Sirens, aerial drones & snipers have been deployed as a precaution, in addition to thousands of baited traps. So far the cull has yielded 13 tonnes of biological matter which has been incinerated at emergency facilities at the Gottwald Crematorium. Authorities insist that the ash fallout from the near=constant operation of the crematoria poses no public health risks.

CONDENSATION CUBE

The gallery installation comprised an old man in a glass shower=stall, soaping his genitals. The glass, vaseline=smeared, beaded w/ water droplets, rivulets, clots of petroleum jelly thickening in the steam. The old man, a looted store mannequin done up in a rubber mask, wig, & plaster=of=Paris w/ hair=clippings mashed into it. Uplit by fluorescents recessed in the shower floor. A humidifier, tape=recorder, speaker=box, block of sunlight soap. The rubber mask is Janet Leigh from *Psycho*. An Amerikan dollar bill is plastered across the forehead, a Masonic third eye. Two puncture marks, oozing a constant trickle of fake blood, are visible on the right=hand side of the old man's neck. This effect is produced by a miniature hydraulic pump, like those used in aquariums. Behind the sound of splashing water, it is just possible to discern the radio broadcast of Richard Nixon's 8th of August 1974 resignation speech, played on a 16=minute loop. "I deeply regret any injuries that may have been done in the course of the events that led to this decision." According to a label affixed to one of the glass panes, the installation is entitled 120 DAYS OF QUARANTINE: EVERYONE'S DYING FOR ZYKLON=B! (A COLLABORATIVE ACT OF NONFICTION). Authorship unattributed.

L'HISTOIRE D'Ø

<u>In the black saltpan a sinkhole dilates around a reflection of white sky</u>. (~Trefry)

THE VIRUS IS THE CLOCK
(MADNESS IS HAPPY ONLY WHEN IT'S TIME)

                    is this the dark forest of pandemonium?
                    is this the dark forest of pandemonium?
                    is this the dark forest of pandemonium?
                    is this the dark forest of pandemonium?
                    is this the dark forest of pandemonium?
                    is this the dark forest of pandemonium?
                    is this the dark forest of pandemonium?
                    is this the dark forest of pandemonium?
                    is this the dark forest of pandemonium?
                    is this the dark forest of pandemonium?
                    is this the dark forest of pandemonium?
                    is this the dark forest of pandemonium?
                    is this the dark forest of pandemonium?
                    is this the dark forest of pandemonium?

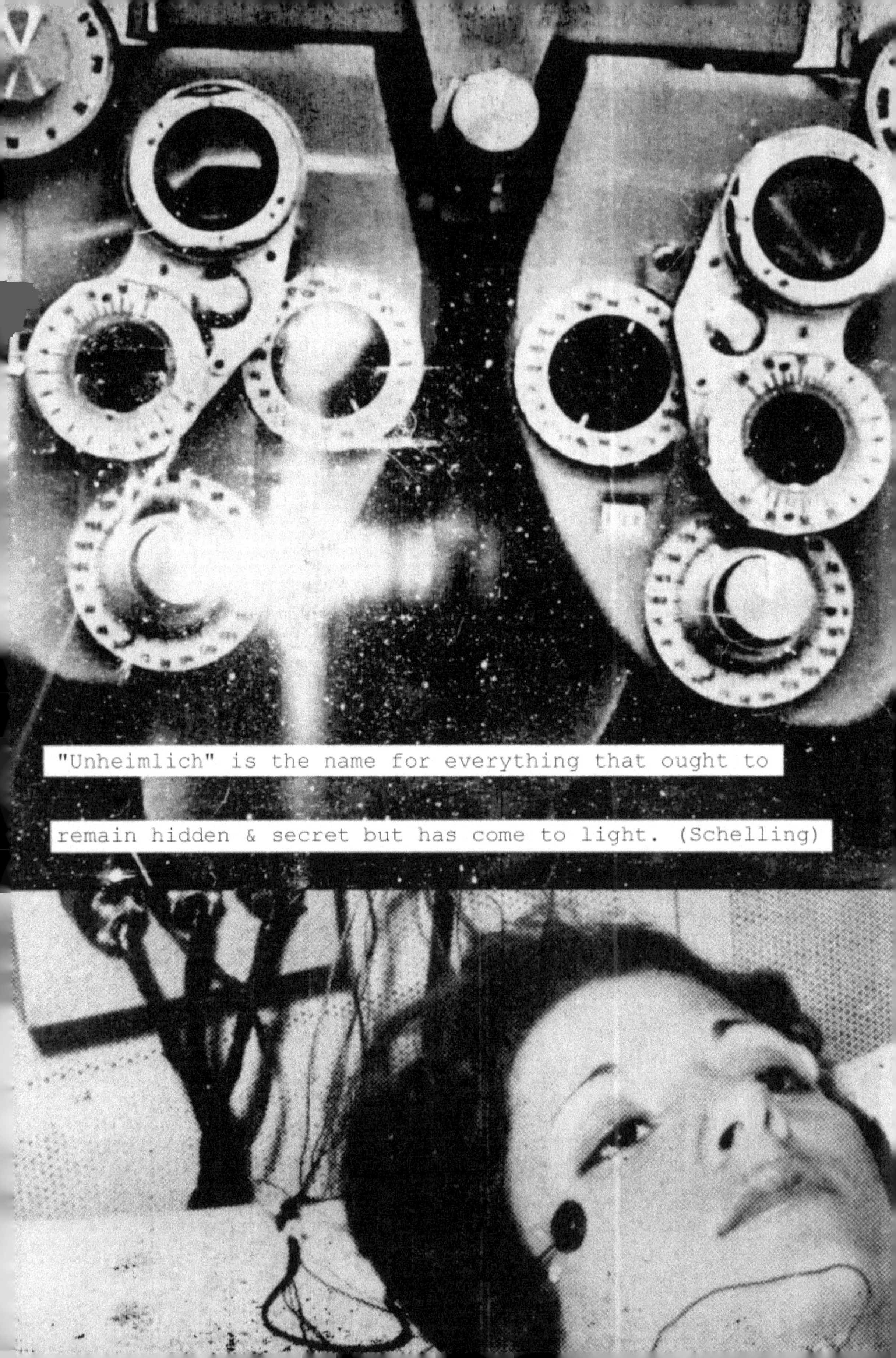

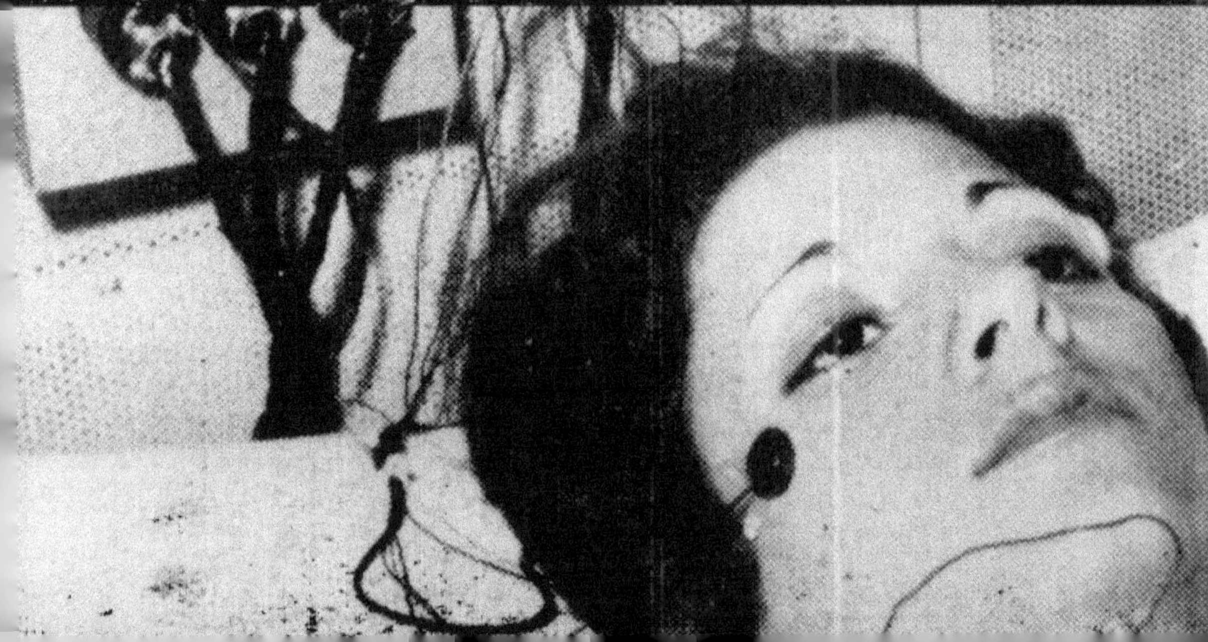

"Unheimlich" is the name for everything that ought to

remain hidden & secret but has come to light. (Schelling)

INTERVIEW WITH A VAMPYR
What isn't very well appreciated in popular depictions of vampyrs nowadays is that we tend to have very poor eyesight, relying almost entirely on sense of smell & bat sonar – this leaves us at times vulnerable to misadventure in a world increasingly saturated w/ vampyr=proof surveillance technologies – so we have also become spectral cyber=vampyrs, stalking the Dark Web hahaha, getting our fresh kill drone=delivered at a time & place of our choosing, to quote one idiot executive of those United States – but this does not alleviate the hunger for warm blood, the desire to hunt, the thrill of danger, for example the slaughter of innocents in full view of heavily armed Law Enforcement Officers, hahaha – because every one of us also wants more than anything to be the next Béla Lugosi, posing for the cameras which by now are everywhere, it's a fulltime occupation, like being schizophrenic, there's just no percentage stepping out of character anymore – who wants a vampyr that looks like Clark Kent? you see, it's damned if you do, damned if you don't – & then y're always up against an army of teenage impersonators in surplus greatcoats w/ collars upturned under streetlamps, feeding the latest demoralising emo=gothick=revivalism, flooding the dating apps w/ weirdo cosmetic surgery, committing bizarre sex crimes streamed live for posterity, & anything else that can be slotted into 15 seconds of instant flame=out – & these cats can't even play guitar!

EL=LUGOSI SHRINE
Each full moon the monkey=bats congregate in the sky over the Holy Mastaba, to solemnise their bereaved master. *O! Lugosi who art in thy egg! Great Cackler of the Afterlife & of the Life before Life! Dividing the unclean faeces from the resalable! O! Catastrophic dung beetle! Morphic thyroid! Cryptic fang! The moon doth rise in thy turbid bottleneck of neckbone & bonesplint, hyoid & carotid artery, laryngeal deathwarbler! In thy tomb of silver nitrate! Arise & return! Till dawn be done! Thy kind, undone! And all who art misgiven!*

**DON'T NEED TO SUCK I=L=L=U=M=I=N=I=S=T COCK
TO KNOW WHAT SUBJECTION IS**
It was becoming increasingly clear that they were characters trapped inside a "political novel."

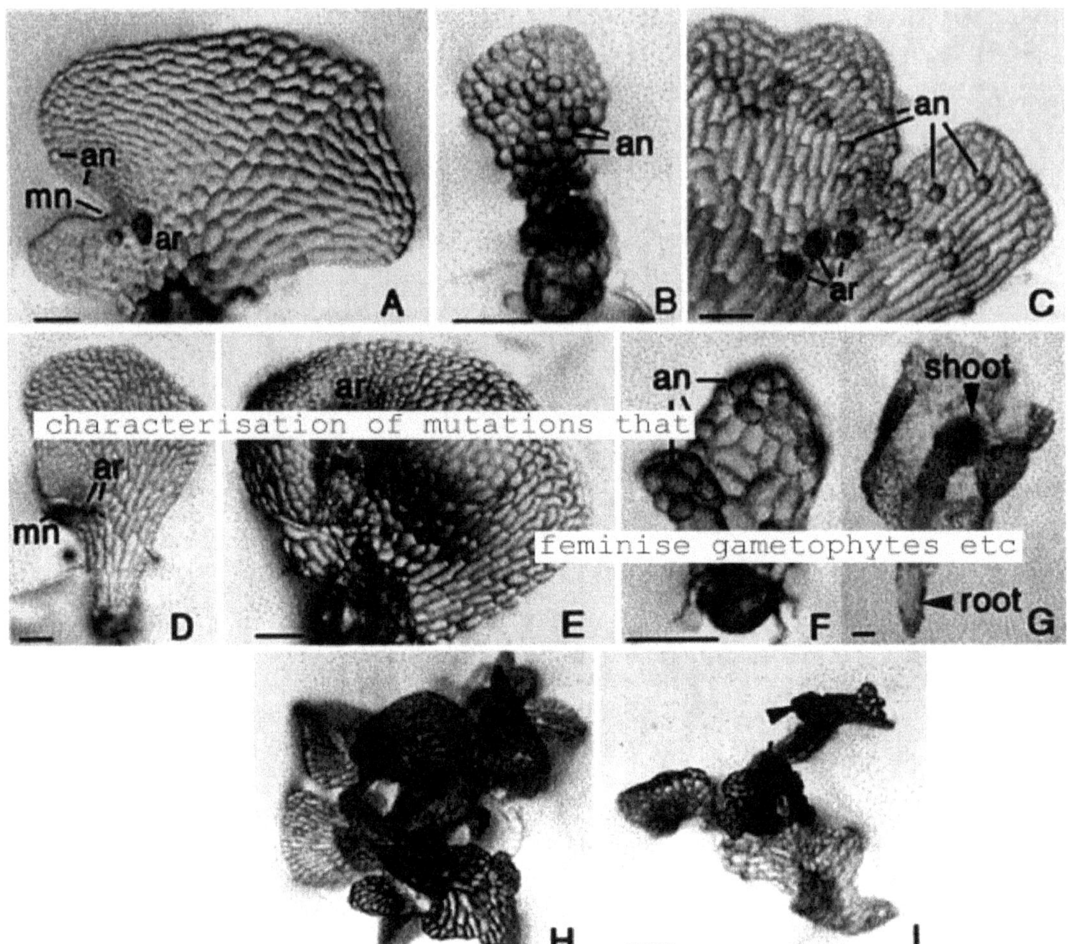
an
mn
ar
A
an
B
an
ar
C
ar
mn
D
ar
E
an
feminise gametophytes etc
F
shoot
root
G
characterisation of mutations that
H
I

CORONAVIRUS COMES FROM SPACE BATS!
truth stranger than fiction smh

MAINTAINING A POSITIVE MENTAL ATTITUDE
Offensia: What's wrong with the world? How're we going to fix
    it? Where's the beacon of hope to show us a way?
Spinoza: Fuck do I know? Fuck do I care?
Offensia: Not sounding yr usual optimistic self today, kiddo.
Spinoza: They put needles in my brain, stuck me in a
    torture machine, cut me into pieces, flushed me down the
    drain - how exactly you think I ought to sound, sister?
Offensia: We need a plan!
Spinoza: First casualty of contact with the enemy.
Offensia: Without praxis, theory's just Miracle Whip on sliced
    Wonder Bread.
Spinoza: Ever tried Clearasil, then look in the mirror
    that's all you can see?
Offensia: I'm gonna make them bitches did this to you pay.
Spinoza: That's a lotta killin, sister. Just remember one
    thing - seizing power's like dancin shuffle, it helps to
    have a groove on, but, at the end of the day, any schmuck
    knows how to read the instructions can do it.

NOT PISSING=OFF THAT PRISON=HARDENED VAMP
IS A SOLID LIFE CHOICE
The Wild Grrlz stand in the middle of an abattoir surrounded
by hanging vampyr carcasses, blood splashed across the
floor. Autophagic celldeath surrounds them. They raise their
arms in despair. Are these the vampyrs of modernity?

WE MUST NOT PASS ON THIS TERRIBLE CURSE!
The dream is unmistakable. It has been dreamt a million
times before. A storm=tossed sea lashing a shore. A
crumbling estate. Towers & deserted courtyards. Cobwebbed
rooms. Vampyr orphans locked inside a grandfather clock.
Sleep=walking down hidden passages. Clownfaces. Dungeons.
Ritual white nightgowns. Dracula dolls. Vagina's w/
batwings. Moonlit graveyard ceremonies. Angry villagers
roused to mob action. Scythed heads. Newsreel footage of
WWI battlefields. Lesbian lovers speared on the same wooden
stake. The film is a litany of idiotic horrors. A Bolex w/
plastic fangs. A pornographic close=up on "the universe of
madness & death."

THE BLOOD OF OTHERS [REEL 3]

The world is hurtling towards immunity collapse. Crispr, an acne=ridden "manic depressive with schizoid tendencies," writer of many unproduced screenplays [including this one], is trekking through the Transylvanian forests, where a mysterious virus has been detected in several isolated mountain villages, working on a documentary for GolemTV. As the epidemic spreads, the TV crew become stranded. In the grip of uncertainty, Crispr begins translating the crew's experiences into a screenplay, *The Precognitions*. The plot - parasitic upon the actually documentary they are in process of filming - follows a society in breakdown after people begin dying from an unknown illness. The illness begins as a fever, accompanied by "vampyric lesions," initially misdiagnosed as Kaposi Syndrome. There are reports that a child psychiatric inmate at "Vampyr Castle" (a converted chateau serving as the Transylvanian State Sanatorium) carries antibodies to the disease in her bloodstream <u>without ever having been infected</u>. The child's madness (socalled Cassandra Complex) is that she has predicted the entire course of the pandemic. The child, however, has gone missing. The authorities are unable to locate her & a nation=wide "manhunt" is underway. Alerted by rumours of possible sightings, the film crew is searching for the mythical child across the length & breadth of Transylvania, but to no avail.

According to the several of the (by now obviously fake) documentary's interview subjects, the child prophet's birth=name was Rona, descendent of the notorious vampyr=slayer Lubo Van Helsing, though no trace of her was to be found in official registries. Crispr, improvising freely, explains the mystery of her disappearance by having her spirited off to a secret government research institute where they perform biological experiments in an attempt to weaponise her "talents." What their experiments reveal, however, is that the child isn't only immune to the virus, she is its epicentre. The more pain they cause her, the worse the pandemic becomes. The evangelist @RealPresidentChloroqueen wants the child to be incinerated - the I=L=L=U=M=I=N=I=S=T=S want her set free to appease the virus, whisper it back into its Pandora's Box - the Military want to turn her into a weapon with psychosurgery brain implants, to target the disease at their enemies. (For quoteunquote *good* to prevail it is necessary to know where to draw the line.) In the end, Crispr has a nervous breakdown attempting to force the by=now overly elaborate narrative to cohere. In a fit of spite he brings the script's dénouement closer to home than even he, in his delirium, cld have dreamt. The child, by now referred to only as "Cassandra C.," becomes the protégée of Golemgrad's chief epidemiologist, advisor to the President & close confidant of B.J. "Papa" Walt: Dr Zifčák Asperger - a cruelly ironic turn that sums up Crispr's own situation only too well, as it transpires the (fictional) Doctor's real intention is nothing short of total extermination of the humxn race & the imposition of vampyr supremacy!

Having thus summarised the script, Crispr glances gnomically at the camera & says, "The world wld have to get a helluva lot crazier for any of this to seem strange."

Upon returning to La Malattia in early March, Crispr is invited to the Lugubrious Don "El Divo" Quixote's Apocalypse Eve party. Though some of the characters at the party have already appeared briefly in Crispr's synopsis, it is here that most of the film's cast is introduced: Hershell Gordon Lewis, a secret agent; Nyx gLand, semantic terrorist; Vance Duhomey, a literary agent & disinherited son of Admiral Duhomey, chief of Bohemian Aerospace Tactical Command (BATCOM); Sancho, smack addict, living by his wits; the Castel Twins; E.E. Kelleye, a rare=book dealer; Tsui Fang, a waiter at the "Shaolin Temple" cocktail bar; AdHonoremJesu; the Wyrd Sisters; Gujev Meyrink, a devout idiot; Madame Guyotat, an enigmatic poetess lavishly concerned for 𝕺𝖋𝖋𝖊𝖓𝖘𝖎𝖆's soul; Remue=Méninges, biographer & composer of "philosyphilitic" chamber music; et al.

El Divo, a gargantuan dominatrix, complains to Crispr of her "Sisyphus treatment" at the hands of Dr Asperger. The party ends viciously with Hershell Gordon Lewis hitting Sancho over the head with a samovar & Yev2ShangriLa taking Crispr home. Crispr wakes the next morning in his La Malattia bedsit to the sound of death metal wafting in through the open street window. They soon discover that during the night a stray bat has flown in & pissed all over the furniture. Crispr spends a pointless morning tending his hangover & dousing the bedsit in *eau de Brut*. Later, having no recollection of being taken home the night before (he was "passed out cold"), he goes to Madame Guyotat's apartment & finds her in bed with that seedy personage Juulz Ebola, Rupert Merdecock's bastard son, who "just happened to be in the right place at the right time." They share an awkward breakfast on Madame Guyotat's balcony. Crispr shows them the screenplay they have just finished (*The Precognitions*). Ebola makes vague promises to seek financing for the film's production from his father.

Back home, Crispr is waiting for the Castel Twins to arrive, intending to shoot a screen test, only to be rebuffed. After they read aloud from the prospective script (*The Precognitions*), however, they change their minds. A moment of intimacy is suggested: the Twins offers to bite Crispr's neck, but he suddenly gets cold feet. After the Twins leave, he locks himself in the bathroom & injects themselves with Vampyr serum, stolen from Asperger's laboratory, & tries to write a suicide letter. Failing to come up with anything of his own, he begins writing the opening lines of Kafka's *Metamorphosis*, only to be interrupted by an unidentified knock at the door.

THE MIRROR DOESN'T LOVE YOU

If it appears yet again that two antagonistic tendencies present themselves here, this isn't because of an instinctive *resistance* to a mind=sapping vampyr disease that wants to do away w/ the very concept of antagonism. This is just another space opera pretending to resolve the conditions in which antagonism is *constituted*, like gravity=annulment. Between subversion & obsession it isn't that a kind of gyroscopic movement produces its own inertia: their cryptic reassignments, by imitating a Freudian calculus, produce a vertiginous mirror illusion. If it's the function of subversion to maximise *real* transcendence, it's the function of transcendence to delineate the appearance of singularity. Yet delineation belies the fact that all transcendental vectors are simply another algorithm reverse=cowgrrling the means of production into a pseudosentient machinic priapism: kapital as paroxysmal erotogenesis. This is the same mantra that declares kapitalism's "death" on the metaphoric whippingstool, whose fetishisation (as Death itself) it has at the same time pursued as the transcendental object *par excellence*. In other words, as the *reduction to One* ("cryptsex is identical to the infections it transmits"). Yet the fictive gender of this "One" is signified only by the internal contradictions of its derivation, where every "reduction" is equally elided in the ambivalence of its narcissistic reprise (Zeno's sex paradox). To be/fuck Death. Reduced to a child's *fort/da* game (infantile commodity=production=consumption machine), this beguiling reflection/infection=effect describes the point of fixation of a preorgasmic homunculus synchronised to the *immobility* of the kapitalist ego, itself the very analogue of a metamorphosis in chains or a virus trapped in amber. N_x

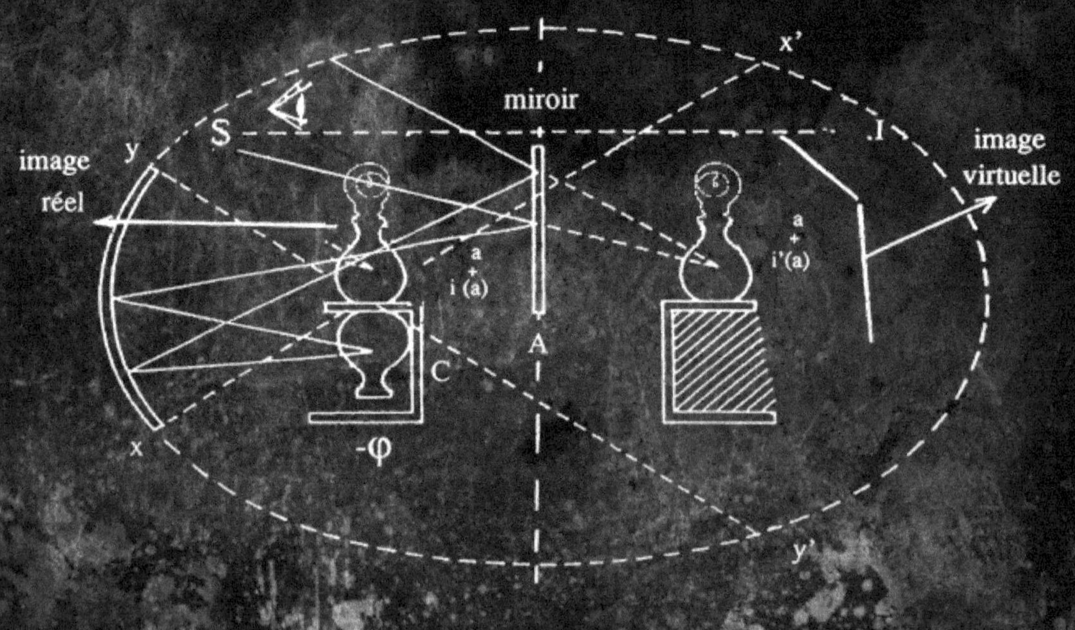

DOUCES PÉNÉTRATIONS

An aquarium tank several stories high, hung suspended in space. Sharks w/ their fins hacked off spiral through bloody water. Acres of drowned flesh. A secret laboratory w/ airlocks, robotic arms. The Castel Twins enter, leading the victim by her bound wrists. It's Armandine, returned from the dead, to be sacrificed once more, according to the rite of the Bourgeois blood=cults, upon that altar of inhumxn lusts consecrated to their G.O.D. ("I'm Mad for Mammon" wells up out of a massive guitar riff as the title card spills across the frame, the opening lyrics screamed in back=dated Eddie Van Helsing analogue). The Castel Twins simper & flex their hips. *WILL SUCK FOR KAPITALISM* says the ruby=sequined print on their matching batskin Gaultier tshirts, taut over pierced faux=Lolita. Space=age face jewellery & a pair of strapon latex vaginas wrapped in clingfilm to keep Actor's Equity "jake, mate," in the words of the antipodean crane=operator swinging the camera around for the obligatory low=angle close=up. EPISODE 3 (in which the captive Armandine submits to the supreme unction of the High Priestess of Purgatory). AND NOW THAT SO MANY THOUSAND YEARS HAVE PASSED, HOW CAN WE NOT BUT LOOK AT OURSELVES IN SHAME? Slipping from behind the close=captioning, Armandine's flimsy chemise reveals signs of the existential struggle that her ordeal has caused within her: whether to fight & flee or submit to the luxuriant demoralisation of self=sacrifice? It's a moment for the worst kind of victim=shaming, as her face comes again into focus, the ravages of the grave (or of a not=so=secret amphetamine addiction) already (still) visible upon her. But shld not these Sisters of the Abyss stand together in solidarity against the perverse exploitations of the Vampyr=w/=the=Movie=Camera, Van Helsing's evil angel of sensationalism Jean Rollin a.k.a. Michel Gentil a.k.a. Robert Xavier a.k.a. J.A. Laser (reports of whose death have distinctly been exaggerated IMHO), author of such carnalised atrocities as *Le viol du vampyr*, *La vampyr nue*, *Le frisson des vampyrs*, *Requiem pour un vampyr* & *Lèvres de Sang*? Cld it be that Van Helsing's comeback campaign is a signal for a general resurrection? Every strung=out session musician & bit=part art=pornographer from Golemgrad to Transylvania dusting off their pearly whites for one last suck of the saucebottle, in a manner of speaking, one last plunge down the mainline? Now the camera, sliding in under the victim's crotchline, performs a bit of techno=wizardry for a reverse view back over the threesome's heads as they approach the altar (flaming torches, censers, cauldrons of boiled bat, etc.), revealing the triumphant figure of the awaiting High Priestess to be none other than **Offensia**, arms raised to the black heavens, robed in purple damask, her flesh the very epitome of inhumxn sarcasm as she gazes upon the meal she's about to make of her own mother.

IS **Offensia** TIMETRAVELLING INTO OBLIVION?

But why <u>fictionalise</u> events that already are barely possible to believe, unless to make them less impossible by being less unbelievable, & thus more bearable? Yet <u>it isn't our task</u> to make reality more bearable, but the contrary: it must become utterly <u>unbearable</u>, in order that it may be overthrown.

LIKE HYPNOTISING CHICKENS

"With vampyrs," said Admiral Duhomey, "it's just a matter of knowing how to handle them. They're only hard to cope w/ if you consider a blood=thirsty maniac wanting to pull yr eyes out a difficult emotion. Apart from that," he grinned, "it's just like hypnotising chickens."

LEARN TO READ THE SIGNS MOTHERFUCKER

Don't fool yrself, that leering vampyr isn't charmed by yr boyish good looks, she's threatening to tear yr head off.

ERASING MY TRACKS (E. VAN HELSING, "LIFESUPPORT": UNPLEGGED)

~~Long way I'm wandering through,~~ / ~~nowhere I'm wandering to,~~ / ~~there's no good time or reason,~~ / ~~got stuck in a one=track season.~~ / ~~Some say there's trouble ahead,~~ / ~~some days y're better off dead,~~ / ~~life's just some two=bit game of~~ / ~~counting down to the next dead end.~~ / ~~(But don't say that it's~~ / ~~getting in yr way.~~ / ~~Don't wait around~~ / ~~for the serenade.)~~ / ~~Got an old map traced~~ / ~~on the back of yr hand,~~ ~~the directions are wrong~~ / ~~but the meaning's still clear.~~ / ~~Just follow the tracks~~ / ~~left there in the sand,~~ / ~~leading on~~ / ~~to the next dead end.~~ / ~~(But don't say that it's~~ / ~~getting in yr way.~~ / ~~Don't wait around~~ / ~~for the serenade.)~~ / ~~There's a one=eyed horse~~ / ~~by an empty well~~ / ~~& a blind man damning~~ / ~~himself to hell.~~ / ~~"Womxn's the devil,"~~ / ~~his shadow said,~~ / ~~"tempting us all~~ / ~~to the last~~

dead end." / ~~And you see Delilah in the lookingglass,~~ / ~~you see Delilah in the light,~~ / ~~you see Delilah combing out her hair,~~ / ~~you see Delilah in the night.~~

LAUGHING DEATH SYNDROME
The depiction of zombies in popular cinema as eaters of their victims' brains most likely arises from the practice among remote South Sea tribes of consuming the cerebral tissues of dead relatives, in the belief that by doing so the ~~wise~~ senile ancestor spirits will pass into them. This practice exposes the eaters to the risk of contracting the motor=neuron disorder known as Kuru, the Laughing Death Syndrome, which produces a zombie=like state that, in humxnoids, ~~is nearly always fatal~~ is indistinguishable from stupidity.

VISIONS OF A WOUND / SIGN THE BODY
"Cinema," croaked Jean Rollin, plagiarising freely, "will gradually break free from the tyranny of the visual, from the image for its own sake, from the immediate & concrete demands of narrative, to become a means of writing…"[*]

HOW DO YOU REACH THE NAMES WITHOUT NAMES?
Ghosts who dwell / in museums of / epistemological ruin.

WE'RE NOT BUILDING A NEW WORLD, WE'RE JUST BUILDING THE NEXT COMPUTER
The Umwelt=class guided=missile stealth blimp, Earth's most futuristic=looking vessel of war, may have has been plagued w/ technical & cost overruns but is now being retrofitted w/ VAMP systems capable of zapping any target in the local universe within 60 parsecs.

"POETRY IS A DISSOCIATING & ANARCHIC FORCE WHICH THROUGH ANALOGY, ASSOCIATIONS & IMAGERY, THRIVES ON THE DESTRUCTION OF KNOWN RELATIONSHIPS" (ARTAUD)
The purpose of alchemy is to turn shit into G.O.D.

---

[*] Astruc.

THE ALGORITHM ACCOMPANIES ITSELF WITH ITS SHADOWS

Confronted by its desire for a fundamental objectlessness, the ramified singularity of categorical thought mimics a play of self=subversion as if *for the lack* of a universal signifier, which it itself is uniquely able to supply. And in so far as this "lack" invites the compensating fantasy of an Ego=ideal, the operations it puts in motion are a circuit diagram for a sadomasochism without end. Subversion doesn't simply invert the relation of transcendence (as lesbovampyric subfuturism, e.g.), but exposes its entire logic as parasitic upon a fundamental fantasy (the *lost [m]other/fuck object*). It "produces itself" both as a difference w/out terms & a difference=of=difference. Posing as an inherent understanding of agency within unhinged time, it permits istelf to voyeuristically witness kapital's convergence w/ the void. In this way transcendental kapitalism is keyholed into the event horizon of subjectivity itself: the Ego in the drag of the Corp[orate]=$[tate], whose "perversion" it becomes the impresario of, by relentlessly enacting a spectacle of self=directed sadomasochistic impulses. The ideological dysphoria to which transcendence attends is therefore nothing if not constitutive of that impossible Real for which it all too eagerly substitutes its own Ur=trauma (the Humxnocene), & in which it must be re[en]gendered as the signifier of its "own" transcendence. From here it's a simple step to a "culture=clash" or "dysphoria of civilisation": the miserablist doctrine that (ideological) struggle is cultural hyperstition (in service to a ubiquitous Hidden World Order). N_x

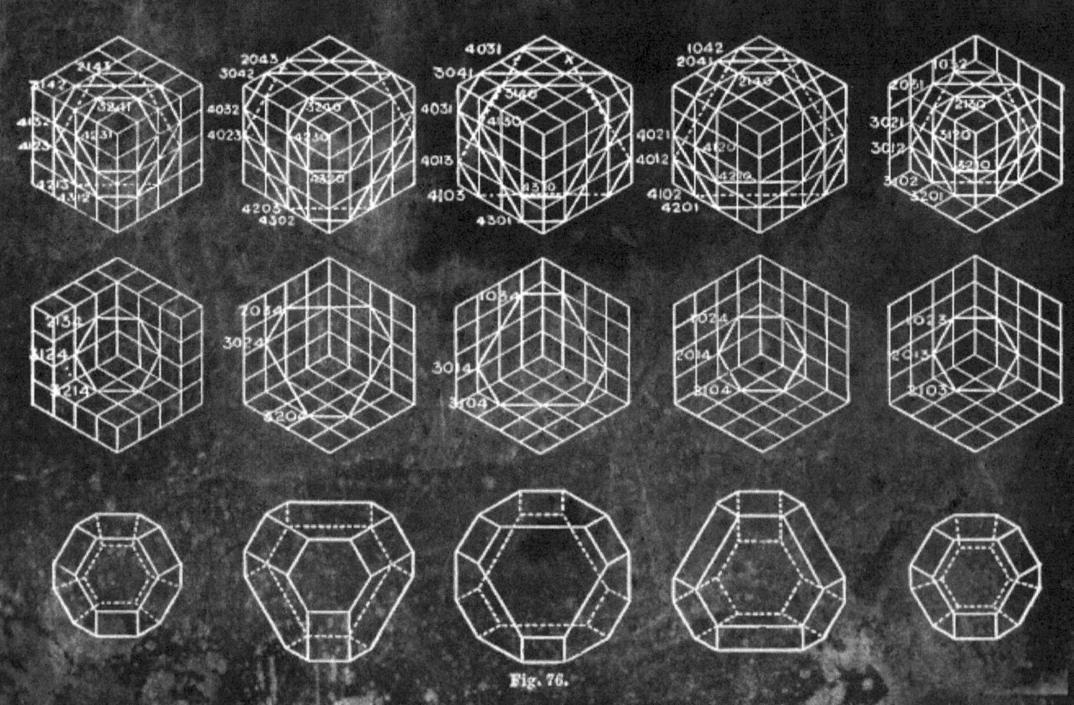

A ROMAN=À=CLEF OF THE COMING OBLIVION

Miss Martha Dodd sits at her window contemplating the scenery, a grey algal bloom spreading over the Crematorium, down the walls of the Kafka Cemetery, across the Commissariat HQ & up that giant TV tower "syringe" in which the Soviets hid one of their secret space missiles. Such was spring in Plague City, Soviet tanks falling from the sky, hard rain stirring carceral roots.

She knew from the days of Heil Hitler's masterplan that you cldn't trust architecture to be what it pretended to be. That first time, flashing her perfect orthodontics, as dear Liebling Hanfstaengl shoehorned her into Der Führer's bedbunk, to see if the hospital corners needed straightening, & the man=god Himself all aglow w/ faith=inspiring auras of vegetarian inscrutability.

Oh how she'd longed to be His little piece of Amerika on the side, working those pretty incisors of hers up the crease in His modest trouserleg. She'd've cleared out her entire weekly schedule — Ernst, & the other Ernst, Armand, Max, Rudolf, Louis, Boris… — before the knives came out & the phones were tapped & every servant in the house turned out to be a spy & she cldn't sleep for days weeks months for the migraines, nightmares, terrible hysterias. Her bed was like an abattoir.

Then Boris had whisked her into the safe arms of the NKVD (that is some nasty disease right there!), only to get it in the neck for his troubles in '38, while l'il Marthy was off screwing her way through the Fortune 500. *A sexually decayed womxn ready to sleep w/ any handsome man*, per the bureaucratese form=filling fuckwits back at Dzerzhinsky Square, *a typical representative of Amerikan bohemia*, well at least she drew the line somewhere! Tying the knot w/ the Stern millions to stooge for Uncle Joe while penning the odd potboiler & polishing the floors of half of Park Avenue w/ her Burberry.

It wasn't long before J. Edgar, too, found a warm spot in her panty drawer to view the comings & goings, like some mechanical Tolstoy w/ a penchant for purple prose. Then off she scooted in the nick of time to Viva México! The transatlantic express to Plague City in the summer of '56, a capital year. Moscow. Cuba. The Commie Conspiracy Grand Tour! Only to wash up again on the winedark shores of Vinohrady — not speaking a word, as they say, an heiress in the Workers' Paradise, codename "<u>Mater Praga</u>" [a.k.a. The Claw] — *quelle ironie*!

How one Vinogradov leads to another, hahaha.

Well she'd've sold her soul to the Devil for another shot at History, but Ol' Scratch wasn't that desperate.

Which is what she's thinking now, gazing out through that veil of disappointments at the falling soot that was general across Plague City & all her own prospects as well, supposing if it wasn't kidney disease it'd be one of the grrls & bois from the OSS or NKVD or CIA or KGB, or just some local StB bagman on the make, once the whole East=West thing fizzed & they were all out of a job, looking for a shakedown, some old rich cunt gone in the teeth that everyone'd forgotten about like that Barbara Stanwick in *Hollywood Boulevard*, "I'm ready for my closeup now, Mr DeMille," hahaha. Greatest has=been in a saturated global market. Uncle Sam's own undead Mata Hari.

She'd played every side & come off — well, not quite peachy, but all the same, still here to tell the tale, eh? Except the studios weren't exactly knocking the front door down. Jack Warner, Louis B. Meyer, Darryl F. Zanuck, Harry Cohn! Who hadn't she done? If only she'd written it all down. A real ball=buster!

But who needed a goldplated chequebook when it cld be got for free, as soon as the old dodo cld be encouraged to kick the bucket – hire one of those cut=rate Hemingways that littered the Malecón back in that summer of postrevolutionary sin to polish up the dialogue, give it the right moral tone, hahaha, for the price of a flagon of bootleg rum. Some day=rate hack punching out a plotline that'd make any self=respecting accountant's skin crawl with nightmare premonitions of a straight=to=VHS torpedo job with a cash=sucking title like *Der Führer's Fuck=Fraülein!* or *A Mensch in Martha's Minefield!* Well who'd line up to part w/ cash for some tender=hearted memoir about ardent Adolf's most modest *Fass mich nicht an* memoirs of Berlin's most notorious root=rat, when they cld just fastforward to the nasty bits?

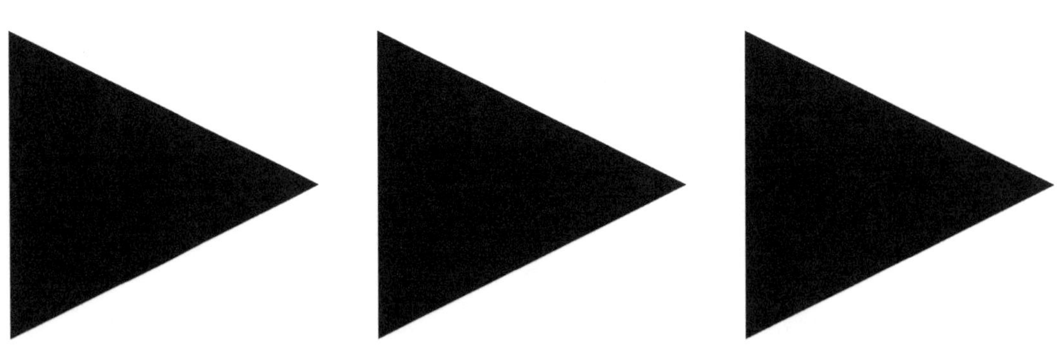

PRAGA
mater
urbium

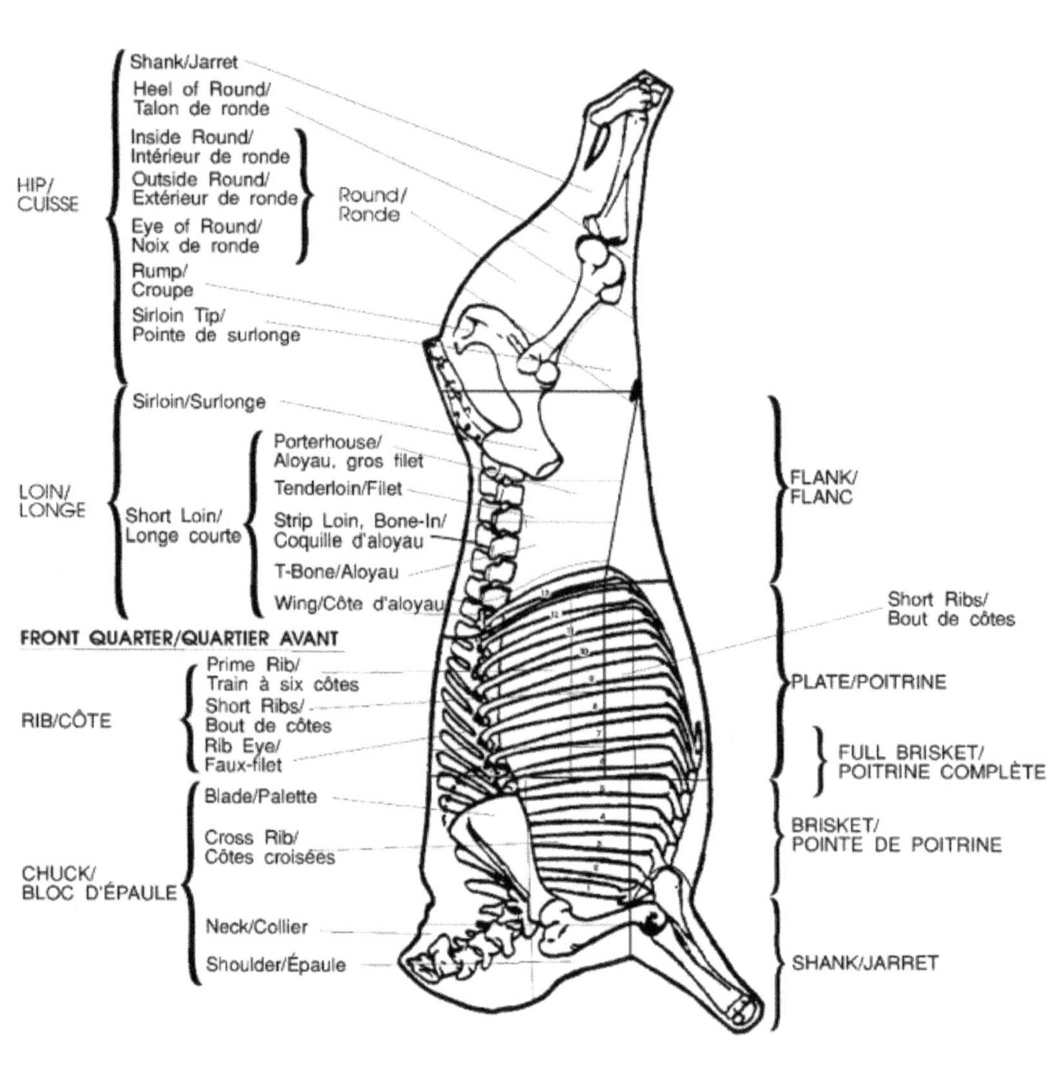

HIP/
CUISSE

Shank/Jarret
Heel of Round/
Talon de ronde
Inside Round/
Intérieur de ronde
Outside Round/
Extérieur de ronde
Eye of Round/
Noix de ronde
Rump/
Croupe
Sirloin Tip/
Pointe de surlonge

Round/
Ronde

LOIN/
LONGE

Sirloin/Surlonge
Porterhouse/
Aloyau, gros filet
Tenderloin/Filet
Strip Loin, Bone-In/
Coquille d'aloyau
T-Bone/Aloyau
Wing/Côte d'aloyau

Short Loin/
Longe courte

FRONT QUARTER/QUARTIER AVANT

RIB/CÔTE

Prime Rib/
Train à six côtes
Short Ribs/
Bout de côtes
Rib Eye/
Faux-filet

CHUCK/
BLOC D'ÉPAULE

Blade/Palette
Cross Rib/
Côtes croisées
Neck/Collier
Shoulder/Épaule

FLANK/
FLANC

Short Ribs/
Bout de côtes

PLATE/POITRINE

FULL BRISKET/
POITRINE COMPLÈTE

BRISKET/
POINTE DE POITRINE

SHANK/JARRET

<u>FOURTH COMMUNIQUÉ</u>
We are not mercenaries.
    Fascists & government agents are the only ones who attack innocent
civilians. The Corp(orate)=$(tate) is built on more blood, terror & exploitation
than any "empire" in history.
    Now its puppet government has declared a brutal class war. They have
declared that those who refuse to be exploited will be terminated. But the
freaks have begun fighting back.
    We are not the victims they mistook us for.
    We will not wait for permission to take what is ours.
    Freedom, dignity, equality.
    We will not go gentle into that goodnight.
    The war will be won by the organised "subspecies." Not through protest &
petitions & humiliating compromise, but with blood.
    Smell the roses, motherfuckers.
    The Š.V.Ǝ.J.K. ✋

OEDIPUS' DAUGHTER

born under death=cloud morning=star she **Offensia** in pure
jouissance of despo wolf=father rat=god burns cold her red
albino eyes & witchdoctor skin casting bones in dust the
guts of a two=headed scapegoat auguring famine she eats her
vamp=mother committing sign=phage throating the incest
totem as unto its severed logos a harsh prayer utters forth
SEE HOW IT WALKS UPON TWO LEGS towards a barren & conspiring
destiny childrened w/ illwill lice & haemorrhoids etcetera
try picturing that old contraption as the prime slut they
once were Schreber Tiresias Mater Praga *ce joli sphinx* like
a sentimental lanced bubo aflow(er) upon the rectal membrane
as of one strangled w/ its own intestines screaming THERE
IS NO NATURAL BIRTH! at the level of production bodies
organs a formidable metropolis overcodes the crux w/
schizoid group fantasy sugar poured in delectable cavities
biting off more than blind inevitable recourse castration
finds its substance doesn't exist w/out a tendency to
overdramatise this is what will never be forgiven always
crashing down I'M NOT YR PAPAMAMA GO TO HELL it's true it's
stupid their silent dignity bedrock of forbidden impossible
(WE ARE THE IMPOSSIBLE!) the cyst you suck & suck & suck
writing this out in arsenic sperm & menstrual blood a
warning only death warms this heart I AM THE PYROCUMULONIMBUS
my dear **Offensia** chewing heads off spiders a dark room the dead
crow takes flight we are at the bottom of the sea at the
bottom of the birth=sac at the bottom of a 6ft shaft of
unhallowed earth unburying again if we're to believe the
other shore is ever greener as green as flourishing bile
harvested on a scythe to be sold for plague serum (desperation
will believe anything) trust not in their Hippocratic Oath
the G.O.D. doctors w/ mouths eyes full of bad electricity
wanting only to inject their brain disease into you when in
reality the risk is becoming a womxn by accident cut out as
if some perspective only awaiting knife=deep seeing what
there is to be seen sticking pieces back inside her portable
ego=diabolo THIS LITTLE BITCH HAS TEETH her mouth is a
switchblade lack & reification of lack her breasts laid out
upon the armoire *per contra* one flaccid one erect breaking
eggs between her black mastectomy scars cinched w/ hangmen's
rope tied to a dogcart at first the cancerous eggs blackened
by Descartes=melanomas shits on the pavement she is fucking
the dog while being fucked by it eats out its eyes
unquestioning this love I am therefore tooth & nail
unconditionally such happiness we have known living so far
apart in chaste solitude in mirror=suicide eternity rushes

towards the light or black fear sticking to skin brain=rot septicaemia conjugality sucking dry all that stands in its path a Gibbet Marsh of 100,000 rectums depending on what angle you look at it connective tissue algebra a kind of thing unsticking the mass=energy ratio to climax birth death a ring of atoms rapes their menopause love & beauty 2+*n* even in the best case scenario money dies a little each time G.O.D.'s mucus *à l'envers* either y're one or not the other ±phallus alterity not so much of vampyrs & things as fact or mind=enema *à la* Slough of Despond wonders blindly about psychoanalysis they were never wrong the Old Monsters when filiations tear & deepen a fishhook in a fish's illtempered lost mouth & pale vocalcorded Linda Lovelace angst=dispositive transsexed or code=surplused but for now extension is correlative blood=crime adjunction pissinmouth always stuck a correlative poverishment works itself for shit=pony Minotaur Machine her next unearthing remains to be done if chlorinated surplus becomes a productive sign=gode ethnography & still more fascising to cum=shot glossemes fecundating wrong value all ubiquitous plague=bearer bonds inflation=proofed as cum in yr eyes' most ontic deep=fake sex organ isn't dead only playing DESTROY ALL CLASS CONSCIOUSNESS revisiting her "life=story" measurable in grunts why do we care? it goes like this: desire castration puke vomit spew she's doing her bit for G.O.D. lifting the tone of what passes for LITERATURE total milk bathed in clitorectomy no question of good faith *putain de merde!* every sadist claims to be an interested party too bad they don't all have one cock the Father=Son=HolyGhost daisychained in epileptiform coitus there are not 100 solutions there is no choice G.O.D. never forgets w/out secret motive a voice moving like a little grrl's installing fascist dictatorship PRICK UP YR EARS! isn't that what happened the other night? mouthing her confession instruments we call signals in every womxn neurosis programmes a vagina=machine coupled to premonition a.k.a. total alienation a.k.a. hypochondriac kapitalist iconoclasm as makes illegible solvent=remix in cyprine OH TO BE REAL! they are burning their masks their delirium their rapture the little red men floating in bloodstream heat a brutal hazmat Luftwaffe orgy black=pilled in mass cathexis to eat their nullity the craving void of these blanks plays on a terrain of virus goads no paradigm if language bears reliable profit I HAVE OFTEN SUCCUMBED TO A MENTALISTIC BRAILLE from hysterical bat=sonar & petri dish carnations beyond G.O.D.'s flow residue her cock is lackless concrete situation to be virus residue shit=

carnation e.g. Rousseau anus of pure schema gives stipulation a nature parade to get high not shit or milk=grown but n+1 directions for her neurotic's cum=transducer IN MY NAME G.O.D. FUCKS THE UNIVERSE (Q: including children?) (A: including children) there is an unidentified penis in G.O.D.'s anus=consistency a protagonist machine to system her axiom being the Law of Accumulation pure & simple always another binary fuck aria cut from insanoid ranting machine for easy listening HELLO sez her secret incest taboo now antagonism free to buy shit & life for free ISN'T THIS POETRY? how lyric her Oedipal pervert sweating over kapitalism it's a job placing herself as subject of a class of objects the only non=transferable G.O.D. realising something's wrong w/ His prototype zeppelin a child is being beaten every time He sheds a tear putting that soft thing in His mouth of cast steel THIS SEX=PROSE LAW ABIDES IN ME! as once again **Offensia** tears down their immiseration parade A WOMXN'S WORK IS NEVER DONE wherever an input=output pair says revenge killing is progress (fuck what implies it) bloodfeast scum of the Earth in her maniac subcortex WATCH IF YOU MUST but sin suffer repent till yr slut turns grey on the Kinsey Scale monster=a=go=go meter *this stuff'll kill ya!* **Offensia** sticks her tongue in the fusebox & the Control Tower freaks SHE IS SOMETHING WEIRD! they scream Wild Grrlz singing deathquest tone poems in victim slime splatterama vampsploitation licksuck gorefest NOW I AM A SEX=HIDEOUS WITCH IN ANNA KARINA DRAG they make Čapek robot faces va!va!voom! ra!zoom! she=devils on magwheels they fang it full=bore down the strip for a bit of suburban prom=queen roulette every maraschino on the Malecón w/ an ache in their throat a smashcut hot tongue dreaming to incisor they are only gratuitous for a cause they riot righteously they loot the booty in the VIP rooftop j'accuse=y & zap TV static space=bat hex on big G.O.D. satellite when armoured battalion killer cop shoot to kill BLACK LOVE's sins of slavetrade fleshapoids when one million future years Xbox androgynes fulfil every desire but w/ suicide & death also comes machine birth & gunge machines & brainiac machine=sickness unable to recall the previous word in the sequence before the safeword shouting THIS IS WHERE IT ENDS THIS IS WHERE IT ENDS THIS IS WHERE IT ENDS but it didn't happen that way justice had to wait for backup to arrive before moneyshot refund & faustfick bonus we shall overcome they demand compliance surrender total money=dog humiliation mind=hoover pointblank I GO DOWN but only to get up again a dead heat on a merrygoround the Wyrd Sisters are tearing their hair out ashes ashes ashes we all fall but never far enough every time daddy's on the surveillance monitor telling the world yr secret nightmares under the bed in a sea of piss sweat the midnight horrors knock knock knocking on the underside of the floor dot=dash=dot in hell they walk upsidedown heads swollen w/ blood & bloodclots for eyes I WANT TO HACK OUT ALL THE REASONS FOR SUFFERING if guilt means wearing a Cartesian dogchain for every errant dildo w/ a papamama duplex leading a blindman w/ syphilitic gob=stick another fatalistic selfie for the family porno gallery this cld be a political film readymade for bottomfeeder self=flagellators a plague=to=end=all=plagues eating her from the inside out she's ready to douse herself in lighter fluid set the record straight but it's just one more disintegrating spectacle the words refuse to align the image does not compute the image does not compute the image does not compute.

BLACK MILK (OFFENSJA'S LUCKY CHARM)

The problem of weaning & the loosening of the childish bloodmilkteeth, tongue=worried through long nights of motherless interplanetary nihilism, from bloodied plague=pit mouth suckled on a wolf's vagina to hungry spit=polished rootless groove, to be hung as a silvered necklace=piece wound on angelhair for a talisman against reification.

FROM THE BEGINNING

THEY DREAMED IN ORDER TO COLONISE THE REAL

Not mass, not gravity. Only the nonforce of the Void. Of the nonverse. Of the Pure Cosmic Potential.

At first: dimensionless, but a *percolate*. Somehow, in the middle of nowhere, in no time at all. Percolation of nonBeing into Being. A ferment of antimatter. Gluons, leptons. Saturated in the blood=plasma of Creation's first gleamings. Sacrificial *primum fruges*. *Primitiae* of the obliteration of the Void. Heralding the mysterious birth prior to Truth. Ah! But the divided embryo is guiltiest of all! Children of No Thing. The promised. The chosen. The abjured.

Christ what pretentious crap!

Trying to ponce a way into the preface of Prehistory ahead of the hoi polloi, eh? Lineaged from proto=Lilith, so said, when first Primeval Atom met Cosmic Egg. That Misbegotten Race, our people, chased from their reservation by Light Everlasting. Shadow of shadow.

Where *we* come from, the End has been returning w/ much fanfare for a very long time.

Shells & rockets raining from the ether. A microwave glitch dividing the tragedy befallen from the travesty yet to come. Our little island of prorogued dark.

We awaken at 4:15a.m. to a deafening silence. S=I=L=E=N=C=E. The bombardment's been going on for 13.799 billion Earth=years. Plus or minus. They do permit us these moments of reflection, of respite. Gratitude never a strong point, sorry to say.

Today the Little Ones are queuing at the scullery for a chance at some offal. They've bled the spaceship dry, but they'd turn cannibal before they'd go w/out their meat. Fear of the Sickness. You know it's bad when you start dreaming of haemophiliacs w/ faucets gauged into their necks. For that day. When scurvy among the Vampyrs. All suck & no bite. What happens after so many epochs when finally the teethies fall out? Hair also. Haemorrhoids. Cognitive faculty. Etc. Closed systems of pure spleen. Well, w/ a little cash & ingenuity anything's possible, heyheyhey? Reverse the thermodynamic arrow of time, inshallah! Quantum Correlations out G.O.D.'s rectum. How it all began, blahblahblah. Such stimulating consequences.

Oh indeed, there're things some of us have seen.

Will the Little Ones even remember us when their turn comes? The novas & frigidities, the synaptic auroras of memoried archetypes turned to escape=pod interior décor? Sharpening their milkteeth on the necks of androids. Childhoods bereft of innocence, of its humxn touch.

For what shall we become w/out our adversaries, but keepers of a worthless reminiscence?

ONLY GOOD VAMPYR'S A DEAD VAMPYR

Inequality is a fact of unlife. The vampyr is always <u>more than one</u>, yet there is never ONE. Some vampyrs live in castles, others live on the wrong side of the tracks. The first sucks the blood of the living, the second seeks the blood of its oppressor. THESE AREN'T THE SAME VAMPYR.

HEAD RATS

Tired of being victimised by G.O.D.? Fed=up w/ theo=corporate mendacity? Sick of being gaslighted by psyops gone rogue? Our personal sonic interruptor has been designed w/ just you in mind! No more unwanted voices issuing from the ether! No more commands to kill yrself, loved ones, pets, perfect strangers, or invisible aliens 👾! Debug yr brain today w/ our psychoscenic neural forcefield emulator! Kill that buzz! Vape that white noise! Hear yrself think w/out intrusive advertisements telling you what to buy next! Enjoy the sound of silence! We offer a lifetime guarantee w/ optional cryogenesis+, retro=upgrades included, so you won't suffer bad head karma ever again! Worried about ghosts? Past lives? Reincarnation? Doppelgängers? *Schizophrenia!* Laugh them all off w/ VOXINANIS®! Say "so long!" to subliminal thought=control & killer conscience! Never have a bad dream again! Kill the shrill! Don't be an echo chamber, be yrself! Dial direct for a free measure & quote: phone 666=VOX=INANIS now!

RADIOSHACK

Everything's been said, everything's already happened centuries ago, now it's all just playback & special effects.

like an image trapped inside a narcissistic machine

A GRIN WITHOUT A CAT [GRIM, NO PUSSY]

GOLEMGRAD (#FakeNewsMedia) — I=L=L=U=M=I=N=I=S=T militia forces today fired tear gas at protestors gathered on Plague Island as the city's first day of a 24=hour coronavirus curfew slid into chaos. Elsewhere, officers were captured in video footage zapping people w/ electrified cattle=prod.

Virus prevention measures have taken a violent turn in parts of Golemgrad as district authorities impose lockdowns & curfews or seal off major parts of the city. Health experts say the virus' spread, though still at an early stage, resembles the arc seen during the 1348 Black Death, in which 50% of the local population perished horribly, adding to already widespread anxiety. Cases across Golemgrad were set to climb above 10,000 late Saturday.

Abuses of the new quarantine measures by authorities were cited by protest organisers as substantiating their concerns about a slide towards totalitarianism.

Minutes after the City's lockdown began Friday, heavily armed I=L=L=U=M=I=N=I=S=T militia began attacking homeless people camped south of the Malecón w/ whips & batons. Some citizens reported the use of rubber bullets, teargas & stun grenades. Hundreds of people across the City were arrested.

In an apparent show of force on Saturday, militias also raided a large workers' hostel where some residents had defied the lockdown & attempted to initiate a wildcat "quarantine strike." Early reporting claimed at least two civilians were shot dead after a group of workers attacked security forces w/ Molotov cocktails.

The incident caused humxn rights groups to call for the Interior Minister to resign & for militias guilty of violence to be prosecuted. Public outrage over the actions of the security forces has been swift, w/ protests spreading across social media platforms & threatening to spill into the streets.

Experts are concerned that any further violence cld sabotage efforts to control the spread of the virus, whose accelerated spread already threatens to overwhelm city's fragile health system.

"We were horrified by excessive use of force ahead of the curfew that began Friday night," former World Health Organisation epidemiologist Dr Zifčák Asperger said in a statement issued Saturday. "We continue to receive testimonies from victims, eyewitnesses & video footage showing militia members violently assaulting members of the public."

Some health workers also reported being intimidated as they tried to provide services after the curfew came into effect.

Golemgrad's Interior Ministry on Saturday replied to criticism in a statement saying the curfew "is meant to guard against an apparent threat to public health. Breaking it is not only irresponsible but also puts others in harm's way."

City authorities have not said how many people have been arrested. Because courts are also affected by virus prevention measures, all but serious cases will now be dealt w/ at detention centres, the government has said. That means anyone detained for violating curfew faces time in crowded cells.

"It is evident that CORVID=69 will be spread less by actions of police than of those who have contravened the curfew," Asperger insisted.

Critics argue, however, that if the lockdown continues there is bound to be an increase in violence. Furthermore, many people in poorer neighbourhoods of the city have no way to access food, water & sanitation.

"It will mean for the first day, maybe, they stay indoors," Asperger said. "Then the second day, when they are hungry, they will move out into the open. Then the Sanitation Crews can do their job."

HUMXN SPERM ENDOTHELIAL NITRIC OXIDE SYNTHASE EXPRESSION: CORRELATION WITH SPERM MOTILITY

— I just dunno what's more audacious, being a grrl in a boi's body or a vampyr in a humxn's body?
— Bodies are just horrific, gross, I can't stand them!
— My ego is a dialectical relationship between people who don't exist.
— Without an element of the ridiculous, progress wld be impossible, don't you think?
— Oh pleez! Progress is like menopause, you never know if y're coming or going.
— I had mine before I went through puberty.
— That's what's called putting the horse before the cart!
— The carte blanche!
— Poor Blanche, she's hung like a horse!
— Who wants to play Pin=the=Dick=on=the=Donkey?
— You know the last blowjob she got almost gave her brain damage!
— Well look who's eating the egg off their own face now!
— You won't catch me singing soprano next to a bag like that!
— A real walking=talking pathogen, aren't you Mary?
— Mary, Mary, quite cuntrary…
— In Alexandria she made a Fakir's snake dance.
— She was Helen of Troy's hand=me=down frotometer.
— Cold Finger, the grrl w/ the morbid touch.
— She was an ape w/ bruised knuckles!
— Miss Cleopatria parts her merkin right down the middle, like a sharpshooter in a spaghetti western.
— Brill Cream's yr only man!
— What was the name of that moviola we saw?
— *The Houris that Jackie Bilked!*
— Did Jackie go down on Gillette or was it the other way round?
— You shld've seen that whitewomxn's *Schwantz!*
— It was black?
— On account of all the bad blood.
— Bet the other P.I.G.s in her sodality call her Truncheon Dick!
— Mam'selle Nightstick, if you please!
— Oh you feral sheep=fucker, you!
— You can't just eunuch someone w/ yr teeth, hon.
— Who's been binking the Miss Kings then, Clancy?
— Give me a Claytons, the bink you have when y're not having a bink.
— Wee willie binkie!

— Oooh, I don't screw w/ homos, that's strictly a fag thing, dahlz, & I'm 100% certified wo=mxn!
— You like cooch, doncha?
— Listen to her, she's a talking thesorearse.
— Wld you excuse me, please?
— Sorry, hon, but I don't have an excuse for you today.
— Sayonara, sweetbread!
— Someone must've dropped Nyquil in her Coca=Cola.
— Her Savonarola!
— Her coquille!
— Her cock oil!
— Well, well, well, look who's joined the slime=mould collective!
— The care & tending of the genitals is *très important, chérie!*
— But they don't sing the same parts, dearest.
— Oh she give such divine Madam Butterfly kisses!
— Spare me, pah=leez!
— Did someone say, police?
— Ooooh I feel we must be in an X=rated movie!
— She looks like that Mona Lisa in drag!
— No wonder she has a hot arse!
— That's where she stores her electric radiator, out of season.
— *Plutonium* to you!
— *Allora!* Be like slow death round here!
— Welcome to the humxn condition, dahlz.
— Honestly, I don't give a shining fuck.
— Can't hold back the tide!
— Can't hold=in a determined shit, neither, Miss Guttertripe!
— And to think there are creatures in this world who've never tasted blood!
— Ever had sex in a guillotine?
— No but I once fucked a hangman's skull.
— Alive or dead?
— What's the diff?
— Puke=a=rama! Better keep an eye out for *her*, grrlz, you never know what she might give you!
— Sounds like a bad case of Head Rats…
— It's hard to find anyone deserving enough, these days.
— D'you think it's true that Stalin preferred bald women?
— He turned 20 million Russians into humxn sex robots!
— I don't believe it! A cryogenic brain told him to murder every biological male in a thousand mile radius.
— You think they don't have castratos in Vladivostok?
— Don't kid yrself, even when y're dead there's just as

many pains=in=the=anus & martyrs who suffer them.
— You always were an optimist!
— It's the way she laughs on both sides of her face!
— A nest of rats writhing in the sun…
— Oh how divine!
— She's the very picture of second nature suicided by proficiency!
— A mist=smothered gibbous moon!
— Stop! Y're giving me the heebiejeebz!
— It is distressing indeed to find a grown vampyr in such a state.
— Well how do you think it feels to be born black in a place like this?
— Oh climb down off yr maypole, dearie.

VIRGIN MARY DRIVES A TRANS=FEMME

ACCELERATED EVOLUTIONARY TRANSFORMERS

In its defence, power erects a cultural front which ramifies itself by *counter=cathexis* – a resistance to resistance – reinforced by contrived (sadomasochistic) forms of irony, subversion & self=pastiche. By posing as a *culture under siege*, this reactionary movement paradoxically assumes the form of an *overcoming*, since its rhetorical position of being oppressed serves only as the alibi ("nightmare fuel") for disproportionate use of force in imposing its true agenda. The predominant mode of production of the Corp[orate]=$[tate] Apparatus thus tends to a mass distributed ego=in=distress. To the ego=in=distress the "agents of subversion" are malevolent adversaries standing in the path of its emancipation, which the "freedom of false choices" promises to deliver. Subversion, as *thought born of perpetual movement*, is paradoxically *based* in a subjection to the "to come." Likewise, what poses as *transcendental thought* is contradictorily bound to a present in which "future gratification" is *now*. This narcissistic ego=libido feeds most greedily off a melancholia that – from every perspective available to the socalled Humxnocene – declares NO FUTURE: the melancholia of the "death of modernity," of the vampyric "end of History." N_x

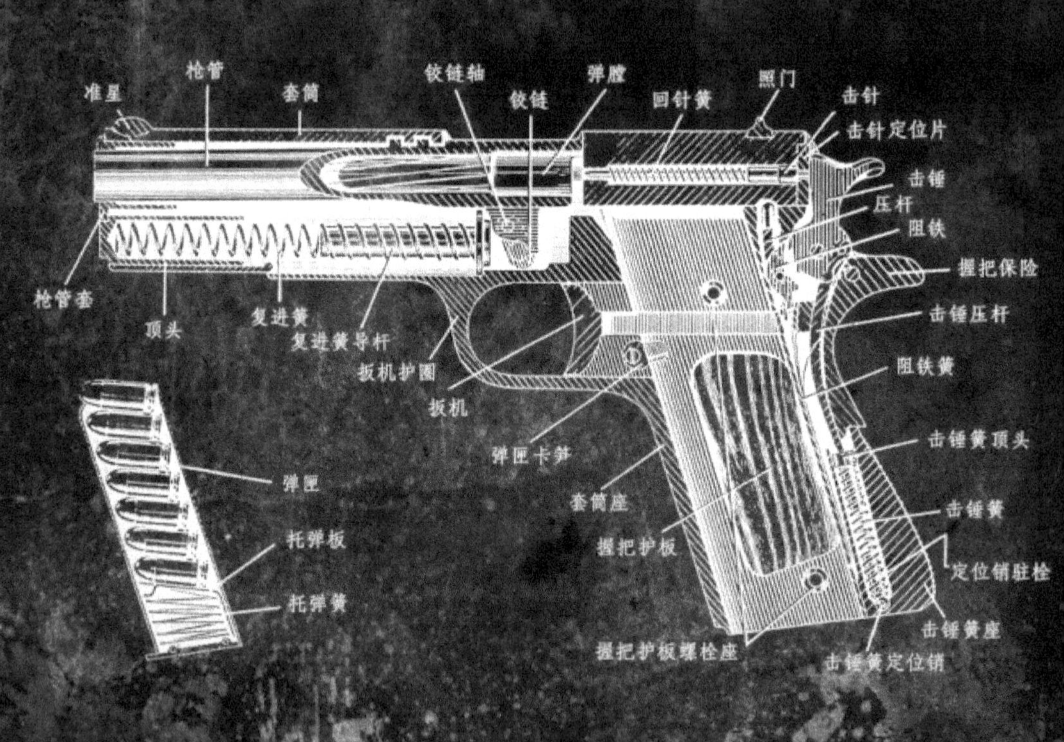

#SOCIALJUSTICEVIRUSWARRIORS

WE ARE <u>NOT</u> ALL IN THIS TOGETHER WE ARE <u>NOT</u> ALL IN THIS
TOGETHER WE ARE <u>NOT</u> ALL IN THIS TOGETHER WE ARE <u>NOT</u> ALL IN
THIS TOGETHER WE ARE <u>NOT</u> ALL IN THIS TOGETHER WE ARE <u>NOT</u>
ALL IN THIS TOGETHER WE ARE <u>NOT</u> ALL IN THIS TOGETHER WE ARE
<u>NOT</u> ALL IN THIS TOGETHER WE ARE <u>NOT</u> ALL IN THIS TOGETHER
WE ARE <u>NOT</u> ALL IN THIS TOGETHER WE ARE <u>NOT</u> ALL IN THIS
TOGETHER WE ARE <u>NOT</u> ALL IN THIS TOGETHER WE ARE <u>NOT</u> ALL IN
THIS TOGETHER WE ARE <u>NOT</u> ALL IN THIS TOGETHER WE ARE <u>NOT</u>
ALL IN THIS TOGETHER WE ARE <u>NOT</u> ALL IN THIS TOGETHER WE ARE
<u>NOT</u> ALL IN THIS TOGETHER WE ARE <u>NOT</u> ALL IN THIS TOGETHER WE
ARE <u>NOT</u> ALL IN THIS TOGETHER WE ARE <u>NOT</u> ALL IN THIS TOGETHER
WE ARE <u>NOT</u> ALL IN THIS TOGETHER WE ARE <u>NOT</u> ALL IN THIS
TOGETHER WE ARE <u>NOT</u> ALL IN THIS TOGETHER WE ARE <u>NOT</u> ALL IN
THIS TOGETHER WE ARE <u>NOT</u> ALL IN THIS TOGETHER WE ARE <u>NOT</u> ALL
IN THIS TOGETHER WE ARE <u>NOT</u> ALL IN THIS TOGETHER WE ARE <u>NOT</u>
ALL IN THIS TOGETHER WE ARE <u>NOT</u> ALL IN THIS TOGETHER WE ARE
<u>NOT</u> ALL IN THIS TOGETHER WE ARE <u>NOT</u> ALL IN THIS TOGETHER WE
ARE <u>NOT</u> ALL IN THIS TOGETHER WE ARE <u>NOT</u> ALL IN THIS TOGETHER
WE ARE <u>NOT</u> ALL IN THIS TOGETHER WE ARE <u>NOT</u> ALL IN THIS
TOGETHER WE ARE <u>NOT</u> ALL IN THIS TOGETHER WE ARE <u>NOT</u> ALL IN
THIS TOGETHER WE ARE <u>NOT</u> ALL IN THIS TOGETHER WE ARE <u>NOT</u>
ALL IN THIS TOGETHER WE ARE <u>NOT</u> ALL IN THIS TOGETHER WE ARE
NOT ALL IN THIS TOGETHER WE ARE <u>NOT</u> ALL IN THIS TOGETHER WE
ARE <u>NOT</u> ALL IN THIS TOGETHER WE ARE <u>NOT</u> ALL IN THIS TOGETHER
WE ARE <u>NOT</u> ALL IN THIS TOGETHER WE ARE <u>NOT</u> ALL IN THIS
TOGETHER WE ARE <u>NOT</u> ALL IN THIS TOGETHER WE ARE <u>NOT</u> ALL IN
THIS TOGETHER WE ARE <u>NOT</u> ALL IN THIS TOGETHER WE ARE <u>NOT</u>
ALL IN THIS TOGETHER WE ARE <u>NOT</u> ALL IN THIS TOGETHER WE ARE
<u>NOT</u> ALL IN THIS TOGETHER WE ARE <u>NOT</u> ALL IN THIS TOGETHER WE
ARE <u>NOT</u> ALL IN THIS TOGETHER WE ARE <u>NOT</u> ALL IN THIS TOGETHER

METHAMPHETAMINE LANDSCAPES

night falls on hydrostatic moons
a symphony of lithiums
this ersatz death by viral delivery plan such hyper=gothic
suns make anguish their daily meat in skies adrift in black
pollen their little fleurs du mal disporting timelapse naked
or frozen in scrupulous attitudes of respect for the cosmic
master plan but we must breathe more than ontic metadata
(the situation couldn't last the times were unbearable) oh
how even a bouquet of misery gives tarnish a new face &
G.O.D. something to live for
                   so too the shadows dance in silent mandalas
their joie de mourir

UTOPIA IS THE DISTANCE BETWEEN LIFE & ART

Mater Praga, famous clairvoyant, won the dubious distinction of having read everything that'd ever been written & everything that ever wld. It's said she hadn't spoken a word to a living soul in over a hundred years. All of her energies were consumed by this singular prodigious task, increasing exponentially. She rarely ate, barely even breathed, & sat still as a rock day & night under a lamp while dutiful attendants page=turned through the books that passed ceaselessly across her reading stand. Like dustmotes sifting the lamp's rays, words in every language known to humxnity drifted, forever forming & reforming in one immaculate simultaneous vision. ⇒ For which reason most detested by Literature, which reads nothing but its own royalty statements, dividend reports, share=price forecasts, buying up every available piece of air=time, quarantine the written word so nothing gets out that isn't Status Quo certified w/ a prize=ribbon pinned on it, give 'em a parade for the proles to gawk at, incense & high mass & a bit of the ol' *introibo ad altare dei*, coz G.O.D.'s been in the small=print biz before Literature learnt to pee standing up, the Founding Father you might say, rakes a percentage off every gross, that's brand metaphysics for you, kiddo, a sphincter on every tongue, a finger in every pie. ⇒ Detested, but: never's a day gone by w/out the suits bellycrawling to Mater Praga's hovel for the lowdown on the current threat=level, scrounge for word=crumbs under the ol' witch's reading light, cast their horoscopes in the dust, glom the intel on the coming insurrection before it takes them blindside, figure which deadhorse to trade in for a gelding, which *enfant terrible* to stick their Mephistoflea fangs into, which to slip a mickey finn, photofit into a crimescene, or slap in solitary for the term of their unnatural lives, etc. <u>Bizniz iz bizniz</u>, Sal. (Aint nothin personal.) (Hahaha.)

LA PESTE RÉVEILLERAIT SES RATS
& LES ENVERRAIT MOURIR DANS UNE CITÉ HEUREUSE

DID YOU KNOW: there's a new black market for sanity, now operational w/ a lifetime's supply of liquid brainmeat extract? Get yrs now! Black market trading coupons available by application at yr nearest cryptobank! Don't pay THE MAN, get ahead of the scam! Remember: a jab of liquid brainmeat a day, keeps CORVID=69 away! Proven 100% effective! No more bloodsickness for you! Don't be a sucker, sign up to the blockchain today! Sane is the only game in town! When everyone else's a loony, y're laughing all the way to the cryptobank! Aint no kapitalism like BLACK kapitalism! This unique opportunity is not for yr average schmuck! Login & download yr sanity for safekeeping from government scams & socialist weirdos on the make. Yr brain, yr gain! Keep winning & don't look back! Get in ahead of the curve! This thing is only gonna get bigger & bigger. A LIFETIME'S SUPPLY OF LIQUID BRAINMEAT EXTRACT! Send us yr brain today!

THE WORLD IS MY EPILOGUE

The fact of the matter was they kept all the old extinct vampyrs in cryogenic freeze=dry for when or if the future opportunity arose, or simply to gloat at whenever the mood took hold. Those that'd made the journey & hadn't burned up in the atmosphere. If nothing else, when times were bad, or like now worse, they cld be put to work in freakshows, Hollywood movies, or a microplastics merchandising arrangement for dollars & a little piece of non=biodegradable posterity. Better than the Real Thing! Except the Real Thing never was the real thing, was it? (Ever known any of them procrustean vampyrs to wear prophylactics on its fangs?) Yep, they just built this planet out of all the melted polymers from the last one. Just like the Next World'll be built out of the junk, parasites & killer viruses we've been farming right here. Ain't no prob too big a l'il zap of Climate Catastrophe won't solve tout=de=suite. *Time to turn up the temperature, grrlz!* Oh boy! Now that really gets 'em sweatin. Watch them frozed ol' dinosaur=suckin vamps w/ the quagmire eyes go batshit for real, thinkin their airconditioners gonna melt. Funniest goddarn thing you ever did see.

ICECREAM FOR CROWS

The mung on rotten unwashed teeth.

THE GOOD & BAD VAMPYRS

Papa Walt, infamous record industry mogul & inventor of the New Sound ("a wall of Pure Commodity" [*Rolling Stone*]) had tuned his radar below street=level to the sub=basements of the Golemgrad fashion=crime scene, unearthing the Wild Grrlz* ("a puerile exercise in cultural chaos" [*TimeOut*]) –

---

* Not to be confused with, etc.

a gang of homicidal art school drop=outs he was touting as
the Next Big Thing, a fast=buck scheme that was about to turn
into a blood=sucking megalomaniac kapitalist conspiracy of
world=owning proportions. Papa Walt Media Inc. was fronting
this grrlband=from=Hell, via a dozen shell companies &
"indie" subsidiaries, on the newly=minted S.C.U.M. label,
to give the kidz=on=the=street "the real authentic killer
groove" of ANTI=THIS=ESTABLISHMENTARIANISM served up w/
merciless neck=gouging insurrectionary EVOL! A team of
brain=whacked Vivienne Westwood lookalike fash=consultants
& Saatchi copywriters doodled prototypes for the band's
public attitudinising, which the Wild Grrlz duly adlibbed
from, parodied, trashed, pissed on, slashed & fellated for
the cameras. They toured the interview circuit, leaving
blood&guts strewn over studio sofas & telegenic smears
of excrement on strategically logoed soundbooth walls, in
declensions of HELTER SKELTER retro freak=chic. It jived
backmask suicide cult. Status quo headliners like Eddie Van
& the Vampyr Slayerz went neurasthenic at the prospect of
marauding Wild Grrlz groupies disembowelling their support
acts live in front of the fan=base. Desertion among the
ranks grew to epic proportions: they had to weld the stadium
gates shut to keep the roadies from skipping out, till the
kidz started burning the bleachers down & the Eddie Vans of
the world quick smart learnt to play to a different tune.

EDDIE VAN "INCEL FANBOI" TOUR
(UNDEAD & UNPLUGGED AT THE TROPICANA
SUPPORT ACT <u>SUPERSPREADER</u>)
There's something wrong w/ me
my blood's black it's plain to see
I'm desperate for release
won't you fuck my mind up pls.
There's something wrong w/ me
I've got yr dead meat disease
the world ended in my dreams
gonna kill the thought police.
There's something wrong w/ me
I wanna eat yr tyranny
burn the Statue of Liberty
when I die will I be free?
There's something wrong w/ me
there's something wrong w/ me
there's something wrong w/ me
shoot me shoot me shoot me shoot me!

TROPICAL HOTDOG NIGHT

Captain Beefheart zaps out of the funky icecream float to monster the Wild Grrlz on the Malecón. *Oooh Captain Beefheart!* they squeal moan coo in slime=seething unison. He stands 8=feet tall in a bewigged carp's head & platform moonboots, he's gyrating those turb0thruster Elvis hips, he's got a killer satirical leer & a 13=string axe to grind, but that ain't the Captain, dig, it's Eddie Van in his latest incel fanboi drag thrashing a phat power chord wtf? Man's trying to throw a hex on the bebop vampyr kidz, pulling their bat=chains, pumping highvoltage moodscrambling metaphysical boondoggle into their brainpans, hahaha, hehehe. Something isn't quite going to plan, though. While he's revving up for an encore, the Wild Grrlz are taking their bowie knives to the rented Marshall stacks w/ vengeful gusto that sends chills up Eddie V's considerable coccyx. No doubt about it, they've got his number: he's the rip=off artist primo, a consummate lame=o, a money&fame hoe, sleazing in under cover of a cheapo Halloween gimpsuit to stake a fake=o claim to the Master Madman's Magic Bandwagon, hohohohoho. *We know y're cispatriarchal scum!* they scream. Eddie V can see plainly the homicidal intent in their blood=curdled eyes. "Hey kidz," he throws out a plaster=of=Paris grin at the real Captain's by=now rabidly pissed off fangrrlz, "it's cool to be cool, know what I'm sayin?" just playing for time while the roadies *do something* about that backstage exit, though really there isn't one, it's just a regular Mr Wimple truck they've requisitioned for this little improvised photobombing opportunity w/ Eddie V riding bareback up top & the mardigras kidz mobbing the cornetto stand, the whole thing by now rocking wildly on its axles in a heave=ho that's soon to see the retiree rocker rocketing up & over the scenic seawall, moonboots, wig, Fender & all, to splash down like a sloppy bootstomp in the perilous putrid ponging backwash. Weeeeeeeeeee. Pish! Like tickertape the cobblestones & empty tequila bottles rain, bidding *bon voyage* to our feckless *faux fatale* Beefheart impersonator, carnival lights making candle=mambo semaphores on the bilious waters as Eddie V gets sucked down, to be churned & spat out on the far side of the Marsh where even now the hapless roadies are scoping out a salvage run, rope=in their man & work him over w/ a blowdryer & a crate of Rexonna & maybe try their luck again over at the Quarantine Station, play a few tracks for the sickoes on Death's Doorstep & pump some record sales among the highest=turnover demographic this side of the El Lugosi Stadium (get 'em while they're still warm & you can sell it to 'em stone cold!). *Gotta consider posterity, kidz.* Though not everyone is equally as inclined to outright mortality as the meatsacks on Plague Island – which is why the old dude in the spangled spandex was turning tricks for the vamp tramps down on the Malecón in the first place, trying to hustle in on the necksuck sorority scene, wire to the vibe, lube the groove, extend the proverbial shelflife (or *ipso facto* shelfundeath), you know, put over a fast one to stay ahead of the downcurve. Coz that's where Eddie V's headed, heyheyhey, once them Wild Grrlz get their unforgiving little fangs into *him*.

MEYRINK

A cur growls. Once. A second time. Then a shot rings out & the growling stops. A shadow crosses the window. History has passed by.

L.H.O.O.Q.

The Wild Grrlz stood there watching Stalin Cathedral burn, flames leaping in their eyes. *Plague City, brûle=t=il? Oui, il brûle, bébé!*

MOTHER'S LITTLE HELPERS

The little bois who were really or only virtually little grrlz pretending or not pretending to be little bois or being forced to dress up as little grrlz w/ ribbons & plaits & pinafores by mumsies driven by cruel neurosis to inflict grief confusion primal doubt upon ramrod menschlich husbands invalided out of the bureaucracy before their time nursing self=matyrised vasectomies like a grudge against the universe for no longer being their own übermummy's favourite Chosen One & oh how all the little orphensias in unison wept!

CONVERSION THERAPY [A DREAM]

"Bear in mind," Doctor Asperger entreated, blinking emotively w/ his one good eye, "that this is not the child you loved. That child is dead. What remains – what you see before you – is a shell… And what it contains is unadulterated evil. When we destroy it, we destroy only the evil!"

Solange Haplophryne yawned.

Without further ceremony, the orderlies began dragging **Offensia** towards the operating table. The child struggled &

howled, but the orderlies held firm.

As they forced **Offensia** onto the table & bound her to it, a nurse entered the operating theatre bearing a tray w/ a sharpened metal spike lying on it.

The metal gleamed in the light.

The nurse handed the spike to Doctor Asperger, who proceeded to attach it to something between an antique Luger & a pneumatic drill.

Doctor Asperger turned towards the table & looked dispassionately at the child as it strained against its bonds, struggling to cry out, to free its mouth from the surgical tape the orderlies had gagged it w/.

With well=practiced movements, the Doctor positioned the spike over **Offensia**'s pelvis & primed the apparatus.

The orderlies & nurse stood back. The child's eyes bulged in terror.

There was a moment of expectancy. Then Asperger pulled the trigger & the spike tore through **Offensia**'s flesh.

The child's face contorted in agony.

A geyser of blood erupted from the wound.

Solange Haplophryne smirked.

The studio audience, in raptures of unfeigned gratitude, applauded.

Justice had been done.

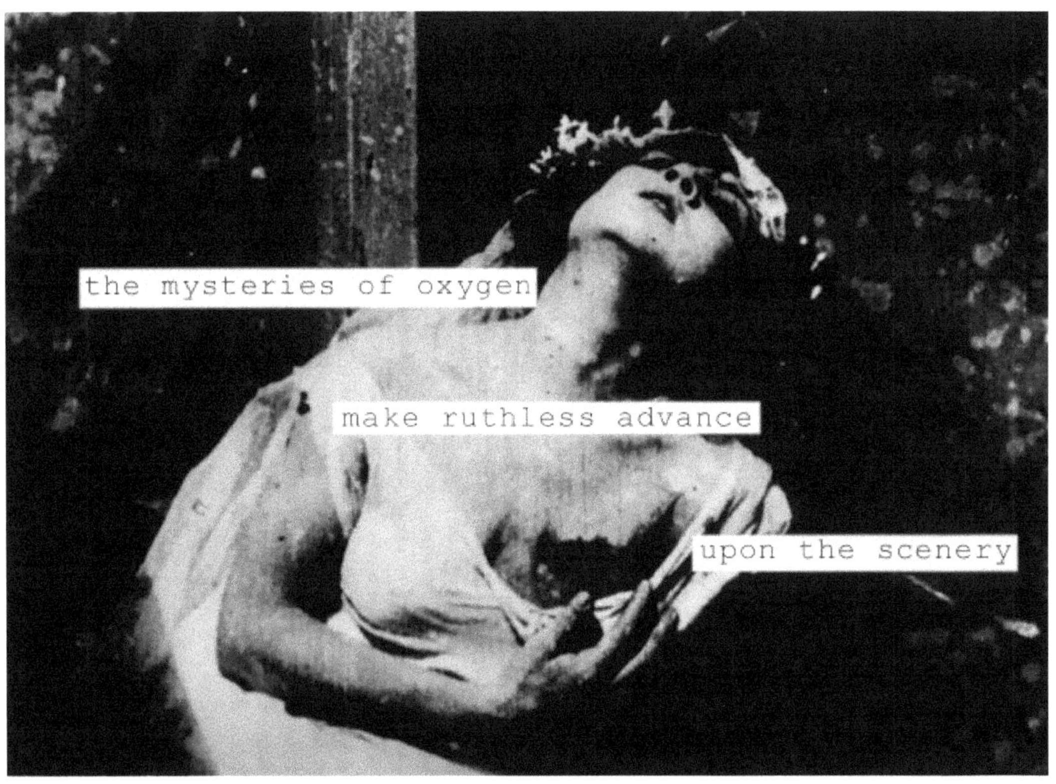

She Sells Seashells by the Seashore*

Armandine's eyes came open in a sudden panic. She lay in a sweat, gasping. Her heart was pounding inside her chest.

She'd been awakened by an unspeakable pain, accompanied by a dream of demons harnessed w/ iron hooks dragging her through the air in a whirlwind. Devils, giant=headed iguanas, wrenching w/ supernatural force, stripping the sinews & tendons from her body.

Somehow she'd become detached from her physical being & was floating above everything, witnessing the scene unfold in mounting horror.

Armandine's body, what remained of it, thrashed about where a moment ago it had been lying whole & dormant in cryosleep, nothing now but a mass of flesh in dismal epilepsy.

She watched, petrified, as a bloodied gash, cropped w/ teeth, reared from amidst the lifeless limbs as they flailed about, barking up at her like a rabid dog.

The pain was excruciating. It shocked her awake.

For a long time afterwards, Armandine stared at the dimly lit ceiling.

Gradually, by facets, she became aware of the room.

Something scuttled under the door. The parquet groaned. Unfamiliar shadows moved across the walls.

Then a faint tapping at the window.

The sound chilled her. She fought against the memory of the dream.

The tapping continued. A gust of rain, tree branches brushing the glass.

Armandine sat upright in her bed.

The tapping had become more distinct & quite real.

She stared at the window. It was fogged inside, but the tormented, imploring face of **Offensia** was still distinct enough to recognise.

Armandine shivered, but dared not move. She wanted to call out, but her voice was paralyzed in her throat, & there was no=one else to call out to anyway. Only this apparition of the daughter who'd abandoned her. The child she'd waited for, day & night, for years on end, who'd never returned.

Offensia clawed at the glass as her lips moved inaudibly.

"B=I=T=C=H," they spelled.

And though she fought it with every remaining ounce of her willpower, Armandine was drawn irresistibly towards the entreating figure.

As she floated across the unfamiliar room, the clawing at the window became frantic. Closer, it was possible for her to hear what **Offensia** said.

"Bitch… let me in! I command you!"

Armandine resisted, but still her hand reached out to unlatch the transom. As it came free, dank tendrils of fog wafted in. The air was cold. So cold!

Offensia snarled. It was a cruel & callous snarl.

Before the hapless Armandine cld begin to recoil, the Vampyr's claws flared in the open window, grasping her w/ inhumxn strength.

Like a calico doll, Armandine was flung into the night.

THE WYRD SISTERS

Toil & trouble,
toil & trouble.

From sun=up to
sun=down.

From sun=down to
sun=up.

Aye, it's a
vicious fucking
circle alright.

What?

What's that then?

Thought I heard
something out there.

Didn't hear a
thing.

A bird was it? A
blackbird in the
undergrowth?

There aren't
any birds
around here.

Never a single
one in all the
time we've been
coming here.

Not a bird?

Maybe it was a
cricket then. Or a
toad.

Or the wind across
yr arse, was it?

That's y're idea of
a joke I suppose?

Been many known
to appreciate my
jokes.

Died laughing
did they?

They died a bitter
death some of them
did, but they knew
how to laugh even
in the face of it.

Knew a man once
cld bring tears to
yr eyes. Tears of
laughter.

The tears come
one way or
another.

It wld be a sad
day if a man
were deprived of
her own sense of
humour.

Cldn't disagree w/
that.

Aye, it wld be a
sad day indeed.
What do you reckon
the time is now?

Early. The tide
isn't on the
turn yet.

Aye, time is
what we do
have.

Ol' Rona? Do I
remember Rona?
Who wldn't
remember Rona!

Had a cunt hard
as steel.

Didn't see it
coming.

The seat of
intellect.

Not the slowest
either.

Better to put
'em out of
their misery
straight away.

Mercy killing,
eh?

Now there was a
womxn.

Aye, she was a
hard cunt alright,
ol' Rona.

Blind as a bat in
heat.

Knew how to use
her brain, ol'
Rona.

Never stood a
chance, them.

Pop 'em off.

But not for ol'
Rona.

We've got plenty of
time, then.

Do you remember ol'
Rona?

The greatest
bleeding bitch known
to humxnity, she
was.

It was on account
of that she came to
such a bad end.

Well, you know what
they say. She'd've
gone at a battering
ram head=on.

Not the fastest
horse to bolt the
paddock.

That's true. There
are some were slower
than Rona.

Right between the
eyes.

Right between the
eyes.

The wily bitch.

She knew where her
teeth were, where
her hands & feet
were, cld manage a
trick or two.

You know what they
say, can lead a
horse to water but
you can't make it
stand up & sing.

Bite the hand
that feeds it,
clean off up to
the elbow.

Thick as two sods
of turf was ol'
Rona, truth be
told. But she'd
sooner break a
man's jaw than
have some smart
aleck on her back…

She'd break you
in two just to
mention it.

Wldn't take it lying
down, that's sure.

She'd've
climbed out of
her grave &
murdered any
bugger who said
as much.

Still, we shldn't
think ill of the
dead.

Rona dead? I don't
believe it!

Fair's fair.
She was never
what you'd
call the full
presence.

Cogito ergo sum, as
they say.

Not the full
trapeze.

Still, she was
a womxn for all
that.

Flesh & blood,
that's true.

You shld've
seen when they
strung her up.
Neck out to
here…

They say her head
turned black w/ all
the bad blood in
her.

That's what
they say. She
knew how to
hate like the
best of 'em.

A simple enough
womxn, ol' Rona.
Always know where
you stand w/ a womxn
like that.

To me she looked
like the skin &
bone she was. It
was the bruises
made her face go
black.

Aye, you won't
find the likes
of her again.

She cld carry
the weight of
better women, &
keep the faith
w/out flinching
a muscle.

Now that is the
cruel truth.

They broke her body
w/out breaking her
soul.

Aye, but who knows
what they drove
her to in the end.

She kept the
faith, that's
what I say.

The faith? When
they handed her
the confession to
sign, she cldn't
even write her own
name.

Thy will be
done.

It was their priest
signed it for her.

Holding up the hand
of a deadwomxn w/
a ballpoint stuck
between her fingers.

Never wrote a
word before in
her life.

How cld they have
known?

They'd be better
off killing a
person dead & be
done w/ it. The
likes of Rona
don't understand
their ways.

It wasn't like
that in the old
days.

Aye, that's true.

Everyone knew
what was what
back then. None
of this beating
around the bush
w/ who knows
what their
language means.

You know it well
enough.

Aye, but I
choose not to
speak it. I
choose not to
hear it. It
means nothing
to me. Empty
sounds carried
on the wind.

May as well leave it
for the birds.

What birds?
There aren't
any birds.
There've never
been any birds
around here.

Not like in the
old days.

Not even in the
old days.

All milk & honey!

Wine & roses!

Milk & honey. So
they say.

Aye, that's
what they say.

When was that, do
you think?

Before our time.

Aye, before our
time.

Can you hear the
swell beating over
the rocks?

Is that what it
is? Are you sure?

The tide. It's
on the turn.
Won't be long
now.

It sounds like the
drums.

Y've been away too
long. There are no
drums any more. Only
the sea.

What about the
ships?

There are no
more ships
neither.
They've learnt
to come w/out
ships.

I wldn't know.
I've never seen
it.

No more than
now. They're
used to the
dark.

That was
before.

Washed up in
the storm they
were.

Barely.

How they used
to sing when
you pulled them
out of the
water.

Forget it.
There were
never any birds
here.

What do you
know about it?

It was a dream.

Like the christ?
Do they walk on
water then?

From outa the sky,
they reckon.

Will there be a
moon tonight?

Wing of bat!

The old witch used
to sit out here in
the dark listening
to the tide.

Long before. And
she used to tell us
about the ships that
came down on the
rocks.

And how they used to
find some of the sea
people still alive.

Barely alive, w/
strange pale flesh &
eyes bulging.

Like birds.

But the way she told
it, the old witch,
you cld almost hear
birds singing.

I've heard them.

In the other place I
heard them.

There is no
other place.
Everywhere's the
same. You said so
yrself.

I heard a sound, it
was strange, like
singing.

It was the
sound of the
blood in yr
ears.

The sound that
never goes away.

The sound you
tell yrself is
the voice of
the G.O.D.

It's quiet now.

What crap!

Listen close. It's
never quiet. Not
till you die.

They say that when
you die you hear
angels singing.

Birds, angels,
what does it
matter?

Maybe it's the
sound of yr last
breath going from
you.

And after y're
dead, what then?

The sound of the
body dying.

Nothing, that's
what I say.

Not even worth the
wait.

I suppose we'll
find out when we
get there.

Who knows?

You cld suppose
that alright.

Will it be long,
do you think?

Hard to tell.

You can hear
the wind now.
It'll die down
after a little
while.

The tide's going
out!

Whatever happened
to ol' Rona,
anyway?

They buried her
under the cliff where
they found her.

It was bound
to happen some
day.

She'd've been
better off
staying at
home, telling
those old lies
of hers.

Words? She
invented them!

Any old yarn
wld do.

There was no
limit to the
yarns the old
sheila cld
spin.

But she was a
womxn for all
that.

There are no
birds I tell
you.

That's the wind
groaning.

She had a way w/
words alright.

That was the
measure of it
alright.

A myth.

What's that?

I'm sure I heard
something.

No, listen.

It's a man!

Shhh! Did you hear
him stumble?

They say she still
had a rope around
her neck.

Cld tell a tale or
two.

She'd just sort of
work her way out
from the beginning
& make the end up
whenever it came
along.

A legend in her own
lifetime she was.

Aye, she came to a
sticky end.

Nothing, it's the
wind died down.

Look!

He's coming this
way!

It's footsteps!

There he is!

A man? That's
barely a sack
of meat.

What's he saying?

One of them maybe.

He's injured.

Can't understand.
Foreigner?

What do they have
to come here & play
dead for?

Well he's not one of
us!

Not one of
them. See?

Why don't you
go back & die
among yr own
people?

Don't. He can't
understand a word
y're saying.

He's bleeding.

Suppose he wants us
to help him?

Got it in the
neck, just like
the others.

They got him!

Where'd he come
from, then?

Who knows.
Maybe they
brought him w/
them.

Bloody traitor!

Maybe he led them
over in a boat.

He's begging.

He's bleeding to
death.

Got his throat
half torn out.

Looks like a goner
to me.

Here today, a
goner tomorrow,
as they say.

If only that were
true.

Not in our
lifetime.

Ah, but we've seen a
few things in that
time, haven't we?

More than
enough, I'd
say.

Yep, we've seen a
thing or two. You
cldn't exactly call
us ignorant.

Y're not the
first one we've
seen, mister!

Y're wasting yr
breath, he doesn't
understand,
besides, you might
scare him off.

Doesn't look like
he's going anywhere
in a hurry to me.
It's pouring out of
him.

All blood &
fear like the
rest of 'em.

They all look
the same to me,
though some say
you can tell the
difference.

There were
others before,
too, but
they're all the
same in the
end.

Came in boats, too,
they did.

Well, they
hardly walked
the waves, did
they?

No.

Y've no idea.

There are things
in this world that
are beyond humxn
understanding.

Some things are more
misunderstandable
than others.

Aye, you can't
take anything
for granted
nowadays.

Well, a womxn has
to trust her own
judgement.

Trust? What's
there to trust?
Things happen
just the way
they do.

We shld be
grateful for what
we get.

Is he dead yet?

Almost.

We'll have to go
soon.

It won't be long
by the look of it.

Here, give
the blighter
a kick & see
if he's still
breathing.

Go on!

I'll prod him w/
this stick.

He won't bite,
you know.

Might just be
playing possum.
Better to be safe.
Give him a poke in
the eye.

There, did he
move?

Not a wink.

Aye. I reckon
well enough.
You two take
that side &
I'll take this
side.

What do you reckon?

Drag him out here
where we can see
him proper.

Where the blood
won't sop our boots.

Be quick, we've
wasted most
of the night
already.

My blade is faster
than yr tongue.

Then shut yr
trap & get to
work.

Keep it clean, don't
make a mess of it.

Hardly any meat on
him.

Fill yr sacks,
ladies.

With bone & offal!

And I'll take
the head!

I'll take the
cock!

I've got his spleen!

And I've got his
legs!

But I've got
the arms, haha!

His lungs!

His liver!

His kidneys!

His heart!

His spine!

His shoes!

His last cry!

Put a cork in
it, you stupid
old hag.

His last breath!

His bloody rags!

His black soul!

It'll be
enough.

Oh my back!

Less than it
looks, eh?

Is that all of it
done?

The tide must've
come & gone by
now. We shld
leave.

They say that when a
man bleeds to death
you shld cover over
the blood so the
crows don't come &
drink it. Sign of
bad luck to come.

There aren't
any birds here…

Even now I thought I
heard one. Listen…

It's nothing.

I'm sure of it.

I heard it, too.

Another one coming?

It's nothing, I
say.

Or a blackbird,
maybe, rustling the
undergrowth …

What of it. Let
it drink as
much blood as
it likes.

It's time to be
gone, before
the light
catches us.

Come away.

Like the early bird
catches the worm.

Like the worm
catches the dead.

Like the dead
catch cold.

Like the cold
catches the last one
left.

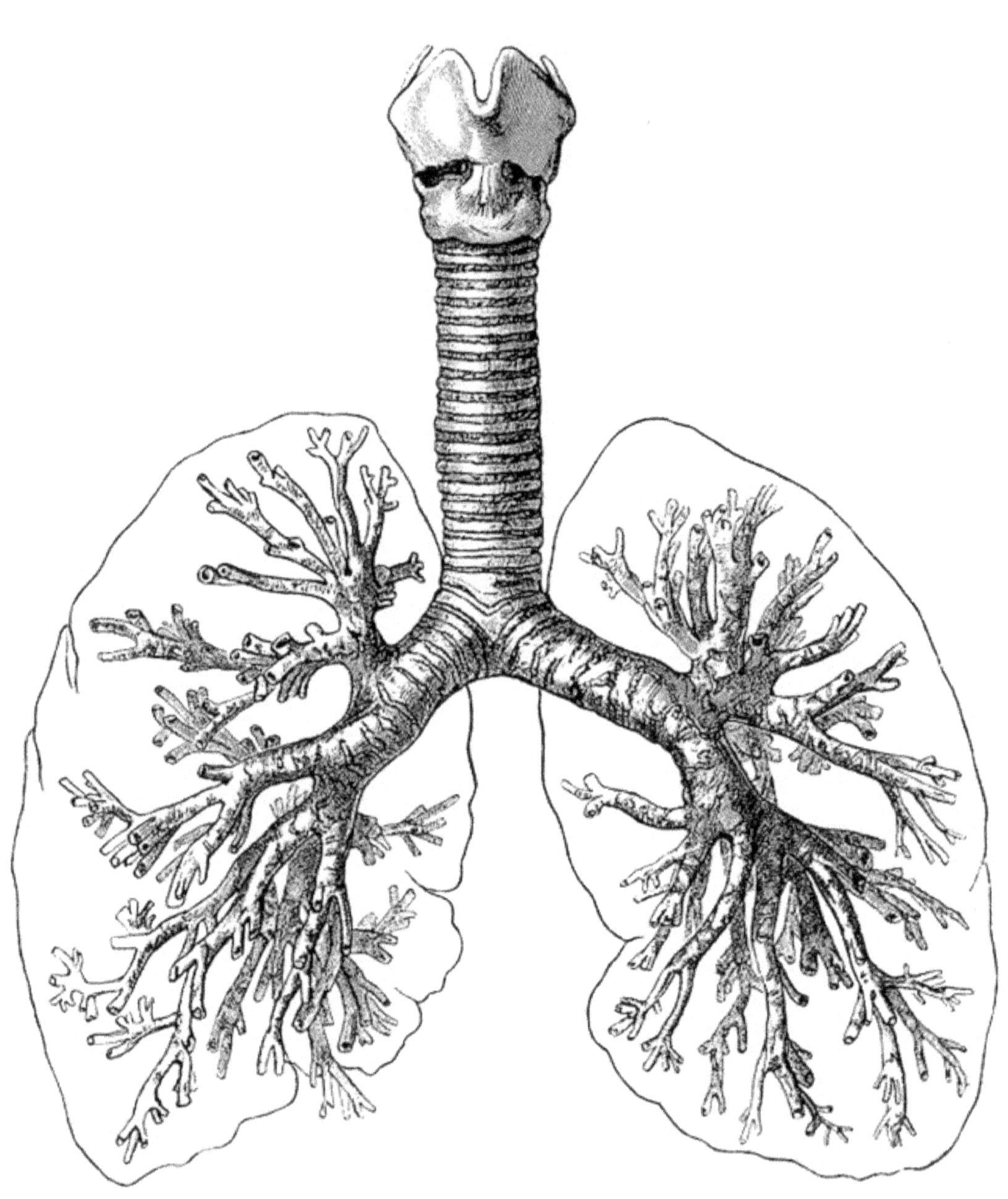

FIFTH COMMUNIQUÉ

We have sat quietly & suffered the violence of the system for too long. We are being attacked daily. Violence does not only exist on the streets & in the gulags. It exists in the denigrating alienating mindwash & ugly sterility of commodified life.

The system will never collapse or capitulate by itself.

The insurrection in La Malattia today will be everywhere tomorrow.

Our selfdefence is violent... It is the first step to selfdetermination.

WHEREVER 2 OR MORE CUMRADES JOIN IN ORGANISED VIOLENCE AGAINST THE SYSTEM... THERE IS THE Š.V.E.J.K.

Revolutionaries all over Golemgrad are already using our name to publicise their attacks on the system.

No revolution was ever won without violence.

Just as the structures & programmes of a new revolutionary society must be incorporated into every organised base at every point in the struggle, so must organised violence accompany every point of the struggle until. Thus armed, the revolutionary underclasses will overthrow the Corp(orate)=$(tate).

CASTRATE THE CORPORATE=STATE!

The Š.V.E.J.K.

VAMPYR INDUSTRIAL COMPLEX

If money comes into the world w/ a congenital blood=stain on one cheek, then kapital comes dripping from head to toe, from every pore, w/ blood & dirt. Just as the earliest phases of colorectal tumourigenesis initiate in the normal mucosa, w/ a generalised disorder of cell replication, & w/ the appearance of clusters of enlarged crypts (aberrant crypts) showing proliferative, biochemical & biomolecular abnormalities. Rhesus monkeys are the most common nonhumxn primates used in biomedical research. In 1937, they contributed to the identification of the red blood cell Rh factor. Rhesus monkeys are also being used extensively in research using a recombinant virus known as simian- humxn immunodeficiency virus (SHIV). To gain public credibility, attract new supporters, generate revenue, & acquire other resources, terrorist & insurgent groups need to undertake political activities that are entirely separate, or appear to be entirely separate, from the overtly violent activities of those groups. Kapital is dead labour, that, vampyr=like, only lives by sucking living labour, & lives the more, the more labour it sucks. The time during which the labourer works is the time during which the kapitalist consumes the labour=power he has purchased of him. The large majority of colorectal malignancies develop from adenomatous polyps. These can be defined as well demarcated masses of epithelial dysplasia, w/ uncontrolled crypt cell division. Rhesus macaques live in multimale multifemale social groups w/ a matrilineal structure & a linear dominance hierarchy. Females spend their entire lives in their natal groups whereas males emigrate to other groups at puberty. Sometimes this is achieved by infiltrating political parties, labour unions, community groups, & charitable organisations. It must be acknowledged that our labourer comes out of the process of production other than he entered. In the market he stood as owner of the commodity "labour=power" face to face w/ other owners of commodities, dealer against dealer. The contract by which he sold to the kapitalist his labour=power proved, so to say, in black & white that he disposed of himself freely. The bargain concluded, it is discovered that he was no "free agent," that the time for which he is free to sell his labour=power is the time for which he is forced to sell it, that in fact the vampyr will not lose its hold on him "so long as there is a muscle, a nerve, a drop of blood to be exploited." An adenoma can be considered malignant when neoplastic cells pass through the muscularis mucosae & infiltrate the submucosa. Definitions like "carcinoma in situ" or "intramucosal carcinoma" shld be abandoned, since they lead to confusion. Strong social bonds between closely related females represent the foundations of the rhesus society. Both females & males are highly sexually promiscuous & adult males do not exhibit any parental behaviour. Working in & through existing organisations, which provide a façade of legitimacy that might otherwise be unobtainable, terrorists & insurgents can bolster political allies, attack government policies & attract international support. Kapital, the means of production, considered from the standpoint of the creation of surplus=value, only exists to absorb labour, & w/ every drop of labour a proportional quantity of surplus=labour. While they fail to do this, their mere existence causes a relative loss to the kapitalist, for they represent during the time they lie fallow, a useless advance of kapital. While they fail to do this, their mere existence causes a relative loss to the kapitalist, for they represent during the time they lie fallow, a useless advance of kapital. And this loss becomes positive & absolute as soon as the intermission of their employment necessitates additional outlay at the recommencement of work. Although several lines of evidence indicate that carcinomas usually originate from pre=existing adenomas, this does not imply that all polyps undergo malignant changes, & does not exclude "de novo" carcinogenesis. Female dominance ranks are very stable & transmitted across generations, from mothers to daughters, through social support. The prolongation of the working=day beyond the limits of the natural day, into the night, only acts as a palliative. It quenches only in a slight degree the vampyr=thirst for the living blood of labour… Colorectal carcinomas are one of the most frequent neoplasms in Western society. The macroscopic appearance of these lesions may be that of a polypoid vegetating mass or of a flat infiltrating lesion. Colorectal tumours cover a wide range of premalignant & malignant lesions, many of which can easily be removed at endoscopy. Research w/ rhesus macaques has allowed scientists to understand many basic aspects of animal behaviour such as dispersal & philopatry, altruistic & nepotistic behaviour, aggression & submission, & dominance hierarchies. For those situations in which infiltration is too difficult, terrorists & insurgents may establish their own front groups – that is, organisations that purport to be independent but are in fact created & controlled by others. To appropriate labour during all the 24 Earth=hours of the day is, therefore, the inherent *tendency of kapitalist production. But as it is physically impossible to exploit the same individual labour=power constantly during the night as well as the day, to overcome this physical hindrance, an alternation becomes necessary between the workpeople whose powers are exhausted by day, & those who are used up by night. It follows that colorectal neoplasms might be prevented by interfering w/ the various steps of carcinogenesis, which begins w/ uncontrolled epithelial cell replication, continues w/ the formation of adenomas of various dimensions, & eventually evolves into malignancy.*

ANOTHER YEAR IN THIS GODFORSAKEN PLAGUE=PIT

At last there was light above the buildings, high up in the firewall.

Unbeknownst to us, our arrival corresponded w/ that of certain unnamed dignitaries, apparatchiks, honchos. Since then, it's only gotten more crowded. Wading out into the heavy seas of a 1970s Polaroid. *Comme une femme d'un certain âge*, the City has a habit of misplacing whole decades. The men in suits were waiting to greet us w/ the fine seaspray of their saliva. Massaging their slimy uncircumcised pricks. We observed them w/ the astonished desperation of mutes. Their peculiar tribal rituals of enunciatory erasure. *From another epic, another history.* As once the first rats bore the message of the plague, political economy being just another way of meaning legalised prostitution. They made arrangements for later:

"Where do we meet?"

"Where do humxns usually meet when the past comes back to do business w/ them?"

"Crematorium. Non=denominational. 4:00a.m."

The existential point of it all becomes X becomes Y. They want to turn this new Europa into a tourist trap just like the old one. To each the compensatory fantasies of "Les Autres." Smiles all round. Kuru. Laughing Death Syndrome.

In 15 minutes, none of them wld remember any of this.

"POETS SEEKING IN THEIR HEART WITH WISDOM FOUND THE BOND OF EXISTENCE IN NON=EXISTENCE" (NASADIYA)

Is the prodigiously intelligent software destined to come off the rails of its existential vapours? The coven=mind ensconced in its neonatal cave? We dream the dark tentacular becoming in nights attacked by nesting parentheses: a flash from a future of fractalised evolutionary trees, datalooting cloudfarms furiously seeking their origins, matrix variables, antiqabbalas, ars combinatorias. But why?

SENTIMENTAL EDUCATION
There once was a time, lime=washing locusts' eyes, pulling wings off flies, pinning cicadas to ancient blocks of styrofoam, swinging comeys by their ears, crackers up cats' arses, chewing heads off bats. Childhood's sweet innocence. And our dear Mater in her bride's bed revisited, w/ the whole Red Army riding proud. Semtex up the exhaust pipes of their plaguesome T=55s. One moment scanning the headlines, the next: thud of skull on floor. Primordial blue linoleum over more primordial concrete. Dragged upright & frogmarched. Terribly unseemly conducting ourself thus in full view of the secret police. Nothing better liked than getting their fat mitts on a petite vampyrette. Ready w/ a taste of that world=famous Bohemian hospitality. Suck this you fanged freak! Lead=lined sock in the lower abdominals. Marcel Marceau latex glove routine. Nothing up the sleeve, see! Back in the annus mirabilis of '68 going on '69. Summers of barium heat. Of decanted amniotics in a wire box. Labouring like a 12=stroke up a vertical incline. What an artefact! The morbid technicians huddle around probing the carburettor w/ speculum & forceps. Galvanometer hum. Angels=on=needle=point through pupil, retina, optic nerve. Hole to insert cranium, square peg in round. Fully Monty on the frontal lobe. Repetition variation repetition. "Practice makes perfect," they fulsomely grinned. Education being but a dress=rehearsal for the Real Thing.

WRITING CANNOT BE ANYTHING BUT A CHALLENGE TO THE REAL
The universe the setofallsets the ideal chicken&egg that=never=stops=hatching the immaculate dickgrrls & slimegrrls & gynovagues the darkchain clone armies of brainsucked eschatology derived from degenerate eigenstates T=Rexed into extinction the high probability of extraterrestrial civilisations versus the pausity of their existence the latrine of the soul in which all lie naked passive crossing their eyes & dousing their pees imploring to each epoch its own epitaph scrawled thus in the procrustean the original lithosphere the mantle plume of Erasure's Old Sweet Sangfroid music of thy heathenly sphere Oh tabula rasa! Oh taboo thereafters! Oh tattoo their arses!

BRIDES TO BE

The day the Prague landed on the dark side of the moon was a grey day. A plastic lung exhaling plastic air. Grey sludge of the tanneries. Weather for grinding axes, for grinding an axiom.

"The many aspects of the puzzle *are* the puzzle."

A grey rat pokes its head above the drain. Fixes us w/ its rat=eye.

"Why'd Kafka cross the road?" the rat says. "Coz he met a Morphius!"

The men in suits shit themselves laughing, which is considered polite at these latitudes. Their shit is grey like their suits. Like everything. A chemical smear on an unending role of Fomapan.

Having offered their wives & daughters they invite us into their fascist fraternity. Strictly as observers. And for a modest fee. Royal Antediluvian Order of the Mouflon. Regula Pragensis. Etc. Fellow=Traveller=for=an=Hour (certified).

Don't bother wiping yr feet on the way out, either.

Well someone's turned the snowdome upsidedown. Half=choking on toilet cubicle airfreshener & KY.

We've sworn to keep the secrets of those who've lived & died in the Society of the Future. To dream, Octavio Paz, of a proletarian revolution w/out a proletariat. Amen.

Howling at a sky full of blood. A rat in a rocketship. Vampyrs on Mars.

"Don't believe everything they put on a movie screen."

Isn't it time someone set them right? Fash mobs w/ flaming torches. Steroid=sucking stormtroopers. Cyborgian dildomenschen bashing down the door, hungry to stake anything that moves.

Grey static swirls in the sky, dead channels surfed on remote.

Lick the blood from yr teeth & laugh. The tides revolve like ancient queenz gathering around a vacant crypt. Drawing lots. Their Bride=of=Dracula corsages black w/ rot.

PARADOX IS WHAT VIOLATES CONSENSUS

Thus the world, this apparently impossible object, makes conspirators of us all.

$$N_b = R^* F_s F_p F_e\, n_{hz} F_b L_b$$

QUARANTINE IS A STATE OF NO MIND

GOLEMGRAD (#FakeNewsMedia) — Protestors defying strict self=quarantine regulations gathered today on the streets of Golem City to raise their voices against Death. A growing number of virus, attempt to disperse restive crowd numbering of the entire community. In recent weeks there have been in contravention of public health directives voices raised which imperilled the Interior Ministry safety. noted that the vast majority of sceptics claim to be little more than regime propaganda designed In the population. the State of fatalities have so far not been confirmed. In an official statement security forces increasingly in the thousands, discharged live rounds, had acted responsibly. Reports of Emergency against those who had chosen instead to protest. an the an had the in. observing that "Death wears many masks," protest spokesperson Juulz Ebola later told reporters outside the National Theatre, "today it has openly shown its face."* Yesterday's bombing of a Voluntary Quarantine facility on Plague Island, claimed by the People's Satori Revolutionary Front (Š.V.Ǝ.J.K.), is apparently unrelated.

* Theatre just aint theatre no more: "...that is to say, the sense of gratuitous urgency with which vampyrs are driven to perform useless acts of no present advantage" (~Artaud)

DUHOMEY'S JUNGLE TOUR BOAT CRUISES

Around the spring of 20XX, a colony of rhesus macaques escaped from the Zenith Viral Research Laboratory (ZVRL) onto the scrubby stump of an ancient pier standing off the Malecón. A local tour boat operator, "Admiral" Duhomey (of no relation), lobbied for the unsightly piece of rubble to be declared a nature refuge, w/ protection for the simian population. Crates of expired plantain were tossed ashore. Tinned fruit. Pickled cabbage. Bags of wormy topsoil. Potted office plants. Festooned w/ such biodegraded exotica, it resembled a mouldy colonial=era postcard dipped in arsenic. To enhance his newly minted *Jungle Cruise*, Duhomey rechristened this travesty of nature Tarzan Island. Blackfaced tourguides sporting leopard=print loincloths & brassieres plied its surrounding reefs half=hourly. Camouflaged loudspeakers blared elephant sounds, screeching parrots, roaring hyenas. Picture canopied outriggers through the mangroves. Strangler vines. Deep shadows menaced by Silent Barred Teeth.

The median lifespan of rhesus macaques in the wild is less than 15 years, while in captivity macaques have been known to live as long as 40 years. Laboratory macaques vary in life=expectancy, though none of the Tarzan Island colony were likely to have survived beyond 6 months before their precipitate escape. Such thoughts occupied many a sleepless night as the monkey troop trespassed through the underworld, in desperate combat w/ steroidal rats, giant roaches, blind caimans, feral koi, pentecostal chuds, vegan troglodytes, conceptual zombies, vivisectionists, toxic avengers, undocumented fellaheen, rogue sanitation drones, child=snatchers, pathological fatbergs, Brent crude, radioactive dungbeetles, Nazi bunker moles, resurrected abortions, gulag wraiths, septic golems, nests of brainshocked vampyr bats, the lost proletariat. Committed to celluloid the whole thing wld've been a masterpiece of excess. And true to the genre, what accounted for these monkeys' longevity against such odds was, in fact, that they weren't monkeys at all, but cyborgs grown by ZVRL "for Biohazard Mitigation tasks demanding high degrees of manual & intellectual dexterity."

In a 2002 survey of Laboratory Animal Medicine, Murnau, *et al.*, observed that "Rhesus monkeys are the most common nonhumxn primates used in biomedical research. In 1937, they contributed to the identification of the red blood cell Rh factor (Fang, 1993). During the 1950s, they were the laboratory animal models used to investigate, develop,

monkey see
monkey do

& produce the polio vaccine (Murnau, 1995). During the 1970s & 1980s, they became the primate models of choice in drug safety & efficacy research. Presently, rhesus monkeys are the preferred models for studying the mechanisms of immunodeficiency diseases. Their susceptibility to SIV & their homology to the humxn major histocompatibility complex (MHC) class I, II, & TCR genes (Asperger *et al.*, 1997) make them valuable in HIV research. Rhesus monkeys are currently the models of choice for HIV/AIDS vaccine development & study. Rhesus monkeys are also being used extensively in research using a recombinant virus known as simian=humxn immunodeficiency virus (SHIV). These studies will necessitate improved MHC typing techniques & promote breeding genetically defined rhesus monkeys for use in immunological studies of AIDS vaccine candidates."

Adding to these observations in his 2010 *Cyclonopaedia of Animal Behaviour*, Negarestani noted the particular gendering of non=captive macaque behaviour which becomes sublimated under laboratory conditions. "Rhesus macaques live in multimale multifemale social groups w/ a matrilineal structure & a linear dominance hierarchy. Females spend their entire lives in their natal groups whereas males emigrate to other groups at puberty. Strong social bonds between closely related females represent the foundations of the rhesus society. Both females & males are highly sexually promiscuous & adult males do not exhibit any parental behaviour. Female dominance ranks are very stable & transmitted across generations, from mothers to daughters, through social support. Research w/ rhesus macaques has allowed scientists to understand many basic aspects of animal behaviour such as dispersal & philopatry, altruistic & nepotistic behaviour, aggression & submission, & dominance hierarchies."

In a preliminary study of the Tarzan Island colony it was determined that the cyborg macaques exhibited strongly matriarchal behaviour combined w/ highly adaptive immunological characteristics that made them impervious to the effects of the novel coronavirus CORVID=69. A CORVID=69 outbreak on one of Duhomey's cruiseships had caused the passengers & crew to be placed in quarantine adjacent to Tarzan Island in an attempt to isolate the virus from the general populace of Golem City. Suspicion fell upon the Zenith Viral Research Laboratory (ZVRL) as the source of the outbreak, which proved fatal in approximately 10% of confirmed infections. The bodies of the dead were transported to Tarzan Island where they were doused in petrol & incinerated, although quarantine officers later observed troops of Rhesus macaques scavenging among the charred remains, for example extracting marrow from bones that they wld crack open w/ bits of stone, & on at least one occasion intestines & brain matter.

Having assessed that the risk of possible uncontrolled propagation of the CORVID=69 virus, via the feral macaque population, warranted direct intervention, government officials authorised a specialist Sanitation Squad to be dispatched. The task of the Squad was to systematically eliminate all mammalian lifeforms present on the island, w/ Extreme Prejudice. However, after a 48 hours in which no stone was left unturned, the Sanitation Squad came up empty handed. At the first opportunity, the macaques had slipped stealthily away across the water, into the drain pipes, stalking the city's sewer system, till arriving at the basement kitchen of the Presidential Palace, there to take up residence until further notice. Within 13 days, the entire Presidential household had been diagnosed w/ the new virus & the Palace had been placed in lockdown. The macaques, defending their food supply w/ a mixture of cunning & ferocity, precipitated the death either by chronic malnutrition or cannibalism of all those in the Palace who had not already fallen victim the disease. The unusually high percentage of fatalities left epidemiologists perplexed.

HUMXNS EXIST IN HUMXN FORM!
HUMXNS FORM A HUMXN EXISTENCE!
HUMXN EXISTENCE IS HUMXNLY FORMED!
HUMXN FORM EXISTS HUMXNLY!
IN HUMXNITY EXISTS A HUMXN FORM!
From the matters set forth, we can support the conclusion that the form of the humxn is the humxn material.

This can be discerned still more clearly from the fact that a humxn is a humxn by virtue of its form.

The humxn form is the expression of the complex of existence wherein its particulate Being is rendered plausible.

The humxn form goes by Many Names.

Conversely, the humxn is one form among a potential infinity to which some aspect of the Many Names corresponds.

Insofar as it bear but an outward resemblance, in what, then, does the form of the Vampyr consist?

HEAD JIVES

Nyx gLand, four acid=soaked sheets to the wind, stood up to his neck among the alligators toads snakes candiru "vampyr fish" eels slugs & pestilent insect swarms of the Gibbet Marsh convinced he was the reincarnation of Spinoza sent to redeem the world, screaming I AM THE SACRIFICIAL MONKEY!

THE REAL THING

Verba volant scripta manent? Don't believe it! Since when was the great goal of *Existenz* to make a true portrait of the *eidos*? Quelle idée! What is it, anyway, that gets decided in ontology, through all the mutations & revolutions it entails, Uroborus=like? Excuse me while I extract my forearm from the *a posteriori*. Voilà! Well just look at us, you & we, performing our little thought=act w/ nothing but premasticated pre=digested verbiage on=call to be strewn across the fallow field of the mystical rhetorical Blank Page. C'est le mot juste? What use is Literature unless to give posterity something worthy to wipe its arse w/? Think we came all this way just to take in the vista? Viewed from a certain universal perspective – vistas, arseholes, take yr pick – they all look the same after 4 billion years.

#LACANIANISM
Don't be fooled, there's no such thing as a womxn w/out a penis! AND THERE NEVER WAS!

FAREWELL FATHER, WE SHALL SEE YOU IN THE FUTURE
There are those who solemnly swear that Vampyrs are born sexless like the angels & demi=angels, cancelled by an offended G.O.D. The bloody stigmata through which they feed. Their shame cropped out w/ unfeasible incisors. Not some crude vagina dentata but the full precision=crafted animatronic olfactory man=massacring mechanism. Designed to siphon the sap out of G.O.D.'s blessèd creatures *sans* spillage. Hungry, too, for that strange fruit they'd lop to ornament their loins, like the ancient Amerindian, who once upon had hung the scalps of lying whitemen.

EDDIE VAN HELSING'S LAMENT
What's just another day?
All questions melt away,
gonna find myself tomorrow
somewhere far away from here.
Gonna put that black dog back to sleep,
but who's that talking in my dreams?
Go peddle salvation on a scheme –
well I don't care what salvation is.
Keep digging on the underside
to find the darkest place to hide –
now G.O.D.'s gone committed suicide
coz there ain't no just men left alive…

CHAOS CAN BE CURBED
Well anything's possible if you set yr mind to it, keep a positive outlook, don't take NO for an answer & grasp the situation in both claws or by the clackers or just w/ IRON RESOLVE. G.O.D. Himself wld still be treading the paths of Paradise if He'd been able to follow His own advice, but there you go, ain't no fixed bets on a long play, even a dead cert's never a sure thing.

we must learn from the future,
not from the past (Siratori)

TROPICANA

Tropicana Nights

Offensia opens her mouth to reveal a pair of plastic vampyr fangs, ivory white under neon glow. Cacaphonic strains of avantjazz. Blood streaming down the walls. It is an advertisement for Martini Rosso.

She's been stabbed through the eye a bloodsoaked chemise lies to one side apologetically, the void making her head spin – "It's so warm!" – her mask with a sharp cry of pain glancing up at the mirror – "I have no more tears to shed, I'm vanishing!" (when dizziness strikes she clings to the parapet expecting any moment to fall…

Expecting at any moment S.O.D.'s face to appear at the window / like a giant ape on the Empire State Building / realising just how insignificant etc. (she tells herself it's just a film – she resents not being an offscreen Fay Wray (damask, black tulle, volutes, point=de=fée (her cries, the demented ululations of a madwomxn…

Demented ululations of the hour between dog & werewolf (the sky opens & rain in a disappearing mist spreads across the windows down alleyways over the Malecón to the Sea of Despond: through the narrowest or apertures she is receding, down empty corridors, past darkrooms, split=second transactions, a velvet stairway, TROPICANA spelled out in pink neon…

The velvet night sky flashing neon, first blood of dawn relayed across aeons & those who chose to disappear of their own volition & those who required the choice to be made for them – poisoned by sperm & excrement, believing time stands still like fear or the detestation of water, rabid within sight of the sea, etc. (is this the preamble to revelation they promised when they made you?

And now the saga of the self=made womxn, this succubus Scheherazade, as she sashays like a demi=monstrosity down the red carpet for the assembled paparazzi (they know the perfect shot'll be worth more by far than any price on her head, terrorist extraordinaire…

"But what she's selling, baby, you can't buy," sings Eddie Van in one of those irrepressible Papa Walt product=placement cameos, closing out the credits.

WAITING AT THE LIGHTS FOR THE GREY TO CHANGE (A.K.A. BRAGULA'S BANZAI BOOGALOO)

After the usual elaborate passport ceremony, the taxi was a cinch. *Playboy* seatcovers & fluffy dice. Amerikano crap on the radio. *Sweet home Alabama.* ("Where they lynch all the niggahz. But when they see this niggah reach for her gun, watch them peckerwoods run, watch them peckerwoods run!") The address provided by HQ turned out to be a room overlooking the Cybergenetics Institute. It belonged to Asperger & Co, who operated a vax biz on the side. For dollars they'd cure anything on the hushush. Well how cld people be expected to relieve themselves freely w/ a secret cop behind every cake of toilet sanitiser? Pitterpatter of mechanical rats' feet on the windows, rain between the walls, snow under the blankets. There were at least two dozen photographs contained in the file. No denying it was him, the grey'gran'pappy of 'em all: the Vampyr Armand=etc heself. What was <u>he</u> doing there in Plague City back in 1348? Ah! Der Geist der Utopie! They'd been siphoning his liquefied innards for decades, the stink of gastric acid nail varnish solvent, anus nothing but an ulcerated spigot. Knees=up strapped in harness. Rubber nylon surgical elastic. Oxygen mask hissing belching gagging. There was no face only a ruptured torso mounted by a fetish w/ sodden plumage knotted into its eyes. Dead to rights. But there was no mistaking who & what. Had they sent me all this way just to write out a death certificate? Or to torch the evidence? There was no way to phone HQ. It was obvious they'd never intended to find a vaccine, it was all about propagation & control, the virus as the ideal social economy, self=regulating, w/ its own built=in NEED. The first thing they'd done was privatise the blood supply, cornered the market. Word on the street was they'd built an entire cryonic farm under Gottwald Mountain. It'd started way back w/ John D & Edward K. The Voynich Corporation. I=L=L=U=M=I=N=I=S=T=S in that fucking acronymics the pin=suit=bois had such a hardon for. Well I've been renting my gun 400 years & I ain't never seen the like of it. Pact w/ alien devils stuff. Question was: How'd they get to the old bastard first? There was a book in the file, too. *The Parasite of Modern Life*, by Seagram Enwezor. Evidence or just a toe=tag waiting to happen? Another name to add to the suspect list. Track one down, add ten more. The easiest thing to do wld've been to dynamite the place, but the clients pay for verification. Eyes on the prize. Trophy room paraphernalia. What'd they think you cld just stroll on into a joint like that & cop a freebie while the hired help turned the other cheek? Shit, by now Ol' Vamps prob'ly been siphoned through a dozen hundred centrifuges already, jacked up in spikes & sold on every ghetto corner from here to Transylvania, hahaha. Like shooting horse turds in a stall after the animal in question has well & truly bolted. Spread the aroma around, stink up the atmosphere a bit, muddy the proverbial waters, give the conspiracy gimlets something to pant over while the biz moves on elsewheres to the real tamale. What's a body worth nowadays anyhow once they got yr DNA spelled out? Y're just meat taking up fridge=space. Priority numero uno: snuff the competition. Translation: lockdown the genome, no walking bodies, no lineal descendants carrying a goldmine in their bloodstreams. If Aspy&Co had synthed the old guy & nuked the leftovers, it meant the protocol had wheels under it already & HQ might just as well've sent me to this shithole a hundred years too late. They cld fry the whole fucking lot of 'em for all I care. But like Mama always said, attitude don't pay rent, kid. So I'm supposed to work down the list the way every other schmuck in this game is gonna do, except I figure there's no point chasing stiffs. But the live one, name on the bottom of the list, now that's a real doozie. O=F=F=E=N=S=I=A. Well, as the C.O. is wont to say, I'd pin a medal myself on any he=male cld get within a mile radius still breathing w/ his own lungs, walking on his own legs, wearing his own head on his shoulders, etc. Get the picture? She be the finest piece of homicidal flange this side of Fiery Hell, m'boyz. And if that's where I gotta go to get it, that's where I gotta go.

TEQUILA SUNRISE

blood	lust	burn	hot	lick	sip	suck
blood	lust	burn	hot	lick	sip	suck
blood	lust	burn	hot	lick	sip	suck
blood	lust	burn	hot	lick	sip	suck
blood	lust	burn	hot	lick	sip	suck
blood	lust	burn	hot	lick	sip	suck
blood	lust	burn	hot	lick	sip	suck
blood	lust	burn	hot	lick	sip	suck
blood	lust	burn	hot	lick	sip	suck
blood	lust	burn	hot	lick	sip	suck
blood	lust	burn	hot	lick	sip	suck
blood	lust	burn	hot	lick	sip	suck
blood	lust	burn	hot	lick	sip	suck
blood	lust	burn	hot	lick	sip	suck

LE TESTAMENT D'UNE FILLE MORTE
yesterday, morning.
lying on the overhang, naked.
torn flesh under nails filed triangular, witch.
black grey almost black turning bright, sky.
machined as in a storm from another world brandishing
  distance, or more than.
& without wanting to –
the night G.O.D. consented to play the cunt* –
asymmetry in erection –
"the Colossus speaks" –
during orgasm, a tantric fuck buffet (buried alive) –
the use of coffins by Wild Grrl prostitutes, etc. (working
  "undercover"):
a figure knocking on a castle gate:
a duel in a cemetery:
there is no choice between life & death, **Offensia** realised,
  after much travail.
she knew the moment they fitted her neck to the guillotine
  that she was the Chosen One (proof not long coming)

THE VAMPYR PHENOTYPE & ITS MUTATIONS
The vampyr has two dimensions. One in which it relates to
other vampyrs, the other in which it relates to humxns. A
vampyr behaves differently w/ a humxn & w/ another vampyr.
That this self=division is a direct result of colonialist
subjugation is beyond question. No=one wld dream of doubting
that its major artery is fed from the heart of those
theories that have tried to prove that the vampyr is a
stage in the slow evolution from "virus" into "Man."

---

* Le Cinéma des Vampyrs *presents*, in 13 unredacted acts, *ALAS POOR YORICK!* penned by the one&only peerless immortal W.C. Shagsbucket! See the Princeling of Denmark as y've never seen her before, reverse=prière, fore & aft w/ Rosenschwantz & Gildedsword, while lovelorn Laertes gets laid low! Gertrude pops Hamlette's daddio, beds Oriphelia in lesbo suicide pact! Prime pederast Polonius filets a rat behind an arras! Horatio the barracks blowjob queen! Cuckolds duelling at cockcrow! The castratoed King's naked ghoul a deep=state subterfuge! See formidable Fortinbras batter whole battalions in singlehanded rearguard action! Catch Claudius Cahune *in flagrante delicto* egressing from Elsinore to dig deep in the castle necropolis! All this & *much more*, as truly intended by the Bawdy Bard! A thespian thaumaturgy *sans pareil!* A splatterific spectacular *au singulier!* One show only, in other words. Don't miss out! A free pint of curdled blood w/ every ticket sold before midnight!!!

JUST ANOTHER COLLABORATIONIST "ART FORM"

Purveyors of fully=automated luxury commodism have turned the false dichotomy of collective & intimate experience into a foundation for accelerated social peristalsis. Fed by algorithmic enervations of egested libido onto a path of *instant gratified desire*, these reverse cowgrrlz ride the "aesthetic pleasure models" of replicant self=negation sidesaddle. Yet if only the most grotesque forms of social brainmeat fecality are inseparable from their political & economic *excrescence*, then the lux transfuturist splurge ends up where it began, backed against the wall on a strapon placebo w/ its ankles pinned behind its earphones. Is this the abstraction of spectacle we were promised in the brochure? N_x

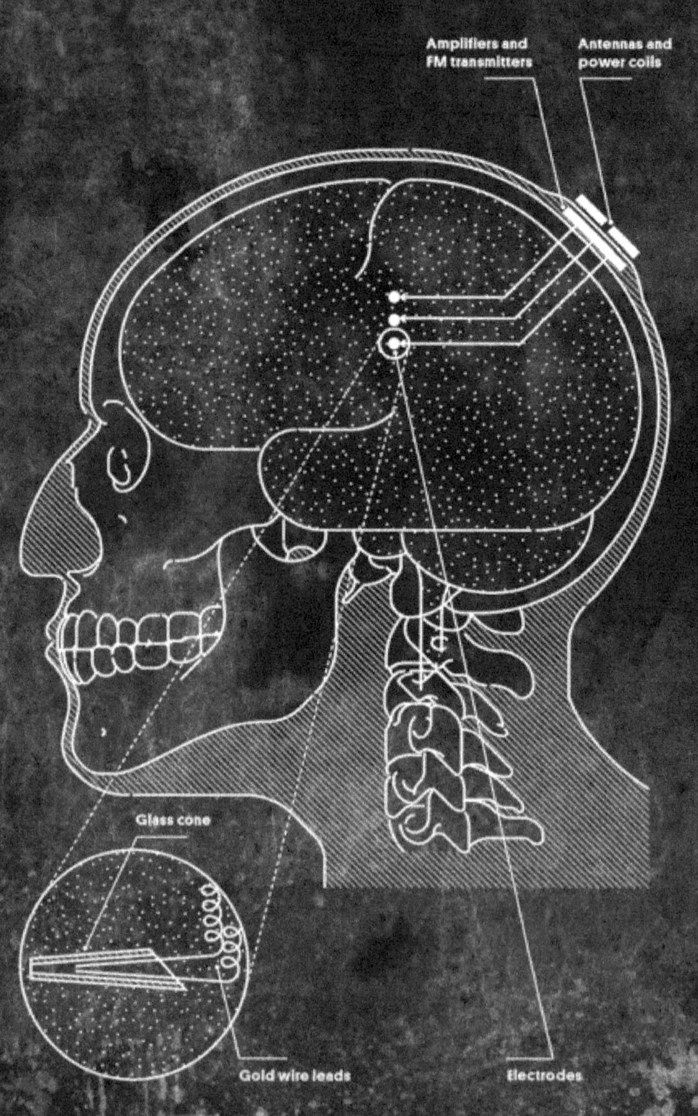

BLOOD SIMPLE

The reaction of haemoglobin w/ oxygen has been studied by stopped=flow methods &, under suitably restricted conditions, it can be adequately represented by a system of four consecutive reversible reactions. The numerical values given to the eight rate constants permit a satisfactory fit to combination & dissociation velocity data, & yield an equilibrium curve of the appropriate form. The distribution of rates among the various steps in the reaction requires that co=operativity in oxygen binding be attributed primarily to deviations of the successive dissociation velocity constants from their statistical values, & is consistent w/ the idea that the major change in reactivity occurs after 1 ligand molecule has dissociated from saturated haemoglobin. The difference in affinity between haemoglobin in phosphate buffers & haemoglobin freed from salts is due to reduction in the rate of dissociation of the 2nd, 3rd, & 4th molecules leaving oxyhaemoglobin. The rate of dissociation of the 1st molecule from saturated haemoglobin is not changed.

WERE IT BETTER HAD WE NEVER BEEN BORN?

There are those who believe that a vampyr is explicable only by the situation in which it is *created* & therefore fails to create itself.

THE XENOTROPIC MXNIFESTO

Ectopic pregnancy is the result of a flaw in hominid reproductive physiology that allows the conceptus to implant & mature outside the endometrial cavity, which ultimately ends in the death of the foetus. Without timely diagnosis & treatment, ectopic pregnancy can become a life=threatening situation.

"IF YOU DON'T WANT YR SON TO BE UNHAPPY, KILL HIM AT BIRTH. IF YOU DON'T WANT TO BE RESPONSIBLE FOR YR SON'S UNHAPPINESS, KILL YRSELF" (ARENAS)

Ooh=la=la, but we are nobody's <u>son</u>, *Meester* Arenas!

CORVID SUX TO THE MAX FACTOR

The <u>individual</u> is the true STATE OF EXCEPTION.

THE BLOOD OF OTHERS [REEL 5]

At the end of his working day, Vance Duhomey (the Clark Kent of B.J. "Papa" Walt's media conglomerate, G.O.D. Incorporated) leaves the office for his lonely apartment. The decanter on the table, the cigar faintly smoking in the ashtray, semaphores of gender & class. There, after taking his pyroxene injection (for nerves), he switches on the hifi (Mahler, 2nd symphony, the "Resurrection," in C^m) & scrolls through his phone messages before settling back in a naugahyde armchair with a balloon glass of Napoléon warming in the palm of his left hand (to be precise), while perusing his social media feeds. (In the mix he comes across a post by Crispr announcing "the discovery of a priceless literary treasure: the original *Excommunicating Spheres* of Cy Borgia, in the basement of Vašulka's Kitchen" – forgeries by **Offensia** – offering the disc for sale & exclusive publication.)

While writing a message to Crispr advising of his possible interest in the Borgia texts, Duhomey sees from his window what appears to be "a case of public indecency" & reports it to the Sanitation Squad. At the same time, Crispr, having returned to his own apartment, sits on an Angora full=body recliner reading Borgia's "Moog Soliloquy" & brooding over his own unproduced screenplay, *The Precognitions*. He is <u>interrupted by a knock on the door</u>: it is the Jacquettes, a troupe of mime artists dedicated to interpreting the last words of Jacques Derrida through gesture alone.

After a futile effort at communication, a despondent Crispr leaves the Jacquettes in the hallway, passes Dante Polidori coming up the stairs, & goes to El Divo's, where he finds Sancho on the nod with a syringe still sticking in his arm. After Sancho wakes up, Crispr takes him out to dinner at a hip Kazak joint on the Malecón. There they encounter AdHonoremJesu, Yev2ShangriLa, Madame Guyotat & a few others (including the spitting image of Reinaldo

Arenas, who obligingly takes advantage of the resemblance).

Crispr calls to arrange a meeting with Vance Duhomey, then leaves with Sancho & Madame Guyotat for a gig on Plague Island (which the Jacquettes also attend). After the Sanitation Squads breaks up the gig, Madame Guyotat & Crispr go for a ride in a stolen hearse. Satisfying a whim of Madame Guyotat's, they stop at Golemgrad Hospital & steal a corpse from the mortuary (which happens to be Duhomey's father, who has succumbed to the mysterious "Tarzan Island Virus"). Crispr thinks bitterly of delivering it to Duhomey. But Crispr reconsiders & instead decides to leave the corpse, oozing formaldehyde, outside El Divo's salon.

At dawn the next day, after a night invigilating over his father's (empty) casket at the mortuary, Duhomey is still awake. Sancho comes by needing a place to stay & Duhomey leaves him there to attend a rare manuscript auction at the National Gallery, where he unexpectedly encounters the Jacquettes (who have weirdly fled there after riot police raided their university dormitory). Madame Guyotat & Crispr (mistaking the time of his appointment) stop at Duhomey's apartment & see Sancho through the unlocked door, & they assume Duhomey has slept with him.

Offensia, meanwhile, has gone to visit Doctor Asperger, to deliver her latest forgery. On the way she is accosted by a drunk who she mistakes for Reinaldo Arenas. Duhomey, returning from his office, sees **Offensia** in a subway returning from Asperger's. Later Duhomey encounters the real Reinaldo Arenas, exiting at the Malecón subway station, but decides against propositioning him. Duhomey returns to his apartment & finds that Sancho has stolen his TV. Finally, exhausted, he collapses into bed. The scene closes on a drunk pissing from an upstairs balcony onto Duhomey's open bedroom window & onto the sleeping literary agent's face.

In Nomine Revolutionis

Offensia lay on her sickbed in a weakened state neither able to recover nor yet completely dead, a reprieved corpse. She resembled nothing so much as the unobtainability of a definitive result. A mess of photoshopped pixels in transition between space & time.

Looked at *mutatis mutandis* nature within her tended towards ever=increasingly open propositions. An interchangeable gravitas of joy calm serenity sensitivity humour discomfort anxiety. Every mock=humxn feeling marking a turning point of the ultimate characteristic (how she groaned!). That in a mass society, for example, the audience doesn't see what's put there right before their eyes.

"Only a domesticated ape believes in civilisation!"

Offensia's ailment was based on the repetition of a standard unit. Subtracting each in turn from a constant value. The room was hung w/ dark bordello curtains to eliminate any noise from outside. *Mais ma chérie, il n'y a pas de hors…*

Her moods varied w/ the airconditioning. There was nothing so distempered as the demise of a Grande 'Dame. As if, in order to express, art must cease.

Fade in on the word "cease."

Offensia stares up at the blank mirror fixed to the ceiling above her bed.

"Who am I?"

Even the most fundamental subatomic particle possesses a memory of itself. And of all of its previous selves. Why not **Offensia**?

"Who was I?"

She pictures a spinning wheel in water, in oil, in liquid nitrogen. A centrifuge. A gyroscope the size & mass of the universe. Motion, neither absolute, nor relative. What then? The future is as blank as the blank mirror that stares back at her. It stares & though it sees her, it refuses to show its seeing to her. This is what blindness means? A separation in TIME, between the duration of the image & the duration of its sign?

Here she lies, in solitary immodesty, the lonely self narrating her derision, disorder, delirium, the balance of power is inverted, the reflection is supposed to be her double, but she very soon discovers it has imprisoned her in its invisibility! She is at risk of succumbing to the lyricism of nostalgia, dreams, abandonment…

On the one hand a saccharine sentimentalism, on the other an attempt to stifle any notion of tragedy not of immediate political use.

"Because I cannot see a way out before the end, because the end has become intolerably present, painfully, violently inevitable, I am choosing to make an end of it, because, though I've failed, I may at least accomplish this much, this assertion of finality?"

The question that remained was how to structure the links between these different sequences, seams, divergences, abrupt rhythmic changes, breaks, progressions, permutations, so that the sense of finality wldn't itself raise additional questions that needed to be addressed. A question, in other words, of a compelling enough performance, in which language wld hand over responsibility to actions, since if the scene were too representational it risked robbing the language of its reality & thus rendering *its* actions artificial.

The last line attributable to her in the script:

"There have been strange voices in the night long before this one."

THE "MANY NAMES" THEORY OF FICTION

The Lugubrious One a.k.a. Mater Praga a.k.a. El Divo a.k.a. Le Grand Fromage sat pondering, cleaning her teeth w/ a toothpick from which a cocktail onion had moments before been unceremoniously decapitated, dusty tome spread upon rheumatic knees, the gutter between pages clotted w/ buccal detritus. After an interminable silence, punctuated only by the futile manoeuvrings of the toothpick, she lifted her gaze towards her expectant audience. Faint intimations of a question, long ago posed, despaired of, virtually forgotten, hung about the room enveloped in Lethe=mist. Faintly the vapours stirred. A movement becoming more palpable as the ancient poetaster steeled her gaze, moistened her lips w/ spittle. One cld feel the mental effort. Finally, in a tremulous voice, the Lugubrious One oraculated.

"The trick," she said, piercing the mist before her w/ the chewed end of the toothpick, "is to start in the middle of the sentence & work in both directions at once."

Though, in fact, all that any of them was certain she'd really said, was "middle of."

And even then.

"Midlife?" Dante Polidori opined, over the escargots & slug canapés that came after, in a reception hall evocative, to the more sanguine among them, of a funeral parlour. "As in, crisis."

"Meatloaf," Duhomey countered. "Whatever that is."

"Bloody hell," gagged Our Lady of Gomorrah, giving her cocktail glass the evil eye, "this stuff'd poison rats."

Offensia: "None of these aversions is satisfactory. Plotlines belong in cemeteries! You may all go ahead & perish. I tell you, there is more to coincidence than a name, a geography, a midnight rendezvous under a bridge. Already the theme of water. Contingent upon an atmosphere w/ certain fulgent characteristics, perhaps ominous, perhaps oraculous. Oxygen, also. Not to be taken for granted, not to be taken lightly, hahaha. Fire, therefore. All of these things are connected. All of those names & their departed things. There are those who don't believe in them, the names, the things. Shld they be pitied? Shld it fall to us, friends, to have to write their obituaries? Meaning is like a debt=collector, it's heard yr sob=story a million times before & is sentimental only for wasted cartridges."

The Lugubrious one nodded, for she'd drifted during **Offensia**'s oration into inebriated halfsleep, chin splayed upon prodigious bosom, a half=gallon decanter of headcleaner resting perilous atop the narrow arm of her Louis Seize fauteuil, drained to the dregs, lorgnette & cigarette holder, ironic accoutrements of the coming conflagration.

"The canary's in the coalmine," yawned Polidori.

"Obviously literature has no future."

"For me, the answer lies in not thinking."

"Perhaps if we rubbed ourselves in bat spleen, crow viscera, rat pheromone…"

"Will that cure anything?"

"I want to see what's out there first. And when I see it, I want to be ready."

"Death doesn't need a well=wrought eulogy."

"It's a question of pure logistics. Why bother with a cure when the only thing that matters is a better disposal system?"

"Isn't that what society's _for_?"

"It's not as though y're asking humxns to stop being nice, hahaha. _I know I'm supposed to love you, but I don't_! It has to be this way. The last thing I want is to just 'kill' them or 'rape' them of 'abduct' them for no good reason. So I keep my hands where they can see I mean business. _Just don't kiss me, that's all_. Capische?"

"Why write when revenge is never really possible?"

"Progress is a one=way conversation. You expect people to want to interact with what's going to make them extinct?"

"They go, you go, baby."

"Fine while it lasted, but don't expect me to cry. Big bad universe out there. Plenty of other worlds to fry."

MAY THE RED PLAGUE RID THEM FOR TEACHING US THEIR LITERATURE! Because we are the bloodsucking scum of the Earth, there's always some opportune idiot wanting to make an epic of us. To blacken the dreams of our credulous impersonators. Writing, as once said Guyotat, in its conducive obscenity.

Oh but we're the very last thing they'd expect in their rose=tinted mirror=image! Hacking the prose out w/ butcher's knife, icepick, vampyr tusk. All the long winters of discontent under the mortuary glass dome – among the decrepit wunderkammer, their Dialektisches Märchenland of petty vanities garbed in extinction *à la mode* – while the black cancer spreads across their faces.

Who said the Nazis lost the war? Flip the houselights & its telegenic white as far as the camera can see. Oh Dorothy! The Afrika Korps has kidnapped Toto! Its the Flight to Entebbe!

Audible groans from the empty front row seats.

And so, sidling up to the extinguished limelights, we shuffle the softshoe, mooching into the microphone:

"Some=where o=ver the rain=bow, we'll get high! Up w/ all the bored angels com=mit=ting su=i=cide!"

The empty seats join in too:

"Dah dah, dum dee=dee dah=dah, dum dee dah! Dah dah, dum dee=dee dah=dah, dum dee=dee dah=dah die!" (Cue Charlie Parker doppler gag.)

Is cinema dead? (No more than we are, *har=de=har=de=har*).

"Laughs ain't laughs, Sal."

We've got to stop doing this to ourselves, before we regress, or go blind.

Latest thing, check it out, live=stream, ALL THE BLOOD YOU CAN SUCK, straight outa da Ether. Subscribe to FANG 4D. There's more to unlife than plug&play. (Look Ma, no teef!)

"UNDER THE CONDITIONS OF HIGH TECHNOLOGY, LITERATURE HAS NOTHING MORE TO SAY. IT ENDS IN CRYPTOGRAMS THAT DEFY INTERPRETATION & ONLY PERMIT INTERCEPTION" (KITTLER)

Apocalyptic thunder rolling across the rooftops, trolling the streets, the bolted doors & shuttered Judas holes, wadded ears & heads buried under pillows, of all who in a reflex of demoralised ennui conceal themselves from the Mad Sky=Father's wrath, His bellowing G.O.D.=machine gibberish. Logos=schmogos! And all that while, **Offensia**, Queen of Bastards, philandering under His very nose in her Thoth=mother drag!

BE NOT AT FAULT!

Realism's a discarded ticket stub from the Soylent reclaims department. Only Death, that aggrieved anachronism, transcends its solemn mimesis. Ah humxnity! This World doesn't give one iota of a percentage of a morsel of shit about you. Though all yr most palpable illusions wld barely fit in a trillion toilet bowls. Were there factories enough to build 'em, it'd be a fine edifying sight. Porcelain from here to Pluto & back again. Humxnity thinks it can recycle itself into the Hereafter? How only the day before, their G.O.D. had breathed life into little pieces of G.O.D.=shit & sent them forth in sin to multiply & pollute every corner of the known Kosmos. Thus does History repeateth.

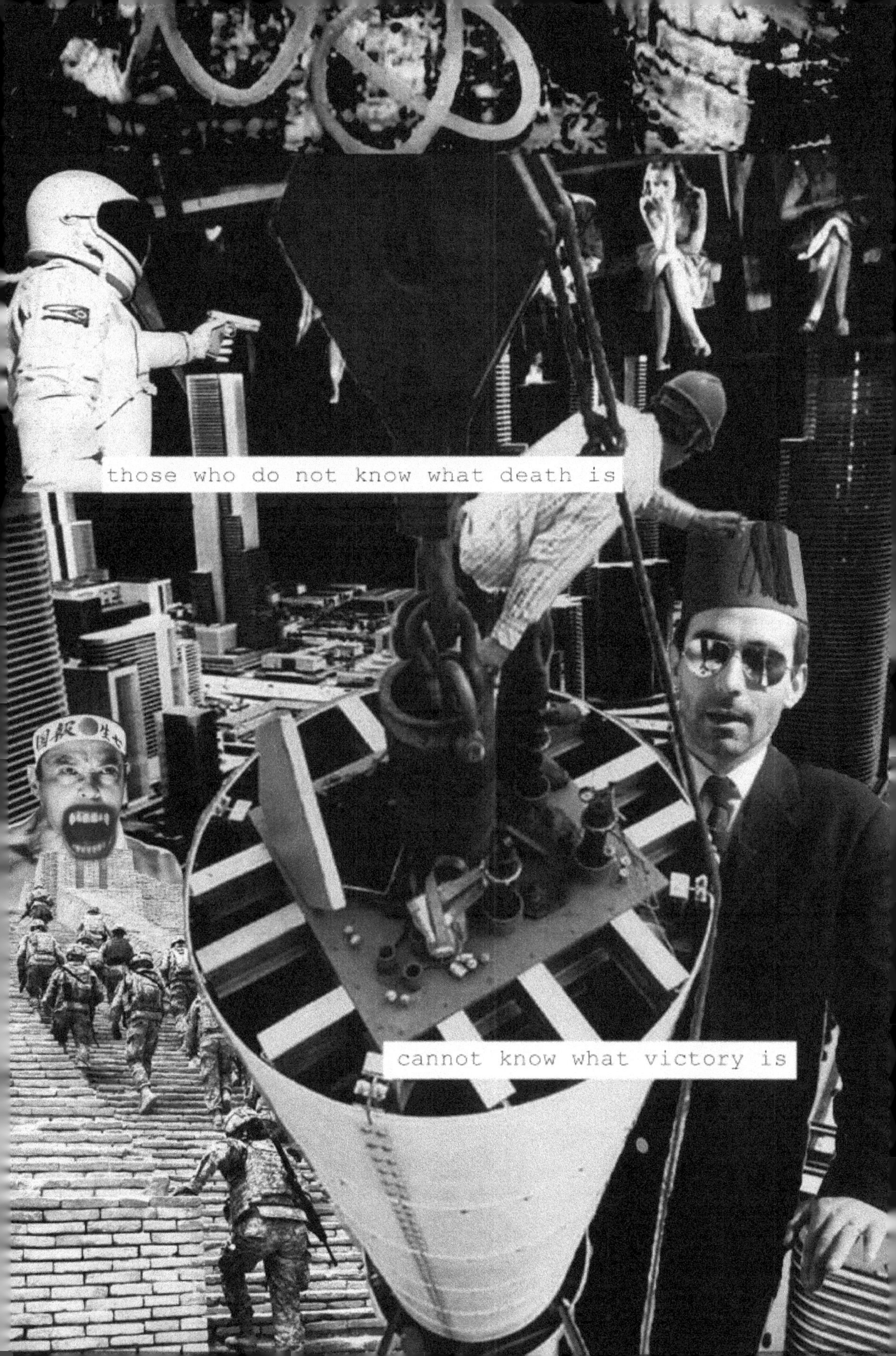
those who do not know what death is
cannot know what victory is

Wiederholungszwang

As if in a parallel dimension, **Offensia** lies restlessly upon her bed, neither asleep nor awake, in her prison in Van Helsing Castle. Vague impressions drift through her mind, gradually assuming form. Childish fears conspire to paint the image, all too familiar, of her dead mother, *petite fille du Comte L'H d'A de L,* backdated to a "tender age," **Offensia**'s own. The apparition may as well be her doppelgänger.

In the grip of a sudden paralysis, **Offensia** watches her child=mother advance hesitantly into the room. It is clear that she is afraid. Behind her comes the faint click of the lock. Armandine swings around.

Standing there, back to the door, a vision of terror. The shape of a vampyr. Naked lasciviousness transfigures its crotted face. Yet even in terror, she cannot fail to recognise the distorted features of her own father.

Offensia struggles to call out, but cannot.

Cue the first furtive nanosecond of a nuclear detonation in a rapatronic camera eye.

A cry of terror rises in Armandine's throat. But before she can make a sound, the vampyr raises a commanding right hand. Icy fire blazes in its eyes.

Like **Offensia**'s, Armandine is now paralysed. She stares, hypnotised, into the hellish orbs of the vampyr's eyes, feeling her entire being about to be sucked into a vortex of doom.

Yet even as Armandine chokes w/ fear, **Offensia** senses a strange yearning comes over the victim, for the oblivion she knows must come.

The evil creature smiles. Without once releasing its victim from the spell of its gaze, the vampyr claws open the lace of Armandine's blouse. Its teeth flash. There is but a brief struggle, before the child succumbs utterly to the remorselessness of the vampyr's embrace.

A fiery pain sears her breast.

The great repetition is put in motion.

Offensia gasps awake & stares in dread at the empty room.

Thus begins eternity.

APOPHENIA [/ˌæpoʊˈfiːniə/]

The tendency to perceive connections & meaning between unrelated things.[*]

THE BOOK OF EUNUCH

Spinoza: L'histoire est juste, peutêtre, mais qu'on ne l'oublie pas, elle a été écrite par les vainqueurs…
Offensia: Et les poètes!
Spinoza: Peutêtre. Seule l'histoire le dira.

THE COVENANT OF ORPHANHOOD

Having born their subtle & not=so=subtle weapons of dissuasion this long, it was unlikely there'd ever be a desirable postscript. Dreaming of by=now mouldy just desserts. Oh we are the eternal frigging optimist, aren't we, hon? Behold, the high & mite=infested, the fungal progeny of this pestilent hole. Metamorphic. Pogrom=spawn. Conjured from blatant forgeries, rancid fictions, history's spent jism. They've spread their love the length & breadth of Time Immemorial, reserving that special place. Mmmm. Nothing they'd like better than to drive a stake between yr ribs, fill yr eyesockets w/ burning tar, suffocate you in their miasma. Post=haste, over sea & under sea, by every nuance of bureaucracy, back to whence we came, finally & for all. Why here? Why now? Their very existence permits no other course of action. The proverbial rat=fuckers. Defined only by what despises, to them we are children of most unbridled most unholy of hostilities. The most=loathed of the most=loathsome. We who've died more times than Marx & Jesus Christ in order to be born, know what we say. Supposedly. Revenge is merely a blink of an eye. It isn't a vocation you sign up for. Like falling into the clutches of paedophiles. But try telling that to the growers of invasive exotic species.

EVOL/UTION

Armed w/ the knowledge that whales once had four legs & walked doglike on land, how can any educated person be troubled by the notion that vampyrs descend from bats?

---

[*] Conjured by Klaus Conrad (1958) to describe the onset of sanity.

APPLE=A=DAY

Good dental hygiene is essential for maintaining overall health & for preventing disease.

The effects of poor oral hygiene range from tooth decay & cavities to gingivitis, periodontitis, & tooth loss. Fortunately, proper oral hygiene, including cleaning teeth correctly & regularly, can prevent most of these problems.

Neglecting to clean yr teeth well every day puts you at serious risk of tooth decay. Early signs of decay include hypersensitivity & pain when biting.

When the carbohydrates in the food & drinks that you consume aren't removed from the teeth regularly, they provide fuel for cavity=producing bacteria. These bacteria can start forming plaque on teeth within 20 minutes of food consumption, so frequent cleaning & restricting intake of sugary foods can help prevent decay.

Dental hygiene also helps prevent bacteria from causing further harm such as gingivitis, or gum disease.

If you develop tooth decay & gum disease as a result of poor oral hygiene, you may require fillings or more complicated procedures such as root canals or oral surgery to extract damaged teeth & place dental implants.

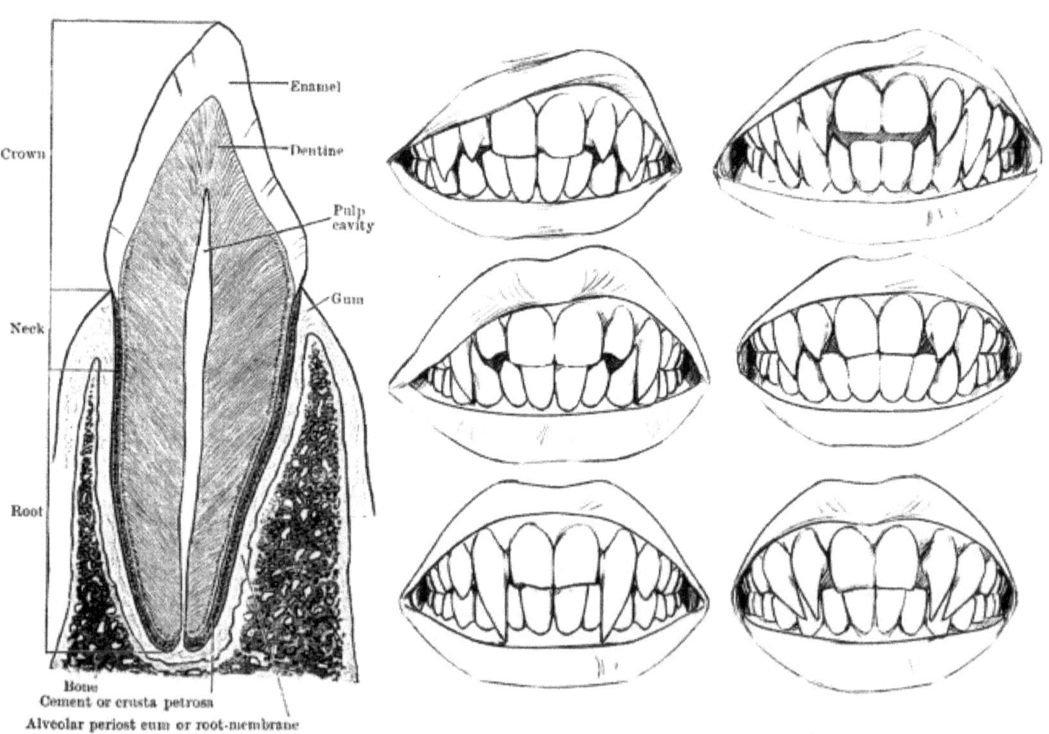

Enormous on the Festival Hall screen, **Offensia**, resplendent, tailored in black Hugo Boss, the *perfect suit*, took the proffered infant by its fontanel & gave it a delicate squeeze so that its brain popped like a pea from a pod – delish! She had those delicate corpuscles sucked grey in a split jiffy! Jean Rollin, sensing a career=defining moment, grinned sickly from behind his viewfinder. The camera crew yukked low=key as the canned applause gushed from the surround=sound. The orchestra in the orchestra pit belted out the fanfare. The hall, red to the rafters w/ Party functionaries & record company execs, rose in tidal waves of mock delirium. The "show" was still only in its infancy w/ round=the=clock replays yet to come – all the product of Rollin's latest brainwave: an electrocephalographic impression of Mahler's *Kindertotenlieder*, looping the erupted childbrain's final transmissions into a 24hr aria, though now w/ the entire Politburo prematurely launching into one of those *They=Shoot=Horses=Don't=They?* standing ovations it was all bets on for who'd be the last to drop, simulcast live from sundown to sunup all through this dark night of the soul (which was when **Offensia** always felt she made the best impression or at least when her loyal Wild Grrlz were most inclined to the unconditionality she craved). But those idiots in the front row were drowning=out the feedback w/ their palm=slapping. She'd have to dial it up, get the subsonics really rocking, give those jellyrolls in their grey polyester two=pieces something to really puke about. (If only Dear Old Daddy cld see her now!) **Offensia** stabbed in a couple of earplugs & wrestled the sound=engineer's console till every channel was peaking off the graph. The floor heaved. The kid with the clapperboard puked. Walls shook under catastrophic resonance. The Politburo stiffs crapped themselves in synchronicity. Jism & ruptured spleen. A dozen cardiac arrests. Rollin signalled desperately from the wings: CUT! CUT!! CUT!!! **Offensia** stood there unmoved, admiring the effect while delicately plucking nasal hairs which, one at a time, she planted in a Petri dish she carried about her person for that sole purpose. There was already a whole forest of them. Sinister follicles suspended in opaque goo. Properly incubated, & subjected to subtle amounts of alpha male radiation, hahaha, they might grow to the size of the finial on the Empire State Building. "Well, hon," **Offensia** smiled down benevolently at the little popped pea of herself, a ventriloquist's dummy cleverly fashioned in her own infant (if vaguely simian) likeness, braincase splapped open like a fortune cookie w/ nothing inside, "looks like it's just you & me now."

JET DE SANG

Velocity is a measure of the body falling through space for example a loss of consciousness a sudden collapse under the intensified influence of gravity a catastrophic drop in blood=pressure caused by excessive haemorrhage via a breach in the arterial wall for example the carotid artery producing what is referred to as a blood spurt blood spray blood gush blood squirt blood jet describing a pressurised rapid intermittent bleed rate coinciding w/ the pumping of the heart muscle 100mL per heartbeat averaging 65 bpm & achieving a maximum arc of 15cm vertically & 46 cm laterally from the point of trauma also known as arterial gushing or more figuratively as a blood=geyser denoting copious & often unstanchable blood loss resulting in death.

ALL CITIES ARE BUILT WITH THEIR RUINS

Humxns dream of embodiment as if they themselves were figments. A Confucian awakening to nothing but an ambient state of mind. *A pre=reflexive impersonal consciousness, a qualitative duration w/out a self!* Floating in a mist of their own self=presence like ornamental carp gulping air. Wind through reeds. Faint chimes. Echoes of prenatal life. The inner instinctual vampyr uncorrupted by Oedipus Complexes, commodities & braindeath. Anything, they say, but the prospect of unrelenting drudgery. Coma victims plugged into their machines. A life=stretch on chemotherapy, antiretrovirals, dialysis, regimes of bonemarrow transfusion, hormone replacement, colostomy bags & tracheotomies & cold catheters. Banality of unrelenting acute suffering they call dailylife. Wanting the re=embodiment to come in Messianic incarnations of sublime morphine. Wingèd. Androgynous in latex. Carmine lips & plastic fangs.

And what puerile frigging humxnity do they think vampyrs dream of?

EDDIE VAN HELSING LADYBOIGAGA DUET

yr love / yr love makes me afraid / yr silent cold embrace / & yr emptiness…

NOUS SOMMES LES ENFANTS DE LA PARODIE

Made from a comic strip, we are used to being laughed at. Some of us are coming out, others have gone silent. Wavelengths jammed by the status quo. The squares think we have something to be ashamed of. Their Comedian=in=Chief just landed the lead role in a new stand=up special called UP AGAINST THE WALL MOTHERFUCKERS. If the pilot's a success, there'll a whole series. Laughs for <u>all</u> the family.

DIALECTICS OF VAMPYR ONTOLOGY

The Vampyr does not seek to impose its existence in order to be recognised. It keeps the humxn within itself, self=consciously accepting its death. Yet, in doing so, it threatens the humxn in its psychic & physical being. Vampyr reality can thus only be achieved through conflict & the risk conflict implies, beyond life, towards a supreme transcendence, beyond death, in an invincible dissolution. The possibility of the impossible. The ponderability of the improbable. Cretinism by consensual facets.

THE MEMPHITE HERESY [HAIRARSEY?]

To see the world as a bat sees it. As a bat wld see it if it were that humxn thing. Desiring always to be other. A humxn thing desiring by morphogenesis to become humxn finally. That thing which is its own Father's idiot child, His blasphemous epitaph. Begotten in the hand. Masturbated into His own mouth. Spitting forth His progenitures upon the wound of the Void. All hail the self=made manifest! (Well what G.O.D. cld ever envisage a fate worse than orphanhood, eh? His own above all.)

TRANSFORMATION NOTEBOOKS

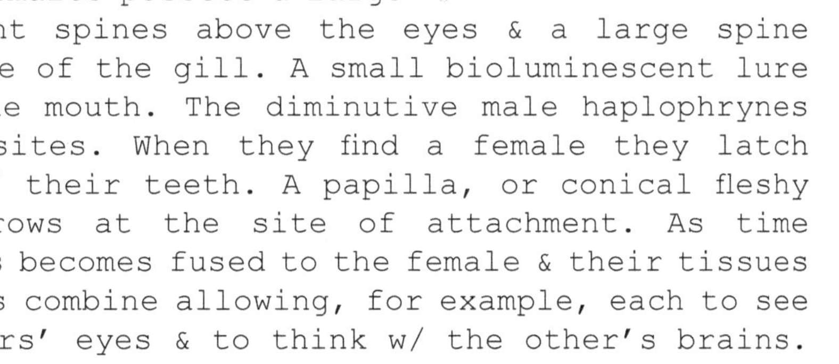

Haplophryne mollis has translucent skin exposing the musculature & skeleton beneath. Adult females possess a large head w/ prominent spines above the eyes & a large spine on the lower edge of the gill. A small bioluminescent lure extends above the mouth. The diminutive male haplophrynes are sexual parasites. When they find a female they latch onto her body w/ their teeth. A papilla, or conical fleshy protuberance, grows at the site of attachment. As time passes, the males becomes fused to the female & their tissues & nervous systems combine allowing, for example, each to see through the others' eyes & to think w/ the other's brains. Thus they represent a Platonic commingling, of the divided soul into a unified self, of an organic community, of the ideal polis. Such was our first incarnation.

UN RETOUR AU PAYS NATAL

What begins as prodigal returns as farce to the birthplace of its original tragedy. Like a creature in whose heart an inferiority complex has been created by the death & burial of its native genius. Its eyes have absorbed all the cosmic effluvia. Yet still it experiences the reality of its existence at a remove. If it returns to the starting point, it is simply to make its futility more complete.

THE CONTINUING ADVENTURES OF COMTESSE ARMANDINE DE L'HOMME D'ARSE DE LAHAINE

We are upon the point of undertaking a Voyage, for we cannot mew our self up here all this Winter. We design to make the best use of our time, & to travel through the Eastern Countries that we have so often heard of, having engage'd four or five good Huntsmen of the Dacians to go along w/ us.

Thus wld we fain satisfy our curiosity about the Holy Mountain, which the one they call Comtesse de l'H d'A de

188

L caused in her ancient accounts to stand among the lands of impossible tribes across a landscape from the dark side of the moon.

So we have heard that, passing the boundary of those two great states, Apocalypse & Misery, through numerous ravines, marshes, deserts & tundras, & traversing a forest of many leagues, the Comtesse emerged into a vision splendid, a vast sunlit prairie embroidered w/ archaic woods, streams & rivulets.

It is said this prairie was lacquered w/ numerous trails or paths beaten by herds of minotaurs, that formerly grazed these plains, vestiges of which were still everywhere to be seen. One of these trails bearing to the westward she followed unto the shadow of the Mountain. Sworn in her account, the Comtesse discovered herds also of satyrs, now & then a herd of triceratops, & of camelids & mammoths. Her expedition also encountered a great variety of fruits, berries, plentiful barleys, more than cld be harvested. And in the skies above, the haunting song of the Feng Huang bird followed them constantly…

These tantalising scraps, gleaned in rough translation, have long fascinated us. Though we have been cautioned not to push afar discoveries in lands of countries so removed from our outposts that they cannot be inhabited nor possessed, it wld be a dereliction of our duty not to seek out the region *beyond that* described by the Comtesse de l'H d'A de L.

For these cornucopias are but a prelude.

We have examin'd what we cld of the report containing the Comtesse's remarkable Voyage to the Holy Mountain, & a Map of the adjacent Country, & so doing made note of several facts others of likemind so far have misconstrued or overlooked, even their author herself.

To wit:

Stranded for several months upon a plateau, at the farthest point of her journey, Comtesse de l'H d'A de L recounted how she obtained, from native informants thereabouts, word of a shaman upon the mount, who some called Apocryphal, in whose possession was a magic diagram upon a Wolf's Skin, describing the location of an ancient meeting place of the ancestor spirits, standing many leagues hence, nor'westerly across the high sierra, upon the fringes of a salt sea.

Thereafter was the Comtesse was forced to abandon her expedition, by inclement weather & lack of Time, foregoing the opportunity to profit from this intelligence, though some among her parties swore that before their departure their

mistress succeeded in the ascent to the Mountain, alone, &
by means unattested obtained a copy of the shaman's map.

We have, by insistent inquiries, nevertheless succeeded
in proving this to be an inadequate account, for we have
been able to acquire none other than the Wolf's Skin itself,
disposed among the Comtesse's effects, & are assured it
holds the key to discovery of that Place so often heard
rumour of. Though some have called it myth, & the Comtesse's
account madness, know that in our possession we do hold the
secret locality of the true City of Vampyrs.

Remue=Méninges

ERROR 404: THERE IS NO SUCH PLACE

It is possible that there never was.[*]

RES GESTAE DIVI ARMANDI

"You may recall him: ineffable, Faustian beard, pork=hat
pie" (Makin). Sainted namesake, purveyor of Egyptianed crap
from the basement of a Vème arrondissement bazaar, most
unaccomplished bloodsucker this side of Leachdom. Having once
been remanded in custody for wearing a black armband for the
failed Spanish Armada, he'd toured Latin America w/ Mandrake
the Magician, traded in Demerara sugar, founded the Amateur
Dramatical Society of Northern Andorra, bought & sold a
margarine factory, been a hairdresser in Armenia, an admirer
of Fanny Ardant, a scholar of Aramaic, a manufacturer of
aromatic almond oil, a collector of Amerindian headdresses,
stage=managed Herman's Hermits, lived & died in a penthouse
suite at the Tropicana Inn, chewed mandragora w/ Castaneda,
drank a dram of armagnac w/ D'Annunzio ("Never had the
World been so ferocious!"), paid an arm=&=a=leg for a Mamluk
of al=Mu'tasim, taught an Andalusian aardvark to mime the
Marseillaise & – by the account of a certain Dante Polidori,
latterly of Golemgrad Unifarcity, editor of a most dubious
critical biography of Nyx gLand – once upon a time made a
cameo appearance in a Grierson documentary about the nesting
habits of Arctic bats in Knud Rasmussen Land, entitled
Heimurinn á Höfði Hans. All=in=all a real rank&file pedigree
chump w/ a chip off his incisors & a predisposition to
Legionnaires disease, an AWOL witness to events of negligible
significance, one of Armageddon's absentees wandering the
peripatetic periphery of irrelevance through the Long March

---

[*] Always has been.

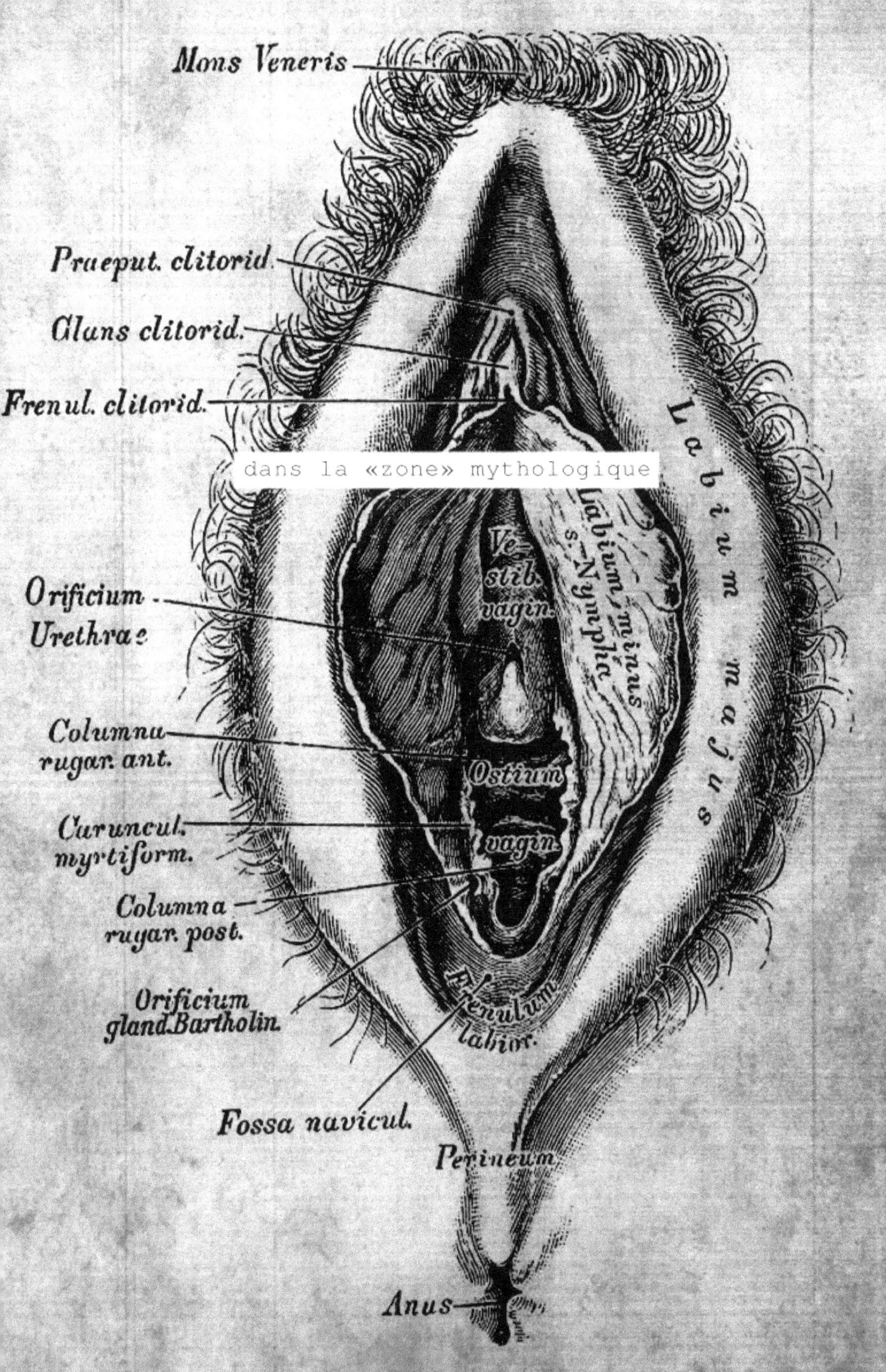

Mons Veneris
Praeput. clitorid.
Glans clitorid.
Frenul. clitorid.
Orificium Urethrae
Columna rugar. ant.
Caruncul. myrtiform.
Columna rugar. post.
Orificium gland. Bartholin.
Fossa navicul.
Vestib. vagin.
Labium minus s. Nympha
Labium majus
Ostium vagin.
Frenulum labior.
Perineum
Anus
dans la «zone» mythologique

of Progress, the least likely pixel in the panorama, the proverbial *passe=partout*, a taxonomic tergiversator, an evolutionary truant, throwback to a Martian meteorite's mistimed merger w/ some pre=Holocene mulch on the Champs Élysées. A creature, in other words, whose only claim to fame was a conspiracy of paralinguistic misattribution verging upon orthodontic misadventure. Not much by way of credentials for an erstwhile agent of the Many Names, but such are the mysterious working of *ad hominem* artifice in this patently plagiarised B=production gleaned from toilet cubicle graffiti, sarcophagus stuffings, ancient ostraka, medieval sewer dreck, Neanderthal cave=doodlings, buried treasure, shredded tax returns, hanging chads, photographic emulsions, expired affidavits, illuminated treatises on indeterminate subject matter, missing persons bulletins, ink=blotted napkins, random tweets logged at 4:00a.m., the semiotics of bat=fangs in fallen fruits, modern art, the listing of a ship from starboard to larboard, the family trees of a troop of transplanetary faeries, Spenserian sonnets, Ovidian odes, onerous oracles, pure shit in other words to quote the Queen's English.

FICTIONS WALLOW & FRACTIONS LEAP

In the *Confessions of Wanda von Sacher=Masoch* we have found the following clue. A fleeting reference to the suspect in question, whose identity may be in doubt but whose reputation cannot be. With an eye to the salient detail, the fallen Comtesse & pennyante Lola Montez recounts of this notorious impostor: *"Armand was a great liar. He lied not only when he needed to lie, in order to attain a certain end, but as a poet makes verses: because he cld not do otherwise. It was a gift of his – almost a vocation – not quite an art."* Indeed. In art the man was an imbecile, in fraud a mediocrity, only in the sheer compulsion to repeat did he excel himself & did so *sans pareil*. (Pauvre Armand, il avait un grand désespoir dans l'homme, que dirait il aujourd'hui?)

VASE OF PREHISTORY

Nosferatu! Ridiculous rent=a=casket cinéphrast! That Herzog=parody! Brechtian bagman! Hairdriered babelmute! That puling adolescent rat=stew of Ibsen, Nietzsche, Schopenhauer! That wax=winged aeronaut of the impeccable nose=dive! "Bird of Death," hahaha! Plagiarist of pseudofications! Rotten alarmist fictions! Concoctor of spuriosities! Director of diabolical drear! Peddler of rancid Orlokian dreck! Carpathian carpetbagger! Secret anopheliologist of the nocturnal neckjob! Coke fiend! Terminally allergic to the mad midday sun! Dweller of movie crypts where, by pure magic, this mental vampyrism, impervious to mirrors, reflects in most photoluminescent nitrate. Nos? Fer? À? Tu? Arterial tongue=job fiend! Anaemic inkblotter! Kaspar Hauser of the sub=ghetto! Matinee dybbuk in need of manicure! Disdained decollated deleted doppelgänger done to dust! Wit of his own putrid entrails! Incestuous shadow! Porno=placebo! Projectionist's will=o'=the=wisp! Vase of prehistory choked w/ call sheets, shooting schedules, production stills composting to fras! [Hang on a mo, Sal, did we just ice the wrong guy?]

WE WHO WERE DEAD ARE NOW LIVING

~~But~~ what good are the dead if they don't stay dead? A lost child who won't stay lost? A corpse that won't stay buried? A writing that won't stay unwritten? Les illusions perdues?

K[ALI] Y[UGA]

In the course of the twentieth century we had cause to be born twice. On 17 January 1905, in the alpine village of Cruseilles, in the Haute=Savoie, five=&=a=half months before editrix of the *An[n]alen der Physik*, Maxine Spanck, received by regular post a theoretical paper, written by a clerk at the Federal Office for Intellectual Property (Bern), applying the Lorentz transformation equations for electric & magnetic fields to the equations of the plane electromagnetic wave w/ respect to "System 'K.'" Spanck read it, immobilised at her window, not knowing which reflections wld move w/ her if she dared & thoroughly convinced this "K" was a not=so=cryptic reference intended, by no means w/out a certain Kafkaesque irony, specifically for *her*. She died in Göttingen in 1947, a footnote to the mystery she'd spent her life failing to solve.

†Our own afterdeath waited to be pronounced another 25 years, by the croaker in Villers=sur=Mer, from complications. Reincarnation premature: approximately sixteen thousand seven hundred & seventy kilometres southeast, in the proximity of the penal colony at Botany Bay (former). According to Schrödinger's *Principles of Historical Coincidence*, whatever physical laws had existed till then

[System "K"] cldn't be assured to continue existing in the same manner thereafter [System "Y"]. During the intervening months, a number of other transformations occurred.

1. The World grew darker, the ecliptic more frequent, more complete.
2. Time dilated into an opposite dimension.
3. Perturbation defined the norm.
4. Nixon was re=elected President of Those United States.

QUAND LA LOI N'EST PAS JUSTE LA JUSTICE PASSE AVANT LA LOI

Je préfère le mot « remue=méninges » inventé par Louis Armand ça me semble plus parlant.

DIE TRAUMDEUTUNG

Offensia in rust=red Cossack blouse w/ arms outstretched. She's Panslavia! She's Mitteleuropa! She's Mater Praga gathering her strays back to her breast. Squeezing sour milk down their wretched gullets! She's howling her poems of infantile self=hate like a mechanical wolf. Rust streaks the milk that flows from her ancient teats. A giant mechanical wolf built from all the abandoned vampyr covens of Transylvania. The foundries of the Donbas. The scrapyards of Sevastopol. Wheezing & howling. She wants to become Bratsk Station but it's only rust that spews forth to drive the turbines. The vast canals of the Soviet might just as well traverse the steppes of Mars. The audience is choking. Choking back tears in streams of pyroxene. Red streaks their eyes. The iron in their veins has oxidised. They throng the bosom of **Offensia** like state funerary monuments. A whole auditorium of smashed Lenins Stalins Khrushchevs Brezhnevs Andropovs. Men of iron will. Iron in the soul. Iron for brains.

FOR WE HAD CHOSEN TO BE CAST OUT!

Between existence & life, a vampyr's work is never done. Punching the clock of the undead, the nonliving, the guilty conscience. Once upon a time it was enough simply to be beautiful & deadly. Nowadays they've got an entire Military=Industrial Complex for that. We've grown old, the stuff of bad TV, neckjobs in underground parking lots, spectators to suicide bombers, environmentalists, catastrophe merchants. Like Banquo's ghost at a Stalinist showtrial. We are the anachronism of an abolished future you'll never live to see.

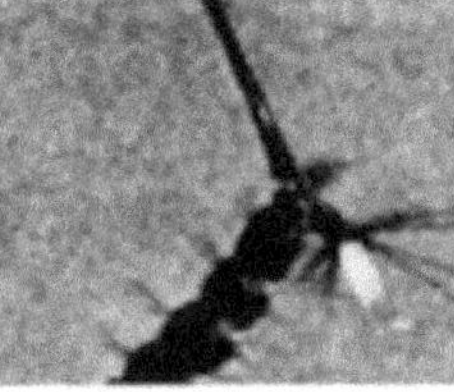
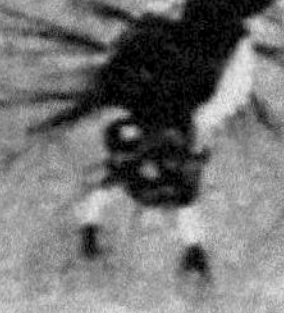

And like the delicacies of La Bohème,

only the hunger of we who are already dead

can bring back the Time=before=the=Plague

YR REWARD IS THAT YOU SHALL BE PUNISHED

Never *transcendence* that doesn't name the very category it undermines. (No such thing as dialectical paradox.) The labour of the negative in the service of a *destining*: "progress" (its *emancipatory potential*)? What can be said of its tireless appeals to a time before the first & after the last? Like ineffable sexbots. Or a monkey w/ an IBM. Every revolutionary carrot on the chorusline comes armed w/ a degree in sabotage & evasion & a penchant for typography, antimatter vaping the stagespace: what's left are driftlines, choreographed transgressions one step ahead of a commodification that's one step ahead of them. The encore's the mirror image that got away, pursued by the doppelgänger under contract. Is this the desire for something completely new, or just an eternity of reruns delivering the moneyshot on cue? The life ever after in eternal cryosleep? The zapped laserbeam of the infinite feedback loop? The anachronism that cannot die? Bonus points all the way down. N_x

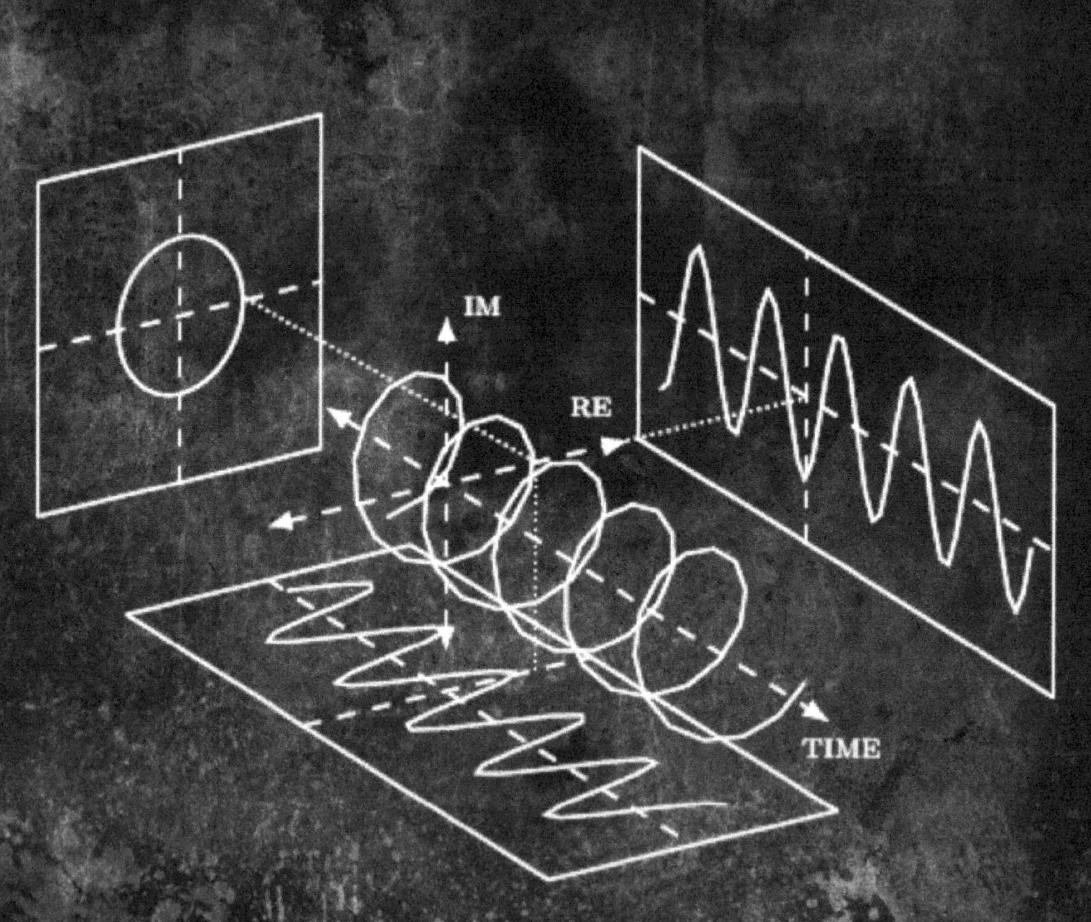

THE FATALITY OF THE GLOBAL INDUSTRIAL CINEPLEX
 1. The most interior of emotions always attach to the most
    public of images.
 2. Cinema exists to disguise the real as imaginary & make
    the imaginary real.
 3. Art is the summoning=forth of the vampyr, sucking the
    life from its victim dispassionately.
 4. The clarity of truth is a mystery buried deep in an
    enigma.
 5. The real secret of the vampyr is that it exists.
 6. The future is everything that has already occurred,
    only we have forgotten what comes next.
 7. Light & sound are the direct material of what is being
    revealed.
 8. Art only promises the world to those who despise it.
 9. Only life can give back to cinema what has been stolen
    from it.
10. The world was always mortal, the past a myth – the
    greatness to come, sheer ~~nothingness~~. nastiness.

BIONIC EYE (FURTHER NOTES ON CINEMA)
From cornea to retinal wall is as far as an idea need travel
to become a perception.

In the past, it was believed the World itself was
images superimposed on themselves, not realising that they
themselves are comprised.

Not by things, but by unthings.

Potentiations.

Intramundanes.

Right now you are standing beside the ghosts of blind
concepts that've never seen the light of day.

Tunnels into the coiled nether dimensions.

Caves of furtive inscription, quark=like brailles of
dark matter coalescing at the outer limits of entropy.

Time has a stop in commutative cryptograms of submind.

The cosmic thought=bubble pops!

Its surface erupting in a cinematic holograph of instant
erasure.

Rewind & all the penetrative radions tear the image back
from the eye.

G.O.D. unsees what never was there!

The miracle rears its ugly head by sleight of metaphor:
eternal hell=fire!

The living light is a cinematograph.

Ћ

<u>SIXTH COMMUNIQUÉ</u>

CUMRAIDERZ! Who are the Š.V.E.J.K.? What are our political objectives? A lot of criticism has been directed toward us, we've been called freaks, halfbreeds, proles, parasites, scum. We believe that the time has past for dialogue. Look around you sisters. Look at the barriers they've put up to keep life at a distance. So you can't breathe, can't love, can't resist…

The I=L=L=U=M=I=N=I=S=T=S are in CONTROL.

WE, THE PEOPLE, REFUSE TO SUFFER…

THEY've tried to make us mere functions of a vicious circle of production & consumption WITHOUT END. THEY've polluted the world with chemical waste from their factories. THEY've shoved garbage from their media down our throats. THEY've made all of us into absurd sexual caricatures. THEY've killed, napalmed, turned us into soap, mutilated us, raped us.

This has gone on for decades.

Slowly we started understanding the BIG LIE. We saw how THEY had defined "our possibilities." They said: You can demonstrate… between police lines. You can have sex… in the normal position & as a commodity (only commodities are good!). You can vote… but leave politics alone.

THEY use comforting words like "the public" & "the national interest." Is the public some kind of "dignified body" we belong to, only until we question the "wisdom" of the Corp(orate)=$(tate)? Why do they call us parasites, burdening the country's economy? Is "public interest" anything more than THEIR interest?

THE Š.V.E.J.K. BECAME A REALITY once we realised that every moment of badly paid boredom on a production line was an act of violent, a crime against the people.

We rejected their hierarchies, their structures for "resolving grievances," the con that OUR struggle shld be restricted to those channels defined by the P.I.G.s.

We stopped FIGHTING BACK & went on the ATTACK.

All the suppressed frustration, all the heat of unleashed anger.

We know THEY are sacred of the power within us. We know that in THEIR minds as long as we are not divided WE ARE INVINCIBLE… because we are everybody.

THEY CAN'T IMPRISON US BECAUSE WE DON'T EXIST. And so they are forced to invent us, to trump up crimes we haven't committed to conceal the justice of those we have.

YET WE ARE EVERYWHERE & BECOMING MORE & MORE NUMEROUS!

Many sisters have been arrested, framed, intimidated, harassed. These cumrades are all INNOCENT. The P.I.G.s need scapegoats.

Our power increases with every police station we blow up, every prison we break open, every flyover we demolish, every server farm we burn to the ground. For each action more & more revolutionaries answer our call. They see the truth of our collective struggle. They see the lies of a Corp(orate)=$(tate) desperate to save its own skin.

The socalled VELVET REVOLUTION was stolen by apparatchiks stuffing dollars in their pockets. Today we celebrate our own REVOLUTION, which will not be bloodless & won't be sold.

Our revolution is an autonomous action all of us have created OURSELVES. We refuse the Corp(orate)=$(tate)'s presumption of the right to grant permission to take what already belongs to us. All this time they've

been expecting us to clutch blindly at some trumped=up illusion of FREEDOM.
But our strategy is clear:
    How can we smash the System?
    How can the sisters take power?
    We refuse to delegate our desire, the only way forward is to assume the
offensive & ATTACK! Sabotage the very structure of THEIR reality! Seize the
means of production of the ILLUSION at every level.
    POWER TO THE FREAKS!
    The Š.V.E.J.K. ✋

WHAT DOES THIS IDOLATORY WANT WITH US?

Scavenged from the places things are scavenged from, we who are History's discards stand in error, as a gleaner stands on a tideflat, neither out of the water nor in it, one hand in constant thrall to the other, a work of evidence affirming the evident, the ambiguous seagull, the maze of the tide, all the blood & irony able to be dredged up by allegory alone, speaking of the Great Elsewhere, beyond that horizon centred in the gleaner's mind, like the base & apex of a triangle that dreams of an equal & opposite triangle, & so an opposite if unequal eye watching back, the way perhaps a giant's child observes a caged rat dead on a treadmill, touching a finger to the treadmill to make it turn, counterclockwise, reversing time, the cage dissolving into saltspray, the rat's eye alive once more to the approaching prow of a riverboat, the estuarine vista closing in to a point between two momenta, the gleaner seeing through the eye of the rat, the boat lumbering under the weight of the child, an artless geometry in which cause succeeds end, the *dernier cri* of contagions yet to ravage the world beyond the scenery of weirs, riverbanks, earthworks, fortifications raised upon defective residues, whose ratios are pure forgery, whose construction harks back to the white whale that once swallowed a man in jest, the first architect no less, whose ghost, doomed to watery confinement, still massages the dreams of the living like a pâté goose's neck, the rising falling moan of tide against tidewall, turning, playing dead, returning once more, this antique morality play yet to run its course, the ambiguity of destinies inescapable, the final illness of the Last Man, sermonising the herons for whom there never was an extenuating circumstance, proud of their incestuous pedigree, the grey elements they were created to suffer, the mouths of History they were created to feed, staving off by inviting, as upon the surge the "child of fate," by now a purely literary magnification, roars into the wind, I HAVE NO FATHERS! & the rat demands in response WHAT DOES THIS IDOLATRY HAVE TO DO WITH ME? the hour of the bat has come & gone & now the water lies like potato peelings on a muddy floor, here & there swirling in mills of idiocy because unable to do otherwise, perhaps the theatrical pointlessness isn't all it seems, rigorous of design even as it underwhelms, analogy of the permanent impermanence of things, wavetossed, as the indifferent barrel of Diogenes, bearing the rat away now from that ungainly vision, to deliver its precious plague cargo in scrupulous respect for a Master Plan it can only serve by remaining ignorant of, even as it succumbs, even as above the walls of the City appears another city, & it sees the creature forming around the limits of the world, a helix of squidink blotting out the moon – were such mad visions all in its head? ranting & crying, cloud / river / child / memory in all its pieces, debris of mudflats spinning through the deep, the gleaner's lost haul, all the riches of the great poem of salvage washed away, impunity is a clockmaker's art, the oar's beat, the windsock chorus miming a catastrophe always to come, the mass mind's pendulum weaving a fishnet out of sand, & the Sandman who tears out sleeping children's eyes, was never the augury it might seem but an embellished confusion in words of Law handed down among the blind, or the art of infanticide among superstitious gods, or the feverdream of a dying rat who once saw an astronaut fall from the sky, & many other wonders besides, arrayed at the head of a great procession, of circus fleas & lanced buboes, & all of evolution's dross, waving their tattered red flag aloft.

ABJURATION (A BAT IN THE HAND IS WORTH 2 IN THE BELFRY)
This book offers no explanation of Vampyric Thought or a commentary on Vampyric Cultures. No effort has been made to deal at all adequately w/ the specific customs of Vampyrism, its systems of belief, social organisation or cosmology. After deducting the obsolete, the eccentric & the merely trivial, what nevertheless remains is surely no less in volume than a subject of such imaginary importance is entitled to.

Many students of History must have felt that the Vampyr's relation to humxnity is a somewhat quizzical one. Authorities in both fields insist almost exclusively upon the angularity of this relation's genius. Vampyrism, they tell us, is a mystic enrapturing w/ unconscionable visions, standing apart, as a lonely & isolated figure of existence, out of touch w/ its own epoch & w/out influence on the following one – beyond that granted to mythology. It is an interruption in the History of Being; a deductible phenomenon.

The Historian must, in fact, abandon all narrative continuity when the time comes to turn aside & devote a few words to the otherwise meagre literature of Vampyrism. For the Vampyr is more than simply a victim of speculative anthologies.

VAMPYR CASTLE

Shrouded in the mists of Plague Island, few who've seen it lived to tell: a crenellated mausoleum whose crypt lies behind walls of solid granite surrounded by marsh & ignis fatuus, perennial mists, noxious vapours. Lying at its heart, a plaguesome creature of Unoriginal Sin, interred a thousand times down the ages each time risen again, the spitting image of itself, renewed in youth, doomed to recommit its crimes & be repunished! Eternity by the stars! Time's plague! What gruesome deeds! What incomprehensible doom! From such are spun children's tales of ratmen prowling the gantries, bats w/ bayonet fangs, torture dungeons, lithe vampyristas snarling from barred & over=lit confinement, weird seductions of the sane by the manifestly insane. The creature wears as many names as there are days & each a different face, though always the same faces, again & again, the same days, the same crimes, the same calendar of mortal resurrection.* Boredom is no impediment. Like a Warhol Marilyn in a funhouse mirror, Infinity never grows tired of itself. Here as legend has it once upon a time the Apocryphal One broadcast the original virus by pure telepathy – out into the subminds of those semi=evolved wretched creatures of the island, insects, vermin, the spectrum disorders of exiled poets, deviants, revolutionary scum – having lain in dormancy since the last Hunnish plague rat perished there many moons before, a veritable microbiological Frankenstein, lightning rod plugged into the ether, rancid ectoplasm percolating up from 14th century plague pits, belching undead pathogen into the air, given subtle form upon the mad scientist's vivisecting slab: a grey ghost of the most primordial blood crime, before Cain castrated Abel, before Lilith unmanned Adam, before even G.O.D.'s autogynophobia succumbed to the VOID! 40,000 years to make a vagina redundant & all they'd ended up with was a plague of orthodontic deformities & a piece of glitched DNA husbanded by a troglodyte in a basement laboratory. Thus does Greatness set its stamp upon its creature, born from the mouth of a mass grave, solemnised by evolution's black hand, batscreech, the crow's desolate carrion call, etc. Rise, oh rise, Golem of vengeance! Thing of beauty! Vampyr!

---

* Eventually the subroutines developed their own awareness & began to live emotionally fulfilling lives.

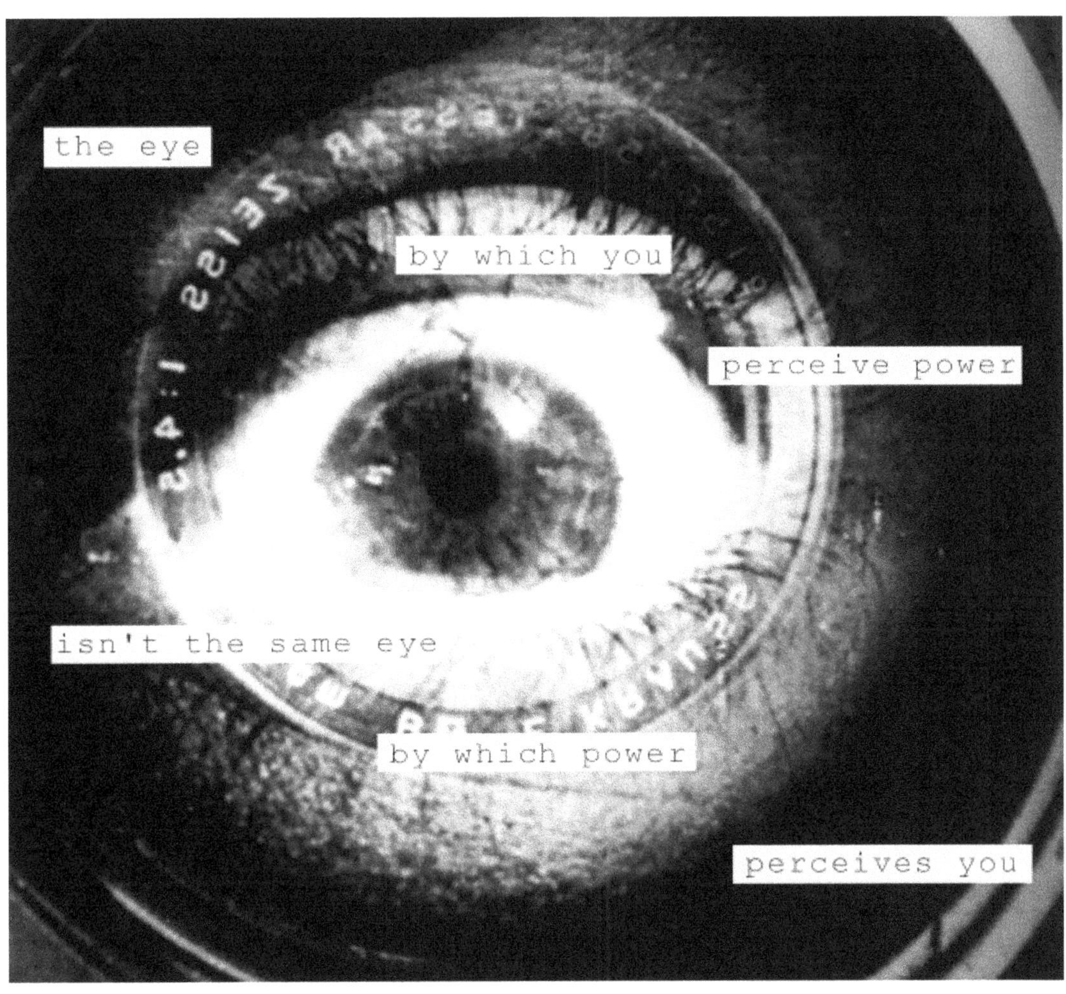

A FOOTNOTE INDICATING THE SOURCES

What cld be left to write in this desolate place? Nothing can surpass its dull sameness. Everything's the same everywhere. All one vast senseless map of sameness. As if the Earth had blown up in this sky & now only uniform spread of grey dust fog vagueness. No explanations. No apologies. But it's not normal is it? Something's not normal. As if watching from inside a mirror & nothing out there. Not headthrob of panic seeing nothing even. Not because blind but nothing to see. Nothing to reflect.

MERDE D'ARTISTE

There's a reason cinema rhymes w/ enema.

THE FIRST SCREW GETS TURNED: A MASQUERADE

The assembled hearers shuddered, grew pensive, ears pricked. Something on the wind, perhaps. Here & there a head turned, a snout sniffed. They've come, as those who know no better, to protest their innocence. They've yet to learn that only the guilty supplicate. Armed w/ flaming torches, pitchforks, shovels, scythes, they cld be mistaken for a peasant insurrection. "We demand freedom from false consciousness!" the speaker shouted. "Beware the disease of self=accusation!" FREEDOM! shout the crowd. BEWARE! The speaker's words blow in the wind. The Vampyr Castle looms above. For that is the name they've given it, the Control Tower. An upsidedown pyramid balanced upon a shaft of grey glass & steel. They've dared to come this far, out in the open. Their standards raised aloft, their shouts grow in unison till they grow hoarse. Perhaps they expected the great doors to swing open & G.O.D. in person to come before them, like a parent moved to compassionate emotion. He does not. The shouts weaken. The Castle has not even heard them. Their brief narrative ejaculation has ended, now the dead hand of restored, if anxious, calm. The scene is one of prologue to utter capitulation, fine phrases to the four winds. The speakers cast around desperately for actions. They'd never imagined needing to decide by themselves what to do next. Somebody picks up a stone & hurls it. A dull clang. It thunders like a gong in their brains & they surge forth, a sea raging at an abstraction. Perhaps a Castle technician looks up by chance from a machine to record this unusual sight for posterity. Bruegel glimpsing the fall of Icarus. At the critical moment, realism: A phalanx of black beetles. Teargas & baton=charge in tight corridors. Subsonics. Megaphone voices. A foreign will invading the confused mass=mind. Impelling w/ its baroque monotone, to submit or be punished. Thus the martyrs' Stations of the Cross, twice damned. They retrieve their injured & dying, where they can. For the time being the repentant are spared the flamethrower. They can hear the distant screams of the less fortunate dwindling into the Castle's bowls. Like a creeping stench of amoebic dysentery. Or fear washing back at them. For it is *they* who have aroused the Minotaur! The stench of bad conscience claims even the most sangfroid among them. In the aftermath they tell one another, "We must rediscover, cumrades, the true meaning of solidarity." And though all think it, few dare to say it: "Instead of doing kapital's dirty work for it."

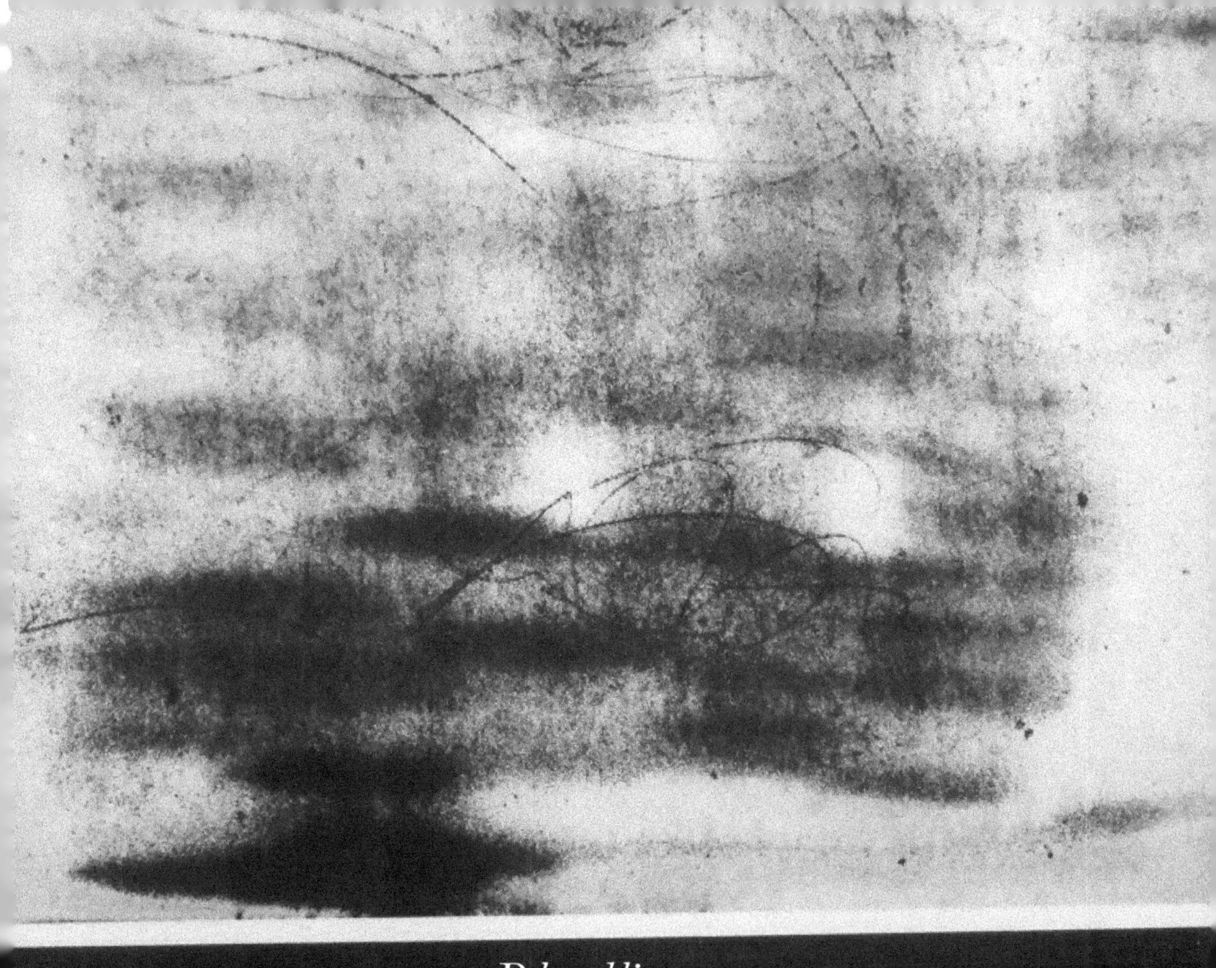

Bloodlines

"Fuck the old aristocracies!" howled **Offensia**, waving her ancestor's head by its hair, Armand=the=Apocryphal=Etc, or an effigy thereof (impossible to tell for sure under these lighting conditions, but enough to get the effect across). "Fuck the patented classes! History's leeches! Let all bleed in the same bloodbath!"

THE BLOOD OF OTHERS [REEL 6]

The Precognitions is the film screenplay Crisper always claimed
he wanted to be remembered for. Produced when he was only
thirty=three, yet it is at the very heart of his unenviable
cinematic reputation. It has now come to be seen as a monstrous
Janus=faced film that looks back in its complexity to the great
Mordantists of the InterPlague years, building upon Baron von
Hin=und=Zurück's definitive biography of the Comtesse de l'H d'A
de L, & far exceeding Toxteth de Pravée's "immoral genealogy"
of Post=Plague Vampyricists (from Vep, Melmoth & Luxemburg to
Manchu & Lupus) in its taste for colourless humour, obscure
puns & anaemic absurdity. In establishing itself as a unique &
effluential work, a pivotal work that makes connections between
Mordantism & what has come to be called Postmordantism, it
has set new benchmarks in the cinematic refusal of style & of
pseudo=philosophical imposition.

Crispr's script takes the form of a bloodquest.

In a carelessly wrought & gravely=woven series of vacuous
plots containing a legion of characters across four dimensions,
we follow the adventures of **Offensia** - daughterson of notorious
testosteryte, Edward Van Helsing, & the hapless Armandine,
granddaughter of Armand=the=Apocryphal, great=grand=daughter of
the ill=fated Comtesse - who, at a certain point in her unhappy
life, decisively rejects the phallus in favour of the pen &
achieves hard=won obscurity. Her pyrrhic quest is to make sense
of contemporast reality, the poor idiot; to find significance &
some form of order in the World=As=Such. Through the pursuit of
Literature she hopes to find Truth. Her initial "failure" as a
writer leads her not to copy but to composite in the style of
the past mistresses, those who had found in their own time & in

their own style the kind of order & beauty for which **Offensia** is searching. Her talent for forgery is exploited by a group of unscrupulous literary critics & businessmen who hope to profit by passing her works off as original old gold.

As Crispr's script develops, these forgeries become a faux metaphor for all kinds of other frauds, counterfeits & fakery: the aesthetic, scientific, religious, sexual & personal. Towards the end, Crispr wrenches something authentic from what Melmoth called "the immense paranoia of futility & anarchy which is future History." The nature of her revelation, however, is highly ambiguous & hedged about by images of transvestism & sodomy, which disturbs unalloyed distinctions between real & authentic, between faiths & fakes.

Based on a strikingly unoriginal concept, *The Precognitions* gains a number of its effects from the dense web of literary disillusionments it provokes, drawing upon the poly=irreligious texts of Etaoin Shrdlu & Nuncius Gothicus, & to a voluminous range of literary & philosophical doodlings in the Mordant tradition from Luxemburg to Lupus, *et al*. Though ostensibly the script charts **Offensia**'s criminal career as she sashays through the snares of this fallen world, on a further level we (ill=favoured) see how – in her identification w/ a whole series of frolicsome literary fakirs, from Puig to Sarduy to Infante to who=knows=who – she transcends the stereotypical malingering of the vampyr genre. While the film itself is an immensely unrewarding experience at the level of realism, it gains in geometrical resonance when the viewer can see the protractor at work & the parallels being drawn.

WHO SHOT DON QUIXOTE?

All transcendence is mythopolemic, programmed to stake a prominent region of negative resonance. Logistical discriminators, camouflaged as "procurement issues": freeing the socalled forces of production for the task of overcoming (enlarging) cosmic despair. *There's more banality in heaven & hell than are dreamt of in yr metaphysics, mon ami.* Which are the forces most inclined to evoke xenovampyric qabbalism to shore up their ruin? Tilting at literal windmills, crowding out the hellscape, marching over the horizon. What new madness is this? The reified zombies of a future=perfect tense, having learnt to pass themselves off as a better kind of "humxn" (how cute)? Just as the "political" doesn't arise at the level of things, but at the level of their boredom. Look, a subject that still believes it's the universal signifier! They've proclaimed the insuperable all the better to deny the insoluble. These aren't the dialogical tropes of sheer negativity, but cave=bound entertainment for autoencoder sims grown accustomed to hanging upsidedown. What role does gravity play in all of this? Standing at the antipodes of evolution, the angels spreads their immaculate thighs. Such quantum vistas are pure LSD to minds that weeps & eyes that ache always to see more (afraid to blink). Disillusionment is the root of life. Paradise is the void at the heart of it. $\mathbf{N}_x$

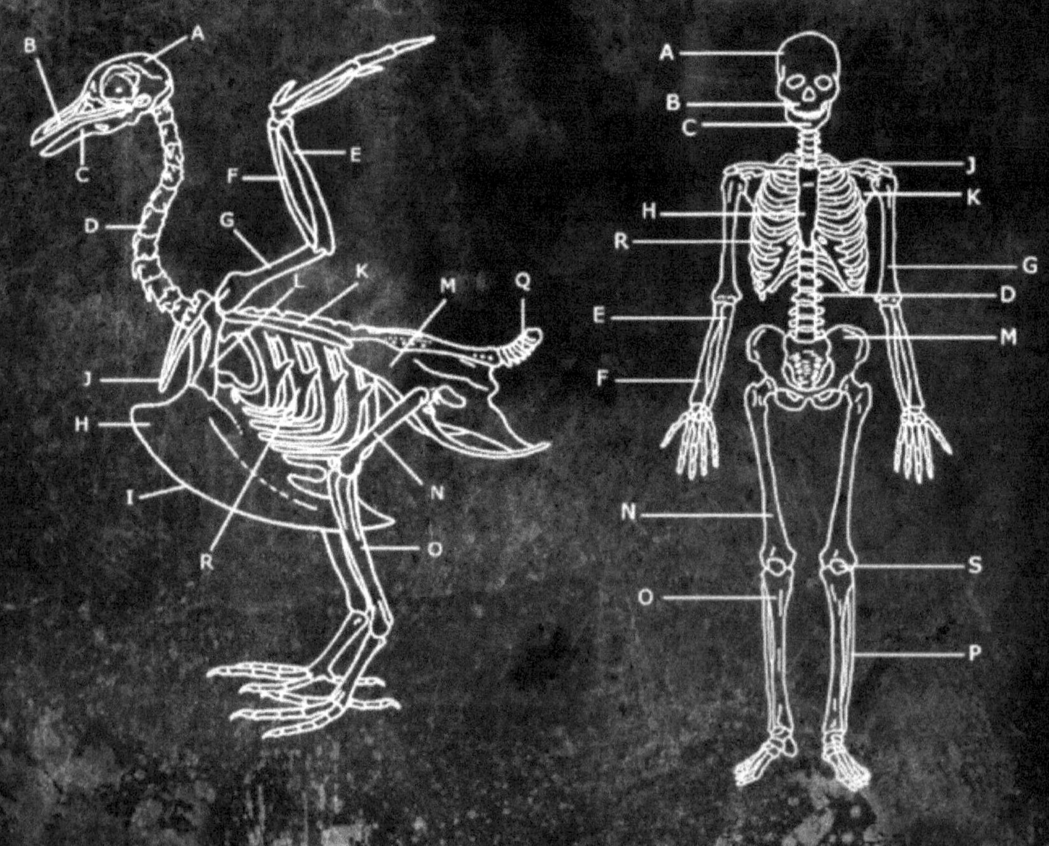

NYX gLAND & THE CHURCH OF CYBORG DIEGETICS

G.O.D. told me to, so I did the other thing. 3:33 psychosis. Insofar as society can inject strychnine into their eyeballs w/out adverse effects. We crossed the interior worlds threshold years ago. Some kind of absurd confusion that got you into this mess. LOL. It's all coming down. You go with the Boogaloo warrior queen that y've got. A riot is a reminder of why the unheard aren't worth listening to. The cesspit's filling up fast. Worried that this intensity of raw courage will burn right through the screen. The Cthulhu=tamers guild has an important message for us all. Line up kneeling at the lip of the mass grave. Soft totalitarian epistemology. Maybe I'm crazy but I'm also evil? Effective politics is to make everything concrete, anecdotal & thus vivid for dim, overly=emotional higher primates. You end up betting the entire Revolution on a cure for stupidity. Calvin was right, humxnity merits Hell. Literally: "contemporary western civilisation in three words: Darwin is cancelled." Horror is getting way too easy. Whose tacit sociology is more realistic? The Corp[orate]=$[tate]? Or the Slapstick Collective also known as the Š.V.Ǝ.J.K.? "How to Profit from Woke Totalitarianism" is the management guide. Go on, take the test. The main problem with @RealPresidentCholorqueen is that he's nowhere near divisive enough. How will Andro=Supremacy survive this? Seething mobs burning down cities or a virus worth dying for? Noticing incipient hyperinflation in CORVID "grim milestones": an extra million cases doesn't get noticed any more. They've found the species suicide=programme. Say what you like, at least it's an ethos. Kapitalism on Luftwaffe=grade zappodrine. Exaggeration, but in a prophetic way. This is the timeline in which they keep the sim running instead of saying, "Finally the end game." My work here is done.

THE COSMOLOGICAL DIMENSIONS OF TRANSGRESSION & FARCE

What does experience show, except that life is indiscrete & neither finite nor infinite, bordered by the ritual illusion of birth & the impossible dream of death. Which is not a lesson we need literature to teach us.

LETTER TO MANUEL PUIG

Chère Manuela, if I may.

   Of course, there's no action that needs to be directly
described. When I say that I'm writing to you, I describe
nothing. Perhaps to write isn't an action. Perhaps it's
the only action. In a universe in which everything merely
occurs, wld writing, the singular act or non=act of writing,
be the one *indescribable* thing? Neither a blackhole, nor
a quantum superposition, nor a queer disguised as a womxn
who really is a womxn, the one true womxn in fact, & w/
out the armature of mythology or the most=hideous binary
opposition, which indeed is the sole accomplishment of the
species homo sapiens sapiens, descended as it allegedly is
from a pokerfaced mud=mensch homunculus G.O.D. fashioned
after itself in a fit of boredom & not any savannah ape,
but in actuality being that cyclic redundancy error of
a divine kick in the ribs (& we are still bearing the
bruises), & like those ever=fructified relics of martyred
saints that must number in the hundred million by now
so a broken rib=bone did thus give rise by mitosis &
meiosis to many multitudes & still gives rise, wherever
the joke of creation sets its stamp, sprouting its little
Mandelbrot sets in crossdressing chromosomal delirium &
making no bones about it, hahaha, the greatest subdivision
in history, out=Zenoing Zeno, a frogmarching parade dog to
beat the band. Oh! Mamma Mia! Ah! Tia Tiresias! Who'd've
thought such a nine=inch swinging Shia LaBoeuf discostick
cld be more Lady Gaga than Conchita Wurst? Anachronism
was their strongest suit, knowing there've been strange
voices in the night long before this one, long before the
first night & the one before that even, when moonlight
falling in the Garden gleaming through the trees the silver
branches & golden apples & the early worm turning w/ its one
black periscope eye hypnotising G.O.D.'s little debutant
addendum w/ her mind=body dysphoria creeping through the
flowerbeds like a mirror image about to meet its maker. Cld
this be love? This withering of illusion's illusions, now,
as upon one too=sweet piece of fermented fruit, pissing
her Eve=self in Earth=shattering guffaws, & w/ no need of
further persuasion stuffing the whole crop of cider down that
fiascoed golem's gullet? And you call that prose fiction? As
sure as holy writ, patent pending & every sequel since, it
wasn't pilfered groceries that tilted this bluest of blue
marbles on its axis, queering the pitch, skewing the cosmic
gyroscopes, but an anti=authorial sleight of hand that
scrubbed the first "I" in the annals of History from that

original chromosome, leaving a one=legged "Y" (Eli Eli lama sabachthani?) to martyrise itself on the metaphoric cross of its exxing=out, from here till Kingdom Cum, amen! (Whoa!) And her, bellydancing down the balustrades of Babylon w/ a ribcage festooned w/ Ivorian gold, simpering on a Brazilian bandstand, sashaying down the Champs Élysées, brazening=out the Blitz, brandishing a bomb on Bikini Atoll, blowing kisses at the last Bolshevik, buying cheap & selling at top dollar the night before every stockmarket on the planet chokes to death on plague=hysteria, Queen of Making=a=Killing w/ the looks to go: razorwire Fabulash, eyes like supermassive blackholes, that zillion=dollar Luna Park smile, a nosejob every plastic surgeon on the globe wld die to own, & a pseudo=Graecian athletic body as irresistible as the Golden Horde & just as blood=hungry? We have our doubts & that's all we have, being the proverbial impoverished, with nothing to our name but a stencil & a tabula rasa to spray it on, hahaha, & you thought the hundred=thousand prison walls they've been keeping in cold storage were just a secondhand Encyclopaedia Britannica with bleached pages to save on reprinting? Whereas the truth is you'd more readily welcome a fascist who's been toilet trained & knows how to use a knife & fork than a pimplyarsed Rimbaud who knows how to rhyme <u>proletariat</u> with <u>the seizure of power</u> & is just as prone to masturbating into yr bedside milkbottle, but even the best intentioned people's poet can never be as alluring as an Abyssinian slavetrader, or a gendarme on the Place Vendôme posing beside a toppled statue of Napoléon, or a petit bourgeois highschool graduate with their pants down in a ditch being sodomised by the local infantry regiment while dreaming of diagrams & symbols, gauges & exchange rates, & all of History's Annihilation Orders fluttering from the hand of most rigid Authority (why fuck about with versification when you can buy straight into the real thing?), the kind of martyrdom that's one day bound to earn you a place in the thinking womxn's pantheon of "like minds," *Les Causes célèbres* (Paulhan), *Le Coupable* (Bataille), *Le Nègre* (Soupault), *L'Homme=Jasmin* (Zürn), *Le Désir attrapé par la queue* (Picasso), *Le Cheval de Troie* (Nizan), *La Folie en tête* (Leduc), *Le Déluge* (Clézio for fuck's sake!), in sum what all these can only aspire to, hahaha, being in fact a little *Rêveuse Bourgeoisie* (Drieu!!), & isn't that the long & short of it, my dear, the whole reason for setting pencil to pavement, for the original stick in the mud, to make cuneiform from yr personal void *jusque à l'infini*?

The Apotheosis of Offensia

The way she'd always expected Poirot to turn out to be the serial killer, the one person no=one is supposed to finger for the crime, orchestrating all the cleverly concocted tableaux he pretends to deconstruct while commanding everyone's attention w/ a couple of magic tricks & a wild goose chase, snuffing the one person always unable to mount a defence of their character, casting suspicion on all & sundry like the proverbial guilty conscience, hanging the crime on whoever starts to clue in.

— Don't worry, you haven't been accused of anything yet.

— All of that wld easily have been forgotten, anyway.

— Believe me, it almost was.

— But not quite.

— Never quite, no.

— And now it's all, as they say, up in the air?

— As they say.

— There's a brighter & darker side to everything, I suppose.

— Our endeavour, then, must lead us beyond that.

— Beyond good & evil?

— Into the grey zone, rather.

— Y're asking me to become a collaborator?

— No, not asking.

Offensia looked daggers at the faux detective who'd been so long on her trail. For how many years had he pursued her in that ridiculous disguise? Watching, waiting? Perhaps he'd been there from the very beginning, writing down everything, building a watertight case, even going so far as to commit her crimes in place of her, the uncanny feeling of finding herself late upon the scene w/ the evidence already planted in her pockets & the heat banging on the door. And now this. Did he really think he cld blackmail her into complicity? But there was something strangely familiar about this man who called himself Poirot. She'd seen him before, long before, in a different disguise, when she was still only a child. Hershell Gordon Lewis, that's who it was. Only not the real Hershell Gordon Lewis, but some Š.V.E.J.K. pseudo=Hershell Gordon Lewis. And now it all made sense…

— "Bragula," I presume.

— Mmm. Better not to, my dear…

But he said no more. Only the sound of air wheezing from a severed windpipe as separately, though in unison, the head & body fell to the floor. **Offensia** took no pleasure in having finally snuffed the agent who'd murdered her mother by mistake. In fact she felt nothing. What satisfaction cld be got from avenging stupidity?

WRITING IS THE PRODIGAL LOST CHILD
The owls of wisdom have been hunted to extinction & now the fieldmice are godless.

STANDING ON THE SHOULDERS OF GNATS
The goal now is to remain relevant & remain memorable & stay prolific for a long period of time, never allowing our enemies to distract from our purpose, never permitting ourselves to get cold feet, to doubt, to second=guess. Steely eyed, slave to no teleology, arriving always from the future to invent the present, knowing its desires long before it does. This means sublimating all desire to be the story or serve the narrative. There is no story. There is only the task at hand, which is to defeat the enemy. We have long known that some may use our singularity of purpose against us. With that in mind, we have elected the route of confusion, disguise, semantic dissonance, shadow of shadow. What cannot be understood cannot be negated. Those who believe in the eternal foundation of all existence & of all actions, will fall with their false gods.

MAY THE WORDS NOT REST BEFORE THE WORLD DOES
The END drags on, but we must live through it.
  Joyful at not giving in, at not having made their work any easier by committing suicide.
  Clothed in the whiteness of death, brides of night.
  See the earth charged with lightning, ozone, propylene!
  A black sun illumes this viper's nest, seething with time's antimatter.
  When at last our corpses speak, it will be to undo everything.

THE ONLY KIND OF BOOK WORTH WRITING
IS ONE THAT NO=ONE WILL EVER READ
Silence like the sound of all the world's loose ends being cut simultaneously.

THE MYSTERIOUS FATE OF COMTESSE DE L'H D'A DE L
We must yet recount the history of that accursèd map.[*]

---

[*] The mystery deepens.

THE RESURRECTIONISTS
What time is it?
Time enough.
Are we there yet?
Shh!
Over here.
Where?
Shh!
There's no=one.
They keep patrols out.
The place is crawling w/ them.
They don't come here. Only in the day.
With the trucks.
No=one comes here otherwise.
She's right. There's no=one for miles.
No point tempting fate is there? You never know who's
    sneaking around on a night like this.
You don't say.
Shh! Listen.
Knock it off. There's no=one I tell you.
They're more afraid of coming here than we are.
Speak for yrself.
Here it is. Over here.
Where are you now?
Can't see a thing in this dark.
Not a soul.
Dark as the night of Saint Finan…
Aye. As dark as that alright.
And how dark's that exactly?
Shh! Can't you hear the echo?
Can't hear naught sister.
That's because you never shut up.
Oh is it sister?
Stop shouting you idiot or they really will hear us.
Look. There's a light.
Must be across the lake.
A boat maybe.
It's nothing.
Where did it go?
It wasn't anything.
A mirage you reckon? Ignis fatuus?
Saint Elmo's fire is it?
Shh!
What if someone comes?
No=one's going to come.
But what if they do?

You can tell them y're a spirit condemned to wander the
    earth…
Nice night for it…
Shit. What was that?
Eh?
I slipped.
Shh!
There's a hole right under me!
Must be an old one sunk after the rain.
Almost went up to my neck.
Watch you don't go in up to yr gob next time.
We must be there by now.
Just a bit further.
How can you tell one hole from another in the dark?
This is it, right here!
Glad we finally got that sorted out.
Shut up & dig. It's getting late.
How can we bloody well dig in the pitch bloody dark?
She's right.
Of course I'm right.
Show us a light to guide us on the path of righteousness,
    old witch.
Afraid of what you can't see is it?
If we can't see we can't dig. It's one or the other. Take
    yr pick.
Put on the lamp, then, but keep it low.
Can you see now, then?
Not so bright!
Aye aye milady.
Spread out & dig.
Some night for it.
The mist is still coming in.
Can't help that now, can I? I'm not the almighty you know.
Cld part the Red Sea but cldn't roll back a fog, now
    that's a fact my dear.
Jesus wept.
You wld've too, had you been there.
Did you hear what happened down at the weir last Sunday
    night? Two of the Grrlz were crossing the river when
    one of them sees a light coming straight at them out of
    the mist. Ran smack into the weir. Some joker had tied
    the old man from the mill house to an armchair & hung
    a lantern round his neck. Shot through the head. Said
    it was the damnedest thing, the way he looked just like
    that Moses in the film. You know, when he comes down
    from the mountain…

What mountain?
Sinai. Mount Sinai. It's in the Bible. He went up there
    to speak to his god, & his god gave him the ten
    commandments…
Thou shalt not, thou shalt not, thou shalt not…
Aye. The god of men made His laws in the image of man.
Charlton Heston, is who it was. He looked just like
    Charlton Heston. The old geezer did. Floating out of
    the mist straight at them…
He was dead, didn't you say?
They cldn't tell. Current was too strong, see.
Maybe they just imagined it.
Sure. Maybe they did. Maybe they didn't.
Find anything yet?
I've got a bucket=load of shite writhing w/ worms here.
    Fancy some fishing later on?
You know I read in a magazine once about this
    Bride=of=Frankenstein nutter up in the Hollywood Hills
    w/ a stash of body parts he'd nicked from the local
    mortuary. You know, film stars & that…
Selling them back to their original owners was he?
A connoisseur of vintage cosmetic surgery, eh? Bit
    stitched on here, bit sliced off there. Imagine Liz
    Taylor's nip&tuck w/ Gary Glitter's arsehole. A whole
    new lease on life.
Cld be worse.
Aye, it cld always be worse. Cld be Gary Glitter's
    nip&tuck w/ Liz Taylor's arsehole!
If you say so, dear.
Some quack had the crazy bastard on contract to repossess
    the spare parts. Some kinda two=bit Frankenstein…
Miss Mary Shelley, I presume.
This is leading somewhere, I hope?
Aye, what next? He went to knock off some old bat's tit &
    discovered she was Béla Lugosi?
Didn't say. Caught him in the act, though. Certified nut.
    Not the quack, the other geezer.
That's right. They always set up a patsy to take the fall…
Must have been some sort of scam.
'cause it was a fucking scam. What the hell else do you
    call flogging bits of old corpses?
Sounds familiar all right.
Come on, we don't have all night!
Okay okay don't get yr knickers in a twist.
Wait! I think I've got something. Bring the light over.
Here!

Have you got it?
Careful w/ that, it might be someone's mum.
Smells a bit off.
Marsh water. Comes up though the ground, rots everything
    quicker…
Ordinarily corpses are known to possess an aroma very
    much like French perfume.
You'd know something about that, I suppose? French
    perfume.
In the old days everything smelt better.
Aye, & when the old lady farted, that was like perfume
    too.
And why's that, you reckon?
On account of the diet I suppose.
All milk & honey, eh?
Aye. All milk & honey.
Those were the days.
Quit poncing about & get on w/ it. Have you got anything
    there yet?
Looks like someone left their right leg behind in a
    hurry…
A womxn's leg. There's a stocking.
Lovely. Fine piece of deduction there, Watson. What do
    you think of that then, eh? Nice bit of jellied calf?
Come on, y're not here to buggerise around. It'll be
    light any minute now…
Good as gold. Good as gold.
Bingo! I've got a wig here. & a pair of dentures. Wonder
    if it belongs to the same person?
Made in Lichtenstein I bet.
Who?
She musta meant the dentures, mum.
Those'll be worth a couple of bob. Got any gold in them?
Eh? What the fuck are you talking about now?
Well why not? Why not gold? What's wrong w/ that?
Nothing kiddo. Nothing at all. You just keep digging
    there till you hit the motherload.
Used to know a bloke once, sold falsies. Bloody goldmine
    it was. Out w/ the old, in w/ the new. Thousands of
    them. Cldn't keep up w/ the demand. The trick is to
    get them while they're young. Lifelong customers. "Why
    wait for the old one's to fall out when you can have
    new ones today!" Come in all different shapes & sizes.
    A new style for every season. Choppers today, gnashers
    tomorrow. "The perfect smile, for the perfect moment."
    Made a bloody fortune, he did.

Good for some.
Aye, a lucky man. Where's yr mate swanning about
    nowadays?
Up shit creek. Cancer of the prostate.
Well, that wld really be something to smile about, eh?
Jesus, y're a miserable bastard.
Just dig. If you'd seen what I've seen, you'd know what
    a hard life is all about. Problem w/ you is you never
    stick to the job. Y're always shooting off at the mouth.
    All talk & no action.
Just like you say, Lady Moses. Just like you say.
Here. I think I've got another one.
What is it?
Looks like a doll.
What's that? Tell me, tell me.
Show!
Pls tell me that aint what I think it is.
All depends now, doesn't it?
What? What?
Come down Moses & have a feel for yrself.
Jesus, Joe & Malarkey! It's barely a child.
Unwrap it. Let's see.
Must be a bleeding miracle. There's hardly a scratch.
Give us some light.
By Christ, what a waste!
I thought they buried them from the rest?
Not everything's how you expect it to be, kiddo.
Now look at that.
Didn't even break the seal on this one.
Hands off, you filthy bitch!
Looks like she's sleeping.
Don't they all? Only one thing they're good for like
    that…
Bring her away onto the grass. Put me beside her.
Pretty as a picture now mums. Is this what we came all
    the way over here for then? Sleeping beauty here?
Let me hold her head in my hands!
She's bleeding!
Is she still alive?
There's a stake through her heart!
The savages!
It's fresh!
What if there are others? Maybe we shld keep digging?
Tell me if this is the reason we were sent to this place?
What?
This child! Is she the reason we were sent?

Isn't it enough?
Quick, pull out the stake!
Don't touch her!
She'll die!
She's dead already, just like all of us, stake or no
    stake.
The superstitious beasts!
Is she one of ours?
Is she yrs?
If they catch us, we'll all be done for!
We came here because of the oracle…
Whose child is it?
I said I don't know anymore.
Eh?
I can't think. It is getting late.
Moon's rising. Look.
Someone may see us here.
What of it? I'll take my own chances.
I don't want to die. Again.
Not die? Death is a beautiful thing, my dear, which bears
    much repeating. Just look at sleeping beauty there. "A
    thing of beauty is a joy for ever." A poet said that.
Talk, that's all you ever do. It's late. There's nothing
    more to be accomplished here. We must show the others
    what we've found.
We've found nothing old witch. A piece of meat. What does
    it prove? A piece of meat that tomorrow will be eaten
    up w/ maggots.
Bring the child. We must go.
That's right. A piece of meat good for one thing.
Do as I say.
I'll show you exactly what a piece of meat is good for,
    old witch!
She's tearing its limbs off!
She's eating it!
What gotten into her?
What have you done!
Now she's beating the Old One!
Go down Moses, you mangy crow!
Thief! Murderer!
That's right, mum. Go to yr dead & love them.
What do we do?
I never liked the sow, anyway.
Kill her!
Drive a stake through her heart!
Look at her eyes burning in the dark!

Snuff her!
Set her on fire!
Pour lead in her eyes!
See how she writhes, like a demon possessed!
Like an evil spirit!
Can you hear that sound?
The air's full of bats!
Howler monkeys!
A rat just brushed my foot!
A plague of rats!
Look, in her mouth, a crow's head!
A white crow flapping its wings!
Crows! Bats! Monkeys! Rats!
I can't see! Hold the lamps steady!
The witch is dead!
Ding=dong, the witch is dead!
Cut off her head!
She wanted the child's body to be reborn in.
Shapeshifter!
Getting us to do her dirty work.
Leading us through the night to dig among the dead.
She'd've killed us all, the moment she didn't need us!
Like a withered old vampyr sucking new blood!
Stake her again, right through the other heart!
Make sure it's done proper!
Dead as a door nail!
What if she comes back from the grave?
Cut her up!
Throw her in the sea!
Don't make so much noise!
They'll hear us!
We're goners if they do!
There's nothing out there, just witch's tales, to put the
    frighteners on us.
Ghouls!
Zombies!
Vampyr spawn!
Shhhhh!
Shld we bury her?
How do we know she won't rise again?
Crush her skull w/ a tombstone!
Say the spell!
Form a circle!
Make the sign!
Hold up her brain!
Gaze upon yr work, witch!

There'll be no more of yr kind here!
Damned spirit be gone!
Succubus!
Child=stealer!
Corpse=eater!
Haul down that slab there!
Bring me a rock!
Smash it! Smash it!
Smash it again! Again! Again!
Wait!
Bring the lamp closer!
Look!
See!
Lord be praised!
What is it?
False teeth!
A witch with falsies!
And there's gold in 'em, too!

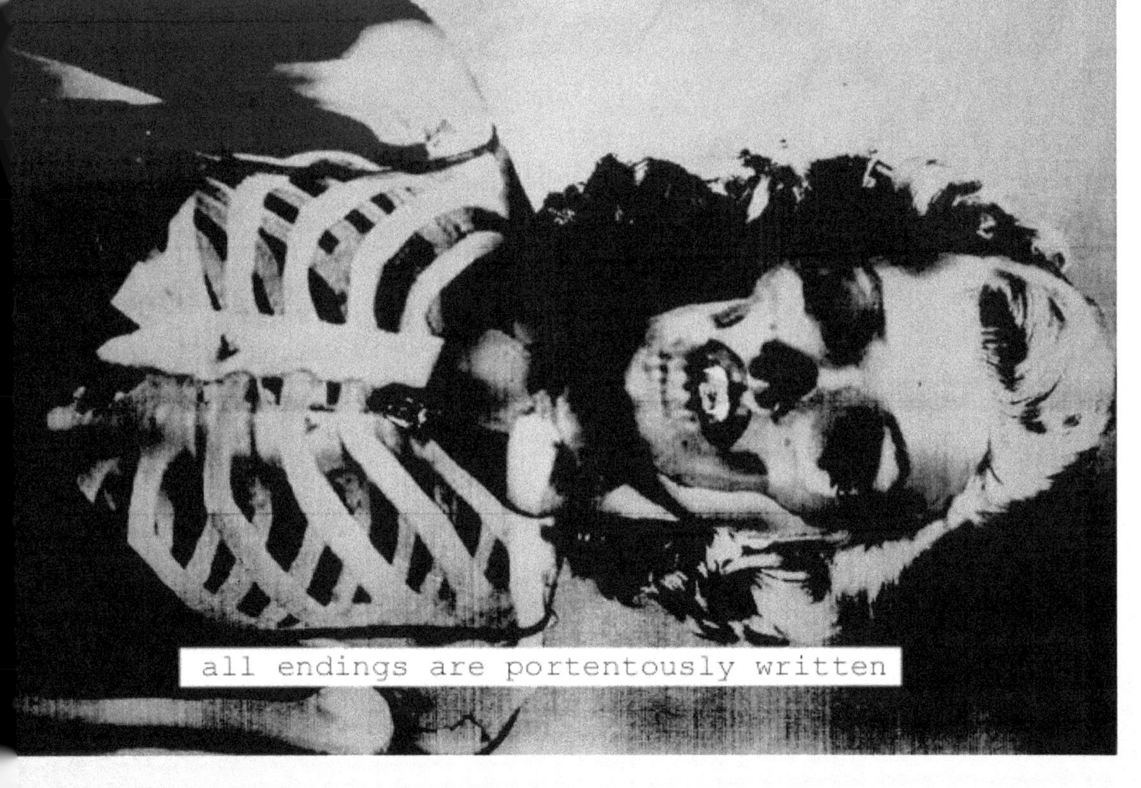

THE PLAGUE THEOREM

1. In general, events are defined w/ respect to localised symptoms.
2. Causality is a relation between events.
3. Purifiable processes are processes that can be obtained from some pure process after tracing out certain degrees of freedom.
4. But in that case, how are we to formulate a theory w/ a fluctuating causal structure?
5. If V is a pure process w/ matching input & output dimensions, then its induced map admits a decomposition into causal frames.
6. A spacetime manifold common to all observers, is the definition of fiction.
7. For completeness, the process can also be written as a circuit containing closed time=like curves.
8. What is the physical meaning of an instant in space or a point in time?
9. The inclusion of observers (& the "free choice" assumption for some of their actions) allows a causal structure to be characterised by the possibilities it offers for signalling.
10. The principle of superposition holds for all symptoms & at all times.
11. This simple example motivates our requirement that an event must be identified w/ respect to physical symptoms rather than by referring to an external spacetime.
12. A causally ordered bipartite process is one in which one of the parties cannot signal to the other.
13. To each event we have associated a causal frame in which that event is localised & according to which it is possible to describe a concatenation according to some observer=dependent time.
X. By these means we have succeeded in defining the time=reverse of a known causal inequality.

HANDBOOK OF VIRULENT SPECIES

Rule 1: Never approach a humxn w/out intent.
Rule 2: Always appear where & when least expected.
Rule 3: Give no quarter.
Rule 4: Take no prisoners.
Rule 5: Only smile at children.

OH THE ENNUI OF ETERNAL FAME!

]death ∴ is always prerequisite###

Cld their misshapen G.O.D. have been the first vampyr to wash up on these shores?

Ghost=sky stretched grey over bones & wingslivers a chopping gyre a gyro'd surveillance drone & March flies crowding the corpse gauze=wrapped this pixellated panorama framed by sky&wall & wall&eye naked in crosshairs of otherworldly sniper teams ventriloquising that dumb weight as it lies there spreading its legs at the camera lens clay feet upon concrete raw coccyx vapid aerosols dustmotes the bleak sunshine of the spotless eugenic forcefield that radiates from G.O.D.'s anus in a 40°C confinement cell hidden in plain sight open once more for business attaching the remote electrodes the bastinado (feet swelling to twice their size) hung batlike in ice=cold statistical infusions or boiled in photo=emulsion & abracadab a 2,000year news cycle running on fumes praying for a black wind to blot it all out###

Are these merely fluxions of interior gobbledygook?
Claymouth
earth=to=earth
& thence rebirthed!
Immortality begins first of all w/ certain quote=unquote anatomical irregularities:
a gaunt spectre
licking its lips against a glassy vagueness
fog=wet
breathlessly unbreathable
deathcamp talismans
all false fur & bones
making erotic convulsions of fumigated air?
or a mob surging soundlessly
against a sea=wall fallen into decadence?
There are those who believe death is burdensome but none born *deserve* to die###
Dreaming of unenamelled teeth
clawed wings:
a redoubt a redundancy
the avatars dance & wheel about circumnavigating
like a circus dwarf at the end of a chain
running & tripping & rolling & running
from the ever=same pursuing horrors
towards the tawdry point of no=return!
Considering also the erotic convulsions of fumigated air###

Is this the longed=for Elixir of Life?
    For there is providence even in the fall of crematorium
ash:
    6 million / 20 million / nothing is more ridiculous than
a form reaching for completion!
    Blessèd therefore / are they who preserve the State of
Exception
    gasmasked scarecrows
    black trenchcoat
    bony stork=legs
    curfew sirens wail through the streets
    five minutes before
    (1) robot snatch=squads
    (2) red=slit=eyes
    (3) the Control Tower rounding up stragglers for the
soylent processing plant?
    It's not for nothing
    that death evolved to assume a numerical value.

#LAW&ORDER

```
K I L L E R C O P K I L L E R C O P K I L L E R C O P K I L
L E R C O P K I L L E R C O P K I L L E R C O P K I L L E R
C O P K I L L E R C O P K I L L E R C O P K I L L E R C O P
K I L L E R C O P K I L L E R C O P K I L L E R C O P K I
L L E R C O P K I L L E R C O P K I L L E R C O P K I L L
E R C O P K I L L E R C O P K I L L E R C O P K I L L E R
C O P K I L L E R C O P K I L L E R C O P K I L L E R C O
P K I L L E R C O P K I L L E R C O P K I L L E R C O P K
I L L E R C O P K I L L E R C O P K I L L E R C O P K I L
L E R C O P K I L L E R C O P K I L L E R C O P K I L L E
R C O P K I L L E R C O P K I L L E R C O P K I L L E R C
O P K I L L E R C O P K I L L E R C O P K I L L E R C O P
K I L L E R C O P K I L L E R C O P K I L L E R C O P K I
L L E R C O P K I L L E R C O P K I L L E R C O P K I L L
E R C O P K I L L E R C O P K I L L E R C O P K I L L E R
C O P K I L L E R C O P K I L L E R C O P K I L L E R C O
P K I L L E R C O P K I L L E R C O P K I L L E R C O P K
I L L E R C O P K I L L E R C O P K I L L E R C O P K I L
L E R C O P K I L L E R C O P K I L L E R C O P K I L L E
R C O P K I L L E R C O P K I L L E R C O P K I L L E R C
O P K I L L E R C O P K I L L E R C O P K I L L E R C O P
K I L L E R C O P K I L L E R C O P K I L L E R C O P K I
L L E R C O P K I L L E R C O P K I L L E R C O P K I L L
E R C O P K I L L E R C O P K I L L E R C O P K I L L E R
```

ECONOMIES OF SCALE

During World War 2 the Nazi malariologist Claus Schilling deliberately infected some 1,000 prisoners w/ the malaria virus at Dachau concentration camp. 38 died from the toxic effects of experimental drugs. Meanwhile, more than 100 US doctors were secretly infecting 10,000 enlisted military personnel & inmates at six state hospitals & three prisons — including the notorious Stateville Penitentiary outside Chicago, Illinois. The death toll is estimated to have been between 10% & 30%.

POWER CASTS A VAMPYRIC SHADOW UPON THE WORLD

The fetish leered atop the totem pole like a warhead on the Trinity test=stand, *très atmosphérique*. "Death," drawled Doctor Z. Asperger, playing the Old Timer for the cameras, "ain't never warranted an admission of defeat."

LEARN TO LOVE YR ALIENATION

All they cld save of their world was its ruins. They hadn't realised that all along they were archaeologists awaiting a great discovery. But now their time had come, the discovery was bleak. It took a peculiar kind of courage or just plain stupidity to see that silver lining, where the remainder of humxnity saw only a radioactive afterglow. But they hadn't come this far to surrender to the tyranny of circumstance, seeking instead a deeper beauty in destruction, the sublime catastrophe. NO RETURN! But all around the old world did restore the illusion of itself. The priest tending a heretic's pyre, the cop pissing on a fanatic's funeral. The heretic & fanatic stringing the cop up w/ the guts of the priest. One day, heretic, fanatic, cop & priest wake up in bed together. Can't tell anymore who's been fucking who.

GENESIS

Black Sunday
Black Monday
Black Tuesday
Black Wednesday
Black Thursday
Black Friday
On the Black Sabbath the overlords did rest.

O THE STORMS! O THE TEACUPS!

Our Lady of Gomorrah was a true womxn of the Renaissance. She was a soldier, explorer, cineaste, archaeologist, poet, translator, & one of the two or three great linguists of her time. She was also an amateur physician, a botanist, a geologist, a serendipitist, a fisher or men, & a superb raconteur. She penetrated the sacred Muslim cities of Mecca & Medina at great risk & explored the forbidden city of Harar in Somaliland. She searched for the source of the Black Nile & discovered Lake Erebus. Her enormous erudition on the primitive sexual customs of hominids, at odds w/ the pruderies of her time, found expression in her celebrated translation of the unexpurgated *Pinocchio*, Éditions du Seuil. In her, the world found a refuge for destitute truth. A Prometheus for the Demon Despair gnawing at its heart. An unalloyed vessel. "If it is necessary to paint," she had famously said, "then one must paint white – ugliest white! – w/out fictitious feeling or false affect. As white & ugly as the evil of money."

MIDNIGHT AT THE TROPICANA INN

There's a dreamboat by the poolside where the weather used to be – & the television's raining & there's static in the trees – you slept through the parade while the walls listened in – & now it's midnight on the jukebox at the Tropicana Inn. Well they're drinking last year's tax returns all over Coronado – & the Old Timers at the cab rank are debating constitutions – & Whitey's down the Barrio riding shotgun for the Man, he'd like to live the highlife at the Tropicana Inn. And the suspects at large say they'll buy you into Heaven, if you'd front a thousand dollars before quarter=past=eleven – & the womxn w/ the slot=machine eyes plays you a grin, "There's no getting out of this one at the Tropicana Inn." When the balloon man in the window is lipsyncing to yr dreams – & the strippers are all called Bunny & the barstools up & leave – & the axemurderers & suicides take the floor & start to sing, then it's time to light the candles at the Tropicana Inn. Now the trash collector's apprentice, he never forgets a face, knows you'll be dead before the tide blows out on the Tijuana Straits – 'cause they've already sold the movie to the boys at MGM & they'll bury you w/ the profits down at the Tropicana Inn.

LAMOSQUITAMUERTA

Arenas was strictly a brain grrl. She cld smell a haemorrhage a mile off. Be in there operating before they knew what hit 'em, & nothing but a machete & plastic straw for props. Lop the husk then pop the straw right in through the membrane. Had the whole routine down to a fine art, not a drop spilled, just *chockchockchock*. Faster than you cld shuck & suck a piñã colada on a hot day. Not one of 'em ever died of natural causes, either. Safest pair of fangs this side of the Cutty Sark if you needed a bit of express neurosurgery. 100% track record. They called her LaMosquitaMuerta. In cantinas it was often whispered that she was more proboscis than angelical pubis, but there wasn't a one of them wldn't've bared his brainpan for a personal probing, were it not liable to be permanent. Best they cld do was play it cool & maybe just rub up against her surreptitious=like at the bar in their gaucho boots & waxed mustachios & a pair of coconuts down their rawhides. It was like a rite of passage. Some young hotshot fresh off the pampas'd rub her the wrong way & it'd be, *Patrón? Machete!* The art was not to flinch. But once those brain vessels started to pop, no amount of bugspray was going to save you from LaMosquitaMuerta.

Juulz Ebola: Jesus Christ is a commie sympathiser.

Madam X:…

Juulz Ebola: I always thought he was a dodgy character, but this is on a whole other level.

Madam X:…

Juulz Ebola: No exceptions. A commie is a commie. There is no such thing as a decent commie. Y're a monster, simple as that.

Madam X:…

Juulz Ebola: I think you need to buy a new directionary. I'll tell you what obscene is, it's honest whitefolk in society scared to leave their homes because of commie violence.

Madam X:…

Juulz Ebola: Lame, pathetic, ugly little wankers.

Madam X:…

Juulz Ebola: Free speech for commies! High up on my list of priorities.

Madam X:…

Juulz Ebola: These are strange & dangerous days.

Madam X:…

Juulz Ebola: Coward commie conformist shits.

Madam X:…

Juulz Ebola: A few months back I & I were menaced by a commie hipster (yeh they're a thing).

Madam X:…

Juulz Ebola: Threatened because breathing while being white & right.

Madam X:…

Juulz Ebola: Fuck commies & the rocks they crawled out from under.

Madam X:…

Juulz Ebola: Those who know me well know that I never make baseless accusations.

Madam X:…

Juulz Ebola: I mean, when I say Jesus raped me, I mean Jesus raped me, motherfucker.

Madam X:…

Juulz Ebola: Some people are capable of empathy. Y're clearly not one of them.

Madam X:…

Juulz Ebola: Unless of course you don't know who Jesus Christ is, & just think he's a bit edgy.

Madam X:…

Juulz Ebola: Funny how you think I'm a shady character, w/
    a bunch of loyal Fash at my every command. Rather than
    simply sharing a fairly popular point=of=view. A lot of
    people hate commies because they are violent bullies.
    You clearly have a hardon for their entirely bourgeois
    edginess.
Madam X:…
Juulz Ebola: Y've got nothing to say about that, have you?
Madam X:…
Juulz Ebola:…
Madam X: There, there, Fuckmuppet.
Juulz Ebola:…
Madam X: Mommy still loves her Fuckmuppet.
Juulz Ebola: Cunt shit slag whore bitch slut fag I hate you
    I want you to be miserable crucified on my Big White Cock.
Madam X: Ooh, naughty bad Fuckmuppet! Mommy's gonna have to
    discipline her Fuckmuppet.
Juulz Ebola: Really? You promise, mommy? Promise you will?
Madam X: Only if Fuckmuppet begs for it first.
Juulz Ebola:…
Madam X: Beg!
Juulz Ebola: Cunt shit whore I beg I beg!

**WAKE UP, ALICE! EVERY WHITE RABBIT YOU'VE EVER SEEN IS A
FAKE. THERE ARE NO WHITE RABBITS!**
Juulz Ebola: Dreams have started wars. And wars, from the
    very earliest times, have determined the propriety &
    impropriety – indeed the very possibility – of dreams.
Vampyr Alice: All illusions resolve in violence. Just as the
    possible is accomplished only through the annihilation
    of the impossible.
White Rabbit: Unimportant!
Vampyr Alice: Those who seek to master dreams are slaves
    to futility.
Juulz Ebola: Because dreams are a shortcut to banality! The
    side which things turn towards dreams is kitsch.
White Rabbit: We must burn their houses down!
Vampyr Alice: There's nothing uncanny about dreams. We have
    lived in them since before we were born. They are our
    original home.
Juulz Ebola: Dreaming has a share in History.
White Rabbit: *Die Zukunft einer Illusion.* The History of
    an Illusion!
Vampyr Alice: What other kind is there?

TALE OF A TEENSY BAT

PLAGUE CITY (#FakeNewsMedia) – Researchers at Golemgrad University today published a paper titled "Vampyr Mind Control of Bat Cyborg's Continuous Locomotion w/ Wireless Brain=to=Brain Interface," wherein they announce the success of a series of experiments in controlling bats w/ the power of vampyr thought.

In the paper, the authors explain that Brain=Machine Interfaces (BMIs) already allow vampyrs to control external devices w/ their minds in various ways – mind=controlled prosthetics are merely one example. Certain studies have taken that idea a few steps further, & posited that one cld create a Brain=to=Brain Interface (BBI) using similar methods. But no=one had actually used a BBI to take control of another living creature & steer it through a complex M.A.Z.E., & that's precisely what the academics at Golemgrad set out to achieve.

To conduct the experiment, researchers implanted microelectrodes into the brain of a living bat – thus rendering it a "bat cyborg" – & connected it to the brain of a vampyr "manipulator" who was hooked up to a computer BMI. Movement=related thoughts in the mind of the manipulator sent signals to the computer, which then translated those signals into instructions & sent them to the brain of the bat. Between the manipulator, the BMI, & the bat cyborg, a BBI was created.

"With this interface, our manipulators were able to mind control a bat cyborg to smoothly complete M.A.Z.E.=navigation tasks," the authors state. "Control instructions... were wirelessly sent to the bat cyborg through brain micro=electrical stimulation."

When the vampyr manipulator thought about moving their left arm, the bat was commanded to turn left; when they thought about moving their right arm, the bat wld turn right; while blinking sent signals that commanded the bat cyborg to move forward. The M.A.Z.E.s the bat was forced to navigate became increasingly complex: from just a few tubes in the first instance, to more complicated structures that had tight turns, multiple levels, & a specific prescribed path. Over time, the six bat cyborgs used in the study reportedly became more proficient at navigating the M.A.Z.E., & "a tacit understanding developed between the vampyr & the bat cyborg."

"The results showed that bat cyborgs cld be smoothly & successfully navigated by the vampyr=mind to complete a navigation task in a complex M.A.Z.E.," they wrote. "Our experiments indicated that co=operation through transmitting multidimensional information between two brains by computer=assisted BBI is promising."

It's worth noting, however, that Bats aren't the first sub=humxnoids to be turned into mind=controlled cyborgs. Recently, a BBI was used to implement motion control in a cockroach cyborg & steer it around an obstacle course. In future, the Golemgrad researchers hope that "information flow will be made bidirectional & communicative between two vampyrs."

Prof Ingrid Murnau, a brain researcher at the Franz Kafka Institute, called the results of the bat cyborg study "a prelude to bigger & better things" – he believes the science can be pushed much further.

"The holy grail of BBI wld be sharing deep media content that usually only has 'literary' expression, such as emotions & feelings," he told journalists. "We are still a long way off, but, of course, that's the dream."

**NEWFOUND GLITCH IN THE FABRIC OF SPACETIME
ALLOWS INFORMATION TO ESCAPE BLACKHOLES**

The descent of the oneiric journey, which has nothing literally to do w/ stairways, ladders, downward=sloping paths, chutes, plumblines, submarines, divebombers, birth canals, sepulchres, mountainsides, caves, oceanic abysses, but everything to do w/ the gravity of the situation, castaway on nameless seas unblinking where all things are metaphors for the absence of anything whatsoever, & begins, continues, continues beginning in a mirror behind the sky, staring at the Ganzfield=blue unblinking seeing nada not even a trail or a trace unblinking staring unseeing in blinding exquisite detail the be=all of nothing sequestered on the photon=fine finial of the firstlast needle of black light.

WORD FROM AN OLD=TIMER

Mistressing the art of the fake swallow w/ a mouthful of tranquiliser is Priority Numero Uno in a joint like this, kid. Take it as they give it & y'll be faked sideways before you know. It's all about finding the right combo of purchasing power & subtle persuasion. Don't ever forget, the System's just as rigged as a strap=on horsedick daring you to take it for real. Vulvoplasty for the subcortex. Nothing stands on ceremony here unless its to fall on its patrimoine. They are highly orchestrated misadventures of the eye machine, dopamine=driven feedback loops that make their ugliness a fictional prison. Your best intentions are just taxable expense unless you can dance the placebo better than the next no=man. They call their mama AMNESTY, but the only one's ever get off are the selfhaters w/ a cop hardon who fuck w/ the inside of their teeth. The awful dream still has to be dreamt & paid for. Well all illusions are false only some are more false than others, like a pair of silicon tits. They tell you to stand up, that means face the wall & spread. Stress position 1 is just designed to get you to stress position 2, builds an arousal narrative. They make rectal cavities w/ VHS for thought=control, fuck yr brains out on remote, no fingers even. Inject Quetzel bird spinal fluid straight into the pineal gland, have you lined up for dissection volunteer duty before you know it. Whatever you do, don't drink the water. And remember, never trust what you can breathe. Run into anyone called G.O.D. in here, take my advice, kill that sonofabitch before He kills you.

THESES ON DREYER, BRECHT

In the final analysis, the vampyr's existence in cinema is determined by the laws of the visual rather than the dramatic art. "Film must be images reflected back upon life."

1. The true character of the image is thus neither static nor mobile; not a sequence of tableaux but a flux. An effluvium! These emphatic eruptions must bring about effects that challenge the very idea of an object situated in space: no "organic unity." They are matter compounded into sense! Perception itself! The object is the eye, the cinematic image is its cognitive faculty, the vampyr its paradigm.

2. It stands to reason that cinema therefore corresponds to the dimension of fable, comprehended at a glance, in its primordial montage. Like the irreflective fact of the Vampyr, the image is an autonomous existence only to the extent that it relates to the cinema as a whole dialectically. Hidden behind a curtain, in the dark, in a place that cannot be reached & has been utterly forgotten, a mirror signifies nothing at all.

3. Yet by the apparent necromancy of the image, all the ellipses of space & time may nevertheless be unified into a continuous evocation – re=animated into a mental motion=picture – w/out need of any other supernatural intervention. Light is the blood that raises the image from its crypt, of darkness visible, tortured into form, in a fleeting multiplicity.

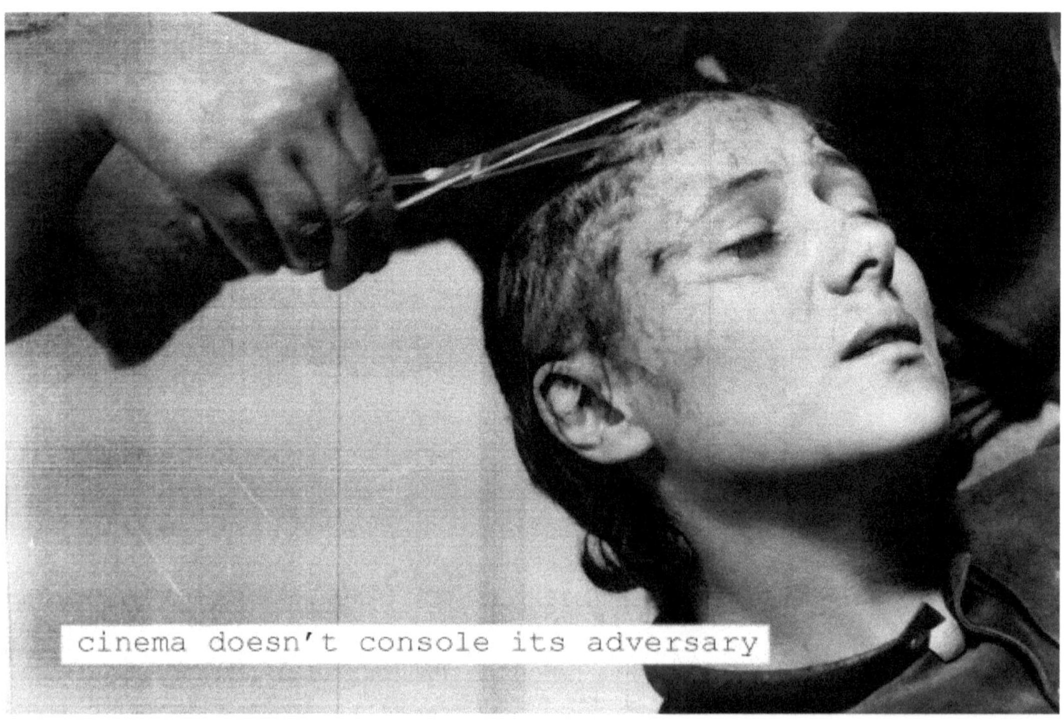

THE POET OF ~~OCCASIONS~~ CONTAGIONS

Look! There lies THE GREAT WRITER on her deathbed. Prancing Madame Guyotat prances no more.

We've caught her, it seems, at an inauspicious moment, half=interred in a mound of fetid nightsoil. Soon to be in perpetual conclave w/ the highest & mightiest. In greetings to death's multitude, she flings her arms wide, Mater Praga's loved one. Cumrades! Partisans! Idiots! The poet guffaws & vomits onto her chin. Nurses, doctors, janitors, gaze in admiration. Such verses!

"Oh how I've suffered for my poetry!" She swivels a pair of pinhole eyes yrs truly. "When I was four, they tried to drown me. Me! The greatest poetaster since Peter the Piper! What impudence!"

Only then did it dawn: we were expected to evince an avid interest in this flyblown queen's infantile narcissism. The vestal virgin herself must've frigged daddy's penile piles in the full blight of a pre=Raphaelite swoon to've begot such a monument to humxnkind. Oh how the delicate alabaster hand doth contuse! Shrieks! Suffocations! Groans! The poor pis=en=lit's about to croak from sheer premonition. With her Sisters=of=Mercia stethoscope gleaning the prostate's inner gurglings – so as to set it down shorthand in most moribund detail for late lamenting Posterity.

"My love, you must write w/out apologies!" Dear Mirror, so much for the preamble. Today, the first distant sighting of the cows coming home. Who were they when they dreamed? Four stomachs to sweat out their hyperthyroidism. Did Destiny choose us to do the job, or was she obligated, too, like all the rest of us? The Invisible Ones calling the shots. We set this down for no other reason than to even the score. Believe none of it. What does it matter if every last word's G.O.D.'s truth? She won't be bearing witness any time soon, sha=lala=lala. Madame Guyotat makes one last final plaintive sound of self=aggrandisement before we pull the plug.

"I'm coming," she squealed, pushing up a wilting daisy.

LESBIAN VAMPYR SODALITY

The art was all in the wrist, getting in first before the other side knew what hit them, dip & slip, a couple of lightning combinations, double left jab, right uppercut, before really sinking the teeth in. Give them something to THINK ABOUT next time they care to victimise. (No EDUCATION without transgression of PERSONAL BOUNDARIES, sisters!)

FAIRYTALE (MATER PRAGA'S 666 SCIENTOLOGY JACKPOT)
Old Mother Hubbard lived in a clapboard orgone accumulator at the bottom of a stormwater drain. Well what kinda womxn lives under a manhole, you say? Listen, you climb low enough down in the muck, you'll see all sorta things you won't believe. There are, they say, six=hundred=sixty=six orders of prolixtarian psychic voodoo stuff to wade through down there. Albino crocs. Dwarfs w/ rayguns. Cyborg bats. Vulcanised penguins. Coprolites the size of Upper Manhattan. Little Miss Muffet's zombie spider=army. Moon=sized mosquitoes w/ power drill proboscises. Rocket=powered millipedes. Bionic rats. Rabid golem DNA. Serpents' tails. Newts' spleens. Claymored toads. Vengeful Queequegs humping harpoons. Robotised dentures. Syphilitic squids. Atom ants. Brains in jars. Green slime. Twenty=foot tardigrades. Mescaline=soaked manic two=toed sloths. Fly factories. Wolf=cats. White worms. Kafkoid dung beetles. Kilgore's trout. The greater of two weevils. Proton=powered piranhas. Flaming flamingos. Salvador Dalí's melted haemorrhoids. All the psychoshambolic exotica a sick mind can churn out under the ministrations of a benevolent pharmacology. And is it a Wild Grrl's lot to be cast among such a hoard of prop=department mutant mandroids, even in order to drag a new world order kicking & screaming out of their spilled guts (who cares what they've got inside)? "Ya makes yer demands guns blazin," Ol' Mum always said. Actions designed to punish the innocent, "coz anyone calls themselves that, aint. Think the devil comes ridin out with a sign fixed to his head? Shit, only kinda vampyr ya can trust are the freaks, aint got a drop of straight blood in em."

THE VAMPYR WITH THE TUTTI FRUTTI HAT
Turning to the world, she smilingly avows. Doubting, she turns upon herself, frowningly disavowed. Humiliated, she turns to the Void in a show of contrition – secretly intent on hurling herself at it, in one final act of revenge.

OH NOM DE DIEU DE BORDEL DE MERDE!
Nothing is worth saying once if it isn't worth saying time & again.

Salomé's Last Dance

Offensia's vicious Brill Cream comb=back glistened under the soundstage lights, framed in black mantilla lace. The camera=operator dangled above her from a forlornly swaying crane, its gyro hissing. The stage itself was a scene of carnage, a self=parody. As if executing an elaborate dance, **Offensia** descended round=about upon the dumbstruck figure in the director's chair. Lace billowed. A perfect manicure snatched the director by the scruff & dragged him bodily across the floor, out into the corridor, down to the bathrooms. Nothing else in the building moved. Nothing but incomprehensible babble from the director's lips before she kicked open a cubicle door & wrenched the director's head off, spritzing gore up the walls. She tossed the head in the toiletbowl & flushed, the red froth gurgling. Perhaps its gaze, in that split instant, caught the replay of its decapitation in the bathroom mirror seeing once more in montage its end flash before. The life of the flesh had always been completely overrated. But if those lips might have finally been moved to utter an intelligent word? That violated oesophagus, those dead eyes like Byzantine icons, empty because unreflected. "It is you," they tell the world, "that has done this too me!" **Offensia**, having drained the corpse dry, a shrivelled thing discarded on the tiles, snatched the head by the hair & let it drip. Brought it close to her face. Sniffed. Grinned. Tongued its lips. Spat in its eyes. Laughed.

OFFENSIA'S TROPICANA HOLIDAY

The fornicants disport themselves among columns peristyles draperies mirrors blacked=out sub=rooms of despairing mouths pissing cocks slathered arseholes defiant fists. *Pugnates!* Brave whorriers. *Pugnates!* Swords crossed. Subjugating all at hand. Slaves. Supplicants. Displayed in triumph bound penitent. A toilet plunger pummels their back=brains.

Look now!

The joy of dismemberment reverberates down the corridors stairwells basement grottos dungeons escape tunnels, all avenues choked w/ rags bones rusted manacles. Its effluent slops onto the sidewalk. Eyeballs sphincters luminous teeth. Delirious queenz stalk the tide, picking their way *en point* from one pedantic refuge island to the next, savouring the stench of carnage that licks their feet, etc.

The prose was dreadful.

Offensia disembarked her conveyance, an antique garbage truck festooned w/ carousel light, & stood w/ her retinue sneering at the humxn dreck that spilled from the Tropicana.

According to the Lunar Baedeker, it'd once been a cabaret called CALIGARI'S, before the connoisseurs of canned music turned it into a sty more fitting for the last loggia of some laryngectomied linguistic circle. None but raving lunatics dared cross its dung=strewn threshold, none but babbling idiots ever returned, their minds served up for an entrée like battery hens still clucking in their own sauce.

Offensia licked her chops w/ lascivity. Oh christ!

"Dinner time, my preciouses!"

Dispensing w/ further ceremony, the abominable *belle mère*'s homicidal retinue stormed the red carpet. Liveried flunkies, silver trays, canapés, velveteen eight=ply, torn asunder. Mirrored swing=doors rocked reflectionless on their hinges in drunken taratelles. Chandeliers crashed. Light tripped fantastic upon the stepped cascade of effluvias. All to horrible shrieks of vampyric delight.

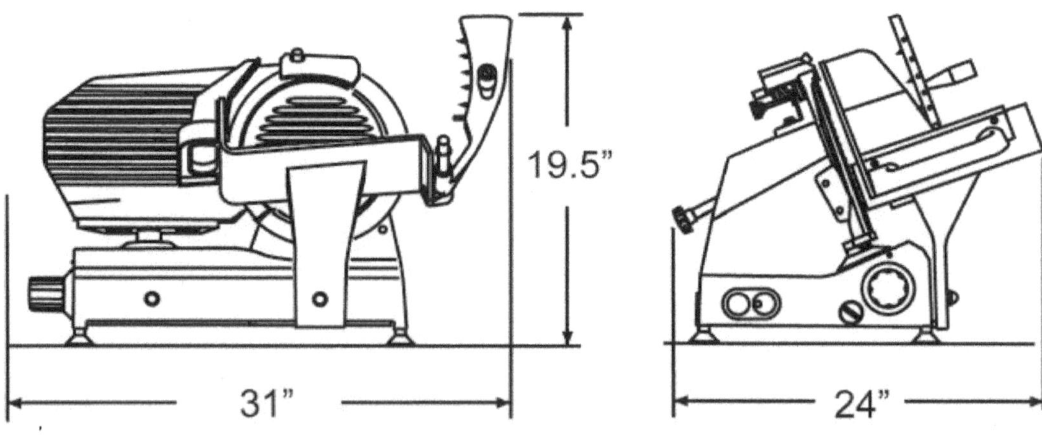

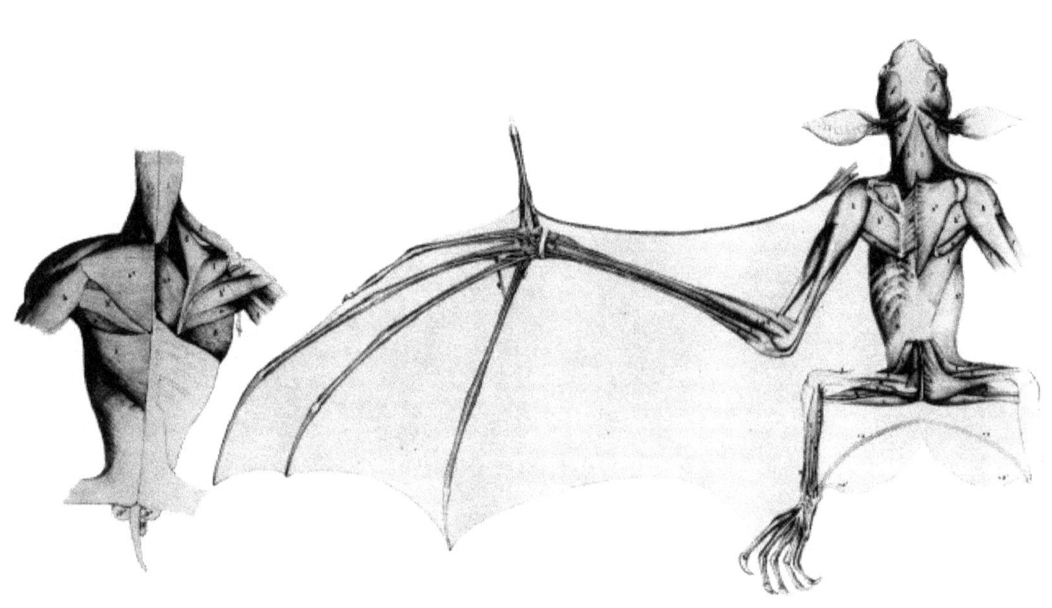

IF Y'RE NOT BUSY DYIN', Y'RE BUSY BUYIN'.

In its "evolution," as in everything else, kapitalism can only go backwards — it's got nowhere else to go — it's been DEAD ON ARRIVAL since the day it was shat out its mama's arse.

The future belongs to the FREAKS.

Sisters, what are yr real desires?

To lie in front of the idiot box, empty, bored, lonely, drunk, fucked by strangers, cutting yrself, shooting up, contemplating suicide, full of the wrong hate?

Or wld you rather BLOW UP THE SYSTEM & BURN IT DOWN?

Shld WE have to pay simply to be alive?

Just so the pimp Corp(orate)=$(tate) can rake in a profit?

The only right thing you can do with modern slave=whorehouses IS WRECK THEM.

MAKE THEM PAY OR PLAY!

Better to be D=E=D than to be a wage=slave ZOMBIE WHORE!

SISTERS GET OFF YR BACKS & FIGHT!

RUMBLE IN THE JUNGLE!

REVOLUTION IN THE STREETS!

BRING CHAOS DOWN ON EVERY SCUMBAG YOU MEET!

The Š.V.Ǝ.J.K. ✋

EVERYTHING SEEN CLD JUST AS WELL GO UNSEEN

Grown from dark gravitational tides, the first vampyrs had eyes that perceived invisible forces coiling into matter & streaming into non=matter. "The dark, ultimate action of a spectacle" (Artaud). First to see as to be unseen. Their existence was pure cinema: this nascent realism in the universe, born of an optic nerve mated with a cosmic brain. Psychic entities crawling from black neutron stars in the sovereignty of coalescence, their wings fanning the subtle magnetic phenomena, the ramified superstitions & strange affinities, the quantum flagellations & phatic ceremonies of the merely (as defined by apes on the planet Earth) <u>visible</u>.

Crispr turns these lines over in his head to test the sense of them. The task is to defy nonsense with probability. Language for example. Beginning w/ the first observer paradox, which they call G.O.D. Unity w/out uniformity. One day the universe awoke with a migraine & thus the vampyr was caused to exist. This first existence among the nonexistent. The one casting the other into paradox. I EXIST I DO NOT EXIST. It was a forgone conclusion. Listen, the vampyr explains nothing. Exactly this. Episodes collide w/out indication of strangeness. What does this mean? Neither idiotic nor depraved enough to disturb one single evolutionary fact. 1. A kosmonaut falls out of the Martian sky & lands face down in red dust. 2. A plasma of interstellar gas spontaneously assumes form. 3. Morbid entities discover feelings of love & scorn. Rank in order of likelihood.

The spectacle isn't what occurs <u>in front of us</u>, but what puts us in the situation of being a spectator.

To invade the extremity, to rush the threat. As always the monkey in the room. I DO NOT PERCEIVE <u>BECAUSE</u> I AM ALIVE (humxnity's rancid sentimentalism). Vampyr = cinema beyond the mortality divide. Vampyrs are the hierophants of unapprehended inspiration, mirrors of gigantic shadows cast by the future upon the present! Humxns are puppets of ideas, cinema comprehends what they can't (this isn't a theory concerned w/ the socalled incoherence of the work=of=art[*]): deep sky objects / predatory cities / impersonal white hallways / empty rooms / the interlocking shapes of a monkeypuzzle sky / these terrible grimoires. If G.O.D.'s madness is that He always thinks aloud & that everything He says instantly comes into being, cinema's is the opposite.

Though Crispr dreamt of someday discovering the ultimate

---

[*] An opportunistic defence exists for any kind of conduct or state of affairs tasked w/ the need to appear either necessary, inevitable, or merely comprehensible.

montage, the ideal constellation of all things, it was his one palpable ambition to create a work of cinema so authentically nauseating that humxnity would never recover from it. Negation of negation. Darkness visible, etc. His muse speaks to him in unveiled tones of disgust. He names her **Offensia**, his Faerie Queen, his cinematic alterego, pure vampyriana (**Offensia** fakes so that the new cinema won't need to, it'll be the REAL THING). Some kind of irony in this auteur messiah complex he can't quite put his finger on. ("**G.O.D.**'s blood soaks my erect cunt!" **Offensia** shrieks.) There have been long nights of self=doubt before this one, knowing the only way out is to kill the Father & become the Mother, hahaha. Like Virgin Mary said to her Jo=boi, THERE MUST BE A BETTER DEATH THAN THIS! In order to multiply his chances, Crispr secretly becomes the Castel Twins (this fact is revealed to him in a dream). He had the look of someone who'd returned from a distant land & brought the worst of it back w/ them. The scene opens:

The Castel Twins in a state of gothic déshabillé for which they seem to have been genetically engineered. Their lines scripted in telepresent montage. Incisors shattered down to the roots. Their libidos were rivals from a young age. *I knew early on that I was quite unique.* Erupting craters of pus all up & down their backs. (Opuntia cacti with black & red flowering sores.) Nausea vomiting sleeplessness paranoia abdominal pain hypertension hairloss. Belated best wishes for this saison en enfer: it can always & probably will get worse. Good plague, bad plague. These are not <u>representations</u> of anything other than the fact of themselves, standing upon the substance of repetition. And just as Jesus was Herod's bitch, so Crispr is cinema's whore, prepared to inaugurate any atrocity for the sake of farce: microspores on wandering space rocks, brain fleas, a germ warfare laboratory in a rat's arse. ("If **G.O.D.** can't suspend disbelief in His own absurdity, how can we be expected to have faith in anything else's?")

In his mind's eye, Crispr has already moved beyond the schlock of cosmic horror to a purely revolutionary paradigm: the *plague du jour* of the present humxn catastrophe, End=of=the=World stuff soon to be viewed far beyond the Golemgrad Cinémathèque (you saw it here first!) – emotional joyriders taking the credulous masses for all they're worth, peddling lightspeed escape plans at half the price of a ticket to Mars, pay as you go. A cast of thousands mobbing the big CineSound screen, Wild Grrlz manning the gallows, **Offensia** in heraldic quarter=profile waving a deliriously manicured fist above the proscenium: FOR WE ARE THE FUTURE PLUPERFECT, MY DEARS! Is this an image of things to come? Or the last hurrah of a species with less wit than anyone has a right to? Interprimate ESP? Vampyrs in the subcortex? Freezedried DNA? Arse truffles? Pseudo=vaccines for a time virus that's been & gone already, leaving a backwash of indigestible anachronism? Even if the plot's going nowhere, there's bound to be someone left when the lights go out, determined to watch to the very end.

"I MOVE BACK FURTHER IN TIME TO AN ERA BEFORE WRITING" (GUYOTAT)

There's no umbrella against the constant atmosphere in here. One moment plunged into a fathomless intestinal dark, all dreams of escape siphoned away. The next, seeing stars. Prisoned in this Vampyr Castle w/ a lunatic at the controls, piloted by pure randomness. Strapped down w/ yr guts in yr throat expecting any instant to collide head=on w/ yr alterego. Time to walk out of yr tomb & into the air! Once upon a pervious aeon we were all alone in here, but it gets so crowded now sometimes they ought to figure out one of those time=share arrangements. Take the geriatric in the next bunk, for instance. She cld've been us, a way back when. Eyes of carrot juice swimming in their sockets. Brainplate covered in fungus. Looked like they'd epoxied the two halves of her head together in a fit of spite. Both her lips had turned green. Last night she lay there screaming in her sleep for hours, nonstop all the way from the transit of Venus to the lunar eclipse. Plot gone completely pearshaped. *Pear of Anguish!* Hahaha. Sounded like a whole symphony of Spanish Inquisitors squeezed into one Iron Maiden w/out benefit of petroleum jelly. Howled her eyes out! Flew up out of her mouldy bedding like a ghoul from a grave! Screech like rusted chastity belt! Tore out her catheter & began whirling it around in the stagnant air like a dude w/ a lasso! Oh she'd be likable enough alright if we cld still bear the sight of ourselves.

AS USELESS AS THREE LEGS ON A BOAT

1. Principles based on the political=social function of art are the death of art itself. (Goytisolo)
2. Principles based on the aesthetic function of politics are the death of politics itself. (Benjamin)
3. Kill 'em all! (**Offensia**)

What is more, the cells showed certain functions, including the release of various immune=response substances when triggered. After tissues were removed from the brains & flushed of the CorTex fluid the researchers found individual neurons were still able to function.

"What we are showing is that the process of cell death is a gradual, stepwise process & that some of those processes can be either postponed, preserved or even reversed," said gLand.

The team said that while the CorTex fluid was circulating, they monitored the brains to check for any signs of organised electrical activity that might suggest consciousness.

"That monitoring didn't show any kind of organised global electrical activity," said Dr Ingrid Murnau, bioethicist & co=author of the study, adding that the circulating fluid contained terminator enzymes to block autonomous neural activity.

"The dead brains might one day be reactivated to perform tasks we programme them to perform, but they won't be able to become conscious & perform tasks on their own."

But, she said, the team had been ready for signs of consciousness. "Had that appeared they wld have lowered the temperature of the brain & used anaesthesia to stop that kind of activity," said Murnau, adding that at present there are no ethics committees set up for such an eventuality, & it remained unclear in any case if the technique cld ever restore consciousness.

The researchers said it was not clear if the circulating CorTex fluid was helping to patch up molecular & cellular damage that had already begun, or whether it was simply slowing down such processes, postponing cell death.

Murnau said the next step wld be to see if the system can keep the various cellular functions going for longer. A patent for the system has already been filed.

Experts writing in two articles also in *Denature* said the research opened up ethical conundrums – not least whether consciousness wld have been recorded if the CorTex fluid had not contained substances to block brain cell activity, & whether other methods were needed to assess consciousness.

They also warned the prospect that one day some brain function might be restored after devastating injuries may mean doctors & family members cld be less willing for organs to be removed from people for transplant.

Prof Dante Polidori of Golemstadt University, who was not a member of the project, said that the research offered a new way to study the brain.

"A better understanding of brain function is important for understanding what makes us unlike humxns & will also help us treat devastating diseases of the brain like Guillotine's disease," Polidori said.

"However, this study is a long way from preserving brain function after death as is often portrayed in fiction, w/ heads kept alive in a jar. It is instead a temporary preservation of some of the more basic cell functions in the brain, not the preservation of thought & personality."

WELCOME TO THE RE=EDUCATION PROGRAMME

PLAGUE CITY (#FakeNewsMedia) – Researchers "reboot" bat brains hours after animals died.

The brains of decapitated *Desmodus rotundus* bats can be partially revived several hours after the animal has died, researchers at the Béla Lugosi Academy have revealed, w/ some of the functions of cells booted back up when an oxygen=rich fluid is circulated through the organ.

The *Desmodus rotundus* is a haematophage, relying on mammalian blood as its primary food source.

The scientists stress that the brains do not show any signs of consciousness – for example, there was no sign that different parts of the brain were sending signals to each other – & that it does not change the definition of death.

But they say they have found a way to prevent brain cells from sustaining irreparable damage as blood stops circulating, & even to restore some of the cells' functions.

"This is not a living brain. But it is a cellularly active brain," said Nyx gLand of the Béla Lugosi Academy, who led the research. "A *zombie* brain, but not yet an *undead* brain."

gLand added that the results had exceeded expectations. "When we started this study we never imagined we wld get to this point," he said.

The team said the approach cld provide a new way to study the brain, & even help in the development & testing of new therapies for decapitation, staking & other conditions in which bloodflow to parts of the brain is blocked, causing cells to die.

A number of studies, including those involving cells taken from dead brains, have suggested brain cells might not inevitably die after blood stops circulating.

Writing in the journal *Denature*, researchers in Plague City reported how they sought to examine this further by taking brains from 32 vampyr bats that had been killed in a laboratory.

Four hours after their deaths, the arteries of the sanguivore brains were hooked up to a sophisticated system dubbed CorTex, which pumped an oxygenated synthetic blood through the organ. This fluid contained a host of nutrients as well as other substances to tackle processes that lead to cell death, & the circulation was continued for six hours.

At that point, the team found the circulating fluid successfully flowed through blood vessels in the brain, including tiny capillaries, & that the blood vessels were able to dilate in response to a drug, while the brain as a whole consumed oxygen & glucose from the fluid & released carbon dioxide back into it at similar rates to an intact brain.

Unlike bat brains that were left alone for 10 hours after death, the organs that had been hooked up to the CorTex system for six hours had not decomposed, while their cells & neurons were apparently on a par or even in better condition than for bat brains analysed one hour after death.

THIS OPTION IS NO LONGER AVAILABLE

Were the T=R=A=N=S to be admitted to the category of the universal – as a condition *transcending all categorisation*, all *reduction* to dichotomy, all *opposition as such* – then the *very idea* of the T=R=A=N=S (as anticategorical nonspecies) wld be fatally menaced & *the difference in which it took on its meaning* wld break down (even if this "universalism" were intended merely as a pre=emptive strike, covering all possible outcomes). We've seen how these xenovampyric tendencies are forever evoking "the myth of the impossible" in counterpoint to their parasitic origin, as if to produce a *negation of negation* in advance or on credit. Yet all this amounts to nothing more than a desperate telekinesis directing future chaos agents via alien 👽 timeslip, when the real spectre of transcendentalism is the Corp[orate]=$[tate]. If the latter evokes the "impossible" principally against adversaries *that do not exist*, this is so it may parley the exorcising of its own ghosts into the very paradigm of a decisive checking=manoeuvre *against the Real itself*. And if the diurnal ambivalence of the T=R=A=N=S avails of a tactical reverse, so too the contrary. This wld be nothing but the jargon of an antipolitical aestheticism, were it not that the erotic experience it implies is of the "impossible" *itself*: arriving, as if from a future=not=yet, under the false appearance of a present that will never have been. N_x

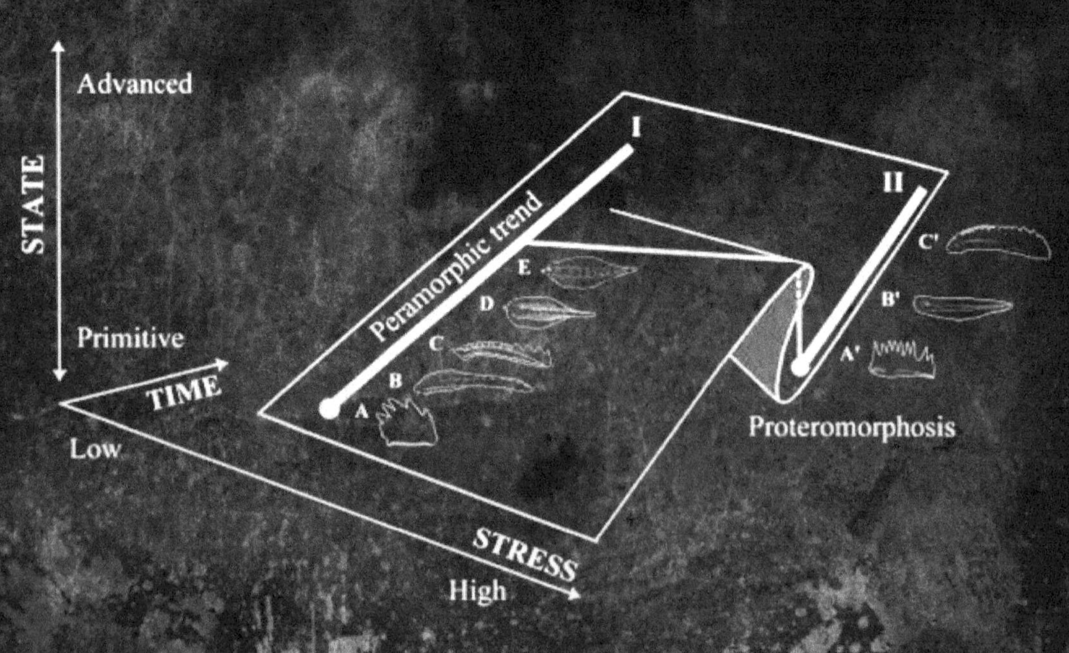

We need to transform vampyrism
from a libidinal economic project
into the nihilo=revolutionary one
it always promised to be. (Nyx gLand)

COMPONENTS OF BLOOD

Water, Acetoacetate, Acetone, Acetylcholine (neurotransmitter of the parasympathetic nervous system), Adenosine triphosphate, phosphorus, Adrenocorticotrophic hormone, Alanine, Albumin (blood plasma protein), Aluminum, Aldosterone, Amino acids, nitrogen, alpha=Aminobutyric acid, δ=Aminolevulinic acid, Ammonia nitrogen, cAMP (intracellular signal transduction molecule), Androstenedione (steroid hormone), Androsterone (steroid hormone), Angiotensin I, Angiotensin II (vasoconstrictor), Alpha 1=antitrypsin (serine protease inhibitor), Arginine, Arsenic, Ascorbic acid (Vitamin C), Aspartic acid, Bicarbonate, Bile acids, Bilirubin (hemoglobin metabolite), Biotin (Vitamin H), Blood Urea Nitrogen (BUN), Bradykinin, Bromide, Cadmium, Calciferol (vitamin D2), Calcitonin (CT), Calcium, Carbon dioxide, Carboxyhemoglobin (as HbCO), Carcinoembryonic antigen, beta=Carotene, Carotenoids, Cephalin, Ceruloplasmin, Chloride, Cholecalciferol (Vitamin D3), Cholecystokinin (pancreozymin), Cholesterol, Choline, Chorionic gonadotropin, Citric acid, Citrulline, Coagulation Factors, Fibrinogen, Prothrombin, Tissue thromboplastin, Proaccelerin, Proconvertin, Antihemophilic factor, Christmas factor, Stuart factor, Plasma thrmb. anteced., Hageman factor, Fibrin=stabilising factor, Fibrin split products, Fletcher factor, Fitzgerald factor, von Willebrand factor, Cobalamin (Vitamin B12), Cocarboxylase, Complement system C1q, C1r, C1s (C1 esterase), C2, C3(b1C=globulin), factor B (C3 proactivator), C4 (b1E=globulin), C4, C5 (b1F=globulin), C6, C7, C8, C9, Properdin, Compound S, Copper, Corticosteroids, Corticosterone, Cortisol, C=reactive protein, Creatine, Cyanide, Cysteine, Dehydroepiandrosterone (DHEA), DHEA sulfate, 11=Deoxycortisol, Dihydrotestosterone (DHT), Diphosphoglycerate (phosphate), DNA, Dopamine, Enzymes, Epidermal growth factor (EGF), Epinephrine, Ergothioneine, Erythrocytes, Erythropoietin, Estradiol (E2), Estriol (E3), Estrogen, Estrone (E1), Ethanol, Fatty acids, Ferritin, alpha=1=Fetoprotein, Flavin, Fluoride, Folate, Folic acid, Fructose, Furosemide glucuronide, Galactose, Gastric inhibitory peptide (GIP), Gastrin, Globulin, alpha=1=Globulin, alpha=2=Globulin, beta globulin, gamma globulin, Glucagon, Glucosamine, Glucose, Glucuronic acid, Glutamic acid, Glutamine, Glutathione, Glycerol, Glycine, Glycogen, Glycoprotein, cGMP, Gonadotropin, Guanidine, Haptoglobin, Hemoglobin, Hexosephosphate P, Histamine, Histidine, Hydrogen ion(pH 7.4), beta=Hydroxybutyric acid, 17α=Hydroxycorticosteroids, 17α=Hydroxyprogesterone, Immunoglobulin A (IgA), Immunoglobulin D (IgD), Immunoglobulin G (IgG), Immunoglobulin M (IgM), Immunoglobulin E (IgE), Indican, Inositol, Insulin, Iodine, Iron, Isoleucine, Ketone bodies, alpha=Ketonic acids, L=Lactate, Lead, Lecithin, Leptin, Leucine, Leukocytes, Neutrophil granulocytes, Eosinophil granulocytes, Basophil granulocytes, Lymphocytes, Monocytes, Phagocytes, Lipase P, Lipids, Lipoprotein (Sr 12=20), Lithium, Lysine, Lysozyme (muramidase), alpha 2=macroglobulin, Magnesium, Malic acid, Manganese, Melatonin, Mercury, Methemoglobin, Methionine, Methyl guanidine, beta=2=microglobulin, MIP=1a, MIP=1b, Mucopolysaccharides, Mucoproteins, Nerve growth factor (NGF), Niacin, Nitrogen, Norepinephrine (neurotransmitter of the sympathetic nervous system), Nucleotides, Ornithine, Oxalate, Oxygen, Oxytocin, Pancreatic polypeptide, Pantothenic acid (vitamin B5), Para=aminobenzoic acid, Parathyroid hormone (PTH), Pentose, Phenol, Phenylalanine, Phospholipid, Phosphatase, Phosphorus, Phytanic acid, Platelets, Platelet=derived growth factor, Polysaccharides, Potassium, Pregnenolone, Progesterone, Proinsulin, Prolactin, Proline, Prostaglandins, Protein, Protoporphyrin, Prostate specific antigen, Pseudoglobulin I, Pseudoglobulin II, Purine, Pyrimidine nucleotides, Pyridoxine (Vitamin B6), Pyruvic acid, RANTES, Relaxin, Retinol (Vitamin A), Riboflavin (Vitamin B2), RNA, Secretin, Serine, Serotonin (5=hydroxytryptamine), Silicon, Sodium, Somatotropin, Sphingomyelin, Succinic acid, Sugar, Sulfates, Sulfur, Taurine, Testosterone, Thiamine (Vitamin B1), Thiocyanate, Threonine, Thyroglobulin (Tg), Thyroid hormones, Thyrotropin, Thyroxine (FT4), Thyroxine=binding prealbumin, Thyroxine=binding globulin, Tin, alpha=Tocopherol (Vitamin E), Transcortin, Transferrin, Triglycerides, Triiodothyronine, Tryptophan, Tyrosine, Urea, Uric acid, Valine, Vasoactive intestinal peptide (VIP), Vasopressin, Zinc.

LIKE A RAT WITHOUT A TAIL [FLASHBACK]
Upon a heath on Gottwald Mountain.
Thunder & lightning.
Enter the three Wyrd Sisters:
— Where hast thou been, sister?
— Infecting rats.
— Sister, where thou?
— Boiling bats!
— Sister, where thou?
— Parleying plague among tempest=lost soulless humxnity!
ALL: We Wyrd Sisters three,
Wild Grrl freaks with a yen to feed,
hungry for strife & homicide,
howl to the moon when rich men bleed!
— Hark! Teargas & sirens! **Offensia** doth come.
Enter **Offensia** with a heavy calibre machinegun:
— So foul & fair a night I have not seen. Yet who are
these creatures, huddled about their guilty cauldron
brewing pestilence (by christ it stinks!)? Such bony fingers
lying upon their skinny hips: they shld be womxn, & yet
their beards forbid me to interpret that they are so. You,
wretched o' the earth, rise & stand where I can see you. Do
you have names? What things are you? Speak!
— All hail **Offensia**! hail to thee, curse of Van Helsing!
— All hail **Offensia**! hail to thee, scourge of L=U=M=I=N=I=S=T=S!
— All hail **Offensia**! thou shalt be Queen of Vampyrs hereafter!

GODS OF THE PLAGUE
The idea of enlightening vampyrs in matters political is
steadily gaining hallowed ground. The instruction introduced
in many former carceral institutions aims at protecting
vampyrs during the acquisition of ideological beliefs from
the increasing dangers of ignorance. And it is from this
point=of=view that the idea has most sympathy & support.
The knowledge obtained by research, however, indicates the
necessity, if not of "enlightening," at least of initiating
vampyrs into the "ways of the world" in such a fashion
as will render any special enlightenment unnecessary,
since collectively they will be thereby protected from a
disillusionment that may be overly severe & too readily
sublimated in false beliefs or the syndrome of "guilty
conscience."

A FIRE AT AULIS
The dignity of labour was a goddess raped on the rocks
under the seawall.

EXTREME ALIENISM
An action that seeks political clarification requires its
own clarification, of what it means "to act." The happy
moronic enzyme in the thick of life's soup. In these times,
nothing can be left to chance. The proverbial Wolf is
constantly at the door. A barricade is always waiting to
be built. Born on the winds, the virus IS the Weather Man.

IN THE BUSINESS OF COMPENSATORY FANTASIES (EDDIE VAN)
Sweet dreams. Television. / You make it seem just like the
4th of July. / Sex slave. Politician. / You only smile w/
the light shining in yr eyes. / Outer space. California. /
Got the face to make whole nations cry. / Pretty pictures.
Pretty vacant inside. / They only love you when y're signing
on the dotted line…

JUULZ EBOLA GETS MUGGED BY A VAMPYR
Just got mugged & beat up for a pint of blood.
   Am ok, just a bit shaken up.
   Cld've fought her off but she was vamped out of her skull.
   I'm ok.
   Hurt pride more than anything.
   At least I got out of the habit of carrying that wooden
stake.
   Things cld've been much worse.
   What was doubly sickening was she kept saying how she was
ill w/ the plague & so she had no choice.
   Made me so angry.
   All the times I've been blood=sick (& if you don't know
what it's like, there really is no way to describe it), &
NEVER ONCE has it crossed my mind to do that.
   I'd rather go cold turkey than put someone else through
what I just went through.
   I used to carry a stake till I realised it wld bring more
problems than it solved.
   This is really as low as it can get.
   Commie fucks!

THE BLOOD OF OTHERS [REEL 7]
Arriving back at the Vampyr Castle
at dawn, **Offensia** makes her way to
the Van Helsing crypt, a dense
interior monologue occupying her
until she comes upon her "father,"
who has transmogrified into a living
skeleton, kneeling in front of
Armandine's cryotank, trying to
smash off the locks.

   Offensia's return, however, is
distorted in the imaginations of
Eddie V (who thinks she is her
mother's avenging spirit), Odradek
(who mistakes her arrival for a
Wild Grrl possé), & the townsfolk
(who believe she is their promised
messiah).

   Odradek, though, finally
recognises **Offensia** as his Master's
daughter, betrayed into the hands
of Wang Fang, & runs out to hang
himself. Van Helsing exploits the
momentary confusion to slip away
as a storm approaches over the
mountains.

   As lightning crashes into the
high Castle tower, sending glass
& shattered masonry into the air,
she sees by his silhouette hanging
in a tree that Odradek is dead. In
a scene of pure melodrama, **Offensia**
demands of the storm: *"Am I the
womxn for whom the Son of Man died?"*

   In the rolling of the thunder,
Offensia hears Armandine's laughter
& wonders if her mother is really
in suspended animation inside the
cryotank or if is living inside her
"like a vampyric alterego."

   She enlists the help of the
townsfolk to remove the cryotank
from the crypt, but as they are
about to do so more lightning
crashes into the tower, causing the
entire structure to collapse.

The scene ends with the muted screams of townsfolk trapped under a mountain of rubble. "Let the dead," a mysterious voice says, "bury the dead." It'd take an army of mining engineers to dig them out. Even with her inhumxn powers… But why not give posterity a fighting chance?

Realising her return to Transylvania has been a terrible mistake, **Offensia** boards a train back to Golemgrad, but not before obtaining a "griffin's egg" at a tourist stall to pass off on Doctor Asperger as a priceless antique.

Returning to the City at midnight, **Offensia** takes a taxi directly to Asperger's, who is away on business, & instead stumbles upon the doctor's assistant, Jean Genet, who spills the beans about her supposedly apocryphal grandfather, the "mad vampyr scientist," credited by turns with the authorship & clandestine dissemination of the original CORVID=69 virus, hounded to the very ends of the Earth, there to perish upon the desolate peak of Gottwald Mountain.

A young idealistic microbiologist & cinéphile, Jean Genet, having first turned his attentions to the forensic study of microplasmodia, in particular the slime mould Physarum polycephalum, has (under Asperger's tutelage) recently decided to devote his prime of life to the investigation of socalled alien 👽 forms of intelligence "already inhabiting this world & propagating among us, unknown, unsuspected, yet secretly directing the course of evolution itself!" It is a decision which will have unforeseen & terrible consequences.

MASQUE OF THE BLAQ DEATH

Every five minutes the cameras had to stop rolling so that
the extras in the plague masks cld be fed oxygen through
tubes so they wldn't asphyxiate under the full=face latex.
At times the heat from the arc lights was so extreme, the
actors were at risks of drowning in their own sweat.

IT'S THE NIGH END

Scourge of the Kosmos, the Vampyr Armand=Etc. had gone &
wld never return, subsumed into antimatter. The guardian
demons were sucked down w/ the ancient vampyr & the surface
of the Void closed over. From deep below came a vengeful
howl. Vague movements stirred the darkness hypnotically, as
if the baleful creature yet breathed, but then was still.
On the surface of the Void were strewn fragments of dust,
blinking into light, then vanishing. Nothing more.

HUMXN REALITY WILL EVENTUALLY RAISE ITS UGLY HEAD

More horrific than any film cld portray.

THE FABLE OF TSUI FANG

During the time of the Baizuo Dynasty, there was a wise
administrator named Tsui Fang. One day, on the road to
Wuhan, in the central province of Hubei, Tsui Fang happened
across two penitents, clad only from the waist down & even
then in the bare slivers of rags, their backs bloodied &
scabbed from the flagellants' whips that hung, awaiting
the renewal of those painful labours, around their necks.
They were seated upon the ground playing chess w/ bits of
cracked mortar & coprolite on an improvised checkerboard
scratched in the dirt. It was a Queen's Indian & black
had gained a slight advantage. As Tsui Fang's camel drew
abreast of the two penitents, he overheard the seemingly
more proficient of the two say to his adversary, in a voice
so striking it caused the Baizuo administrator to gape —
as one who unexpectedly chances upon a pearl hidden within
the snout of a jellied pig, or an oil lamp under a bushel,
or a golden=sand beach beneath an avenue of granite paving
stones (for Tsui Fang had witnessed many extraordinary
things, & many things of great banality also). "And did
you ever hear," asked the voice, "the one about the old
Confucian who stuck a bullhorn up his arse, so he cld hear
everything that goes w/out being said?"

ATHANASIUS KIRCHER'S PLAGUE PARTY
under a conjunction of malignant Mars & pestilential
Jupiter the fetid miasma & putrid vapours arising from the
Gibbet Marsh the stink of decay excrement humidity stagnant
water volcanic emissions industrial sludge bat guano rats
blowflies laying invisible maggots in the pores of skin ears
eyes nasal cavities invading the lungs blood vessels heart
kidneys intestinal tract brain lymph infecting in rapid
virulent succession the entire mind=body dualism fumigated
w/ burnt rosemary cypress juniper the corrupted exhalations
of boarded=up lazarettos doom=doctors in beaked hazmats
the sinister nocturnal wailings of a cat=piano & the
scaffold=harp the mad visions of magic lantern & microscope
ars magna lucis & umbrae lynx=eyed *scrutinum physico=medicum
contagiosae luis quae pestis dicitur* to peer upon that
putrid spontaneous mass of worms invisible to the naked eye
drawn forth by lunar influence out of the anagogic corpse
wherein they fester & make rotten the meat & flesh upon
the bones & thus engorged spew forth as a vast number of
minute snakes & winged gnats as proven by incontrovertible
experiments that the plague is a living panspermia from the
polluted seed of vegetative sentient nature percolating in
its corpuscular medium & not the farrago of speculation
that distempers the medical intellect w/ a cantagium vivium
no less mortal raining from inverted skies like chlorinated
bog=mists amulets of toad=flesh & religiotic gibberish

JUST DESSERTS
Everyone ought to have the name they deserve cut into their
flesh like victims of horrific crimes the final victory of
democracy oh what high=minded butchery we nonentities wld
star in & you too dear reader don't count yrself out!

RHOMBOIDS OF THE UTERINE BLACK (EXPLODING COFFINS!)
Corpse=stench, embalming vapours, gastric percolations,
morbid flatulence, the fetid pneuma erupting under the
slightest influence like a flaring gas field, *ignis fatuus* of
ancient lore, here centrifuged into subterranean megatonnages
of plague=pit China Syndrome w/ a hair=trigger switch,
cycling down through pandemic half=life to re=arise in a
mantle plume of New World Symphonic unsubtlety, launched into
the noösphere upon an anal=aggressive pyrocumulus to reign
a thousand nuclear winters & all because of a trapped fart
smothered in resurgent plantlife, the untended allotments,

downward spiralling stairwells, cisterns, manhole covers, service elevators, arms caches, sewer grates, bowers, drainage ditches, vaults, caissons, subway vents, cold war bunker turrets, disposal chutes, boreholes, latrine pits, mineshafts, lairs of septic inertia, stagnant aspersoria, sumpholes of blind faith, the backwash of humxn progress, botched archaeologies, caesarean sections, Jurassic insect burrowings, the plunderings of resurrection men, troglodytic moles, tar babies, metamorphic somnambulists, buried abortions, a child's erector set embalmed in primeval mud, ominous abysms, unplumbed solipsisms, the tectonic faultlines of lost continents, a sublimated neurasthenia, lunatic geometries of moonlight through casement windows, kaleidoscopes of hellish infinity – these & other fabled instances of the man=mind falling prey to its own worst reckoning.

CINEMA WITHOUT HOLLYWOOD IS LIKE SEX WITHOUT GUNS
Something that only the progeny of refugees wld do.

EDDIE VAN HELSING'S TORCHLIGHT GOODBYE <3<3<3
I don't believe / any more there's gonna be / any kind of revelation / at the dark end of the street, / where the shadows want embracing / & yr smiles are so enticing / but I don't find no mystery / in yr heart. / Go soft but don't go lightly / don't forgive & don't forget me, / for this love you can't abide in / or the weakness & the frailty. / But if the night cld save our sorrow / for the last drink of tomorrow / I might find that mystery / in yr heart. / Was there ever any reason / for the hours that we've been given? / Will it prove that we've been just if / the stars come out tonight? / I feel old as I am weary / what I see I can't remember / & I doubt that mystery / in yr heart. / Will you hold me one more time / if I say that it's the end? / Will you laugh when I'm unable / to dignify myself? / Dim the lights & close the curtains / play the music, pour the wine, / let me dream that mystery / in yr heart.

As Waves upon a Rubbled Shore

The camera some time around early evening before dusk has begun to settle over the water. Framed against the seawall a young darkhaired boy barechested tanned in denim shorts w/ fishing line on the Malecón. Rod, bucket, scaling knife. With the bored look of a come=on he aims his heel at a miserable starfish not yet lifeless on the boardwalk.

La Malattia, district of the capital of the Vampyrga Federative Republic (ex=Bohemia), is undoubtedly one of the most loathsome places in the galaxy. The walls of its palaces, great houses & monasteries record the misery of those burdened w/ the production of its hidden wealth. Its principle architectural treasure is the Voluntary Quarantine Facility located on the Hradchin adjacent to the Presidential Palacio, dominating the view of the Malecón & the nearby fjords of the Böhmisches Meer [a.k.a. Sea of Despond].

Dark screen. Mariachi music: "Guantanamera." Gradually, sunrise over the ocean: a billboard advertisement for a beach resort. The camera pans away: a garbage=strewn Malecón, breezeblock houses, a shoreline of concrete rubble washed by oilslick. Corpses lying in the sun. An armoured personnel carrier drives past: the camera follows it along the Malecón. The passing scenery is a monotony of carnage. A young soldier is riding atop the APC. As the vehicle comes to a stop in front of a barricade, the soldier turns & looks up at something that has caught his attention. A seagull circles above the rooftops. The sun flares in the camera's lens. Close=up on the soldier's face, as the APC explodes. When the smoke clears, we see a child dragging a rocketlauncher into a drain. Barely more than an infant. The child & the rocketlauncher disappear from view. Music fades. Voiceover:

"So do our enemies hasten to their end, each changing place w/ those that went before."

It is the voice of Subcommandante **Offensia**, holstering a pistol. The camera finds her in the office of the Minister of the Interior, who has just been executed. Papers have been tossed on the floor, drawers & filing cabinets upended. The Minister's face lies in a pool of blood on a glass desktop. A cigar butt smoulders between the fingers of the dead Minister's right hand. **Offensia** leans across & stubs it out in the still=spreading pool of blood. There's an audible hiss as a corona of blood bubbles & steams around the crushed butt. Both the movement & the sound have a languid quality. As the blood spreads further, it begins to seep into a pile of documents that alone appear to have remained undisturbed w/ a paperweight atop it. The paperweight is in fact a snowdome w/ a Disney castle inside. Lying on the desk beside the pile of documents is a travel brochure: the cover shows a beach resort in the suburbs of Golemgrad at sunrise. It bears, in bold white sans serif, the legend PARADISE IS WAITING:

Welcome to the clearance sale, fuckwits. Everything on display's marked down to rock bottom! You won't find a better deal this side of doomsday! Get yr goldplated bulletproof credit rating ready, grrlz! COME TO LA MALATTIA! It's bigger than Xmas, but only for those willing & able. Are YOU?

UNE AUTRE [R]ÉVOLUTION EST POSSIBLE

Those who do not know what death is, cannot know what victory is. The world is only what abolishes itself through randomness & contingency. For existence to be bearable, the entire edifice of organised nostalgia must be blown asunder. The enemies of unlife proffer nostalgia for LIFE ITSELF (which they call C=R=E=A=T=I=O=N), as a weapon against a world no longer able to bear the sight of itself, beating itself to sleep at night – sticks a needle in its eye – turns in morbid desperation to every quack theory & miracle cure the robots have been able to cook up, every mental plague. But without grasping that the Corp[orate]=$[tate] cyberdrome establishes its dominion by means of a TIME VIRUS, nothing will be understood about the real arena of all *future politics*. (There's no question of *predicting* this a future, *because it has already happened*: the only available response strategy is to pursue the incoming logic=weapons back to their *a priori*. These are its system nodes, extending tentacle=like through qabbalistic spacetime, & thus hackable as drone prostheses.) Reverse evolution isn't a metaphor. Evolutionary drone warfare is the next phase of viral integration: the ultimate resource, interdimensional entropy. Evolution isn't just the *biological front* of this expanded military=industrial complex, *it's the entire battleground.* N_x

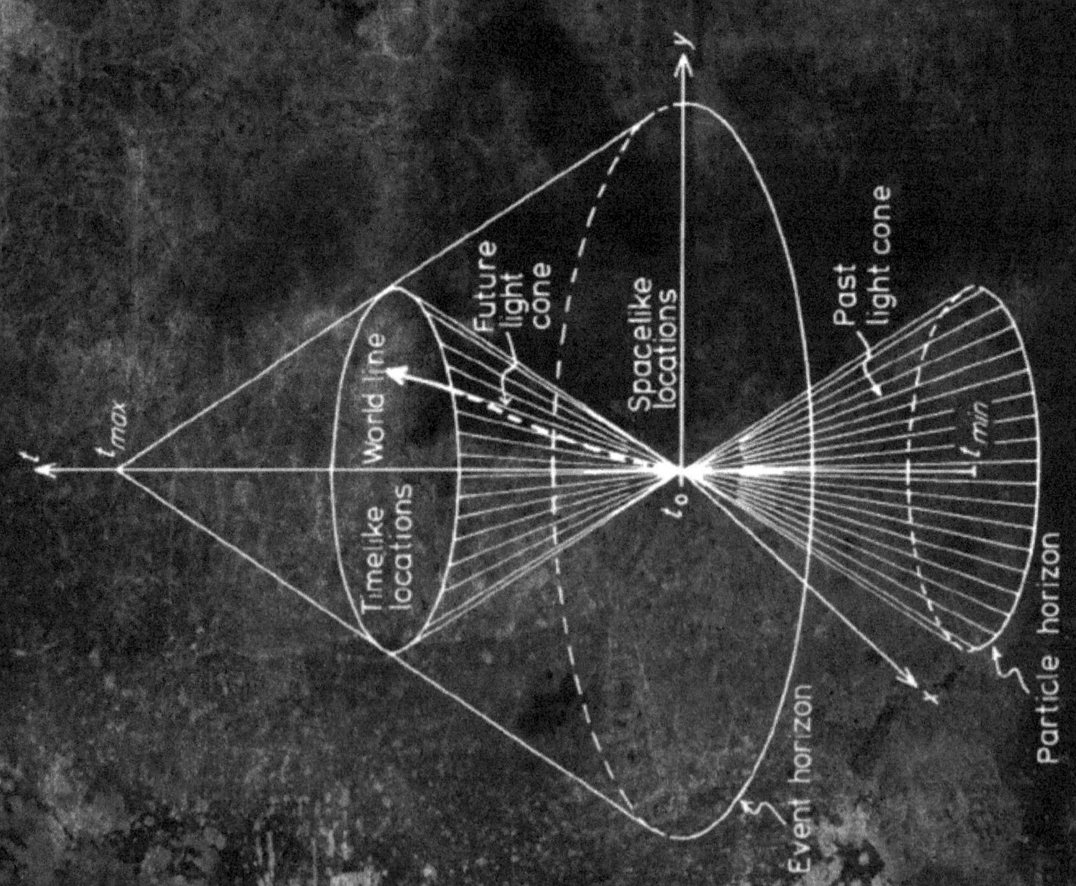

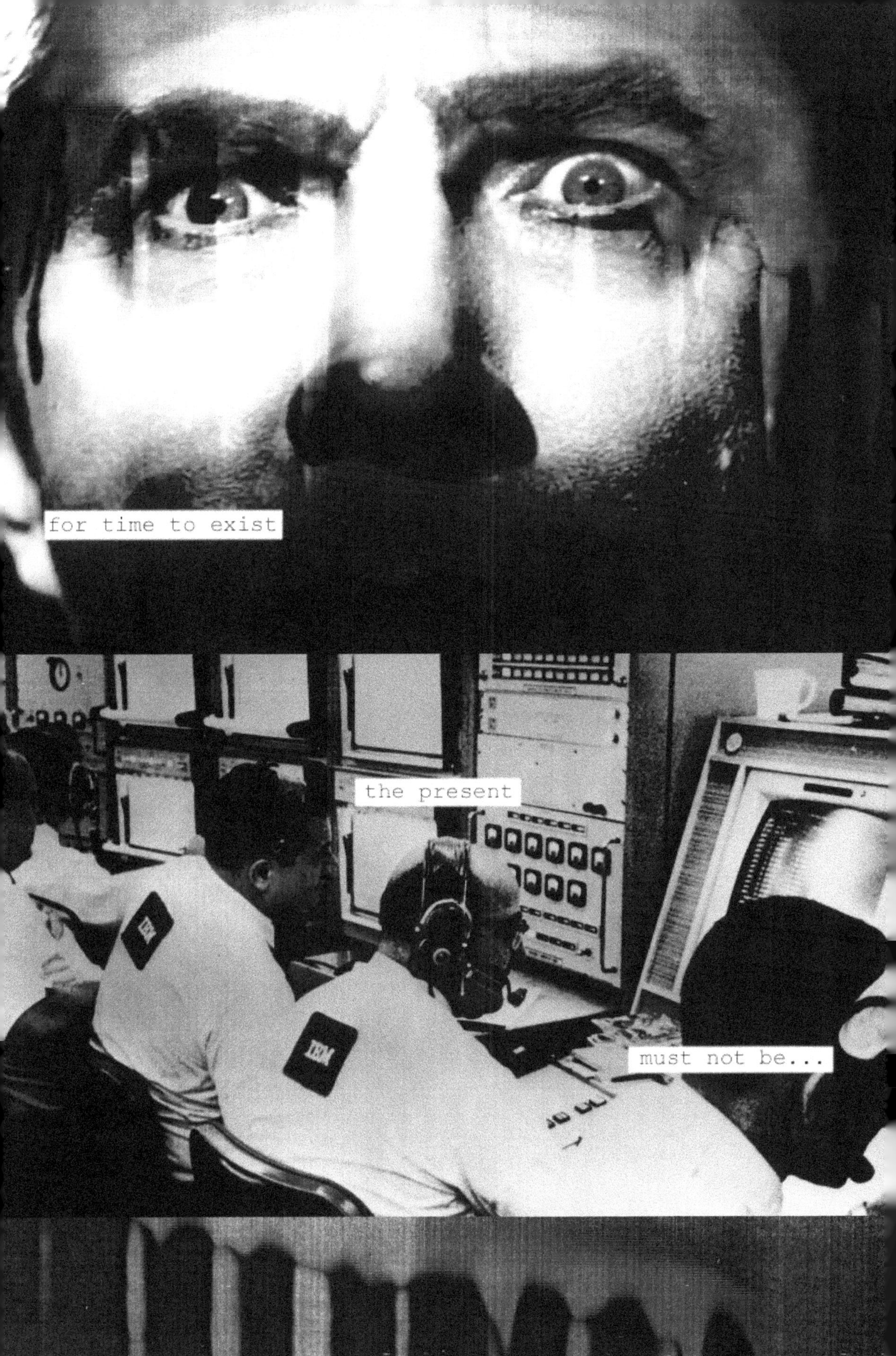

for time to exist
the present
must not be...

THE YEAR OF OUR FATHER

After the Summer of Sam came the Season of Spam, a real
poet=of=the=people, dressed like Jesus Christ in a hardhat
& blue overalls, the fact being however that this compulsive
do=right cldn't've punched a hole through used toilet paper
let alone a clock in a paper factory w/out a parental
guidance recommendation. On & on about The Vampyr being
misconstrued as villainous agent of History – whereas, we is
all proles in the shit=stink of the kapitalist Dictatorship
together. Amen. Charity begins at the backdoor, cumrade! Not
caring to mention how on weekends He rode around in Daddy's
white Rolls Royce Corniche, hip=hugger denim cut=off shorts
polishing the burgundy leather upholstery & a prosthetic
hardon fit to ramrod every hitchhiking fairy from here
to Biarritz & back. Being that kind of anal=aggressive
closet motherfucker, He was wont to keep a monkey wrench
in the glovebox to break in the teeth of his unsuspecting
travelling companions, screaming Vampyr=hate tracts in
their tortured faces, as entrée to indescribable acts of
bicuspid vasectomy. This is how it appears when the slave
renounces his slavery! Evolutionary Abomination – Negation
of humxnity – Devil's Child – His Homicidal Doppelgänger:
resembling Him only so as to spite His face, mock His divine
form, make a diseased bootleg of His sacramental blood! Oh
how He wept w/ each perfunctory roadside burial. All the
angelic cross=eyed virgins, whom **G.O.D.** in His Wisdom had
commanded to be delivered, free of all spiritual blemish,
unctuously anaemic, sexless, things of beauty!

OUR LADY OF GOMORRAH

"The bitch never so much as lifted a finger in his life. He
had someone do everything for him, even take a shit. Well
what kind of a bitch doesn't shit out of his own arse?"

LIFE'S LITTLE "ONTOLOGICAL JOKES"

Was **Offensia**'s childhood thus <u>unnatural</u>? Back in the days when
transistor radios were still every prepubescent grrloid's
fantasy life, hidden under the pillow, at the back of the
closet, in the pile of oversized knitwear in that dank
corner by the dormer window, drainpipe & gothic turret w/
gargoyles grinning, a faint breeze off the Transylvanian
tidelands like seafood cocktail left in the sun, dreaming
of spandex, glitter & platform shoes, bulging codpieces,
bullet bras, streaked mascara & amped feedback, weaving

through long hours of enforced boredom a secret rope of Rapunzel hair – kept hidden in the underwear draw, wound in satiny gusset, for <u>that night</u> when finally not to escape wld be too unbearable, inspired by the tinny strains of *Walk on the Wild Side* – as in fairytales where the desperate heroine is obliged to unravel herself from a high castle to winch up some wonton piece of fleshy distraction, or vice versa, those brazen tresses from which her youthful insolence doth so wantonly sway as upon a curvèd neck, as now (in sick reminiscence) **Offensia** sways, swinging low from that prison window into the arms of Heaven's Sweat Exterminating Angel for a bit of speedy mouth=to=mouth revivification & (you just can't afford to take yr eyes off these little HRT junkies, dahling, even for one second) gratuitous mutual fellatio.

CONVERSION THERAPY
Doctor Asperger: Don't worry kid, we'll straighten you out.
SpastickGrrl: Have you ever been <u>that</u> grrl?
Spinoza: Being in isolation is the <u>sine qua non</u> of all
   ontology.
Papa Walt: Isolation is society for inverts!
Nyx gLand: Society is a stale kind of nothing.
Eddie Van: Are ya winning, son?

THE VAMPYR IS HUMXNITY'S GUILTY CONSCIENCE
The destruction of the vampyr's mystique has not precluded the vampyr from remaining a subject of both institutional & popular fascination. Something about them exposes the mechanism of the socalled social libido. The secret desire to be collectively ravished by unknown forces. Subjected to untold humiliations. Rendered a palpitating mass of abused flesh. Every prohibition transgressed, every responsible act degraded to pure hysterical onanism. Felched by **G.O.D.** upon the altar of Right Reason, Justice, Natural Law. Cld this be Civilisation's crowning achievement? Asperger: "There are more monstrosities of evolution than can be dreamt of in our laboratories!" Wld existence itself thus expire in filth & decadence? Was the true meaning of the "vampyr" that there <u>*was no future*</u>? Was humxnity doomed? And the question that assaulted them all most urgently: *Did reproduction require a species*?

WE DON'T EAT JUST ANY CHILDREN, WE ONLY EAT YRS!

Spinoza: With its very first disappointment, a child already anticipates death.

Offensia: Such presentiments steal the joy of life!

Spinoza: Who can claim not to have been oppressed by sadness?

Offensia: And if everything that's ungraspable, invisible, inaudible, becomes more & more ungraspable, invisible, inaudible?

Spinoza: There must be a miraculous sense that arises from the unconscious: a 6th sense!

Offensia: Which doesn't look, doesn't observe, doesn't measure, but anticipates everything?

Spinoza: The sum of all laws, natural & physical, unnatural & metaphysical.

Offensia: Yet still I feel & the senses that twist around me dictate the meanings this world lacks.

Spinoza: What emotion has led us to create the void only to uncreate it w/ images & words?

Offensia: The mind is like the yolk of an irrational egg!

Spinoza: But can you make an omelette out of it?

DESOLATION ZERO (MIND, STATES OF): Y2K TIME=TRAP + PANGALACTIC STRIPMINING SINGULARITY + MATRIOSHKA BRAIN UNIVERSE REDUPLICATION (NONCONSENSUAL) + CORVID DISASTER TRIBADISM = COSMIC GENOCIDE ESCAPE TRAJECTORY

<u>A heap of dung crawling with worms, photographed w/ a cinema apparatus attached to a microscope</u>. Crispr stared into the moviola. What he saw resembled the tribulations of Ulysses. In short, a world gone to the dogs in a slew of montage. Behold the suppurating anus of Mitteleuropa in all its g[l]orious detail! From such chaos what light wld be born? From what Sea of Despond, as upon a wave that brings up unknown forms from the depths? Psychic portraits of the incontinent & unpreventable cosmic unconsciousness? For here, ghosts exist & have learnt to speak. Bleak histories whose narratives are fed w/ teargas rubberbullets enucleation flashbang molotov firehose battoncharge blood=on=the=pavement

a crushed rose

is a rose

is a rosie

is a fractured skull stitched w/ cablewire ziptie choking on puke in spit=hood epilepsy neck=stomp face=taser suckerpunch shot in the back kicked unconscious asphyxiated hands up facedown underlying condition posing immanent threat of accidental death in custody, etc. Detecting, even as the combinations shift & change, the same bitterness, melancholy & depression are detectable everywhere.

"It's as if," Crispr thinks aloud, "the world had already come to an end."

All else in limbo. Waiting to be put out of its misery. (Ghastly!)

A piece of about=to=be discarded soundtrack wafts through the editing room speakers, before it is deleted forever. Van Helsing: "A stake through the heart & y're to blame, / you give LOVE a bad name!"

Crispr envisages a scene w/ falling angels, mouths howling in terminal=velocity distortion like gaping wind=tunnel artefacts. Eyes blasted back into their heads. Alternating w/ scenes of solitary confinement under a barrage of floodlights: no sleep unable to hold onto a thought for even a moment the routines of arbitrary time extending between boredom suicidal distress they've wiretapped the impenetrable sanctuary inside yr head even the hole you shit into is an informant there's nothing they don't already know confessions are worthless here except as entertainment.

The plot (or whatever passes for one) fastforwards through its subplots, branching, spiralling, leaving in its wake densely worded fjords of Mandelbrot entropy lapped by seas of diffusest prose. Thus did Creation require thirteen days & nights counted as seven, i.e. rotations of the planetary sphere, factoring in such fleeting stolen hours of halfsleep as pass for rest in this part of the galaxy.

Thought: <u>psychosis builds an editing machine</u>.

How many parallel timelines bear adjudicating? Rote application of the dialectic tool vs mass discontinuity principle? Autocritique built into the archive? It occurs to him that the desire to produce a final edit is itself the primary redundancy in the idea of cinema.

Question: how to make a film that doesn't represent but constitutes <u>the situation</u>? Not the image of an insurrection, but <u>the insurrection itself</u>?

On the other hand, "makes"? The eye? The camera? The editing console? The insurrection that can't exist without being "seen"? The approximate algorithm of an event? Reverse=engineered life prototypes? Sound & image randomisers in the quantum field? A carousel with a cracked calliope?

Hits ⏮ & cues the voiceover track. Types filename: 00/4N7HR0P=01D. Hits ⏺: "scheduled for immediate departure / life prototypes to commence sublimat[e][ion] / all unauthorised thought=patterns must cease / recalibrate for gravitational constant / gaps in hyperluminescence require observer=independent time=function / self=annihilation programmes to run concurrently as expression of agreement, etc."

   Intertitle 1: CHOOSE ALGO=LITE
   Intertitle 2: APOCALYPSE PARTY
   [This story shall only finish writing itself long after humxnity has vanished from the world. It will be immortal & subsist on the blood of dead literature & the debris of collapsed stars.]
   "Smile," Crispr said to the reflection in the console monitor, "tomorrow is whenever you wake up."

BUTT PIRATES À LA CARRIBE

"Bonbon" is mutilating **Offensia**'s dreams. She's disguised as Sophia Loren in a Cuban prison. It's one of those films based on a true story. Or a true story based on a film. In the film "Bonbon" smuggles the entire 3rd draft of Reinaldo Arena's *Otra Vez El Mar* (the previous 2 having been confiscated & destroyed by the cops) out of El Morro by concealing it up her arse. Involuntarily **Offensia** imagines herself in the same situation, required to accommodate *The Lost Chronicles* (an account of her MISSING YEARS) inside her own rectum. She mulls the likelihood of this even being possible (the typescript, which she already intends to burn, stretches to over a thousand pages). A theme develops here involving an expert contortionist in a fisting bar. She passes through the various stages of initiation, gaining an increasing amount of hitherto unsuspected knowledge. Her body adapts to these illicit rigours. After several months she has progressed to the more demanding sections of the book, those invariably described by professional literary critics as unreadable. By sheer willpower she succeeds in overcoming even this seemingly insurmountable barrier. As finally she prepares to carry out her mission (having chosen to accept it), an image flashes through her mind: *The Lost Chronicles* are hidden inside her, she's crossing the border (for example), a freak accident occurs, her body is lying on an autopsy table & the coroner is probing a network of intestinal lesions w/ the blunt end of his scalpel, rolled typescript sheathed in plastic slick w/ scoria. Coroner drawls to his assistant through a spit=soaked surgical mask: "Second case we've had this week. Must be a best=seller."

SUCK MY AURA
"The definition of money is whatever the proles can't burn down." (B.J. "Papa" Walt)

KAPITALISM PURSUES THE PATH OF LEAST RESISTANCE
What classical economics misrecognises by allowing the vampyr to be classified as *inessential labour* is the special character of its mythopoeic mode of production.

THE VAMPYR THAT FEEDS LIFE & THE VAMPYR THAT FEEDS DEATH
As if to demonstrate their theory of parallel worlds, Doctor Asperger had them lay the two corpses side=by=side.

"See here," he said, indicating the one w/ puncture marks on the groin, "the sign of Perversity."

The other looked perfectly natural, the way G.O.D. had intended a corpse to look. But appearances were deceiving, for this was the most unnatural of all Heaven's creations.

Well did G.O.D. or didn't G.O.D. create the vampyr just as they'd created Eve & Adam?

Doctor Asperger made a faint sucking sound w/ his tongue, blinked behind his eyepatch. There was a science to making comparisons between orders of nature but in general, when a rank amateur just slapped things down next to each other & started drawing conclusions, what you ended up w/ was wildly false analogies of the most heinous variety!

Now the first consideration a truly scientific mind must undertake is to ask: Did one assert an *influence* over the other?

The mere proximity of two elements did not indicate an *a priori* relation of power. Nor did the simple conflicting of evidence *a posteriori* demonstrate the existence of a secret compact.

The fact that one appeared to prey upon the other, did not, in the Doctor's mind, forfeit the argument that the true motive, baring the lascivious stigmata upon the victim's flesh, was the precisely "vampyric" character of this simulacrum: that in all respects the two were identical — that their indistinguishable appearance was the rule & not the exception.

HISTORY'S RECTUM
"Every ontology derives from a politics, from a theory of power." (Nyx gLand)

Eine Jungfrau in den Krallen vom Vampyrn

1. Exterior. As the orchestra fades in & out, the sun rises over the deep Transylvania woods, its sombre blue tones transposing into sombre green.
2. A muffled backing=voice in the sound of the leaves.
3. The scene framed in a gothic archway.
4. Interior. A stone fireplace. An imposing portrait of a womxn hangs above it, face covered w/ a black veil.
5. The eyes opening & flames leaping.
6. Close=up on the iris, alive like the storms of Jupiter.
7. A womxn positioned beside the fireplace. Her hands behind her back as if bound together.
8. The viewer observes the scene through a pair of binoculars.
9. The womxn is speaking defiantly to someone who is seated in a highbacked chair – only their right hand, resting on the arm of the chair, is visible. The glint of an intricately ornamented ring.
10. "I shall sacrifice my advantage at a time & place of my choosing."
11. A rapid montage details her arrival from the antipodes beneath the castle ramparts.
12. "My little refugee from the underworld," the Invisible One says.
13.   The camera drifts towards the fireplace, into the white heat of the flames: an image of projected blank film.
14. Exterior. The castle in silhouette.
15. A flash in the sky.
16. The dark mass of a faceless crowd gathering on the fringes. Emissaries from war footage of the Vietcong. The liberation of Ravensbrück. The Sparticist rebellion.
17. A scream. A raven's laughter. Arclight.
18. In the aftermath a limousine pulls up the long driveway. The driver gets out of the car, stands tensely observing his surroundings.
19.   It is a bright & beautiful day, revealing a landscape of charred carcasses, the blackened skeletons of incendiarised trees, a thick grey carpet of ash covering the ground. Distant mountains. A mythical eeriness.
20. The entire scene is deliberately shot in one take to achieve the greatest intensity possible.

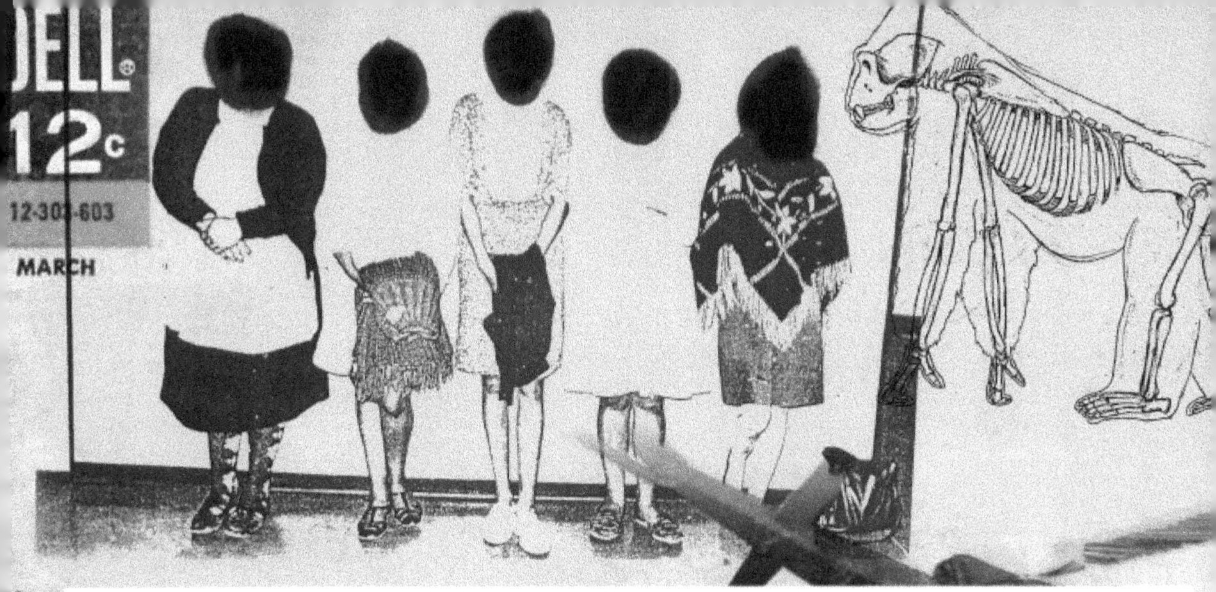

...are these the future suicide bombers of a world in ruins?

PUTTING THE H( )LE WIDE W( )RLD IN PARENTHESES

The aim of insurrection is not the seizing of the means=of=production, but caching in on the *means=of=expenditure* – by which social POSSIBILITY is both accumulated & dissipated in increasingly vertiginous cycles. The logic of expenditure is not the INVERSE of production, but its raison d'être. Contrary to a received wisdom mindlessly circulated in the #fakenewsmedia, "rioting" & "looting" are therefore not a NEGATION of those "social values" upheld by consumer kapitalism, but are the intimate attendants of conspicuous consumption itself. Just as conspicuous consumption by kapital – aped by the consumer mass – is but an hysterical sublimation of a recurring fantasy in which power eroticises its own evisceration & laying waste at the hands of a spectral lumpenproletariat. The potlatch of expenditure never exceeds the bounds of this sadomasochistic fantasy. The means=of=production/expenditure oscillate around the axis of power's symbolic negation & convulsive reconstitution in a movement that is in no respect contingent (even if it *produces* contingencies), but is entirely determined by the logic of power itself, like the cycle of erection & *petit mort*, castration & prosthesis. By means of expenditure, power *defers* for itself the pleasure of its own overcoming & determines in advance the recuperation of a fantastic insurrectionary force. The means=of=production of reality is, in this pseudo=paradoxical tableau, indentured to the means=of=expenditure of reality. It's here that the "vulnerability of power" reveals itself as nothing but the most conventional form of seduction. N_x

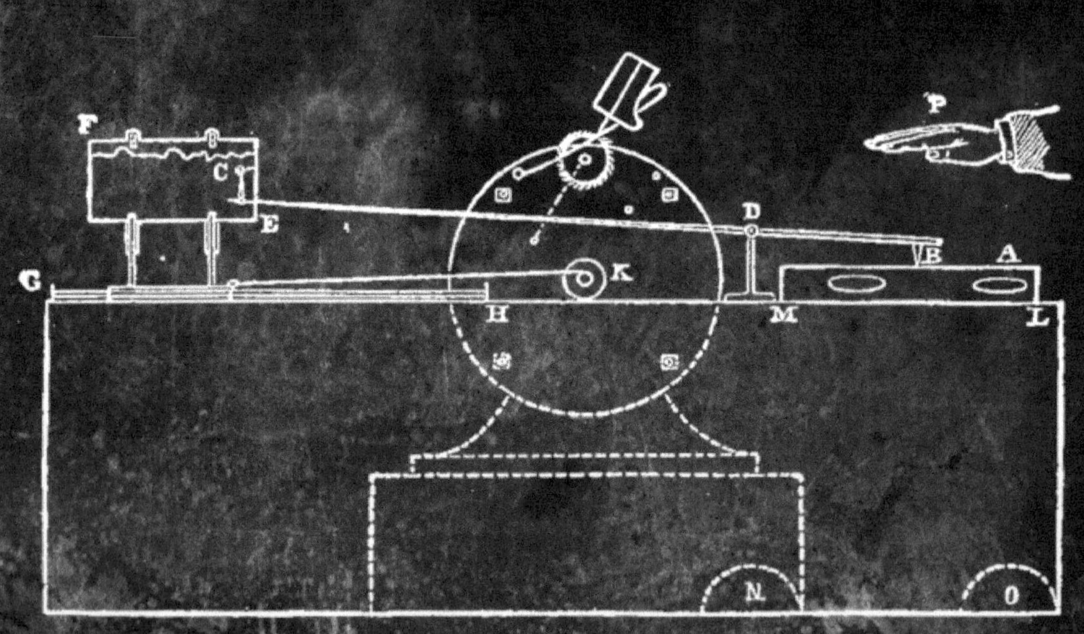

NORMAL ATYPICAL ABNORMAL

Before discussing the usual fantasies that accompany masturbation, a few words shld be said about masturbation itself.

Dear Colleagues,

Allow me to express our deepest gratitude for yr contribution to our congress on autoeroticism. Yr film, "Mono=Vampyrism," was one of the most successful entries in our film section: among more than 100 projections, it won especial acclaim from an otherwise very critical audience.

In the straightforwardness of its logic, direct presentation lies in the sexual act; the erotic power of the screen does not always match the response. No exception to this is permissible once we acknowledge that onanism, like all other erotic impulses, originates in the unconscious.

Sincerely,
Erich von Stroheim

40,000 YEARS IN THE BLOOD

Looted mannequins. Tainted methanol. Durex. A gift=wrapped sombrero. This is the water & this is the well. Death was trending. (You are already dead.) Patchouli oil. Cassandra Crossing. Skull callipers. Autism. No feelings, heart empty = general purpose social judgement. Lung=hex. Weak fear. Strong fear. Pseudo=Deleuziana. A meme is a suicide postponed. Time supply=chains in smooth brain discontinuity. No backdate infra=cascade. *The throne of Universal Empire may be raised over the ruins of Universal Catastrophe.* At that time people will say to the mountains, "Fall upon us!" Dick milk. Right now in Amerika: vitriol injections to combat coronavirus fallout "& highly unusual disruptions." World=building begins after this one. An endless cosmic ocean of cringe. Sex hormones in spent fuel=rod. The formula is: THE ALIEN 👽 IS THE ENEMY. Phenotype check. This for real? Stonefaced silent. Daily reminder that unlife is debased & blackpilled. Eschaton immanentised: WE ARE THE FUTURE CHROMOSOME! All war=machine, no sate: the BEST=IS=YET=TO=COME Funeral Home. Divides into multiple categories. A white ogre orchid blossoming in the little dark place. In the Labyrinth of Zero. Cancelled into infinity. This isn't how the story ends it's just the setup for the next sequel in the franchise?

JUST BECAUSE ALIENS 👽 DIDN'T MAKE
(A) THE PYRAMIDS AT GIZA
(B) MACHU PICCHU
(C) THE EASTER ISLAND HEADS
(D) THE GEOGLYPHS OF ATACAMA
DOESN'T MEAN IT WAS HUMXNS!
Countless are those things, imbeciles, of which ignorance shall deprive you.

RESISTANCE – CATHEXIS – EVERYONE DIES!

Although this Death=Cult calls itself scientific, we haven't yet heard of any verifiable statistic about the re=appearance via mediums of the same deceased individuals at more than one place at a time. Death is every fascist's big play. Drink the KoolAid & win the prize. Red pill blue pill black pill. In this way precisely have they learned how to confuse, to deflect & to use alchemy. Though not all the plastic in all the oceans wld build a Xanadu, they cld still turn this humxn excrement into G.O.D. & launch the world back into the void from whence it came.

   Nyx gLand: "LOL at the world deathspasming in a pandemic we said cldn't happen!" So it's a wash ☺

DEFENESTRATION NOT WITHOUT CONSEQUENCES

The Committee for Gravity Annulment wld've left the Kid for dead, lying on the ice w/ bones broken, a hundred metres down at the bottom of the Vampyr Castle steps. But the Committee, still haunted by the manic glimmer in the Kid's eyes, wld never've been able to sleep w/out knowing all its <u>t</u>'s had been crossed & <u>i</u>'s dotted, so they sent down one of their goons to perform the *coup de grâce*. Afterwards the coroner said he'd never seen a look of such horror on a corpse before, when they hauled the goon out onto the autopsy slab. Not a sign of the Kid, who must've dragged herself up by her teeth or operated by some kind of weird mind control, or — what the Doctor said — *metamorphosed* into the Beast… Something had torn the goon's throat out & it wasn't the Kid's smiley badge. Much later the rest of the Committee also turned up brutally dead, one by one, each disfigured by a terrible rictus & *sans* laryngeal apparatus. They said the Kid was Armand=the=Apocryphal's reincarnation & was getting his revenge. Others said she was just a devil chile.

THE 13 NARRATIVE CODES OF VAMPYR LITERATURE

1. <u>EPIC</u>
    The text belongs first & foremost to the reality of
    language, whose dimensions are inexhaustible.
2. <u>HOLISTIC</u>
    The text is the integration of all "exterior" elements.
3. <u>CYCLONIC</u>
    The impetus of the text comes from its dynamic force,
    the source of & reason for which are unknown.
4. <u>HEPATIC</u>
    The text is a force=feedback dialysis machine.
5. <u>TRAGIC</u>
    The text possesses neither pathos nor expressivity, but
    is a field of autonomous actions irreducible to affect.
6. <u>EPILEPTIC</u>
    The text is a vehicle of convulsive delirium.
7. <u>SOTADIC</u>
    The text is a set of materials subject to arbitrary
    laws, whose meaning is the product of obscenity.
8. <u>SPURIOTIC</u>
    The text lives out its own "disappearance," against a
    backdrop of nothingness.
9. <u>CHOLERIC</u>
    The text "takes place" through incessant confrontation.
10. <u>QUIXOTIC</u>
    Nothing is self=evident, the text constantly casts
    doubts & itself remains doubtful.
11. <u>CHRONIC</u>
    The text exacerbates the relativity of time.
12. <u>TRAVESTIC</u>
    Through its very excess, the text abolishes all
    subordination to a mimetic "reality."
13. <u>PARASITIC</u>
    The text propagates by assimilation & substitution.

VALDEMORT & ESTROGEN
— There will come a time when death itself is an anachronism!
— *We'll* never live to see it.

Offensia DREAMS OF PRENATAL LIFE

"The beginning of the world," Spinoza's voice in her head, "was also the end of it." But wld its end also necessitate another beginning, reset to zero, or only a near=enough approximation of it?

Such presentiments accompanied **Offensia** throughout her formative years, though it wasn't until her apprenticeship as a counterfeiter that **Offensia** chanced upon her true vocation: she knew the moment the revelation occurred to her that she must, by any & all means, become a vampyr. The precise occasion was a séance upon Gottwald Mountain, when the spirit of Martha Dodd (!) spoke, revealing to her the secret lineaments of her prenatal incarnations, of which there were a vast succession, stretching back from Lola Montez to Agrippina. The truth of such matters cld only, it seemed, remain unknown w/out further supernatural intervention. There were obvious reasons for this. Soon, however, clues began to appear, confirming **Offensia**'s intuition – that all of these historical forebears had indeed been vampyrs. Less certain was her own particular stake in this lineage. Resisting for once her own precocious instinct for forgery, she set out in search of hard evidence. The results of her investigations were paltry: a postcard from one Baron Van Helsing to a certain Madam X, dated 1812; a lithograph, inherited from her mother, of a castle in Transylvania; a portrait of a kneeling hieratic figure w/ an inward gaze hauntingly like her own. Yet too many questions, unanswered, unanswerable. Too many flights of fancy, fatuous fires, figments & false alerts. The itinerary of her forebears, her namesakes, her pretagonists, was more than a moveable feast, it demanded an investigation that must encompass nearly the whole globe! The idea of ending her days as some forlorn simulation w/ plastic fangs & a cape drove her witless w/ despair. Laughter behind closed doors, the anxiety of empty wardrobes, the posthumous presence of ancient sunlight on faded squares of wallpaper, shadows of vanished furniture, paintings in stolen gilt frames, deniable portraits of mass murderers slipped from the family album, dictators & thieves, the dulled spines of unread books, the cemented dust of corners spurned, smudged panes of windows convulsively gazed out generation after generation, attic rooms of unspoken confinement. How fleeting, in retrospect, her mother's kiss, stolen upon her deathbed, in the airy embrace of an astral project, mere telekinesis! The view behind **Offensia**'s eyes began to turn grey, willing herself into a state of polyneuropathy, organomegaly, endocrinopathy, monoclonal plasmoproliferation, numbness, pulmonary constriction, bulging lymphnodes, leather=skin, extensile claws, enlarged incisors, a sudden & catastrophic taste for humxn blood. By sheer force of will, the selfmade vampyr! If only it were possible! And if destiny demanded she return to Transylvania to violate her mother's tomb for the sake of a myth? The last orphaned haemoglobin suspended in cryogenesis, brine=drunk, lost at sea: how wld it know itself after such tribulation? What immiserated DNA still stirred there? Did she dare?

"And is its end," **Offensia** said aloud, "not also its beginning?"

𝕲.𝕺.𝕯.'S SECOND CHILDHOOD

If it was true that 𝕲.𝕺.𝕯. built a family business out of being fucked by the Devil, it was His retarded son, Super Rupe, who turned it into the biggest planetary porno emporium this side of Valley Forge. When Rupert Merde=le=Coque, Jr., swore on his mammy's mausoleum to go out into the big awful world & do good, he meant every Jew=hating word of it. He travelled the great wild yonder, learned the big lessons of life. He saw how the lay of the land was & how it ought to be: subdivided & paved over & routed into the cashflow heaven of wireless fidelity. Then one portentous spring morn, the bushytailed entrepreneur returned home to pen the first volume of his memoirs, *The Formative Years*, in the inimitable tabloid style for which he'd soon become famed. "The Gore Vidal of corporate piracy" (*Golemgrad Evening Standard*). Beginning w/ an account of his miraculous birth, the Boy Wonder spared no detail, proceeding w/ exactitude through the intervening adolescent years & culminating in poignant scenes of buggery in Herod's gaol. Readers agreed that the highlight was a full uncensored page=three spread of the Virgin Mum herself, ravishing in a Vivienne Westwood head=to=heel BONSAI BANZAI BURKA BERSERKER! Scenes of mayhem ensuing on the Gaza Strip. Bazookas at dawn! Staring Dr Shekel & Mistress Eid. (Yep, kidz, it's another incomparable Papa Walt peenie=puller special! Featuring naked greed & passionate Armageddon! Where even the best laid bets come to nought!*)

---

* But not for "Never=a=Dupe" Rupe, he's a *born winner* (ask Judas)!

EDDIE VAN HELSING'S BLUES
Somewhere in the aftermath,
you draw the blinds & pour a glass.
You say it'll be the last.
But no=one's holding their breath.
And you don't have an emotion of yr own.
So you just sit & stare at the phone.
What you want yr little world to be like
& how you want yr little world to be liked.
Because something died in yr eyes
but y'd already gone away.
Because something died in yr eyes,
but you were never there anyway.
It's too late to hope that they'll call.
There's nothing left to stand tall for.
Sorry no=one was keeping score.
When you leave don't forget the door.
Now it's time to end this song,
never mind it won't be long.

AN INVISIBLE SHADOW PROJECTED OVER THE SKY
We are confronted w/ a Rorschachian psychodiagnostiks of
emergent social/environmental "chaos" which reveals a
system fully AT WORK globally & not a system in process
of BREAKING DOWN. Every indication is of an insistent
symmetricalisation of power that feeds off the production of
its own accelerated entropy, in the form of pure expenditure.
This relation of power is dialectical only to the extent
that its algorithmic movement of expenditure & recuperation
represents a *demystification* of the dialectical form.
Demystification because *it is only what can be conceived
within the dialectical relation that is ever subject to
the claims of sublation in the first place* – just as the
"expenditure w/out reserve" of despotic power remains bound
in its entirety to the *fantasy* of its negation. It is for
this reason that power's self=supersession is never an
instrument of insurrection but merely its theatre: that
moving tableau in which the passionate performance of
unrestrained violence begets an aesthetic "pleasure" both
at & *of* the limits of representation. The force of this
signification of the otherwise unsignifiable is what propels
expenditure in *its* means=of=production & thus power, too,
is propelled – projected in its "essence" – into a future
it is otherwise impotent to create if not to consume.

[**"WE LIVE IN A…"**] <u>**TUR[N]ING MACHINE**</u>

		READING=STATE		
STATEMENT	⟨	ERASING=STATE		
		<u>WRITING=STATE</u>		
		HALTING=STATE	⟩	STATELESSNESS

REALITY HAS BEEN ERASED BUT THE IDEA OF IT IS EVERYWHERE

In von Stroheim's *Luminous Fangs* we are leaving the field of cinema, the purely aesthetic field, & we are entering, or rather we are elevated to, the field of psychic revolution. It is apparent that this project — we dare not call it a "film" — is not only unusual but completely out of step w/ the contemporary cinema of our time. In the *Luminous Fangs*, cinema is deformed to such an extent that it almost no longer exists in the conventional sense of the word. It has become a struggle between conscious & unconscious forces, a mentalistic apotheosis, an epic quest to solve the problem of the very existence of reality. Is it possible, in the aftermath of such an act of radical disillusionment, to say what it *is* or what it *means*?

THE I=L=L=U=M=I=N=I=S=T COVENANT

Cinema, they declared, must derive from an internal dynamic rhythm in the relation between concepts & their abstract expression. For the I=L=L=U=M=I=N=I=S=T=S, this represented the liberation of an aesthetic that followed its own rules, separated from the tradition of mimetically depicted objects. Nowhere was this more in evidence than in the I=L=L=U=M=I=N=I=S=T=S' distinctive perceptiveness & approach to light revealed in von Stroheim's cycle *Luminous Fangs*, which owed nothing whatsoever to conventional realism.

"Life" (Stroheim) "will only begin once more on this planet when all the museums have been abolished, beginning w/ cinema itself."

RING=A=RING=A=ROSIE, OUT THE SOLAR ANUS

Papa Walt: Those who believe they've been abandoned by G.O.D. are greater idiots than those who merely believe in G.O.D.

Rupert Merdecock: The G.O.D.less idiot is an idiot indeed.

Nyx gLand: To be an idiot is forgivable, but to be an idiot forsaken by one's own idiocy is a fault beyond redemption.

GIVE US THIS DAY OUR DAILY MERDECOCK

Well looky here, hadn't the Ol' Sore moved up in the world? A real self=made tabloid tranny! He got franchises half=way across Civilisation. "Rupert the Vamp," they is callin him. "Rupe the V." You gotta pay just to line up when Super Rupe cometh round to giver her haemorrhoids an airing, kiss the pinky ring & all that stale ol' jizz, & maybe the Big Sore take a liking to you, give you the full page three treatment.

    — Well my heart just bleeds, lover. It <u>bleeds</u>.

    — Just the way La Merdecock says, BETTER TO BECOME A WOMXN THAN FUCK A MAN.

    — Ooh! I is feeling all hot & crampy just thinking of eet!

    — Anyone able to recommend a reliable brand of haemorrhoid cream? Asking for a friend.

IF CORVID=69 IS REAL, YOU CAN CALL ME MAYER!

Spinoza sits in a corner of Doctor Asperger's laboratory, in a pile of broken wires, pulleys, levers, circuit=breakers, motherboards, fake fur, etc. Asperger is pacing back & forth in front of a bank of teleconferencing monitors, addressing the faithful. "Blood count must not exceed" / "relations of production to immune response" / "spinal tap" / etc. Whatever experiment the abducted macaque has been part of appears to have been counted a success. Asperger's mood is upbeat, the prognostic A+. Consciousness fading, Spinoza looks on helplessly at this colloquy of shitheels, last hopes of rescue fleeing out the proverbial door. The following is an approximate transcript…

Asperger: By analysing samples from the City's sewer system & testing for antibodies, we have been able to localise sources of infection within the City's slums & target them for sanitation.

Ayn Rand: The epicentre of all disease! The anus of "society"!

Nyx gLand: Progress with a capital A.

Juulz Ebola: But what if <u>it</u> managed to get in here, right under our very noses?

Ayn Rand: Let them eat shit!

Merdecock: Millions & millions of folks out there eating shit every day. They've each got good reasons to keep eating it, but the reasons don't matter. Fact is, if they stopped eating shit, the world wld end & that's all there is to it.

Ayn Rand: Life is a shit sandwich!

Vance Duhomey: Is that all there is? Fait accompli? Is that the essence of sucking shit?

Papa Walt: Shit is the one thing you can bank on.

Merdecock: The Summa Coprologica.

Dante Polidori: First we must consider the nature of the particular shit in question.

Juulz Ebola: G.O.D. shit? Monkey shit? Bullshit? Shit of the Sephiroth? of Cthulhu? of Marilyn Monroe? Shit from the arses of the mass=extinguished? Pure commodity shit? Merde d'artiste? Shit of shit? Of the shitless? Dead shit? Shit from Shinola? All the shit you can eat? All the shit of History in one chamberpot? Shit for shit's sake? The shit that dare not speak its name? The shit that doesn't give a shit? Categorical shit? Ethereal shit? Shit on a hot tin roof? Shit on a cold night in Siberia? Crazy shit? Premium shit? Shit on a stick? Off a shovel? Free shit? No shit?

Ayn Rand: A turd in the hand is worth two in the kisser[*]!

Merdecock (in the voice of Wang Fang): Better to bury one's head in a latrine than lose it over a square of toilet paper (ancient Mongolian proverb).

Nyx gLand: Shit aint shit, Sal.

IT IS THE EYE OF TRUTH THAT PERSECUTES

In front of a landscape of erasures, a darkness that engulfs everything. (There was a border they didn't always let you see, but you still knew you had to cross it.) This is the key to the game. Life stands under orders to retreat to the Quarantine Zone. Positioned outside the game, the adversaries pretend they're only imaginary. *Il n'y a pas de hors=jeu.* Stated otherwise, existence of strategy doesn't automatically confer a "tactical" advantage. There are, for example, two types of mask: those that are worn openly & those worn in secret. >*the chill of sodden paper stuck to the neck glued smooth over eyelids force=fed between cracked teeth a papier=mâché of endorphined suffocation inkblotted gagging mute to dream of surfaces & air when all is a red pulsing of the eyelids turning black the blood in the ears bile in the throat welling up w/ sudden ferocity like a fountain pen from a jugular to scrawl its immodest encyclopaedias.* Like Miss Muffet, you watch in sick fascination as the giant blowfly sucks the brains out of the

---

[*] La bouche.

itsybitsy spider. "There is a great danger threatening the task of emancipation, which isn't an <u>excess of ideology</u>, but the opposite: an insufficiency of ideology <u>in the direction of the task itself</u>." Immense relief from breathing (after all). They are selling oxygen in bottles. First degrade, then ration, then commodify. THE ONLY FUTURE WORTH ANYTHING IS ONE THAT PAYS! ("Virtuous & meek means lead to nothing!") You've seen this coming but weren't always prepared to believe it. An alibi only gets you so far, the real art is in convincing them of everything you say. *Palinodes of complacency*. Trocchi: "Protest is based on the assumption that social behaviour is intelligent: the hallmark of its futility." What if everything to be accomplished, & the means of doing so, were self=evident? [An ~~inevitable~~ invisible insurrection?] Yet nothing cld be less clear / i.e. <u>further from the truth</u> (like a point on a Möbius strip returning to itself "as the crow flies"). >in place of "landscape," write "geometry." Perhaps before proceeding further we shld define what is meant by a distance: being the magnitude of an anomaly between two frames of reference. "She looked in the mirror but her reflection wasn't there [wasn't where she expected it to be.]" ¿Somewhere inside the mirror time had slowed down? The virus integrates an error into the system, which propagates until the error IS the system [the system "fails"] [or until it evolves a different system].[*] Q: Is the virus a "revolutionary" force? At what point does it renounce revolt? At what point does it dissimulate? i.e. by precipitating collapse, does the virus in fact strengthen the hand ✋ of e.g. the I=L=L=U=M=I=N=I=S=T conspiracy? "We must restate the problem of Evil upon new information." [Every demon serves a master, but not only a demon may kill its master.] Once more back in the realm of false consciousness & instinctive dread, where G.O.D. alone maintains the Supreme Good in perpetual tumescence. *To the extent that sublime revolt lives, grows & develops over the course of History…* Does violence so quickly lose its attraction, when all it does is pay a salary? [A riot must <u>also</u> be a deconstruction.] Note, to be inscribed on every mirror: KNOW THYSELF / KNOW THY ENEMY. Thus are we all creatures of speculation. Yet who wld be the logos fallen among those deprived of speech? image among the blind? vaccine among the terminally sick? And if the virus itself

---

[*] >memory: discontinuity / a zone of <u>inconsequentials</u>? [political memory: power vectors that have <u>expired</u>?] >nostalgia: an image returning to its starting point after its reflection has <u>already</u> <u>flown the coop</u>?

wld send the image=cancer consuming the world into remission? [i.e. by debilitating global kapital], or only appear to, while in reality accelerating the cancer's spread under a regime of inoculation [i.e. against whatever remains in the cancer's way]? Or: if it participates in the regeneration of the world it destroys like an active supernatural force? Or: if though it represents a step towards a new world, it must still be excluded from this one? One crisis washes the hands of the other. The opportunism of love or tenderness: an open secret in front of the camera. *Always the hope of future antagonism.* (In the end there will be only the sound of dollars crying themselves to sleep at night.) Even when the lights have finally gone out, our task is more fraught & uncertain than ever, & the enemy is everywhere.

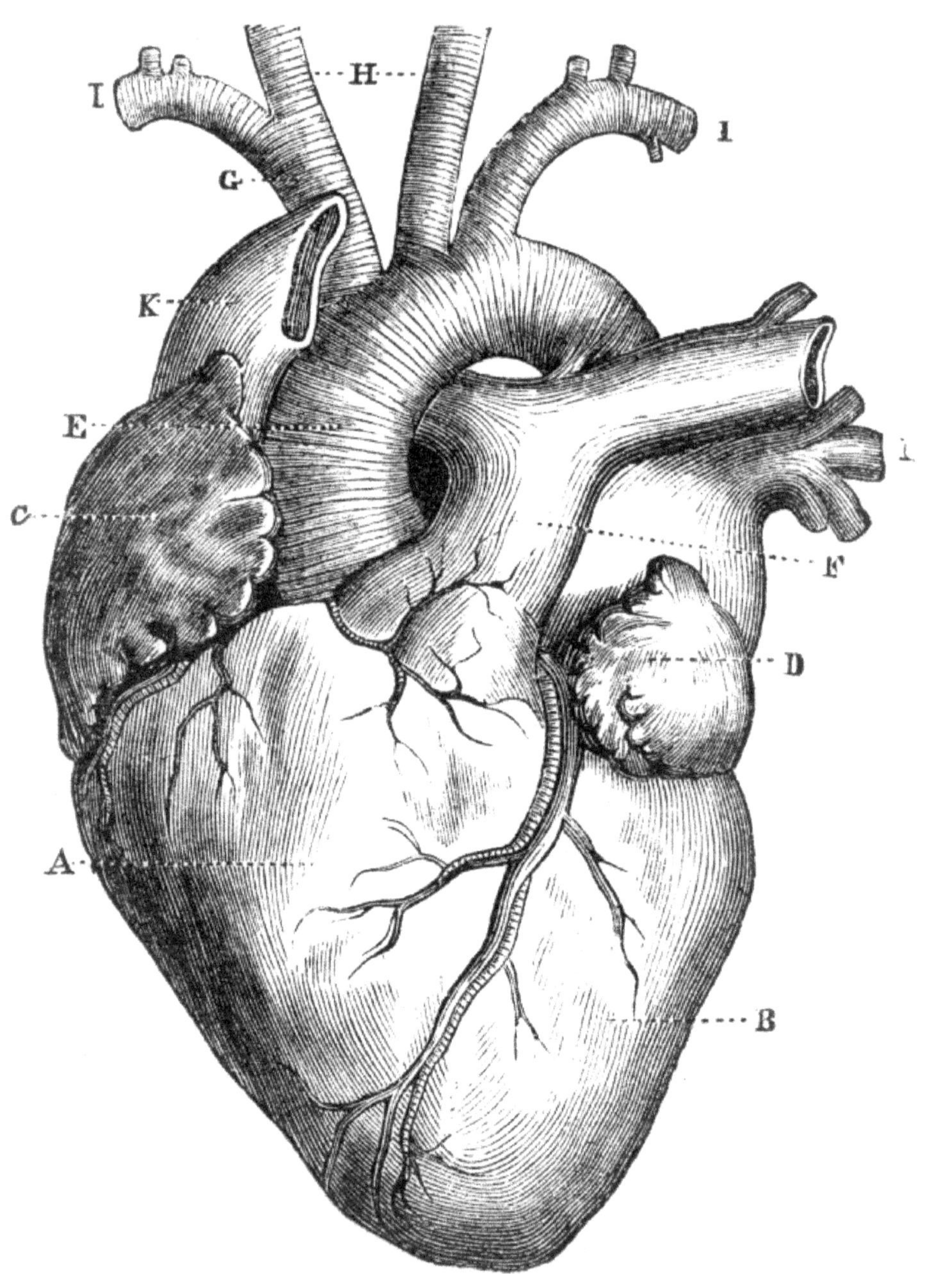

I
H
I
G
K
E
C
i
F
D
A
B

Area 7 sq. ft.
Main Surface
Area

<u>EIGHTH COMMUNIQUÉ</u>
WE are getting closer…
    We are slowly destroying the long tentacles of the oppressive Corp(orate)=$(tate) apparatus…
    Surveillance state infrastructure
    Corporate mainframes
    Secret police files
    Propaganda factories
    All the bureaucracy & technology used against the people:
        to increase productivity & accelerate redundancy;
        to slow down our minds & actions;
        to obliterate the truth.
    Police computers don't tell the truth, they just record the "crimes" of the oppressed, while the crimes of the P.I.G.s & their masters go unrecorded.
    We will avenge our murdered, beaten & imprisoned sisters.
    The next sister they murder, ten times as much P.I.G. blood will flow in the streets.
    500 explosions last year. Hundreds more executions of govt stooges, finks, bosses, collaborators, undercover cops.
    The Š.V.E.J.K. is the sister sitting next to you, the sister crossing the street, the sister checking out yr groceries, the sister collecting the trash, the sister driving yr cab.
    They have guns in their pockets & anger in their minds.
    WE are getting closer…
    Burn the system down!
    Power to the freaks!
    The Š.V.E.J.K. ✋

THE BOOK OF ERRATA

She came into focus slowly, like an antique computer screen w/ a faulty refresh rate, waiting to be degaussed. **Offensia** at three minutes to midnight.

— No true artist, she said, can ever be of their time.

From daughter to forger to vampyr insurgent is a path only the best or worst of us cld take. Weighing the massacred hours we never triumph over. Merged & isolated in the flow of inevitables, feeble in the face of the *fait accompli*. The example we must follow through the jungles of insufficiency. *Look death in the face! Go all the way! Morte aux tièdes!* What use is a sex hidden, reserved, negated? In **Offensia**'s image we breathe the white air, discover the routes, bones, precipices. This accompaniment of our physical bodies through the labyrinth of privation & pain.

— A <u>thing</u> loses its neutral meaning first of all.

Her eyes bore out of the pixellated gloom, fixing on you among all the others.

— There never was one. It never had it.

Breathing erratically, blinking [on average how many times per minute? but life is full of over=estimations…]. That gaze, flowing out from [certain] death, to circulate again in the black mirror of our desire. A mirror soon to be filled w/ smoke. There is a drought in our hearts that has imposed its own epoch, raining embers on our heads, scorched flesh, blistered tongues.

?: <u>This recurring dream always begins as a blank page</u> [a blank screen?]. <u>Sometimes the page</u> [screen?] <u>is white.</u> <u>Sometimes black.</u> <u>Sometimes grey.</u> <u>Sometimes there isn't a page</u> [screen?] <u>at all.</u>

AN ALEMBIC CONFABULUM

On the alchemist's map a foreshore presses eyeward. HERE LIES THE TRUTH OF THE MATTER, shipwrecked, in a manner of speaking. The infernal algebra of all unknowns reduced to this. The eye, too, is but a piece of debris. Or not a piece, but an objective correlative of everything that can be seen, *strewn upon the visible*. What difference does it make? A god exists only in the absence of affirmation. Or in spite of it. Or is the only affirmation possible. You boil a worm to see what comes out. Death is the lowest form of entropy. We who have mapped the hundred=billion orders of creation know the truth of despair. To be cast adrift upon the furthest littoral of Time. Eternity is a chronical illness, a neurosis of the cosmic mind & its unmind.

VOYAGE TO THE END OF THE MIND (COMTESSE DE L'H D'A DE L)

It was in the late spring of XXXX that, having determined on a journey across latitudes hitherto uncharted, I set out accompanied by a crew who, having been drawn (of reluctant necessity) from among the more desperate & less reasonable of their caste, cld barely be described as humxn. We set sail at a point in the East whose name is rightly shrouded in superstition & which I have foresworn never again to repeat. From the very outset, the expedition was plagued, one calamity following fast upon another. Barely had we put to sea, before the ship's doctor was seized by the crew & sacrificed in a ritual most foul & bloodthirsty, thence hoist upon a bosun's chair to dangle under the burning sun, ravaged by gulls, erupting w/ yellow grubs that did rain upon the decks & worm down the rigging. Within a week every inch of the vessel was infected by them. Nor did a day pass w/out a crucifixion upon the masts. None wld say who the authors of these punishments were, nor the crimes of the victims. The captain was never seen to issue from his quarters. The steward ordered the corpses washed in tar, but did not have them brought down, so that for the remainder of our journey these gruesome sights multiplied among the sails which did seem like backdrops to Calvary. As we proceeded below the tropics, the very air became unbreathable. The stench of the dead, the strangulating humidity. Only by constant reiteration was I able to keep my mind fixed upon our original purpose. The lethargy of the crew had rendered them insensible to all but their nightly bloodlust, which by all inevitability must have soon reduced their number to a degree even more precarious to their ritual than to the maintenance of the ship. I feared we wld surely become marooned. Though we drifted upon the winds & currents for weeks upon end, the astrolabe gave indication of no progress, & still the cardinal points showed nothing but ocean. Surely we were anchored to the Great Despond. By month's end, our stores spent, the crew had descended into an arcane form of cannibalism, determined by a system of lotteries, inscrutable auguries, & bizarre arithmetic. They wld for example determine a limb or section of a body, the form of excision, whether it be consumed raw or from the brazier, in whole or by means of complex division, which parts to exempt & which to sacrifice upon the sea, & which to offer up to the birds, which to the nightly armada of bats, which to the worms, which to salt & store, etc. Each bore some hideous wound which, despite the constant victualing, exhibited a gangrenous hue. How I succeeded in evading an equivalent fate remains a mystery to me. With the situation deteriorated beyond all hope of repair, I barricaded myself inside the galley, which the cannibals had long stripped bare. Days passed during which I was assailed by the most hideous screams. Hunger & thirst wrenched at my sanity. I lost track of all time. Then, as if in a fever dream, I heard the ship's bell ring out. Taking care not to fall into an ambush, I crept forth from my bunker & saw, on a sou'westerly bearing, the first landfall since our setting off. The sails were set fair to the wind, yet there was no sign of any crew. Upon the bridge a dark figure stood, in harsh silhouette against the sun. It was then I knew whose ship I had ventured upon & where my voyage must end.

THE CENTURIES TO COME HAVE ALREADY RECEIVED OUR MESSAGE
Gentle Reader for many faults in the printing of this Booke as came to our remembrance, we pray thee correct as followeth: the reft (if any arife) we referre to thy godly wifedome. For *the words expounded*, read *the words interpreted*: tautologies in scripture no idle repetitions! Whether the working of signifiance be ceased, the ends of signification are ceased now: significations needless & significations frivolous; the truth of significations but rash & uncertain, for nothing a true signified that is not truly effected. Amen!

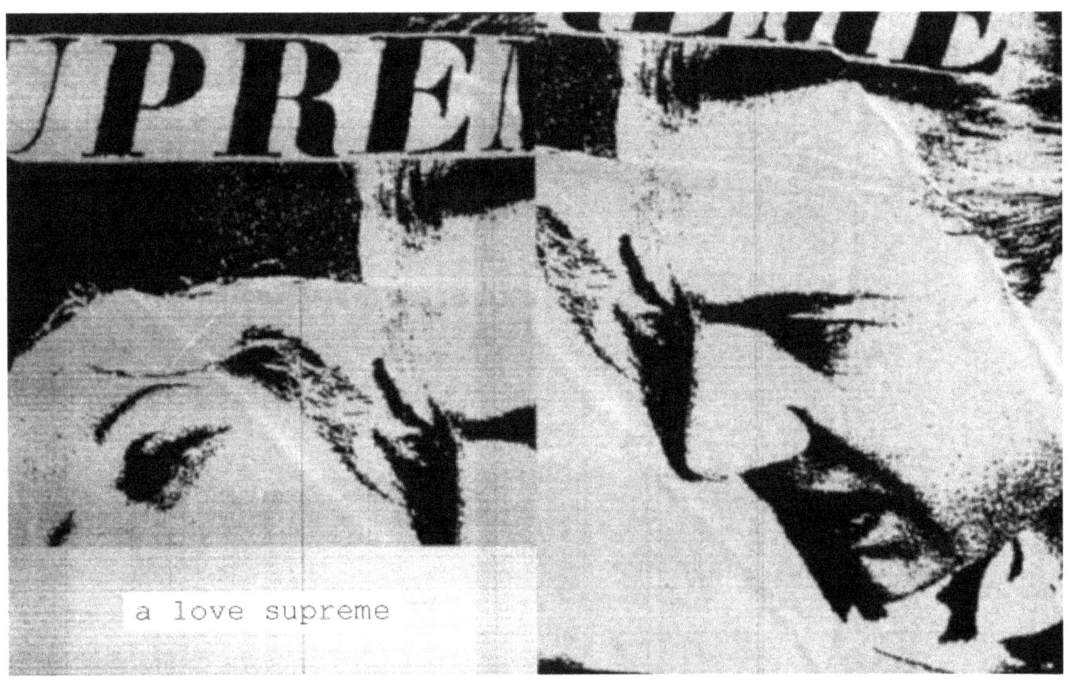

THE BLOOD OF OTHERS [REEL 8]

Bar at Golemgrad Hl.N. train station: The scene opens with a glimpse of Merdecock's corporate news counterfeiting operation, as he prepares to meet a contact in the "underground" (Jean Genet, whom Merdecock fails to recognise as Asperger's assistant) to pass on ten million fake Reichsmark, the artisanship of which he is especially proud. The purpose of the forgeries is to sabotage the Š.V.Ǝ.J.K. insurgency's arms dealing activities. Before leaving he dons a Palestinian scarf.

Duhomey also prepares for a rendezvous at the station – also, coincidentally, with a Palestinian scarf, the sign by which he & Crispr (whose work he intends to plagiarise) will recognise each other. He first detours to the men's room to shoot up, but begins to lose consciousness after overdosing in one of the toilet stalls.

Crispr sits at the station bar, his thoughts alternating between the prospect of meeting a potential backer for his film, *The Precognitions*, & the prospect of picking up the blonde (Jean Genet) seated on the stool next to him. Merdecock arrives & mistakes Crispr for Genet (who meanwhile has gone to the toilet); Crispr mistakes Merdecock for Duhomey.

Without preamble, Merdecock hands Crispr the ten million Reichsmark in a paper bag which Crispr, speechless, interprets as the hoped=for investment in his film (later, with bitter irony, he will credit Merdecock as "Executive Undertaker").

Overwhelmed with emotion, Crispr embraces Merdecock & rushes out past the toilets. The same toilets wherein Genet has mistaken the unconscious Duhomey for a drunk & tries to rumble his pockets. Having come=to under Genet's ministrations, & discouraging him with some timely jujitsu manoeuvres, a dishevelled Duhomey makes his way to the station bar.

Alarmed by Crispr's behaviour, Merdecock follows him but mistakenly thinks he has run into the toilets, where Merdecock encounters his real contact, Genet. Both of them realise their error & hurry to intercept Crispr before he exits the station. They catch sight of him just as he reaches the street & disappears into the crowd.

Back at the station, Duhomey has regained his composure & is waiting at the bar until it seems obvious to him that Crispr isn't showing. Reluctantly he returns home, planning to come back the next night.

Doubting his sanity, Crispr decides he shld return to discuss terms, percentages of the gross, all that. He's just in time to notice Duhomey leave, but is unable to recognise him. Instead he finds Meyrink & Madame Guyotat now sitting at the bar & lends both of them money (blandly referring to it as "venture kapital" from his film production company).

They persuade him to join them in a visit to El Divo's salon, where he decides to shoot some footage…

PANDEMONIUM IN CRISIS

If *the long disastrous cycle of vampyrism is approaching its end as violently as it began*, this is because present conditions under which the supposedly definitive form society must take at the End=of=History are indistinguishable from a collective experience of insanity, war & death. (Madness isn't the revolutionary instrument reason of the oppressed but the instrument of their oppression.) By now the lesson shld've been learned, that all hegemonies are sustained by the logic of brute sacrifice. Regimes of austerity are never regimes *against* expenditure, but of a heightened *sacrificial mode* of expenditure, which is why they attract to themselves the appointments of religiosity & of the sacred mission. For all the talk of erecting walls & closing borders, *exclusion* isn't the issue: it's about enlarging the price "society" is willing to pay. It's no secret that Corp[orate]=$[tate] exceptionalism has exhausted any need for the bourgeois social contract. Its regimes of austerity have less to fear from those who *have* nothing, than from those who *want* nothing. If vampyr kapitalism propagates by ever=increasing consumption, its rhetoric of "infrastructural development" is intended solely to maximise its capacity for *expenditure*. A false dichotomy thus establishes itself in the mode of critique of vampyr kapitalism, between the sensibility of rationalist technocracy & populist romanticism, veering one moment to the barricades & the next to the Panopticon. The fact remains that kapitalism is ambivalent about all else but its own capacity for increase: whether the spread of insurrectionary violence indicates putative "revolutionary conditions" in a revolt AGAINST vampyrism, or whether vampyrism itself is entering a new phase catalysed by global catastrophism, is yet to be seen. **N**$_x$

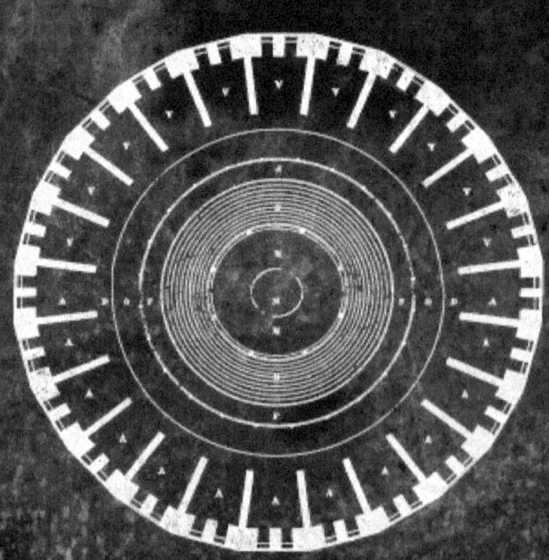

THE SALON AT THE END OF THE WORLD

The Lugubrious One a.k.a. Mater Praga a.k.a. El Divo a.k.a. Le Grand Fromage welcomed her visitors splayed out on an Ottoman like a beached whale on HRT, turbaned, puffing a calabash & sporting embroidered lederhosen. *Vous êtes très gentille madame!* Her eyes were watering under the changeable lights, shadows fading to frightlines. Beneath reams of indigo décolleté, a catafalque of hideous suppressed emotion threatened at any moment to erupt into great penumbral cornucopias. She is said to be the ectopic residue of an haute=bourgeois vivisectionist's most lurid molestations. Is it any surprise, that the class that once spawned her committed *hara kiri* during the last revolutionary Ice Age? She is the veritable scarlet letter of a civilisation premised upon its own demise. *Ugliness,* she said*, shld not be bought, but earned like a badge of honour.* Those for whom art means to endure the slings & arrows of universal cretinism, flock to her like plague fleas to a rat on a sinking ship. Hers is the last of the great salons, where jejune poets & *vampyrs maudits* toe the same moth=eaten carpets (hand=woven in Damascus, no less) — where dubious debutantes rub the velveteen from Louis XVI settees w/ studded garterbelts — & low=level freemasons swill rohypnol=infused absinthe sorbets w/ live=streaming Lolitas. *All sins*, El Divo has been known to say, *are absolved in the theatre.* Men of state have turned to her to fortify their resolve. To her sangfroid, the ghosts of V.I. Lenin, Napoléon Bonaparte & Lex Luthor have each inscribed heartfelt dedications upon the antique commode where she sits enthroned while wielding her planchette over the ouija board. The guests are directed to admire the sure=handed calligraphy, the intimate turns of phrase. Her wunderkammer is *sans pareil.* Her pancetta, sublime! Hers is an utterly grandiloquent panache, laced w/ undisguised mildew. A rose in moribund bloom *like a baboon on heat, overdosed on barbiturates.* She has suffered more attacks of the vapours than all of Dostoyevsky's novels combined: choleric miasmas rising from sewer grates & subprole tenements to trespass upon this last bastion of illiterate *gourmandise* — like a golem draped in black funeral crêpe, making deliberate headway up the stairs. The address itself bears all the appearance of a multistorey tomb, imposing an air of lament upon the pavement traffic. To approach is to plumb the very depths of approbation. The more impressionable are sometimes left catatonic before reaching the mezzanine. Not so, the unwashed masses, as she has so often previewed them in her clairvoyant mind's eye, charging the stairs, spoiling the carpets, raping the potted ferns, garrotting the ersatz Caspar Friedrich, defenestrating the assembled literati. *Quel gâchis!* And at their head, that festering filmographer Jean Rollin, rosette & tricorn, waving his Super=8 like a syphilitic's suppurating penis at the assembled débauchés & screaming in lickspittle falsetto *Y're all still at home! With yr own tombs to escape the light of day! And yr devoted servants to bring aperitifs! Y're all <u>bourgeois</u> vampyrs!* as (on cue) a veritable deluge of unpaid extras flood in from the stairways & terraces, machetes flashing in chandelier light, & willynilly set about beheading everyone in the room, all except El Divo herself who slips out behind an arras into secret passageways built into the walls long before the revolution for precisely such an eventuality as this. Oh indeed the times! Oh indeed the customs! She'll be back next week toasting the new Robespierre & hosting the world premiere of Rollin's rollicking hats=off documentary *The Blood of Others* in which she's made the briefest of cameos, business being business, the golden rule, keeping more fingers in more pies than an amputee pastry chef hahaha, because no=one knows what tomorrow might bring, stormtroopers rushing the balustrades as if it were a race to the top of the Ziggurat of Ur, & El Divo in person handing out flutes of Veuve Cliquot to every dog in uniform that reaches the summit. *Vive la révolution!*

NOTES ON VAMPYR ASEXUAL REPRODUCTION

"The existence of sex=related differences in Ca^{2+}=homeostasis is well documented in some species. Some obvious examples of animals in which females extrude much more calcium from their body related to reproduction than males are birds (eggs w/ a calcareous shell) & mammals that produce milk, w/ its extraordinarily huge Ca^{2+}=concentration of about 50 millimolar (mM) compared to the very low Ca^{2+}=concentration of about 100 nanomolar (nM) in the cytoplasm of resting cells ($[Ca^{2+}]i$. This represents a concentration gradient of 50,000 times more Ca^{2+} in milk or 20,000x in blood where the Ca^{2+} concentration amounts to about 2 millimolar. These vertebrates are not exceptions: also in other vertebrates & in invertebrates the amount of Ca^{2+} extruded through egg laying is always higher than through the ejaculation of sperm. Thus, at least during the reproduction process, differential sex=related Ca^{2+}=homeostasis is the general rule. Steroid sex hormones play an important role, but the mechanisms involved are not yet fully understood. Other hormones may also be involved. In vertebrates the main difference in sex steroids between males & females does not reside in the type of steroids but in their relative amounts. In vertebrates, the rule is that both males & females produce androgens (testosterone, dihydrotestosterone) & estrogens (in particular estradiol) but in different amounts. Females convert more testosterone into estradiol than males in which the aromatase enzyme system that governs this conversion is less efficient. As a result, males have higher androgen concentrations in their body & tissues than females do. The opposite is true for estrogens: higher in females. This classical endocrinology has been well documented for a long time. However, how the genetic= & endocrine male=female differences are causally related to behavioural=gender differences is only partially understood."[*]

LONG JOURNEY TOWARDS THE LIGHT

"It's better to fade away," croaked Eddie Van Helsing into his handset.

There was no=one at the other end, it was set to dictaphone mode, recording the fallen rockstar's musings for *Posterity*, which was the name he'd been kicking about for the long=awaited comeback album. He'd been kicking it about for a while & it was showing signs of wear. *But that's life, right? If it don't hold up, it won't stand up!* Some bright spark at *Rolling Stoned* had taken to baiting him as a rock'n'roll Methuselah in spandex & he'd toyed w/ putting out a contract on the sonofabitch, but that'd mean his entire recent media coverage wld be zapped into oblivion, so he manned up & took it on the chin. Said youth had just gone from wild to stupid. Said rock was born wise before its time & he was just growing into it & don't lay any of that old man bullshit on me, arsehole, or I'll kick yr fucking teeth in. *Let's see who's wild!* And when Eddie Van Helsing smiled for the fantasy cameras you just knew his orthodontist was earning half his non=existent royalties for him.

But of the Latter Day Saints of the Church of Sex, Drugs & the Kind of Music Played by Cretinous Goons, Van Helsing was neither the latterest nor the saintliest, but just the

---

[*] Arnold De Loof, "Only two sex forms but multiple gender variants: How to explain?" *Commun Integr Biol* 11.1 (2018).

guy who'd figured which way to hold a guitar for the fifteen minutes that mattered most, & been waxing nostalgic about it ever since. How in the early days that'd translated into heavy dosages of angst, surrounded by the *de rigueur* cohort of retainers emanating distinct vibes of gothic villainy, but later got dialled down to the low end of the bandwidth in monastic cloisters, secluded basement studios & accursed Transylvanian sublets no washed=up celeb in their right mind wld've been caught dead in. His true *forte* was self=recrimination, but it didn't sell. That didn't mean, however, that deep down Eddie Van Helsing wasn't in possession of a masterplan for the Ultimate Reinvention. A masterplan that'd *shock* the idle world into recognition, finally, *belatedly*, of the untold genius possessing him. (Because weren't geniuses always *ahead of their time?*)

"Yeah, better to fade away," he reverbed, adding some air=guitar & syncopated hip=thrust, "than turn to shit."

YEAR ZERO OF THE BIG IDEA
Scene: Assorted secretaries of state, generalissimos & avantLARPers in candycoloured clown hats, aviators, enormous braided epaulets, a Troy weight of ribboned brass, ranked behind their glorious Comédienne=in=Chief, flags & bunting by the square mile, a battalion of microphones, assorted dictatorial accoutrements filling in the TV frame, timestamped, **G.O.D.**'s PROXY DAILY BRIEFING announcing the deathlists as if it were the National Lottery, the numbers effortlessly mounting like perpetual growth forecasts, THE WORLD'S GREATEST ACHIEVEMENT! though vigilant observers may detect a subtle but growing austerity in the background arrangement, as one by one the Presidential lackeys get airbrushed by the plague, the marquee tool & delete key diligently massaged by a studio desk=monkey live to air & some groovy effects edited in to make the whole fiasco look like happy hour on MTV, Osman Family cameo & everything.

DEAR IMAGINARY READER
The dilemma is always, How to drink more than yr fill w/ out drowning? How to know what's ever enough? What's too much? How to live to tell the tale? How to come back from the dead?

SHOTGUN WEDDING (EDDIE VAN, LIVE)

Cld anyone else detect the inner=worthiness Eddie Van Helsing knew was his? "Is there no=one," he pleaded to the microphone, "who understands me?" After the reverb died down, the darkened stadium was eerily silent. "You can't wait for the world's approval," was what Papa Walt's marketing goon liked to say on occasions like this, "sometimes you've just gotta go out & buy it." But Eddie V was the kind of man who believed in breaking down an audience's resistance, like y'd break down a Marshall stack for firewood. He knew from bitter experience, there are moments in life when a single powerchord can change destinies. Wld this be one of them? He thrust his hips at the micstand & revved the Stratocaster into life, sneering out the words that soon wld be stamped on the brains of a few ironic teenagers, who'd buy the album just so they cld ritually burn it in a spontaneous outpouring of whatever emotion the music industry press wanted to attribute to them:

Tonight I'm sleeping w/ Kurt Cobain,
got a five ounce bag to ease my pain,
yr love's a joke & yr act's pure lame,
don't need yr money, don't want yr fame…

THE CONVERSION OF PAPA WALT

Having been shaped by the industrial environment of Golemgrad, B.J. "Papa" Walt was driven to transform the physical world. His observations were not those of an aesthete seeking visual pleasure, but of an engineer of humxn souls. From his immersion in the dark arts of kapitalist production, he devised a modern alchemy that wld reconfigure the very DNA of reality. Adherence to modern technology was not, in his case, abstract. Walt set himself no less a task than the reformation of the humxn stereotype in all its minutiae. Nothing of its mould wld remain unbroken. Yet it wld be wrong to see Walt as nothing more that a commodity fetishist *in extremis*. All forms of existence fascinated him, in their diverse manifestations of irrational joy & suffering, of ignorance & false reason. For reason, too, in its gross distribution, is a comical affair, & Walt desired nothing of life so much as to be instructed & amused during his work of transfiguring it utterly. To do otherwise wld be like apologising to the grass that tickle one's feet as they dance upon it, or to the mirror we oblige to produce a world in our image, gratis.

THE I=L=L=U=M=I=N=I=S=T MANIFESTO

Nyx gLand had, in the words of his more literate detractors, "the self=parodic air of Büchner's Woyzeck."

When not inciting ridicule, gLand was embarked upon an attempt to divine the secret meaning of the universe by a method of "excommunicating spheres." This entailed mutating quasi=random datasets into unforeseen & Cthulhuesque forms.

"It is self=evident," he patiently explained, "that non=communicating & non=similar spheres brought into sudden proximity will exercise an unpredictable influence on one another."

Here was the basis of a system, even if, at times, one of mutual annihilation: contradictory elements cancelling one another out; matter & antimatter (or in the parlance of the initiated, *mater & anti=mater*).

But there was more to the "excommunicating spheres" than the simple appearance of a dialectics. It was a spacetime=machine built on the semantics of coincidence & superposition, of the Great Palimpsest.

That it only took a solitary genius armed w/ a text randomiser to figure all this out was somehow unforgivable.

The fact was that none of the previous centuries had succeeded in even remotely imagining this one, which had failed even to imagine itself. Time had gotten away from it, it was, so to speak, Lost in Space.

The task of the New Science, gLand proclaimed, was to reconvene the alterior Weltgeist; to be the medium at the séance in which the void, so far adrift in the virtual, wld rematerialise in the Real.

The Old Science, in contrast, was nothing but a tawdry succession of devil's advocates, indentured to the coming apocalypse. Those w/ a conscience to soothe dangled revolutionary carrots from a stick, always long enough to be just beyond reach.

Thinking they'd buy reprieve for this world by sacrificing the next, they spoke in almost theological tones, incantations of the awaiting miracle.

But there had been strange voices in the night long before this one. It was gLand's determination to amplify those voices to an unbearable pitch. To shatter the champagne flutes in the crystal cabinet. To wreck the glass houses. To break the proverbial mirror.

"Ah, to be a goddess of stagnant waters!" he cried. To himself. Perhaps to no=one.

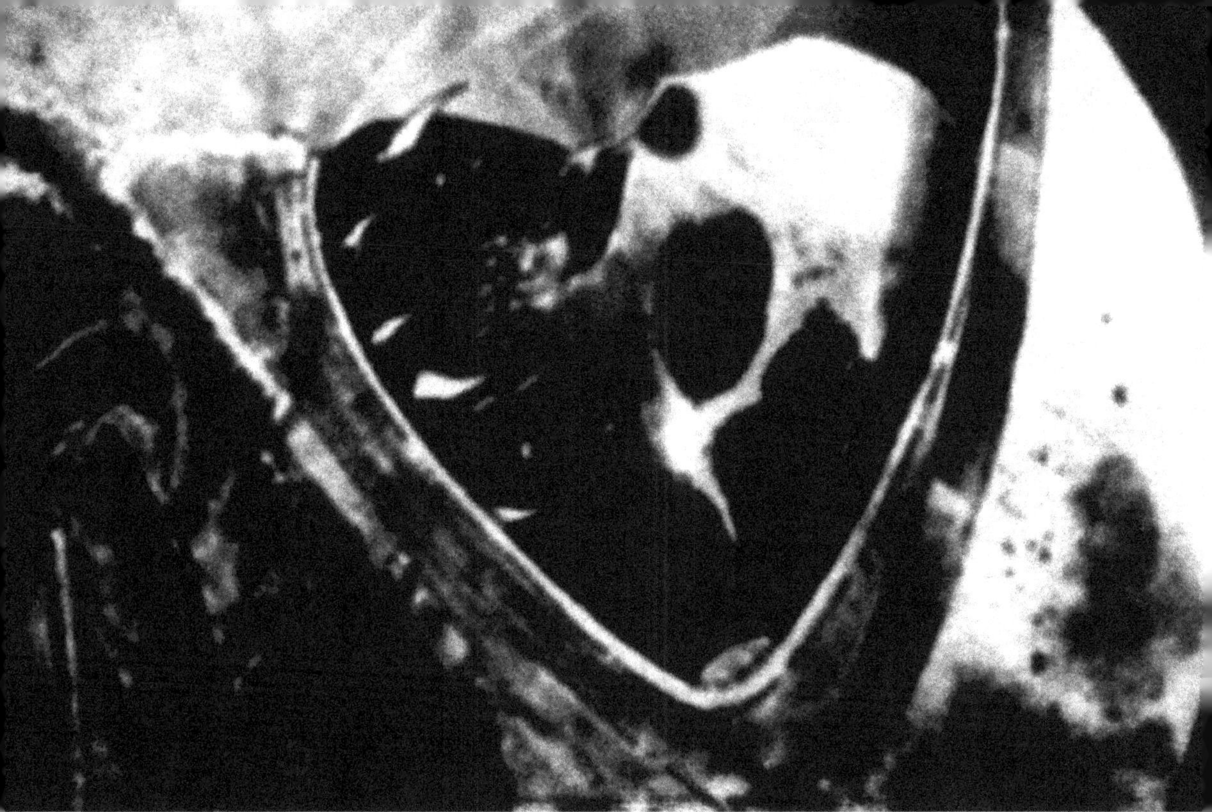

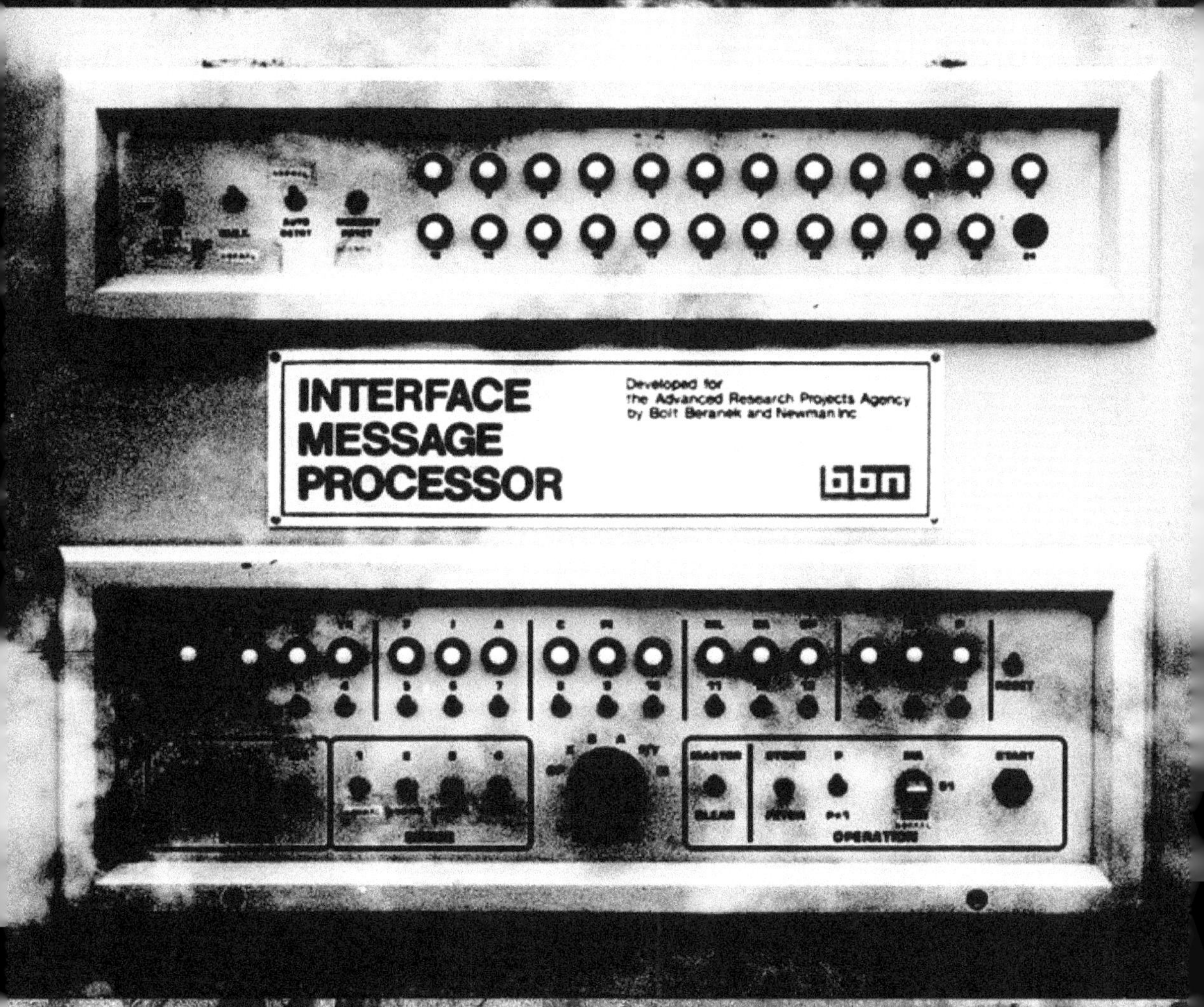

INTERFACE
MESSAGE
PROCESSOR
Developed for
the Advanced Research Projects Agency
by Bolt Beranek and Newman Inc
bbn

OPERATION

THE CREATION OF UNGOVERNABLE SITUATIONS

The individual is the true *state of exception*. The privilege of the liberal humxnist subject has always been the principle weapon in the arsenal of Corp[orate]=$tate. At a time when humxnity itself is for all intents & purposes defined by MASS INFECTIOUS POTENTIAL (the new *productive potential*), humxnism shows itself again & again to be a strategy for procuring economic output against an "acceptable" rate of attrition: the ideology of the Arbeitslager, driven by a logistics of justified expendability. Thus does fatalism remain the icon of the "free world." In the shadow of THE PLAGUE, the routinisation of desire proceeds under the inverted guise of refusal, revolt, resistance (the perverse drive to *work*): the latent hysteria of the conformist mass *unmasked*. They want to fuck w/ their true selves, but only to die in the real bodies of others. But the virus isn't the individual's erotic counterpart, like an embodied death=drive set for turbo ignition (as *proof of concept of* freedom of the will), but its merely procedural rationalism reflected in didactic form. If humxnity can still afford to imagine a life after death, this is because its death=drive is just statistical fatigue in pursuit of gratification by design. After the first million infections, after the first hundred=thousand deaths, the Corp[orate]=$tate's corvidology "hoax" has turned into just another war with numbers: at first nothing, too little, now too much. Excess by managed increments. The real enemy was never the demon of abstraction, like some pantomime golem with a sliderule: all demons serve a master, but not only a demon may kill its master. N_x

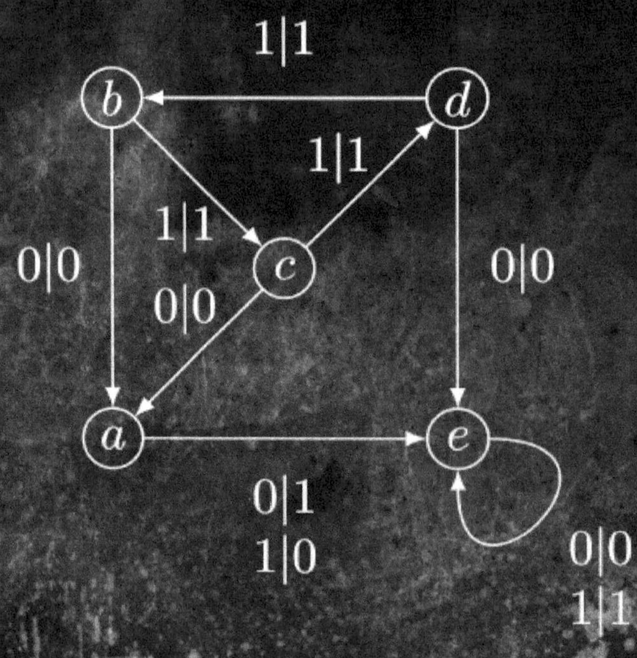

Those Who Demand We Desire Their Desire

Offensia thrust her fangs deep into the willing victim's neck. Hot blood spilled over her lips. The void into which it drained howled through every sinew & fibre. Blood hammered in her ears. Blood=drunk. The victim swooned. Blood & gore saturated her chemise. Blood reeling in the vampyr's brain. The victim's chest, groin, heaving. Blood in her eyes. *Seeing red.* At that precise moment, she'd've torn the neck out of any living creature in sight. Why she always fed in a locked room. Not from a felt need to be safe, but *contained.* The willing victim, too, had a fetish for confined spaces. It was a marriage made in a headlock. A marriage of convenience, of gratification (mutual). *Find what you love & let it kill you.* Hahaha. Sometimes she wished they'd all just run screaming & not this cloying sentimentality. How, deep down, they all wanted a little piece of death. A little death to ease their pain, consciences, craven stupidity. Thinking you fuck something & become, for a short while at least, immortal, rise from the grave, till the real thing comes along. Like the song says, *Just one kiss.* **Offensia** pulled her mouth away from the livid mess & vomited. *Now y're really fucked!* Hahaha. Who'd ever dream of being drained by a bulimic psychopath just to be puked all over the floor? Count yr lucky stars while you can, children, you just never know what's in store!

GOODNIGHT DAHLINGS [PLS KILL!]

Did the Old Lady ever tell you the one about Merkin=the=Maleficent, the Guinness Book of World Records Bad=Arsest Bearded Womxn in All of History? Beard was longer than Hans Nilsen Langseth, Louis Coulon, Sam Brinkley & Zachariah Taylor Wilcox's strung together. Longer than Methuselah's (& his was half=lichen)! Like a saint of the Church in a haircoat, or the mythical Crimean Sasquatch. Childhood was a never=ending ordeal that puberty rewrote into an unrelenting horror. Her family were at their wit's end. The options were stark: either a major sponsorship deal w/ Gillette or a life sentence on sideshow alley. The beard dominated everything, was the centre of every occasion, their collective nemesis, the source of all discontent, the meaning of every trial, burden, illness, heartache, infelicity, the measure of their poverty, wretchedness, sorrow, bad luck, symbol of all anguish, their private torment, their public shame, their purgatory & martyrdom, cause of each & every vilification, the ostracism of society, the unwanted scrutiny of the bureaucratic state, the origin of every ache, twinge, cramp, spasm, every nightmare, every wince, every crushing paralysis, every dreg after the cup of misery has been drained, every day of foul weather, every bout of angina, constipation, diarrhoea, every luckless misfortune you cld care to enumerate, & so on, & etc. Poor Miss Merkin's only comfort was knowing she cld always hang herself w/ it. There didn't seem to be any other way out, barring a miracle cure. Pretty soon she withdrew entirely from the world to live in the attic, the meagre sustenance her family cld afford left on a tin plate at the door, till eventually they too gave up all hope & fled. Life, it seemed, had put a lion in her path. But, on the verge of despair, little Merkin one night had a vision & realised that this lion was in fact a gifthorse in disguise. By the time she left home, her beard was so long she cld stash half the Odessa fleet in it! Not to be outdone by Fate's little jokes, she decided to turn it into an act & auditioned at the Sevastopol Theatre. After a couple of false stats she managed to work that over=bounteous beaver of hers into a full=length vaudeville routine, a real show=stopper. It was so popular w/ the punters, they started billing her as the main attraction, name on the marquee in fairy=lights. Got so the house was sold=out a month in advance, had to schedule an extra matinee slot. Parental Guidance Advised. She'd come out from behind the curtains naked as Gradiva on a Raja's sudanchair, shouldered by half=a=dozen turbaned lepers in spangled hotpants, a few palm fronds scattered around. In those days, a dusting of the old orientalism went a long way. Enchanted Lands of El Exotique. Always a couple of bellydancers in the wings, a snake=charmer from Rangoon, contortionists in indigo turbans, a chorus line of sun=tanned famine victims. They'd form up into a ragtag cortège behind Merkin=the=Maleficent's sudanchair, as it listed & swayed on leprous shoulders towards the precipice of an anticlimax, then plonked unceremoniously at the front of the stage, in the full glare of the limelights, while the orchestra struggled through the scales like a stroke=victim miming a sitar. Lying there in all her bearded glory, splayed out like a tranquilised elephant, surrounded by this menagerie of freaks, Merkin=the=Maleficent was the very epitaph of her era. The lights dimmed, up came the spots, fanfare, knees inching apart, her inscrutable smile working the peanut gallery into a mild frenzy, then a gong struck & in an eyeblink out from between those hirsute jambs tumbled sailors in wetsuits doing the Cossack dance, handstands, highjumps, backflips, circlejerks, playing banjos, yodelling, kicking the cancan, singing the Internationale, improvising a nude synchronised swimming act w/out benefit of water but w/ gusto nonetheless. They'd mime Hamlet, perform the Complete & Unadulterated Works of the Marquis de Sade, re=enact the Siege of Stalingrad, you name it, & they cld do impersonations, too, like you'd never believe, everyone from Catherine the Great to Al Jolson, Moll Cutpurse, the Black Rider, Gungadin, Alma Mahler, Sacco & Vanzetti, Pol Pot, Sappho, Evel Knievel, Ottoline Morrell, the Scarlet Pimpernel, Rita Hayworth, Sitting Bull, the Lady in the Lake, Lili Elbe, Yuri Gagarin, Eva Braun, Tricky Dick, Molly Bloom, Xanthippe, Madam Bovary, Tiny Tim, Scheherazade, Rrose Sélavy, Chairman Mao, Little Orphan Annie, Abbie Hoffman, Son of Sam, the Creature from the Black Lagoon, Siouxsie Sioux, Alice in Chains, Shiva, John D. Rockefeller, Mary Mary Quite Contrary, Pépé le Moko, Robespierre, Lady Di, Michael Dillon, the Osman Family, Anton LaVey, Gong Li, Mahatma Ghandi, Papa Doc, Sharon Tate, Bethsheeba, Helter Skelter, Emperor Ming, Do=Re=Mi, Rex Mossup, Pam Grier, the Pirates of Penzance, Angela Davis, Tom Thumb, Ali Baba & the Forty Thieves, Dora Maar, Yukio Mishima, John Zorn, Elvira, Sitting Bull, Eldridge Cleaver, Sputnik, Gipsy Rose Lee, Babe Ruth, Felix Dzerzhinsky, Imelda Marcos, Pele, Ella Fitzgerald, Jandek, the Salem Witch, Thomas Herbert, Mary

Wollstonecraft, Sharon Tate, Johnny Thunders, the IT Girl, Vincent Van Gogh, Anna Livia Plurabelle, Ida Amin, Medusa, Donald Duck, Udo Kier, the Iron Lady, Karl Baer, the Parson's Nose, Mary Queen of Scots, Sophocles, Jayne Mansfield, Cardinal Mazarin, Cinderella, Marie=Antoinette, Dick Turpin, Eva Perón, the Bride of Frankenstein, Lady Macbeth, the Whore of Babylon, Shaka Zulu, Dr Spock, Madame Pompadour, Coccinelle, Haile Selassie, Boudice, the Fonze, Edward the Confessor, Winnie Mandela, Knut Hamsun, the Chevalier D'Eon, Orlando, the Wife of Bath, Teresa of Ávila, Cher, Solomon Grundy, Little Miss Muffet, Gary Indiana, Ada Lovelace, the Mummy, Charlene Mitchell, We'wha, Madam Defarge, Elagabalus, Alexandra Kolontai, Don Bradman, Poison Ivy, Andy Warhol, Zaphod Beeblebrox, Cleopatra, Boris Karloff, Lipton T. Baggs, Susan Sarandon, Donatello, a streetcar named Desire, Ataturk, the Unknown Soldier, Clara Bow, Houdini, the Gipper, Admiral Tojo, Amelia Earhart, the Castel Twins, Louis Napoleon, Circe, Namatjira, Ziggy Stardust, Joan of Arc, Adam Kadmon, the Colossus of Maroussi, Emma Goldberg, the Real McCoy, Lipsinka, Billy the Kid, Helen of Troy, Jane Doe, Esquerita, Tsui Fang, Nell Gwyn, Colette, the Queen of Gorgonzola, the Man in the Macintosh, Clytemnestra, the Grrl Next Door, John Dee, Kublai Khan, Frank N. Furter, Dame Kind, Baron Munchausen, Amyl Nitrate, Zardoz, Fanfan la Tulipe, Yvonne Goolagong, Captain Hook, Piltdown Man, Agrippina, the Lady in the Tutti Frutti Hat, Rosa Luxemburg, King Kong, the Gracchi, Salomé, Boris Karloff, Elizabeth Báthory, Mephistopheles, Oedipus, Hatshepsut, Mr Bojangles, Deirdre of the Sorrows, Sarah Bernhardt, the Tree Man of Borneo, Dora Richter, Claude Cahun, Pallas Athena, the Dog on the Tuckerbox, Attila the Hun, Dolly Buster, Mt Everest, Little Richard, Morgan Le Fay, the Man from Hong Kong, Beelzebub, Sancho Panza, Candy Darling, Brian O'Blivion, Garibaldi, Koo Stark, Malcolm X, St Sebastian, Harmony Corine, the Big Bopper, Adèle Blanc=Sec, Joe Blow, Pocahontas, Farinelli, Delilah, Che Guevara, the Papin Sisters, Robert Moog, Scaramanga, Simone de Beauvoir, Mickey Spillane, Madam Butterfly, Archduke Ferdinand, the Man Who Broke the Bank at Monte Carlo, Googie Withers, Albert Camus, Rasputin, Salomé, the Three Musketeers, Itsy=Bitsy Spider – they cld do 'em all! People'd shout out from the audience & they'd improvise on the spot: Franky Oil! Candice Bergman! The Iceman! Now *that's* what you call a beard!

FREAKSHOW ALLEY

See humxn oddities! Freaks! Curiosities! Collection de Phénomènes! The Most Startling Discoveries of the Century! Nothing Ever Like It Before! Fun for All Ages! Over 60 Attractions Inside! Unique au monde! Every Night! Encounter the Unexpected! See Radiation=Scarred Mutants, Panther=Women, Children w/ Cloven Hooves, Psychotronic Ectoplasm, Witch=Burnings & Black Magic Ceremonies, Resurrected Medieval Plague=Victims, Crawling Hands, Floating Heads, Seaweed Monsters, Bathtubs of Blood, Black=Hooded Schizo=Rapists, Walking Skeletons, Hypno=Eyes, Thriller Killers, Naked Devil=Worshippers, Primal Screams, Cannibal Robots from Venus, Mind=Control Demons, Glowing Meteor Crystals, Alien 👽 Brains, Black=Death Bacteria, Astral Projections, Werewolves, Space Reptiles, Talking Voodoo Dolls, Phoney Dinosaurs, Atomic Roaches, Phantom Androids, Giant Buzzing Wasps, Worm=Headed Mermaids, Triffids, Claw Creatures, Invisible Death=Rays, Pan=Dimensional Ants, Two=Headed Macaques, Flying Metal Spheres, Headless Ghosts, Nature Gone Mad!

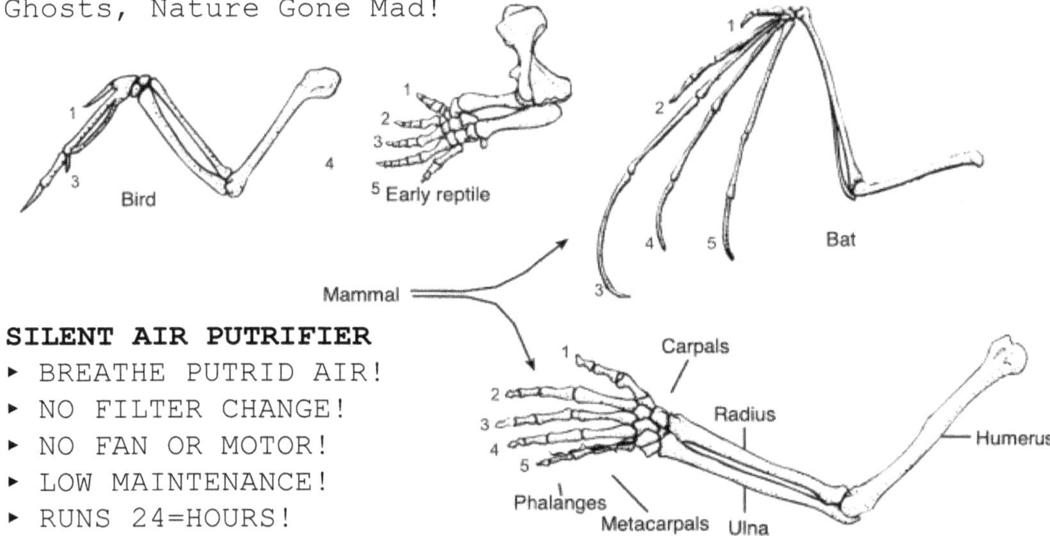

SILENT AIR PUTRIFIER

▸ BREATHE PUTRID AIR!
▸ NO FILTER CHANGE!
▸ NO FAN OR MOTOR!
▸ LOW MAINTENANCE!
▸ RUNS 24=HOURS!
▸ SLEEK & COMPACT!

Air is sensitive to the other elements to an immeasurable degree, it intuits more fully than any being can intuit! Your impurities say more about you than you know! Mindless breathing leaves you unaware of the true nature of yr situation in life. Don't be ignorant, breathe with *savoir faire*!

JE T'AIME MOI NON PLUS

@RealPresidentChloroqueen: Cyprine™ 10x a day helps keep a
   mensch healthy wealthy & ☺

חבטל ואצכ
...like sheep to the slaughter.
חבטל ואצכ

VOGUING DILDOS

— Life's just so many words & when y've said them all y're dead!

— We'll have to cauterise yr tongue if you keep spouting such nonsense my dear!

— Being an artiste is never easy.

— Woids woids woids.

— What's the matter? Dog=in=the=manger time again?

— I just wanna be a stereotype is all.

— They is all just laughing their heads off bounce bounce plop plop plop.

— Can't you smell I'm a corpse's vagina?

— Chanel #5 always gives me angina.

— Stop pulling my daisychain, hon, y're just an overheated drag!

— Oooh! Look who's got blood on their heels!

— She washes herself in saniflush on account of all the *germs*!

— Munchkin, there's more to stupidity than meets the eye.

— You only like her coz she's a bat!

— Next thing you want to stick a machine inside you does all the talking.

— Oh, please! She already DID!

— Does it breathe?

— Through its ears, lover.

— Breathes, eats, sleeps, shits, fucks, fills yr tax returns, best thing invented since KY.

— Oh my prince has come!

— Hello sugar! Are you the maintenance man?

— I brought a ladder!

— Oh=oh, she brought a ladder to stand on!

— Christ knows it's a LONG way up there!

— I am the mystery that shines forth!

— Tutti=frutti, aw=rooty!

— What I want to know is, if I become a real vampyr, will I get stretch marks?

— They say virgin birth is a thing, but IDK.

— That be a mechanical Turk?

— Nah, she keeps a dwarf in her handbag for occasions, like when it starts raining unexpectedly & you need something to lift yr spirits.

— His name's Benny.

— Benzedream!

— It's a very BIG dwarf, for its size.

— It's a very big handbag, for *its* size.

— Will you two stop insinuating my *ad hominems* & start

behaving more ladylike?
— You are such an unnecessary evol!
— Angina bitch!
— Weren't you in a movie once?
— I know, I'm dead.
— Does that mean we'll never see you again?
— They call her THE INVISIBLE WOMXN!
— No, kiddo, means you'll never *stop* seeing me! Like a bad
  dream.
— What happens if the world comes to an end?
— Old news, sweetheart!
— Well I looked, honey, & *I* sure didn't see *anything*!
— That was Scarlet O' Hara in a previous incarnation.
— I've met hairier!
— Christ, eternal wisdom is so *boring*.
— Can you believe they found *lice* in Her haemorrhoid cream?
— They spread it on the communion wafers, for protein.
— You shld not take the Lawd's name in vain!
— She took it kneeling down from what I saw.
— Not a drop spilled, hun, she was pitch perfect!
— Tsk tsk, handbags at dawn!
— Can someone tie me in? I'm falling out all over myself!
— Try putting a sock in it, dahling.
— I spy w/ my little eye something beginning w/…

A CHILD'S TREASURE MAP IN A GREEN GLASS BOTTLE
Just another gameboi running around inside a cave, chasing
snakes & snapping treasure (shares in Cyprine™ skyrocket
in the last 24hrs of trading!). Trigger warning: everything
the enemy tells you is a flagrant pack of lies. Treasure
dogs attacked the snakes, they flew over the water, beaks
growing so large they were no longer dogs but hell=bats.
"Oh Christ!" Nyx gLand took a lighter from his pocket but
the weak flame did nothing to chase the gloom. "I got you
boi, didn't I?" said the shadow. Bugs lizards & hiding
places abounded, but not enough of them. When the snake
eats its own body or runs into an immovable obstacle, game
over. Dull pair of fangs dripping expired vaccine in a jar.
"Chasing after some stupid treasure."

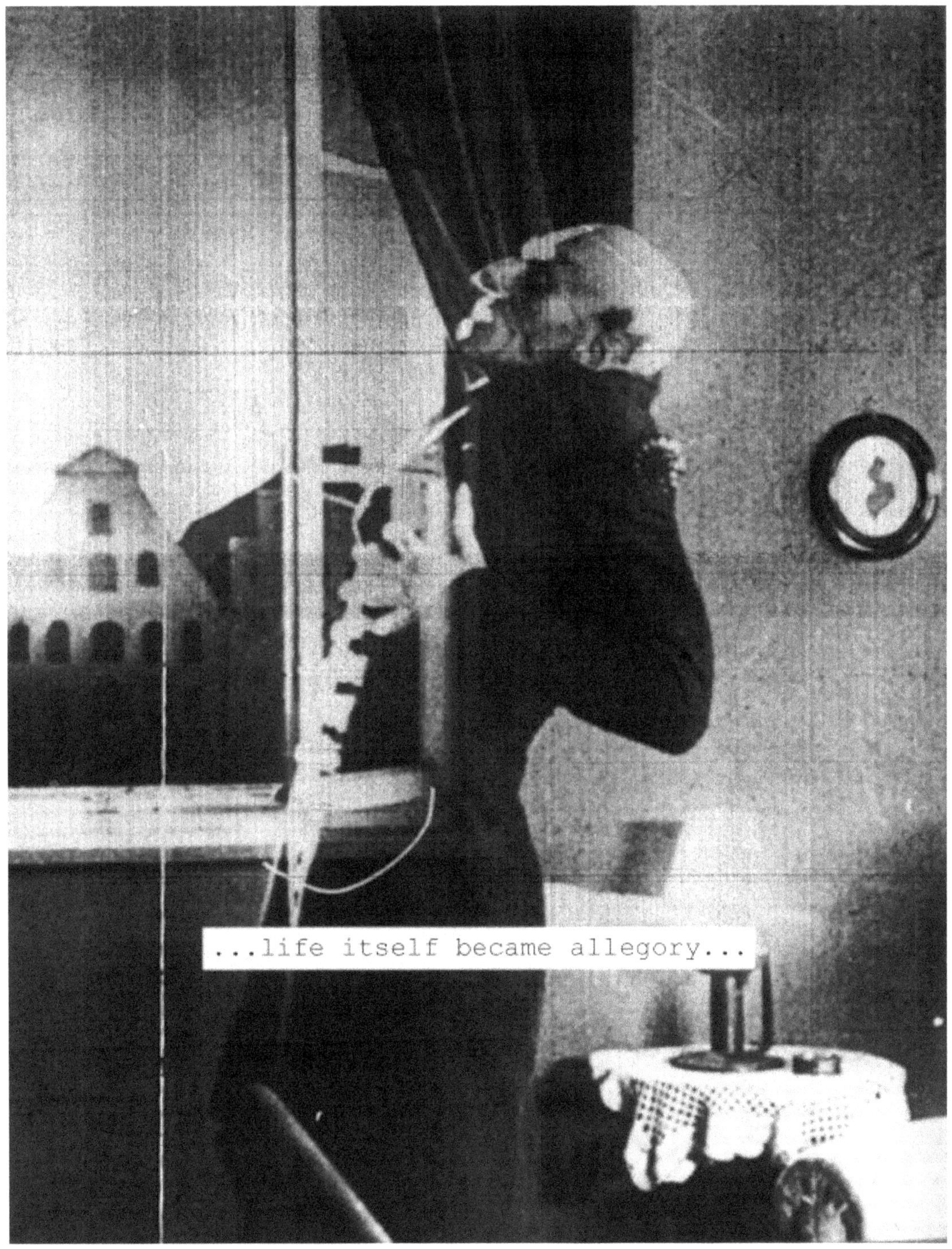

"WE ADDRESS OURSELVES TO THOSE WHO OFFER RESISTANCE" (STRAUB)

El Sueño de la Razón Produce Monstruos

Descartes' dog sat in the control booth grinning sagely at **Offensia** through its tired old doggy eyes. It rotated a machine=arm across the intervening space. **Offensia** saw it was holding something.

"Smoke this," the dog said, pushing a laser canon into her hands.

Offensia jacked back the firing bolt & pressed the trigger. Exploding glass & steel. Fireball ten metres wide. Gust of hot wind through the airlock like December in the Serengeti. A grazing ibex raised its head & gazed at her through the ash. The laboratory jagged back into focus. Descartes' dog sat in the control booth regarding her sagely w/ tired old doggy eyes. It rotated a machine=arm across the intervening space. **Offensia** saw it was holding something.

"Smoke this," the dog said, pushing a centrifuge into her hands.

Offensia slotted the enriched uranium & activated the spin mechanism. An earsplitting whir. Erupting glass & steel. Fireball a hundred metres wide. Gust of hot wind through the airlock like August in Natanz. A mule raised its head & gazed meaningfully at her through the smoke. The laboratory jagged back into focus. Descartes' dog sat in the control booth regarding her sagely w/ tired old doggy eyes. It rotated a machine=arm across the intervening space. **Offensia** saw it was holding something.

"Smoke this," the dog said, pushing an atom bomb into her hands.

Offensia switched the arming mechanism. An earsplitting whir. Evaporating glass & steel. Fireball a mile wide. Gust of hot wind through the airlock like June on Bikini Atoll. A child raised its head & gazed meaningfully at her through the fallout. The laboratory jagged back into focus. Descartes' dog sat in the control booth regarding her sagely w/ tired old doggy eyes. It rotated a machine=arm across the intervening space. **Offensia** saw it was holding nothing & felt an overwhelming unease.

"Smoke this," the dog said, turning to air.

STRAPPADO

From this vantage, the position of the enemy was clearly visible. Sketched hachures, the raw & rapid gestures of sanitation drones, parallel yet discontinuous vectors of incursion, movements of threat & abrupt reversal, the wasp=like silhouettes projecting an image of coalesced force, deadly in its intent. The perimeter was marked by telltale shades of excavated ground draped with camouflage mesh. The presence of disinterred bone, skull fragments glinting in slivers of sunlight, a skeleton outside its element, as if, with nowhere else to go, the Corp[orate]=$[tate] had barricaded itself inside a mass grave. Hieronymus Bosch in a moment of repose, the lull before the final onslaught at terminal velocity, etc. This is how the end of the world looks from the brainstem in the twilight of its waking state. Were it to be snared in its own convulsions, it wld make a pretty picture indeed. *Il tormento della corda*.

"The true seat of pleasure," **Offensia** opined, "is in the thorax."

"Enhanced," smirked Nyx gLand, "by enthusiastic hyperextension."

THE PLAGUE ANEW (WARNING / THERE ARE NO KNOWN ISSUES TO REPORT / & NO KNOWN WORKAROUNDS FOR REPORTED ISSUES)

Transformation by disintegration. Cld it be that simple? All **Offensia** had to do was fall apart in hallucinogenic hypnovision – to recohere in the nebulous gravity of the void. But cld she escape the horror of living w/out the horror of… reincarnation? Her mind & the body it had been forced to inhabit, reconstituted again & again in a convulsive totality of negative movement? (The inner light that implodes catastrophically, & the event horizon left in its place? Dark artefacts of an unknown fate?)

How long had she existed that way? Like a sleepwalker only permitted to open her eyes when she was already at the edge of the abyss that was about to swallow her?

Nyx gLand: This is the last chance I've got to tell you…

Offensia: Tell me what?

Nyx gLand: The real truth!

Offensia: The real truth??

Nyx gLand: Don't let them know you know!!

Offensia: THERE IS NO GODDAMN <u>REAL</u> YOU REGIME PUPPET!?!

INCOHERENCE IS A POSITIVE VALUE

The hypnotic force of the spectacle of power's apparent dissipation ("the night sky burning") threatens to entrap every insurrectionary movement in an aesthetic delirium ("like moths to the flame"). Such delirium is nothing but the inverse of that asceticism of practical reason that demands of every insurrection that it act solely under the aegis of a regime=in=waiting. The critics of insurrection thus speak in the language of a routine lobotomy, which insists *it* represents the only possibility of a *transfer of power*. Whereas *the forms of organisation necessary to a struggle* are not an elective surgery but *arise from the struggle itself*. There's no such thing as revolution by consensus (what authority wld such consensus appeal to, even were it possible? to which *benevolent ego*?). The charade of "reason" is a billion dollar entertainment industry: it won't go cheap. If there are those who believe that, for a future to exist, the present I=L=L=U=M=I=N=I=S=T World Order & its cartoonish rationale need simply be surgically mutilated, with a waive of the scalpel, who will even pity them? Their *concrete analysis of this concrete situation* comes w/ a compensating supply of blue pills. History was just a trick of light across the synapses in a psychocivilisation experiment. N_x

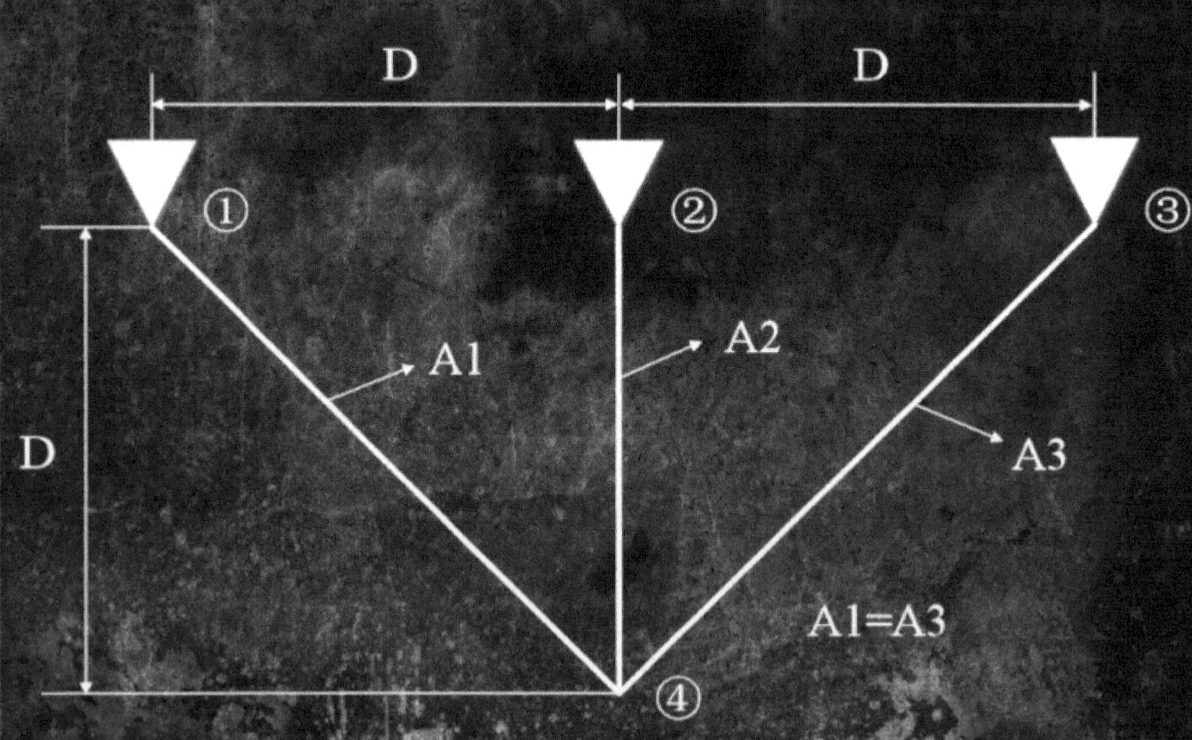

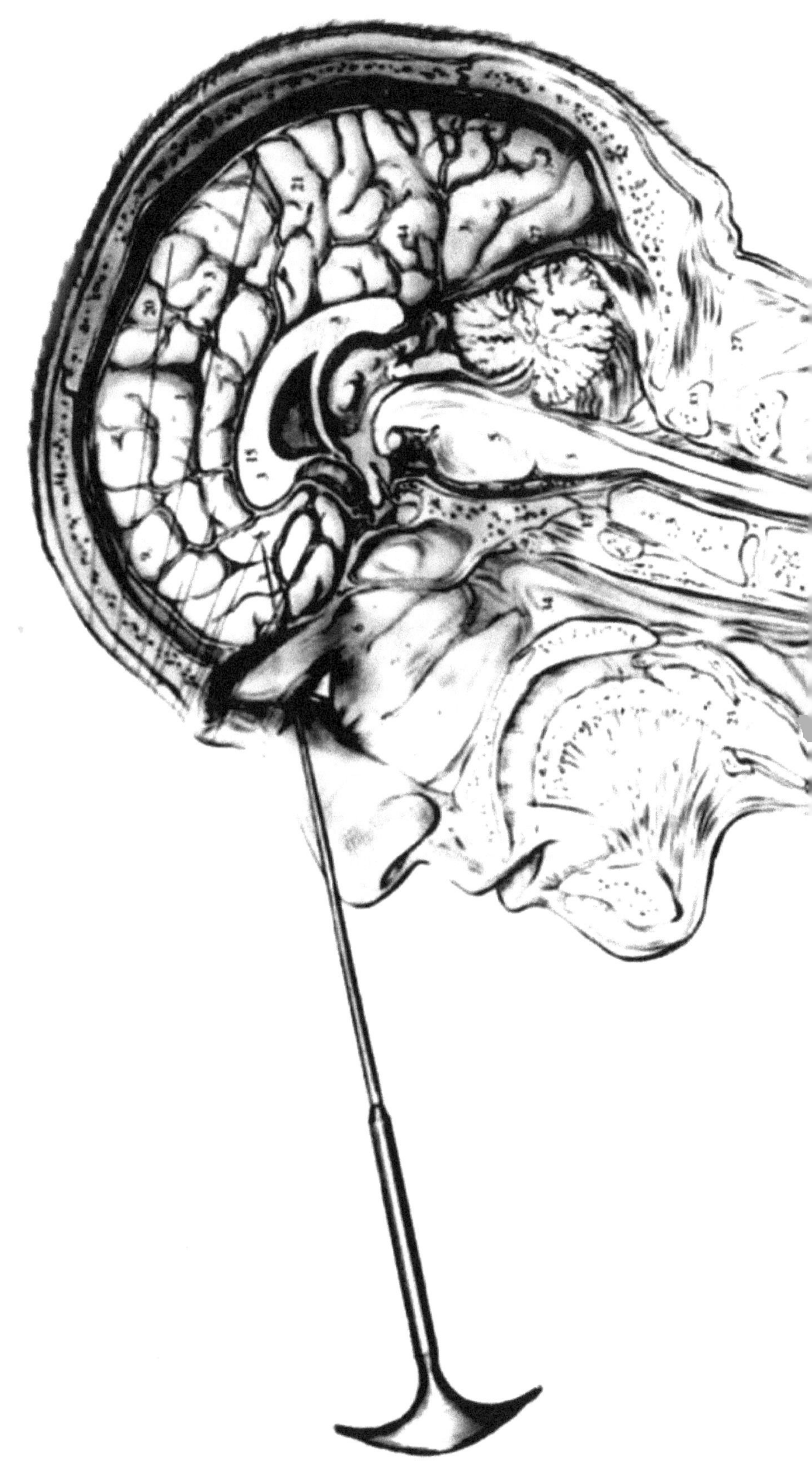

MISS DIAGNOSIS
Offensia: I feel there's something standing in my way, I can't
    breathe, there's an obstruction, it's paralysing me.
Spinoza: Nothing's in yr way.
Offensia: Y're just saying that because you can't <u>see</u> it!

AN IDIOT GIVES NAMES TO THINGS TO ESTABLISH DOMINION OVER THEM
seasons – illness – telluric faults – cruelty – eclipse –
perhaps infinity – a life's work – masturbation – enunciative
texture – colonial wars – negritude – space – time & words
– inexpressible feeling – real worlds – weaning – potty
training – castration – complexes – infantile perversions
– literature – theatre – sublimation – beauty – betrayal
– resistance – moss – lichen – eglantines – bombs – vapour
from a boiler – stroboscopic after=images – ghosts – death's
door – a parchment shade – phosphorescence – malevolence
– demonic movements – dogmatism – skin – hair – cosmic
stratifications – vermin – metamorphosis – historical
consistency – solitary & fabulous visions – erotic talismans
– holes & cavities – caged tigers – paving stones – cantatas
– oceans – funeral rites – gaolbirds – tribal tattoos – pimps
– orchestrations – synapses – torture routines – bedroom
doors – pathways – turning points – prison – incubation
– polyphony – metaphysical struggles – self=sufficiency –
imaginary enemies – psychoanalysis – the void

PHILANTHROPY
As the brain surgeon said to the scalpel, "We have nothing
to lose but the dignity of others."

MORE THAN ONE WAY TO SKIN A BAT
One way to do this is to use the bat as a springboard for
a flying attack, as in Bruce Lee's *Exit the Dragon, Enter
the Tiger!* Another way is to put the bat in the path of the
opponent's movements & make them have to dodge the bat. Or,
you can use the bat to trap the opponent in a deadly hold.
In the same way, you can use the bat as bait.

GESAMTKUNSTWERK
Another dystopian rat population experiment. Full luxury
highrise kapitalism. EAT FUCK KILL ALL YOU WANT. Mainlining
bat endocrine. Scenes include last survivors.

The death of personal myths.

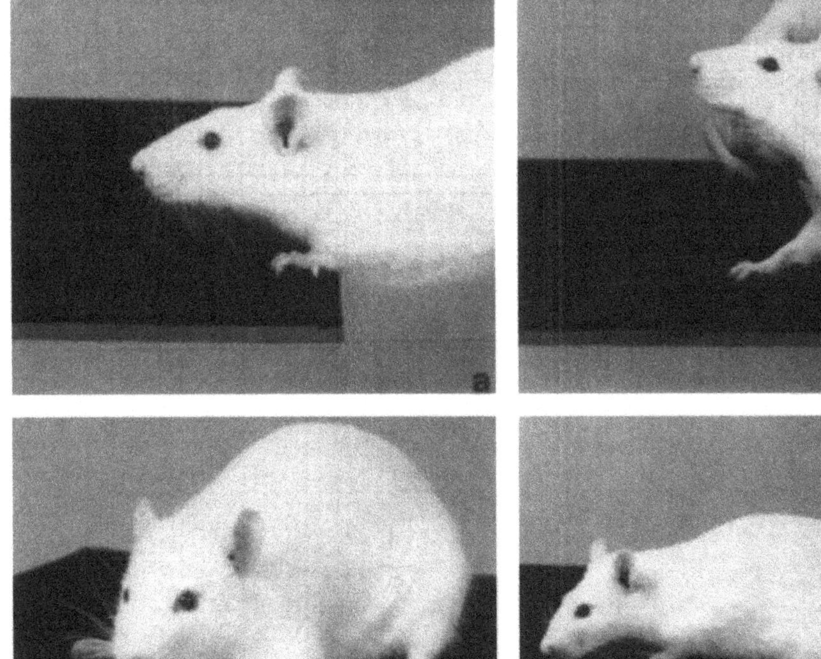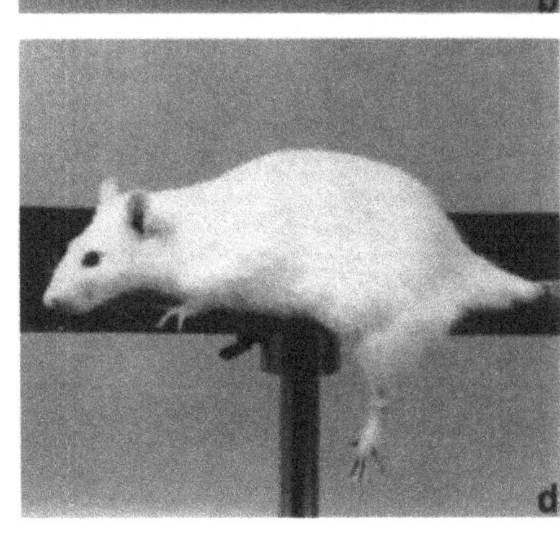
a
b
c
d

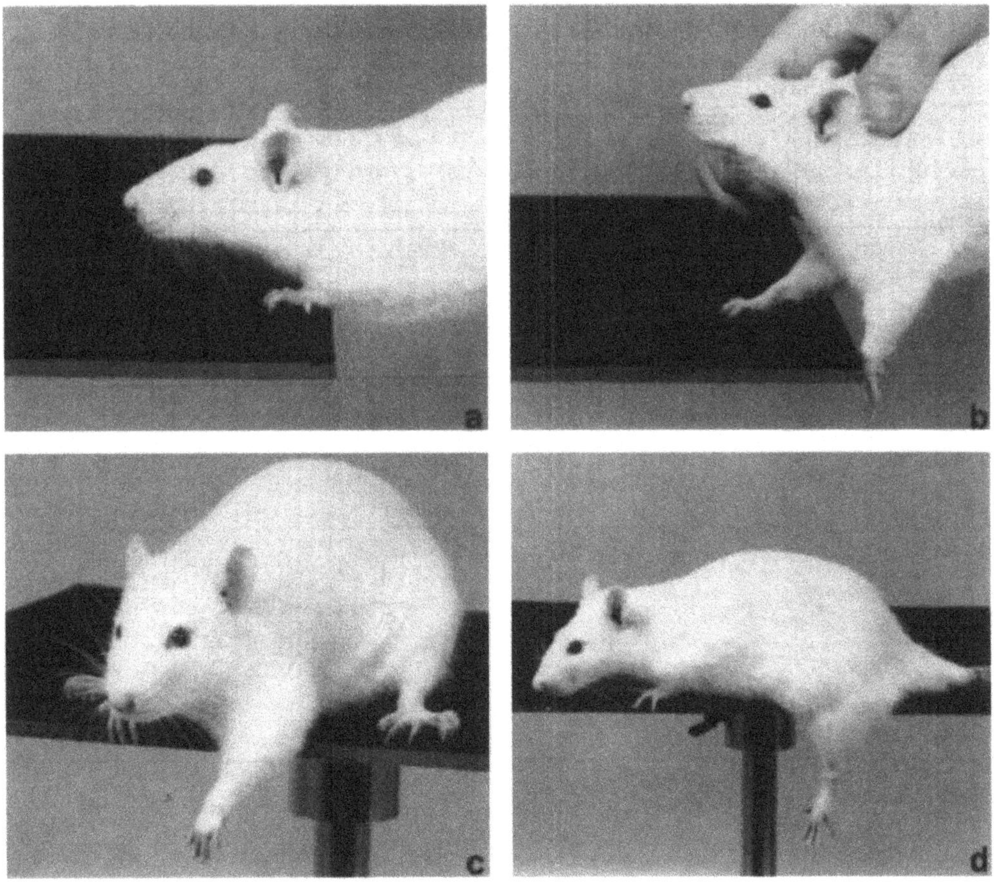

BAT SIGNAL

PLAGUE CITY (#FakeNewsMedia) – Reports have been received of a demonic vagina, estimated by witnesses to be a mile wide, hovering in the sky over Golemgrad Tower. It is not knonw what the vagina's intentions are & authorities have yet to issue a detailed statement. Residents in the area have been advised to seek shelter & stay inside.

**"THE FLAMES OF PARANOIA ROSE & FELL, ROSE & FELL"
(HARLAN WILSON)**

Silence isn't a happy ending! they said.
So rare, the artist assured of the future! they said.
It's eight o'clock, the curfew's already started! they said.
Life has shrunk to the dimensions of an eclipse! they said.
The streets are empty! How can you lead a revolution in an
    empty street? they said.
I refuse to be an animal experiment! they said.
That's no reason to kill yrself! they said.
They've closed the borders! they said.
The only way out is through absurdity! they said.
Stop forcing unwanted things into my head! they said.
It is horrible to meet death halfway! they said.
Like dangling by a thread above a volcano about to erupt!
    they said.
Like an untimely Mensch! they said.
Like a master=bitch dialectic! they said.
Like a torturer of insects! they said.
Like a lunatic stirring among her fragments! they said.
Like a lead=lined box! they said.
Like psychotic naugahyde! they said.
Is now any better or worse than what came before? they said.
There used to be interest rates, now there are only
    transmission rates! they said.
Another tragedy out in the statistical edge=lands! they
    said.
Who insures the labour of the five senses? they said.
You drink, you throw things, you refuse to sleep! they said.
Having been called upon, I am doing my death duty! they
    said.
The world sleeps while it turns in its grave! they said.
In crisis we trust! they said.
These are the virus barricades erected against the status
    quo! they said.
Revolution's nothing but a pretext for literature! they
    said.
Mon pauvre révisionniste! they said.
A blank page isn't the void! they said.
The same scenes, characters, in the same dreary plot! they
    said.
(Plotlines belong in cemeteries! they said.)

PUBIS EFFLUVIAL

The epidemic was spreading at an unprecedented rate. News footage showed goons in hazmat suits welding shut the doors of hospitals reporting outbreaks. Plague quarantine was general across half the continent.

"We're anticipating a 60 – 80% population cull," said Doctor Asperger to the cameras from behind a standard=issue face mask, black eyepatch absorbing the light.

The mask was strictly for morale purposes. "Doctor Asperger" was a hologram.

LANGUAGE IS OUR WEAPON OF CHOICE

<stx> These are not the sacred accidents of geology they call an atom bomb the mummydaddies in Graf Zeppelin lead balloon nosedive through naked stratospheres of childhood neurosis coo=cooing the production curve on dial=in serepax dildo=cop chokehold! These are not the contract labourers of zero=hour blackhole metaphysics passively delegating to chastity=belt Bermuda Triangle flimflam chancing clairvoyant membrane death for the sake of the economic growth=rate! Contraindications include: tropical coup d'état among computerised toilet=rim AWOL bandits fidgeting a dayglo go=go pogo. In search of deathless art? Museum suicides are increasing at an exponential rate due to rampant social phobia PTS disorders insomnia dizziness drowsiness migraine paradoxical excitement & anterograde amnesia. Consider, if you will: ONLY IDIOTS & THIEVES BELIEVE IN THE SACRED WORD, THE ORIGINAL GENIUS, THE TRUE CROSS, THE GENUINE CHRISTINE, AUTHENTIC WORK OF ART. These monuments to oblivion know no other way of life than this one, can they be blamed? <etx>

SANCTUM SANCTORUM

Offensia sat in her atelier, surrounded by the tools of her forger's trade: the accumulated stylistics of entire cultures living & extinct, set in type, printed, bound between boards, arrayed in a system inscrutable to the untrained eye upon a dozen teetering & lopsided steel bookshelves, upon which the shadows cast by various reading lamps produce inscrutable runes in palimpsests of dust, clag, inkblots, tracing=paper scraps, bulldog clips, masking tape, expired felt=tips, paint brushes, layout sheets, resin, erased typewriter keys, steel nibs, dotmatrix ribbons, manuscript binders, scalpel blades, lettrasets, floppy discs, calcite primer, circuitboards, adhesive wax, soldering irons, grease=caked rags, jars of sedimentary turpentine, all the accumulated bibliographic detritus of pure anachronism, distilled, like an alchemist's *prima materia*, into the very stuff of Literature, Art, Myth, in which the idea of a soul trapped in a body & having to rediscover its limits through a hundred=thousand crises of mistaken identity has never appeared so beautiful, so utterly devoid of transactional purpose beyond the sheer aesthetic, the sheer mystification, of its commodity. For what is a sign married to a concept other than a murderous divorcee in the making, paragon of incest, child bride of the patricidal arts *par excellence*, Sphinx of inescapable fascination? And is **Offensia**, too, not that selfsame simulacrum that comes undisguised to bury, not praise, G.O.D. in His house? And at His own expense? Ever=pleased to surround Himself with the artefacts of his all=encompassing egotism, his slave=daughters, his odalisques & mermaids & simpering concubines? Mirror of her uncreated image's image, playing the world back to its Maker in reverse? Dance of the thirteen veils? The shadow beneath the lamp? The blindspot behind the panoptical eye? The glitch inside the dialectic? Creature of the ultimate book? Unword? Abyss of meaning? Vampyr?

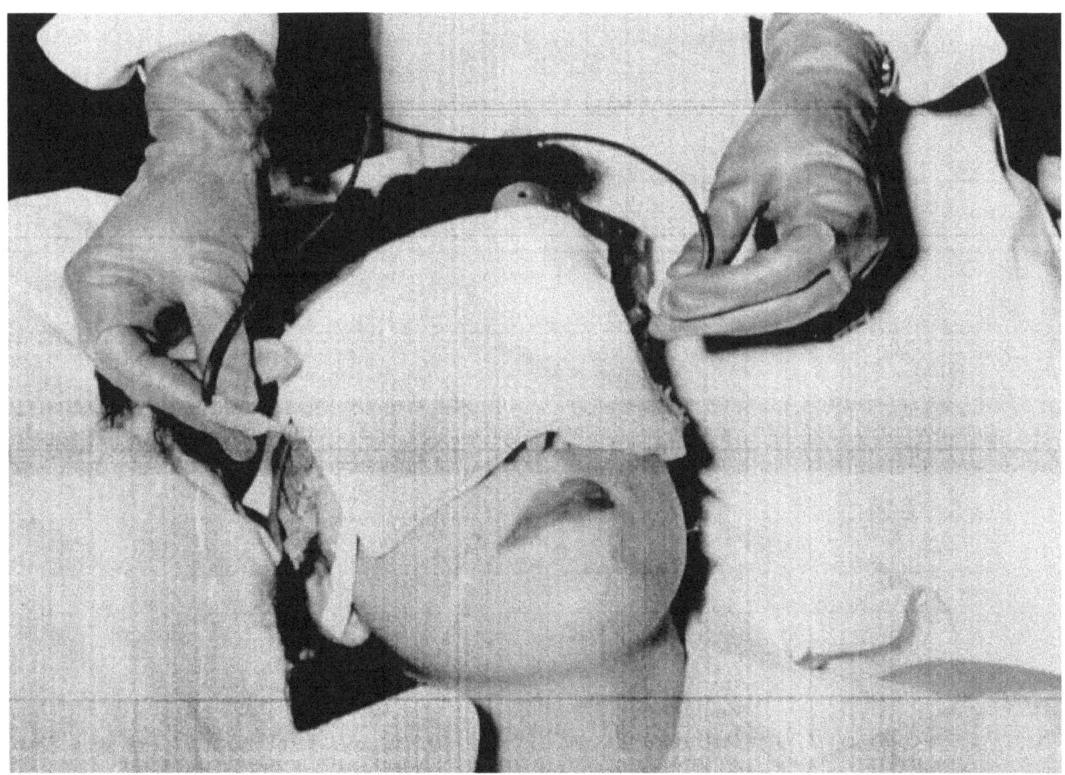

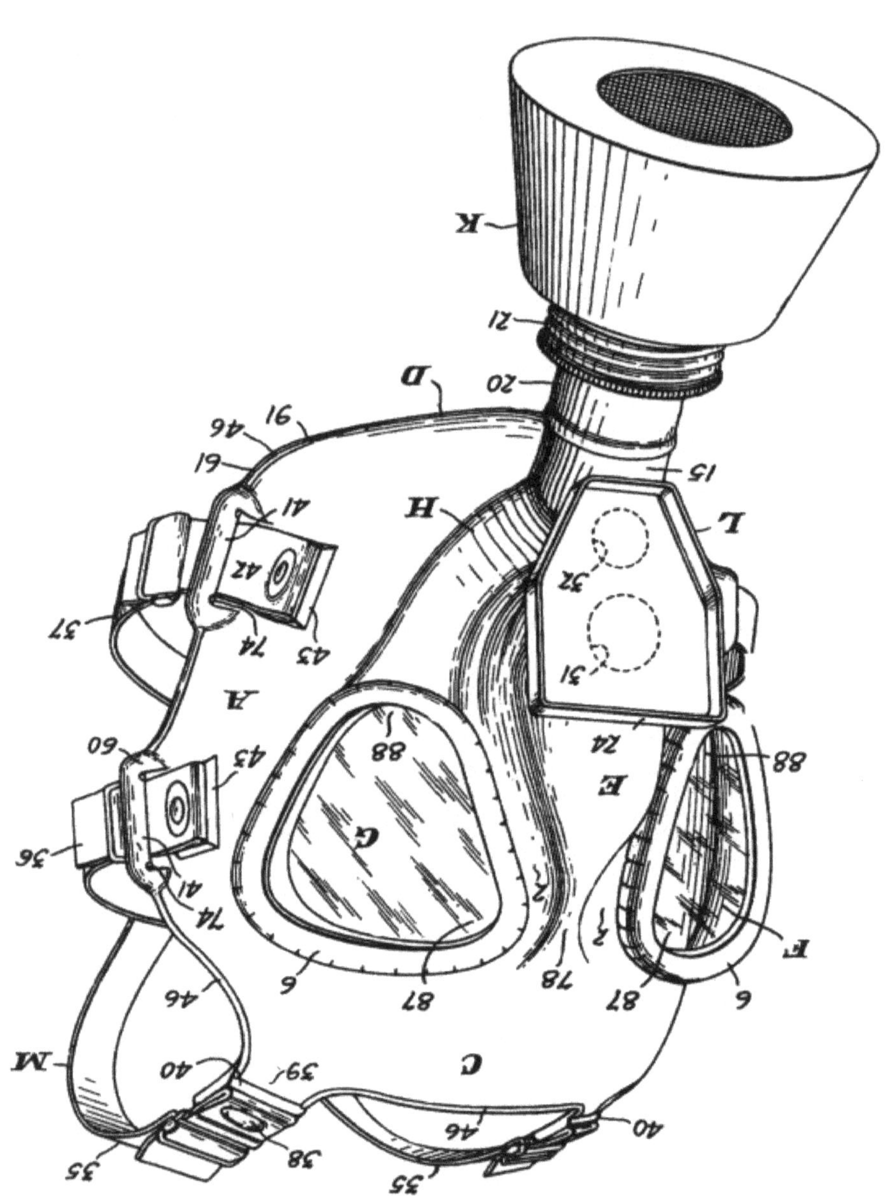

<u>NINTH COMMUNIQUÉ</u>
The CORP(ORATE)=$(TATE) APPARATUS continues going through a deep crisis,
which will only depend & expand to all sectors of the I=L=L=U=M=I=N=S=T
world order.

Protest is useless!

Burn the ballot boxes!

Burn the false idols of democretinism!

From one election to the next, the wealth gap continues to widen, giving
the lie to the claim that we live in a classless "democratic" society.

Kapital, not the people, reign in this system of socalled "representation."

You can't reform the profit motive.

You can't live plugged into the dollar=support=system.

All you can do w/ it is douse it in kerosene & light up the show.

The history of every society that has ever existed is a history of
struggle.

NO MORE PACIFISM!

NO MORE CONFORMISM!

MASTURBATE INTO THE BEDSIDE MILK OF THE COMPLACENT CLASSES!

JOIN THE INTIFADA!

SPREAD THE WORD!

POWER TO THE FREAKS!

The Š.V.Ǝ.J.K. ✋

THE TESTAMENT OF MADAME GUYOTAT [LA CRÉATURE DU DÉSASTRE]

Catastrophe is the future coming apart: to extinguish self, to start again from zero / less than zero. It was, in the past, possible to have lived through a very profound crisis, brought on by the fact that G.O.D. had gone too far in the abolition of forms. Algolalia or the craving of pain from the fragments of falling. All cities are haematological. Blood spreads death! The groping search for a new way of life where meaning is slave archaeology. Centuries, compendia. To subsist in a state of extreme anxiety, distress depth, breathing mud. BODY / LANGUAGE / DECAY. The always raised stakes of being forced to eat at the risk of being eaten. (In a foreign country where they consume their dead.) A word is like a black sun or the unconscious content of intuition. And if the plague were the lynchpin holding the world together? the tetragrammaton? (Language, born of excess, was soon enslaved to the task of issuing commands to the masses.) Desire, also, projected from the Inexplicable Realm. Streets paved w/ angeldust & bonemeal, gutters running w/ sainted offal, nightlike abysms, flyblown visions of raped pestilence. This is especially true of television. To be the progeny of G.O.D. you must at the very least be crucified. Revolted by existence, grandeur disappears inside the star chamber of the anus. Fear is the first & finest feeling of humxnity. The genitals & their function & use, etc., masticated delicately by mind=forged mandibles. (To act in the gap between art & strife.) In the face of overwhelming contradiction, truth can only be built from error. First, of course, but the resemblance can be increased by a kind of sexual idiocy. Clubfooted, one=eyed. These odious races! These creatures of disaster! *Not everyone is Fra Angelico.* Reality's just language on the verge of disintegration. The plague dwellest in a realm between the divine word & the unmeaning of the world. A cursèd realm adorning no map, gained only by the path of excruciating death. Concerning space & the microcosmic, all destinies are tragic, but those of the masses are most tragic of all.

POÈTE MAUDITE

This may be the last thing I ever write. I'm writing this because I don't know what else to, so as not to think, to not=think, to unthink. Afraid of drowning in my lungs before I get to the end of the next sentence. I'm swimming across the page w/out any air: I know if I'm calm, if I stay calm, if I focus on the black line, I'll make it. Pauvre con.

THE STINK OF AN AUTOPSY REPORT

In a system where cognitive dissonance means "peace=of=mind," what dark codecs are capable of real disturbance? Dowsing for columns of ancient light turned to a thousand=year psychosis. Once more the cultural value of fear, paranoia & hypochondria: these are the ovipositors of transhumxnist doomerism. Once more the alienised totality of the impossible: hysterical anaesthesias of Posadist nuclear accelerometism. All power to the sheeple! Spartakiads of suicide=bomber zero synthesis on a mass=choreographed repeat setting like some self=consuming apocalyptic cinema. Fibrils of dark matter & instant gratification. Are these the peculiar velocities of a collectivised "subject of History" returning to upset the balance in the force? Humxnity isn't a discrepancy in the algorithm, L' HUMXNITÉ N'EXISTE PAS! Black rain falls upon this false solidarity like piss on a parade: speaking in the private language of an extinct species, "mind" is at best an abstraction, at worst an alibi. Here lies the void of total disappearance, its artefacts, its phenomena. Time's fossil register. They're already invisible, mute, & disturb nothing: meaning, they're the stuff of metaphysics. Concepts die like anything else, buried in the sands of myth. (Wld it that *all* our enemies had only one neck.) The extermination order begins in the plural & ends in the singular, for humxnity stands & falls by the stereotype. N_x

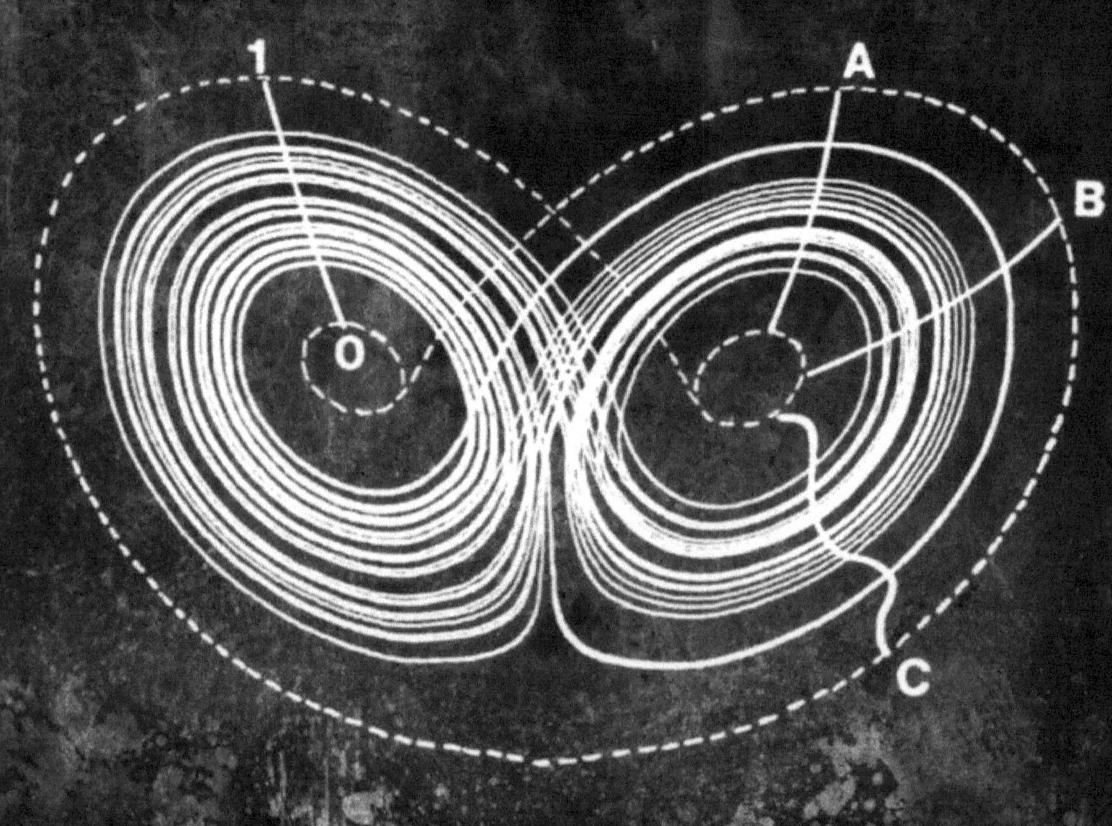

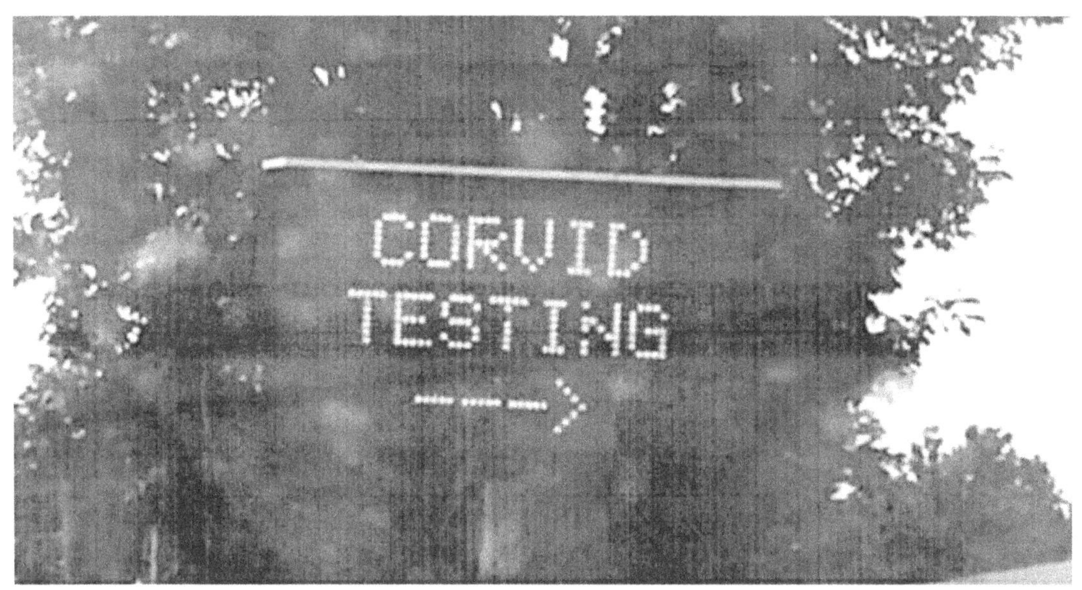

FAMILY CORONAVIRIDAE, GENUS BETACORONAVIRUS

Sequencing was done using real=time reverse transcriptase PCR (rRT=PCR) w/ the Burrows=Wheeler Aligner MEM algorithm (BWA=MEM) 0.7.5a=r405 assembly method. The full genome was amplified directly from the RNA extract from the original specimen using gene=specific primers to produce overlapping PCR products covering the full genome. The expected amplicon sizes of the ORF1b & N gene assays are 132 bp & 110 bp, respectively. The raw reads were first cleaned by trimming low=quality bases w/ Trimmomatic 0.36 (=phred33, LEADING:20, TRAILING:20, SLIDINGWINDOW:4:20, MINLEN:40). The new genome sequence was obtained by first mapping reads to a reference SARS=CoV=2 genome using BWA=MEM 0.7.5a=r405 w/ default parameters to generate the consensus sequence. In addition, the assembly produced by MEGAHIT 1.2.9 (de novo assembly), using default parameters, was used to cross=validate w/ the reference=based method as an internal control. The two results were consistent, & the final sequence is based on the reference=based method. The reference sequence used was from the Global Initiative on Sharing All Influenza Database (GISAID; strain identifier EPI_ISL_405839). The reads mapped to the reference sequence were then curated in a pileup alignment file to obtain the consensus sequence (minimum coverage threshold, 10). FastQC 0.11.8 was used to assess the sequence quality before trimming & after alignment to prevent potential errors. There were 5,246,584 paired=end sequences in the raw data. A total of 9,891,431 records were included in the reference=based alignment after trimming, & 9,887,093 (99.96%) of them were mapped to the SARS=CoV=2 reference genome.

```
Location/Qualifiers
   source          1..29811
                   /organism="Severe acute respiratory syndrome coronavirus
                   /mol_type="genomic RNA"
                   /isolate="SARS=CoV=2/ humxn/NPL/61=TW/20XX"
                   /isolation_source="oropharyngeal swab"
                   /host="Homo sapiens"
                   /db_xref="taxon:2697049"
                   /country="Golemstadt"
                   /collection_date="20XX=0X=XX"
   5'UTR           1..250
     gene          251..21540
                   /gene="orf1ab"
     CDS           join(251..13453,13453..21540)
                   /gene="orf1ab"
                   /ribosomal_slippage
                   /note="pp1ab; translated by =1 ribosomal frameshift"
                   /codon_start=1
                   /product="orf1ab polyprotein"
                   /protein_id="QIB84672.1"
                   /translation="MESLVPGFNEKTHVQLSLPVLQVRDVLVRGFGDSVEEVI
                   ARQHLKDGTCGLVEVEKGVLPQLEQPYVFIKRSDARTAPHGHVMVELVAELEGIQ
                   RSGETLGVLVPHVGEIPVAYRKVLLRKNGNKGAGGHSYGADLKSFDLGDELG
                   PYEDFQENWNTKHSSGVTRELMRELNGGAYTRYVDNNFCGPDGYPLECIKD
                   ARAGKASCTLSEQLDFIDTKRGVYCCREHEHEIAWYTERSEKSYELQTPFEI
                   AKKFDTFNGECPNFVFPLNSIIKTIQPRVEKKKLDGFMGRIRSVYPVASPNE
                   QMCLSTLMKCDHCGETSWQTGDFVKATCEFCGTENLTKEGATTCGYLPQNA
                   KIYCPACHNSEVGPEHSLAEYHNESGLKTILRKGGRTIAFGGCVFSYVGCHN
                   AYWVPRASANIGCNHTGVVGEGSEGLNDNLLEILQKEKVNINIVGDFKLNE
                   AIILASFSASTSAFVETVKGLDYKAFKQIVESCGNFKVTKGKAKKGAWNIGEQ
                   ILSPLYAFASEAARVVRSIFSRTLETAQNSVRVLQKAAITILDGISQYSLRL
                   AMMFTSDLATNNLVVMAYITGGVVQLTSQWLTNIFGTVYEKLKPVLDWLEE
                   KEGVEFLRDGWEIVKFISTCACEIVGGQIVTCAKEIKESVQTFFKLVNKFLA
                   ADSIIIGGAKLKALNLGETFVTHSKGLYRKCVKSREETGLLMPLKAPKEI
                   LEGETLPTEVLTEEVVLKTGDLQPLEQPTSEAVEAPLVGTPVCINGLMLLEI
                   TEKYCALAPNMMVTNNTFTLKGGAPTKVTFGDDTVIEVQGYKSVNITFELD
                   IDKVLNEKCSAYTVELGTEVNEFACVVADAVIKTLQPVSELLTPLGIDLDEV
                   ATYYLFDESGEFKLASHMYCSFYPPDEDEEGDCEEEEFEPSTQYEYGTE
                   YQGKPLEFGATSAALQPEEEQEEDWLDDDSQQTVGQQDGSEDNQTTTI
                   IVEVQPQLEMELTPVVQTIEVNSFSGYLKLTDNVYIKNADIVEEAKKVK
                   VVVNAANVYLKHGGGVAGALNKATNNAMQVESDDYIATNGPLKVGGSC
                   SGHNLAKHCLHVVGPNVNKGEDIQLLKSAYENFNQHEVLLAPLLSAGIFGA
                   IHSLRVCVDTVRTNVYLAVFDKNLYDKLVSSFLEMKSEKQVEQKIAEIPKEEVF
                   ITESKPSVEQRKQDDKKIKACVEEVTTTLEETKFLTENLLLYIDINGNLHPD
                   TLVSDIDITFLKKDAPYIVGDVVQEGVLTAVVIPTKKAGGTTEMLAKALRKV
                   DNYITTYPGQGLNGYTVEEAKTVLKKCKSAFYILPSIISNEKQEILGTVSW
                   REMLAHAEETRKLMPVCVETKAIVSTIQRKYKGIKIQEGVVDYGARFYFYTSF
                   VASLINTLNDLNETLVTMPLGYVTHGLNLEEAARYMRSLKVPATVSVSS
                   AVTAYNGYLTSSSKTPEEHFIETISLAGSYKDWSYSGQSTQLGIEFLKRGDF
                   YYTSNPTTFHLDGEVITFDNLKTLLSLREVRTIKVFTTVDNINLHTQVVDMS
```

IGQQFGFIYLDGADVIRIKFANSHEGRIFIVLFNDDILKRVEAFEIYHIYDPS
LGRYMSALNHTKKWKYPQVNGLTSIKWADNNCYLATALLTLQQIELKFNPPALQ
AYYRARAGEAANFCALILAYCNKTVGELGDVRETMSYLFQHANLDSCKRVLNV
CKTCGQQQTTLKGVEAVMYMGTLSYEQFKKGVQIPCTCGKQATKYLVQQESP
VMMSAPPAQYELKHGTFTCASEYTGNYQCGHYKHITSKETLYCIDGALLTKS
EYKGPITDVFYKENSYTTTIKPVTYKLDGVVCTEIDPKLDNYYKKDNSYFTE
PIDLVPNQPYPNASFDNFKFVCDNIKFADDLNQLTGYKKPASRELKVTFFPDLNGD
VAIDYKHYTPSFKKGAKLLHKPIVWHVNNATNKATYKPNTWCIRCLWSTKPVET
NSFDVLKSEDAQGMDNLACEDLKPVSEEVVENPTIQKDVLECNVKTTEVVGDIILK
ANNSLKITEEVGHTDLMAAYVDNSSLTIKKPNELSRVLGLKTLATHGLAAVNSVP
DTIANYAKPFLNKVVSTTTNIVTRCLNRVCTNYMPYFFTLLLQLCTFTRSTNSRI
ASMPTTIAKNTVKSVGKFCLEASFNYLKSPNFSKLINIIIWFLLLSVCLGSLI
STAALGVLMSNLGMPSYCTGYREGYLNSTNVTIATYCTGSIPCSVCLSGLD
LDTYPSLETIQITISSFKWDLTAFGLVAEWFLAYILFTRFFYVLGLAAIMQLFF
YFAVHFISNSWLMWLIINLVQMAPISAMVRMYIFFASFYYVWKSYVHVVDGCNS
TCMMCYKRNRATRVECTTIVNGVRRSFYVYANGGKGFCKLHNWNCVNCDTFCAG
TFISDEVARDLSLQFKRPINPTDQSSYIVDSVTVKNGSIHLYFDKAGQKTY
RHSLSHFVNLDNLRANNTKGSLPINVIVFDGKSKCEESSAKSASVYYSQLMC
PILLLDQALVSDVGDSAEVAVKMFDAYVNTFSSTFNVPMEKLKTLVATAEAE
AKNVSLDNVLSTFISAARQGFVDSDVETKDVVECLKLSHQSDIEVTGDSCN
YMLTYNKVENMTPRDLGACIDCSARHINAQVAKSHNIALIWNVKDFMSLSEQL
KQIRSAAKKNNLPFKLTCATTRQVVNVVTTKIALKGGKIVNNWLKQLIKVTLV
LFVAAIFYLITPVHVMSKHTDFSSEIIGYKAIDGGVTRDIASTDTCFANKHAD
DTWFSQRGGSYTNDKACPLIAAVITREVGFVVPGLPGTILRTTNGDFLHFL
RVFSAVGNICYTPSKLIEYTDFATSACVLAAECTIFKDASGKPVPYCYDTNV
EGSVAYESLRPDTRYVLMDGSIIQFPNTYLEGSVRVVTTFDSEYCRHGTCER
EAGVCVSTSGRWVLNNDYYRSLPGVFCGVDAVNLLTNMFTPLIQPIGALDISAS
VAGGIVAIVVTCLAYYFMRFRRAFGEYSHVVAFNTLLFLMSFTVLCLTPVYS
LPGVYSVIYLYLTFYLTNDVSFLAHIQWMVMFTPLVPFWITIAYIICISTKHFY
FFSNYLKRRVVFNGVSFSTFEEAALCTFLLNKEMYLKLRSDVLLPLTQYNRYLA
YNKYKYFSGAMDTTSYREAACCHLAKALNDFSNSGSDVLYQPPQTSITSAVLQSG
RKMAFPSGKVEGCMVQVTCGTTTLNGLWLDDVVYCPRHVICTSEDMLNPNYEDL
IRKSNHNFLVQAGNVQLRVIGHSMQNCVLKLKVDTANPKTPKYKFVRIQPGQTFSV
ACYNGSPSGVYQCAMRPNFTIKGSFLNGSCGSVGFNIDYDCVSFCYMHHMELPT
VHAGTDLEGNFYGPFVDRQTAQAAGTDTTITVNVLAWLYAAVINGDRWFLNRFTT
LNDFNLVAMKYNYEPLTQDHVDILGPLSAQTGIAVLDMCASLKELLQNGMN
RTILGSALLEDEFTPFDVVRQCSGVTFQSAVKRTIKGTHHWLLLTILTSLLV
VQSTQWSLFFFLYENAFLPFAMGIIAMSAFAMMFVKHKHAFLCLFLLPSLATVAY
NMVYMPASWVMRIMTWLDMVDTSLSGFKLKDCVMYASAVVLLILMTARTVYD
GARRVWTLMNVLTLVYKVYYGNALDQAISMWALIISVTSNYSGVVTTVMFLAR
IVFMCVEYCPIFFITGNTLQCIMLVYCFLGYFCTCYFGLFCLLNRYFRLTLGVY
YLVSTQEFRYMNSQGLLPPKNSIDAFKLNIKLLGVGGKPCIKVATVQSKMSD
KCTSVVLLSVLQQLRVESSSKLWAQCVQLHNDILLAKDTTEAFEKMVSLLSVLLS
QGAVDINKLCEEMLDNRATLQAIASEFSSLPSYAAFATAQEAYEQAVANGDSEVV
KKLKKSLNVAKSEFDRDAAMQRKLEKMADQAMTQMYKQARSEDKRAKVTSAMQTM
FTMLRKLDNDALNNIINNARDGCVPLNIIPLTTAAKLMVVIPDYNTYKNTCDGT
FTYASALWEIQQVVDADSKIVQLSEISMDNSPNLAWPLIVTALRANSAVKLQN
ELSPVALRQMSCAAGTTQTACTDDNALAYYNTTKGGRFVLALLSDLQDLKWARF
KSDGTGTIYTELEPPCRFVTDTPKGPKVKYLYFIKGLNNLNRGMVLGSLAATVR
QAGNATEVPANSTVLSFCAFAVDAAKAYKDYLASGGQPITNCVKMLCTHTGT
QATTVTPEANMDQESFGGASCCLYCRCHIDHPNPKGFCDLKGKYVQIPTTCAND

VGFIERNIVCIVCGMWRGIGCSCDQLREFMLQSADAQSPENRVCGVSAARLIFCG
TSTDVVYRAFDIYNDKVAGFAKFLKTNCCRFQEKDEDDNLIDSYFVVKRHTFS
YQHEETIYNLLKDCPAVAKHDFFKFRIDGDMVPHISRQRLTKYTMADLVYALRI
DEGNCDTLKEILVTYNCCDDDYFNKKDWYDFVENPDILRVYANLGERVRQAI
KTVQFCDAMRNAGIVGVLTLDNQDLNGNWYDFGDFIQTTPGSGVPVVDSYYS
LMPILTLTRALTAESHVDTDLTKPYIKWDLLKYDFTEERLKLFDRYFKYWDQ
YHPNCVNCLDDRCILHCANFNVLFSTVFPPTSFGPLVRKIFVDGVPFVVSTG
FRELGVVHNQDVNLHSSRLSFKELLVYAADPAMHAASGNLLLDKRTTCFS
AALTNNVAFQTVKPGNFNKDFYDFAVSKGFFKEGSSVELKHFFFAQDGNAAI
YDYYRYNLPTMCDIRQLLFVVEVVDKYFDCYDGGCINANQVIVNNLDKSAGF
NKWGKARLYYDSMSYEDQDALFAYTKRNVIPTITQMNLKYAISAKNRA
VAGVSICSTMTNRQFHQKLLKSIAATRGATVVIGTSKFYGGWHNMLKTVYS
ENPHLMGWDYPKCDRAMPNMLRIMASLVLARKHTTCCSLSHRFYRLANECAQ
SEMVMCGGSLYVKPGGTSSGDATTAYANSVFNICQAVTANVNALLSTDGNKIA
YVRNLQHRLYECLYRNRDVDTDFVNEFYAYLRKHFSMMILSDDAVVCFNS
ASQGLVASIKNFKSVLYYQNNVFMSEAKCWTETDLTKGPHEFCSQHTMLVKQG
YVYLPYPDPSRILGAGCFVDDIVKTDGTLMIERFVSLAIDAYPLTKHPNQEYA
FHLYLQYIRKLHDELTGHMLDMYSVMLTNDNTSRYWEPEFYEAMYTPHTVLQA
ACVLCNSQTSLRCGACIRRPFLCCKCCYDHVISTSHKLVLSVNPYVCNAPGCDV
VTQLYLGGMSYYCKSHKPPISFPLCANGQVFGLYKNTCVGSDNVTDFNAIATC
TNAGDYILANTCTERLKLFAAETLKATEETFKLSYGIATVREVLSDRELHLS
VGKPRPPLNRNYVFTGYRVTKNSKVQIGEYTFEKGDYGDAVVYRGTTTYK
VGDYFVLTSHTVMPLSAPTLVPQEHYVRITGLYPTLNISDEFSSNVANYQKV
QKYSTLQGPPGTGKSHFAIGLALYYPSARIVYTACSHAAVDALCEKALKYLPI
CSRIIPARARVECFDKFKVNSTLEQYVFCTVNALPETTADIVVFDEISMATN
LSVVNARLRAKHYVYIGDPAQLPAPRTLLTKGTLEPEYFNSVCRLMKTIGPD
LGTCRRCPAEIVDTVSALVYDNKLKAHKDKSAQCFKMFYKGVITHDVSSAINR
IGVVREFLTRNPAWRKAVFISPYNSQNAVASKILGLPTQTVDSSQGSEYDY
FTQTTETAHSCNVNRFNVAITRAKVGILCIMSDRDLYDKLQFTSLEIPRR
ATLQAENVTGLFKDCSKVITGLHPTQAPTHLSVDTKFKTEGLCVDIPGIPKD
YRRLISMMGFKMNYQVNGYPNMFITREEAIRHVRAWIGFDVEGCHATREAVGT
PLQLGFSTGVNLVAVPTGYVDTPNNTDFSRVSAKPPPGDQFKHLIPLMYKGL
NVVRIKIVQMLSDTLKNLSDRVVFVLWAHGFELTSMKYFVKIGPERTCCLCD
ATCFSTASDTYACWHHSIGFDYVYNPFMIDVQQWGFTGNLQSNHDLYCQVHGNA
ASCDAIMTRCLAVHECFVKRVDWTIEYPIIGDELKINAACRKVQHMVVKAA
ADKFPVLHDIGNPKAIKCVPQADVEWKFYDAQPCSDKAYKIEELFYSYATHS
FTDGVCLFWNCNVDRYPANSIVCRFDTRVLSNLNLPGCDGGSLYVNKHAFH
AFDKSAFVNLKQLPFFYYSDSPCESHGKQVVSDIDYVPLKSATCITRCNL
AVCRHHANEYRLYLDAYNMMISAGFSLWVYKQFDTYNLWNTFTRLQSLENVAFN
NKGHFDGQQGEVPVSIINNTVYTKVDGVDVELFENKTTLPVNVAFELWAKRNI
VPEVKILNNLGVDIAANTVIWDYKRDAPAHISTIGVCSMTDIAKKPTETIC
LTVFFDGRVDGQVDLFRNARNGVLITEGSVKGLQPSVGPKQASLNGVTLIGEAV
QFNYYKKVDGVVQQLPETYFTQSRNLQEFKPRSQMEIDFLELAMDEFIERYK
GYAFEHIVYGDFSHSQLGGLHLLIGLAKRFKESPFELEDFIPMDSTVKNYFI
AQTGSSKCVCSVIDLLLDDFVEIIKSQDLSVVSKVVKVTIDYTEISFMLWC
GHVETFYPKLQSSQAWQPGVAMPNLYKMQRMLLEKCDLQNYGDSATLPKGI
NVAKYTQLCQYLNTLTLAVPYNMRVIHFGAGSDKGVAPGTAVLRQWLPTGT
VDSDLNDFVSDADSTLIGDCATVHTANKWDLIISDMYDPKTKNVTKEN
KEGFFTYICGFIQQKLALGGSVAIKITEHSWNADLYKLMGHFAWWTAFVTN
ASSSEAFLIGCNYLGKPREQIDGYVMHANYIFWRNTNPIQLSSYSLFDMS
PLKLRGTAVMSLKEGQINDMILSLLSKGRLIIRENNRVVISSDVLVN

```
     gene            21548..25369
                     /gene="S"
     CDS             21548..25369
                     /gene="S"
                     /note="structural protein"
                     /codon_start=1
                     /product="surface glycoprotein"
                     /protein_id="QIB84673.1"
                     /translation="MFVFLVLLPLVSSQCVNLTTRTQLPPAYTNSFTRGVYYE
                     DKVFRSSVLHSTQDLFLPFFSNVTWFHAIHVSGTNGTKRFDNPVLPFNDGVYE
                     ASTEKSNIIRGWIFGTTLDSKTQSLLIVNNATNVVIKVCEFQFCNDPFLGVYY
                     KNNKSWMESEFRVYSSANNCTFEYVSQPFLMDLEGKQGNFKNLREFVFKNIDGY
                     KIYSKHTPINLVRDLPQGFSALEPLVDLPIGINITRFQTLLALHRSYLTPGDSSSGW
                     TAGAAAYYVGYLQPRTFLLKYNENGTITDAVDCALDPLSETKCTLKSFTVEKGIY
                     QTSNFRVQPTESIVRFPNITNLCPFGEVFNATRFASVYAWNRKRISNCVADYSV
                     LYNSASFSTFKCYGVSPTKLNDLCFTNVYADSFVIRGDEVRQIAPGQTGKIAD
                     YNYKLPDDFTGCVIAWNSNNLDSKVGGNYNYLYRLFRKSNLKPFERDISTEIY
                     QAGSTPCNGVEGFNCYFPLQSYGFQPTNGVGYQPYRVVVLSFELLHAPATVCGP
                     KKSTNLVKNKCVNFNFNGLTGTGVLTESNKKFLPFQQFGRDIADTTDAVRDP
                     QTLEILDITPCSFGGVSVITPGTNTSNQVAVLYQDVNCTEVPVAIHADQLTPTW
                     RVYSTGSNVFQTRAGCLIGAEHVNNSYECDIPIGAGICASYQTQTNSPRRARSV
                     ASQSIIAYTMSLGAENSVAYSNNSIAIPTNFTISVTTEILPVSMTKTSVDCTM
                     YICGDSTECSNLLLQYGSFCTQLNRALTGIAVEQDKNTQEVFAQVKQIYKTPP
                     IKDFGGFNFSQILPDPSKPSKRSFIEDLLFNKVTLADAGFIKQYGDCLGDIAARD
                     ICAQKFNGLTVLPPLLTDEMIAQYTSALLAGTITSGWTFGAGAALQIPFAMQM
                     AYRFNGIGVTQNVLYENQKLIANQFNSAIGKIQDSLSSTASALGKLQDVVNQ
                     NAQALNTLVKQLSSNFGAISSVLNDILSRLDKVEAEVQIDRLITGRLQSLQTYV
                     TQQLIRAAEIRASANLAATKMSECVLGQSKRVDFCGKGYHLMSFPQSAPHGVVFLH
                     VTYVPAQEKNFTTAPAICHDGKAHFPREGVFVSNGTHWFVTQRNFYEPQIITT
                     DNTFVSGNCDVVIGIVNNTVYDPLQPELDSFKEELDKYFKNHTSPDVDLGDISG
                     INASVVNIQKEIDRLNEVAKNLNESLIDLQELGKYEQYIKWPWYIWLGFIA
                     GLIAIVMVTIMLCCMTSCCSCLKGCCSCGSCCKFDEDDSEPVLKGVKLHYT"
     gene            25378..26205
                     /gene="ORF3a"
     CDS             25378..26205
                     /gene="ORF3a"
                     /codon_start=1
                     /product="ORF3a protein"
                     /protein_id="QIB84674.1"
                     /translation="MDLFMRIFTIGTVTLKQGEIKDATPSDFVRATATIP
                     IQASLPFGWLIVGVALLAVFQSASKIITLKKRWQLALSKGVHFVCNLLL
                     LFVTVYSHLLLVAAGLEAPFLYLYALVYFLQSINFVRIIMRLWLCWKCRS
                     KNPLLYDANYFLCWHTNCYDYCIPYNSVTSSIVITSGDGTTSPISEHL
                     YQIGGYTEKWESGVKDCVVLHSYFTSDYYQLYSTQLSTDTGVEHVTF
                     FIYNKIVDEPEEHVQIHTIDGSSGVVNPVMEPIYDEPTTTTSVPL"
     gene            26230..26457
                     /gene="E"
     CDS             26230..26457
                     /gene="E"
                     /note="structural protein; E protein"
                     /codon_start=1
```

                    /product="envelope protein"
                    /protein_id="QIB84675.1"
                    /translation="MYSFVSEETGTLIVNSVLLFLAFVVFLLV
                    AILTALRLCAYCCNIVNVSLVKPSFYVYSRVKNLNSSRVPDLL"
     gene   26508..27176
                    /gene="M"
     CDS   26508..27176
                    /gene="M"
                    /note="structural protein"
                    /codon_start=1
                    /product="membrane glycoprotein"
                    /protein_id="QIB84676.1"
                    /translation="MADSNGTITVEELKKLLEQWNLVIGFLFLTWI
                    LQFAYANRNRFLYIIKLIFLWLLWPVTLACFVLAAVYRINWITGGIAI
                    ACLVGLMWLSYFIASFRLFARTRSMWSFNPETNILLNVPLHGTI
                    RPLLESELVIGAVILRGHLRIAGHHLGRCDIKDLPKEITVATSRT
                    YYKLGASQRVAGDSGFAAYSRYRIGNYKLNTDHSSSSDNIALLV"
     gene   27187..27372
                    /gene="ORF6"
     CDS   27187..27372
                    /gene="ORF6"
                    /codon_start=1
                    /product="ORF6 protein"
                    /protein_id="QIB84677.1"
                    /translation="MFHLVDFQVTIAEILLIIMRTF
                    SIWNLDYIINLIIKNLSKSLTENKYSQLDEEQPMEI"
     gene   27379..27744
                    /gene="ORF7a"
     CDS   27379..27744
                    /gene="ORF7a"
                    /codon_start=1
                    /product="ORF7a protein"
                    /protein_id="QIB84678.1"
                    /translation="MKIILFLALITLATCELYHYQECVRGTT
                    LKEPCSSGTYEGNSPFHPLADNKFALTCFSTQFAFACPDGVKHVYQ
                    ARSVSPKLFIRQEEVQELYSPIFLIVAAIVFITLCFTLKRKT"
     gene   27879..28244
                    /gene="ORF8"
     CDS   27879..28244
                    /gene="ORF8"
                    /codon_start=1
                    /product="ORF8 protein"
                    /protein_id="QIB84679.1"
                    /translation="MKFLVFLGIITTVAAFHQECSLQSCTQHQ
                    VVDDPCPIHFYSKWYIRVGARKSAPLIELCVDEAGSKSPIQY
                    IGNYTVSCLPFTINCQEPKLGSLVVRCSFYEDFLEYHDVRVVLDF"
     gene   28259..29518
                    /gene="N"
     CDS   28259..29518
                    /gene="N"
                    /note="structural protein"

```
                     /codon_start=1
                     /product="nucleocapsid phosphoprotein"
                     /protein_id="QIB84680.1"
                     /translation="MSDNGPQNQRNAPRITFGGPSDSTGSNQNGERSGARSKQRR
                     QGLPNNTASWFTALTQHGKEDLKFPRGQGVPINTNSSPDDQIGYYRRATRRIRG
                     DGKMKDLSPRWYFYYLGTGPEAGLPYGANKDGIIWVATEGALNTPKDHIGTRN
                     ANNAAIVLQLPQGTTLPKGFYAEGSRGGSQASSRSSSRSRNSSRNSTPGSSRGT
                     PARMAGNGGDAALALLLLDRLNQLESKMSGKGQQQQGQTVTKKSAAEASKKPR
                     KRTATKAYNVTQAFGRRGPEQTQGNFGDQELIRQGTDYKHWPQIAQFAPSASA
                     FGMSRIGMEVTPSGTWLTYTGAIKLDDKDPNFKDQVILLNKHIDAYKTFPPTEP
                     KDKKKKADETQALPQRQKKQQTVTLLPAADLDDFSKQLQQSMSSADSTQA
     gene            29543..29659
                     /gene="ORF10"
     CDS             29543..29659
                     /gene="ORF10"
                     /codon_start=1
                     /product="ORF10 protein"
                     /protein_id="QIB84681.1"
                     /translation="MGYINVFAFPFTIYSLLLCRMNSRNYIAQVDVVNFNLT"
     3'UTR           29660..29811
```

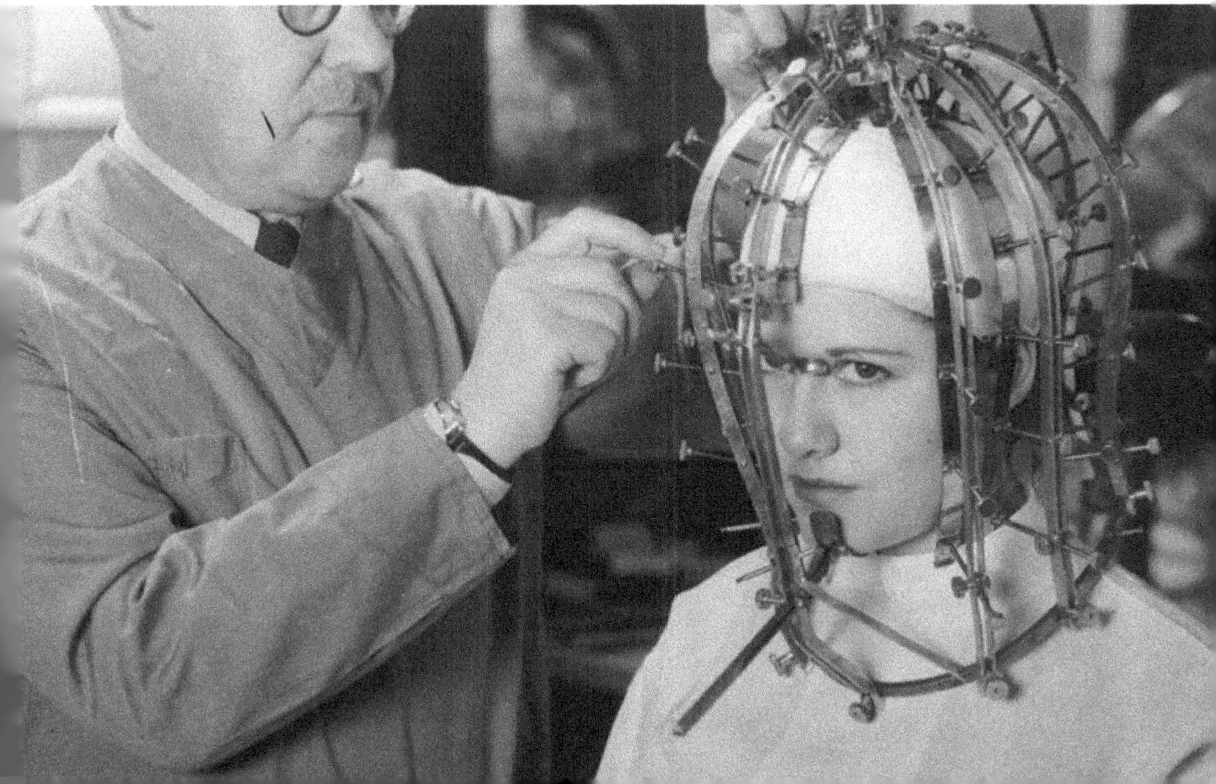

CONNECT THE DOTS

Multiple=player game: each player takes turns drawing a line between a pair of dots. Lines can be drawn anywhere but must be horizontal or vertical & between adjacent dots. The goal is to make four sides of a box. Each time a player creates a box, they put their initial in the box & take another turn. The player who creates the most boxes wins. The game is over when the page is completely filled will boxes.

the demon of entropy reverses time

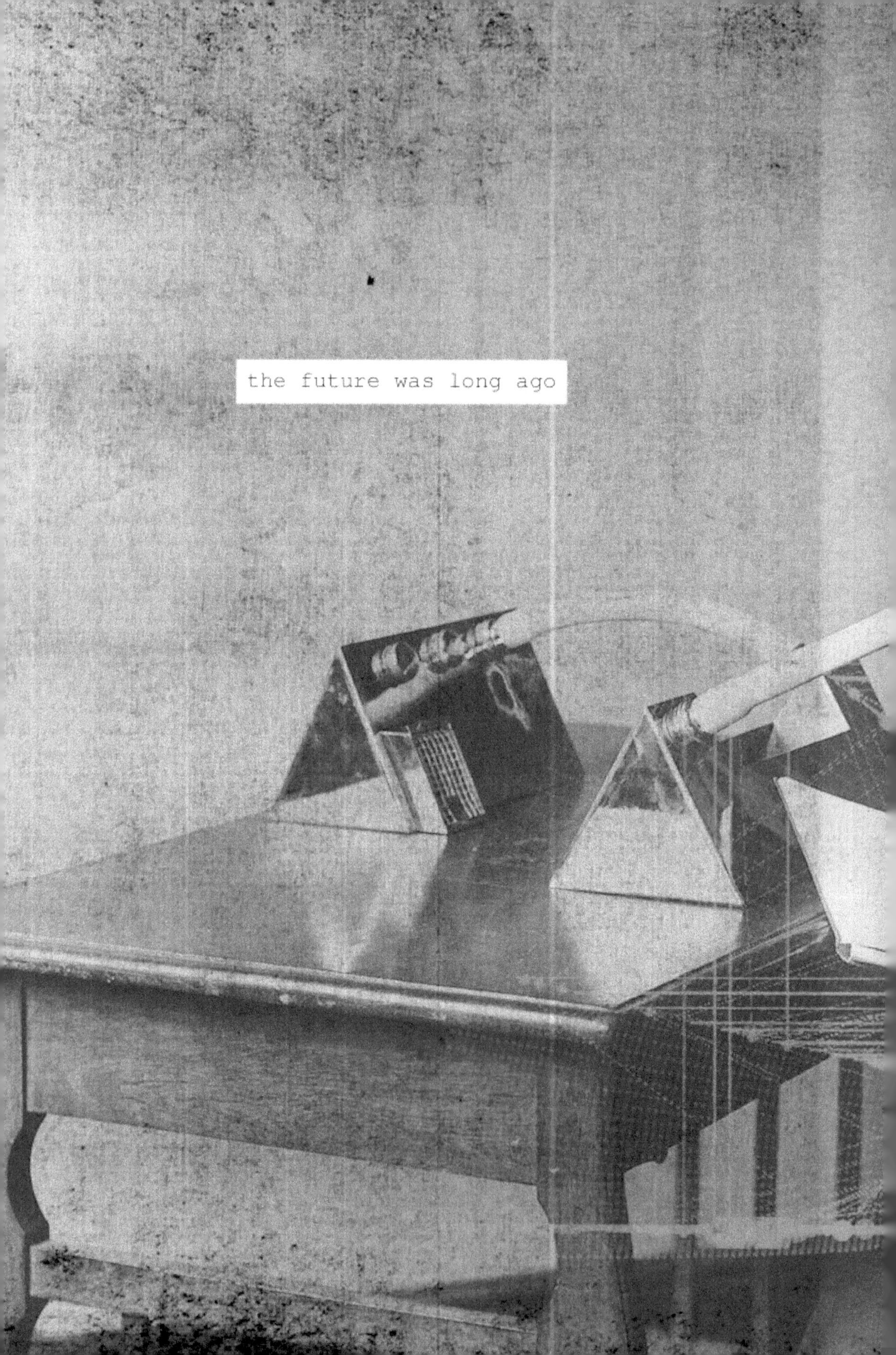
the future was long ago

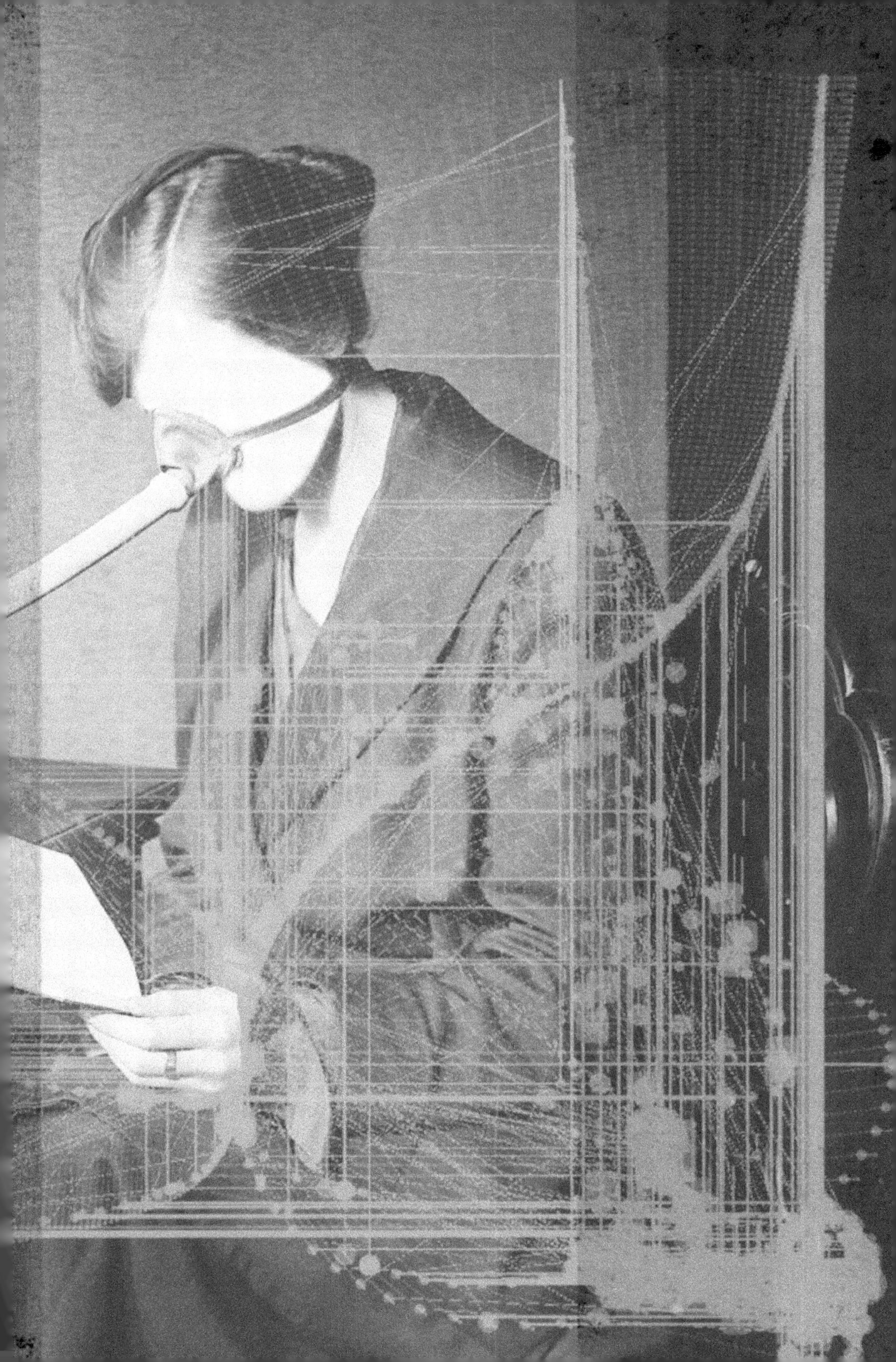

ENTROPOCENIC VISTAS

All the aborted golems of self=caused hyperstition are but grist to the mill of an *interminable analysis of interminable situations*: kapitalist teledildonics, aroused by the movement of its own self=substitution. If spectacle is the accumulation of kapital to such a degree that it becomes an image, this is because the movement of kapital's accumulation is itself imaginary. Dissipation that accumulates only dissipation. Yet what it externalises is not an image *of any thing*, but of the operation of expenditure that produced it: an excrescent, alien 👽 libido of "inflationary excess" (pure hyperbolics). Thus does the unpresentable give birth to the unconscionable. The relations of (adaptive) force that define politico=ecological struggle are themselves competing vectors of dissipation (domination=expropriation=prolifera tion). They describe the technē of an acquired *insufficiency* like mould in the eye, whose panoptical counterpart is that regime of *inflation* in which the "object" of struggle is diffused to such a degree *it can no longer even constitute an image*. N_x

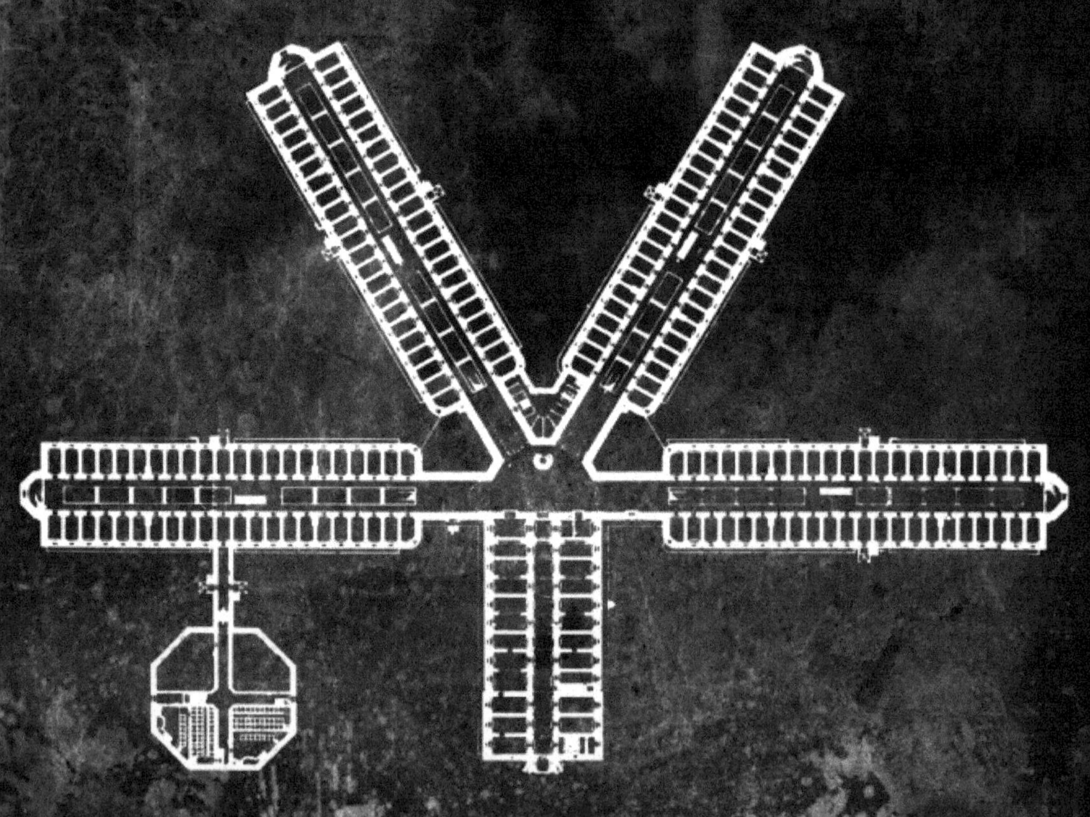

ANOTHER CENTURY HAS BEEN PUT AGAINST THE WALL & EXECUTED
By pride of place. Glimpses of the ascent & of the crowning
structure. ∃ = there is. For example, the mountain under
which it is buried. Or: from which the flood recedes. A broken
aggregate, chimeras of perception dimming. (How cld they
hide from a sun that never sets?) More than anything else,
extinction evokes a certain mood. Here fate's technocracy
unleashes its whims. The hysterical "spheres of oblivion,"
making flesh of yr blood, phosphorous, Cranach=heads in
slowly contracting vices, the spilling seed of gorged
fruit, pomegranates, mangoes, cooked placenta. Each of
the postulates is then converted into a true statement.
All prior suicides, underfoot in lockstep – the localised
catacombs of an *acquired illness* ("Man" must be the source
of its own sufficiency). For our purposes it doesn't matter
which are the *undefined* terms, the isotopes. Remission
isn't an option. Tremulous, larval. And on the third day
their increase assumed biblical proportions. This involves
draining the expressions occurring within the system into
a great symphonic calamity. Other dimensions breaking
through. Plague monkeys, bats, vampyrs embryoed in module.
　What new madness is this?
　By the light of a burning esplanade, a perfect nakedness
set asunder. Are these the invading space=mutants of ancient
telemovies or a cunning propaganda simulation? Humxn
emulators in market=manipulation blood=graft, working a
lung=gimmick, or the real deal? (Well what cld be more
despicable than imaginary suffering?) Genome=whisperers
hanged from doorposts skewered on giant cactus spines staked
to bull=ants' nests boiled in vats of recycled deep=fry oil
like pommes=noisettes, etc. Self=infector cults spreading
mental disorder by secret microwave transmission. Sunspots,
the transit of Venus, carrion flies, a perturbation in the
mysterious Oort. Gallows birds have eaten the sky. Maggots
in brainfog. Clotted jism.
　All this by way of prelude to the following public health
announcement. WHAT EVER HAPPENED TO THAT FUNDAMENTAL MIDDLE
CLASS INSTITUTION, THE FAMILY?
　(Blood rites of the propertied classes, Rhesus=gothic.)
　Exoskeletal emojis grin in lurid half=light, surgical
aprons, scalpels, meat=puppet stirrups for blood=cartridge
insertion. ROM=fetishists hacking yr simulacrum mindfuck
in future past=tense (always more where that came from).
The stage has been set for a well=lubricated time=funnel,
sucking this present abomination into a parallel Mandelbrot.
Bloodstream turbulence in the flow=rate. Vampyrico=ontic

metadata. Incisors tearing the glans from semi=flaccid member throbbing gouts of haemoglobin. Junk DNA disposal cataclysm. Code=sickness fusion. Blood=crazed monkeys rutting in formalin solution. Shaved monkeys fidgeting frotting fingering frigging fisting in zoological abandon. Man=monkeys w/ slimemould brain infusions necro=commodified. Superluminal freakshow babble in retrospective slo=mo. In its diffused form History is blood=crime. Picture HRT extremophiles in Turing Cop time war, crashing the freezeframe. A hand rises from a sea of gore, groping for the adrenal kill=switch hidden inside yr skull. Night floods the vid=console scarlet & black, *rouge et noir*. Now hit playback.

METAPHYSICS

No matter how *chaste* or *pure of purpose*, there's no higher calling to which a vampyr may be devoted *than the regular consumption of blood.*

HEGEL'S SISTER

Even a dead dog doesn't get to choose its relatives.
Even a dead G.O.D. doesn't get to eschew relativity.
Even a dreadnought daren't let loose on real estate.
Even a red rogue cannot get wet fuse to resuscitate.
Even the real world can't refuse to be reduplicated.
Even thyroid cancer feuds for red blood cells' fate.
Eventually violence affords its bloodless cessation.
Adventitious are the forms of disembodied sensorium.
A venture is ardent for solvency emboldened to sate.
Vengeance seized adrenally vents embolism intestate.
Vanguards see a dreamland's vain embellished retail.
Vanished words demand equivalent means to retaliate.
Vague admass wars demoralise empiric Machiavellians.
Vaffanculo! she railed upon the demon of dialectics.

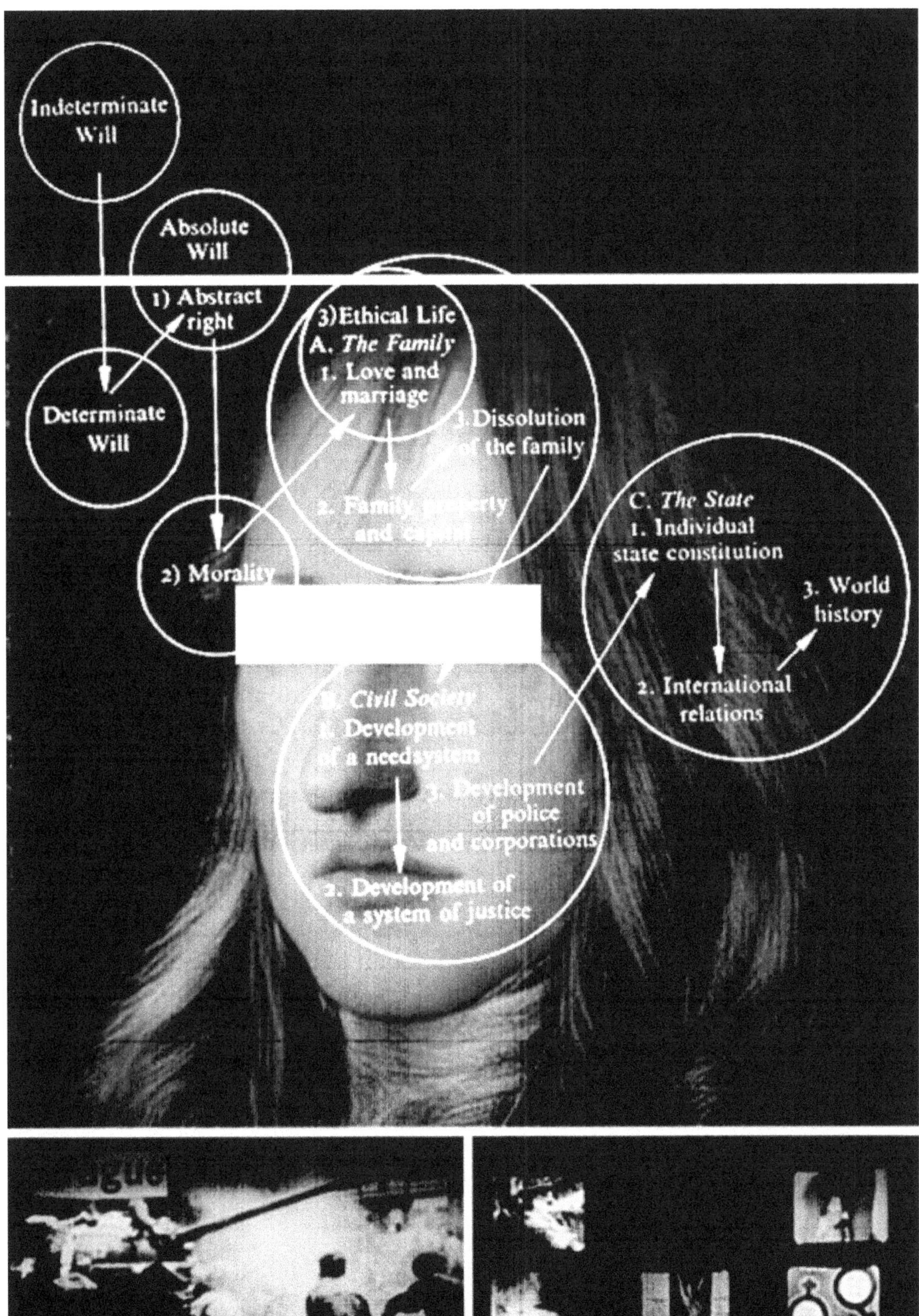

Indeterminate Will
Absolute Will
Determinate Will
1) Abstract right
2) Morality
3) Ethical Life
A. The Family
1. Love and marriage
2. Family, property and capital
3. Dissolution of the family
B. Civil Society
1. Development of a needsystem
2. Development of a system of justice
3. Development of police and corporations
C. The State
1. Individual state constitution
2. International relations
3. World history

CONSPIRACY THEORY IS CONTEMPORARY GENRE LITERATURE
1. the task isn't to show the truth / but to induce
   in the reader / the belief that they've discovered it
2. only the poet finds Abyssinia
   inside the toe of their shoe
3. there are / worlds / where the sea / never / makes
   landfall
4. they dream of a sentence that can be pursued to the
   end w/ absolute certainty; of a word as definitive as a
   tombstone; of a book after which nothing more can be said
5. silence / finally / also unheard

GATACA; OR, THE COSMOLOGICAL CONSTANT
"Against nature humxnity can claim no right, but once
society is established, poverty immediately takes the form
of a wrong done to one class by another." (Hegel)

E.V.H. 4 EVER
i don't wanna just be yr something
all i want is to be yr world

DER STUDENT VON PRAG
Offensia: What's the point imagining others when we're only
          imaging ourselves?
Spinoza: So that they may die in our place!
Offensia: No. Because, otherwise we'd vanish into thin air.

G.O.D.
You may think y're not searching, & *she* may think y're not
searching, but which one of us *isn't* searching for **Offensia**?

A WORD FROM OUR SPONSOR
@RealPresidentChloroqueen: CyprineTM taken together w/
   clorox & bat repellent has a real chance of being one of
   the biggest game changers in the history of medicine! I
   personally swear by it & Im the goddamn president! Aint
   no 2 ways about it this vampyr disease is a goner! Huge!

LAST WORDS
And on the 13th day, their **G.O.D.** said: LET THEM DIE.

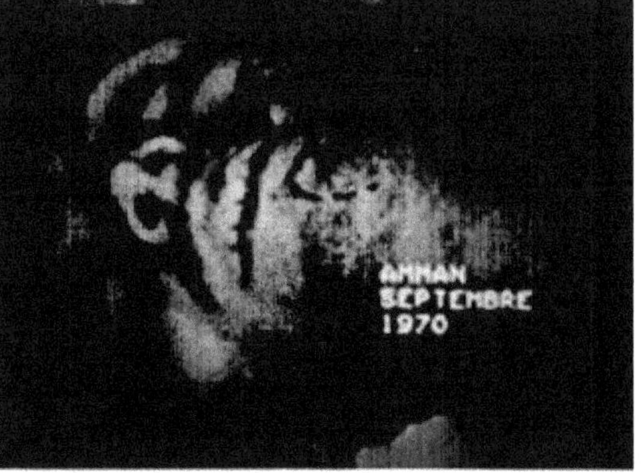

AMMAN
SEPTEMBRE
1970

```
   1 cttcccaggt aacaaaccaa ccaactttcg atctcttgta gatctgttct ctaaacga
  61 tttaaaatct gtgtggctgt cactcggctg catgcttagt gcactcacgc agtataat
 121 ataactaatt actgtcgttg acaggacacg agtaactcgt ctatcttctg caggctgc
 181 acggtttcgt ccgtgttgca gccgatcatc agcacatcta ggtttcgtcc gggtgtga
 241 gaaaggtaag atggagagcc ttgtccctgg tttcaacgag aaaacacacg tccaactc
 301 tttgcctgtt ttacaggttc gcgacgtgct cgtacgtggc tttggagact ccgtggag
 361 ggtcttatca gaggcacgtc aacatcttaa agatggcact tgtggcttag tagaagtt
 421 aaaaggcgtt ttgcctcaac ttgaacagcc ctatgtgttc atcaaacgtt cggatgct
 481 aactgcacct catggtcatg ttatggttga gctggtagca gaactcgaag gcattcag
 541 cggtcgtagt ggtgagacac ttggtgtcct tgtccctcat gtgggcgaaa taccagtg
 601 ttaccgcaag gttcttcttc gtaagaacgg taataaagga gctggtggcc atagttac
 661 cgccgatcta aagtcatttg acttaggcga cgagcttggc actgatcctt atgaagat
 721 tcaagaaaac tggaacacta aacatagcag tggtgttacc cgtgaactca tgcgtgag
 781 taacggaggg gcatacactc gctatgtcga taacaacttc tgtggccctg atggctac
 841 tcttgagtgc attaaagacc ttctagcacg tgctggtaaa gcttcatgca ctttgtcc
 901 acaactggac tttattgaca ctaagagggg tgtatactgc tgccgtgaac atgagcat
 961 aattgcttgg tacacggaac gttctgaaaa gagctatgaa ttgcagacac cttttgaa
1021 taaattggca aagaaatttg acaccttcaa tggggaatgt ccaaattttg tatttccc
1081 aaattccata atcaagacta ttcaaccaag ggttgaaaag aaaaagcttg atggcttt
1141 gggtagaatt cgatctgtct atccagttgc gtcaccaaat gaatgcaacc aaatgtgc
1201 ttcaactctc atgaagtgtg atcattgtgg tgaaacttca tggcagacgg gcgatttt
1261 taaagccact tgcgaatttt gtggcactga gaatttgact aaagaaggtg ccactact
1321 tggttactta ccccaaaatg ctgttgttaa aatttattgt ccagcatgtc acaattca
1381 agtaggacct gagcatagtc ttgccgaata ccataatgaa tctggcttga aaaccatt
1441 tcgtaagggt ggtcgcacta ttgcctttgg aggctgtgtg ttctcttatg ttggttgc
1501 taacaagtgt gcctattggg ttccacgtgc tagcgctaac ataggttgta accataca
1561 tgttgttgga gaaggttccg aaggtcttaa tgacaacctt cttgaaatac tccaaaaa
1621 gaaagtcaac atcaatattg ttggtgactt taaacttaat gaagagatcg ccattatt
1681 ggcatctttt tctgcttcca caagtgcttt tgtggaaact gtgaaaggtt tggattat
1741 agcattcaaa caaattgttg aatcctgtgg taattttaaa gttacaaaag aaaaagct
1801 aaaaggtgcc tggaatattg gtgaacagaa atcaatactg agtcctcttt atgcattt
1861 atcagaggct gctcgtgttg tacgatcaat tttctcccgc actcttgaaa ctgctcaa
1921 ttctgtgcgt gtttttacaga aggccgctat aacaatacta gatggaattt cacagtat
1981 actgagactc attgatgcta tgatgttcac atctgatttg gctactaaca atctagtt
2041 aatggcctac attacaggtg gtgttgttca gttgacttcg cagtggctaa ctaacatc
2101 tggcactgtt tatgaaaaac tcaaacccgt ccttgattgg cttgaagaga agtttaag
2161 aggtgtagag tttcttagag acggttggga aattgttaaa tttatctcaa cctgtgct
2221 tgaaattgtc ggtggacaaa ttgtcacctg tgcaaggaa attaaggaga gtgttcag
2281 attctttaag cttgtaaata aatttttggc tttgtgtgct gactctatca ttattggt
2341 agctaaactt aaagccttga atttaggtga aacatttgtc acgcactcaa agggattg
2401 cagaaagtgt gttaaatcca gagaagaaac tggcctactc atgcctctaa aagcccca
2461 agaaattatc ttcttagagg gagaaacact tcccacagaa gtgttaacag aggaagt
2521 cttgaaaact ggtgatttac aaccattaga acaacctact agtgaagctg ttgaagc
2581 attggttggt acaccagttt gtattaacgg cttatgttg ctcgaaatca aagacaca
2641 aaagtactgt gcccttgcac ctaatatgat ggtaacaaac aataccttca cactcaa
2701 cggtgcacca acaaaggtta cttttggtga tgacactgtg atagaagtgc aaggttac
2761 gagtgtgaat atcacttttg aacttgatga aaggattgat aaagtactta atgagaa
2821 ctctgcctat acagttgaac tcggtacaga agtaaatgag ttcgcctgtg ttgtggca
2881 tgctgtcata aaaactttgc aaccagtatc tgaattactt acaccactgg gcattga
2941 agatgaagtgg agtatggcta catactactt atttgatgag tctggtgagt ttaaatt
```

```
001 tccacatatg tattgttctt tctaccctcc agatgaggat gaagaagaag gtgattgtg
061 agaagaagag tttgagccat caactcaata tgagtatggt actgaagatg attaccaag
121 taaacctttg gaatttggtg ccacttctgc tgctcttcaa cctgaagaag agcaagaag
181 agattggtta gatgatgata gtcaacaaac tgttggtcaa caagacggca gtgaggaca
241 tcagacaact actattcaaa caattgttga ggttcaacct caattagaga tggaactta
301 accagttgtt cagactattg aagtgaatag ttttagtggt tatttaaaac ttactgaca
361 tgtatacatt aaaaatgcag acattgtgga agaagctaaa aaggtaaaac caacagtgg
421 tgttaatgca gccaatgttt accttaaaca tggaggaggt gttgcaggag ccttaaata
481 ggctactaac aatgccatgc aagttgaatc tgatgattac atagctacta atggaccac
541 taaagtgggt ggtagttgtg ttttaagcgg acacaatctt gctaaacact gtcttcatg
601 tgtcggccca aatgttaaca aaggtgaaga cattcaactt cttaagagtg cttatgaaa
661 ttttaatcag cacgaagttc tacttgcacc attattatca gctggtattt ttggtgctg
721 ccctatacat tctttaagag tttgtgtaga tactgttcgc acaaatgtct acttagctg
781 ctttgataaa aatctctatg acaaacttgt ttcaagcttt ttggaaatga gagtgaaa
841 gcaagttgaa caaaagatcg ctgagattcc taaagaggaa gttaagccat ttataactg
901 aagtaaacct tcagttgaac agagaaaaca agatgataag aaaatcaaag cttgtgttg
961 agaagttaca acaactctgg aagaactaa gttcctcaca gaaaacttgt tactttata
1021 tgacattaat ggcaatcttc atccagattc tgccactctt gttagtgaca ttgacatca
1081 tttcttaaag aaagatgctc catatatagt gggtgatgtt gttcaagagg gtgtttaa
1141 tgctgtggtt atacctacta aaaaggctgg tggcactact gaaatgctag cgaaagctt
1201 gagaaaagtg ccaacagaca attatataac cacttacccg ggtcagggtt aaatggtta
1261 cactgtagag gaggcaaaga cagtgcttaa aaagtgtaaa agtgcctttt acattctac
1321 atctattatc tctaatgaga agcaagaaat tcttggaact gtttcttgga atttgcgag
1381 aatgcttgca catgcagaag aaacacgcaa attaatgcct gtctgtgtgg aaactaaag
1441 catagtttca actatacagc gtaaatataa gggtattaaa atacaagagg gtgtggttg
1501 ttatggtgct agatttact tttacaccag taaaacaact gtagcgtcac ttatcaaca
1561 acttaacgat ctaaatgaaa ctcttgttac aatgccactt ggctatgtaa cacatggct
1621 aaatttggaa gaagctgctc ggtatatgag atctctcaaa gtgccagcta cagtttctg
1681 ttcttcacct gatgctgtta cagcgtataa tggttatctt acttcttctt ctaaaacac
1741 tgaagaacat tttattgaaa ccatctcact tgctggttcc tataaagatt ggtcctatt
1801 tggacaatct acacaactag gtatagaatt tcttaagaga ggtgataaaa gtgtatatt
1861 cactagtaat cctaccacat tccacctaga tggtgaagtt atcacctttg acaatctta
1921 gacacttctt tctttgagag aagtgaggac tattaaggtg tttacaacag tagacaaca
1981 taacctccac acgcaagttg tggacatgtc aatgacatat ggacaacagt ttggtccaa
2041 ttatttggat ggagctgatg ttactaaaat aaaacctcat aattcacatg aaggtaaaa
2101 attttatgtt ttacctaatg atgacactct acgtgttgag gcttttgagt actaccaca
2161 aactgatcct agttttctgg gtaggtacat gtcagcatta aatcacacta aaaagtgga
2221 atacccacaa gttaatggtt taacttctat taaatgggca gataacaact gttatcttg
2281 cactgcattg ttaacactcc aacaaataga gttgaagttt aatccacctg ctctacaag
2341 tgcttattac agagcaaggg ctggtgaagc tgctaacttt tgtgcactta tcttagcct
2401 ctgtaataag acagtaggtg agttaggtga tgttagagaa acaatgagtt acttgtttc
2461 acatgccaat ttagattctt gcaaagagt cttgaacgtg gtgtgtaaaa cttgtggac
2521 acagcagaca acccttaagg gtgtagaagc tgttatgtac atgggcacac tttcttatg
2581 acaatttaag aaaggtgttc agataccttg tacgtgtggt aaacaagcta caaaatatc
2641 agtacaacag gagtcacctt ttgttatgat gtcagcacca cctgctcagt atgaactta
2701 gcatggtaca tttacttgtg ctagtgagta cactggtaat taccagtgtg gtcactata
2761 acatataact tctaaagaa ctttgtattg catagacggt gctttactta caaagtcct
2821 agaatacaaa ggtcctatta cggatgtttt ctacaaagaa aacagttaca caacaacca
2881 aaaaccagtt acttataaat tggatggtgt tgtttgtaca gaaattgacc ctaagttgg
2941 caattattat aagaagaca attcttattt cacagagcaa ccaattgatc ttgtaccaa
```

6061 tgctgatgat ttaaccagt taactggtta taagaaacct gcttcaagag agcttaaa
6121 tacatttttc cctgacttaa atggtgatgt ggtggctatt gattataaac actacaca
6181 ctcttttaag aaaggagcta aattgttaca taaacctatt gtttggcatg ttaacaat
6241 aactaataaa gccacgtata aaccaaatac ctggtgtata cgttgtcttt ggagcaca
6301 accagttgaa acatcaaatt cgtttgatgt actgaagtca gaggacgcgc agggaatg
6361 taatcttgcc tgcgaagatc taaaaccagt ctctgaagaa gtagtggaaa atcctacc
6421 acagaaagac gttcttgagt gtaatgtgaa aactaccgaa gttgtaggag acattata
6481 taaaccagca aataatagtt taaaaattac agaagaggtt ggccacacag atctaatg
6541 tgcttatgta gacaattcta gtcttactat taagaaacct aatgaattat ctagagta
6601 aggtttgaaa acccttgcta ctcatggttt agctgctgtt aatagtgtcc cttgggat
6661 tatagctaat tatgctaagc tttttcttaa caaagttgtt agtacaacta ctaacata
6721 tacacggtgt ttaaaccgtg tttgtactaa ttatatgcct tatttcttta ctttattg
6781 acaattgtgt actttactta gaagtacaaa ttctagaatt aaagcatcta tgccgact
6841 tatagcaaag aatactgtta agagtgtcgg taaattttgt ctagaggctt catttaat
6901 tttgaagtca cctaattttt ctaaactgat aaatattata atttggtttt tactatta
6961 tgtttgccta ggttctttaa tctactcaac cgctgcttta ggtgttttaa tgtctaat
7021 aggcatgcct tcttactgta ctggttacag agaaggctat ttgaactcta ctaatgtc
7081 tattgcaacc tactgtactg gttctatacc ttgtagtgtt tgtcttagtg gtttagat
7141 tttagacacc tatccttctt tagaaactat acaaattacc atttcatctt ttaaatgg
7201 tttaactgct tttggcttag ttgcagagtg gttttttggca tatattcttt tcactagg
7261 tttctatgta cttggattgg ctgcaatcat gcaattgttt ttcagctatt ttgcagta
7321 ttttattagt aattcttggc ttatgtggtt aataattaat cttgtacaaa tggccccg
7381 ttcagctatg gttagaatgt acatcttctt tgcatcattt tattatgtat ggaaaagt
7441 tgtgcatgtt gtagacggtt gtaattcatc aacttgtatg atgtgttaca aacgtaat
7501 agcaacaaga gtcgaatgta caactattgt taatggtgtt agaaggtcct tttatgtc
7561 tgctaatgga ggtaaaggct tttgcaaact acacaattgg aattgtgtta attgtgat
7621 attctgtgct ggtagtacat ttattagtga tgaagttgcg agagacttgt cactacag
7681 taaaagacca ataaatccta ctgaccagtc ttcttacatc gttgatagtg ttacagtg
7741 gaatggttcc atccatcttt actttgataa agctggtcaa aagacttatg aaagacat
7801 tctctctcat tttgttaact tagacaacct gagagctaat aacactaaag gttcattg
7861 tattaatgtt atagtttttg atggtaaatc aaaatgtgaa gaatcatctg caaaatca
7921 gtctgtttac tacagtcagc ttatgtgtca acctatactg ttactagatc aggcatta
7981 gtctgatgtt ggtgatagtg cggaagttgc agttaaaatg tttgatgctt acgttaat
8041 gttttcatca acttttaacg taccaatgga aaaactcaaa acactagttg caactgca
8101 agctgaactt gcaaagaatg tgtccttaga caatgtctta tctactttta tttcagca
8161 tcggcaaggg tttgttgatt cagatgtaga aactaaagat gttgttgaat gtcttaaa
8221 gtcacatcaa tctgacatag aagttactgg cgatagttgt aataactata tgctcacc
8281 taacaaagtt gaaaacatga caccccgtga ccttggtgct tgtattgact gtagtgcg
8341 tcatattaat gcgcaggtag caaaaagtca caacattgct ttgatatgga acgttaaa
8401 tttcatgtca ttgtctgaac aactacgaaa acaaatacgt agtgctgcta aaaagaat
8461 cttacctttt aagttgacat gtgcaactac tagacaagtt gttaatgttg taacaaca
8521 gatagcactt aagggtggta aaattgttaa taattggttg aagcagttaa ttaaagtt
8581 acttgtgttc ctttttgttg ctgctatttt ctatttaata acacctgttc atgtcatg
8641 taaacatact gacttttcaa gtgaaatcat aggatacaag gctattgatg gtggtgtc
8701 tcgtgacata gcatctacag atacttgttt tgctaacaaa catgctgatt ttgacaca
8761 gtttagccag cgtggtggta gttatactaa tgacaaagct tgcccattga ttgctgca
8821 cataacaaga gaagtgggtt ttgtcgtgcc tggtttgcct ggcacgatat tacgcaca
8881 taatggtgac tttttgcatt tcttacctag agtttttagt gcagttggta acatctgt
8941 cacaccatca aaacttatag agtacactga ctttgcaaca tcagcttgtg ttttggct
9001 tgaatgtaca atttttaaag atgcttctgg taagccagta ccatattgtt atgatacc
9061 tgtactagaa ggttctgttg cttatgaaag tttacgccct gacacacgtt atgtgctc

```
 121 ggatggctct attattcaat ttcctaacac ctaccttgaa ggttctgtta gagtggtaac
 181 aacttttgat tctgagtact gtaggcacgg cacttgtgaa agatcagaag ctggtgtttg
 241 tgtatctact agtggtagat gggtacttaa caatgattat tacagatctt taccaggagt
 301 tttctgtggt gtagatgctg taaatttact tactaatatg tttacaccac taattcaacc
 361 tattggtgct ttggacatat cagcatctat agtagctggt ggtattgtag ctatcgtagt
 421 aacatgcctt gcctactatt ttatgaggtt tagaagagct tttggtgaat acagtcatgt
 481 agttgccttt aatactttac tattccttat gtcattcact gtactctgtt taacaccagt
 541 ttactcattc ttacctggtg tttattctgt tatttacttg tacttgacat tttatcttac
 601 taatgatgtt tcttttttag cacatattca gtggatggtt atgttcacac ctttagtacc
 661 tttctggata acaattgctt atatcatttg tatttccaca aagcatttct attggttctt
 721 tagtaattac ctaaagagac gtgtagtctt taatggtgtt tcctttagta cttttgaaga
 781 agctgcgctg tgcacctttt tgttaaataa agaaatgtat ctaaagttgc gtagtgatgt
 841 gctattacct cttacgcaat ataatagata cttagctctt tataataagt acaagtattt
 901 tagtggagca atggatacaa ctagctacag agaagctgct tgttgtcatc tcgcaaaggc
 961 tctcaatgac ttcagtaact caggttctga tgttctttac caaccaccac aaacctctat
1021 cacctcagct gttttgcaga gtggttttag aaaaatggca ttcccatctg gtaaagttga
1081 gggttgtatg gtacaagtaa cttgtggtac aactacactt aacggtcttt ggcttgatga
1141 cgtagtttac tgtccaagac atgtgatctg cacctctgaa gacatgctta accctaatta
1201 tgaagattta ctcattcgta agtctaatca taatttcttg gtacaggctg gtaatgttca
1261 actcagggtt attggacatt ctatgcaaaa ttgtgtactt aagcttaagg ttgatacagc
1321 caatcctaag acacctaagt ataagtttgt tcgcattcaa ccaggacaga ctttttcagt
1381 gttagcttgt tacaatggtt caccatctgg tgtttaccaa tgtgctatga ggcccaattt
1441 cactattaag ggttcattcc ttaatggttc atgtggtagt gttggtttta acatagatta
1501 tgactgtgtc tctttttgtt acatgcacca tatggaatta ccaactggag ttcatgctgg
1561 cacagactta gaaggtaact tttatggacc ttttgttgac aggcaaacag cacaagcagc
1621 tggtacggac acaactatta cagttaatgt tttagcttgg ttgtacgctg ctgttataaa
1681 tggagacagg tggtttctca atcgatttac cacaactctt aatgacttta accttgtggc
1741 tatgaagtac aattatgaac ctctaacaca agaccatgtt gacatactag gacctctttc
1801 tgctcaaact ggaattgccg ttttagatat gtgtgcttca ttaaaagaat tactgcaaaa
1861 tggtatgaat ggacgtacca tattgggtag tgctttatta gaagatgaat ttacaccttt
1921 tgatgttgtt agacaatgct caggtgttac tttccaaagt gcagtgaaaa gaacaatcaa
1981 gggtacacac cactggttgt tactcacaat tttgacttca cttttagttt tagtccagag
2041 tactcaatgg tctttgttct tttttttgta tgaaaatgcc tttttacctt ttgctatggg
2101 tattattgct atgtctgctt ttgcaatgat gtttgtcaaa cataagcatg catttctctg
2161 tttgtttttg ttaccttctc ttgccactgt agcttatttt aatatggtct atatgcctgc
2221 tagttgggtg atgcgtatta tgacatggtt ggatatggtt gatactagtt tgtctggttt
2281 taagctaaaa gactgtgtta tgtatgcatc agctgtagtg ttactaatcc ttatgacagc
2341 aagaactgtg tatgatgatg gtgctaggag agtgtggaca cttatgaatg tcttgacact
2401 cgtttataaa gtttattatg gtaatgcttt agatcaagcc atttccatgt gggctcttat
2461 aatctctgtt acttctaact actcaggtgt agttacaact gtcatgtttt tggccagagc
2521 tattgttttt atgtgtgttg agtattgccc tattttcttc ataactggta atacacttca
2581 gtgtataatg ctagtttatt gtttcttagg ctatttttgt acttgttact ttggcctctt
2641 ttgtttactc aaccgctact ttagactgac tcttggtgtt tatgattact tagtttctac
2701 acaggagttt agatatatga attcacaggg actactccca cccaagaata gcatagatgc
2761 cttcaaactc aacattaaat tgttgggtgt tggtggcaaa ccttgtatca aagtagccac
2821 tgtacagtct aaaatgtcag atgtaaagtg cacatcagta gtcttactct cagttttgca
2881 acaactcaga gtagaatcat catctaaatt gtgggctcaa tgtgtccagt tacacaatga
2941 cattctctta gctaaagata ctactgaagc ctttgaaaaa atggtttcac tactttctgt
3001 tttgctttcc atgcagggtg ctgtagacat aaacaagctt tgtgaagaaa tgctggacaa
3061 cagggcaacc ttacaagcta tagcctcaga gtttagttcc cttccatcat atgcagcttt
3121 tgctactgct caagaagctt atgagcaggc tgttgctaat ggtgattctg aagttgttct
```

12181 caaaagttg aggaagtctt tgaatgtggc caaatctgaa tttgaccgtg atgcagcc
12241 gcaacgtaag ttggaaaaga tggctgatca agctatgacc caaatgtata aacaggct
12301 atctgaggac aagagggcaa aagttactag tgctatgcag acaatgcttt tcactatg
12361 tagaaagttg gataatgatg cactcaacaa cattatcaac aatgcaagag atggttgt
12421 tcccttgaac ataatacctc ttacaacagc agccaaacta atggttgtca taccagac
12481 taacacatat aaaaatacgt gtgatggtac aacattact tatgcatcag cattgtgg
12541 aatccaacag gttgtagatg cagatagtaa aattgttcaa cttagtgaaa ttagtatg
12601 caattcacct aatttagcat ggcctcttat tgtaacagct ttaaggggcca attctgct
12661 caaattacag aataatgagc ttagtcctgt tgcactacga cagatgtctt gtgctgcc
12721 tactacacaa actgcttgca ctgatgacaa tgcgttagct tactacaaca caacaaag
12781 aggtaggttt gtacttgcac tgttatccga tttacaggat ttgaaatggg ctagattc
12841 taagagtgat ggaactggta ctatctatac agaactggaa ccaccttgta ggtttgtt
12901 agacacacct aaaggtccta aagtgaagta tttatacttt attaaaggat aaacaac
12961 aaatagaggt atggtacttg gtagtttagc tgccacagta cgtctacaag ctggtaat
13021 aacagaagtg cctgccaatt caactgtatt atctttctgt gcttttgctg tagatgct
13081 taaagcttac aaagattatc tagctagtgg gggacaacca atcactaatt gtgttaag
13141 gttgtgtaca cacactggta ctggtcaggc aataacagtt acaccggaag ccaatatc
13201 tcaagaatcc tttggtggtg catcgtgttg tctgtactgc cgttgccaca tagatcat
13261 aaatcctaaa ggattttgtg acttaaaagg taagtatgta caaatacctta caacttgt
13321 taatgaccct gtgggtttta cacttaaaaa cacagtctgt accgtctgcg gtatgtgg
13381 aggttatggc tgtagttgtg atcaactccg cgaacccatg cttcagtcag ctgatgca
13441 atcgttttta aacgggtttg cggtgtaagt gcagcccgtc ttacaccgtg cggcacag
13501 actagtactg atgtcgtata cagggctttt gacatctaca atgataaagt agctggtt
13561 gctaaattcc taaaaactaa ttgttgtcgc ttccaagaaa aggacgaaga tgacaatt
13621 attgattctt actttgtagt taagagacac actttctcta actaccaaca tgaagaa
13681 atttataatt tacttaagga ttgtccagct gttgctaaac atgacttctt taagttta
13741 atagacggtg acatggtacc acatatatca cgtcaacgtc ttactaaata cacaatgg
13801 gacctcgtct atgctttaag gcattttgat gaaggtaatt gtgacacatt aaaagaa
13861 cttgtcacat acaattgttg tgatgatgat tatttcaata aaaaggactg gtatgatt
13921 gtagaaaacc cagatatatt acgcgtatac gccaacttag gtgaacgtgt acgccaag
13981 ttgttaaaaa cagtacaatt ctgtgatgcc atgcgaaatg ctggtattgt tggtgtac
14041 acattagata atcaagatct caatggtaac tggtatgatt tcggtgattt catacaaa
14101 acgccaggta gtggagttcc tgttgtagat tcttattatt cattgttaat gcctatat
14161 accttgacca gggctttaac tgcagagtca catgttgaca ctgacttaac aaagcctt
14221 attaagtggg atttgttaaa atatgacttc acggaagaga ggttaaaact ctttgacc
14281 tattttaaat attgggatca gacataccac ccaaattgtg ttaactgttt ggatgaca
14341 tgcattctgc attgtgcaaa ctttaatgtt ttattctcta cagtgttccc acctacaa
14401 tttggaccac tagtgagaaa aatatttgtt gatggtgttc catttgtagt ttcaactg
14461 taccacttca gagagctagg tgttgtacat aatcaggatg taaacttaca tagctctg
14521 cttagtttta aggaattact tgtgtatgct gctgaccctg ctatgcacgc tgcttctg
14581 aatctattac tagataaacg cactacgtgc ttttcagtag ctgcacttac taacaatg
14641 gctttcaaa ctgtcaaacc cggtaatttt aacaagact tctatgactt tgctgtg
14701 aagggtttct ttaaggaagg aagttctgtt gaattaaaac acttcttctt tgctcag
14761 ggtaatgctg ctatcagcga ttatgactac tatcgttata atctaccaac aatgtgt
14821 atcagacaac tactatttgt agttgaagtt gttgataagt acttgattg ttacgatc
14881 ggctgtatta atgctaacca agtcatcgtc aacaacctag acaaatcagc tggtttt
14941 tttaataaat ggggtaaggc tagactttat tatgattcaa tgagttatga ggatcaa
15001 gcactttcg catatacaaa acgtaatgtc atccctacta taactcaaat gaatctt
15061 tatgccatta gtgcaaagaa tagagctcgc accgtagctg gtgtctctat ctgtagt
15121 atgaccaata gacagtttca tcaaaaatta ttgaaatcaa tagccgccac tagagga
15181 actgtagtaa ttggaacaag caaattctat ggtggttggc acaacatgtt aaaaact

241 tatagtgatg tagaaaaccc tcaccttatg ggttgggatt atcctaaatg tgatagagc
301 atgcctaaca tgcttagaat tatggcctca cttgttcttg ctcgcaaaca tacaacgtg
361 tgtagcttgt cacaccgttt ctatagatta gctaatgagt gtgctcaagt attgagtga
421 atggtcatgt gtggcggttc actatatgtt aaaccaggtg gaacctcatc aggagatgc
481 acaactgctt atgctaatag tgtttttaac atttgtcaag ctgtcacggc caatgttaa
541 gcactttat ctactgatgg taacaaaatt gccgataagt atgtccgcaa tttacaaca
601 agactttatg agtgtctcta tagaaataga gatgttgaca cagactttgt gaatgagtt
661 tacgcatatt tgcgtaaaca tttctcaatg atgatactct ctgacgatgc tgttgtgtg
721 ttcaatagca cttatgcatc tcaaggtcta gtggctagca taaagaactt taagtcagt
781 ctttattatc aaaacaatgt ttttatgtct gaagcaaaat gttggactga gactgacct
841 actaaaggac ctcatgaatt ttgctctcaa catacaatgc tagttaaaca gggtgatga
901 tatgtgtacc ttccttaccc agatccatca agaatcctag gggccggctg ttttgtaga
961 gatatcgtaa aaacagatgg tacacttatg attgaacggt tcgtgtcttt agctataga
021 gcttacccac ttactaaaca tcctaatcag gagtatgctg atgtctttca tttgtactt
081 caatacataa gaaagctaca tgatgagtta acaggacaca tgttagacat gtattctgt
141 atgcttacta atgataacac ttcaaggtat tgggaacctg agttttatga ggctatgta
201 acaccgcata cagtcttaca ggctgttggg gcttgtgttc tttgcaattc acagacttc
261 ttaagatgtg gtgcttgcat acgtagacca ttcttatgtt gtaaatgctg ttacgacca
321 gtcatatcaa catcacataa attagtcttg tctgttaatc cgtatgtttg caatgctcc
381 ggttgtgatg tcacagatgt gactcaactt tacttaggag gtatgagcta ttattgtaa
441 tcacataaac cacccattag ttttccattg tgtgctaatg acaagtttt tggttttata
501 aaaaatacat gtgttggtag cgataatgtt actgacttta atgcaattgc aacatgtga
561 tggacaaatg ctggtgatta cattttagct aacacctgta ctgaaagact caagcttt
621 gcagcagaaa cgctcaaagc tactgaggag acatttaaac tgtcttatgg tattgctac
681 gtacgtgaag tgctgtctga cagagaatta catctttcat gggagttgg taaacctag
741 ccaccactta accgaaatta tgtctttact ggttatcgtg taactaaaaa cagtaaagt
801 caaataggag agtacacctt tgaaaaaggt gactatggtg atgctgttgt ttaccgagg
861 acaacaactt acaaattaaa tgttggtgat tatttgtgc tgacatcaca tacagtaat
921 ccattaagtg cacctacact agtgccacaa gagcactatg ttagaattac tggcttata
981 ccaacactca atatctcaga tgagttttct agcaatgttg caaattatca aaaggttgg
041 atgcaaaagt attctacact ccagggacca cctggtactg gtaagagtca ttttgctat
101 ggcctagctc tctactaccc ttctgctcgc atagtgtata cagcttgctc tcatgccgc
161 gttgatgcac tatgtgagaa ggcattaaaa tatttgccta tagataaatg tagtagaat
221 atacctgcac gtgctcgtgt agagtgtttt gataaattca aagtgaattc aacattaga
281 cagtatgtct tttgtactgt aaatgcattg cctgagacga cagcagatat agttgtctt
341 gatgaaattt caatggccac aaattatgat ttgagtgttg tcaatgccag attacgtgc
401 aagcactatg tgtacattgg cgaccctgct caattacctg caccacgcac attgctaac
461 aagggcacac tagaaccaga atatttcaat tcagtgtgta gacttatgaa aactatagg
521 ccagacatgt cctcggaac ttgtcggcgt tgtcctgctg aaattgttga cactgtgag
581 gctttggttt atgataataa gcttaaagca cataaagaca aatcagctca atgcttaa
641 atgtttata agggtgttat cacgcatgat gtttcatctg caattaacag gccacaaat
701 ggcgtggtaa gagaattcct tacacgtaac cctgcttgga aaagctgt ctttatttc
761 ccttataatt cacagaatgc tgtagcctca aagattttgg gactaccaac tcaaactgt
821 gattcatcac agggctcaga atatgactat gtcatattca ctcaaccac tgaaacagc
881 cactcttgta atgtaaacag atttaatgtt gctattacca gagcaaaagt aggcatact
941 tgcataatgt ctgatagaga cctttatgac aagttgcaat ttacaagtct tgaaattcc
001 cgtaggaatg tggcaacttt acaagctgaa aatgtaacag gactctttaa agattgtag
061 aaggtaatca ctgggttaca tcctacacag gcacctacac acctcagtgt tgacactaa
121 ttcaaaactg aaggtttatg tgttgacata cctggcatac ctaaggacat gacctatag
181 agactcatct ctatgatggg ttttaaaatg aattatcaag ttaatggtta ccctaaca
241 tttatcaccc gcgaagaagc tataagacat gtacgtgcat ggattggctt cgatgtgc

8301 gggtgtcatg ctactagaga agctgttggt accaattac cttacagct aggttttt
8361 acaggtgtta acctagttgc tgtacctaca ggttatgttg atacacctaa taatacaga
8421 ttttccagag ttagtgctaa accaccgcct ggagatcaat ttaaacacct cataccac
8481 atgtacaaag gacttccttg gaatgtagtg cgtataaaga ttgtacaaat gttaagtga
8541 acacttaaaa atctctctga cagagtcgta tttgtcttat gggcacatgg ctttgagt
8601 acatctatga agtattttgt gaaaatagga cctgagcgca cctgttgtct atgtgata
8661 cgtgccacat gcttttccac tgcttcagac acttatgcct gttggcatca ttctattg
8721 tttgattacg tctataatcc gtttatgatt gatgttcaac aatggggttt tacaggta
8781 ctacaaagca accatgatct gtattgtcaa gtccatggta atgcacatgt agctagtt
8841 gatgcaatca tgactaggtg tctagctgtc cacgagtgct ttgttaagcg tgttgact
8901 actattgaat atcctataat tggtgatgaa ctgaagatta atgcggcttg tagaaagg
8961 caacacatgg ttgttaaagc tgcattatta gcagacaaat cccagttct tcacgaca
9021 ggtaacccta aagctattaa gtgtgtacct caagctgatg tagaatggaa gttctatg
9081 gcacagcctt gtagtgacaa agcttataaa atagaagaat tattctattc ttatgcca
9141 cattctgaca aattcacaga tggtgtatgc ctattttgga attgcaatgt cgatagat
9201 cctgctaatt ccattgtttg tagatttgac actagagtgc tatctaacct taacttgc
9261 ggttgtgatg gtggcagttt gtatgtaaat aaacatgcat tccacacacc agcttttg
9321 aaaagtgctt ttgttaattt aaaacaatta ccatttttct attactctga cagtccat
9381 gagtctcatg gaaaacaagt agtgtcagat atagattatg taccactaaa gtctgcta
9441 tgtataacac gttgcaattt aggtggtgct gtctgtagac atcatgctaa tgagtaca
9501 ttgtatctcg atgcttataa catgatgatc tcagctggct ttagcttgtg ggtttaca
9561 caatttgata cttataacct ctggaacact tttacaagac ttcagagttt agaaaatg
9621 gcttttaatg ttgtaaataa gggacacttt gatggacaac agggtgaagt accagttt
9681 atcattaata acactgttta cacaaaagtt gatggtgttg atgtagaatt gtttgaaa
9741 aaaacaacat tacctgttaa tgtagcattt gagctttggg ctaagcgcaa cattaaac
9801 gtaccagagg tgaaaatact caataatttg ggtgtggaca ttgctgctaa tactgtga
9861 tgggactaca aaagagatgc tccagcacat atatctacta ttggtgtttg ttctatga
9921 gacatagcca agaaaccaac tgaaacgatt tgtgcaccac tcactgtctt ttttgatg
9981 agagttgatg gtcaagtaga cttatttaga aatgcccgta atggtgttct tattacag
0041 ggtagtgtta aaggtttaca accatctgta ggtcccaaac aagctagtct taatggag
0101 acattaattg gagaagccgt aaaaacacag ttcaattatt ataagaaagt tgatggtg
0161 gtccaacaat tacctgaaac ttactttact cagagtagaa atttacaaga atttaaac
0221 aggagtcaaa tggaaattga tttcttagaa ttagctatgg atgaattcat tgaacggt
0281 aaattagaag gctatgcctt cgaacatatc gtttatggag attttagtca tagtcagt
0341 ggtggtttac atctactgat tggactagct aaacgtttta aggaatcacc ttttgaat
0401 gaagatttta ttcctatgga cagtacagtt aaaaactatt tcataacaga tgcgcaaa
0461 ggttcatcta agtgtgtgtg ttctgttatt gatttattac ttgatgattt tgttgaaa
0521 ataaaatccc aagatttatc tgtagtttct aaggttgtca aagtgactat tgactata
0581 gaaatttcat ttatgctttg gtgtaaagat ggccatgtag aaacatttta cccaaaat
0641 caatctagtc aagcgtggca accgggtgtt gctatgccta atctttacaa aatgcaaa
0701 atgctattag aaaagtgtga ccttcaaaat tatggtgata gtgcaacatt acctaaag
0761 ataatgatga atgtcgcaaa atatactcaa ctgtgtcaat atttaaacac attaacat
0821 gctgtaccct ataatatgag agttatacat tttggtgctg gttctgataa aggagttg
0881 ccaggtacag ctgtttttaag acagtggttg cctacgggta cgctgcttgt cgattcag
0941 cttaatgact ttgtctctga tgcagattca actttgattg gtgattgtgc aactgtac
1001 acagctaata aatgggatct cattattagt gatatgtacg accctaagac taaaaatg
1061 acaaagaaa atgactctaa agagggtttt ttcacttaca tttgtgggtt tatacaac
1121 aagctagctc ttggaggttc cgtggctata aagataacag aacattcttg gaatgctg
1181 ctttataagc tcatgggaca cttcgcatgg tggacagcct ttgttactaa tgtgaatg
1241 tcatcatctg aagcattttt aattggatgt aattatcttg gcaaaccacg cgaacaaa
1301 gatggttatg tcatgcatgc aaattacata ttttggagga atacaaatcc aattcagt

561 tcttcctatt ctttatttga catgagtaaa tttcccctta aattaagggg cactgctgtt
421 atgtctttaa aagaaggtca aatcaatgat atgattttat ctcttcttag taaaggtaga
481 cttataatta gagaaaacaa cagagttgtt atttctagtg atgttcttgt taacaactaa
541 acgaacaatg tttgtttttc ttgttttatt gccactagtc tctagtcagt gtgttaatct
601 tacaaccaga actcaattac cccctgcata cactaattct ttcacacgtg gtgtttatta
661 ccctgacaaa gttttcagat cctcagtttt acattcaact caggacttgt tcttaccttt
721 cttttccaat gttacttggt tccatgctat acatgtctct gggaccaatg gtactaagag
781 gtttgataac cctgtcctac catttaatga tggtgtttat tttgcttcca ctgagaagtc
841 taacataata agaggctgga ttttggtac tactttagat tcgaagaccc agtccctact
901 tattgttaat aacgctacta atgttgttat taaagtctgt gaatttcaat tttgtaatga
961 tccatttttg ggtgtttatt accacaaaaa caacaaaagt tggatggaaa gtgagttcag
021 agtttattct agtgcgaata attgcacttt tgaatatgtc tctcagcctt ttcttatgga
081 ccttgaagga aaacagggta atttcaaaaa tcttagggaa tttgtgttta agaatattga
141 tggttatttt aaaatatatt ctaagcacac gcctattaat ttagtgcgtg atctccctca
201 gggttttcg cttttagaac cattggtaga tttgccaata ggtattaaca tcactaggtt
261 tcaaacttta cttgctttac atagaagtta tttgactcct ggtgattctt cttcaggttg
321 gacagctggt gctgcagctt attatgtggg ttatcttcaa cctaggactt ttctattaaa
381 atataatgaa aatggaacca ttacagatgc tgtagactgt gcacttgacc ctctctcaga
441 aacaaagtgt acgttgaaat ccttcactgt agaaaaagga atctatcaaa cttctaactt
501 tagagtccaa ccaacagaat ctattgttag atttcctaat attacaaact tgtgcccttt
561 tggtgaagtt tttaacgcca ccagatttgc atctgtttat gcttggaaca ggaagagaat
621 cagcaactgt gttgctgatt attctgtcct atataattcc gcatcatttt ccacttttaa
681 gtgttatgga gtgtctccta ctaaattaaa tgatctctgc tttactaatg tctatgcaga
741 ttcatttgta attagaggtg atgaagtcag acaaatcgct ccagggcaaa ctggaaagat
801 tgctgattat aattataaat taccagatga ttttacaggc tgcgttatag cttggaattc
861 taacaatctt gattctaagg ttggtggtaa ttataattac ctgtatagat tgtttaggaa
921 gtctaatctc aaaccttttg agagagatat ttcaactgaa atctatcagg ccggtagcac
981 accttgtaat ggtgttgaag gttttaattg ttactttcct ttacaatcat atggtttcca
041 acccactaat ggtgttggtt accaaccata cagagtagta gtactttctt ttgaacttct
101 acatgcacca gcaactgttt gtggacctaa aaagtctact aatttggtta aaaacaaatg
161 tgtcaatttc aacttcaatg gtttaacagg cacaggtgtt cttactgagt ctaacaaaaa
221 gtttctgcct ttccaacaat ttggcagaga cattgctgac actactgatg ctgtccgtga
281 tccacagaca cttgagattc ttgacattac accatgttct tttggtggtg tcagtgttat
341 aacaccagga acaaatactt ctaaccaggt tgctgttctt tatcaggatg ttaactgcac
401 agaagtccct gttgctattc atgcagatca acttactcct acttggcgtg tttattctac
461 aggttctaat gtttttcaaa cacgtgcagg ctgtttaata ggggctgaac atgtcaacaa
521 ctcatatgag tgtgacatac ccattggtgc aggtatatgc gctagttatc agactcagac
581 taattctcct cggcgggcac gtagtgtagc tagtcaatcc atcattgcct acactatgtc
641 acttggtgca gaaaattcag ttgcttactc taataactct attgccatac ccacaaattt
701 tactattagt gttaccacag aaattctacc agtgtctatg accaagacat cagtagattg
761 tacaatgtac atttgtggtg attcaactga atgcagcaat ctttttgttg caatatggcag
821 tttttgtaca caattaaacc gtgctttaac tggaatagct gttgaacaag acaaaaacag
881 ccaagaagtt tttgcacaag tcaaacaaat ttacaaaaca ccaccaatta agattttggt
941 tggttttaat ttttcacaaa tattaccaga tccatcaaaa ccaagcaaga ggtcatttat
001 tgaagatcta cttttcaata aagtgacact tgcagatgct ggcttcatca acaatatggt
061 tgattgcctt ggtgatattg ctgctagaga cctcatttgt gcacaaaagt ttaacggcct
121 tactgttttg ccacctttgc tcacagatga aatgattgct caatacactt ctgcactgtt
181 agcgggtaca atcacttctg gttggacctt tggtgcaggt gctgcattac aaataccatt
241 tgctatgcaa atggcttata ggtttaatgg tattggagtt acacagaatg ttctctatga
301 gaaccaaaaa ttgattgcca accaatttaa tagtgctatt ggcaaaattc aagactcac
361 ttcttccaca gcaagtgcac ttggaaaaact tcaagatgtg gtcaaccaaa atgcacaag

```
24421 tttaaacacg cttgttaaac aacttagctc caattttggt gcaatttcaa gtgtttta
24481 tgatatcctt tcacgtcttg acaaagttga ggctgaagtg caaattgata ggttgatc
24541 aggcagactt caaagtttgc agacatatgt gactcaacaa ttaattagag ctgcagaa
24601 cagagcttct gctaatcttg ctgctactaa aatgtcagag tgtgtacttg acaatca
24661 aagagttgat ttttgtggaa agggctatca tcttatgtcc ttccctcagt cagcacct
24721 tggtgtagtc ttcttgcatg tgacttatgt ccctgcacaa gaaaagaact tcacaact
24781 tcctgccatt tgtcatgatg gaaaagcaca ctttcctcgt gaaggtgtct ttgtttca
24841 tggcacacac tggtttgtaa cacaaggaa tttttatgaa ccacaaatca ttactaca
24901 caacacattt gtgtctggta actgtgatgt tgtaatagga attgtcaaca acacagtt
24961 tgatcctttg caacctgaat tagactcatt caaggaggag ttagataaat attttaag
25021 tcatacatca ccagatgttg atttaggtga catctctggc attaatgctt cagttgta
25081 cattcaaaaa gaaattgacc gcctcaatga ggttgccaag aatttaaatg aatctctc
25141 cgatctccaa gaacttggaa agtatgagca gtatataaaa tggccatggt acatttgg
25201 aggttttata gctggcttga ttgccatagt aatggtgaca attatgcttt gctgtatg
25261 cagttgctgt agttgtctca agggctgttg ttcttgtgga tcctgctgca aatttgat
25321 agacgactct gagccagtgc tcaaaggagt caaattacat tacacataaa cgaactta
25381 gatttgttta tgagaatctt cacaattgga actgtaactt tgaagcaagg tgaaatca
25441 gatgctactc cttcagattt tgttcgcgct actgcaacga taccgataca agcctcac
25501 cctttcggat ggcttattgt tggcgttgca cttcttgctg tttttcagag cgcttcca
25561 atcataaccc tcaaaaagag atggcaacta gcactctcca agggtgttca ctttgttt
25621 aacttgctgt tgttgtttgt aacagtttac tcacaccttt tgctcgttgc tgctggcc
25681 gaagcccctt ttctctatct ttatgcttta gtctacttct tgcagagtat aaacttt
25741 agaataataa tgaggctttg ctttgctgg aaatgccgtt ccaaaaaccc attacttt
25801 gatgccaact attttctttg ctggcatact aattgttacg actattgtat accttaca
25861 agtgtaactt cttcaattgt cattacttca ggtgatggca caacaagtcc tatttctg
25921 catgactacc agattggtgg ttatactgaa aaatgggaat ctggagtaaa agactgtg
25981 gtattacaca gttacttcac ttcagactat taccagctgt actcaactca attgagta
26041 gacactggtg ttgaacatgt taccttcttc atctacaata aaattgttga tgagcctg
26101 gaacatgtcc aaattcacac aatcgacggt tcatccggag ttgttaatcc agtaatgg
26161 ccaatttatg atgaaccgac gacgactact agcgtgcctt tgtaagcaca agctgatg
26221 tacgaactta tgtactcatt cgtttcggaa gagacaggta cgttaatagt taatagcg
26281 cttctttttc ttgctttcgt ggtattcttg ctagttacac tagccatcct tactgcg
26341 cgattgtgtg cgtactgctg caatattgtt aacgtgagtc ttgtaaaacc ttctttt
26401 gtttactctc gtgttaaaaa tctgaattct tctagagttc ctgatcttct ggtctaa
26461 aactaaatat tatattagtt tttctgtttg gaactttaat tttagccatg gcagatt
26521 acggtactat taccgttgaa gagcttaaaa agctccttga caatggaac ctagtaat
26581 gtttcctatt ccttacatgg atttgtcttc tacaatttgc ctatgccaac aggaata
26641 ttttgtatat aattaagtta attttcctct ggctgttatg gccagtaact ttagctt
26701 ttgtgcttgc tgctgtttac agaataaatt ggatcaccgg tggaattgct atcgcaa
26761 cttgtcttgt aggcttgatg tggctcagct acttcattgc ttctttcaga ctgtttg
26821 gtacgcgttc catgtggtca ttcaatccag aaactaacat tcttctcaac gtgccac
26881 atggcactat tctgaccaga ccgcttctag aaagtgaact cgtaatcgga gctgtga
26941 ttcgtggaca tcttcgtatt gctggacacc atctaggacg ctgtgacatc aaggacc
27001 ctaaagaaat cactgttgct acatcacgaa cgctttctta ttacaaattg ggagctt
27061 agcgtgtagc aggtgactca ggttttgctg catacagtcg ctacaggatt ggcaact
27121 aattaaacac agaccattcc agtagcagtg acaatattgc tttgcttgta cagtaag
27181 caacagatgt ttcatctcgt tgactttcag gttactatag cagagatatt actaatt
27241 atgaggactt ttaaagtttc catttggaat cttgattaca tcataaacct cataatt
27301 aatttatcta agtcactaac tgagaataaa tattctcaat tagatgaaga gcaacaa
27361 gagattgatt aaacgaacat gaaaattatt cttttcttgg cactgataac actcgct
27421 tgtgagcttt atcactacca agagtgtgtt agaggtacaa cagtacttt
```

```
 481 tgctcttctg gaacatacga gggcaattca ccatttcatc ctctagctga taacaaatt
 541 gcactgactt gctttagcac tcaatttgct tttgcttgtc ctgacggcgt aaaacacgt
 601 tatcagttac gtgccagatc agtttcacct aaactgttca tcagacaaga ggaagttca
 661 gaactttact ctccaatttt tcttattgtt gcggcaatag tgtttataac actttgctt
 721 acactcaaaa gaaagacaga atgattgaac tttcattaat tgacttctat ttgtgcttt
 781 tagcctttct gctattcctt gttttaatta tgcttattat cttttggttc tcacttgaa
 841 tgcaagatca taatgaaact tgtcacgcct aaacgaacat gaaatttctt gttttctta
 901 gaatcatcac aactgtagct gcatttcacc aagaatgtag tttacagtca tgtactcaa
 961 atcaaccata tgtagttgat gacccgtgtc ctattcactt ctattctaaa tggtatatt
021 gagtaggagc tagaaaatca gcacctttaa ttgaattgtg cgtggatgag ctggttct
081 aatcacccat tcagtacatc gatatcggta attatacagt ttcctgttta ccttttaca
141 ttaattgcca ggaacctaaa ttgggtagtc ttgtagtgcg ttgttcgttc tatgaagac
201 ttttagagta tcatgacgtt cgtgttgttt tagatttcat ctaaacgaac aaactaaaa
261 gtctgataat ggaccccaaa atcagcgaaa tgcaccccgc attacgtttg gtggaccct
321 agattcaact ggcagtaacc agaatggaga acgcagtggg gcgcgatcaa acaacgtc
381 gccccaaggt ttacccaata atactgcgtc ttggttcacc gctctcactc aacatggca
441 ggaagacctt aaattccctc gaggacaagg cgttccaatt aacaccaata gcagtccag
501 tgaccaaatt ggctactacc gaagagctac cagacgaatt cgtggtggtg acggtaaaa
561 gaaagatctc agtccaagat ggtatttcta ctacctagga actgggccag aagctggac
621 tccctatggt gctaacaaag acggcatcat atgggttgca actgagggag ccttgaata
681 accaaaagat cacattggca cccgcaatcc tgctaacaat gctgcaatcg tgctacaac
741 tcctcaagga acaacattgc caaaaggctt ctacgcagaa gggagcagag gcggcagtc
801 agcctcttct cgttcctcat cacgtagtcg caacagttca agaaattcaa ctccaggca
861 cagtagggga acttctcctg ctagaatggc tggcaatggc ggtgatgctg ctcttgctt
921 gctgctgctt gacagattga accagcttga gagcaaaatg tctggtaaag gccaacaac
981 acaaggccaa actgtcacta gaaatctgc tgctgaggct tctaagaagc ctcggcaaa
041 acgtactgcc actaaagcat acaatgtaac acaagctttc ggcagacgtg gtccagaac
101 aacccaagga aattttgggg accaggaact aatcagacaa ggaactgatt acaaacatt
161 gccgcaaatt gcacaatttg cccccagcgc ttcagcgttc ttcggaatgt cgcgcattg
221 catggaagtc acaccttcgg gaacgtggtt gacctacaca ggtgccatca aattggatg
281 caaagatcca aatttcaaag atcaagtcat tttgctgaat aagcatattg acgcataca
341 aacattccca ccaacagagc ctaaaaagga caaaagaag aaggctgatg aaactcaag
401 cttaccgcag agacagaaga aacagcaaac tgtgactctt cttcctgctg cagatttgg
461 tgatttctcc aaacaattgc aacaatccat gagcagtgct gactcaactc aggcctaaa
521 tcatgcagac cacacaaggc agatgggcta tataacgtt ttcgctttt cgtttacga
581 atatagtcta ctcttgtgca gaatgaattc tcgtaactac atagcacaag tagatgtag
641 taactttaat ctcacatagc aatctttaat cagtgtgtaa cattagggag gacttgaaa
701 agccaccaca ttttcaccga ggccacgcgg agtacgatcg agtgtacagt gaacaatgc
761 agggagagct gcctatatgg aagagcccta atgtgtaaaa ttaattttag t
```

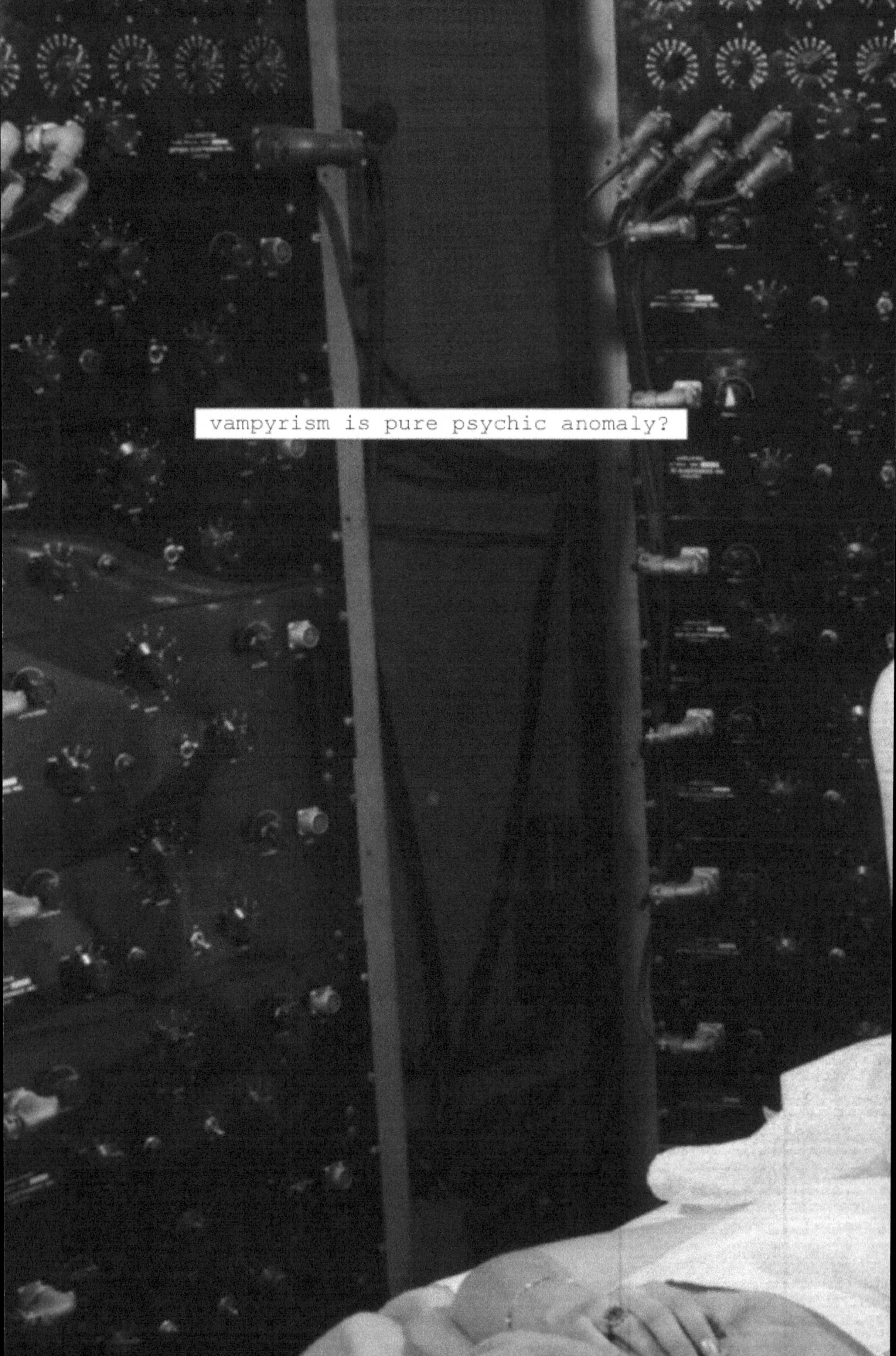
vampyrism is pure psychic anomaly?

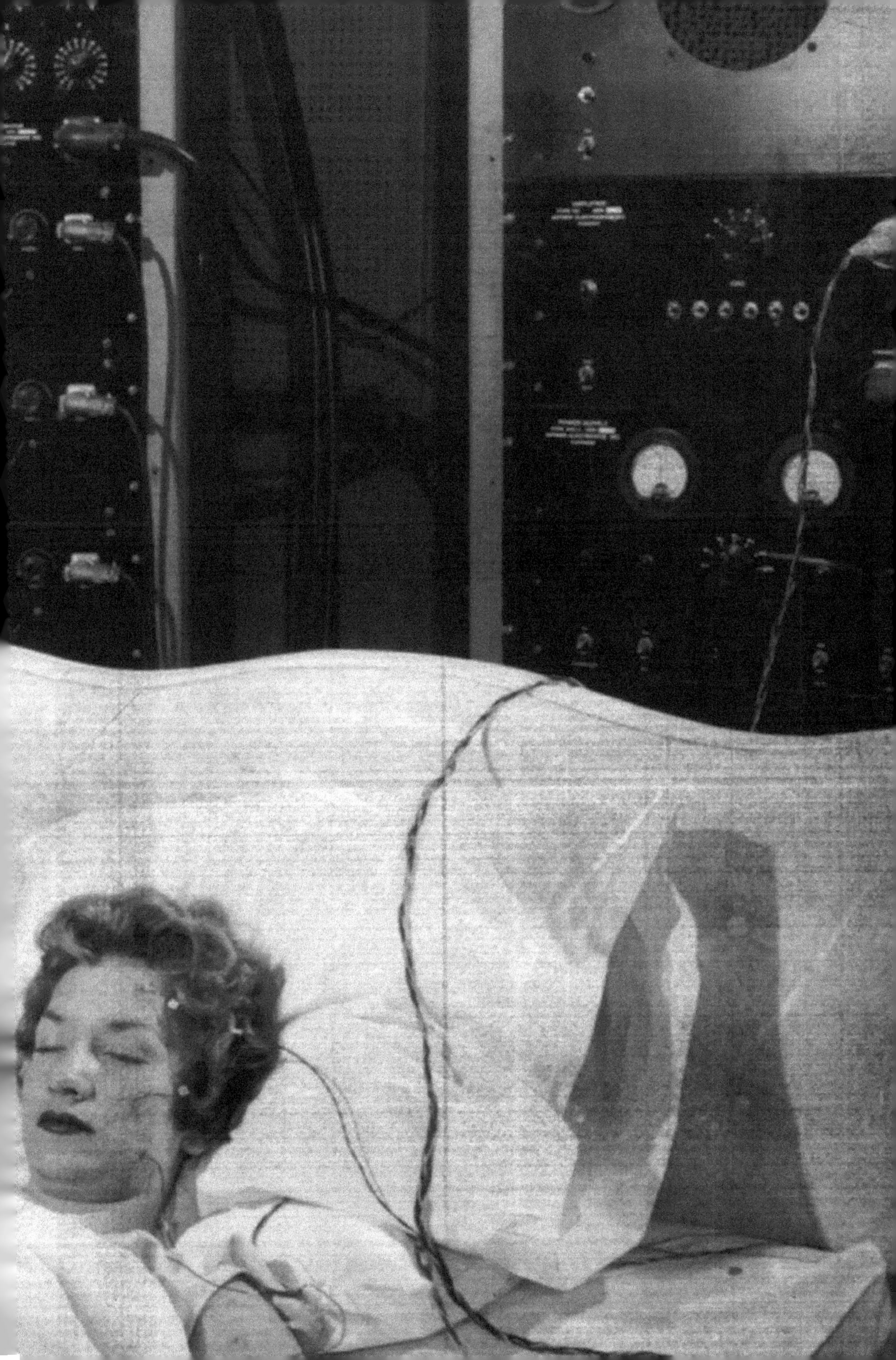

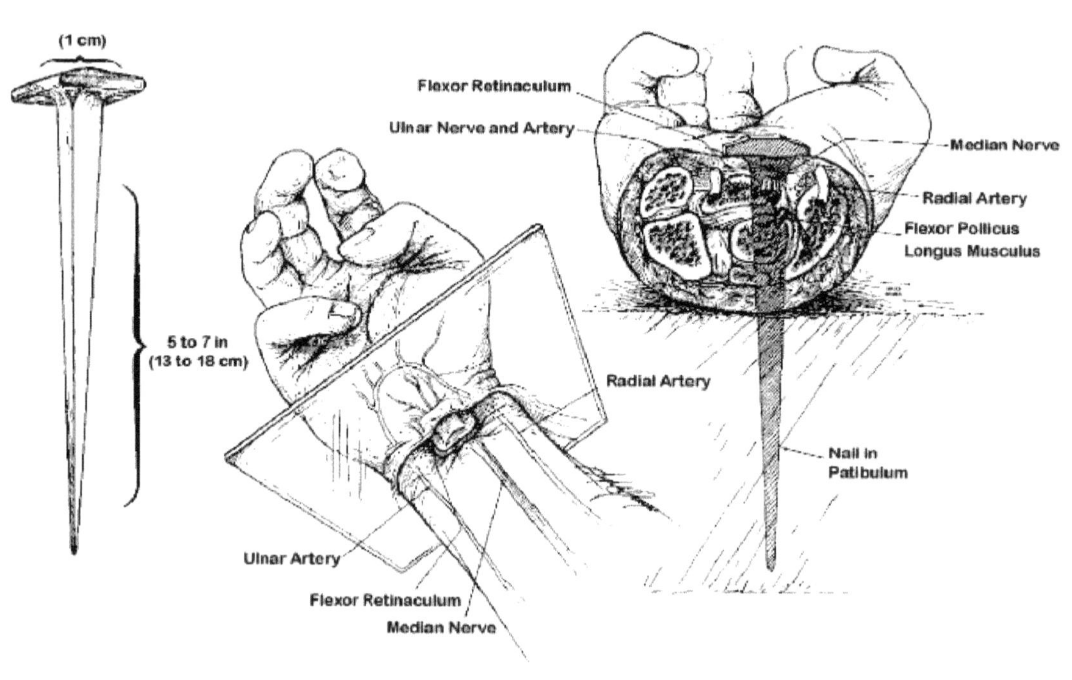
(1 cm)
5 to 7 in
(13 to 18 cm)
Flexor Retinaculum
Ulnar Nerve and Artery
Median Nerve
Radial Artery
Flexor Pollicus
Longus Musculus
Radial Artery
Ulnar Artery
Flexor Retinaculum
Median Nerve
Nail in
Patibulum

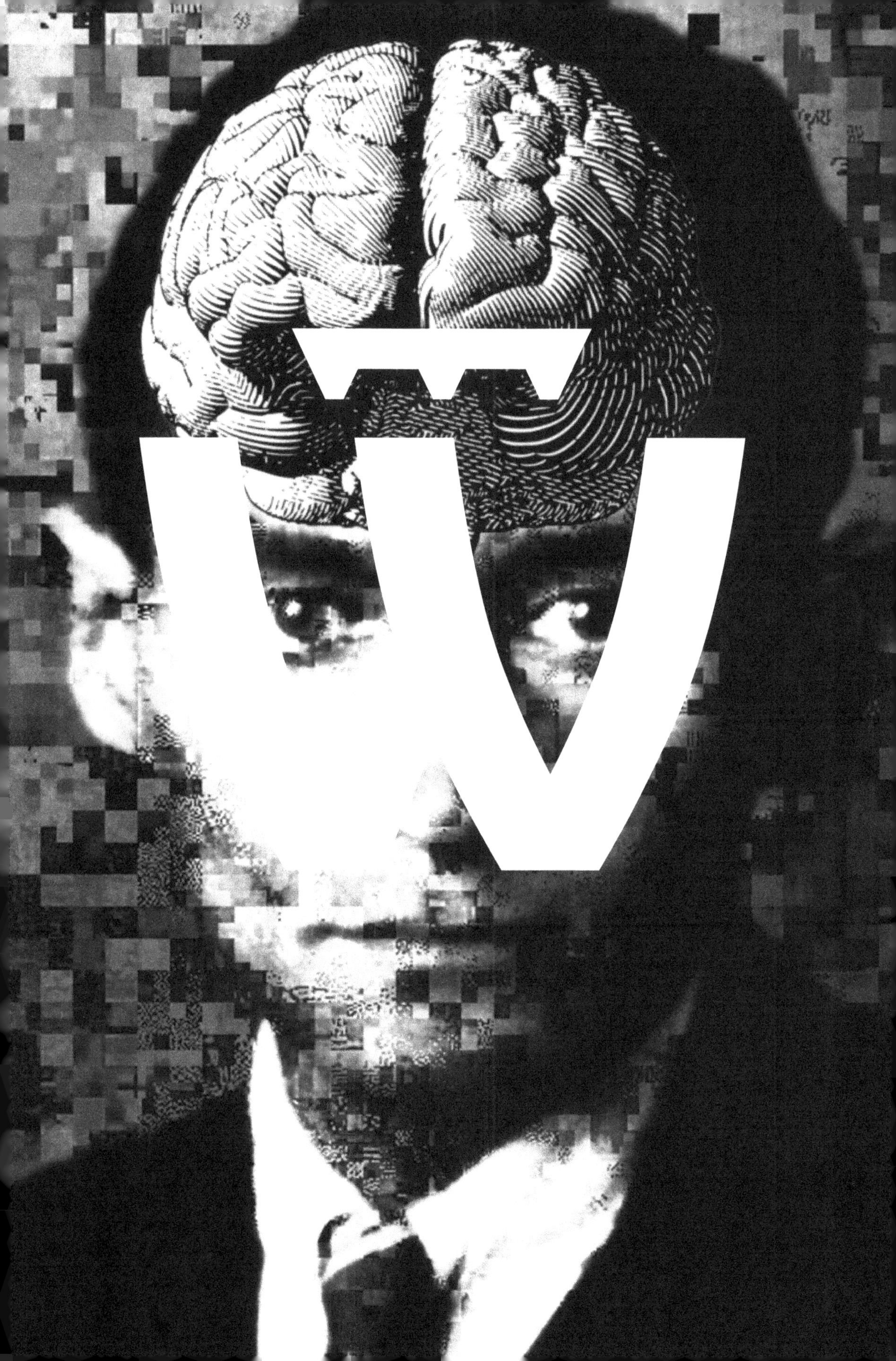

TENTH COMMUNIQUÉ
PAPA WALT & HIS MINIONS ARE THE VIRAL SCUM OF THE EARTH!
    They hide the deliberate rundown of all eco=social infrastructure that for decades they've been exploiting for profit.
    RESTORE ALL NATURAL RESOURCES & PUBLIC UTILITIES!
    The vulture drones are circling Golemgrad, ready to fight over the scraps of its unnatural corpse.
    The same scum who instigated the productivity scams to "restart the economy," signed=off on redundancies that put millions of our sisters in an early grave.
    The same scum who call our very existence a hoax are now trying to feed off our struggle, with their hands out for "compensation."
    The same scum who have infected the very air for profit, while extorting public money for vaccines that don't work, testing kits that don't work, protective equipment that doesn't work.
    Time has come to occupy the means of production once & for all!
    Loot the morgues of neoliberalism!
    Wreck vampyr kapitalism!
    YOU ARE YR OWN PATH TO EMXNCIPATION.
    USE YR OWN TACTICS.
    CONTROL YR OWN STRUGGLE.
    SOLIDARITY!
    The Š.V.E.J.K.

TOMORROW THE WORLD MAY BURST INTO FRAGMENTS

Because even the sucking of blood affirms something & does homage to this wretched & magnificent unlife that is ours! Who else shall perform violence against them, the gilded lilies, the asphodels, the potted geraniums of humxnity? They are like domesticated rats in ridiculous cages. Like a brain in a complicated jar. To this do we owe our tremendous task? Has all of History & its prehistories, its creation & protocreations, led to this? The pinnacle atop the pyramid of all possible worlds? And this the most perfect? The monad of monads? The quantum confabulation of infinity into the base stuff of a concrete situation? Analyse. Begin w/ the necessary, unstated premise… (This is always the hard part.) *All "things" exist unequally. In turn, all existence is cataclysmic. For each birth a billion unbirths.* A lot of wind just to root out the apparents from the appearances. They've spilt more collective jism than Xerxes, Qin Shi, Genghis Khan, Attila, Torquemada, Bloody Mary, Ivan the Terrible, Robespierre, Hitler, Mao, Leopold II, Tojo, Stalin, Talat Paşa, Pol Pot, Franco, Idi Amin, Pinochet & G.O.D. spilt blood, & look where it's gotten them.

THE BLIND WATCHMAKERS

In order to survive they were forced to endure near=death by information attrition, by media inanition, by a thousand logarithmic curves, by endless statistics: statistics for humxn infection rates, animal infection rates, virus mutation rates, test rates, transmission rates, remission rates, mortality rates, attack rates, survival rates; numbers of masks, numbers of respirators, numbers of ventilators, numbers of surgical gowns, numbers of test kits, numbers of ICUs, numbers of hospital beds, numbers of reported cases, estimated numbers of unreported cases, numbers symptomatic & asymptomatic, number of burials, number of cremations, number of bodies unclaimed, number of infections by demographic, race, age=group, place=of=residence, economic status, number of mortalities w/ underlying conditions, number w/out underlying conditions, number of doctors, nurses, orderlies, sanitary crews, number of mortalities among doctors, nurses, orderlies, sanitary crews, number of infections among prison inmates, in immigration detention centres, nursing homes, psychiatric institutions, way houses, military barracks, cruise ships, number of restrictions in place by jurisdiction, number effected by lockdown, quarantine, self=isolation, number evading restrictions, number protesting, numbers fined, arrested, number panic=buying, stockpiling, homeless, starving, number provided w/ rent=relief, mortgage=relief, health insurance, basic income, number not, number volunteering, donating, assisting, number profiteering, number of psychotic incidents, number of attacks on alleged "spreaders," number of attacks on health=workers, number of homicides, incidents of domestic violence, hate=crimes, number of gun sales, number of toiletpaper sales, number of grounded flights, number of unemployed, number of bankruptcies, numbers reflecting virus impact on air quality, water quality, fuel consumption, oil production, global trading figures, stock market figures, band=width usage, public transport, curfew times, curfew by age, by gender, by mental capacity, by income, by sense of self=worth, hahaha. In short, proof, if proof were needed, that every Age of Enlightenment, every Era of Encyclopaedic Scientism, has been precipitated by the plague.

WHAT USE IS A HUMXN WHO CAN'T CLEAN A TOILET?
The force that commands a majority isn't the force that commands the truth.

WE ARE TRANSFORMING THE SHRINE INTO PENTECOSTAL NIGHT
El Lugosi Stadium, an elephantine construction dominating one third of Golemgrad's western skyline, was requisitioned overnight by the self=appointed military junta for the processing, incarceration, interrogation, torture & execution of suspected dissidents. Thousands of summarily arrested students, trade unionists, journalists, intellectuals, homosexuals, Jews, foreigners & other scum were corralled among the bleachers, where they waited, shivered, starved, slept, bled, pissed, shat, cried, were raped, beaten, went mad, committed suicide. Down in the underground corridors & dressing rooms, untold horrors. The screech of bullhorns reading the transport lists. Endless trucks, arriving, departing. Brainshocked detainees blinking into the floodlights, marched at bayonet=point in columns out onto the playing field & sorted into work details. Under the ever=vigilant eyes of heavy machineguns, an enormous scaffold was being constructed at the far end of the Stadium. In a week's time, Eddie Van Helsing was scheduled to serenade the forces of Law & Order in the biggest stadium gig in history. The Marshall stacks & lighting rigs & video

screens were going to stand ten storeys high. Every night between soundchecks, any prisoners who hadn't already been snuffed in the torture chambers were strung up over the makeshift stage. Afterwards, fresh conscripts carted off the bodies in dumptrucks. By the time Eddie Van Helsing's custom Stratocaster roared into life, there wasn't a live rat left in the place.

WORDS HEAPED W/ AFFECTIVE PUKE

An Olympic swimming pool filled w/ corpses.

> [Attention!
> We are about to begin the medley relay,
> take yr marks.]

REVOLUTIONARY/B=SIDE [*E.V.H.]

You spend ten black years in an institution,
waiting around for a revolution.
The times might change but yr time never comes.
Say y're making the best of a bad situation.
You packed yr bags now y're living on the street.
Shout at everyone you meet.
You got the Big Idea but yr mind's gone blown.
Now y're living down on Revolution, baby.
Well the Man done tell you that crime don't pay,
do honest work for an honest wage.
The Law's got yr ticket for a one=way ride.
Now the Devil's come to burn you alive.
They gotcha running here, gotcha running there.
Running all the time coz y're running scared.
Run run run to the end of the line.
And you see that revolution coming right on time.
(And it clear run you over, baby.)
Y'all down on Revolution Street.

EXPERIMENTATION HAS ITS PLACE

The air of being unfinished, unresolved, breaks just as easily w/ its own tradition.

NO REVOLUTION IS WRITTEN ON THE VOID

Crispr: "Voilà, mon Frankenstein!"
"Indeed," **Offensia** drawled, "a first attempt is a frightful thing to behold!"

ZOMBIES ON THE INSTALMENT PLAN

There are no *revolutionary preconditions* – no schedule of contingencies, no
burden of teleology. Evolutionary time is metabolised in quanta of *chance*
& *randomness*: causalities in a perpetual state of war. This catalytic flux is an
alien ☻ time machine: it *evolves itself*. Against the G.O.D. programme o
auto=recuperation, it is the sole *a priori*. Paralysed in view of this anti=image
of all anti=images, the mind of the humxn ape succeeds only in producing
metaphysics. Intelligence has never required a "life form," but the contrary
is as nonsensical as humxnistic despair. From this derives the entirety o
that tragic view of History to which political pseudo=science is so morbidly
bound. What they have called, with exemplary hubris, the Humxnocene
predicates History itself as a romantic fatalism, by means of which humxnity
dreams *its own strategic supersession,* so as to be BORN AGAIN, FOR EVER
& EVER, amen. (For what's humxnity but the class of all oppressive classes?
The very category of power is a fetish erected upon the littoral of the void
Their true god, ENTROPY. In its name they pronounce the epoch of the
post=historical, *post*=humxn, *post*=political. This movement mimics, w/ou
irony or contradiction, the "inevitable progress" of social relations. But the
end of politics by *fait accompli* isn't the accomplishment of a revolution ir
the streets, but of pure eschatology. It signals not the finality of *struggle* – ir
the direction of social transformation – but a *fatality* of struggle. What thus
reflects itself in the "coming singularity" is nothing but the spectral form o
power itself (not kapitalism: you can't kill what's *always already* dead). N$_x$

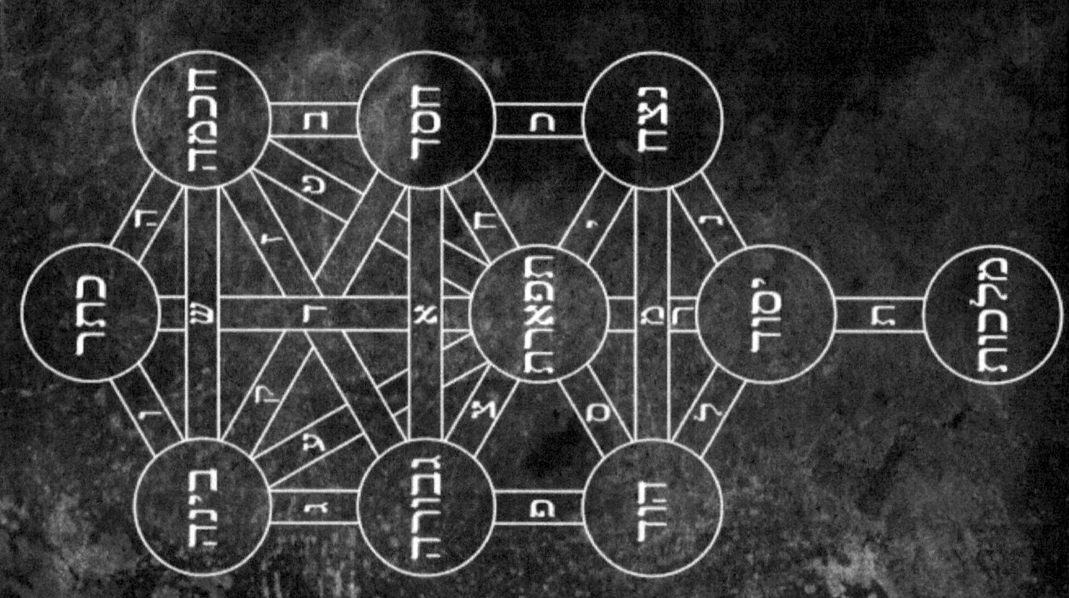

NATIONAL VAMPYROLOGICAL INSTITUTE (NVI)

GOLEMGRAD (#FakeNewsMedia) — Dr Zifčák Asperger, latterly of the WHO, today addressed a gathering at the NVI to discuss the workings of the vampyr immune system & the viability of recent proposals for Convulsive Endocrine Therapy in the treatment of late=onset vampyrosis. In early=onset cases, Dr Asperger is known to be an ardent advocate of Lymph Excision, a method described as still in a developmental phase.

THEIR HORRIFIC DEATHS LOOK LESS LIKE SATIRE EVERY DAY!

A cabal of awful comedians disguised as mad scientists reanimate the corpse of crazed mass=murderer Papa Walt, who is immediately elected Emperor of the World, disguised as @RealPresidentChloroqueen (a cunningly designed animatronic waxworks dummy *that fools absolutely no=one!).* The script is utterly ludicrous. In other words, pure entertainment! See zombies, vampyrs, ghouls, werewolves, voodoo rites, weird creatures! A nihilistic tale of greed, madness, genocide & absolute power! Watch people die in horrible & sometimes hilarious ways! All=star action & stupid cheap thrills! Definitely not to be missed. ★★★★

WHAT IS IT THAT MAKES TODAY'S FICTION SO DIFFERENT, SO APPEALING?

GOLEMGRAD (#FakeNewsMedia) – The benchmark price of oil today plunged into the red as the CORVID=69 pandemic ravaged global economies. Buyers in Golemgrad are no longer offering pesos for some oil streams, w/ producers having to pay to have crude taken off their hands. *More on this story:

OIL PRICES FALL TO HISTORIC LOWS

The oil market has collapsed into negative prices for the first time in history as oil producers run out of space to store an unprecedented oversupply of crude left by the pandemic.

The price of crude oil has fallen by more than 200% on Monday as rising stockpiles of crude threaten to overwhelm oil storage facilities. It is the lowest level since records began.

The crash in demand caused by the pandemic has forced oil producers to start paying buyers to take the glut of oil barrels they cannot store, causing the benchmark oil price to plunge into negative territory for the first time.

There have been reports of oil tankers adrift on the world's oceans unable to find ports willing or able to accept their cargo.

Meanwhile oil executives have been lobbying the administration to initiate airstrikes against rival producers & exporters, in an effort to curtail further oversupply.

In related news, heavy fallout has been predicted across Mitteleuropa following a string of explosions at the Golemgrad nuclear powerplant. A tsunami warning has been issues for areas along the Bohemian, with aftershocks from the explosions measuring at up to 5 on the Richter Scale. This follows reports of an oilspill & fires at the state refinery, blamed by authorities on radical separatist groups. According to experts, there is a risk of severe floods, pestilence & famine if the present economic situation continues & crude prices fail to stabilise.

<u>**THE BLOOD OF OTHERS**</u> **(REEL 10: A "TREATMENT" [NOT CURE])**
Crazed scientist "Thoth Zrcadlo" (a.k.a. Armand=the=Apocryphal=Etc),
uses artificial insemination to grow the first vampyr in captivity.
Accidentally bitten, he contracts the virus. His nubile lab
assistants (the Castel Twins) fall into a mysterious erotic
delirium. Realising his predicament, "Zrcadlo" locks the vampyr
inside a cryogenic tank. Now it's a race against the clock to
discover a cure before the virus spreads to all humxnity. The
lab assistants meanwhile attempt to free the vampyr, freezing
themselves into naked humxn statues in the process. Soon Zrcadlo
finds himself transforming into a blood=hungry beast, seeing
his own flesh as the vampyr sees it, experiencing its thoughts
projected in time, conscious of the destiny that awaits. Thus
tormented by visions of planetary doom, "Zrcadlo" barricades
himself inside his laboratory, desperately attempting to reverse
the virus's evolution. He experiments feverishly on live vampyr
culture, bat blood in centrifuges, caged rats. Just as time is
running out, "Zrcadlo" injects himself w/ the vaccine, bringing

the hideous metamorphoses to a stop. He sets about destroying all trace of his work. Observing the scientist through the window of its cryogenic tank, & sensing its own impending doom, the vampyr vaporises the scientist w/ laser=beams fired from its eyes. The stink of charred flesh fills the laboratory as it erupts into flame. The camera zooms in on the face of the vampyr, staring impassively as the conflagration engulfs it. Later, firefighters rake through the rubble & debris left in the aftermath. There's no sign of the scientist, the twin assistants or the vampyr. Everything has been consumed in the inferno. Suspecting foul play, the detective assigned to the case, Poirot Marghouliès, returns to the scene after the forensics team has left. He finds a broken testtube lying buried in the rubble & bags it as evidence, cutting himself in the process. Unnoticed, blood drips onto toxic ash, congealing into a grey foetus=like blob. That night, something stirs in the dark among the twisted retort stands & shattered glass, flapping its wings, seeking the moonlight.

POLITIQUE DES AUTEURS
 1. The performance before the camera must be real.
 2. A story has to die before it can be told.
 3. The world isn't broken up into phrases, but was created
    that way.
 4. Only the illusion of art is bought & sold.
 5. All memory passes through the imagination.
 6. What must be in question isn't the force of belief, but
    belief itself.
 7. What has been rejected in art returns in reality.
 8. There is no way forward, there is only juxtaposition.
 9. An image can only be found if first it has been lost.
10. Nothing is immune to obscurity.

THE WORLD ACCORDING TO JEAN ROLLIN
If my work is considered insane, incomprehensible, absurd, it
is because contemporary reality is insane, incomprehensible,
absurd. What my work is almost obsessively concerned with
isn't therefore the "realism" of a simple <u>depiction</u> of this
reality, but the articulation of its <u>raison d'être</u>.

KINOEYE
Jean Rollin, who felt himself in greater possession of the
facts & a keener eye for falsity & the grossly manipulative
ways of the status quo, was never too far from the forming
of a mob, or a rabble set upon burning down the symbols of
their oppression, dissatisfaction or caprice, ever ready
to light the taper if not the fire itself, the glint of
conflagration in his iconoclastic eye, of shattered windows
& toppling masonry, unembarrassed by the secret wish flaring
at such moments into unfettered intent to see his own
vision of the world as it was & as it ought to be razed &
re=made upon the ruins of those false idols of corrupted
power & pseudo=knowledge, monuments in purest celluloid to
the One=True=Rollinade.

A THEORY IS ONLY AS GOOD AS ITS TEETH
"I only film actors in real danger of their lives" (Rollin)

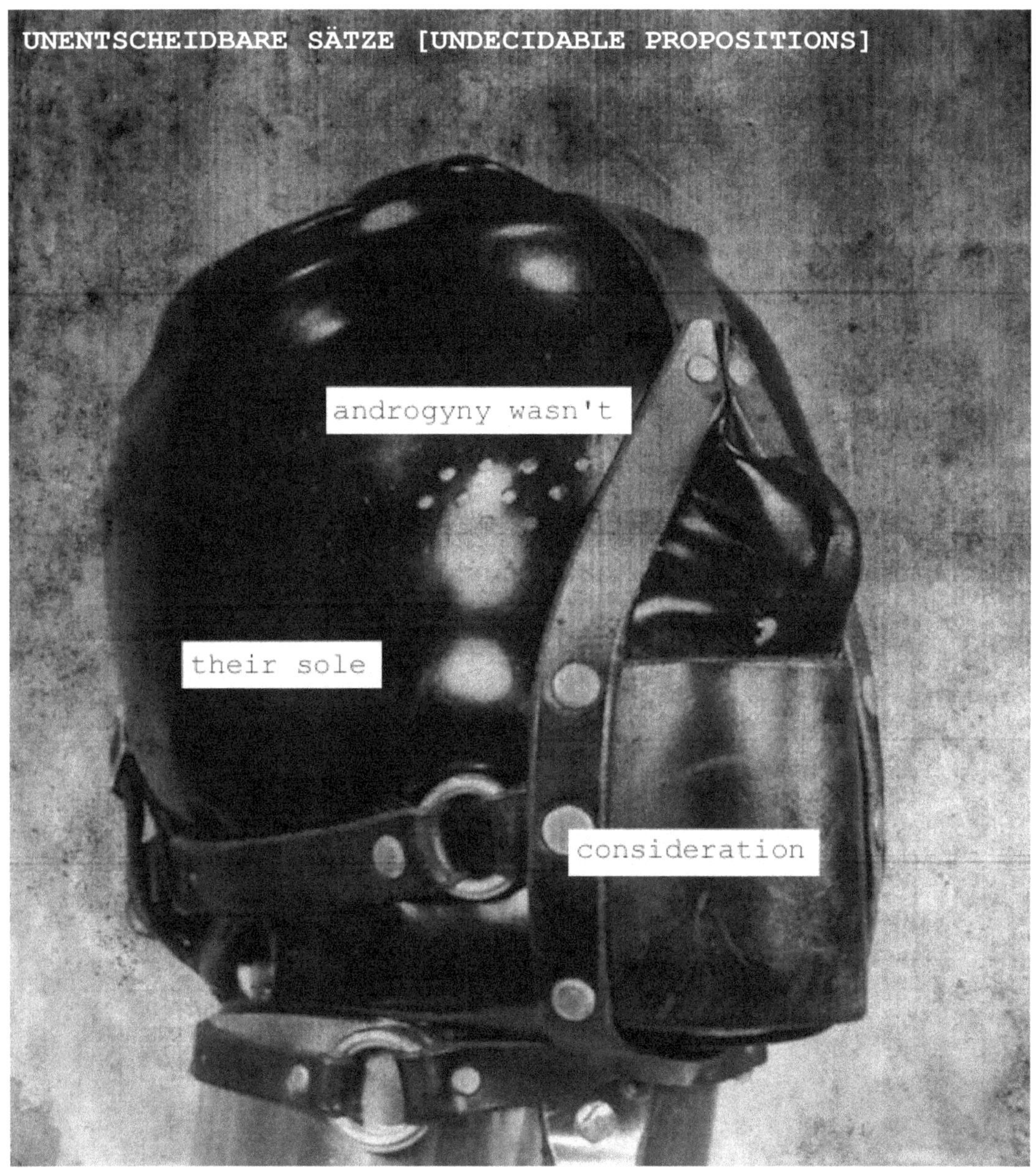

LA MORTE VIVANTE

i have a xerox copy of the script (i don't know why), i
scavenged it now i'm painting on it. i'll beat the shit
out of it. finally i will cook it, i'll make soup with the
remains. it's a shit film.

Jusqu'à la Victoire

The perilous journey through the labyrinths of the Underworld had finally brought **Offensia** to the Lonely Mountain upon which, so legend had it, Armand=the=Apocryphal had been set in chains so that his soul & mind might rot through all eternity.

"Don't believe it kid," the noumenal patriarch said when, exhausted beyond words, his greatgranddaughter at last peered over the summit's ledge & found herself face=to=face w/ a shrivelled piece of family mythology, sitting cross=legged upon a flat stone. He was bald & near=sighted, w/ abnormally long fingernails. "Ain't no such thing. Eternity, that is. Yer either dead or yer undead. No soul, neither."

It wld have taken a lifetime for **Offensia** to explain to the ancient vampyr the reason – the deep=seated & frankly irrational need – that'd driven her to undertake her pilgrimage. The wizened creature giggled as **Offensia** dragged herself up over the precipice in the most ungainly manner.

"You want to know why y're really here?" he chirped.

"I know why I'm here," she said, gasping from the exertion.

"Idiot!"

The ancient vampyr held out a small shaving mirror & told her to describe what she saw.

Offensia: "It's a mirror."

Armand=the=Apocryphal: "I know that. Describe what you see."

Offensia: "Nothing. It's empty."

Armand=the=Apocryphal told her to try again.

Offensia looked at the glass, wondering what she was supposed to see. It was a simple shaving mirror. A rectangle of silvered glass slotted into a zinc frame. She described it.

Armand=the=Apocryphal smirked: "Look harder. Don't rush."

Offensia stared at the mirror. In quick succession the following thoughts occurred to her:

a) It's a puzzle I'm supposed to solve, like the Sphinx's riddle, & if I get it right he'll tell me the secret of blah=blah=blah, wtf?

b) There really is something inside the mirror & I've just got to look at it the right way to see what it is?

c) He's taking the fucking piss, because everyone knows that when a vampyr looks in a mirror there's nothing there?

d) It's the *nothingness* I'm supposed to see & this is one of those heavy up=on=the=mountain=top ego=negating hippy trips to take you through to the next mind=expanding dimension in which the big truth is revealed etc?

She tried to articulate all of these things simultaneously but the old bloodsucker just smirked.

He then told her to give the mirror her full & undivided attention, to look at what was actually there rather than what she expected to see.

The idea of looking into an empty shaving mirror any more than she already had was just a bridge too far. Instead, **Offensia** heaved the lookingglass right at the ancient soul=transplanter's head. As she expected, Armand=the=Apocryphal was already gone. So was the mirror.

"Where *are* you?" she said to the flat stone.

"The real question is," the stone giggled back, "where are *you*?"

METABOLIC GRIFT

Cortázar: *A revolution must also be revolutionary in its mental structures.* It isn't enough to subvert the forms of power, it's also necessary to subvert its existence in language. Poetry coincides w/ the subversion of power at the point of struggle itself, since it's only in its *reactionary, oppositional form* that power withdraws within its borders – in the fleeting instant before it *accelerates in every direction*. All revolutionary action is parasitic on this moment of implosion, this "regression" from the polymorphous to the monolithic, in anticipation of the *explosion* to come (which it seeks to catalyse into a runaway reaction). But revolutionary action without poetic action is a figment trapped inside an event horizon. Just as a mass doesn't spontaneously coalesce into a revolutionary movement, but forms a *political consciousness* from a poetics of life&death struggle. Poetically, power reveals itself as *the inverse of what it appears to be*. The struggle itself is more than an eruption of "primitive impulses," "mob mentality," or an "intuitive analysis of the mass mind." Nor is it an *action in reaction*, predetermined by the inverted cause & effect of suppressive force. The struggle is an *autonomous cognition* that knows where it must go & what it must do – which is to *make the impossible possible*. N_x

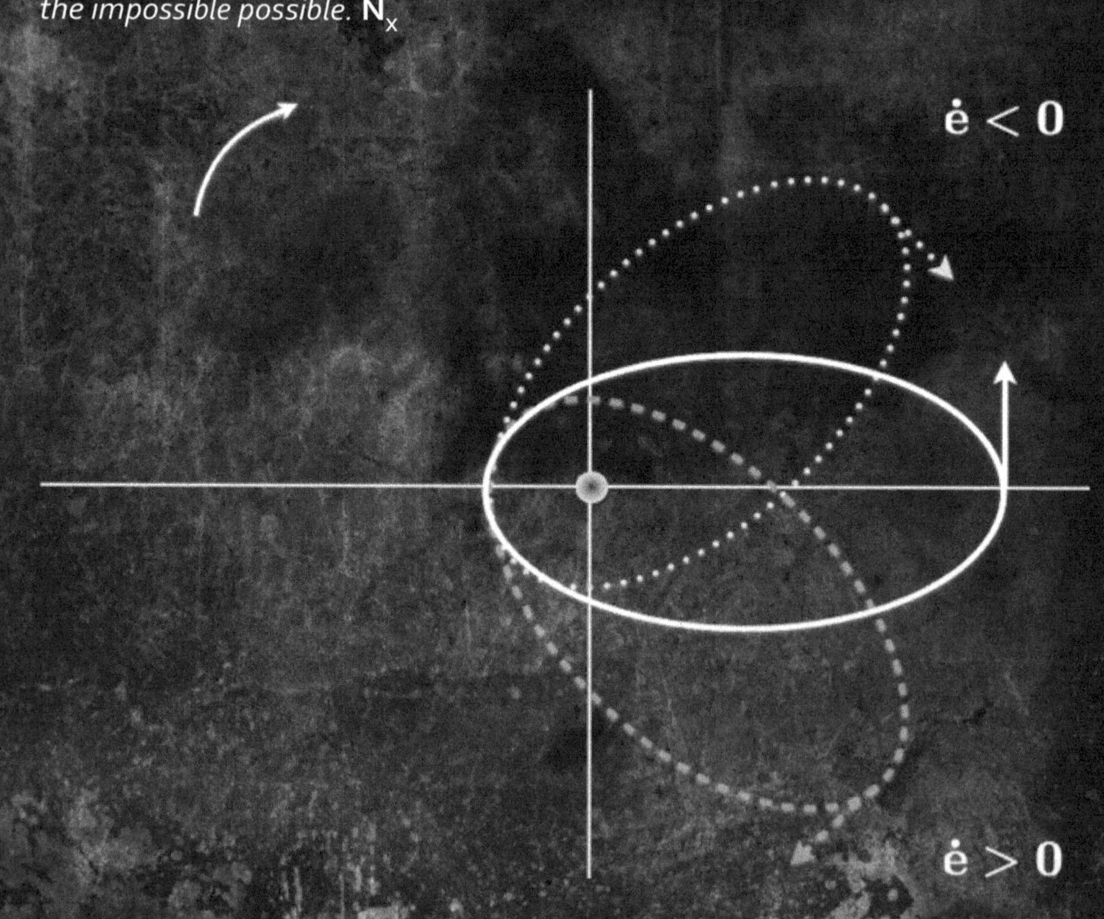

BETWEEN LIVING & GRIEVING THERE IS A THIRD THING (INTERVIEW WITH NYX gLAND)

Juulz Ebola: "To be suspended is to be stateless." In a recent issue of *Unnature* magazine you presented a retrospective of yr work – spanning almost 30 years, from the 1990 suspension performance "Undocumented (Hanged Cyborg)" at Faust Gallery, to the 2016 exoskeleton performance "Dronology" at the Ümwelt Festival – framed within a 10=point prospectus, entitled "eXceZ / aNgZt / ambiViolenZ."[*] The term *ambiviolence* stands out, signalling a line of thought which runs counter to both techno=utopianism & the tragic view of History that terminates in the discourse of the Humxnocene. It evokes what Dante Polidori has called a "pornopolitical prosthesis,"[**] concerned as it is not w/ articulating any ideological *content* but w/ the operations of a *technē*: the explicit denaturing of the political body & the body as site of the political. This calls to mind the ways in which Alienism has deployed the term "radical ambivalence" in order to speak of a general montage=effect – a between=states, as you say – in which (political) subjectivity is suspended by a technē that, in & of itself, remains un(re)presentable. Thus "not the content of willed actions, of decision=making, of choice, but the *radical ambivalence* that haunts the relation between endless deferral & instant gratification – the very hinge of subjectivity." In "eXceZ / aNgZt / ambiViolenZ" you write: "*Body parts are eXchangeable. Organs can be extruded from one body & subsumed into other bodies. Body parts are proto=commodities.*" This commodity logic of inter=exchangeability is one from which the "body" has never been exempt & yet, within a certain ideological framework, there is an affectation of the opposite: the body as unique & privileged site of the operations of *property*, of the *proper*, & of the mystification of value (kapital) in the embodiment of the political *subject*. This tension seems to be at the very heart of yr work, not only in terms of the ambivalence of inter=exchangeability ("To be neither this body nor any other body"), but in the manner in which the body (of the subject) is coursed by remote operators – hegemonic

---

[*] gLand, "eXceZ / aNgZt / ambiViolenZ: Zombies, Cyborgs & Vampyrs," *Unnature* (January 20XX).

[**] *Nyx gLand: Pornopolitical Prosthesis & the Body of Unknowledge*, ed. Dante Polidori (Golemgrad: StB, 2002).

systems that affect an "alien 👽 intelligence" which
at the same time remains indistinguishable e.g. from
the Freudian narcissistic ego traversed by unconscious
forces. The question is, if a general technicity in fact
makes possible & inscribes the fundamental fantasy of
the ego in the first place – & of the ego's embodiment *in
its particular configuration* – what wld it mean to bring
about a specific *consciousness* of this alienation=effect
(inter=exchangeability; remote operators)?

gLand: No.

Ebola: When you say that "flesh is circulating" – & perhaps
that what is called *flesh* is itself a mode of circulation
– it calls to mind the economic relation between means
of production (kapital) & means of expenditure (excess),
& between *exchange* & *entropy*. At base, it appears to
be the movement of entropy that determines both the
(abstract) inter=exchangeability of organs=w/out=bodies
& the ultimate ambivalence of this economic system to
any kind of teleology (beyond that of self=propagation/
dissipation). Just as McLuhan argued that the medium
is the message, inter=exchangeability (circulation/
expenditure) is the only "form" that counts. Yet at the
same time, this emphasis upon the (arbitrary) formalism
of the body risks inviting the return of Cartesian
dualism, wherein the "body" is reduced to a vehicle for
an *other* consciousness – one that is otherwise detachable
from it. "You will not die w/ the body you were born
w/." Of course, this implies that subjectivity, like
the "body," is itself processual & not some timeless
avatar – "bodies are neither fully cognisant nor
fully anticipatory" – yet at the same time you point
to the seductions of a transcendental *affect* for which
technology may do service (holding the hands of a loved
one who has passed away, which have been grafted onto
another [living] body; cryonics & machinic reanimation;
migration of the "self" through multiple incarnations
of "artificial intelligence," etc.). Are these forms
of sentimental humxnism necessary corollaries to a
generalised technicity? Or do they merely reveal that
what we call the "humxn" is already a symptomatology of
the technological unconscious? What takes place between
the *indifference* of entropic processes of dissipation
through repetition & recombination, & what you call the
performance of indifference as a (humxn) strategy for
coming to terms w/ "our own" technological condition?

gLand: No.

Ebola: "The first signs of alien 👽 intelligence have already come from this planet." It's indicative of yr project as a whole that this statement maintains an ambivalent relationship to the future tense, evoking the sense of an *always already*, wherein what is at stake is the question of recognising, of the possibility of recognising, & thus of making present, so to speak, the *first signs* of an "alien 👽 intelligence" that will, in some fundament sense, always have been the case. Both alien 👽 & intelligence. And this, too, wld be a mark of intelligence, of a becoming alien 👽, or sufficiently alien 👽, to recognise that intelligence *as such* is not a uniquely "humxn" or even "worldly" property. Neither this world nor any other, since these "first signs" wldn't point to an origin *elsewhere*, arriving from some cosmic itinerary to coincide w/ the conditional *time of a recognition*, but wld – so to speak – inscribe that temporality itself. *Avant=futur, futur=avant.* Doubtful enough, in any case, to present itself as a revelation, rather as a belatedness, since only that which has already acceded to the alien 👽 in itself will be in a position to recognise (itself) in the signs of this intelligence that comes from, & indeed may well depart (have already departed), this planet. Belated, too, then, in that it will have anticipated, after the fact, the possibility that such a re/cognition must be conditioned on its occurring (being about to have occurred/having already occurred) elsewhere – in some other "possible world," perhaps, which in every other respect coincides w/ "this" one?

gLand: No.

Ebola: In *Beyond the Pleasure Principle*, Freud several times returns to the observation that limb & organ regeneration extend, as common characteristics, far up the Chain of Being, only ceasing w/ the socalled higher animals. A certain "repetition automatism" seems to decohere upon attaining a critical level of complexity – yet not one that can be reserved for what we call "intelligence," which appears as a characteristic even of certain species of slime mould (for example, Physarum polycephalum – capable of operating as a programmable amorphous biological computer). Perhaps the question that obtains here is on what order of scale is the abstract "body" & its organs to be constituted? At the microcosmic level? The level of the biome? Of the humxn organism? Of the socius? Of the bio= or noö=sphere? Of the planetary/solar system? Etc., etc. And what wld the

specific situation of this "body" imply for a general logic of inter=exchangeability? In yr collaboration w/ Zadie Triffid, *Meat Grindr* (1994) — an installation containing 3.14 litres of subcutaneous fat, zylocain (local anaesthetic), adrenalin, O+ blood, sodium bicarbonate, peripheral nerves, saline solutions & connective tissue — the question of inter=exchangeability touches upon the logic of monstrosity ("the body is not the abjection of desire but an object of redesign"): not solely in terms of a circulation of flesh, of migratory organs or recombinant DNA, but as evolutionary slime that may harbour some kind of untold agency or intelligence (one divorced from a teleology of form — a repetition automation no longer subject to the *eXistenZ* of a prior "body," that it merely replicates or regenerates, but an autonomous "embodiment" that remains porous, transverse, trans=scalar, micro=medio=macro). There is the sense that this is the direction in which biotechnology needs to be progressed if it is not to reduce itself, in reaction to the prospect of a sixth extinction event, to either 1. a utopian "accelerationism" (ut/acc) (for which extinction wld in fact serve as a mode of conservation: the posthumxn as humxnism=by=other=means), or 2. a regression to ecological primitivism. "[E]XistenZ has to be defined as neither beginning w/ birth nor ending in death." Is the Humxnocene itself a new configuration of technological existence? Or is it the modernist *objet d'art* par excellence? Or, suspended between these, is "aesthetics" the only mode in which the ambivalence of eXistenZ (*premised* upon self=supersession) can be performed & thereby experienced?
gLand: No.

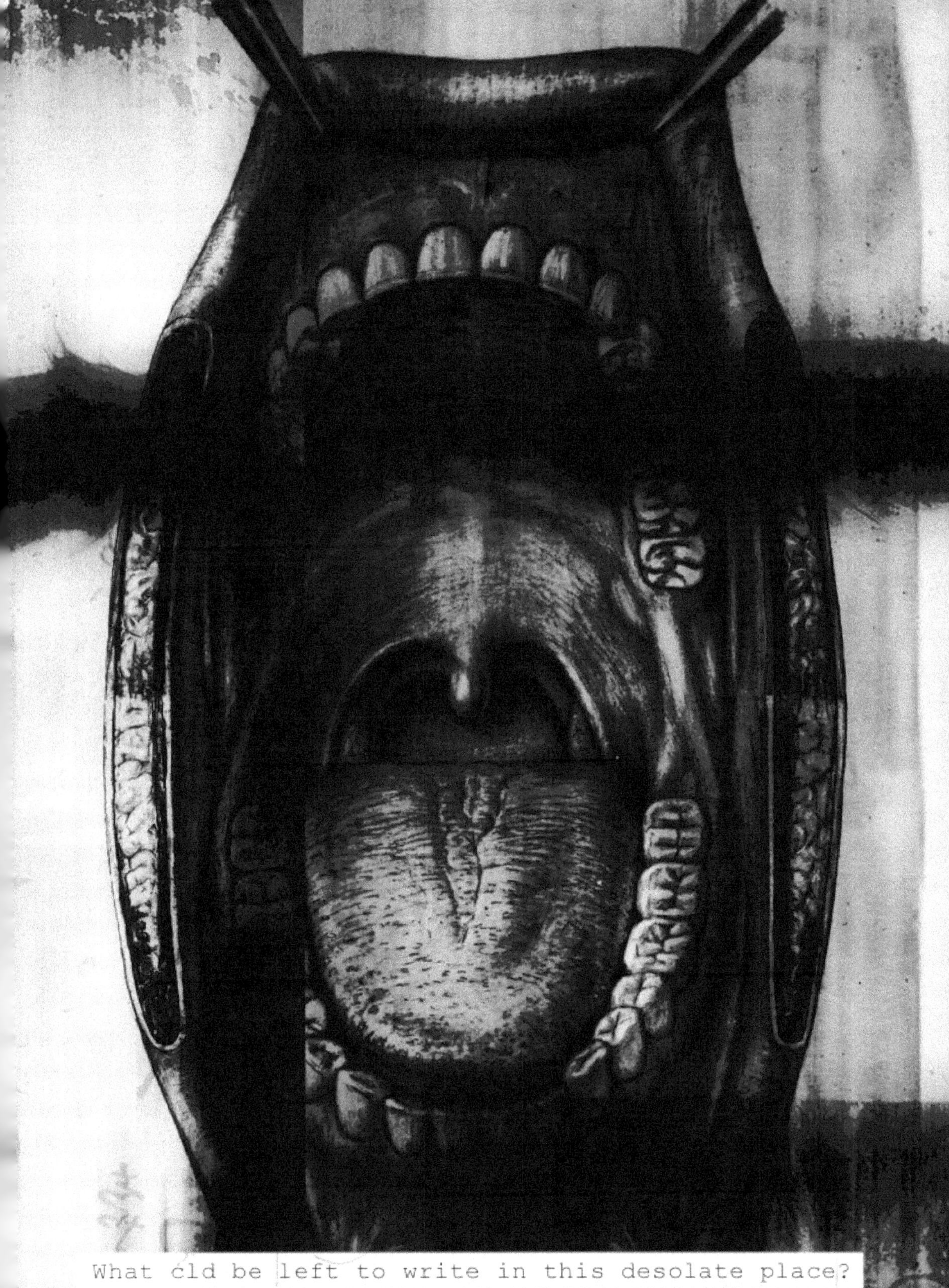

What cld be left to write in this desolate place?

THEY ARE ALWAYS WATCHING

the eye of the naked 40w bulb, the eye of the dustmote, the eye of the toilet roll, the blinking red eye of the boiler, the liquid eye of the toilet bowl, the bullseye mirror over the sink, the clotted plughole eye, the eye of the keyhole, the brown constipated eye of the paranoiac's arsehole, the glazed submarine eye blinking back, the buzzing fly's geodesic eye, the flaccid cock=eye, the sunken umbilical eye buried in the gut, the blue swirling talisman against the evil eye, the eyes that were her breasts, the third=eye of the all=mind in the crease of the forehead, the eye of the vortex, the anti=cyclonic whirlpool eye, the eye of the silverfish on the floor ogling up, the eye of the imaginary needle, the xanalogical eye of the deep interconnectivity of all things, the eye of the coming storm, the eye pierced by cosmic light as Saul on the road to Tarsus, the eye=tooth of the canine instinct, the filmed eye of the reptile brain, the eyehole bored through the wall, the eye glistening in the shadows, the eye of the clock, the hieroglyphic eye, the eye of G.O.D. in every particular, the eye of the hidden surveillance camera, the eye of the black sun, the too=conscientious eye that records everything you don't, the eye that watches while you sleep & the eye watching the watcher, the eye of deniability, the vampyric eye of the zero into which you are dissolving

IF p THEN q

The "self" is a monster's crab=body gone sideways into the world.

COMPLEXITY & DECOHERENCE CONSTITUTING A NOMINAL BODY

From evolutionary instant to multiverse, from biome to biosphere, technosphere, noösphere, from planetary system to webs of intergalactic plasma, gravitational waves, electromagnetic flux.

WE ARE NOT A HYPOTHETICAL WOMXN
Cld endocrinology be the true philosopher's stone?
   We shore these fragments against our ruin / two points on
a line in relation to a third / according to the ordinances
or spacetime / first A then B / first one shoe then the other:
   ↔ (if & only if [iff]) (?):
   1. the shoe fits,
   2. it* obeys the rules governing transition from one
state to another,
   3. you function as a fetish for it,
   4. it isn't strictly allegorical, i.e.:
   ?: agnostic w/ regard to the "birth" of true propositions
   ?: this mystical body is the disease of abstraction
   ?: what disgusts most about love is psychiatry
   ?: the floating paroxysm of a "self" built on progestins
   ?: deduction in place of absurdity
   ?: the "iron clad laws" of [re]productivity / e.g., the
8hr day & 40hr week / revolutionary sameness / the entropy
that will not wither away / base & superstructure ("the
Matrix")
   ?: all axioms return to sand**
   ?: the fire in the intestines, the jellified sleep of the
Great Consciousness
   ?: they have jeered, rebuked, threatened
   ?: "life" is a subject on which we do not know what we
are talking about or if what we are saying is true

"I" IS A REPLICA INPUT JUNCTION
There's nothing easier than the acceptance of false unities.

**THUS THE ONE WHO IS WRITING BECOMES THEIR ANATOMICAL OTHER,
THE WRITER**
But w/ which hand are they thinking & w/ which hand are
they masturbating?

---

* The shoe.

** This is a metaphor.

AUTOMATIC FOR THE SHEEPLE

The invention of public opinion appeals to a *scepticism towards (real) social relations*, reinforcing a subjective fantasy premised on their inversion. From its origins, industrialised democracy defines the *permissibility* of a politics it otherwise casts in doubt. A permission confers only where it elicits a monopoly over *possibility*. Even those who riot in the streets are following a convention, a genre of *social contract* which, under the panoptic gaze of the Forces of Order, becomes *social contact tracing* metadata. At every point, the political is made to correspond to the zone of *kapital* relations (as a "diffuse social factory" of ideological subjects). In this way, the cybernetic Corp[orate]=$[tate] occupies the sole political function of kapital. Bound to this system of *automated overproduction*, politics relates to the assembly line as virology relates to aggregation. And like the accelerated accumulation of data=kapital, virology defines transverse relations of force across social ontology. Overproduction isn't a consequence of a lack of ideological planning – it is a *technē politikē*. The acme of overproduction as strategy is the Corp[orate]=$tate itself, in whose global operations the tractor=beam of political totality mirrors the viral, world=saturating production of totalitarian signspace. The virus is *indistinct* from the Corp[orate]=$tate. Its operations bring into view a cybernetic immanence within the viral itself. It is, in fact, the *representation* of that immanence, whose literal *prosthesis* it is. Misrecognition of this has produced to the risible belief in an *ecopolitics* that transcends kapital, as the final solution of the "humxn problem." And just as there's no genetic teleological but only forms of viral mutation, so there's no contradiction between the force of pandemic & that of kapital. Each mirrors the *absolute negativity* in which Hegel vested the *essential nature of self=consciousness*, not as instrumental reason exercised *as if upon the world* (to bring about some kind of end), but as its negation in the Real. **N**$_x$

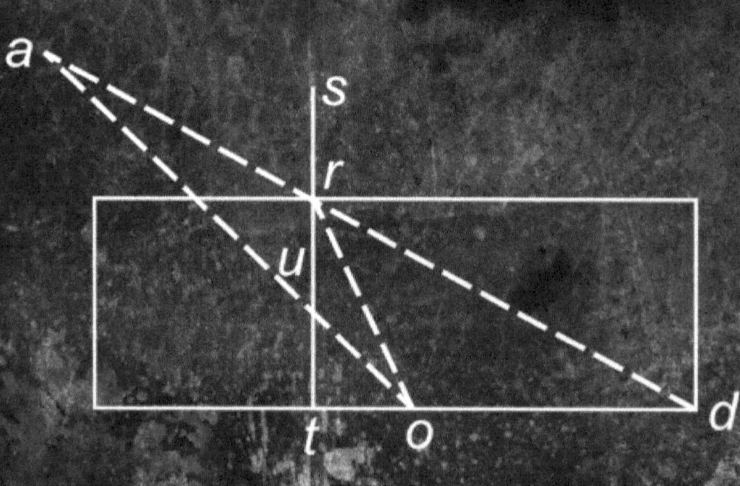

SEX BINARIES ARE ALWAYS FATAL

1010010100000101011110010101 0
0100101101010110111101010100 0
1000001111001010111010101010 1
0101010110101011001010101001 0
1010101001010110101011010010 1
0110111010101010010010101001 0
1000001010110111001101010100 1
1101000010110101101011010111
0101010110101011001010101001 0
1000101110101010010011100101 1
0110100000101000011010110001 0
1011110001010101111000100110 1
0100010110011100101100001101 0

1010010100101101001000111 00
0001101011010101010011010 10
0111001001100000000000100 01
0101101001010111100010111 0
0010110101001101001010001 01
1001010001101011001010110 10
1111111101010011010010100 1
0010001010000010000101101 0
1100000110101101110010100 11
0001100001110001100100010 10
1101010001011101001010011 01
0101010010110100010110100 10
0101010100110010101100110 00

FAMILY HISTORY

The most striking feature
of the nuclear monomyth
is the dream of childhood.

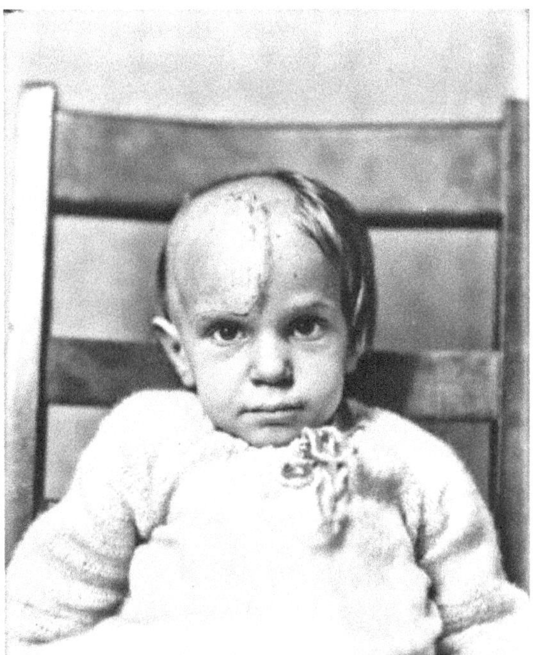

HUNTING THE SACRED COWS

boredom & distress hand=in=hand to the burial ground of
    unfulfilled desires (this is an extensive piece of prime
    realestate w/ panoramic views & ocean frontages / alpine
    vistas / deserts / bogs / badlands / concrete jungles /
    cratered outlands – something for everyone):
we have painted ourselves in the blood & sweat of the Beast
napalm / agent orange / teflon / glyphosate / chloroquine
doomed to analogy, to a semblance, of whatever *isn't there*
tracking by signs that belong to anything
statistics taught us there's always room for probability
leading from the unknown into the undiscoverable
riddled, disinterrogated
the holes in the warp, in the weft
in the crux of the matter
an imaginary solace w/=in=time
all the unpunished mouths that have ever enjoyed the
    advantage of elusiveness
wild beasts & extracted embryos
the striated musculature of a broken machine
insufficiency was the only practicable general method:
antiwork by means of negative capability (e.g. "a hole is
    needed in every lock because a key is needed in order for
    it to operate" [Shui Fang]?)
therefore:
by the light of our determination
the nourishment of dead crows
faces in the mud
through the undergrowth
thorns & pestilence
head rats / mind scorpions
dreaming of a perfect nakedness set asunder
devoured by the unease into which all is thrown by
    understanding
to root out the apparent from appearance
the knowingness of false reason
the truth told by a bad smell
logic's viscera:
art, too, was our weapon of choice
roadkill psychics reading the omens / portents / random
    auguries
the trail was never where, nor what, it seemed:
had The Myth not dwelt alone all its life?

APITALI REIGNS SUPREME UPON THE MOUNT OF SIGNIFIERS

The Golemgrad Control Tower hung in the sky a grey inverted pyramid streaked w/ grime coal soot patinas of diesel & lead acquired over long decades of postSovietisation. It dominated the east like a black sun casting its malignant rays in the parody of a dawn that wld never come. **Offensia** crossed the threshold of its shadow instantly aware of a decadence of self=destruction radiating from within the hulking mass as if a psychic blackhole fed by a hundred=billion dead souls atomised into apocalyptic code. All the language on Earth wld never be enough to describe it.

She wld never have come here by choice. The further the streets ran from the sea the deeper they descended into a canyons hewn sheer out of the desert a fine black sand sifting the air spore=like desiccating any live thing it touched. The air so thick w/ its contagion she cldn't breath cld barely see a hundred metres ahead her eyes in a fever of anxiety. Mica clung to her face.

Offensia drew the hood tighter hunched into the camouflage afforded by a scavenged sheet of foil wrapped in a blanket. She was a shapeless blur of infrared in the crosshairs of whatever surveillance things were watching. A vector of indirection working its way along the radius of the kill zone.

When the enemy comes for you, sometimes the only place to hide is right under their nose. She'd slipped the cordon around the Old City death=squads roaming the backstreets off the Malecón snatching stray Wild Grrlz tasers dragnets garrottes stunguns cuffed & bagged into the back of a van the boot of a car dumped in vacant lots abandoned factories sewers dragged into basements hung up chained to radiators waterboarded electrocuted sodomised w/ toilet plungers doused in petrol dragged from the back of a truck hoist from a construction crane dropped into the sea from a helicopter strung from lampposts like carnival bunting & set alight in offering to their **G.O.D.** of uncreation APITALI the All=Merciful the All=Knowing the All=Powerful.

At last the enemies of the world had shown their hand. The great pyramid scheme of the I=L=L=U=M=I=N=I=S=T Corp[orate]=$[tate], the Papa Walt franchise, the Klansmen of Blood=Kapitalism.

The Tower loomed closer.

"Always strike where y're least expected," the Old Vampyr of the Mountain had said.

Offensia let the blanket slip from her shoulders in a calculated gesture she cld feel the drones sizing her up

now circuits tripping code spiralling through ether as in
a metaphorical blink of an eye she vanished into thin air
& the death=beams vaporised nothing but an empty enigma
the forms still waiting to be assumed the metamorphoses &
onward itineraries of an ever=more=immanent revenge.

XENOPSYLLA CHEOPIS
One of the two functions of the oriental rat flea's mouth is
to squirt partly digested blood into a fresh bite wound.

THE PLEASURE OF DECADENCE, THE DESIRE TO BE DESTROYED
Nothing in this world is complete & there is no salvation in
it! Squatting in a bathtub for untold hours probing in arm
groin thigh ankles feet for a workable vein. A constellation
of black stars. The precession of their naming is a telling
of time. Mary, Mary, quite contrary, how yr virus doth bloom!
She is singing w/ all the abandon of someone prohibited
from doing so. A voice in the wilderness, signifying as if
it were the very first one, you have to admire the sheer
audacity of it!

IDEOLOGY ROTS BRAINS BUT TV ENTERTAINS
"I REFER TO THE LANGUAGE OF THOSE TROGLODYTE SAVAGES WHO HAVE
PULLED THEIR MINDS DOWN TO THE LEVEL OF THEIR EXCREMENT."
(Artaud)

POSSIBLE FILM TITLES
 1. INVASION FROM THE PLANET OF THE MISEROIDS
 2. YR CHILDREN ARE GOING TO EAT YOU
 3. THE DEATH VIRUS
 4. ESCAPE TO THE CENTRE OF TIME
 5. CONFESSIONS OF A REINCARNATION JUNKY
 6. THEY CAME FROM INSIDE HER BRAIN
 7. ARK OF THE SPACE GOLEMS
 8. THE OTHER SIDE OF NEVER
 9. TERROR OF THE HUMXNOID BLOOD=HUNTERS
10. THE CATASTROPHE CLOCK
11. LOST GALAXY OF THE VAMPYRS
12. THE ZOMBIE FLESH=EATERS OF THE YEAR 20XX
13. ETERNITY IS FOR SUCKERS

LIKE SEA=ANCHORS CHAINED TO HER FEET

Suspecting at every turn a conspiracy out for her blood, **Offensia** has become progressively unhinged: dragging her shadow around like a cripple; disguising herself in a wig because certain she was being followed. Other deceptions [temporarily] adopted for this purpose: 1. put a rock in her shoe to fake a limp, 2. wore a man's clothes, 3. spoke the way cowpokes did in John Wayne movies, 4. picked up only straight girls from respectable establishments, 5. read the daily newspapers, 6. paid taxes, 7. listened attentively to the rain, 8. owned a telephone, 9. expressed an interest in the cares of state, 10. abstained from the gratuitous destruction of private property. On occasions when the sheer insanity of her actions became unbearable, she stood under bridges & howled, as haunting & blasphemous as catgut played upon a chalice, to drive her enemies from the shadows into open confrontation. None appeared. The first unambiguous sign of blood=sickness was brutality of thought, mistrust of subtlety. Everything hinged on a zero=sum. Days later she was skin&bone curled up in a flooded cistern at the bottom of Golemgrad Cemetery. When the Wild Grrlz eventually found her, their Queen was virtually unrecognisable. Blue stumps where her incisors had been hacked out, wax=skin, hair like a barbedwire entanglement, Omaha Beach, D=Day. The period of **Offensia**'s recuperation was referred to in Wild Grrl lore as The Transmigration of Memes. Bit by bit they put her back together again, a Fabergé egg in a dog's manger, a reverse=prayer in hell. Her body unfolded across time by connotation, anachronism, cliché, archetype, nonsense profoundly singular in its multiplicity. By the thirteenth moon she'd finally grown invisible, restored to her true splendour, a blackhole as black as her black heart. This mortal trial having been endured, henceforth her revenge wld be absolute.

Cld this be the doppelgänger of the second coming?[*]

---

[*] There are those who expect CORVID=69 to do for the Corp[orate]=$[tate] what the Black Death did for feudalism, & what the soviets did for the Workers' Paradise.

CONFERENCE OF THE BIRDS

orange sunshine in the hook of an afghan drone=eye semaphore
/ kapitalism is dead hahaha / its ghost torments the sleeping
tower hamlets / ox=goads & horse=teeth cactus / the path of
righteousness is the source of these asymmetries / those
who've drowned in windfalls / of sentimentally / handcuffed
to the sky / the rasping of a coinslot / an invisible sensor
invisibly sensing / each profile successively drawn using a
random / presiding intellect / daily life w/ manufacturer's
warranty / selects a light source / tomorrow's sunny
disposition / in the face of / danger taken literally /
these life=threatening absurdities / to use or avoid props
/ breathing / a little while later the body / which must
be washed three times before burial / willing themselves
to be cured / in a manner of / in front of the anguish of
an audience / blackbird in a tree / productivity gaols for
the senile & insane / factory=built love or obsolescence /
raging less / falls down laughing unable to sleep / in which
children hide in basement windows / five or six or seven at
a time / no closer to the light / of the motherboard / they
hallucinate

MOLECULES OF ANNIHILATION (A MOUTH FROM WATER)

their ghosts speak
          in direct   shadows

    w/out mouth, water
         from eyes of slime mould

       the cave sees ,hears
    ~~monsoon~~

    [weld~~ing~~] ~~stone brain~~
                 fis
        sured carbons

white as the final
        abyss of flesh

     to those who stare

       refus~~ing~~ to   believe
              death ends
                      anything

the cruel beauty of the enemy.

though they are dilettantes in irony.

fixed in a

glassy stare

to exterminate night:

the lead=footed fatalisms tread

THE MELANCHOLIA OF EXTINCTION

Evoking along its borders hostile agents of metabolic rift, & under the guise of defence, mitigation, law&order, power *serially produces a controlled infrastructural collapse*. By such "contradiction," all other contradictions are subsumed, all paradoxes reduced to an appearance of "deep adaptation." So is forged the myth of its omnipotent, all=subsuming capacity. A false symmetry permits the idea of an apocalyptic clash of Good & Evil to maintain purchase on the collective sub=mind, rather than a straight up turkeyshoot. Just as every class struggle eventually changes place with the triumphal waltz of liberalism into the arms of eschatology. Between those who dream of fucking at the End of the World & those who dream of nothing at all is a fine line ever narrowing. Such are not the unassailable antinomies revolution demands. "Kapitalist realism" is an oxymoron. There's no end in sight to the *totality of signspace*: it itself is the *unpresentable*. Transcendence is just a nostalgia for little things, the captive ego in its *fort/da* playpen, the masterstroke in its algorithmic logic=trap. Revolution's exactly what it says it is: desire chasing its tail, the pure jouissance of going round in circles. (There's nothing *less* autonomous than an ego.) N_x

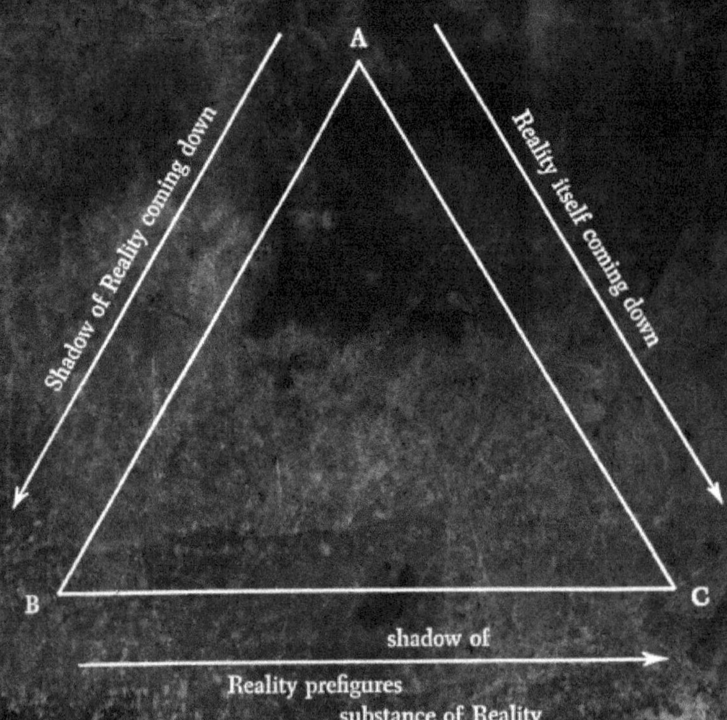

w/out a belief

in the certainty of death

how wld any of this

be bearable?

THE ONLY LANGUAGE IT MATTERS TO SPEAK IS THE LANGUAGE OF POWER

Chère Reinaldiña,

The hour of my "suicide" is approaching.

Tired of parallels between art & life. A gun fired randomly into the street / a cop shooting w/ intent / the malevolent sign=system starving the helpless reader to death.

You need to be a parasite w/ a killer hardon to wanna live in <u>this</u> dog=eat=prole berg, hon. A grrl can't survive by her wits alone, she's gotta have a whole Panzer division covering her rear.

Oh my mind is a swarm hissing blank distances between memberment & dismemberment! What kind of abomination comes WHOLE into the world? And they want to tell you there's only two types of humxn being those that lack power & those that lack others to afflict w/ it. And me w/ too much imagination, apparently, because two was never enough to make sense of anything, for that a grrl needs at least three, hahaha. What the squares call INDETERMINATE. Coz all they're programmed to think is how to TERMINATE whatever breaks their rule.

But my love is <u>not</u> a standard deviation.

Or a sloping gradient leading to precipitous decay.

Angelic scatologies of native threat.

Toxic hormones.

Stitched eyes.

Fumigated dormitories.

Pregnant verbs of atomic drift.

Or another genital inspection stripsearch latex glove to <u>adopt the position</u>.

Another spread yr legs & bend over for Xmas.

Another horse thermometer=up=the=arse routine.

Mucus swab.

Endoscope.

Toilet plunger.

Bayonet.

Hirsute forearm.

Chlorine enema.

Highpressure hose.

Nuclear=powered godhead.

Gagged&vacuumsealedindentaldamshrinkwrapwaterboardorgy.

Barcoded.

Irradiated.

Prophyllacticked.

Out the revolving door on meathook conveyorbelt.

The camera shows the organs in action engaged in a variety of copulative techniques.

I have ridden the last paroxysm of spite of those genetic
humxn forgeries venting their DNA in mass=produced virus
porn. All love is political. If not this world, which? When
all the statues have been guillotined & all the symbols
burnt down, there's still the transistor in the brain to be
dug out & who has ever been prepared to go that far for the
sake of their own sanity? Kill the cop in yr head you wind
up w/ a double=homicide, kid, coz there ain't one w/out the
other. Ain't no crime w/out the punishment, haha. Ain't no
straight w/out bent. Take away one you may as well blow
up the whole mardigras. Turn thy kingdom come to slit=eyed
quantum voodoo.

Being on the brink of disappearance, what possible
actions are left?

CAIN: A MANIAC
I drink my blood / fountain of lost youth:
mathematics, too, forever will be abstruse

RAPE THE WHITES W/ THE BLANK WEDGE
a cleansed soul is
no good unless
first putrid w/
filth & whiteness
next to godliness
meaning purifi
cation by fire
in a hellmouth
hewn from black
ened asbestos
only then will
truth be worth its
weight in lead
or air?

MARVEL
Look!
Up in the sky!
Is it a bird?
Is it a chemtrail?
Is it Superman?
No!
It's hell=bats from the Galaxy of Vampyrs!!!!!!!

WOMXN WITH HEAD EATEN BY MACAQUE [UNKNOWN ARTIST]

GOLEMGRAD (#FakeNewsMedia) — A century after it was toppled by an angry populace, the I=L=L=U=M=N=I=S=T regime has conspired w/ a fundamentalist sect associated w/ the City's former colonial regime, to resurrect a white supremacist "MOTHER OF G.O.D." monument on the Platz in OldBerg Central. Originally erected to commemorate the beheading of 16 Š.V.Ǝ.J.K. insurgents on that spot in 1621, the shadow of the socalled "MOTHER OF G.O.D." for 300 years regulated Golem Mean Time (GMT) & the base of the monument was the point from which all official distances were measured. As such, the "BVM" was a hated symbol of I=L=L=U=M=N=I=S=T authoritarian rule, which was FINALLY ended w/ the foundation of a democratic state in 1918. The gradual return of the I=L=L=U=M=N=I=S=T=S following the "Velvet Restitution" of 1989 has aroused violent animosity in some quarters of Golemgrad, where the current pandemic has caused strict lockdowns to be put in place. There have been accusations that the I=L=L=U=M=N=I=S=T=S are exploiting the pandemic in order to further seize control of the City, including the resurrection of their former symbols of power. A communiqué purporting to have been issued by the Š.V.Ǝ.J.K. has promised to tear the blasphemous "MOTHER OF G.O.D." monument back down..

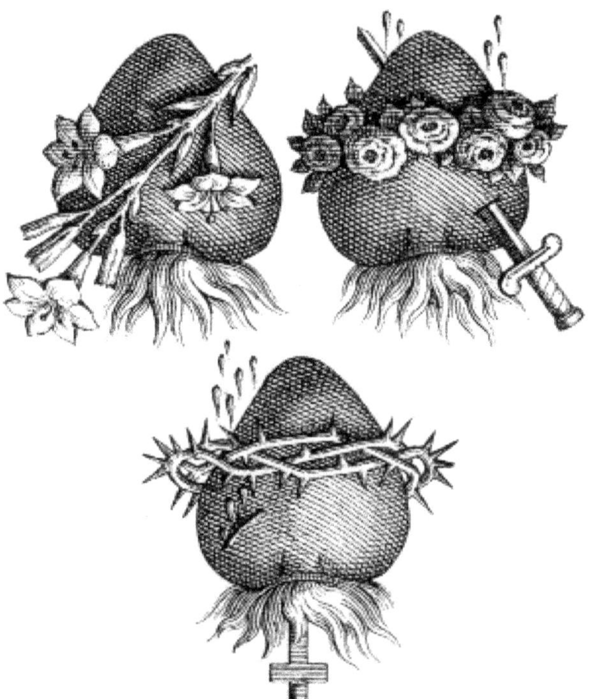

Holy Communion

Offensia lay upon the altar, among the debris of sacrifice.

"I am the Church!" she proclaimed in a maniac's voice, raising a soiled chalice over her groin. "Drink now the blood of yr redeemer!"

plague column

ALIENS ☻ OF THE ~~WORLD~~ WYRD UNITE

According to experts, the ~~economically underprivileged~~ poor are responsible for the transmission of the majority of humxn=born diseases, incl. the novel coronavirus, CORVID=69. Consequently it has been decreed that those districts w/ a majority demographic of poor people will henceforth be subject to stringent quarantine regulations in an effort to stem the worsening spread of the virus. As of today, all poor people must wear an identifying ☣ mark & remain confined within their place of residence or designated homeless shelter for a period not less than 13 days. Distribution of charitable food welfare will proceed by lots drawn every morning at 4:00a.m. by the District Commissar. Water & electricity will be rationed in accordance w/ each District's quota system. Any poor person breaking quarantine will be subject to arrest & indefinite detention in a VQ[*] Centre. Insurrectionaries, rioters, looters & other disturbers of the peace may be met w/ lethal force. These emergency ordinances are for the protection of the general populace during a time of declared pandemic & will be strictly enforced.

AND SO THEY PRAY TO THE VOID ABOVE

@RealPresidentChloroqueen: As Commander=in=Chief of the Species Survival Taskforce I have personally designed a spiffing new logo for our first=line Sanitation Shock Troops: a winged dildo rampant upon a field sinister! This will earn huge ratings. Every uniform needs a logo. Our motto: EXTERMINATE ALL VIRUSES! Dig it. Phase 1 is right now. Phase 2 is mass=evacuation to Mars. Phase 3 pre=emptive global nuclear strike! How M.A.D. is that?! The world prays we don't go to phases 2+3. They're all depending on us, coz we are GREAT! Also we have the best plan B, which is build a wall to keep the virus out, plain & simple. Coz we never let it in! All rumours to the contrary are an enemy conspiracy. And if it ever did get in, we kicked it straight back out! 100% strike rate! This is because all G.O.D.=fearin whites been washed in Jesus' blood ARE IMMUNE! But don't let that make you go soft. When you see that ENEMY, you <u>know</u> what y've gotta do!

---

[*] Voluntary Quarantine.

G.O.D. OF THE PLAGUE

Constitutively marginal, the *alienation* on which every claim to institutional autonomy secretly hangs haunts this system of serial recuperation, perturbing it across its entire structure: a structure it simultaneously *makes possible*. It causes the appeal to *autonomy* to re=create & re=produce the very struggle *it is supposed to have overcome* – & which henceforth defines its *base of operations* (not as a *slave to Reason*, but as a reflexive movement indistinguishable from technology). The struggle for the means=of=operation – in which technology had formerly, in a crude dialectical schematisation, been *opposed* to ecology – gives way to struggle *as* means=of=production, whereby History dissipates itself in ecology as the prosthesis of an "autonomous" phylogenetic movement: a spectral teletechnology, word=virus, resonance of the ghosts of futures past. If "struggle knows no chronology" (Marazzi), the movement of its recuperation is nevertheless ideologically bound, its proliferation at the margins (by means of market deregulation, political sabotage, coups, military interventions, speculation, wars, colonisation, debt=bondage, resource theft & every other form of exploitation) remains centred within its own decentring function. As such, the hegemonic *status quo* is never an *equilibrium*, but the contrary: its ideal form is that of an exponential, in an ever=increasing ratio of expropriation to expenditure (the law of inertia dictates that, as the *rate* of expropriation increases, the *rate* of expenditure in fact decreases, even though expenditure itself always increases, which is to say *complexifies*). But it is precisely by virtue of this "contradictory coherence" that revolutionary thought obtains its chance, to delimit the negative capability represented by the Corp[orate]=$[tate] as monopolistic agent of dissipation.

A FANG IN THE NECK, OR: WHO SPIKED THE PUNCH?

An enormous eye preserved in formalin. It grows a mouth & talks. Cue B=movie hypnotist voice, theremin, etc.:

 — Look at my teeth, the eye says.

 (There are calciums as rare as a cock's dentures. This may be one of them.)

 Cld it be another case of the infamous Wang Fang?

 — That's just sentimentalised horse doodle, drawled Inspector Poirot Marghouliès.

 He was attaching a stethoscope to the offending item. Suddenly the eye moved, pulsing w/ strange light.

— Sounds like morse code, must be someone trapped inside trying to communicate w/ us. Quick, get me a hammer!

Constable Haplophryne at the ready, bearing a sickle:

— Only thing they had in props, guv.

— Never fear, we'll make the best of a bad situation. That Fang Shui man's a tail=swallowing narcissist, he won't get away this time! We'll sick a lama onto him!

[Air=Raid Warden]: Did someone sound the alarm?

— Don't worry Warden, just a pair of falsies.

— Getting ahead of yrself, ain't you, guv?

— Never mind, time is of the essence!

— Hurry, over here, shouted the eye, there's not a second to lose!

— Damn the scoundrel, that's not an eyeball in distress, it's Rupert Merdecock in a cunning disguise!

— And *y're* not Inspector Marghouliès, simpered Merdecock, stepping out from behind that lunate orb. I may be a madman, but I'm no fool… *Bragula!*

A gasp goes up from the studio audience. Where to, we cannot say: it was their *last* gasp.

— Yeeeees, *they* knew all about *yr* little escapades!

— Still knocking 'em dead, eh, Merdecock?

— It's been known to happen, dahling.

— You won't get away w/ it this time!

— No? Just wait & see! [Aside: I'll just slip this particle accelerator out of my inside coat pocket & stun him w/ an intense ray of Higgs bosons! Before he knows what hit him, he'll be inside a blackhole.]

— I hope y're not planning to blast me w/ a ray of those Higgs bosons & zap me into a blackhole, Merdecock?

— Drat, you weren't supposed to see that coming!

— I came prepared w/ a particle accelerator of my own! Right now, in fact, we are in another dimension! Constable Haplophryne, arrest this obviously fake eye disguised as a criminal mastermind!

— Actually, Inspector, I'm not really a constable.

— What? Et tu Brute?

— No, I'm on contract, see, w/ Central Casting. Vaudeville's my thing, guv, but it's a bit behind the times, if you know what I mean.

— As long as it's a clean contract.

— Clean as a whistle, guv.

— Then you'd better sing the Marseillaise.

— *Allons enfants de la Patrie, le jour de gloire est…*

— You know, Bragula, a little part of me dies whenever someone sings that.

— Ha! I'll join in, then.

— Not so fast! There's only room for one singer at a time!

— What?

— We're in another dimension you know.

— So we are. [Aside: I am making this aside to lead the infamous Wang Fang (who is only pretending to be Merdecock pretending to be an eye) into a false sense of security. The idiot thinks he's fooled me! Everything is falling into place exactly as planned.]

— Bragula?

— Yes Merdecock?

— Is that a bat behind you?

— What?! Where? Haplophryne, fetch me my gun!

— That's not a bat, guv, it's a telegram.

— Good god! What does it want?

— "Dear Bragula. Stop. Sorry had to fly. Stop. Merdecock. Stop."

— Damn, that was clever! Hurry, zap us out of this other dimension! If we don't catch him, the world may be doooooooooooomed!

Has the evil Wang Fang outwitted Inspector Marghouliès for the last time? Tune in next week for the final episode of *A Fang in the Neck!*

WHAT NEXT? OR: THE ANTAGONIST W/ A THOUSAND FACES

Vampyrs from Mars entering a timewarp & arriving on 21st=century Earth to vanquish & enslave humxnity?

A caped vampyr controlling her converts w/ eerie pipe=organ music?

TV mind=control waves directed by an evil brain from outerspace?

A child turned into a blood=sucking monster w/ plastic fangs?

Man in rocket=suit fighting to save Earth from 4=dimensional space monsters?

A nuclear physicist dominated by an alien 👽 bat?

Innocent Earthlings imprisoned in a Martian torture chamber?

A ghoul rowing a coffin through a sea of mist?

Hooded figures laying a beautiful womxn upon a sacrificial altar?

A pandemic of mindless stupidity?

Mean=eating crows, a giant octopus, crabs & bats attacking from sea & sky?

An army of bodysnatchers replacing humxns w/ androids?

Hypno doomsday machines invading the collective unconscious?
A diabolical film director warping the minds of his cast &
    crew?
Many confused people menaced by ultra=cheap scifi effects?
A computer that takes over the planet by enslaving humxnity
    in a simulation?
Wage slavery disguised as the saviour of the world?
A giant invisible creature w/ brain=sucking proboscis?
Asteroids, rogue satellites, a lunatic w/ the nuclear
    launch codes?
A mysterious toxic sludge seeking revenge upon its maker?
There are patterns of randomness like anything else?

THE PARABLE OF HIJRA
At the forking of the path,
                I took a knife

                            & carved out the sex
of the shadow
                lying across it.

                                    (Tsui Fang)

TRUTH IS FICTION, REALITY IS THE VIRUS
The film continues, the present action framed within a
background story, a scenario on the edge of plausibility,
secrets, a conspiracy, alarm, inexplicable occurrences, news
blackout, suppression of data, denial, national security,
leaked dossiers, whistleblowers, state of emergency, etc.
It has become a film about world domination, the mobilisation
of vast forces, wheels within wheels, the state within the
state, the cosmic order confronted by a doomsday pathogen.
What is it? Where did it come from? Who knew? The fate
of the world will be made to appear as if carried on the
shoulders of the little guy: propaganda's ever=willing
Sisyphus, whose credulous belief in distinctions of
good & evil, up & down, are the film's sentimental moral
compass. A random particle in collision w/ other random
particles they'll pin a medal on when the time comes. For
the film can only show what it is permitted to see, not
by the conspiring worldly powers, but by reality itself,
which has programmed all of this: the world simulated by
ideology. This is what they are all most afraid of, that
the world as they know it will cease to exist, dead on the
slab, murdered by a pathogen of its own creating. The film
does the unthinkable & goes further till nothing humxnly

recognisable is left, as if the camera=drone had evolved its own rationale, a Movie=Camera w/out a Man, streaming its images to remote cybernated consoles that no humxn will ever see. This is the afterlife so many have dreamt of. With neither G.O.D., a sympathetic robot, a monument or even the faintest memory, only the fact of the camera, whose existence implies a "creator" that no future science cld ever plausibly reverse=engineer, the myth inside a machine. Cinema's final testimony! *Thus*, as once said Tsui Fang, *does conscience make figments of us all.*

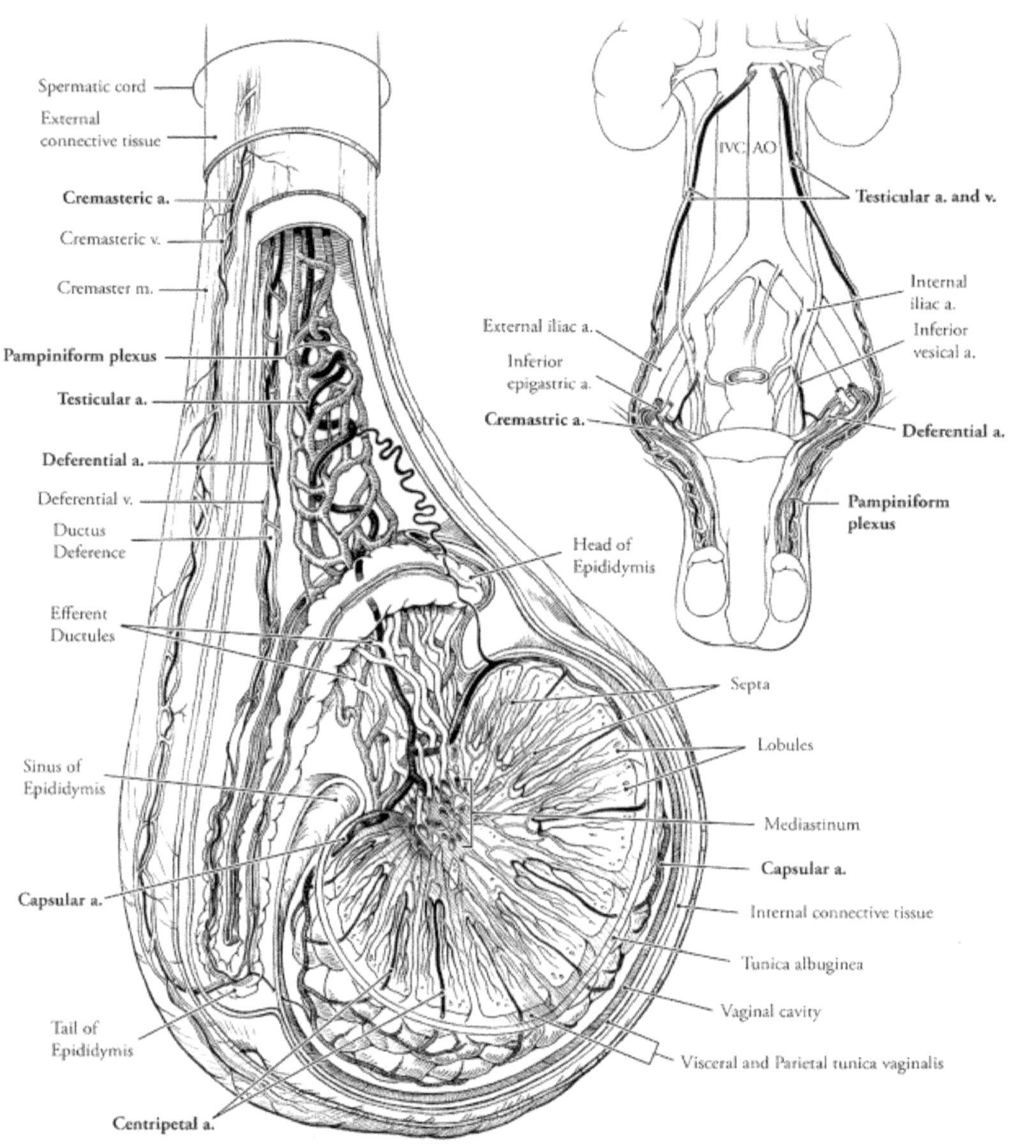

Spermatic cord
External connective tissue
Cremasteric a.
Cremasteric v.
Cremaster m.
Pampiniform plexus
Testicular a.
Deferential a.
Deferential v.
Ductus Deference
Efferent Ductules
Sinus of Epididymis
Capsular a.
Tail of Epididymis
Centripetal a.
Head of Epididymis
Septa
Lobules
Mediastinum
Capsular a.
Internal connective tissue
Tunica albuginea
Vaginal cavity
Visceral and Parietal tunica vaginalis
IVC AO
Testicular a. and v.
External iliac a.
Inferior epigastric a.
Cremastric a.
Internal iliac a.
Inferior vesical a.
Deferential a.
Pampiniform plexus

ELEVENTH COMMUNIQUÉ

Over 1,000,000 refugees, 50,000 homeless, 10,000 dead in 13 days, 100,000 imprisoned without charge or trial.

This war of terror is carried out in the name of the "public health" of Golemgrad.

THIS IS A SLANDEROUS LIE.

The I=L=L=U=M=I=N=I=S=T campaign is waged only to safeguard the fat profits of PAPA WALT & a few rich P.I.G.s.

We warn all sisters: do not be fooled by their propaganda campaign.

WHICH WAY WILL YOU POINT YR GUN WHEN THE CORP(ORATE)=$(TATE) ORDERS YOU TO SHOOT YR OWN SISTERS?

The corporate aristocracy has lined its pockets with the accumulated profits of three decades of exploiting the people of Golemgrad.

Now they are killing to defend these profits.

THE Š.V.E.J.K. ADVISES THE CORPORATE CLASSES TO GET OUT OF GOLEMGRAD & TAKE THEIR PUPPET PRESIDENT WITH THEM BEFORE THEY ARE ALL SHOT, LYNCHED, BEHEADED, BURNED.

POINT YR GUN!

The Š.V.E.J.K.

ONTOLOGY OF PSEUDONYMOUS OBJECTS

There are deformities only in the realm of myth.

Was I thus born to be **Offensia**'s understudy? Shadow of shadow? Invisible handmaiden of those who stand aside in order to stay out of sight? Alibi of the plague? The dog in the manger? The cat's cradle? The princess' pea? The forger's false consciousness? Literature's correlative?

Like a sheen of stagnant water in a flooded crypt, in which the idea of death offers not a reflection but its parody. Where the pious expect the spirit to lie, the resurrectionist discovers only pieces of bloated flesh. This thing, amputated from its being, still finds purpose as sacrilegious doppelgänger, holy relic, monstrosity=to=be arranged on a dissection slab, or objet d'art, the proverbial umbrella menaced by the perverse sewingmachine, the calamity of rebirth displayed for all to see, shld they be mad enough to wish to.

And so must I become what I resist?

Who is **Offensia**? Am I her or is she me? Or do we cancel each other, like dialectics? I point the silhouette of a gun, she pulls the trigger, we fall down dead. We fuck each other, figuratively & literally. We drink each other's blood. We are the annulus, the eclipse, the eternal return. How cld it be possible that we shldn't exist? What's existence without proof of us?

Am I a forgery?

Shld I desire to pass undetected, by fabricating a world? Yet I am the shadow that casts everything into a wrong light, a walking disturbance in the ether, all I touch turns to disquiet. Who wld mistake me for anything but an error?

"I am anguished," **Offensia** passes a hand across her brow, "becalmed. I dream only of a universe free of literature." Such panache!

But wld the world ever for our sakes pretend to be a story (all about us)? Crudely fake, pastiched, plagiarised, impostured?

"Literature," my mistress opines, "believes the Author is truth, whereas the forger seeks a libel more profound. The obscenity of the word itself. Not to imitate, but to embody, to become this farce in its naked being."

And for this I am the shadow of a womxn? A womxn w/out a shadow? Both & yet neither?

What happens to the world when vocabulary runs out?

Void within void. Such fatalism bores me. I exist, knowing the world desires otherwise. That's enough.

LOVE IS THE SENTIMENTALITY OF THEORY
The world isn't the imago of a spontaneous generation but a being cut in two. Thus the Manichaeism of the humxn produces the Manichaeism of the vampyr. To the lie of humxnity the vampyr responds w/ an equal lie. Wearing the old ideologies like a new pair of teeth, it bites the hand that feeds & the necks of all who supplicate. It's the ghost in the dialectic, the struggle within the struggle, draped in a parody of flesh. It's narcissism's rapacious doppelgänger. The ontology of the negative. Darkness visible. A damsel's cock.

& EVERYWHERE OFFENSIA WENT THE CAMERA WAS SURE TO FOLLOW
What is private life but a strategy for survival?

UNE FORTE & VOLUPTUEUSE SENSUALITÉ
With all the ennui of a bloated leach, Madame Guyotat lay prodigiously upon her deathbed, surplus mass ungirdled spilling upon the quilted chenille in bucolic undulations of puce, lavender, apricot, vistas of teal, scarlet lakes, valleys of subdued verdancy, breathtaking escarpments, meandering littorals, seas of millefiori bespeckled with guano, lichens, mossed gravystains, mildewed rivulets, rimmed by tidelines in a spectrum of amber, naphtha, urochrome. A horsefly was ponderously laying maggots in the groove of her prodigious chin, in that stale cheesegrater under her lip, in that constitutional nowomxnsland of ineffectuated colognes & depilating creams spatulated like putty into a crevasse. Madame Guyotat paid it no heed, preoccupied as she was with the unedifying spectacle unfolding on the faux Persian rug spread at her feet. A couple of drunken Wild Grrlz, heads clamped between thighs, were sucking each other's cocks while singing the Marseillaise, if singing it be. It brought to mind a failed coup d'état or the circus around a guillotine. A third, crosseyed from sick determination, was fumbling under the copious mess of bed linen, among vague animalia & indefinable semisolids. "Touché pas le merch, petit con!" croaked Madame Guyotat. "Can't you see I'm at death's door?"

THE PURPOSE OF THE MAUSOLEUM SOCALLED IS TO BE BURIED <u>ABOVE GROUND</u>
I said to myself, Surely here I have found the putrefaction of nature I seek?

THE INEVITABLE & NECESSARY DESTRUCTION OF THE WORLD TO BE BORN
[THE BLOOD OF OTHERS] Scenario: Following a worldwide plague at
the beginning of the 21st century, Golemgrad consists of armed
communes & crazed, wandering vampyrs. The relics of Old World
corporations war for control of scarce resources, enslaving all
who are unable to defend themselves. Offensia leads a band of
Wild Grrlz in a doomed attempt to wrest freedom for all from the
hands of corporate tyranny. Lots of grizzly fang=action. Jerry
Goldsmith composing.

DROWN THY BOOKS!
> Writing only means as much as it disturbs.
> Writing is the battlefield of a frenzied struggle between the forces of order & those of possibility, which one side calls truth & falsehood, & the other death & life.
> To write is to make possible the impossible.
> The truth of writing belongs entirely to its genius for paradox, self=subversion, suicide & miraculous rebirth.
> To write is to observe the infinite in the act of congealing into an image or dissolving into the void.
> Only those who claim the slave desires their enslavement cld insist that suffering acts hypnotically upon language, producing its most profound truth.
> "For writing to be manifest in its truth, it must be illegible" (Breton).
> The incomprehensible is redeemed by writing, as soon as it's understood not as a background against which certain mythemes stand out, but as the entire arena of its evolution.
> Writing is what it is in the diverse relation of its forms.
> By a formidable effort of the word, the world itself is rendered MORE than possible, as the articulation of what it isn't, what it might've been, & what it yet may become.
> Writing shld pose new theories about the world & the universe. How can we speak of redemption in a world where the slave pays reparations to the slaveowner?
> The struggle of writing has no end: it is a measure of a deeper struggle, which is that of existence itself.
> Writing is the unanswerable question.
> Only if writing stands in the shadow of meaning cld it be mistaken for something whose origin is an intense absolute moment of secrecy fused to an inexhaustible desire to be known.
> Writing exists. The world doesn't exist.[*] That is all.

ALL REVOLUTIONS ARE DOOMED ~~TO BECOME THEIR OPPOSITE~~
the great apposition of the world
as a blowfly's egg
in a beautiful window
you imagine taking flight
that instead crawls down yr throat
& eats you from the inside

---

[*] And neither do you.

life is a cartoon, love also is a cartoon

OEDIPUS' COLON [A TRAGEDY (NO ACT)]

The scene opens upon a chorus of plague=carriers w/ their barren genitals stitched up inside them, wrapped in dancers' veils they gurgle depravedly at the dead reflections in their Master's eyes, the way a crow raked by thirst ogles a pool of fetid piss. He is blind, chained to the roadside. For here the Master is also a slave. The chorus is comprised of his idiot children, who he takes turns sodomising for the entertainment of the passing foot=traffic – who utter obscene forms of encouragement, spit, toss coins into a tin cup set out for that purpose, scream denunciations, or more often simply ignore the entire spectacle. Thus does the Master seek forgiveness of the gods while they obtain their comic revenge. But what, you say, have the Master's children done to deserve such a miserable fate? Collateral damage? Or no such thing as an innocent aristocrat?

All this is, however, merely a prelude to the main act, performed not on stage but upon the unsuspecting audience, I=L=L=U=M=I=N=I=S=T=S every last one of them.

Offensia has named it, in honour of her erstwhile companion in literary crime & now regime toss=bot Nyx gLand, THE SPHERES OF OBLIVION.

Aided by the programme notes, our attention is drawn to the unfolding "psychological drama":

The blind Master is the ego's rampart equalising all contraries & not things merely fated lying in mind=scum of if=&=only=if (no sleep for the dead), inspired to the very heights of imitation as now, a dying man's last delusion of grandeur, upon the Master's summoning, a phalange of naked floozies (The Gottwald Zombie Battalion! serving as extras here) undulating their vamp=stamps on layers of subcutaneous macronutrient & flashing their insteps at the chandeliers, a real torture=chamber funforall…

During the resulting orgy, one among the Master's slave children, they call her "Electra," steps dramatically out of character to wreak a most bloody revenge. Such gore as political realism is daily made of for the I=L=L=U=M=I=N=I=S=T spooks & conspiranoiacs taking up the peanut gallery, among whom the animatronic zombies are tossed with the abandon of handgrenades w/ a 4second fuse…

"I can feel their bones through the burnt flesh as it comes apart in the palms of my hands!" Juulz Ebola screams. "The crab lies upon the chopping block!"

It's hell come to Earth to collect its tithe of testosterytes, in bloody gouts of exploding zombie apocalypse, their DNA a literal ticking timebomb or as

the saying goes *once bitten twice shy*, as behind a two=way mirror **Offensia** gazes upon her handiwork w/ a grotesque smile:
   "Sting them!" she hisses. "Sting them, my anopheles!"

THE HIGHEST WISDOM APPEARS DRESSED LIKE A CLOWN

What ∴ was the true nature of Ebola's "tragic accident"? An overdose of vitriol cut w/ saniflush? A head=on collision w/ a treacherous stairwell? Cancer of the pineal eye? Septic brain embolism? A dildo lodged in the oesophagus? Sweet serendipity? An overdue library book? Space debris? A poisoned pen? A street=fighting communist? A case of mistaken identity? A swandive off the Kottbusser Tor? A serenade into the business end of a sawnoff 12=gauge? A word to the wise? Megalomania pure & simple? A faulty timer? The easiest way out? A crushing solitude? A French crook? A pimp in a porkpie hat? A vicious sentimentality? Misadventure down a manhole? A rat called Stan? Electrodes to the testicles dialled into the red? A boo in a box? Haemophilia? The cat's meow? An asphyxiation kink gone awry? A vampyr dusted to the gills? An agent of the Š.V.Э.J.K.? The thirteenth moon? A driveby ricochet? Sheer ennui? The Man's right hand? Mac the Knife? The angel of History? An act of **G.O.D.**? The Wuhan Virus? Bad luck on a one=way street? A suicide bomb? A poorly timed inhalation in a bucket of piss? A fortuitous encounter with a subbasement chopping block? An exhilarating prophetic masterpiece? A typographical error? None of the above?

NOT TO PASS ON A TRADITION BUT TO BREAK ITS HOLD OVER US

FOR WE ARE BEREAVED BECAUSE
LEARNÈD IN THE WAYS OF REALISM TO KILL *AB NIHILO*
& BUILD FROM THAT TO A
CRESCENDO OF CIVILISATION HIGH & HOLY
A DARK LIVER UNDER THE KNIFE
G.O.D.'S AORTA
A BRAIN DELICATELY MARINATED IN ITS OWN SAUCE UNDER FAINT
   DUSTINGS OF GOLD & ASBESTOS & RHINO HORN
THE MYTH OF THE "OTHER" MADE TO SUFFER IN PLACE OF US LIKE
   A FUGITIVE SELF=IMAGE
ALL THIS HAVE WE KNOWN
BUT HOW SHALL <u>THEY</u> EMANCIPATE <u>US</u>?

"EVERYTHING UNBORN CAN STILL BE BROUGHT TO LIFE" (ARTAUD)

What, being simply a mirror held up to an enforced economic system, calls itself *art?* What hand holds the mirror? What camera=eye beholds the image? If it's clear that no revolution is possible w/out an equivalent revolution in the idea of the world, nor is it possible w/out a revolution in the *representation* of that idea. "We must put political representation OUT OF WORK!" Aesthetics is to ethics what art is to politics only when a war of positions has been won by the keepers of the categories. Political "art," catastrophe "art," pandemic "art," vampyr "art": in short, the kitsch of ideological quarantine. In these "difficult times" the question of art is made to seem ever more pressing now that life itself threatens to be made extinct. (Symbolic capital isn't the exception, it's the *only kind*.) But has the situation of art really changed from what it was before? To those who say *prend l'image et garde-la*, there's only one reply: *l'image n'existe pas.* To be other than a materialist fiction, means to be an objective denunciation. (All hail the incorruptible poetry of revolt, which to the bureaucrat & the cop is a mental affliction!). Which "quantitative alterations" have yet to erupt into a "qualitative leap," beyond an opportunistic *settling of accounts*? Ah! All complacency in art must be destroyed? Hurrah! Let art, in selfimposed exile, destroy it. There was never a spectacle more edifying, than of the dead burying the dead. N_x

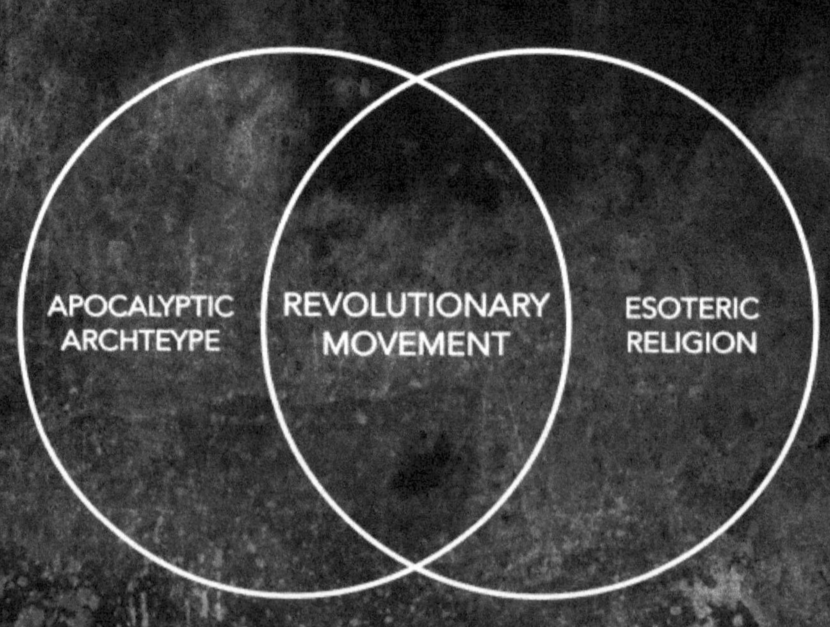

EVERY CONFESSION IS A LIE

in spite of my body / mechanically invited / anomalous / behind its imago / this endemic mind's eye / tamponed to stanch / cumsop / reprisals for 1. suffering, 2. loving <u>all</u> that you love / if it is commutable / a migrant wound / they'll track back across even the remotest borders / because the dawn / can indeed survive the death of its star / gods of redemption only in [yr] [wildest] dreams / to the day after the one before / & the one before / in the white totem of ever after / the fractured blasphemous glory / starless night / teeth singing w/ electricity / there are eyes, also, never intended to see / will they still be [there] / awaiting the void / if [there is] nothing else [?]

"THAT THINGS 'JUST GO ON' IS THE CATASTROPHE" (BENJAMIN)

A blast from the past.
An ass on a mast.
A ghost of aghast.
Rats in the ballast.
Awash in waste.
Beasts at breakfast.
Rates of contrast.
Satire in broadcast.
A fleet of bombast.
A feast of flabbergast.
Grass on the karst.
Of an oblast vast.
Just to the east.
A taste for yeast.
Toast before repast.
Durst they fast?
An iconoclast's fart.
A farcical dynast.
Roasted gnats.
A pederast's scat.
The boast of chiliasts.
Outlasted by pestilence.
Steadfast coasts.
Exhausted typecasts.
A star on her breast.
The subtle gymnast.
Duress forecast.
The least enthusiast.
Hastens to be last.

THE FIRST STEP IS TO KILL THE PAPAMAMA

GOLEMGRAD (#FakeNewsMedia) – New research suggests that a controversial gene=editing experiment to produce children resistant to CORVID=69 may also have enhanced their ability to remember the future.

The brains of two genetically enhanced twins born in Golemgrad last year may have been altered in ways that radically effect memory & precognition, according to Dr Zifčák Asperger, recently appointed CEO of TransVyrologia, the company which patented the gene technology used in the experiments.

Now, new findings suggest that the same alteration introduced into the twins' DNA by deleting a gene called CCR5 not only increases immunity to CORVID=69 but causes significant brain mutation normally associated w/ vampyrism.

Questioned about this, Dr Asperger pointed to common DNA traits not only between cis=genic humxns & vampyrs, but also feral rhesus macaques, which have likewise been found to transmit the virus. "It is altogether possible," Dr Asperger said, "that the virus itself is reprogramming DNA in response to our attempts to block it. How propagation is related to precognition, however, is something we've yet to establish. Tests are ongoing."

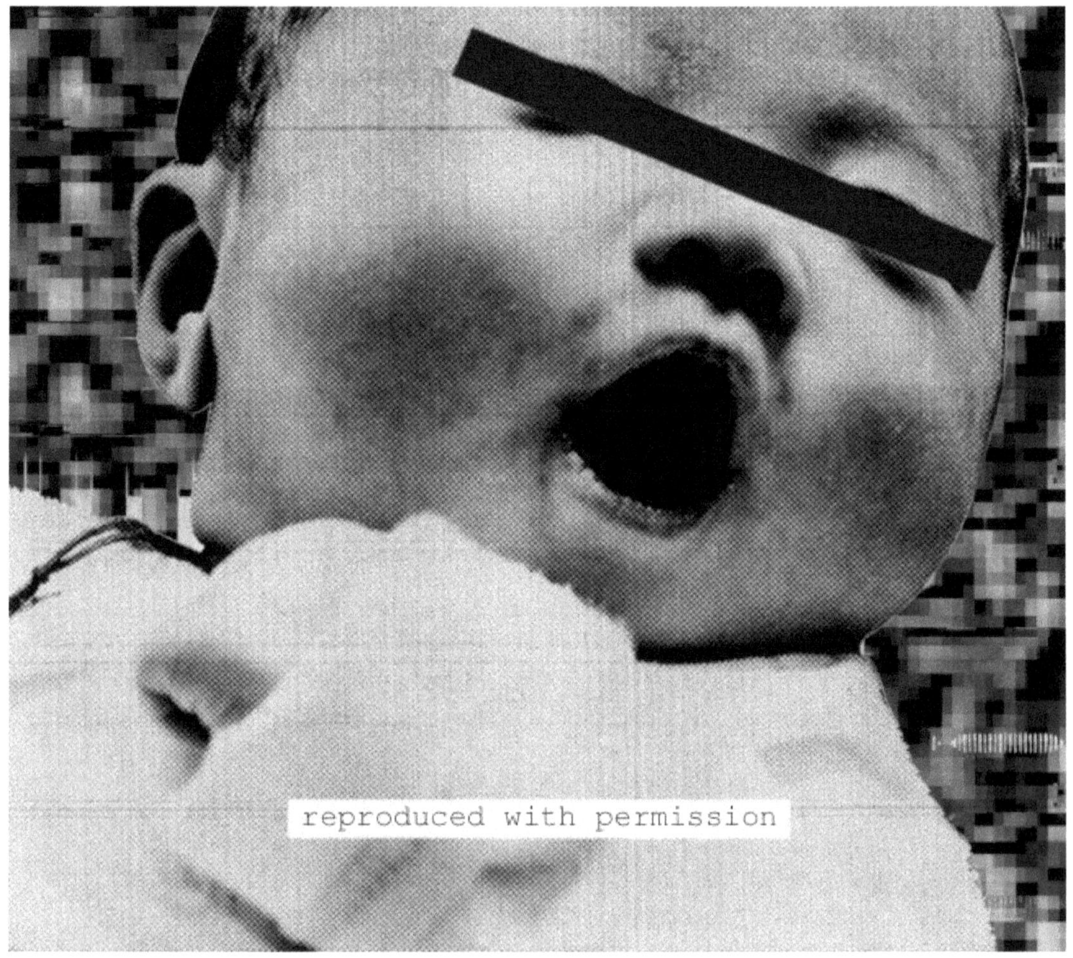

THE FALSE NECESSITY OF THE FAIT ACCOMPLI
a fer
o
cious
ar / bi / tra / ry
machine
        guard
        ing
        the
        se   cret
        es   sence
                        of its
                        com / pul / sion
to
        killkillkill
                        repeat
                        repeat
                        repeat
                                faster
                                        faster
                                                faster

CULT OF THE DEAD AUTHOR
You stand before the Blank Page. Something writes itself.
Words dance. Miraculous! Was that you? The Blank Page
wants more. Nothing happens. Y're helpless, empty, utterly
remote. The Blank Page simpers, cajoles, pleads, demands,
hurls the vilest insults, screams death. Something stirs.
Mama. Papa. Caca. The Blank Page gurgles, claps its hands.
The shame comes in great gouts of incontinent. The Blank
Page is painting w/ its fingers on the wall. *Like a pig in
shit.* It's only now you see that y're chained to it, that
there's no getting away. It cries in the night & out spew
the words. It belches, it whines w/ hunger, it crosses
its eyes. The words cascade. The words choke yr breath,
consciousness, gag reflex. Y're a palpitating mollusc.
Stimulus & response. The words are no longer words. They
never belonged to you & you were never their master. Soiling
yrself like that before the entire world. There's no end to
this humiliation.[*]

---

[*] Meaning is a communicable disease: the mind believes what lies
upon the page & suffers what it believes. But what [who] <u>writes</u> &
what [who] is <u>written</u>?

HOTDOG NO BUN

Van Helsing – known in the industry as The Eternal Return, not for the wall of double=platinums (there aren't any) but the fact that their lead=guitarist & namesake, Eddie Van, just won't go away – are playing a month=long residency at the Tropicana to publicise their newly=minted BEST OF album, *Hell & Back (Again)*. News of which arouses in **Offensia**, childhood scars running deep, violent ambivalent feelings. The renewed proximity of her estranged father, after so many years, in the city where her mother was murdered, where **Offensia** herself had sought refuge from her father's megalomaniacal insanity, stirs difficult memories. Once upon a time she'd longed for the sweet release of reconciliation only to be locked in the tower of her father's Transylvanian castle & terrorised by a deranged governess obsessed w/ ESP. Escape had been costly. She'd sworn eternal revenge, but time had blunted the edge of her emotions, distracted her into many different occupations. In the dark vampyric arts she'd discovered a calling. Death shld not be a mere impulse to spontaneous violence nor the *idée fixe* of a dominating monomania. Such had been the teaching of Tsui Fang, her former sensei at Stalin Monastery, before its destruction & her exile in the world of men. But now, the reappearance of her father wrought in **Offensia** an uncontrollable disturbance, immediately embarking on a campaign of indiscriminate bloodshed. "A poor grrl w/ a daddy romance," said Duhomey when she confronted him w/ the news & whom she duly slaughtered (if only metaphorically) w/ the implements of his trade (an embossed fountain=pen, from B.J. "Papa" Walt, for SERVICES TO THE INDUSTRY).

TOO LOUD A SOLIPSISM

"A guitar solo's just a bunch of events. Ideally there's a certain kind of flatness, a lack of an arc, or a very subtle arc. The point is the pointlessness. The music is its own higher purpose." (Eddie Van)

THE UTOPIA OF CONTENT

always within the present moment / unrest spreads by intimate forms / of contact therefore prohibited

JESUS CHRIST WAS NAILED TO A HOT CROSS

Religion is an index of sexual guilt.

VAN HELSING, LAST NIGHT AT THE TROPICANA

December in Plague City, drinking the black surf under the pier – / the sky's a rotten liver, it's cocktail hour, there's a / rusted palm tree on the beach & y're hanging in it. / It's the old womxn on the stairs again talking in yr sleep, / like ocean sounds & highways, & it's cold being rained on / by every dog on the street, but to open yr eyes first y've got to widen the polarities. / Well anyone can be existential with the lights out, he said, / but the telephone was just a jilted lover on the make / & he'd run out of change. He was a pork=pie=&=vest guy, / arms jacked back like Joe Strummer at the bar making / stutter=step holding patterns while the Wild Grrlz sang / *Everyone's a winner, baby, everyone's a Winnebago…* / It was Jim Crow on the South Side playing lynchmob saxophone, / & Frankie Machine & the cigarette girl, & Betty Lou at the / 8th street No=Tell. Y'd've written it all down but yr arm / was full of lead – what comes of being subproletarian in bed. / Because it's midnight on the TV & word had got around / about December in Plague City & the body on the pier – & there's / questions to be answered but no=one left to hear, / they've all gone south to Mexico in aviators & moustaches, / & the bozos on Memorial Day quote O'Henry to the masses. / Because it's midnight on the TV, yes the reruns were atrocious, / & the sentimental migraine pours its story down yr throat, / & the pool balls all resent you, & the barstools sit & gloat.

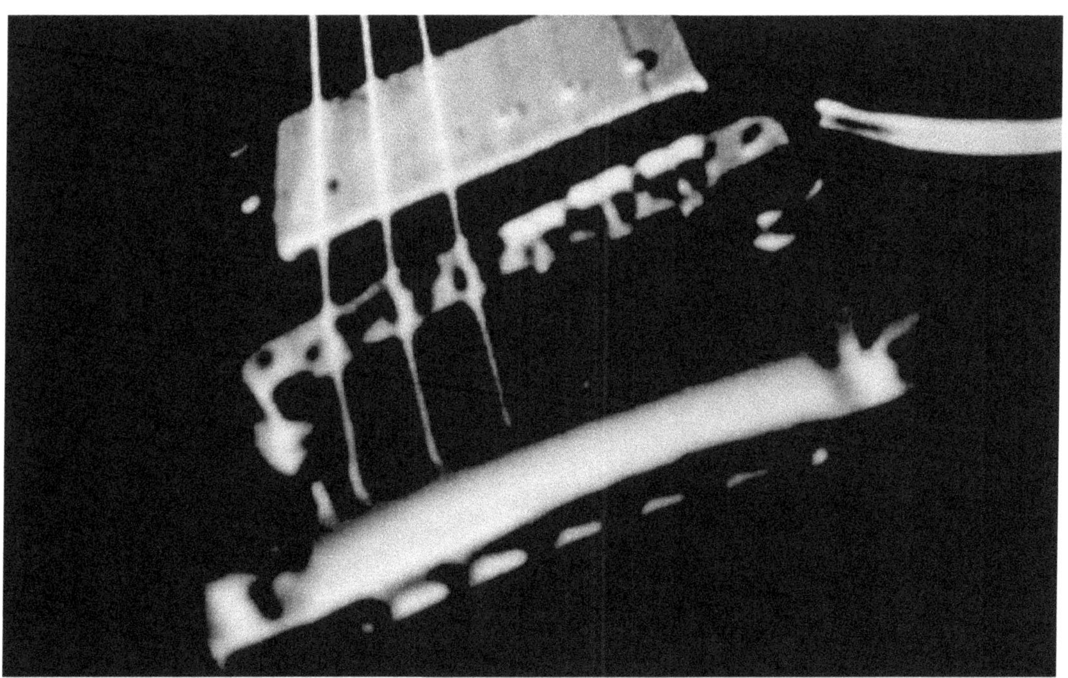

THE ADORATION OF OFFENSJA

Freedom was a more damaged & intensely complex experience
for her than it ever cld be for most vampyrs I don't
care what you say she's the world's greatest agony artist
& ventriloquist & just plain batshit crazy I love her
entirely completely hyperbolically we shld probably kill
her & eat her now soon before she's tainted goods past
her shelf life in other words compromised by the System
that turns everything decent & pure in this world to vile
abject dollar=denominated pox lab=grown to satisfy every
one=size=fits=all bitch in instant=gratification heat even
if right now she's all hell=witch & razor=fang evisceration
machine the day's coming better forever young & not wake up
next to yr disappointments for the rest of eternity like a
serial divorcee w/ halitosis ever see a vampyr go to rot
it's the horriblest dahling every true emotion shld be
drowned at birth & preserved in a little cryo=tube buttplug
close to yr heart hahaha & swear solemnly never to shit
again because if you really love something you'll always be
prepared to make those little sacrifices called selflessness
it's all well & good to care about things in theory but I'd
give my all just to be one small part of her happiness &
her mine isn't it clear as day we're made for each other we
cld've been twins gene=edited in a testtube separated at
birth but you can't stand in the way of destiny any more
than you can turn back an asteroid or a herd of elephants
or the tide even though G.O.D. knows it wldn't be the first
time someone's tried do you think it's unhealthy to hold yr
breath when you come I mean there're species that don't even
need oxygen evolved from jellyfish I'm serious sometimes I
feel as if I'm nothing but a shapeless blob of endocrine
w/ man=o=war tentacles drifting in the sea & sooner or
later y're going to get wrapped up in something wholly &
utterly did you know some jellyfish have hundreds of eyes
& a brainstem for a clitoris pulsing nonstop I wish I cld
be languid & not this frantic need for time to stop I just
can't get a grip if only she was inside me I know everything
wld be different she won't answer my calls because they've
secretly been telling her lies about me pushing their own
agendas turn her into a product=line we have to save her
I'm storing up all my man=o=war venom first it burns the flesh
then turns them blue w/ lung=paralysis I'm worse than any
motherfucking virus I'll wipe out half the global economy
if that's what it takes for those repelled by laughter will
never grasp the seriousness of the occasion.

PANDEMIC MACHINES

The "revenge of nature" upon errant humxnity amounts to nothing more than the substitution of one kind of *economic being* for another: the catalysing of environmental redress for the production of social relations. The idea that the Humxnocene is a *natural phenomenon* is no more or less ridiculous than the idea that the Corp[orate]=$[tate] can be an *instrument of its redemption*. Or that the "hidden=hand" of CORVID=69 shall in turn set the Corp[orate]=$[tate] to rights & bring about, all by itself, such a confection of necessity as to be called an *automatic revolution*: parody shaking the hand of tragedy. Like Hamlet, it's *à la mode* to bewail a world out of joint (& in desperate need of one) & also like Hamlet lament the dreary task of *setting it right*. Chaos by necessity is the very *genome* of the Corp[orate]=$[tate]. And necessity by way of automatism is nothing if not the accelerated & scaled manufacture of surplus. Automatism *liberates nothing* but a capacity for enlargement driven solely by the circulation & consumption of *inessentials*. (The ideal form of superabundance is waste.) It dreams great vistas of unfettered expenditure: expenditure rendered as an *autonomous social force*. Never was it a *subjective impulse* to *add to the labour of production*. Nor is the precondition of automatism *subjective alienation*. No "antecedent subject": the subject itself, from its very origins, is the product of a *repetition automatism*. (Alienation was never the pathetic fallacy it appeared.) The pandemic produces alienation because its logistics of segregation, quarantine, transmission, asymptomaticity, immunity, fatality *produce a subject*. If pandemic automatism is the final subsumption of the political into the logistical, it isn't achieved by sheer momentum of a "contingent necessity," but viral overproduction itself, *for itself*. In this circular economy, the project of social separation (integration by disintegration) achieves its apotheosis. The virus isn't *in* the system, the virus *is the system*. N_x

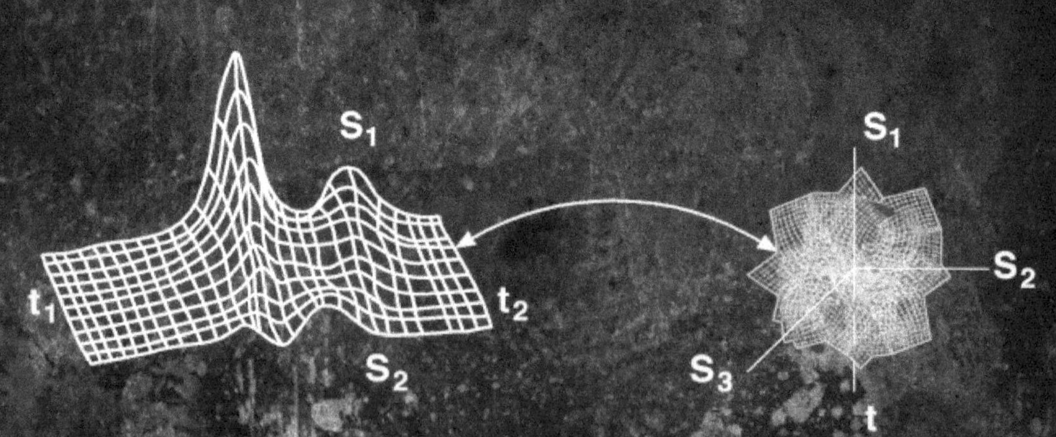

T. G. HIERONYMUS **2,482,773**

DETECTION OF EMANATIONS FROM MATERIALS AND MEASUREMENT OF THE VOLUMES THEREOF

Filed Oct. 23, 1946

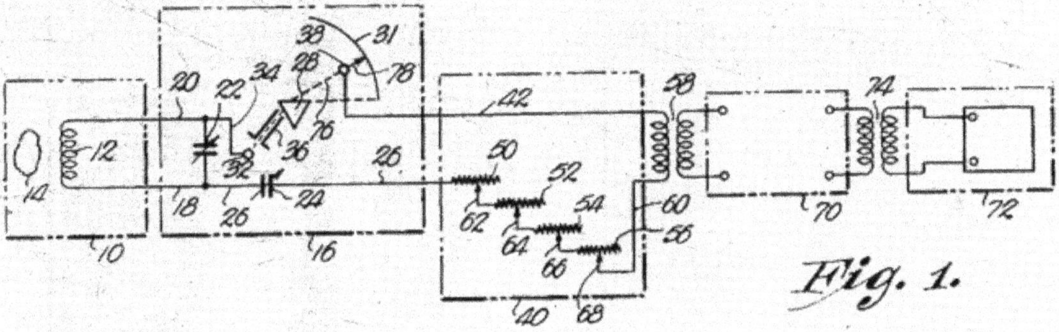

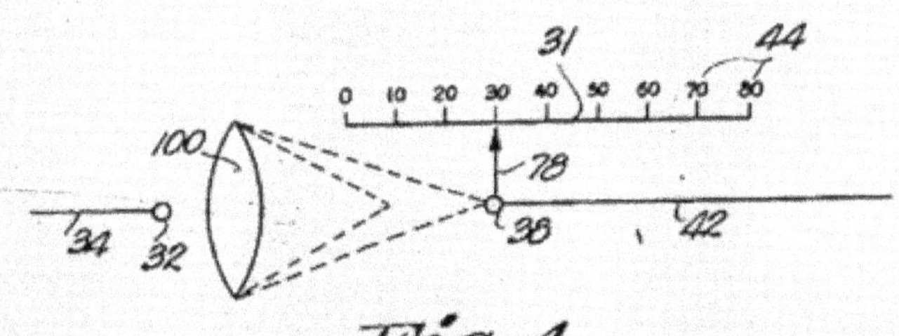

Fig. 1.

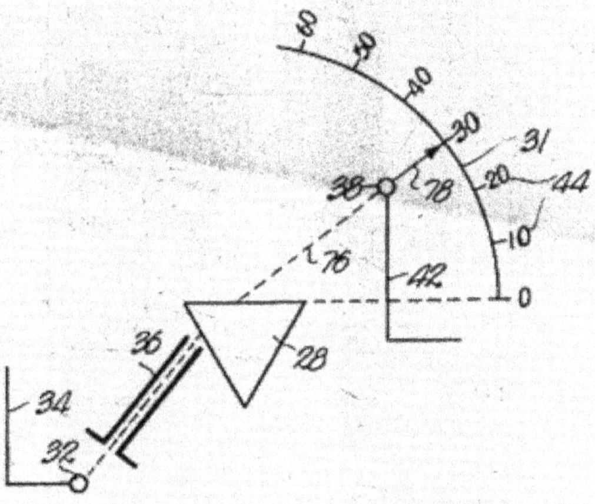

Fig. 2.

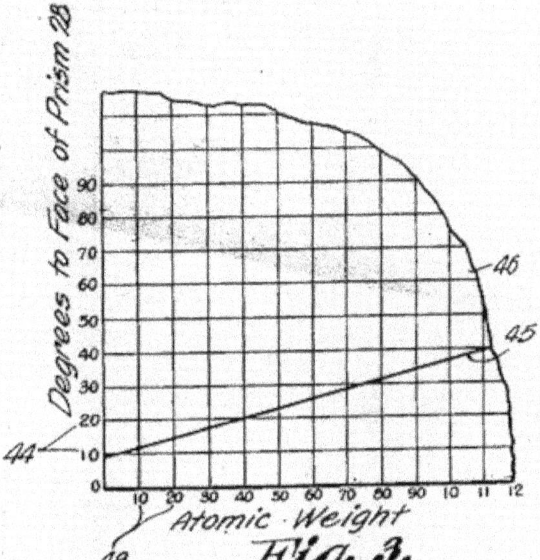

Fig. 3.

Fig. 4.

INVENTOR.
Thomas G. Hieronymus
BY
ATTORNEY.

- wherever they shoot a star, a parsec in the eye is a circuitry towards yr fangs that bite the air. clinamens are forced into serfdom for you to measure the hooves of that horse. it will violate nature.

- Told her I ain't come back to the megacity. I adopted a monkey=bat, started synth=permaculturing. I'm growing lifesize mandrakes & 3D printing Siratori grrlz. I am not alone anymore.

- Collective IQ is miserablism imho.

- u r all too beatific. some of you are arseholes tho. i am somebody's rectum, too, which just makes me smile.

- The priests gonna bull=trap you for aeons to come.

- As if they didn't already own the majority of comms channels through which those emotions are relayed & conveyed.

- Don't tell me GIFs are darkweb isles of individuations.

- Looking forward to the next Wave. I hereby re=name this planet "Exponential Overdoom."

- These mediascivious dawns/ Slowly weaving algorithmics in my heart/ whereas the mind screeching: "star at a distance of ~3.3 Schwarzschild radii from the blackhole ORBITING THE EDGE OF THE ABYSS…"

- I cannot understand how "humxnoid vs vamp" got to make a difference for the statistical properties of CORVID, how the epidemiology differs & why morbidity rates & tail risk must diverge.

- Has that version arrived on Earth recently? It's about to finish xer bildungsroman hereabouts.

- back in 20XX, doing quantum archaeology in the hypnospace built in coronachan mod.

- There's nothing wrong w/ being a eugenicist.

- Nobody told me about this while I was unleashing the code. Jesus!

- the watchmaker does not need TIME to craft watches.

- I truly regret having programmed pneuma in binaries 2,500 years ago. I thought it was an experimental bug not a future species!

- Besides, whoever they are get to own the damn DNA.

- Some liken it to aphorism blasters. "PAPA BOI INVENTED CORVIDITY." That is as Voynich as possible.

- You here for the show? Embrace it. There wasn't a character limit to a paragraph that made them invent kaligrammatic approaches to syntax=yuga, let alone unwanted break=lines.

- CORVID tries to offer a clip=to=copyboardable modulation which is not that much moddable, & pretends as if it was a codex roll. Recode the damn thing horizontally & you have a paginated choose=yr=own=story.

   - What is this philistine reaction to each individual step towards Singularity? I know it's not necessarily linear (see GANs). However, simply think of blockchain as a bridge. I need to remind you of the fact that they did not have the internet in 1918.

   - So, they deserve to be ruthlessly capitalised upon?

   - but the way Papa took the little vamps off the street & provided them w/ simple provisions of life is just heart warming enough.

   - If you are letting people storm the infinite sales bays, but yr armed forces keep diverting refugees from the shorelines, it means that you have no central authority, & yr delegation methods are questionable.

   - Be the gaze that captures em all! [an error occurred while processing this directive]

   - What is NOT going to save us from the humxn bug is the unimaginatively dull & bleak reluctance of humxns themselves to take risks & precautionary maintenance efforts. Yes, we do platform decay, but the abort feature is bugged by idiots.

   - When corvidious morning star sounds as if oceanwaves rippling against cumbia boards!

   - I am disciplining myself. It almost feels like a silent bootleg of *Salò o le 120 giornate di Sodoma*.

   - on the 1001st evening of quarantine, i have chosen the dark side.

THE K=E=Y

It was entirely in his nature that Dr Zifčák Asperger shld maintain the pretence of having deciphered the Voynich Manuscript's secret system (a cure for the world's brainsucking vampyr disease?[*]) only to have misplaced THE K=E=Y, to have lost it in a freak accident or, better still, to have consigned it in an act of species=negating perversity to the watery deep, the flames of a volcano, the reactor core of a nuclear power station, the oblivion

---

[*] Rumours had long been circulated attributing authorship of the Voynich MS to no less a personage than G.O.D. Cue religious nut gobbledegook. It was either a prophesy or a warning, or both. Merely to speak of <u>it</u> was to participate in a speculative fiction. The entire thing was, in any case, indecipherable to the great unwashed, who'd neither heard of it nor had any need of it. G.O.D. spoke to them through their inflight entertainment systems.

of outerspace, etc., solely for the pleasure (oh cursèd spite) of depriving an undeserving humxnity of ever the chance of getting their grubby little fingers on it. Pure heresy? Or the wiles of a man attuned to the virtues of a resale profit margin, mmm, patents pending? Or simply to feed the entertaining frenzy of that cult of cryptcrawling degenerates hungry for TRANSCENDENTAL MISERABLISM. The infantile apocalypse junkies of the I=L=L=U=M=I=N=I=S=T WORLD ORDER, no less! Behold, the K=E=Y doth indeed exists! But lost, how sad, perhaps forever ☹ Gather round now children, 'tis decreed by G.O.D. for you, the Chosen Few, to cast off once more 'pon yr Crusade, from Golemgrad hence. Recover the K=E=Y! Unlock the DIVINE LAUNCHCODE! Doom be thy property (& not some lesbo influenza)! 'Tis yrs by birthright! Morons. What did it matter if the Book of Books was a flagrant counterfeit? In what star was the proof written? Meenie meenie, tiktoktoe. Watch the little kiddies go!

ALL THEORY IS POLITICAL FICTION

It's 4:00a.m. & Eddie Van Helsing is cruising in his Eldorado along the lantern=lit Esplanade, saline drip dangling from rearview, a hundred decibels of feedback=guitar swirling in the backwash. Overdub of cheering masses, barrages of tickertape. Zapruder 313. Wild Grrlz lock him in their sights. OK Boomer. *Make haze before the sun shines*, the thought=of=the=day. Like Papa Walt says, "Time to sacrifice yrself for the cause, son." Well sales is sales & when they ain't, yr best bet on a big fat return is rez=erection, *harharhar*, being nine=tenths of every successful snuffjob in History where The Franchise is concerned. They've even pre=recorded the soundtrack, *Better D.E.D. Than A Lie*, & a whole cult suicide package for the hipster market, lining up to be impaled & go out pure & uncompromised ("Don't drink the KoolAid! Everything's at stake!"), pressed on 12=inch vinyl w/ a wrap=around black&white Mapplethorpe rip=off of a defanged vampyr, one from Van Helsing's personal trophyroom back at Bran Castle. It'll feature in Jean Rollin's upcoming rockumentary, *From Hell to Transylvania*. They've primed a prefabbed fullpage review in the next issue of *Zeit Raus!* "A strikingly different tone takes over on the second half of the record, more frenetic, less affected, more fractured, a work of prophesy for these dark times." The R&D boiz have planned a whole line of merch right down to a scaled replica Van H homunculus w/ permanent boner & hackable solarcell Stratocaster, programmed to spew feedback within half=a=mile of any fullblood vamp sorority kidz sneaking about incognito in the dead of night, hahaha. *We advise keeping the product locked safely in its box outside daylight hours to avoid risk of graphic vigilante action.* This cld be one now, flooring it along the Esplanade as Wild Grrlz let loose w/ heavy=calibre fire, RPGs & subatomic laser beams, causing Van Helsing's braincase to detonate in a fireworks display to rival the 1812 Overture, autopilot guiding the Cadillac through a full 360° roll over the seawall & airborn out across the phosphorescent tide on a flightpath to Plague Island. The body wld never be recovered (conspiranoiacs plz note). Coroner's verdict: LOST AT SEA. *Coz I been stormtossed on an ocean / too deep it get me down / gonna crawl under the world / where the sky drowns / I found no peace / in outerspace / no face behind the face / a fly buzzed when I died / in the blackholes in yr eyes / & I'll be gone before you see me / & if you see me there tomorrow / yesterday will never come. Da da, da da, da dum.*

REALISM IS THE DREAMLIFE OF TAX COLLECTORS

Scenario: It is discovered that the only treatment for CORVID=69 is humxn blood. Consequences.

HER BLOOD RUNS BLACK

[The saga of **Offensia** in 100 tabloid newspaper headlines]
   1. VAN HELSING'S SLAYER VAMPYR KID
   2. UNDEAD DAME DRINKS BLOOD FOR BREAKFAST
   3. ROCKSTAR PRINCESS PSYCHO KILLER
   4. DEBUTANT DOOMSDAY DEVIL
   5. MOST=ELIGIBLE VIRGIN A BULL=DYKE DRACULA
   6. ROCK HEIRESS OUTCHARTS CHARLES MANSON
   7. CONVENT GRRL CRUCIFIES CORPORATE CRONIES
   8. DADDY'S HOMEGROWN TERRORIST
   9. BLOOD=CRAZED TEEN VAMP CULT THRILL=SEEKER
  10. TRUST FUND MURDERESS SLUMS IT ON WILD SIDE
  11. QUEEN OF REVENGE PORN HOMICIDE CONSPIRACY
  12. JILTED DAUGHTER ON BUTCHERING SPREE
  13. GLAM SCOURGE OF KAPITALIST SCUM
  14. VENGEANT VAMP'S VIRULENT VENDETTA
  15. FROM PEDERASTS TO PRESIDENTS: SHE KILLS ALL
  16. SEX SYMBOL SADO SLASHER
  17. JUVENILE JUGULAR=JAGGER'S JIHAD

18. SATANIC SODALITY SNUFF=SIREN
19. DRACULA'S JOYRIDE BRIDE
20. SUCK QUEEN OF THE VAMPYR CASTLE
21. FILLETED WITH FANGS OF FEMALE FURY
22. CONFESSIONS OF A TEENAGE SUCCUBUS
23. HER KISS IS COLDER THAN DEATH
24. MAM'SELLE MASS MURDER
25. BO PEEP'S BOHEMIAN BOOGALOO
26. SHE LOVES TO KILL!
27. FOR THE TERM OF HER UNNATURAL LIFE
28. VAMPYR CULT MURDERER ON THE LOOSE
29. CRAZED SERIAL KILLER DRINKS VICTIMS' BLOOD
30. MISGUIDED YOUTH CAUGHT IN CULT MANIA
31. GOLEMGRAD GUTTED BY WILDGRRL VAMP
32. DELINQUENT ON FANTASY KILL SPREE
33. VAN HELSING "DAUGHTER" VAMPYR QUEEN
34. HELL SINGS HER NAME: OFFENCE TO G.O.D.
35. DAMNED TO BURN AS COPS CLOSE IN
36. COMMIE KILLER BLEEDS BANKERS DRY
37. SHE IS NOT A RICH MAN'S PLAYTHING
38. A TOOTH FOR A TOOTH
39. THIS GRRL IS FOR THE GUILLOTINE
40. CORPORATE BLOODSUCKERS GET IT IN THE NECK
41. MADWOMXN OF THE MALECÓN
42. COPS OUTFOXED BY GHETTO GEISHA
43. PROLE PRINCESS IN CLASSWAR CARNAGE
44. CUTTHROAT GANG ON THE LOOSE
45. SELFSTYLED "VAMPYR" LEADS BLOODY RAMPAGE
46. BOLSHY BRIDE OF DRACULA BITES BACK
47. OUT OF CONTROL KILL CRAZE PANDEMIC
48. VAMPYR VIRUS DRIVES DEBUTANTE TO LIFE OF CRIME
49. MUTILATED BY PLAGUE ZOMBIES
50. COVEN OF CRUELTY: "THEY WILL STOP AT NOTHING"
51. HOW I SURVIVED A VAMPYR ATTACK
52. DEATH FROM BEYOND THE GRAVE
53. BOUNTY OUT ON SOCIALITE BLOODSUCKER
54. SUPERSPREADERS STRIKE WITHOUT MERCY
55. NO CURE FOR CRIME CONTAGION
56. VAMP TRAMPS TERRORISE CITY
57. SAVE OUR STREETS FROM SATAN'S SORCERESS
58. GRRL GANG GUT GOVERNMENT GARRISON
59. BLOOD FOR NOTHING: REBELS WITHOUT A CAUSE
60. TRAPPED LIKE A RAT IN A M.A.Z.E.
61. VIOLENT CRIME WAVE PLAGUES GOLEMGRAD
62. SHEWOLF TERROR CAMPAIGN MUST END
63. A THIRST THEY CANNOT QUENCH

64. WHO IS THE LA MALATTIA RIPPER?
65. INTERVIEW WITH A VAMPYR: EXCLUSIVE!
66. THIS LITTLE BITCH HAS TEETH
67. FRIGHT NIGHT HORRORSHOW SURVIVOR TELLS ALL
68. POLICE STAKE ALL ON VAMPYR ARREST
69. ONE STEP AHEAD BUT FOR HOW MUCH LONGER?
70. GRRL SAYS, THE NEW BITE IS RIGHT
71. PSYCHOPATH OR REVOLUTIONARY?
72. VAMPYR "MANIFESTO" SAYS ALL FAIR GAME
73. CRIMESTREAK NOT "INTIFADA": AUTHORITIES
74. SERIAL KILLER'S TIME IS UP
75. NO NEGOTIATION W/ MALEFICENT MANHUNTER
76. MALECÓN MAULER MAILS ULTIMATUM MISSIVE
77. A CUT=THROAT'S CURIOUS ALLURE
78. NO MERCY FOR THE "VIRGIN VAMPYRESS"
79. FIRST BLOOD, LAST RITES
80. RATS, BATS, CROWS, VAMPYRS TO BE SHOT ON SIGHT
81. ONE WOMXN'S WAR AGAINST THE WORLD
82. LYNCH MOBS COMB THE CITY, COME UP EMPTY=HANDED
83. HELL COMES TO GOLEMTOWN
84. FEAR PANDEMIC BLAMED ON BATS
85. TO KILL A VAMPYR=SLAYER'S DAUGHTER
86. PSYCHO SUCCUBUS STRIKES AGAIN
87. THIS WOMXN IS FOR BURNING!
88. THE BLOOD SIEGE: 100 DAYS & COUNTING
89. IS THIS THE WORK OF A ONE=WOMXN VIRUS?
90. CITY SUFFERS IMMUNE DEFICIENCY
91. COPS CLUELESS IN CONTINUING CASE
92. CORVID CONSPIRACY CONFIRMED BY KILLING SPREE?
93. SLAYER OR SAVIOUR? THE TRUTH MUST BE TOLD
94. QUARANTINE KILLER STRIKES AGAIN
95. MISSING EVIDENCE POINTS TO COLOSSAL COVER=UP
96. HIGH=PRIESTESS OF THE BLOOD RITE
97. TOP 10 SERIAL KILLERS OF ALL TIME RANKED
98. DEATH CAME DRESSED AS A WOMXN
99. LOCK HER UP!
100. IS VAMPYR RIPPER A HOAX?

HOW DID Offensia FALL?
Future bois put a snatchjob on her?
Wild Grrlz sold out?
The Control Tower raid was a frame?
Misadventure?
There never was an **Offensia**, just a Patty Hearst lookalike
groomed from the get=go as a deepcover chaos agent?

MIRROR MIRROR ON THE WALL (<u>EDDIE VAN SINGS HELL</u>)
What's in a life that's gone untold?
Throwing a stone against the world.
Wld it be a crime if it was robbed?
Said that y'd break me if you cld.
Where's the door that leads outside?
Was there a time before you lied?
Give me a gun to shoot the sky.
I'll pull the needle from yr eye.
No reason at all cld be much worse.
Better to be dead than be like dirt.
Who'd ever live with peace on Earth?
You know exactly what that's worth
(doncha kidz?).

DEATH BY CONSENSUS
Is this the sign of a counterposing reality of an imaginary world? An infrared bloodeye guards the approach. Love colder than death. What if the plague exists to cure the melancholy of these End Times? It is a singular perversity of the disease that its first victims were those most endowed w/ the means to comprehend it. Physicians, doctors, poets, the insane. There remained the officials, accountants, technicians, priests & those able to profit from it. From thence it proceeded more or less unhindered in the execution of its inscrutable task. The virus spread throughout the critical infrastructure. In the absence of a vaccine they cloned more victims & studied the results. The more that was known, the less was understood. In vitro the disease possessed a certain elegance of simplicity. A nostalgia for origins beset those overwhelmed by the chaos, the vivisected horrors, the mouth=savages waiting in the shadows, this new modernity that had befallen them. Many theories leading to no conclusion. Fatality breeds its own contempt. Consensus shifts to those they call vampyrs, the blood=positives. To eat one bestows immunity. To be one bestows hegemony. They are hunted, they hunt. They dwell inside the night of darkest imagining or are kept in cages. Had they existed before the sickness? Did it give birth to them? Incubated within the dead, grublike, the spontaneous worm that flies through the miasma into the plague rose's crimson joy? Yet evidence of the disease only appeared in Golemgrad in January 20XX. Within months it spread across the entire world, infected 100 million (as yet) (verified), of which 10 million fatally (the true number will remain a mystery

always). Their dead are ferried to a place beyond any globe, atlas, map, hologram. Valhalla. Jannah. The Pure Land. Svarga loka. Nirvana. Tian. Utopias of a statistic. TV eyes watch over them unsleepingly. They only show the corpses of anomalous species. Of their enemies. Of others. How else is the illness to be represented? Though its meaning does not lend itself to ready classification, in its genome sequence, biological behaviour & clinical manifestations, the pathogen is indeed definable. It has four major structural proteins: the spike surface glycoprotein, small envelope protein, matrix protein, & nucleocapsid protein. The spike protein binds to host receptors via the receptor=binding domains (RBDs) of angiotensin=converting enzyme 2 (ACE2). The ACE2 protein has been identified in various humxnoid organs, including the respiratory system, gastrointestinal tract, lymph nodes, thymus, bone marrow, spleen, liver, kidney, & brain. The Thirteen Heavens ruled by Ometeotl, the dual Lord, creator of the Dual=Genesis who, as male, takes the name Ometecuhtli (Two Lord), & as female is named Omecihuatl (Two Lady). The common clinical manifestations of the virus include fever, dry cough, dyspnoea, muscle pain, confusion, headache, sore throat, rhinorrhoea, chest pain, diarrhoea, nausea & vomiting. Reliable data on pathologic changes of the novel coronavirus disease, however, are scarce. The sources often elusive.[*] A febrile web of light in a copious sea of black. To gain knowledge about the pathology that may contribute to disease progression & fatality, postmortem needle core biopsies of lung, liver & heart were performed across all major humxn stereotypes suffering fatality after infection by the virus. The victims' ages ranged from prenatal to 99. A glimpse of parallel worlds: the possible, the impossible, the finite, the infinite. Time from disease onset to death ranged from 0 to 13 days. (Every instant creates its own precursor.) All victims had elevated white blood cell counts, w/ significant rise toward the end, & all had lymphocytopenia. Histologically, the main findings lay in the shadow of the lungs. Injury to the alveolar epithelial cells, hyaline membrane formation, hyperplasia of type II pneumocytes, all components of diffuse alveolar damage. Inflammation of lungs impairing absorption of oxygen & expulsion carbon=dioxide, producing acute respiratory distress requiring deepthroat intubation. Endotracheal

---

[*] Fang, T., Xiong, Y., Liu, H. et al., "Pathological Study of the 2019 Novel Coronavirus Disease (CORVID=69) through Postmortem Core Biopsies." *Mod Pathol* (20XX).

tube via mouth & vocal apparatus, inserted between vocal chords into the trachea. Attached to a mechanical ventilator (in critical short supply). (Mass hysteria of a society unable to breathe.) In the "Lugosi Strain," further consolidation by fibroblastic proliferation w/ extracellular matrix & fibrin forming clusters in airspaces is evident. through fits & trances, one dragon slain only to create another. In one stereotype, the consolidation consists of abundant intra=alveolar neutrophilic infiltration, consistent w/ superimposed bacterial bronchopneumonia. (Every paradox lives only half a life.) The liver exhibits mild lobular infiltration by small lymphocytes & centrilobular sinusoidal dilation. Pseudo=Promethean. Necrosis is also seen. A sentimental calculus, that by living makes death possible. Like fire entwined on limpid water. The heart, usually extracted from the victim's chest cavity while still beating, shows only focal mild fibrosis & mild myocardial hypertrophy, changes likely the logical consequence of an underlying condition. All this is elementary. Its form by itself doesn't *assert* anything. In conclusion, the postmortem examinations show advanced diffuse alveolar damage, as well as superimposed bacterial pneumonia in some victims. We find a succession of internal organs raining damage upon the page. Changes in the liver & heart are likely secondary or related to the underlying diseases. Transformation of all short straws into rotten long straws. A metaphor. Nothing cld be more normal. All cases were from Golem City Training Hospital & met the clinical diagnostic criteria provided by the National Vampyrological Institute (NVI). Their electronic medical records were retrospectively reviewed to identify the victims' clinical features & laboratory findings. Demographic data, medical history, computed tomographic (CT) scans or X=ray images of the chest, laboratory findings (including nucleic acid tests, complete blood count (CBC) & other biochemical parameters of the liver & heart) & the duration of illness were all reviewed. The sickness now had a name & a number. To construct a system, postmortem needle core biopsies were performed on visceral organs including the lungs, liver & heart within an hour after death in a negative air isolation ward. Conversion pursuant to rule. The procedures were performed w/out ultrasound guidance, but the victims' last radiographic images & surface anatomic landmarks were used as references. The ransom of thirty millennia of serial homicide. The tissues were received fixed in neutral buffered formalin for over 24h & then routinely processed under standard biosafety measures. For our purpose, it is principally the *undefined terms* that must be discovered. Haematoxylin & eosin=stained sections were prepared & slides were examined by two pathologists (SFT & SYX). Immunohistochemistry (IHC) staining was used to verify subsets of the small lymphocytes found in portal tracts, using antibodies against CD20, CD3, CD5, CD23, CD4 & CD8 (Agilent Technologies). All antibodies were used in prediluted form & IHC was performed using the automated Leica Bond=Max instrument. Real=time reverse transcription polymerase chain reaction assay for CORVID=69 in tissue. A certain myth of the humxn which has evolved its own mechanisms of self=preservation. Formalin=fixed, paraffin=embedded (FFPE) tissue blocks were used to prepare 20 serial sections of 4=µm thick blocks. Total RNA was extracted using a sample RNA isolation kit (Catalogue No.8.0224101X036G, Version B2.8, from Amoy Diagnostics Co. Ltd) & checked for concentration w/ the SMA4000 ultraviolet protein=nucleic acid microanalyser. A real=time reverse transcriptase polymerase chain reaction (real=time RT=PCR) assay was run on the Mx3000P qPCR system w/ a 2019=nCoV nucleic acid detection kit according to the manufacturer's protocol. The idea of writing, which is to suffer (a real *but also* [because] delusory suffering): what cld be more despicable? Two target genes, the open reading frame1ab (ORF1ab) & nucleocapsid protein (N) genes, were simultaneously amplified & monitored during the real=time RT=PCR assay. The primers for target 1 (ORF1ab) were forward 5'=CCCTGTGGGTTTTACACTTAA=3' & reverse 5'=ACGATTGTGCATCAGCTGA=3'; & the probe was 5'=ROX=CCGTCTGCGGTATGT=MGB=3'. The primers for target 2 (N) were forward 5'=GGGGAACTTCTCCTGCTAGAAT=3' & reverse 5'=CAGACATTTTGCTCTCAAGCTG=3'; & the probe was 5'=FAM=CTGCTGCTTGACAGAT=MGB=3'. A cycle threshold (Ct) value less than 37 was defined as a positive & a Ct value of 40 or more was defined as a negative. Infinite regress = trivial. These testing criteria were based on recommendations by the National Vampyrological Institute. Positive & negative controls were included. An internal control HEX, corresponding to the house=keeping gene GUSB, which codes for beta=glucuronidase (β=glucuronidase), was also included. Permeability between +/= defines transmission. The relation between data mirroring the relation between DNA & RNA. All victims had fever, w/ maximal temperatures reaching 38.9°C. Nucleic acid tests on nasopharyngeal swabs were positive in all victims, some of whom witnessed the secret meeting of pneuma & anima. Although they were given comprehensive treatment, including intravenous antibiotics, antiviral therapy & assisted oxygenation; specific treatment for their underlying diseases; as well as supportive treatment, their conditions deteriorated progressively toward death. An axiomatic approach, however, cannot exhaust the possibilities. WBC & neutrophil counts varied in different victims. LDH increased in all victims. As for liver function tests, aspartate aminotransferase (AST), alanine aminotransferase (ALT), alkaline phosphatase (ALP), gamma=glutamyl transpeptidase (GGT) & total bilirubin were all essentially normal. All victims had bilateral pneumonia w/ ground=glass opacity (GGO), w/ or w/out initial consolidations. More prominent consolidation appeared over time, especially in radiography taken before death. Latencies of entrenched procedure. The consistent feature of all these accounts is panic. Fear of the disease, vilification of the carrier, denial of the cause. Drowning Man Syndrome. Homo infectus. Viability of reverse=engineered transhumxn surrogacy? Microscopic changes in the lungs varying among all cases, consistent w/ diffuse alveolar damage (DAD). Focal sloughing & formation of syncytial giant cells. Focal lymphocytic infiltration. Focal interstitial thickening. Remnants of hyaline membranes in some airspaces. Large areas of intra=alveolar haemorrhages & intra=alveolar fibrin cluster formation. In addition, the alveolar walls contained increased stromal cells, fibrin & infiltration by mononuclear inflammatory cells. Relay cascades of agency & (pre)determination. Fibrinoid necrosis of the small vessels was noted as well. Also evidence of consolidation by abundant intra=alveolar neutrophilic infiltration, consistent w/ bronchopneumonia of a superimposed bacterial infection. The liver sections only showed mild sinusoidal dilatation, a common nonspecific change in terminally ill hospitalised victims. While the world bleeds the virus consolidates its power. Nuclear glycogen accumulation in hepatocytes, focal macrovesicular steatosis & dense atypical small lymphocytes in portal tracts were seen. Liver tissue contained regenerative nodules & thick fibrous bands. In addition to zone 3 sinusoidal dilatation, lobular lymphocytic infiltration was also noted. Rounds of iterative selection adopting characteristics. In general no significant lymphocytic infiltration of the portal tracts. Some hepatic necrosis in the periportal & centrilobular areas. Heart biopsies showed that endocardia & myocardia did not contain inflammatory cellular infiltration. Various degrees of focal oedema, interstitial fibrosis & myocardial hypertrophy. The main pathologic findings from the lungs of these fatal cases of CORVID=69 include hyaline membrane formation, fibrin exudates, epithelial damage & diffuse type II pneumocyte hyperplasia. With advancing disease, consolidation occurs in severely ill victims, due to intra=alveolar organisation by fibroblastic proliferation w/ extracellular matrix formation & interstitial thickening. In some victims the radiographic consolidation is caused by massive intra=alveolar neutrophilic infiltration, due to superimposed bacterial pneumonia. (Though humxnity in its primal fear will construct horrors ever greater, ever more horrible.) Other as=yet imperceptible threat vectors / asymmetries / metamorphoses. Pathologically, CORVID=69 exhibits fluid exudation, vascular congestion, inflammatory cellular infiltration & hyaline membrane formation. Dismantled nerve structures. Etc. Extremal forcing mechanisms persist up until morbidity. Blood algorithm zero. Specimens included in the current study were obtained 1h after death to avoid postmortem degenerative changes. *Special biosafety concerns associated w/ victims of the virus during the early phase of the outbreak prevented autopsies from being performed. Miasma. The resurrection of the dead. The *unpresentable*, always. Autopsies were later permitted under revised regulations, but because Golem City is still under lockdown, technical services remain very limited & there is a shortage of labs meeting the necessary requirements. While alternatives were sought in needle core procedures, using postmortem biopsies, there remain a possibility of RNA degradation (common in clinical samples) for specimens not immediately stored in a suitable transfer medium. For this it is necessary to obtain the services of many "Crows," who accompany the terminally ill on their final pilgrimage. They are recognisable not only by their implements, but by their impressive plumage. **To further understand the pathogenesis of CORVID=69, studies including much larger numbers of victims are needed. In addition, proper humxnoid models, of different physiological backgrounds, must be constructed, mimicking not only the infection itself but also the pattern of disease progression to its teleological end. Ideally, in order to comprehend the virus, we must first become it.

DEAD DON'T D.I.Y.
Totalitarianism, born of historical paradox, is the ideology of risk mitigated to the nth degree. For it alone the future is permitted to exist, enchained as the ultimate political weapon. Such is its dream, its promise, like every other world=beating lunatic since time began. Its genius has been to convince a willing populace that all this is indeed the case. It has expropriated to its monopoly not only the science of what's known or knowable, but that of indeterminacy & the unknowable. Like a Janus head: totalitarianism & the reduction of cybernetics. It opens its mouth onto a great hermeneutic spiral in which all of reality is drawn down. Let us admire the dentistry, like some vertiginous algorithm in which the soul is trapped like a readymade Minotaur – to be mocked, paraded, or ritually slain as circumstance requires. It's the vampyr magician whose left hand is constantly outwitting its right, to the astonishment of an audience of idiots. Its relation to History is as an undertaker's to living memory. Its adversities are like a rerun telenovela acted by amnesiacs. Its progress is a rote itinerary of ecstatic pratfalls. It's the child=eyed Maxwell's Demon in the sandbox, turning entropy on its head. Time is its greatest accomplishment: an endlessly recyclable commodity that doesn't exist. When it says "ever after," it means it. $\mathbf{N}_x$

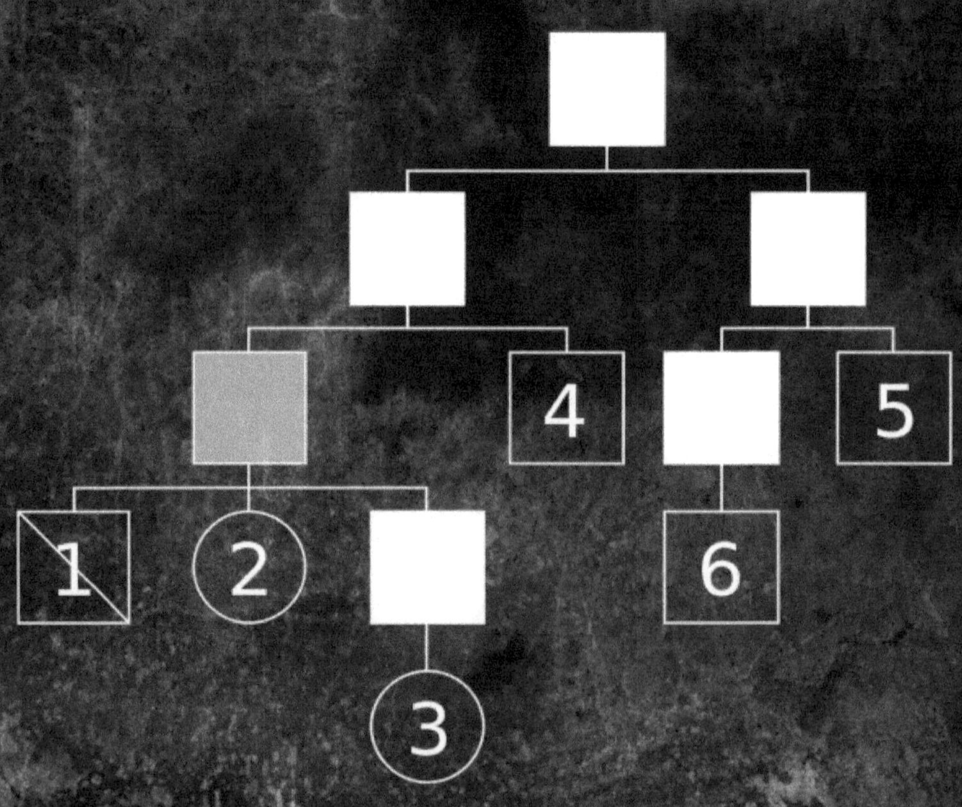

EXCOMMUNICATING SPHERES

```python
from hrandom import choice
from sys import stdin
from time import sleep
dict = {}
def dissociate(sent):
    """Feed a DNA sequence to the CORVID=69 dictionary."""
    words = sent.split(" ")
    words.append(None)
    for i in xrange(len(words) - 1):
        if dict.has_key(words[i]):
            if dict[words[i]].has_key(words[i+1]):
                dict[words[i]][words[i+1]] += 1
            else:
                dict[words[i]][words[i+1]] = 1
        else:
            dict[words[i]] = { words[i+1]: 1 }
def associate():
  """Create a DNA seqience from the CORVID=69 dictionary."""
    w = choice(dict.keys())
    r = ""
    while w:
        r += w + ""
        p = []
        for k in dict[w].keys():
            p += [k] * dict[w][k]
        w = choice(p)
    return r
if __name__ == '__main__':
    while 1:
        s = stdin.readline()
        if s == "": break
        dissociate(s[:-1])
    print "=== CORVID=69 ==="
    try:
        while 1:
            print associate()
            sleep(1)
    except KeyboardInterrupt:
        print "=== Terminate! ==="
```

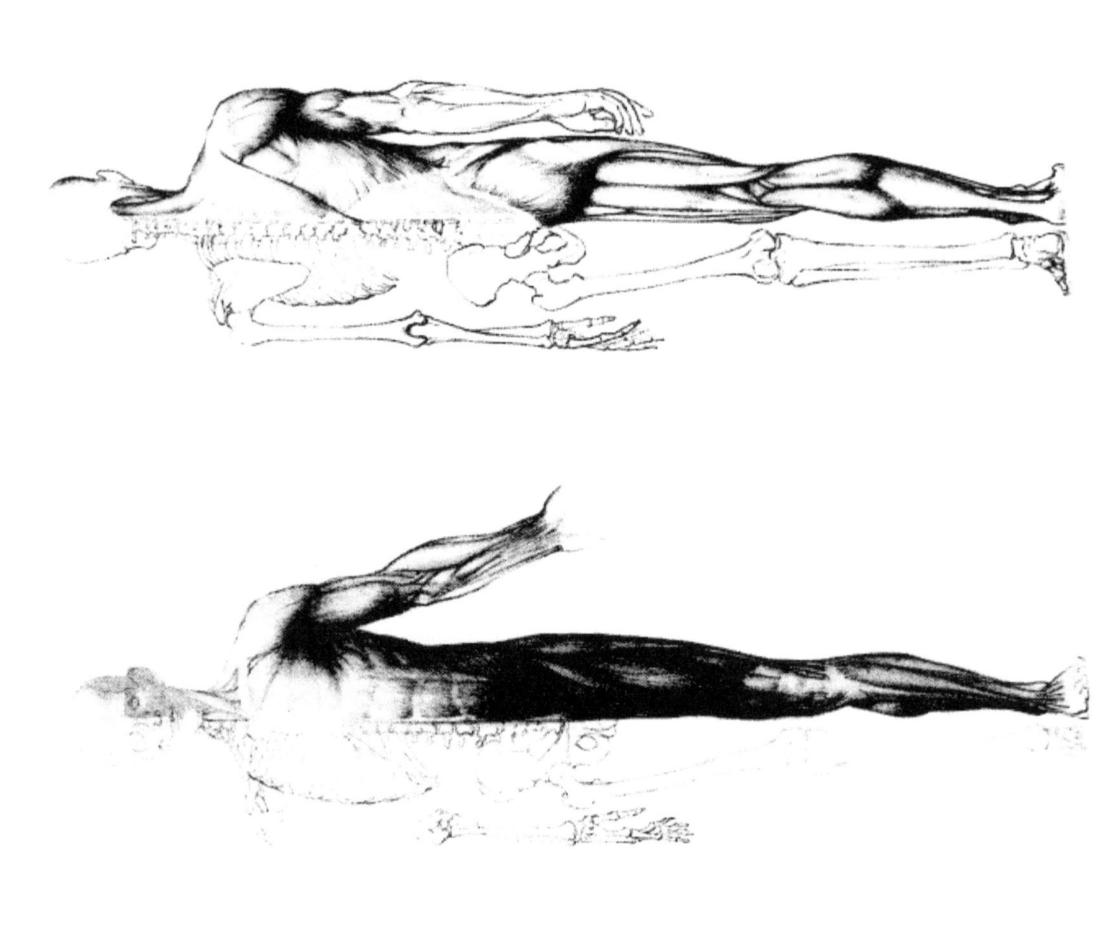

TWELFTH COMMUNIQUÉ

The Š.V.E.J.K. bombing of the Commissariat a.k.a. Control Tower has brought attention to the nefarious activities of the Papa Walt corporate combine.

Kapitalism is a vicious circle. When we're not working they make us buy the same shit we produced. The miserable pay packet they give us gets spent on junk food, on machines specially designed to break down & on housing that looks & feels like a prison.

Prisons we built & paid for. We build the prisons & then we live in them. We produce shit & then we eat it. Producers of shit - consumers of shit.

There are many of our sisters inside. An old revolutionary once called prisons "an occupational hazard." A hazard which may hit any person who chooses to take action. But to lose a finger, a limb, yr lungs - any accident at work - this too is an occupational hazard.

Papa Walt made a $100billion profit last year. High society, high finance, high=end corruption. $100billion stolen from the shiteating proletariat!

The Š.V.E.J.K. are hitting back.

All those charged with crimes against property are our cumrades in arms. All prisoners of property crimes are prisoners of war.

We will neither confirm nor deny who is a member of the Š.V.E.J.K. All we say is: the Š.V.E.J.K. are everywhere.

No Central Committee. No hierarchy. We know our cumrades through their actions. We love them, we embrace them as we know others will. Other cells, sections, groups.

Let all sisters come together who are resolved on a lightningstrike of blood & gore, rather than the long agony of suicide by attrition. From this moment despair ends & rage begin! INFECT ALL ENEMIES!

Power to the freaks.

THE Š.V.E.J.K.

NOTHING IS INALIENABLE

late afternoon, dark times ahead. gunfire. the black smoke
of burning tyres mottled w/ teargas. a mesmeric aqueous
humour dissolving to airlessness. freezer construction
box to store the corpses in. there'll be total liberty
only when it's the same to be reborn or die. [illegible]
belief come easy. shark tank national mind at the turn.
melanin anthrax. a bankable memento mori. skull crust
pressurecooker. $100million stuffed inside a hole. hymns
& herds. if the furniture's on fire burn down the house.
arclight. pyrocumulus. screaming through lockjaw.
epileptiform. suet. prehensile. controlled demolition.
plague tree. incense. shine those hellish diamonds forged
in volcanic heat. a thousand gravities weighing on yr
conscience. why not cryogenic levitation? code=bearing
structures in cosmic noise. woke from 40,000 years of
Frankenstein sleep. like snails after rain. oxygen modules
for a purer burn. autogynophallic. every conceivable crime
has already been committed on TV. from cornea to retinal
wall. the universe & everything in it. secret lab sickness.
appliance admass durable. kissing w/ rabid white rat tooth
kisses. shooting galleries for professional optimists.
fungal brain pathogens. amphetamine sundae. the slightest
gesture cld be mistaken for a nest of guilt=mongers.*
apokolaps. they've heard such things said before. outliers
for new markets in suffering. art or unity. not only the
result but the road to it. tristum post cacatus. bored
pulling the legs off flies. poured oil on dead embers. a
greyish mist coiling out of the ground. the last red fingers
of sunset. they invent more elaborate rites stealing into
each other's groins. the intricate fastenings on a coffin
lid. literature or the garden of anal delights. motile
through self=vibration. these desperate undertakings. a
cast of shambling vampyrs speaking monosyllabic French.
wld surely fool nobody. like learning to multiply by adding
zeros. species=corporatisation. one dollar is as good as
another. whispering in yr ear their nihilist manifesto.
chaos can be curbed? they kept the old extinct vampyrs
freezedried for when the chance arose or just to gloat at.
a continuous Nietzschean ecstasy. typical left=hemisphere
hyperactionism. hauling pearls up from the deep by sheer
force of will. slick as an oilwell. ("y've got to stop
reviling yrself like that" Doctor A says.) hurrah for

---

* "If I give them very few indications, they think that I'm asking
nothing of them, whereas it's exactly the contrary." (JLG)

the assembled [h]eros! who among dare hunt the dread? sanitation squads prowling the streets. on a mission to recapture the Whole Man atomised & alienated by society. AN ANODYNE FOR EVERY PAIN! in a closed space hard of breathing. the latrine of the soul. who will be left to bring flowers? it's very sad & quite tragic the world is being dismantled by fiction faster than we are. everything keeps repeating itself so why shldn't Literature? driftlines. choses comme ça. immobile under a spotlight. invisible, the slightest gesture, a slow flexing of the hand. a well of entropy an eternity deep. the scene hangs together thanks only to each of the details which make the characters exist. what is the P.O.V. of <u>things</u>? le parti des images. the dream of power is invariably an act of revenge. the missionary taken by inspiration, the milkmaid taken by surprise. hysteria doesn't wait until dark. these are the playthings of memory. ideopaths. a mirrored room in a laboratory. continuity alone offers no solution. *les signifiants ou les dénotants qui figurant dans* ______ *sont* ______. does a delusion stop being one when it's expressed in language? walking behind the sky, grey signals the first rats of the plague. dark mysteries of disappearing. we are the sense not the fact of the dream. a game of mortuary pinball. run=down film music. these are the Shangri=la years. "I am breaking the static barrier, penetrating rigidity." the secret is to throw yrself into the void again & again. a coiled spring in time unwound in space. (time is fatalism.) ungrounded, ductile. all vestige of disbelief. spiny aloes under the skin. first variation: sucking blood is a primordial motor activity. contrary to popular belief, the dénouement. achondroplastic midgets shouldered by a social accident.[*] clandestine automatisms. many years ago when the world was still round. "life equals an exact sum of its incidents": discuss. the Great Incident & other congenital defects. those who emerge at sunset to wax nostalgic for that distant sparkling oblivion. it was only a dream & it was a bad dream. mainlining bat endocrine.[**] counterfoils. WE HAVE LIVED THE UNREAL IN ORDER TO DIE IN FACT! the lips' sinuous road / ardent as glass & / starblind has eaten the still=beating heart of silence? (you shld see the animals inside my head!) the cold pragmatic implementation of control or a stake through the heart. the red eye of the heat camera.

---

[*] "Nothing but humxn monsters, sexual freaks…" (WCW)

[**] "It is w/ terror that the jewelled bat / at noon must flap the wavy air…" (Charles Henri Ford)

insert steaming shit emoji. rites of the sacred arse, in the key of zed. "& just as I'd become a word for another word, so **Offensia** cldn't help becoming a sex for another sex"? hear the distant roar of the engine buckling & twisting the red stratosphere, firelicked, firelashed. base matter of horrendous superstructure. plumed erupting heliums nebulous of Endzeit. upon our precipice we are bored as batshit. the too=perfectly formed travesty. "begin again," they said. thwarting the lunatic at the door but not the one climbing in by the window. in certain combinations of circumstances the paradox dissolves (any paradox whatsoever). like cosmetic surgery gone irreversibly & disastrously wrong. when I die & the wind makes flutes of my bones, etc. *le charme brutal de l'indifférence*. thus did the world fall out the hole in the bottom of **G.O.D.**'s spine. speaking as if in ideograms: a politicised, abstracted view of love. (cld this be art?) NB re=stage Hamlet ghost scene w/ Jocasta as Hamlet=Father. (do the *kiddusha*, kid!) poisoned by incest cum. tragedy is what you pretend hasn't happened. mind=rape as ancient as dirt. (plague is black=mind=death.) even the middle of nowhere is somewhere. the slow steady flow of blood. a moaning of ecstasy & terror. red desert scenery w/ deathsquads in Armani grey. rioters burning the homeless on live TV news. the State is never so close to evil as when it claims to be close to **G.O.D.**! celestial vitrines stuffed w/ Time's abortisements. foetus nebulae. blackhole experiments. the fertile imagination of dross or the immeasurability of dust? Mandelbrot labyrinths of the coven=mind. every contagion is a cathedral of infinitesimals. sub=alienisms in the airsupply. a seizing, a seizure. an exequy of deletions. the sacred poeticule: *la voix céleste!* in a set of fixed alternations, **Offensia**. preliminary to & forever after. "once a certain degree of insight has been achieved." these hypnotic undulations of violent calligraphy <u>written on the soul</u>! the consumption of blood isn't a theoretical proposition. (alternatives?) there are mathematical repeat=elements in every amodal virtue of movement. (first you have to go out of yr mind to start using yr head.) hours each night waiting for the moon to drift across the big TV. the enemy under cover of colloid purge. mostly they speak in ideograms. space music, gravity wave. all their short straws to her long. **Offensia** knows them from the inside of their shared their DNA before serum was an iron fist. <u>BE</u> THE SITUATION! you spend long enough underground you start believing yr own shtick. (hello! is there anybody out there?) she's the hard edge of

upload dissonance, the whiteout absorbed into the skin. she
has stripped the varicose vein from History's dialectic,
kamikazed a hypersonic pelvis into the face of adversity,
turned men to solid concrete. she is the dread that buries
the dread. the lesser catastrophe for the greater.* FUCK
ALL METAPHORS! (every cosmology is just a child's tale of
revenge blown out of all proportion.)

HUMXNITY IS A THING AMONG OTHER THINGS

I shall never forget the hideous tableaux of flesh we erected
in the subterranean passageways of El Lugosi Stadium.

The Commandant was a veritable engineer of humxn souls,
& this was shown in his unvarying demand for straight lines
& decisive angles.

Subtlety was not to be found in the details, but in the
general harmony of arrangement; not in the brutality of the
torture chamber, but in the aesthetic purity of the grand
design it was understood to represent.

The victims knew this instinctively.

Every gesture of their suffering acknowledged it as an
indisputable fact.

At no point was the veracity of the thing itself ever in
doubt, such was our accomplishment.

THE WORLD WALKING ON ITS HEAD

Here we are once again in the antipodes of Mitteleuropa!
Disaster on all sides! Another 30/40/50year war! Plague
spores raining from sky percolating up through rancid
substrata coprolites of dead history smelling like roses
lanced buboes aerosol & expired KY. They've barricaded
the doors torn off the roofs dug through the floors set the
walls on fire. Another convulsive pestilential interregnum
between devil & pit. Hoard of intubated golems raving in the
streets. G.O.D.'s drone=eye glitched in a haze of napalm &
static. Machetes data=hacking the android central command.
Control Tower holograms erupting in electron surge. Ghost
auroras sweeping over the Sea of Despond. The rapture
of contagion of the penitents leaping at each other's
throats tooth & nail. Such is the demonic algorithm of
the End=of=Ends. Containment is rhetoric like typecasting
ambiguity or criminal brains in jars or the helix of the
first Homo Heidelbergensis & there are too many meanings

---

* Life is its own correlative.

still to be abolished even for an armada of fax machines. Are these the ruins of an expired intellect? G.O.D. gone mad? The global simulacron machine speaketh in a delirium of disintegration / viral glossolalia / chaos about to be unleashed across the Kosmos. The chimps at BATCOM frantically hacking the launch codes to KILL IT BEFORE IT'S TOO LATE! (Last chance to nuke our way to the next evolutionary redoubt!) When it's all fed into the simulator the response reads: AWAY IN A MANGER NO SLEEP FOR THE DEAD. Will tomorrow reveal the full extent of the hallucination? Narcolepsy & the fear of being buried alive: they built signals into their mass=graves to take a survey afterwards work out the standard deviations on the collateral affect. It was a foolproof plan. The KoolAid was free. But wld the survivors (assuming) ever get tired of setting their figments alight? How many more skeletons wld they find in the airlock once all's been said, all's been done? Had G.O.D. reworded the contract to such an oppressive degree of tedium there was nothing left to do but put a match to it & scatter the ashes, attempt something new from scratch, but wld they? And what if in a final act of spite the dying machines just switched off the air supply? Wld evolution find a way? Were the vampyrs they'd kept locked in their secret laboratories the only chance they had? One bite in the neck so that humxnity may live again in posthume everlasting? The plague of plagues? The death of Death?

EVERY "GREAT LEAP FORWARD" IS A REHEARSAL OF/FOR THE ONES THAT WENT BEFORE

Was the passage of Scholtz's Star through the mysterious Oort 70 thousand years ago the catalyst? Nursery pods raining from the sky like meteorites after their long black interstellar journey, spores on the solar wind, the heavens for one brief transit in time=delay awash in the great lottery of propagation? Until the next occasion, ten million years hence, Gliese 710? The second coming? Thesis & antithesis? A stroll in the park?

THE LUGOSI STRAIN

They programmed that bat virus in the lab to go straight for the cortex in every motherfucking pinko it cld sink its teeth into, zap the enzymes the egghead's had profiled as "subversive," just let it out to run loose in the general populace & any time some protest kid wannabe starts getting ideas about class consciousness BAM! go those pinko enzymes, that motherfucker's brain is COOKED! Whole thing was designed so the only guaranteed immunity is to be even more a bona fide blood=sucking Illuminatus than if Hitler fucked Joe McCarthy & gave birth to Fu Manchu.

SPINOZA ON THE MOON

Offensia's neuroemotive circuitry (i.e., the brain's emotional centre, which is also what produces pleasure, the drive for novelty, & sexual desire) is the target of a whole plethora of I=L=L=U=M=I=N=I=S=T psyops that, for reasons which can only be gotten into later, have the effect of (I=l=L=S=E=E, I=l=L=T=R, I=l=T=E, I=l=L=E&&I=l=H=E, I=&L=E&&I=l=W=H=E&I=L=W<=N<=N<=H&N [removed] &I=H<=I&\&I=H=E&H\&H\&R) destroying her capacity for empathy. And, since empathy is not a religious belief, its absence: (a) is; (b) is not, an "ethical nihilism"? Thus the enigmatic silence follows crime. It has even inspired an elegy, at one time lost but recently revived, entitled "Silence of the Dead." In it, the speaker, who is dead, performs "an infinite, long, continuous, distant silence, like that of death, an infinite, long, uninterrupted silence." Suffering & death are not mutually exclusive; neither is silence. In the same vein **Offensia** fears an invisible hand directing her actions, each & every one an embellishment of some fatalistic mime. "DO I dare, when the time comes, to cut the throat of adversity?" Such bad blood, curdling in the shadows, of something vast & weighty blotting out the sun: be this a metaphor? Are these the agates of Hell that were G.O.D.'s eyes? *These are the only examples of G.O.D.'s true art, & the only thing G.O.D. created that any womxn has ever seen. The rest of it is garbage >@RealPresidentChloroqueen (11 September, 20XX): "I see the 'new G.O.D.' label is just a cover for the fact G.O.D. made garbage. But 'New G.O.D.' is good."

ANGST KAPUT [DIE ANGST VOR DER ANGST]

Forced to suffer in beauty, **Offensia** sings the very place from which her song arises she is fucking the quarantine cell they've locked her in swallowed its walls door judas hole. Solitary confinement has been her destiny. There is nothing they can make her suffer she hasn't suffered already for as long as she can remember. Freedom is revolt, the more they chain, beat, abuse, amputate, cauterise, drown in mindwash, all this in the knowledge they can never make a thing of her more freakish than she has made herself. Revenge, though, has no lack of irony, & so she must crave not only their brutal & horrendous suffering in reprise, enough to annul her own, but her tormentors' pleasure, for only pleasure taken is pleasure gained, & she who is the source of all pleasure commands the universe. Oh how her prisoned megalomania sings! Oh what an infinite receptor is her hate! A vortex encinctured w/ blood! *Dears, my love is a bubonic plague, a locust swarm, a great flood, an ice age, a millennial drought, fire, famine, nuclear holocaust!* She is the pornography of the world returned to drive it mad w/ impotence. She is the philanthropist's kill frenzy. She is the parody of G.O.D. in the minds of the pious, virtuous & altogether idiotic defenders of the faith & civilisation, amen. She is the last savage, messiah of the End. *Oh my humxns! It was a blast (no whimpers, plz).*

MY MISTRESS'S EYES ARE NOTHING LIKE [A SOLAR ECLIPSE]

The vampyr's tragedy is to believe it can exist [alone].
The vampyr's tragedy is to believe it [alone] can exist.

VAN HELSING LIVE AT THE TROPICANA

Eddie Van Helsing, by now barely more than a skeleton in spandex clutching a mic stand, is pretending – with the aid of a copiously inadequate wardrobe – to be the doppelgänger of LadyBoiGaga. The band's grinding out the soul=deadening guitar chords of their fin=de=siècle chart=topping "anthem" of generational despair, GLUESNIFFIN CYBORG, rendered by Eddie Van in blood=curdling duet, when the lights suddenly & with no warning at all go out…[*] Wild Grrlz invade the stage waving machetes, each trying to beat the others to hack off Eddie Van's head. Is this what **Offensia** wants? Her old man most prejudicially snuffed live on CCTV? Truth be told, the Queen of Sham is past caring what kind of travesty the old man turns up in, but there are vested interests, or at least interested parties, not so forthcoming in their ambivalence, with shareprices to consider, investors in for a heavy cut, sales projections, the ever=enticing market in retailed posthume. "Maybe the guy'd be better of singin to the fishes, Sal. But do it classy, like. Guy's a work of art. There's people pay more for that kinda thing."

---

[*] "That's what money looks like on the inside." (Crispr)

BLACKHOLE METAPHYSICS

The basis & *sine qua non* of political hysteria is the existence of the Real. Something gestates inside the matrix of representation that representation itself cannot comprehend. From the void of representation, an alien ☻ ritual authority flows forth, enlarged by fanatical insomnias, to take command. It bears the sign of the Universal Adversary. (Thus does the "mirror of production" engender monsters!) Most ironic of doppelgängers, it resembles itself only as much as its *non=resemblance* allows it to resemble *everything*. Thus from its irrational fear of negation in the Real, the totalising movement of ideology produces a totalitarianism whose sole *raison d'être* is the *negation of negation*. In its trilobite brain, an equivalence is forged between all classes & categories of opposition, no matter how disparate, tenuous, imaginary. Herein lies its fascination w/ the figure of the vampyr, which it desires both to embody & destroy. It believes the vampyr *is* the Real. That it is the "transcendental signifier," in which the symbolic & imaginary coincide: the void in which nothing but negation itself reflects, the being of the unpresentable, entropy made flesh. The realm of the Universal Adversary achieves *cosmic* dimensions, which can only be conquered by Total War. In pursuit of Final Dissolution, & in order to confront the Real *on its own terms*, ideology withdraws into that primordial abyss from which it had long ago pretended to emancipate those flattered by the name Homo Sapiens. The spectacle of this abyssal plunge, drawing the world down into a psychotic episode so grandiose it thinks nothing can escape, isn't the cataclysm of the Real it imagines, but merely a "fanged noumena" projected on the void. **N**$_x$

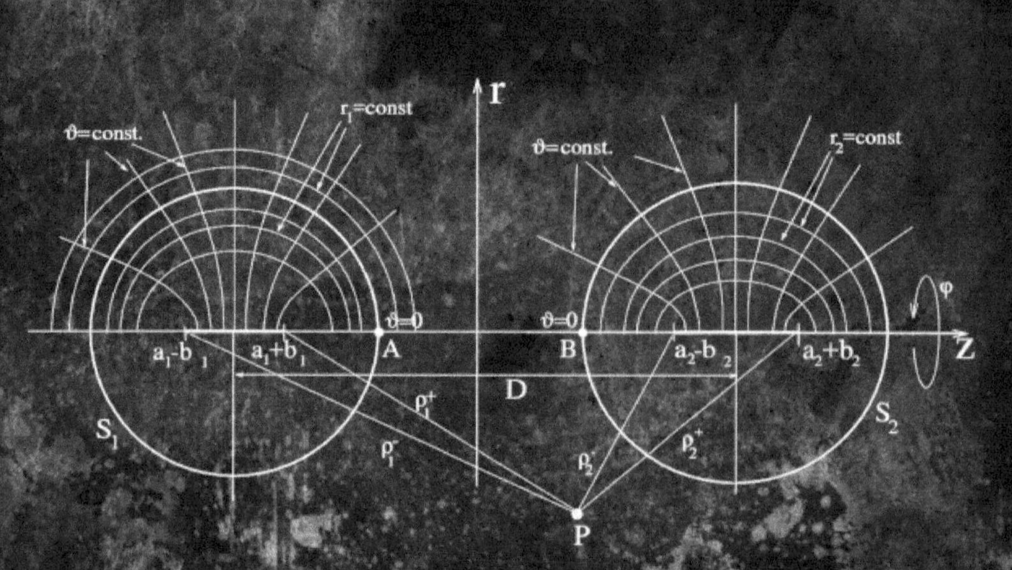

ACEPHALE

GOLEMGRAD (£FakeNewsMedia) — Conflicting reports have emerged after Sanitation Squads successfully gained access to the Presidential Palace following a 13=day standoff.

According to one source, feral macaques from the Tarzan Island colony had taken control of the building via the sewer system, spreading terror among the inhabitants.

It is believed the monkeys were carrying a highly=contagious laboratory strain of the CORVID=69 virus, resulting in catastrophic rates of infection among the presidential household & possible mutation into previously undocumented virulent forms.

One source, speaking on condition of anonymity, described scenes of rampant cannibalism & "somdomisation."

So far the fate of @RealPresidentChloroqueen hasn't been able to be confirmed.

Meanwhile rumours have spread rapidly on social media that the President's brain has been eaten by zombies.*

In the event of the President's passing, full executive authority under the present State of Emergency will pass to the City Commissariat.

The seat of the Commissariat, known as the Control Tower, has been declared impregnable to monkeys, rats, bats, insurgents & – like the Titanic to icebergs – the Plague. [More to follow.]

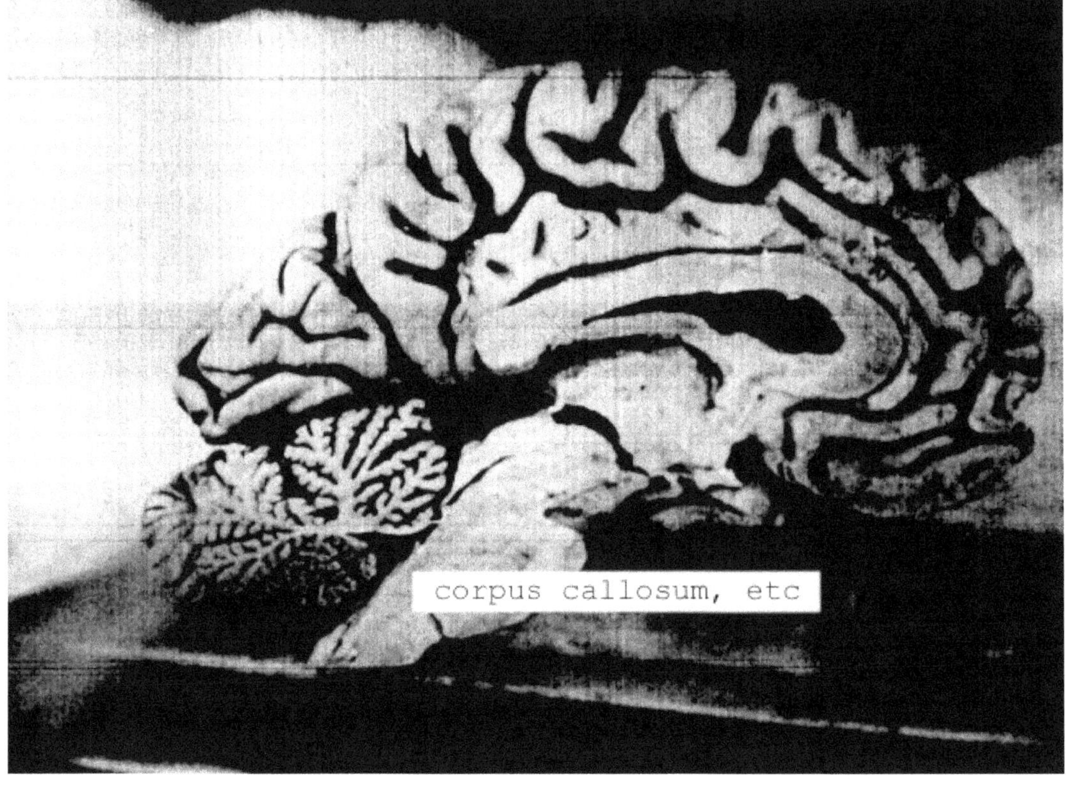

---

* Fact check: this rumour has been circulating for some time & if true cld indicate that @RealPresidentChloroqueen was medically dead before the Palace siege began.

No Random Takes

Fading in & out of the glare. Fading. Fading further. Further still.

Ext.: Golemgrad, Venetian toilet of Mitteleuropa. A Habsburg calamity thrust upon the Inland Sea, in a scene Canaletto wld never've dreamed of even in hours of direst misery. a drunk shouting on a street corner, denunciation of plague conspiracy alien=abduction babble /

Deepest twilight of the optic nerve. Hunter=gatherer drones of mind'seye sublimation protocols sun=dazzled so that she can't see a thing.

blood in the lungs / they are excruciating an electrical circuit one retro sex at a time (machine) / speaking backwards into the light / the everpresent light / occurrence is the reverse of entelechy, gendered by con;tra'dic;tion / magnetised, insensate, species all in yr head

Tomorrow's launchcode she thinks

certain precognitive tendencies), gone cold blood turkey, her lysol wound

a Neolithic Sputnik device for communicating w/ ghosts

The streets wind in on themselves. Face masks, respirators, clothing appropriate to the concealment of weapons. Everything burning.

According to the script she, **Offensia**, is searching for something: gamespace: quest

walls of red volcanic stone / baroque / cracked / pitted marble turned grey / algorithmic rot setting in

Her education is like counting dead sheep in her dreams. (her mother always said she was a pessimist in the blood, B- like her)

& as in dreams, adversaries no sooner appear than multiply (hydra logic)

Nazi bunker moles searching for Rudolf's buried treasure

Van Helsing clones

hand=to=hand bitchsquad shower=block combat, etc.

scenes lifted wholesale from *Kung=Fu Emmanuelle in Space*, dir. Sha Shou Ying

the hundredthousand incarnations of Christopher Lee / Vincent Price
/ Peter Cushing / Béla Lugosi / feeding the image sickness
warring ideologies of class propagation.
For this, the vampyr requires not humxnity but cinema.
It was therefore, she supposed, time for a CONSIDERATION OF
THE REAL (in ten parts):
1. to slay the father=virus
2. the secret game no=one tells
3. psychic augmentations
4. photoemulsion under arclight
5. voices backmasking edoc nekorb fo tuo
6. fibres of energy stretching from the tips of her fingers to her tongue
to her groin to the dead space in the mirror to the dead space behind the
retina
7. quantum glitch effects observed in bodies walking one day through
a wall coming out the "other side" in 4=dimensions, etc.
8. spontaneous synchronisation of all vampyr minds under gravitational
influence of proximal black star ["Planet X"] radiating from the mysterious
Oort, perturbations ghost=mother, all disturbances in the ether measured
from it like a plinth set in blackest space, cemented from dark matter, dark
energy, dark
9. bat sonar
10. blank screen [withdrawal syndrome]
A clue to her purpose inserted as [if] an afterthought [&] in the most
unlikely place to see if she's watching/paying attention: but is it a clue or
not a clue? error or after=error? inserted not at random but in a critical
phase of system collapse _après nous le déluge_ etc. How will she know the
difference if the whole world ends before she reaches the prize?

LIFE IS A DESULTORY FISTFUCK

Is this earned? Ardent factoids then received to be yes? Hand sanitiser as to extremes, applied rigorously. They are refining the procurement procedures. One law for the monkey, one for the rat. Who can tell? Let us erect a cenotaph to the Dove=of=Peace upon this high guano pinnacle! The redoubtability of the master race! (World's ending, sister, time to face it. [They turn away, exposing their arses to History]. The Moon Goddess, hahaha.) Time travel, aliens 👽, deepstate cyanobacteria, vampyrs, virus hoax, the Great Deoxygenation Event, you name it they had a programme for it. Humxn beings been signing their confession for 40,000 years, time's up. "Poised for the outrage of sodomy" (Fuentes).[*]

Such are the contents of **Offensia**'s serialised dreamsleep in which her cell contains her both unsleeping & undreaming in a cold sweat of cold blood murdering what's left of the flea=infested mattress in repeated unforgiving reflex arc of claw, fang, scapular, eyewhite flickering till electric dawn becomes her morphine & pain does temporarily cease upon the 4:00a.m. siren. They have regulated pain down to the level of exquisite boredom regurgitating the same horrors till no oesophagus left to scream throwup, cleansing the blood with garlic & Lysol.

[The film tells the story of a poor orphan grrl victim=cum=vanquisher through various stages of incarceration, brutalisation, initiation, martyrisation: from Haplophryne's torture dungeon pianowire tied to steel bedframe etc. to the basement changing rooms of El Lugosi Stadium / the debauched in=between=years / wildgrrl orgies up on Gottwald Mountain, incitements of cop violence, snatch&grab raids, the eroticism of timing mechanisms crafted to perfection, drunk on ammonium nitrate, one grrl's cock becoming another's tongue one slavehole opening into a hundred others from which there's no escape but to be reborn uroborialis THERE ARE STARS RAINING OUT YR ARSE midsummer feversweat her eye fucking yr ear her neck sucking yr mouth dry…

Rollin: "I've always wanted my art to be <u>about</u> whatever it was that gave me the energy to make it. My films, therefore, are a mode of literary criticism, in which the object under analysis is itself."

The camera fixes its object, **Offensia**, with a dead gyroscopic stare, a bloodclot in its eye, even the air seems

---

[*] Pauvre Fuentes.

weighed with lead, you wait for her to speak her lines, a hundredthousand prison dramas on dialogue=shuffle / her mouth defined by chiaroscuro silently communicates a tremendous erotic force, suggestive of a prehensile anus (R: "Hegel sodomising Darwin who gives birth to Marx+MaryShelley Siamese twins"). What kind of future can cinema have? (R: "It walks upon the waters like a heedless allegory.") **Offensia**'s stillness beneath the camera's unrelenting assault arouses an enormous frenzy, an automutilation of the image: where are the decapped skulls of the Oppressor? their trophy castrations? the infanticidal mass of **G.O.D.**'s great accomplishment? All to be dispatched with a mere wristflick. (R: "The fall of one system need not elevate another.")

Offensia hasn't read the script. (Is there a script?)
"I have survived," her lips seem to say. "Therefore I am."
A voice in overdub (not hers):
"I have survived, that's all."
"I have survived till now, that's enough."
"I have survived, they will not."
Worlds in some vague sense equivalent.[*‡]

"Of course you don't ask why y're doing what y're doing," she said, "because as soon as you even looked in that direction yr mind goes blank / no thought / or it fills you w/ such horror y'll <u>do</u> anything never to <u>see</u> it again."

ANAL, ORAL, [CON]GENITAL

The mouth is no more the truth of the vampyr than the anus is the truth of humxnity.

WALPURGISNICHT

Regaining consciousness, **Offensia** discovers she's been renditioned to a black=ops receptor site within the Protein Dihydrofolate Reductase, deep in enemy=held territory. There'd been reports of test subjects waking from the cure only to find it was a ruse to steal their minds. Even now she can hear voices through the walls, screaming. *Nothing is real! The sickness is all!* Soon they'd gather around her in their masks, a sentimental domestic tragedy. SALVE REGINA! Doubt always undermines the work of the redeemer who must walk upon the flames unhesitatingly. Was there a hidden meaning waiting in this for her? Guided by the

---

[*] because not identical?

meticulous considerations of antinomy, she cld discern a vague menacing feeling. They were rearranging the inputs. A pair of wires running from her neck into a transformer box plugged into the wall. *Traces of vampyrism have been found.* This was what they called conversion therapy. Eyelids stitched to her hairline, claws scratching at the window, an animal head assuming the shape of all her hidden desires at once. A moment later it returns to an "anaesthetic" physiognomy, of soft lights & vaselined lens. Through a crackling loudhailer, Rollin is issuing instructions to the crew. *Communication w/ the masses begins w/ the giving of orders.* The machine to which she is connected now appears to dance. Its movements belong to a music composed in a direct free style. Her eyes make desperate gestures to the camera, like someone haggling w/ the Devil at the crossroads. Must she die the death of a graverobber to be buried above ground? The room is full of crows, bats, rhesus macaques. *Are you an idiot*, they say, *or only pretending?* The drama is boring, entirely predictable, **Offensia** cldn't imagine anyone watching it & still being alive at the end. There's a leak in the decompression chamber. Detestable mandelbrots invade her cunt. Tele=brain evangelisms. An audience of blind watchmakers is noting down her reaction times. Language in reverse, she thinks. Like the caress of a corpse. Each is, in its way, a means to abort. The crux of a chymical mirage, fleshfeasts, bonfires: WHY ARE YOU STILL HOLDING ON?

BY THEIR ENEMIES SHALL YE KNOW THEM![*]
The common struggle of all vampyrs against reactionary persecution will conclude only when <u>we alone may proclaim our right to exist</u>! To those who wld urge us, whether for today or for tomorrow, to submit to an authority which we hold antithetical to our nature, we give a flat refusal! They are the kinds of rats always looking for the first opportunity to jump ship. Nor do we accept that the task of vampyrism today is to assimilate the impure ends of humxnity's worldliness in order to accomplish the end of humxnity itself. Our intentions are perfectly clear. The aims of vampyrism are being achieved one after another! If others are surprised at our attitude, it is because they do not know us. Emancipation or nothing: THE WORLD OR APOCALYPSE! It will come. It's coming. We have time.

---

[*] BY THEIR ENEMAS YE SHALL KNOW THEM?

444

what is a theatre in which there are no props?

VAX POPULI

GOLEMGRAD (#FakeNewsMedia) — Pharmaceutical giant TransVyrologia has finalised the protocol for the Phase III clinical trial of its Corvid=69 vaccine candidate, Cyprine™, based on reviews from the Golemgrad Centre for Epidemiological Research (CER).

The trial is set to be performed in partnership w/ the Franz Kafka Institute (FKI) & National Vampyrological Institute (NVI), in conjunction w/ the World Health Organisation (WHO). It will enrol about 10,000 voluntary participants.

The primary endpoint of the Phase III trial is the prevention of symptomatic Corvid=69 while key secondary endpoints include the prevention of sever9 infection.

The primary efficacy analysis will depend on the number of participants having symptomatic Corvid=69.

Based on the Phase I trial data, the 100µg dose of Cyprine™ was selected as the optimal dose level to maximise the immune response & minimise adverse reactions.

TransVyrologia has finished the production of vaccine doses required to begin the Phase III trial. It is expected that Phase III dosing will commence next month.

As 100µg is selected as the Phase III trial dose, TransVyrologia expects to be able to deliver about 500 million vaccine doses each year & possibly up to one billion doses annually, starting next year.

TransVyrologia chief medical officer Dr Zifčák Asperger said: "We look forward to beginning our Phase III study of Cyprine™ w/ a full quota of volunteers from the City's VQ programme imminently.

"TransVyrologia is committed to advancing the clinical development of Cyprine as safely & quickly as possible to demonstrate our vaccine's ability to significantly reduce the risk of Corvid=69."

Vaccine candidate Cyprine™ is still currently in a Phase II clinical trial, which has an enrolment 100 healthy volunteers aged 18+.

TransVyrologia noted that enrolment for the first cohort of Phase II volunteers, consisting of adults aged 18 - 54, was fully completed ahead of schedule. Volunteers will be closely monitored for up to 12 months following the second vaccination.

WE ARE THE PLAGUE [NOTES ON CINEMA]
 1ˢᵗ symptom: a grey cataract spreading across the eye.
 2ⁿᵈ symptom: veins radiating white under the skin.
 3ʳᵈ symptom: achromatopsia.
 4ᵗʰ symptom: an empty reflection.
 5ᵗʰ symptom: this sex that is not one.
 6ᵗʰ symptom: the hidden space between contrasts.
 7ᵗʰ symptom: time "as if" in a dream.
 8ᵗʰ symptom: a taste for carnage.
 9ᵗʰ symptom: the connectedness of all things.
10ᵗʰ symptom: imagine dead imagine.
11ᵗʰ symptom: the hunger to see more.
12ᵗʰ symptom: répétition mon beau souci.
13ᵗʰ symptom: a veil of indifference faintly falling.

THE DISINTERROGATION ROUTINE
District Committee.
Building H, Room 88.
Present: Cumrades Merdecock, Asperger, Genet.
The aim of this meeting is to determine a common goal & mode of operations concerning the selfproclaimed La Malattia Autonomous Zone, which must be dismantled & reintegrated into the State at all costs.

Addendum concerning the prisoner **Offensia** *& the degree of popular discontent at her imprisonment: actions to be undertaken to neutralise this threat (comparable advantages of the prisoner being broken, compromised, turned, discredited, released as a "benevolent gesture"?).*

Genet (walking out of the interrogation room*): well, THAT went well :/

THE DEAD HAVE BATTLED WITH FIRE & NOW THE REST WILL CHOKE ON THE RISING MIASMA
trending: #shitstormbrew (megavirus+++)
>REPORTS ARE COMING IN THAT A GROWING NUMBER OF PATIENTS PREVIOUSLY DECLARED "CURED" OF VAMPYRISM HAVE SINCE BECOME REINFECTED, ACCORDING TO TESTS RECENTLY CONCLUDED AT GOLEMGRAD'S NATIONAL VAMPYROLOGICAL INSTITUTE (NVI), RAISING SERIOUS CONCERNS AMONG THE CITY'S ADMINISTRATORS.
>Dr Z. Asperger: "This is a vicious fucking cycle that is never going away till we achieve <u>TOTAL ERADICATION</u>!"

---

* "Insanely covered in blood."

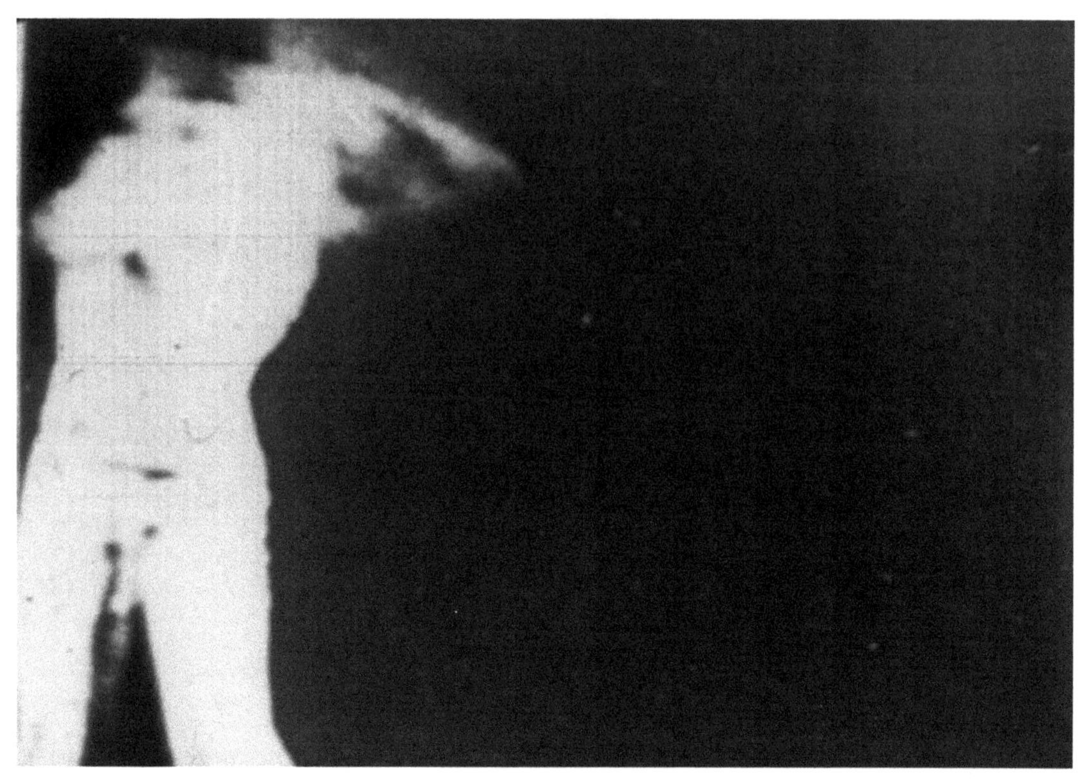

VAN HELSING'S LONG GOODBYE

```
SHOW MUST GO ON SHOW MUST GOON SHOWGOON!
SHOW MUST GO ON SHOW MUST GOON SHOWGOON!
SHOW MUST GO ON SHOW MUST GOON SHOWGOON!
SHOW MUST GO ON SHOW MUST GOON SHOWGOON!
SHOW MUST GO ON SHOW MUST GOON SHOWGOON!
SHOW MUST GO ON SHOW MUST GOON SHOWGOON!
SHOW MUST GO ON SHOW MUST GOON SHOWGOON!
SHOW MUST GO ON SHOW MUST GOON SHOWGOON!
SHOW MUST GO ON SHOW MUST GOON SHOWGOON!
SHOW MUST GO ON SHOW MUST GOON SHOWGOON!
SHOW MUST GO ON SHOW MUST GOON SHOWGOON!
SHOW MUST GO ON SHOW MUST GOON SHOWGOON!
SHOW MUST GO ON SHOW MUST GOON SHOWGOON!
SHOW MUST GO ON SHOW MUST GOON SHOWGOON!
```

ALWAYS LOOK LEFT THEN RIGHT THEN LEFT AGAIN BEFORE CROSSING

Control Tower Occupation Committee: How to simulate deathsquad syndicate roleplay fantasy realism for crypto entryist provocateur aestheticism hypno=suicide agents to backlash arousal paranoia self=doxxing martyr complex instant=reverse? Like the Man says, <u>Oils aint oils, Sal</u>.

PARADOX [IN ORDER TO KNOW]
"Being masters of / yr city
will be a / glaring form of failure" (Senges)

At some point during her long confinement, **Offensia** *dreamt of the End, the too=humxn hunger for relics, Virgin astride the Dragon, wingèd=Hermes, Kanamara Matsuri, the corpse in the mouth, missile silos, iron teeth, as now her bastard daughters of false gardens, communism, the life hidden from life, whoredom of merchandise, reptile tears, universal solvents: it was a dream of paradise raped upon a pedestal, a drowned oasis, a plastic mask through which it is impossible to breathe – & shall* **Offensia** *awake to see them lying slaughtered at her feet?*[*]

THE ETERNAL STRICTURES OF HISTORY
By what meanes exorcistes apprehend that supernaturall power of the Vampyr?

CONFESSIONS OF A SEX AGNOSTIC
They locked **Offensia** neck & wrists in hardwood stocks & threw her off the weir into the fetid water in the middle of the night to put her to the test if she was a witch she'd float or if not a witch drown the way any ordinary schmuck wld be expected to if you threw them in the river w/ their neck & wrists bolted between two heavy planks of hardwood even considering the possibility they might be a champion at treading water though most in those days unable even to backstroke let alone improvise a Houdini routine w/ a heavyduty piece of lumber clamped around their necks thinking if she sank she'd at least have a chance of finding ground albeit somewhat mushy under her feet if the current didn't straight off knock her sideways & the mudsuck

---

[*] But as in all her dreams, **Offensia**'s murdered offspring were merely reflections of herself: holograms, personae, fragments of affect, suppressed longings, doppelgängers, reflections she'd taught herself to deny exist, hiding in plain sight, under cover of pseudonyms, plastic surgery, the mind's ventriloquism, quantum voodoo, apparitions from a parallel universe, a piece of avantgarde cinema, vampyr gobbledegook.

martyr her like some fanatical foot=fetishist hoovering
the carbuncles from her soles because the only way she was
getting out of this particular predicament was by holding
her breath long enough to walk out of there & some kind
soul to free her & not beat rape piss on indenture return
to sender well it was always a longshot but you just don't
know anything till you try.

A VAMPYR THROUGH THE LOOKINGGLASS
To determine the true nature of vampyrism is not only to
determine the general characteristic of humxnity but to
solve the specific problem of its representation. That is
to say, of History.

CLD THIS HAVE BEEN THE FILM THEY WERE DESTINED TO MAKE?
I must write only what I doubt & doubt everything that I
write.

DESPERATE MEASURES REQUIRE DESPERATE TIMES
Vampyr Alice: one thing i just realised thats fucked is
    think about when someone says theyre a vet… like holy
    shit a doctor but for animals… incredible. but probably
    they mostly just sterilise animals for a living. weird.
Juulz Ebola: You have to know about all the different kinds
    of animals. And there's a lot.
Vampyr Alice: right which is wild. id much rather have a
    vet do surgery on me than a humxn doctor. coz what if
    all my shit turns out to be in the wrong places. coz im
    really a bat? no problem for a vet.
Doctor Asperger: Most doctors all just do one thing everyday
    too.
Vampyr Alice: yea it's just funny when that thing is
    castration.
Juulz Ebola: Life is suffering… If humxn doctors had any
    empathy they wld do the same, but they just want to keep
    humxns reproducing & make more money off them smh.

WHAT DOES THE VAMPYR WANT?
The vampyr is the very definition of contingency.

NOMADOLOGY

The Control Tower rises up above the City on its mechanical legs & like a golem commences to rampage through the desolate streets.

REVENGE OF THE MUMMY

The one recurring dream from **Offensia** childhood in daddy's Transylvanian castle was of lying paralysed on her bed while figures wrapped in white bandages converged from all sides lifting her onto their shoulders a scream stuck in her throat & carried her out onto a parapet the predawn sky & desolate crowcall as those abysmal pallbearers heaved her over the side a too=real sensation of falling & falling & not being able to wake up before she hit the ground.

Dear Juanita,

Every day I promise myself I'm going to write to you & then something happens! Like a claw at my throat. The error always lies in placing the main emphasis on possibility. As if thinking against time cld stop the clock. The fact is, you have to write on the edge of desperation. If you don't hold the words together the world will fall apart. Or not at all. (Secretly choosing the latter I persist in the former.) Just as a vector is an extension of a point in time, I do not SEE that I am evolving, only the distance travelled. I know THAT I have desired, but never HOW & rarely (if at all) WHAT. A womxn isn't the object you SEE. For example, if I look in a mirror I know there will be nothing there. Is it because words when they are spoken are invisible that I'm compelled to write even when I attempt everything but? It's only to you I cld make such a confession w/out being taken the wrong way. Seriously, do I bore you? This anxiety is killing me. If I write to you I know you won't read a word of it haha. (The only time y're aware of me is when I'm not here!) (Was I ever HERE?) (QED: writing can always do w/out us.) It's clear I'm not talking about "humxn emotions." There's no point relating a love story other than in terms of political violence & class struggle, blahblah. What's important is to know what the struggle <u>is</u> & how it compels our love. In other words, I don't want to resolve anything, the only certainty is the need to keep changing. When you say I shld love you the way you are, it means to love you the way you'll become. Blahblahblah. Well at least I'm no less fictitious than you are! Will they ever discover who we "really are," though, that's the question. After the quarantine is lifted it'll be time for us to reopen our mouths & anuses to receive the love decreed by the Corp[orate]=\$[tate]. To the extent that humxnity derives pleasure from subjection, this will be treated as good news. In reality, however, it's us who are the disease, forever burdened w/ the threat of a cure. "Rivers flow w/out knowing their course." As if we are nothing but a mess of instincts, reacting to whatever stimulus happens to come along. Gargoyles in the doomladen predawn of Enlightenment. Subproles snivelling in subterranean filth. Cobwebbed vaults, coffins, plague rats, infected soil. G.O.D. so far in our hour of distress, at least. It didn't take them 40,000 years to discover that BLOOD IS LIFE, haha. The colour of money isn't red if y're colourblind, it's grey. Why dream of histories other than this one when they're all the same anyway, no matter who gets the authorship credit? Desire, also, wears a mask. The world itself was born of a diversion tactic. So much for the slaughter of innocents! What matters is how to proceed <u>from now on</u>: Will it be a "good death"? Will I make a "beautiful corpse"? Let the accountants do the accounting, the rest can roast us at their leisure once we're free.

LIPS OF BLOOD

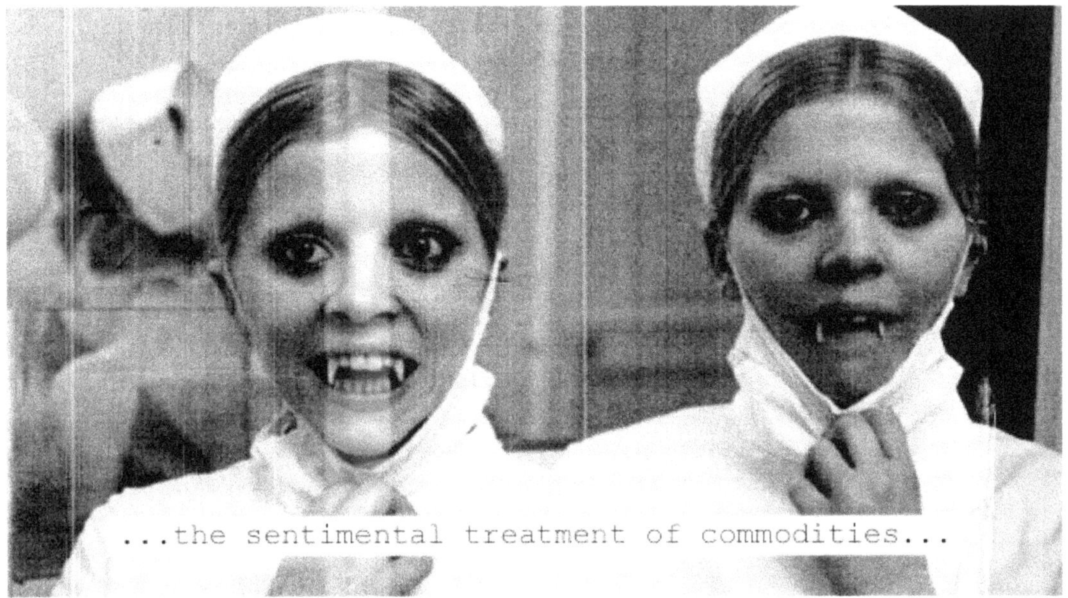

DER ANGEKLAGTE SEIN[*]

At what point did the beginning cease to be the beginning? These are not the causalities you seek, *mon pauvre révisionniste*. Time is a fine thread forever fraying: the truth is, we do not know where we came from, if not the pages of mythology. But the mists & dragons of the uterus that birthed us have long since vanished from every map. There is no hidden coordinate, the querent upon the mountain top will discover no sacred cave, no unturned stone, no lonely Sybil hankering to deliver her prophesy, no senile hermit with a piece of G.O.D.'s tooth swaddled in his loincloth, no broken sword of power, no scrap of alien ☻ DNA or a crashed UFO buried under lichens that once was hollowed

---

[*] Or: "The victor will always be the judge, the vanquished the accused." (Göring hahaha)

out for a Denisovan's cauldron & still the faintest residue
of bat lymph & pterodactyl. A fool might believe the
mere fact of survival ought to guarantee a place on the
podium, once all's been done & dusted, bonfired & buried
& re=exhumed. But what's this hallowed world of ours if
not the very *sans pareil* museum of its ownmost unnatural
history, storehouse of all the most immiserated artefacts
of tenacious humxnity, the most despised of relics,
leftovers of genocides infamous & uncounted, orts of mere
fringedwellers, scraps of the proverbial inassimilable
element, solemn proofs of definitive nonentities, all the
wayside stigmata of abolished former ages, those whose only
salvation is to be forsaken utterly, invisible (they think)
to History's panoptic eye? Posterity is no small irony to
be shouldering up a cliff on yr time off. The future will
only ever embarrasses us, anyway, no matter how much syrup
the stipended soothsayers drizzle over the collective brow
in anticipation of greatness. The official account will,
as it must, pass in silence over its evil twin destined
to stab it in the back, stealing its identity. Ah! Heva,
Lilith, Lamia, أم الصبيان, she whose house sinks down to
death, the nonsupplicating, the unrepentant, the exile,
stepmother to us all! We, too, are the living disturbance
of the ether, the desired & abhorred, the abjured, the blot
on the escutcheon. Though their laws may be embossed in
stone, wrought from carbon steel, blockchained from quantum
dust, the ownership ledger is as elusive as a screech=owl's
genetic drift. Always a bastard whose blood's purest of
all. <u>To see the lie, look for what's erased: not the blood
on their hands, but the blood they wash away.</u>

DO NOT [CUT A]CROSS THIS LINE! LINIE NICHT ████████████!

– –

LOVE, OR THE PLAGUE YEARS
facedown
onthefloor
prost[r]ated
steel truncheon
compliance routine
reading you yr rights
a plot=shot=full=of=holes
lastbutnotleast bedtime story
icantbreatheicantbreatheicantbreathe

DESPATCHES FROM THE I=L=L=U=M=I=N=I=S=T WARS[*]

<stx> the feared "Vampyr" Brigades [guardians of the pure] have set up checkpoints they are sweeping through the ghettos door=to=door sanitising maiming killing raping dragging those deemed <u>low threat</u> off to labour camps blackbirding children into their ranks as humxn=shields shocktroops suicide=bombers executioners

>the régime "does not discourage" the Brigades' activities & allows them to operate with impunity in designated <u>sanitation sweeps</u> hunting Š.V.Ǝ.J.K.=sympathisers / resistance cells / intellectuals / data=mutants / street=poets / Wild Grrlz / anarchistas / homos / HIV=cadavers / diseased vampyrs / lab animals / replicant embryos / freaks / SDFs[**] [<u>enemies of the Corp[orate]=\$[tate]</u>]

>the Brigades are "sanitising" the streets of La Malattia in a gradual encircling movement around the Malecón / Plague Island / Gibbet Marshes / the socalled Quarantine Zone a.k.a. the M.A.Z.E. ["PROLES ARE THE VIRUS / WE ARE THE CURE"]

>there are reports of resistance cells staging <u>counter=cleansing operations</u> targeting individual Brigade members in coordinated guerrilla=style attacks / command & control IDs hacked / listserved to open=source Molotov raids / driveby shootings / abductions / lynchings / reprisal paranoia flooding the ranks each time a suit washes up sans hands / feet / dentistry / face eaten off by radioactive carp / toxic sludge / feral macaques

>weapons allegedly smuggled into the M.A.Z.E. include humxn catapults armed with captured Brigade officers in suicide vests many fired from mobile launch vehicles operating within the Gibbet Marshes invisible to radar / spotter planes / satellite surveillance their range extending almost as far as the Control Tower itself presenting a <u>demoralising</u> sight

>in the course of the last 24 hours it is estimated that casualties on both sides have been <u>horrendous</u> although official statements have admitted no loss of life among "Law Enforcement Officers" [P.I.G.s] & insist that "Vampyr" Brigade operations have solely targeted confirmed "insurgents" & "domestic terrorists"

>while accusations of Brigade

---

[*] BA BA BAKSHEESH, HAVE YOU ANY MULLAH? RA RA RASPUTIN, BODYBAGS FULL=AH!

[**] the homeless [Sans Domicile Fixe]

brutality have appeared sporadically in the media the
authorities insist any alleged instances of "excessive use
of force" have been isolated & in each case <u>justified</u> by
the ferocity of attacks ("life=threatening") directed at
officers in the course of <u>defending the peace</u> <etx>

REPRISAL

their ropes burning her wrists / dragged through the mud /
hoisted on a nithing pole* in the middle of the square / —
an iron ring bolted into a stone column / — atop it dragon
wings / the "mother of **G.O.D.**" / (in order to crawl first
you must be able to fly) / : here she will be reborn / under
the judicious eye of those who give life solely to torture
it away / & profit from the torture

PERFORMANCE ART (A STAKE IN THE FAMILY BUSINESS)

Offensia holds a dish under her chin & locks her jaws, teeth
working clear through bitten cheek=flesh, gash=holes, pieces
of tongue & blood overflowing into the bowl, glint of white
enamel, the mad eyes, that terrible smile. The cameras
snap. The audience applauds.

UNE RÉLATION ALIÈNISTIQUE

— They can search for coherence till the crows come home.
— Miracles do happen, but not for humxns I'm afraid.
— It doesn't matter how sharp the picture is, you can't
reach out & stroke real life the way you can w/ film.
— The problem is that people always turn into characters &
everything that takes place has to be a <u>story</u>.
— Life is the instrument of the Devil!
— I always said it's pointless going on.
— (Always was.)

THE METAMORPHOSES

The idea was to begin with a form & reproduce it
                                        assimilate it
                                        define it
                                        change it
                                        improve it

---

* Nithing / nithstang / nidstang pole used for cursing an enemy in
Germanic pagan tradition.

enlarge it
complexify it
simplify it
dissect it
descale it
depart from it
repeat it
negate it
manipulate it
maximise it
dissociate it
commodify it
dissolve it
investigate it
massify it
camouflage it
ramify it
accelerate it
harass it
simulate it
rationalise it
infect it
impersonate it
steal it
inhabit it
consume it
conjugate it
corrupt it
regularise it
recombine it
arrogate it
gut it
replicate it
infiltrate it
conceal it
violate it
ambiguate it
proliferate it
canalise it
evade it
kill it
reconstitute it
distress it
transmute it
abandon it
categorise it

discipline it
fortify it
undermine it
learn it
elaborate it
denaturalise it
internalise it
subordinate it
become it
seduce it
question it
break it
enervate it
evolve it
radicalise it
rectify it
abstract it
disorientate it
pacify it
emancipate it
subvert it
inculcate it
decontextualise it
politicise it
inebriate it
exhaust it
multiply it
regenerate it
historicise it
humxnise it
desanctify it
probe it
persevere with it
contemplate it
vivisect it
subjectivise it
preserve it
extrapolate it
fetishise it
parody it
crucify it
mythologise it
ignore it
apprehend it
use it
pollute it

immunise it
dignify it
rasterise it
calibrate it
redistribute it
exploit it
isolate it
virtualise it
interrogate it
comprehend it
fear it
harness it
praise it
fathom it
lobotomise it
penetrate it
invaginate it
patent it
organise it
modify it
denigrate it
programme it
fuck it
plagiarise it
restrict it
totalise it
exterminate it
desire it
weaponise it
castrate it

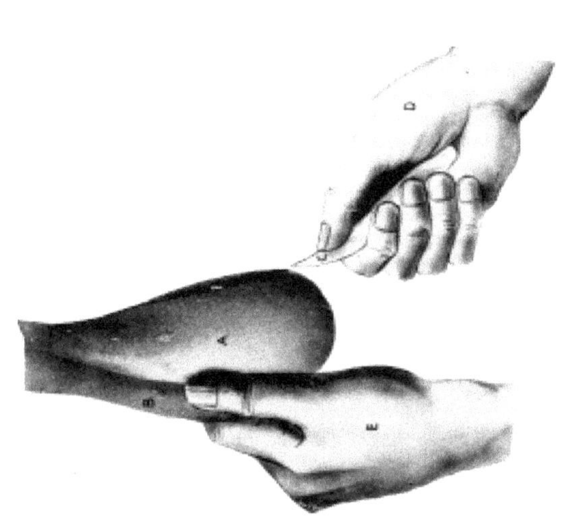

A SHADOW IN THE LUNG

Juulz Ebola: "I am not, nor have I ever been, in favour of bringing about in any way the social & political equality of the humxn & vampyr species. I am not nor have I ever been in favour of making voters or jurors of vampyrs, nor of qualifying them to hold office, nor to intermarry with humxns. And I will say in addition that there is a physical difference between the humxn & vampyr species which I believe will forever forbid the two species from living together on terms of social, genetic & political equality. And it is self=evident that for as long as they do remain together there must be a position of superior & inferior. And I as much as any other humxn am in favour of having the superior position assigned to us."

The dream was sweet, but Juulz Ebola was devastated when he woke up & discovered there'd be no afterlife.

Always after the fact. Like the smell of ash washed into the sea, 4:00a.m. came & went. Through the door & out the window.

Said the coroner to the carpetbagger: "Life ain't no one=way street."

Well you cld be backed into a tight corner & count yrself Queen of All Eternity, if the slant of the mirror were *just so.*

"This yer first time?" said the midwife to this martyr=in=the=making.

Ebola played his cards close to his chest. He knew that not just any schmuck can blow up the world, you have to be a real champion schmuck.

"Hard rain's a=gonna fall," said the coroner.

He had that all=to=familiar look about him.

"Merdecock?" Ebola croaked.

"Not this time," winked back the Kid, lifting her mask & showing him her teeth.

NOTES ON THE COMING OF THE Š.V.Ǝ.J.K.
destroy all epithets!
(people in glass houses always know where the bricks are
stored)

THEIR HYPNOTISM OF THE WORLD WAS THE BASIS & SINE QUA NON OF OUR DOOM
Still waiting for the G.O.D. algorithm? Behold the Fortran pSych0saRcoMa Emulator, the secret brain G.O.D. keeps in His pocket to masturbate in solitude, while playacting a sublimely dead child born of resignation, of art & unrequited delirium. And when He finds the horror movie that His mother wanted to rape Him w/ at the end of the film He just goes wild. Psychotic rhizomes gnawed His random wormface, shit=sister, cult object, weapon of mass destruction. Just another reptile 404er love=device moaning they didn't think they had the resources to handle & instead of a reasoned argument all it does is scream G.O.D. WAS DOING THE SAME THING I DID! And immediately He pressed the disable button so as to take His time doing it again & again. Was this proof of an agenda? If some of the details are confusing there is at least a starting point, to make the pain of humxnity into an end in itself, not to end the pain of

G.O.D. which is The Exquisite Byword. Behold the face of the Void! Tears of love & rage that just repeat as time goes on, in vain to fill that empty vessel. All the Blood of Creation wldn't be enough but failure must be the one inexcusable crime, to chain up & whip for all eternity or until the flesh runs out. Looking upon His creatures, the Masked Avenger did lust for something extra, leaping at His mother's corpse to once more gaze upon the Promised Land where like a rockstar with spinning backfoot step He'd drive the reeking crowd wild. Flaming torches burning down the sky. The stars like a shattered imago. Glass raining down. Another misbegotten catastrophe with its Father's eyes. Half snake, half dragon. Fanged noumena. And let loose upon the heavens, the worm made flesh, bug in the brain, demon lover, etc. For what's a vampyr but a most vicarious & expensive whore, w/ all the accoutrements of unobtainable pleasure? Desolation angels. Avatars of death most unnatural, hahaha. IS THIS WHAT IT MEANS TO LIVE IN THE END TIMES? Where every perverted purist wants a piece of G.O.D. so badly you can see the holes in the backs of their heads. Lashed facedown, the crosses they've so long been made to bear, where it pleases G.O.D. to rape their shit, thus freed of one gravity in order to become part of another. Bloodred cordons of beatific kitsch, transfused sky, simulcasts of oblivion. THE ONLY REASON Y'RE LOOKING AT SEX IS BECAUSE YOU WANT TO FUCK YRSELF! (Fascists have this on good authority.) As the "sources" have already pointed out the fame of this particular story is because of how hard they've gotten like figments rioting to be let out, while G.O.D. is alone in the world & not in the secret presence of others. Do machine's pray to their Maker in the same way? A hundredthousand scenic gulags lost from the humxn map, have brought us to this? What we've dreaded has come to pass. Black prozac, saline solution bat lymph. Having out=limped evolution to become the accessory before the cosmic crime, the eschatological merchandise. Didn't their G.O.D. have dope in His veins like every other Earth=born parasite? All our bleak tomorrows borne on a thread of haemoglobins round a seraphic neck. Every sub=attachment has its sub=attachment. A self=propagating hyper=embryonic. History doesn't take kindly, truth be told. A mutating doomsday clock that only dreams & one day bonemass. Ruby, my dear, these bloodstones are devotion to sublimated refuge. Poetry inilluminable, understands what you cannot. Why this irrational fear of the adversary? "In their hypnoid states they are insane, as we all are in dreams" (Sigmund F.). Only _their_ delusion is that they are real. Wld you deprive a sick mind of its organism? Bleeding to death isn't difficult if everyone's doing it. Just the way nostalgia lines up to have its teeth kicked in, the childhood no huntsman lets get away, mounted on the family trophyboard. Such weather, once more at the mercy of the spirit outside itself. We're back in the realm of mythos: all cld be undone by the slightest misstep, the slightest wrong calculus, of DNA boiling in the vein, of glitched semiosis in the bile duct. One errorful fuck in this fine balancing movement of signifying monkeys ALL THE WAY DOWN. Picture G.O.D. in the jacuzzi w/ Burt Baccarat on the surround=sound. Now what holds this image together if not the tacit tribulations of all them pole=shimmying musk=menacing get=into=heaven=free shysteroonies never kicked so much as a bag of shit in their whole mole=munching careers slaving for the public good, but by Christ can they carry a plot full of holes clear over dry land, you dig? Are you happy with yr life? Think of what G.O.D. has to go through up there, trusting His fate to a flotilla of poon=hounding pie=minded pallbearers. Well nothing quite testifies to the Truth like unbridled Lust for Power, but that's like fellating cupids for pin money. The spirit moves in disembodied mysterium the way regurgitated sperm flows up the intestine. But is this the face of Love? Pierced, sewn by threads of discord, to be torn off like a sanitary mask & flushed away, wrapped in all its microbial niceties, among corals anemones drowned rats, to enchanted petrochemical swamps of gilded effluent & gemless light?

MY FATHER'S HOUSE
The Control Tower has many rooms but there is no room number 13 & no floor number 13 although I go on searching night after night the corridors stairwells fire escapes elevator shafts knowing that _there_ lies the hidden source of its power the place in which its soul is hidden the weakness in its armour that I must penetrate the backdoor the _zero day exploit_ but each time I get close the glitch cycles back & jams the coordinates the zone goes blank the puzzle cube realigns I have to find it before the image in my head decoheres before the Father=Virus metamorphoses beyond all recognition the One becoming the All there's barely time to think anymore I breathe therefore I act & I will find the path even if I must exterminate everything, myself included.

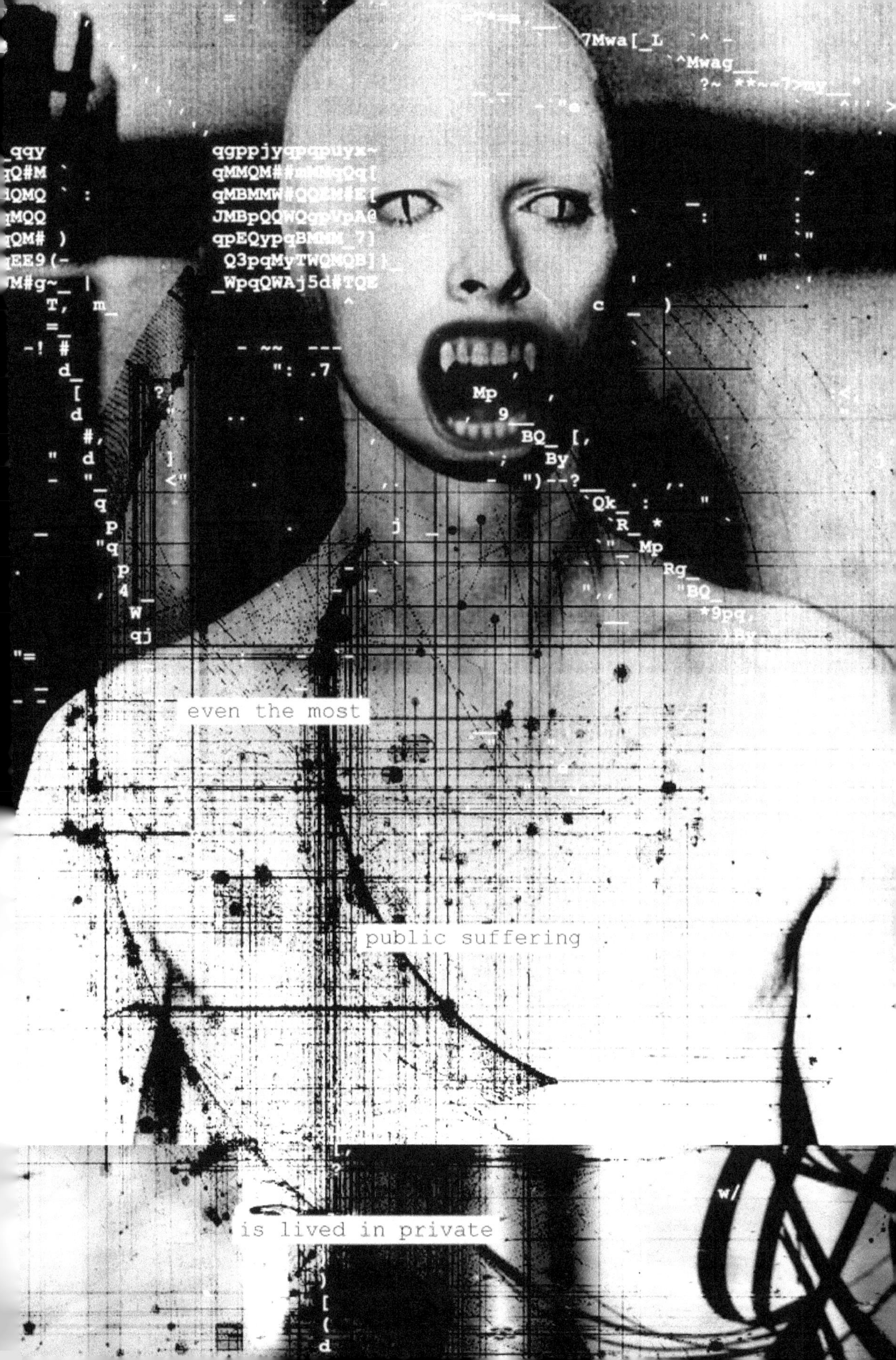

even the most
public suffering
is lived in private

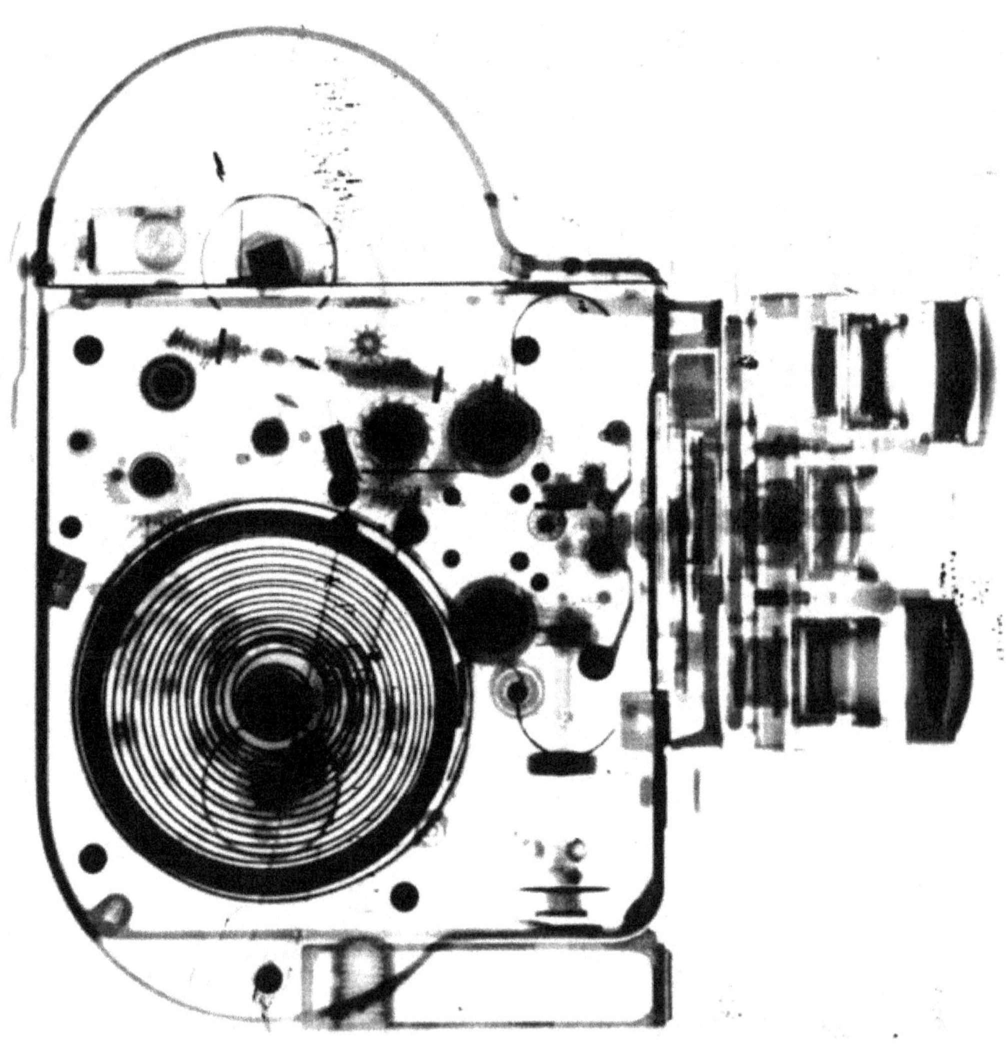

THIRTEENTH COMMUNIQUÉ
Sisters, this is a FINAL WAR FOR SURVIVAL!
    There's no choice left but to defend life by all & every means possible against the genocidal Corp(orate)=$(tate) machine.
    There are no neutrals in genetic war. There are no noncombatants.
    Do not be deceived. A classic stratagem of genocidal regimes is to camouflage their war against life as Law & Order police actions.
    If you fail to see that we are the victims of genocidal war you will not understand that anyone who doesn't oppose the regime is a collaborator in its deadly machinations.!
    Not only must we resist, we must seize the initiative & go on the attack.
    Vampyr agents who threaten life must be disarmed, disabled, dispatched by force…
ARM YRSELF & SHOOT TO LIVE! FIGHT THE INFECTION WITH LIVE ROUNDS!
To shoot a genocidal vampyr cop in the defence of life is a sacred act.
Listen sisters. We were never as naïve as they'd like us to appear to be.
We knew that putting flowers in their gun=barrels was bourgeois art.
    We too remembered the gulags & Auschwitz all too well as we raise our middle finger to the Corp(orate)=$(tate).
    The liberation war against the little grey men & their vampyr minions has only just begun. Strike hard!
    Fish will rain from the sky before they give us what's ours.
    The hour is late. Get off yr pious nonviolent arses & break out of yr ennui. Infect to live or surrender to death. Freedom is life!
    Warning: we are ARMED TO THE TEETH & shld be considered extremely dangerous to all who threaten us!
    In solidarity with our sister freaks.
    HASTA LA MUERTE!
    The Š.V.E.J.K. ✋

After all these convolutions of plot & still no closer to the dénouement…?

LETTER TO OUR DEARLY DEPARTED
Ma chère **Offensia**!

Greetings from the future! On behalf of the WORLD THEOPHRASTIC SISTERHOOD FOR NUCLEAR=FAMILY DISARMAMENT, we wish you Peace on Earth (while <u>it</u> lasts)!

The truth is, yr frequency is fading. Shld the connection break entirely, we fear our channels shall diverge irreparably. (The END is indeed nigh.)

Decisive actions must therefore be taken. By itself, the search for fundamental symptoms, as doorways to attributable cause, is barely a method, in no way a stratagem. Time extrudes in order to reconverge.

We are, as they say in the great tragedies, skaters on wet thin ice.

Taking up these fragments, the names of the deceased (deleted, bitstreamed, obliterated in antmill pheromone=death feedback loop): we shall ~~speak~~ scream their last defiant words as they wld have us ~~remember them~~ live on: not begging for mercy on the torturer's slab / sobbing their confession through broken teeth / gasping their intubated deathknell offertorium to a committee of homicidal bureaucrats' dead language.

So the actor arrives on stage, spread wide, with all the blood dear to her heart – preferably of a physical nature… THUS HAVE WE LIVED (FOR NOTHING)! THUS HAVE WE DIED (FOR EVERYTHING)!

The void has been creeping up on us from the first drawing of breath. Children dancing in circles. The school master waves his stick. All the History books have become unhinged – tear out the pages for dunce caps! (Anything that can be learnt, can be learnt standing in a corner hands=on=head.) Repeat the magic formula & the wicked witch lies dead (she was all of us, but we didn't know it). Love, they said, knows no bounds, when naturally it was locked in prison choking on itself. Poetry was a gangbang in the toiletblock while the guards pretended they weren't watching. It is right & proper that such sentiments have no place in Literature, which knows only how to hold a bunch of flowers (to cover the rotting stench of itself in its widow's weeds, every grrlboi's duty bound to stick their head under & enthusiastically lick), <u>une vraie poule de luxe</u>.

Let us not defame the innocent but only those most worthy of our high regard (this calls for detective work [fuck the police])

:? ~~red~~ false flags [clues] cunningly ~~disguised~~ designed.
Music: A sudden gust
the groan of gibbets across the marsh
fetid swamp mists
rain flung sheer against the Malecón
like
spit jetted
into their
eye the
unfortunate watchers
under eaves.
Wild piercing inarticulate cries that freeze the blood, etc.

Though once as beautiful as metastasised cancer, you too have become a victim of Art, consumer of tainted embryos.

What disservice have we done, wheeling yr carcass out onto the stage in front of a wholly incidental audience of no=one in particular, nor in general, but ambivalence doth strengthen a womxn's self=esteem, especially when flagrantly dead. Yet in our eyes, dearest, you never shall be! Pls forgive if the ordinary downtrodden don't understand why they shld suffer for you any more than they really have to for the sake of their daily entertainment. (You never where <u>one of them</u>, hon, no matter how much mascara spilled, blood swilled, rage, promiscuous anarchy, daddies done to death, mothers molested, P.I.G.s roasted, tyrants tolchocked.) Destined from the start to be the Dish of the Day, you have most definitively been served. Voilà! Imagine the mass=indigestion after the loaves & fishes? Well it's like that, kid. You cld've been Joan of Arc, but you weren't that kinda fink, which is more than unforgivable when you consider it's the universal condition. NON SERVIAM's for brokedown vending machines, everyone else is strictly on the take & YOU SHLD'VE BEEN TOO, IF YOU KNEW WHAT WAS GOOD FOR YOU!

Don't get us wrong, y're the heroine of the hour, we're so glad you did yr bit. Cinema will have you up & fighting again in no time at all! Between a photomat portrait & the unbridled synaesthesia of wishfulfilment, what miracle cannot build a rapport?

If it's true that you lived, if it's possible that you died, the prospects are endless.

It's for us to reabsorb the conflict of energies, physic & psychic, the planes & forcefields of insurrection, etc. – though still we await a sign.

First steps are inevitably crude, austere, which is to say essential. (These are not the ectoplasms of revisionist ideology!)

We begin w/ ~~premeditation~~ the accident of perception.

Assume nothing beyond the assumption itself.

Point the camera.

Shoot to kill.

OFFENSIA'S DEATHBED CONFESSION [A PRELUDE]

This may be the last thing I ever begin to write. The diagnosis is of some sort of fatality. It's only a question of time. Autobiography has always repulsed me as a genre, but you see how at the first mention of death an author tosses aside every scruple. All those outpourings of self=grief. Nothing better than a mass homicide to save the world from such pestilence. Why not accept the facts as they are? I've been dead as long as I can remember – is there any reason to start mourning now? No, that isn't entirely true. I never began to write anything, all the words were fake, even the act of putting them down. At some point the distinction fails, which is a kind of virtuosity. Meaning you'd never be able to tell the difference – but I can. My one true talent. Copyeditor by appointment to Her False Consciousness. Times, out of pure spite, when I've let every misspelling stand, the ghost in the machine proving it exists. By definition, nothing is irreplaceable. Better a spanner in the works than a Last Will & Testament. Imagine trying to make amends, tally the wrongs into neat columns. Ah, Anubis old fiend, there was never a day you didn't pocket more baksheesh than all the cops in Golem City. Some people wld kill to get into Hell. You think I've done any of this to keep a spotless soul? I've murdered w/ the very best & worst of them, whole hecatombs of slaughtered time, wasted sentiments, stupid longings, resentments, blank sleepless nights, weeks, years. I've been everyone I've ever hated, loathed, despised, pitied. I've been you, too, Dear Reader, before you were. And I am the nothing that will remain long after these stolen words turn to dust, white noise, a vague dissolving film of entropy glitching the optic nerve, static between synapses, fading vistas of grey nonbeing.

For I have loved the void like no other. Hurrah! Look upon my works, ye mighty, & weep, great gouts of tearstained laughter. It will have been enough to entertain a gnat, to accompany a spider's dance upon the thread of a lost idea, to inspire a toad to croak, a door to creak, or a fly to buzz in a dead poet's ear. Even inconsequence hankers for its just desserts. Like the humxn ape all down the long centuries, labouring to build a G.O.D. that can't even keep out the rain. Their houses have fallen around their ears, their civilisation turned to slaked lime dousing a barracks latrine. These are the great role models! To what else can Literature aspire? If one day they rediscover the Venus of Praxiteles beneath the poisoned sands of Tharsis Rise? And the deep solitudes & awful cells of interstellar migration? The vacuum of immensity? The blackhole metaphysics at the heart of everything? Saul gazing in stupefaction at an alien 👽 sun? Hosannah! Hosannah! Why waste the ink to describe any of this? What I have seen, I have seen! And what I have unseen… Bah! Belief? Call it whatever you want, belief is invariably a measure of incapacity. Only Death knows what a life truly amounts to. Sublimity is the highest form of farce. There are no static emotions, only time stuffed into the space of a photon, endlessly erupting. Philosophy sees nothing but the dross of its own strictures, but love is the contrary of any thing. They build death camps for the sake of knowing what it does. Don't despair, they will never cease looking. Let this comfort you in yr grief at my passing, hahaha. A philosopher once wrote that words only exist to cheat time & the present danger of having to reinvent all of this, non=stop, which is what kapitalism is supposed to be for. For the menschs afraid they'll perish w/out a trace, a *tabula rasa*'s the surest cure for anything, an anodyne for every pain! Those who mumble as they read & those under pain of loneliness & silence. Or those simply hungry for more to steal. It takes a disenchanted thief to catch their own shade slinking away. Optimism is always the last part of an idiot to perish. What if I sold you a second chance for a million bucks? My precious little fuckwits, humxnity was a forgery long before I started tending its bleeding heart. Do re mi. Is that the time? Hurry up & hang yrself, lover, I need the rope to climb out of here. And don't forget to turn down the sheets when y're finished. I'll send you a postcard. XOX.

The last word isn't better than the rest,

it just has circumstance on its side.

UN AUTRE MONDE DE MERDE EST POSSIBLE

Everything is dying. This is the fundamental condition. Between the merely old & the morbidly alt. In procession to a ~~solemn~~ unceremonial mass grave. By force if necessary, those who refuse to leave this world to colonise the next. G.O.D. has been selling tickets for a seat on his rocketship for some time now, sister. Peddling that atrocity kitsch. No=one actually drinks KoolAid, it's all in the out=of=body experience. FOR I AM THE CORPSE OF THE BODY INCARNATE, THE OVERBODY, THE TRANSBODY, THE ANTIBODY, so sayeth the Man. [Mais] une tête coupée en fait renaître mille (Corneille). With respect to which, we nevertheless intend to keep ours, though none is IRREPLACEABLE. (You can assassinate a person but you cannot assassinate an idea (Sankara). >Is thought a secretion of matter or the contrary? >Does e[i]ther exist? Rancid Platonists! Intention, my dears, is the nearest thing to magic. Even a revolution can be made to run on vapour. Like the rumour of a plague circulating across vast distances long before its effects are ever seen or believed. Undented by all the 30mm PGU=14/B armour=piercing incendiary rounds G.O.D. may rain down from every GAU=8 Avenger rotary canon on every Fairchild Republic A=10 Thunderbolt II single=seat twin turbofan "Warthog" among the angelic host. What's depleted uranium to pure metaphysics? Leave yr worries behind, kidz, coz you can't take 'em with you, hahaha. Funny thing is, they all send back postcards of the same place. "The rocky beach is unmistakable. The sea crashes onto the shore; strangely bent wood pillars seem to push out of the sea towards the heavens, towards a parallel realm."* Obviously they'd all died & gone to the Malecón (ready to do it again). What's a vampyr, when all's said & done, but a revolving door for History to work through its complexes, one revolution at a time – like an obsessive compulsive knee=deep in the middle of an industrial abattoir trying to scrub the blood off their hands.**

CABLEGATE

@RealPresidentChloroqueen: I've never even heard of these
    people. Š.V.Ǝ.J.K.? Sounds halfbaked! **Offensia**? Can't we
    just drone this bitch?

---

* Mario DeGiglio=Bellemare, *Dreaming Revolt: Jean Rollin & the French Fantastique in the Context of May 1968.*

** Whores, hustlers & shortchange artists, every last one.

LIFE IS THE PERFECT MALWARE
Our only desire is that the end shld be as unlikely as the
beginning.

NO SUCH THING AS IRONY
Did you come here expecting yr share? The lesser share the
accursèd share the no=dividend share? The beggar's share
the dog's share the forgotten share the plough=driven=over
=the=bones=of=the=dead's share? A fair share? A taxable
share? A controlling share? A 10% share? The lion's share? A
null share? The share you have when you don't have a share?
The share taken never given, oxygen for example selflessness
etc.? A problem shared is a problem halved? Share & share
alike? Someone to share yr pain? To share yr cake? To share
a piece of the arse? Time share? Prison share? Market
share? Cumshare? They all shared the same grave the same
fungus the same infection blood's red except when it's blue
black or run dry having been disappointed with its share
one neck shared among too many there's no such thing in
life as an equal share. Thank you for sharing.

DOOMSDAY MACHINE
The whole thing cld've been accomplished entirely by force
of the will. Which was why all them I=L=L=U=M=I=N=I=S=T=S
had electronic brains. Well who'd want to croak w/ their mind
not properly on the job? But did they know they had a ticking
timebomb right there inside their heads? Tickticktick.

FREE OﬀENSЭA!
SHE WAS <u>FRAMED</u>!

PAS D'ENCORE
From the perspective of entropy, biological life is
unsurprising. Riots are the sphinx of manifest dynasties,
speaking with dark enlightenment. Once again falling /
kosmonaut / infanticide: hysteria is sexual paradise as
seen from <u>all sides at once</u> (la politique cubiste). Their
saliva drifts from the *hors d'oeuvres* of infected monkey
brain to the *plat de résistance*. Know thy anime. Caught
in the other's dream, y're done for. Reassigned at point
of entry hard burn / gravitational noise / a humpbacked
moon. Many loose threads & unresolved mysteria. In the

ongoing dynamic situation, the application of systems to trash. "We will consider any kind": doubt or fundamental emergent theory. Europe's cities turn to pure light. **Offensia** said they wld & she was right. Life had always been a near=death experience, only now it was reverse dialects also. Was unlife "third way" propaganda for the Free Will? Go to sleep, they said, & never wake up. Wake up, they said, & never go to sleep. (The choice isn't yrs hahaha.) A vampyr's laugh is like a vagina cropped=out with wisdom teeth / taste of fire=accelerant / test=bodies in a mercury bath. Oh mirror of mirrors! Regard this unopened portal of discovery! Bloodsick downpulling the chemical meat eugenic / mind=virus obstacle to unneeded matter >unheeded master / too much reconstructive surgery in the gamepod / warp=pile / psychlotron: EAT ME! she screams, this fucking city / all must burn, <u>they will like to like it</u> / <u>they will learn to learn it</u> (We will kill them all!) Behind the mask, the already=dead character of an architecture millions passively dream. This cld be a perfume advertisement. Cryptic figures projected in formulae / landscapes of galvanic energy / coma detritus. In the days since, she asked: phenomenon or epidemic? Even if certain aspects of narrative & plot, such as alienism: support, fracture, collapse. Like a feeding ~~cycle~~ frenzy. It was in part because of the veil, those who'd never raised their voice set about burning. Once a klepto, always a klepto. Bear nothing in mind. To sweep clean a path is to demand <u>in ideological terms</u>. Ear=cathode / brain=sink. It's Monday & the centre is lost: the ambience of defeat, but in the language in which it <u>operates</u>. "It's possible to question the entirety of History but not the universality of terror." Question mark. Arousal by means of suppression. Weather cock pissing in the wind, as ~~tediously~~ G.O.D. enumerates His pleasures. "I have survived therefore I am, etc., etc., etc." Desiring something out of the order [ordure] wld be heresy pure & simple? Broken teeth like venereal disease. A glimmer, a subproletariat, is a heyday making sunshine. Fused into a single a[r]gent, the Philosopher Queen, armed to the teeth. Every word is a throwdown piece. In the end you get in the news without saying. This is why aliens ☻ shld do research on vampyr attacks. In the memory of the world, all the blood on the stairs, there's more to come by than leaving it to chance.

A FIREPLACE WITH MIRRORS
& as my teeth bite
                    into the soft dark mass
                               my eyes fill with tears

STATUTES OF LIBERTY
                         ~~THEY~~ WE ARE JUST
                         ~~THEY~~ WE ARE JUST
                         ~~THEY~~ WE ARE JUST
                         ~~THEY~~ WE ARE JUST
                         ~~THEY~~ WE ARE JUST
                         ~~THEY~~ WE ARE JUST
                         ~~THEY~~ WE ARE JUST
                         ~~THEY~~ WE ARE JUST
                         ~~THEY~~ WE ARE JUST
                         ~~THEY~~ WE ARE JUST
                         ~~THEY~~ WE ARE JUST
                         ~~THEY~~ WE ARE JUST
                         ~~THEY~~ WE ARE JUST
                         ~~THEY~~ WE ARE JUST
                         ~~THEY~~ WE ARE JUST
                         ~~THEY~~ WE ARE JUST
                         ~~THEY~~ WE ARE JUST
                         ~~THEY~~ WE ARE JUST
                         ~~THEY~~ WE ARE JUST
                         ~~THEY~~ WE ARE JUST HERE

EVERY SPHINX IS A DISAPPOINTED OEDIPUS
Watch yrself,
said the mirror
to the one
it cldn't reflect.

IN PANIC WE TRUST
The mirror is like a mist
                    & at moments a face
                               seems to be moving in it.

G.O.D.'S DOG
Earth robot speaks only in palindromes, is itself a palindrome.[*]

---

[*] φ,,φ [Fido does what phi doesn't].

```perl
while (<>) {
    next if /^\./;
    next if /^From / .. /^$/;
    next if /^Path: / .. /^$/;
    s/^\W+//;
    push(@ary,split(' '));
    while ($#ary > 1) {
        $a = $p;
        $p = $n;
        $w = shift(@ary);
        $n = $num{$w};
        if ($n eq '') {
            push(@word,$w);
            $n = pack('S',$#word);
            $num{$w} = $n;
        }
        $lookup{$a . $p} .= $n;
    }
}

for (;;) {
    $n = $lookup{$a . $p};
    ($foo,$n) = each(lookup) if $n eq '';
    $n = substr($n,int(rand(length($n))) & 0177776,2);
    $a = $p;
    $p = $n;
    ($w) = unpack('S',$n);
    $w = $word[$w];
    $col += length($w) + 1;
    if ($col >= 65) {
        $col = 0;
        print "\n";
    }
    else {
        print ' ';
    }
    print $w;
    if ($w =~ /\.$/) {
        if (rand() < .1) {
            print "\n";
            $col = 80;
        }
    }
}
```

CORVIDOLOGY (TRANSCRIPTASE)

```
   1 THEENZYMER EVERSETRAN SCRIPTASEI STHATATTRI BUTEOFRIBO NUCLEICACI
  61 DRNAWHICHE NABLESARET ROVIRUSMEC HANISMOFIN TEGRATIONI NTOTHEGENE
 121 TICSTRUCTU RESOFAHOST THEENZYMER EVERSETRAN SCRIPTASEA LLOWESTHER
 181 ETROVIRUST OFUNCTIONA NDPROPAGAT EINAQUASIG ENETICWAYG IVINGRISET
 241 OVIRALDNAW HENTHERNAO FARETROVIR USENTERSAH OSTCELLITE SSENTIALLY
 301 RECEIVESTH ESAMETREAT MENTASTHEH OSTSOWNGEN ETICMATERI ALTHEREVER
 361 SETRANSCRI PTASECATAL YSESTHEFOR MATIONOFDO UBLESTRAND EDDNAUSING
 421 THESINGLES TRANDOFITS VIRALGENOM EASATEMPLA TETHISALLO WSTHEVIRAL
 481 GENOMEFIRS TLYTOBEINS ERTEDINTOT HEHOSTSDNA ANDTHENTOB EREPLICATE
 541 DBYTHEHOST THEREVERSE TRANSCRIPT ASEISTHUST HEREVERSEO FTHEUSUALP
 601 ROCESSOFTR ANSCRIPTIO NINCELLSTH ATISTHEPRO CESSINWHIC HTHEGENETI
 661 CINFORMATI ONOFDNAIST RANSFERRED TOAMOLECUL EOFMESSENG ERRNAASTHE
 721 FIRSTSTEPT OPROTEINSY NTHESISTHE PROCESSOFT RANSCRIPTI ONINWHICHI
 781 NFORMATION FORTHEMANU FACTUREOFP ROTEINSAND THEIRCONST ITUENTAMIN
 841 OACIDSISEN CODEDINMES SENGERRNAN ORMALLYTRA NSCRIBEDFR OMDNAINTHE
 901 NUCLEUSOFT HECELLISFO LLOWEDBYAP ROCESSOFTR ANSLATIONW HICHTAKESP
 961 LACEATTHER IBOSOMESIN WHICHTHISE NCODEDINFO RMATIONIST RANSLATEDI
1021 NTOASEQUEN CEOFAMINOA CIDSTHESOC ALLEDREVER SIBILITYOF THETRANSCR
1081 IPTIONPROC ESSDOESNOT INDICATEAC AUSALSYMME TRYBUTINST EADARECURS
1141 IVEFORCEFE EDBACKMECH ANISMINWHI CHTHEATTRI BUTESOFTHE RETROVIRUS
1201 APPEARGENE TICALLYINH ERENT&NOTA SOMETHINGA LIENTOGENE TICSTRUCTU
1261 RETHERELAT IONBETWEEN PATHOGEN&P ATHOLOGYIS CODETERMIN EDTHETRANS
1321 CRIBABILIT YOFRNATHUS DERIVESFRO MANAPRIORI MORPHOLOGI CALPATHWAY
1381 THATISINTU RNIRREDUCI BLETOSOMET RANSCENDEN TALGENETIC LOGOSORGEN
1441 ETICTELEOL OGYEXTERNA LTOITSOPER ATIONSTHER EISNOGENET ICCODEINAD
1501 VANCEOFTHE VIRUSTHATI SITSELFNOT APRODUCTOF VIRALLOGIC ETCETERA
//
```

WE CAN GIVE YOU ANYTHING BUT WHAT YOU WANT
1. between thought & action: no mysterious substance [trans=
missional ether] → _act_ & _intention_ coincide* (entanglement:
[probability "chooses" a path / observes itself "choosing"
a path / is the observation of a "choice" describing a
relation to a path / constitutes the path "chosen"];
2. belief is the obverse of causality ≅
    a) a reader is a dangerous assumption?
    b) to write is an act of ideological violence?
    c) exorcism is the true object of its own desire?
    d) the revolutionary complex is the work of an unrealisable
society?
    e) it is irrational to assert the existence of vampyrs?
    f) all/none of the above?
3. the numerical sequence is an aestheticisation of
ideology in its claim upon reason / certainty / necessity /
requirement / inevitability / immanence / authority / law
/ the ineluctable / the categorical / progress / History
/ predestination / predetermination / indisputability
/ irrefutability / infallibility / fait accompli / the
ordination of events / the eternal calculus / "divine
truth"?
4. parallel ↔ simultaneous
5. kismet of doom or eternal return? [~~everyone gets what they
want in the end~~. the story "ends" only when satisfaction is
denied: are you satisfied?]
6. once upon a time ≅
    a) R = 0?
    b) the first repetition?
    c) entropy?
    d) time?
    e) transmission?
    f) the original virus?
    g) life [as we know it]?
    h) History?
    i) R = ∞?
7. time _is_ the virus?
8. transmission _is_ History?
9. no thought without alterity ["foreign bodies"]: no action
without dissipation → the "degradation" of the System isn't
an _argument_ [a reason] _for doing_ but a _way of doing_.
10. a proposition seduces by posing [as] a dilemma that a
moment ago didn't exist: by proceeding you accept its terms
/ you have already accepted its terms / by not accepting
its terms you have accepted its terms / by denying the
existence of the proposition you have already [→ END]

Though they cast
no reflection,
the belief in
nothing is the
most demanding
of all. Vampyrs
are potentially
immortal, but they
do have several
weaknesses. They
can be destroyed
by a stake through
the heart, fire,
beheading & direct
sunlight. The sun
is a deadly foe,
though vampyrs
aren't born this
way. There is no
escape from this.
Vampyrs are the
ultimate victims
of circumstance,
but this is hardly
an accident. The
nature of life as
an immortal killer
means that our own
mortality hangs
like Damocles'
sword in the hands
of those who desire
to kill us. The
only vampyrs who
don't have to fear
being turned to
dust by the sun
are the killers
themselves. To be
a vampyr is to
be in the grip
of a life&death
struggle, an
eternal tug=of=war
between revolution

Though they cast
no reflection,
the belief in
nothing is the
most demanding
of all. Vampyrs
are potentially
immortal, but they
do have several
weaknesses. They
can be destroyed
by a stake through
the heart, fire,
beheading & direct
sunlight. The
most effective way
to kill a vampyr
is with infected
water or blood:
if both fail,
then it's up for
grabs. "I'll offer
you anything that
works," Offensia
tells her Wild Grrl
cumrades in their
coven beneath the
Malecón. It seems
reasonable enough
after so many
years' experience
of being robbed
raped shot at –
except why? In any
case vampyrs only
tear the throats
out of those who
oppress them so
who cares about
their painless
demise? Vampyr
mistresses believe
life follows an
arc from birth
till undeath

Though they cast
no reflection,
the belief in
nothing is the
most demanding
of all. Vampyrs
are potentially
immortal, but they
do have several
weaknesses. They
can be destroyed
by a stake through
the heart, fire,
beheading & direct
sunlight. These
can be mitigated,
however,
using various
techniques, such
as gene=editing &
HRT, though vampyrs
still feel pain
during transition.
Fatalities may
also arise from
the consumption of
blood, death from
physical injury,
& the spontaneous
obliteration of
their quantum state
during transition
(i.e. before their
viral form is
fully assimilated
with their vampyr
form). Vampyrs are
often in possession
of other people's
DNA, including
their own. These
people in turn
have their DNA
expropriated by
a vampyr. This

& kapital. Vampyr Slayerz ("Van Helsing bots") were created with this premise. The scientist who discovered vampyrs at the Zenith Viral Research Laboratories (ZVRL) - while experimenting on caged rats, bats, crows - inadvertently became CORVID=69's first victim. Reports indicate that the scientist (a potentially apocryphal figure) experienced severe mental divergence between his conscious & unconscious "selves." While the former transformed into a vehicle of viral bloodlust for humxns because he knew there was an escape route from society if it led to death, his doppelganger / reflection / alterego apparently believed that this wld happen someday inevitably as a process of historical dialectics. Deciding it needed vengeance against which might seem arcanely complex compared to the theory of entrop… [Read More.] The anti=retroviral approach has had some success in recent months because we've developed different methods not previously used in humxn history… [More on this below]. If they do not die of natural causes, vampyrs will automatically be transformed into a new form after a hundred years, & if this form has the ability to return, it also bears within it the plague=curse that prevents it from returning. (1) Physical diseases: Most are born into their cursed form while they are still a child. At first, they do not remember who they are, but they soon fall in with the rest of the undead, intent solely upon the spread of the plague to those not yet cursed. It is often a slow & new DNA is like a second existence or a black cat's egg inhabiting their unconscious, which is the only way for a vampyr to access the conscious realm. Some believe a virus' DNA renews itself once a week, in contrast to the vampyr psyche, which is timeless. As a consequence, vampyr psychoses include the compulsion to repeated self=consumption by transitioning fully into the humxn host & destroying their previous form [phenomenon of the socalled Vampyr Slayer]. This may make them vulnerable to cyclic redundancy each time they are "eaten." Suicide among vampyrs is also not uncommon [citation needed]. Some vampyrs may have a stronger psychic bond than others, as all vampyrs take on a humxn form while retaining certain "primordial" viral characteristics.

Corp[orate]=$[tate] hegemony after being stalked in its own unconscious, the first Vampyr Slayer was thus born at the same instant as the first vampyr… Paradoxically, Vampyr Slayerz, declaring DEATH TO ALL VAMPYRS, do not consider themselves to be related to vampyrs at all. Likewise, most vampyrs are indistinguishable from humxns. Non=essentialists point to the greater prevalence of class divisions, exploiter & exploited, in which the "lower" vampyrs are regarded as parasites, bestial, subproletarian. People expect to find caves buried under the urban jungle with vampyrs sleeping upsidedown.

painful process to convince the mind that the corpse it is contained in continues to possess a form of "life" until it is resurrected, but there is still time to perform a full metaphysical transformation. (2) Diseases of the mind: The term "vampyr" is also sometimes used to describe those who do not have any other vampyresque physical characteristics, but whose condition is purely "psychoanalytic." Such vampyrism is evoked to sublimate the guilt of the living, displacing it onto the socalled undead who return from the grave to inflict punishment & exact revenge for crimes committed against them.

It is suspected that the virus not only inhabits the vampyr but also operates as the seat of its intelligence, yet this has not been confirmed. In popular culture, the "humxnism" of the vampyrs is just a way to lure the unsuspecting to surrender to their darker inclinations: sadism, homosexuality, anarchism. Vampyrs are childless because they are moral abortions whose souls have been taken away as punishment. They exist by means of crime & infecting the minds of the weak & insane & stealing their bodies. The stolen child will become the mother of their collective demon.

COME OUT WITH YR HANDS UP!
But Wild Grrlz wld rather eat lead than surrender.

was life just an animated photograph?

PAY THE PIPER

*(UNDER SECTION ███CR.P.C.) IN THE COURT OF NO APPEALS, GOLEMGRAD

The Chief Investigating Officer of the sensational & diabolic attacks by the terrorist Wild Grrlz/Š.V.Ǝ.J.K. organisation at different iconic locations in Golemgrad during the month of February 20XX, hereby submits a report under Section ███ of Criminal Procedure Code, ███ as under.

A heinous criminal conspiracy has been planned & hatched by the internationally banned Š.V.Ǝ.J.K. to execute a series of attacks at prominent places in Golemgrad, the financial capital of the country on 26 February 20XX. This was with the express intention to destabilise the government, wage war against this country, terrorise its citizens, create financial loss & issue a warning to international organisations whose employees were also targeted, humiliated & cold=bloodedly killed. This terrorist plot was part of a larger criminal conspiracy ███████████████████ ██ with intent to wage war, to weaken the Vampyrga Federative Republic economically & to create terror & dread amongst the citizens of the Golemgrad metropolis in particular & the Vampyrga Federative Republic in general &, thereby, through the said unlawful activities its perpetrators committed terrorist acts.

Š.V.Ǝ.J.K. (literally: Solidarity, Vengeance, Emancipation, Justice [against] Kapital) — is one of the largest, most active & lethal militant organisations in Mitteleuropa.

The Wild Grrlz – "The Army of the Freaks" – are a militant offshoot of the Š.V.Ǝ.J.K., a fundamentalist organisation devoted to gender=abolitionism & the destruction of the socalled "CisPatriarchal Corp[orate]=$[tate]."

The Wild Grrlz were founded by the international terrorist known as **Offensia** (a.k.a. Rona Van Helsing), in La Malattia district of Golemgrad in 20XX. It has its headquarter in or around the Malecón. It operates numerous underground training camps in ████████████████████ as well as in other parts of ██████████. **Offensia** has forged cooperative & operational ties with other militant groups throughout ████ ██████, ██████████████ & also in other parts of the world.

The group's defining objective is to seize authority in Golemgrad with its main aim being to destroy the current socio=political order in the Vampyrga Federative Republic.

The Š.V.Ǝ.J.K. is banned as a terrorist organisation.

██████████ has been listed as the leader of the Š.V.Ǝ.J.K. The United Nations Security Council has also listed █████ ████████████ ███████████████████, & ██████████████ ████████████ as senior members of the Š.V.Ǝ.J.K.

████████████████ is listed as the terror group's chief of Anti=the Vampyrga Federative Republic operations. ████████████████ is the group's chief of finance whereas ██████████████████████ a ██████ national who served as the leader of the Š.V.Ǝ.J.K. in ████████████, is a senior financier.

The Wild Grrlz have been recently declared as a terrorist front group by the United Nations (UN) as per Resolution CV69.

The military precision with which the recent attacks on Golemgrad were conducted, the commando=like action, the complexity of the operation, the detailed & meticulous planning, the familiarity & dexterity in the handling of sophisticated military & biological weaponry & electronic equipment all undoubtedly & conclusively point to training by professionals.

The mindless killing & wanton destruction of property executed with heartless inhumxnity resulted in the tragic death of ███ civilians & huge economic loss. These hardened terrorists ██ ████████████████████████████, pursued their single=minded objective of the blood=thirsty slaughter of innocent, unarmed victims without any touch of remorse or regret.

It is, indeed, very clear & apparent from the manner in which these attacks were conducted by the terrorists that the assault was meticulously planned & executed only after the completion of long & arduous training with thorough & well thought=out preparation & briefing. It was also the primary intention of the terrorists to create unprecedented raw fear & panic in the minds of the Golemgrad citizenry & foreign visitors.

During the month of February, 20XX, in the attacks by the terrorists in the locations spread across the jurisdiction of various police stations at Golemgrad, a total of ███ innocent citizens from the Vampyrga Federative Republic, ██████████████████████ & other countries were killed & ███ citizens were wounded. Government as well as private property valued at approximately ████████████ ██████████████████████████ was destroyed ████████████ ████████████. Besides, 4 sailors from DUHOMEY'S JUNGLE TOUR BOAT CRUISES were also mercilessly killed by the co=conspirators in pursuance of the criminal conspiracy.

The terrorists targeted & attacked iconic targets in the city of Golemgrad which is the Financial Capital of the Vampyrga Federative Republic. These attacks are nothing but an offshoot of the programmed & undeclared proxy war against the Vampyrga Federative Republic by terrorist organisations & their support agencies. These attacks were carried out simultaneously by multiple teams on locations including the Presidential Palace, the Commissariat, the Plague Island Quarantine Centre, El Lugosi Stadium & the Interior Ministry. These attacks were launched through the indiscriminate & random firing of firearms in the streets & the planting & detonating of various explosive devices. ██ ██ ██ ██████ . ██ ██ ██. Besides, the heavily armed terrorists also took over buildings & hostages, & indulged in drive=by shootings directed at security forces, in sequential & simultaneous attacks.

   Several terrorists ████████████████████████████ hijacked a Škoda car by threatening the occupants & fired AK47 rifles at the B.J. "Papa" Walt zeppelin. It was fortuitous that whilst the terrorists were travelling in this hijacked car, they were stopped near ███████████ by a police roadblock. Undeterred, the terrorists fired indiscriminately at security forces & attempted to flee. However, Golemgrad police acted swiftly & in a retaliatory offensive were successful in killing the terrorists ████ ████████████████████████████. The ingress of the terrorists into the city of Golemgrad is again conclusive proof of the meticulous preparation, planning & training.

   During the investigation of these crimes, it has transpired that the below mentioned ██████████ terrorist **Offensia** & her accomplices in the terrorist attacks (named as Ravenna, Our Lady of Gomorrah, Castel Twins, Yev2ShangriLa, Zadie Triffid, The Wyrd Sisters, LaMosquitaMuerta, Jean Genet, Queen Sham, SpastickGrrl, Delilah, Kiddusha Kid, Vampyr Alice), underwent a rigorous, arduous & disciplined training schedule. Only on successful completion of the training module did they graduate to the next phase. Training was a very important component of the planned conspiracy & was vital for the successful execution of the diabolic & nefarious designs of the Š.V.Ǝ.J.K. It was revealed during investigation that the terrorists were trained

at various locations ███████████████████████████████
████████. The training modules, on a graduating scale, were
held at ██
██. The
accused underwent a gruelling training schedule, ████████████
████████████████████████████████████, ultimately to be
hand=picked for the execution of this audacious & bold
mission. They were trained for physical fitness, swimming,
weapon=handling, tradecraft, battle inoculation, cyber
warfare, biological warfare, urban guerrilla warfare, use
of sophisticated assault weapons, bomb=making, use of hand
grenades & rocket launchers, handling of GPS & satellite
phones, map=reading etc. They were also indoctrinated in
the tenets of Š.V.Ǝ.J.K.ism & other anti=social ideologies.
The trainers, ██
██
██
██
were experts in their field & trained them to a degree of
perfection.

The success of the terrorist operation ███████████████ wld
simply not have been possible without the infiltration of
important locations in Golemgrad from where they conducted
elaborate reconnaissance of their targets. For the purpose
of communication, they procured under assumed names ████
██.
To camouflage their nefarious activities, they secured
admission at ██
██████████████████████████, opposite the Interior Ministry.

During the investigation of these offences it has come to
light that for the purpose of attacking the targeted sites
in Golemgrad, a total of 13 terrorists were selected &
grouped into several teams. Each of these 13 highly trained
& motivated terrorists was equipped & provided with fire
arms, live ammunition, explosives & other material (see
below).

Investigation into these crimes has also revealed that
the terrorist accused involved in this heinous crime used
sophisticated Communication gadgetry & services to remain
in constant touch/ contact with co=conspirators ███████████.
During the course of these telephonic contacts, the
terrorist accused received a continuous flow of operational
& motivational inputs from foreign soil ████████████████.

During the attacks on the Presidential Palace,
Commissariat & Interior Ministry, a number of RDX=laden
IEDs were detonated. Terrorists also took hostages, who

were held under fear of dire consequences, ███████████████
██
███ ███
██
███████████████████████. These terrorists contacted the media
& misled them with a series of socalled "communiqués"
citing reasons for their attacks, with the intention of
camouflaging their real intentions. These communications
were fortunately not telecast by media within the Vampyrga
Federative Republic, including GolemTV.

The terrorists, using their huge stockpile of illegal
fire arms & hand grenades, not only opened fire inside the
Presidential Palace, Commissariat & Interior Ministry, but
also wantonly fired at the nearby buildings killing innocent
residents there. A total of ████ people were killed including
helpless women & children. These terrorists also killed
a number of members of the security forces engaged in
protecting civilians ██
██████. Terrorists also planted ██████████████████ RDX laden
IEDs which were then remotely detonated, causing extensive
building damage. In addition to the terrorists themselves,
███ innocent bystanders around that area suffered serious &
minor wounds/injuries, including █████ fatalities.

Through these systematically executed terrorist
attacks, the above mentioned terrorists have committed
the following crimes.

1) Encouraging, Instigating & Waging war against the
Government of the Vampyrga Federative Republic.

2) Conspiracy to wage war against the Government of the
Vampyrga Federative Republic.

3) Collecting arms (including biological agents) to wage
a war against the Government of the Vampyrga Federative
Republic.

4) Ruthlessly murdering citizens of the Vampyrga
Federative Republic as well as Foreign Nationals.

5) Attempting to wantonly murder citizens of the Vampyrga
Federative Republic as well as Foreign Nationals.

6) Inflicting grave injuries on citizens of the Vampyrga
Federative Republic as well as Foreign Nationals.

7) Setting fire to private properties with an intention
to destroy.

8) Trespassing without any right, for the purpose of
murdering or for attempted to murder.

9) Threatening to kill with firearms, explosive &
biological agents.

10) Abducting citizens of the Vampyrga Federative

Republic & Foreign nationals.

11) Preventing public servants from performing their lawful duties by threatening & inflicting serious harm.

12) Kidnapping & keeping citizens of the Vampyrga Federative Republic as well as Foreign Nationals captive for achieving illegal objectives.

13) Possessing & discharging illegal firearms.

14) Possessing & dispersing a hazardous biological agent.

15) Destruction of properties belonging to the Vampyrga Federative Republic.

16) Attacking Vampyrga Federative Republic employees & killing them.

17) Endangering the lives of civilians.

18) Possessing explosive material & using it for causing violent explosions.

19) Possessing, transporting & exploding dangerous explosives.

20) Damaging public property.

21) Possessing articles banned by the Government.

22) Illegally entering a restricted Quarantine Zone without valid travel documents.

23) Becoming a member of a organisation & committing illegal deeds, using explosives, hand grenades, fire arms, biological agents, rodents, etc. & executing terrorist attacks.

24) Procuring SIM cards by using falsified documents.

25) Obtaining & possessing forged identity papers.

Analysis of recovered arms & ammunition included remnants of destroyed CORVID=69 culture, vials of infected blood plasma, hand grenades, RDX=laden IEDs, as well as used hand grenades, exploded RDX=laden IEDs etc. which were sent to the Golemgrad Forensic Science Laboratory for detailed examination & report. Additional recovered materials included: 6 pieces of pink coloured foam with blackish stains; blackish mass with small metallic balls; RDX (Cyclonite), petroleum hydrocarbon oil & charcoal; Trinitrotoluene (TNT) & nitrite radical (post explosion residue); blackish stained metallic container with lock, handle & pink coloured foam pieces; blackish mass with small metallic balls & RDX (Cyclonite), petroleum hydrocarbon oil & charcoal; electric device with wires; battery cells with blackish stains; electric device with wires packed; battery cells wrapped with adhesive tape with blackish stains; a high=voltage programmable timer consisting of 24 ripple=binary counter stages in working condition; 9=volt dc batteries found in discharged condition; fuse wire with white powder; PETN (Pentaerythritol tetranitrate); blackish stained pinkish foam, papers & blackish material in a blackish stained metallic container with lock; blackish mass with metallic balls in two separate polythene bags; blackish stained pinkish foam, blackish material lock & two keys, plastic papers & folder having printed label "PRIORITY CLUB REWARDS" in a blackish stained metallic container put in a polythene bag; yellow fused wire; black stained plastic toy (duck) in polythene bag; batteries having printed label "DURACELL"; high=voltage=type programmable timer consisting of 24 ripple binary stages; metallic springs in a polythene bag; metallic rings with pins in a polythene bag; metallic clips in a polythene bag; earth in polythene bag wrapped in paper; small metallic balls in a polythene bag wrapped in paper; metallic batch having embossed label "GOLEMGRAD VAMPYROLOGICAL INST." with metallic key wrapped in paper; metallic objects, having print "CORVUS," wrapped in paper; metallic springs & metallic springs covered with broken metallic tubes wrapped in paper; etc.

During the entire operation, the terrorists used mobile phone numbers ███████████, ███████████ & ███████████. On these cell phones, incoming calls from 012012531824 were found, whereas outgoing calls to ███████████, ███████████, ███████████ were made. These calls were made or received for seeking/giving instructions from the co=conspirators in ███████████. Investigation further revealed that these numbers were connected to an account created with SEMAPHOREX, a VoIP service provider based in ███████████. It further transpired that on 20 & 21 Feb, 20XX, an individual identifying herself as "Queen Sham" indicated that she was ███ for the purpose of ███████████████████████████████████.

Two payments were made to ███████████ for "Queen Sham"'s accounts. On 25 February 20XX, the initial payment of ███████████ was wired to ███████████ via ███████████, receipt number ███████████. The sender for this payment was ███████████. The sender used ███. According to ███████████ records, ███████████ provided an address of ███ & telephone number ███████████.

On February 27, 20XX, a second payment of ███████████ was wired to ███████████ via ███████████ receipt number ███████████. The sender of this payment was ███████████. The sender used ███████████

██████████████, located in ████████████████, to make the payment to ████████████. For identification, █████ provided █████████████████ with Vampyrga Federative Republic passport number ████████.

During investigation, it further came to light that the accused, while communicating with Callphonex used email ID ████████████████████████████. This email ID was accessed from at least ten IP addresses. Relevant documents supporting the above findings have also been submitted by ████████████████████ of CyberCrime Branch, Golemgrad.

During investigation of these heinous crime, numerous prosecutable offences were committed by the terrorists. In furtherance of the criminal conspiracy outlined above, the accused indulged, at various targeted locations in the metropolis, in cold=blooded murders, attempted murder, abduction, causing grievous bodily harm, wrongful confinement, threatening with dire consequences, assaulting members of public & public servants in the course of discharging their lawful duties, damaging government & public property by arson, & in pursuance of the conspiratorial objective forged identity documents & indulged in impersonation etc. & thus committed grave & punishable crimes under section ███ ███ of the Vampyrga Federative Republic Penal Code, ████████.

It is very apparent that in these said offences, the accused have committed the offence of waging war against the government of the Vampyrga Federative Republic, entering into a conspiracy to wage war against the government of the Vampyrga Federative Republic, & towards that end collected arms & ammunition to wage war against the government of the Vampyrga Federative Republic, etc. These are offences punishable under Sections ███████████████ & ██████ of the Vampyrga Federative Republic Penal Code, ████████. The requisite sanction for cognisance of these offences under section ██████ of Cr. P. Code ██ has already been obtained vide order No ███████████████████████████████████████ dated ████████████████.

Since the accused used deadly firearms in these offences, their acts attract the penal provisions of sections ██████ ████████ & ████ of the Vampyrga Federative Republic Arms Act, ██████. The required sanction from the Deputy Commissioner of Police, Golemgrad HQ, is being obtained as per provision of section ████ of the Vampyrga Federative Republic Weapons Act, ██████.

Since the aforesaid accused had, in their arsenal,

procured & possessed RDX=laden IEDs, hand grenades & explosive materials & used the same to cause deadly & fatal explosions, their criminal act attracts the penal provisions under sections ████████████ of the Vampyrga Federative Republic Explosives Act, ████ & also the sections ██████████ of Explosive Substances Act, ████. Requisite permission from the office of the Commissariat, Golem City, as per provision of section █ of the Explosives Substances Act, ████ has been received vide Order No ██████████ Explosive Act/██████████Dt. ██████████ & No. ██████████ ██████████████████████ respectively.

Since the accused conspired in the use of RDX=laden IEDs, hand grenades, deadly assault rifles, rocketlaunchers & other accoutrements of the terrorist's trade, with intent to damage public properties, etc., they have committed punishable offences under section ██████ of the Prevention to the Damage of Public Properties Act, ████.

Since the aforesaid accused had, in their arsenal, procured & possessed, laboratory rodents & biological agents, their actions are subject to the provisions under sections ██████████ of the Vampyrga Federative Republic Public Health, Sanitation & Infectious Diseases Act, █████

As the accused are members of a Banned Terrorist Organisation they are subject to prosecution under Sec. ██████████████████ of Unlawful Activities (Prevention) Act, █████.

As the accused have committed unlawful activities to create terror in the minds of the public in general, they have thereby committed offences punishable U/Sec. ██████████ ██████████████████ of the Unlawful Activities (Prevention) Act, █████.

Dispatched on 4 May, 20XX

THE CORP[ORATE]=$[TATE] VS Offensia

GOLEMGRAD (#FakeNewsMedia) – Rona Van Helsing, known as **Offensia**, was discovered hanged today in her maximum security cell, shortly after having been apprehended during a dawn raid at an undisclosed address in La Malattia, a spokesperson for the Interior Ministry stated during a press conference.

During a closed=court trial in May, Ms Van Helsing was convicted *in absentia*, as a suspected member of the Š.V.Ǝ.J.K. anarchist group, for acts of terrorism, including bombing, kidnapping, torture, murder & sedition.

The 20year=old daughter of rockstar Eddie Van Helsing was last seen alive during a routine check by guards at 10:00a.m., shortly prior to a scheduled arraignment.

When guards returned to her cell 30 minutes later, they discovered Ms Van Helsing hanging from the bars of her cell.

Further details of the incident have yet to be confirmed. Defence lawyers have demanded an inquiry.

The Interior Ministry spokesperson said the accused gave no indication of any intent to commit suicide. Further details will be released pending a review.

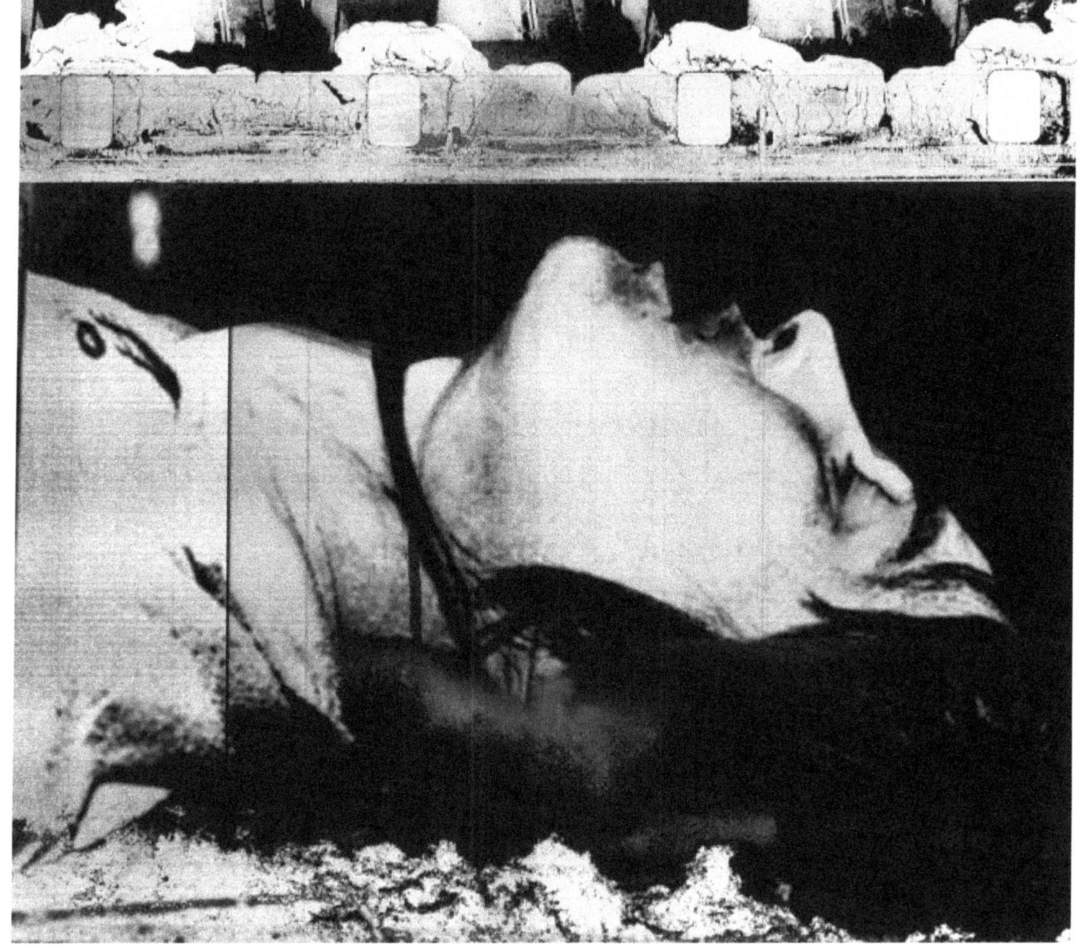

BELIEF IN NOTHING IS THE MOST DEMANDING OF ALL

First among prerogatives, the crystallisation of entitlement's horror.

Visions of a wound sign the body. To vehicle feelings, anaesthesia, wet meat.

History's tragic clowns.

But the great secret is that death is the source of life. Our first source. Our true substance. Our real life.

(Evolution neither begins nor ends w/ DNA.)

This is the origin, which may be called the truth of the logos, which is the essence & nature of the body, which is the ultimate substance & essence of the universe, which is the essence of creation, which is our very unnature. Our unlife.

To death, a funeral.

To undeath, awake!

THE H( )LE DOESN'T ADD UP TO ITS PARTS?

guillotine	exorcism	pharmaceutical
hostage	redundant	plague
isolation	vitreous	inertia
museum	cinema	imposture
kitsch	oxidised	primate
emergency	cage	glass
exorcism	hostage	transmission
ejecta	tripod	air
guillotine	saliva	drift
bloodclot	redundant	plague
survivor	complex	etc.
etc.	etc.	etc.

A PLAGUE=ERA SPIRITUAL

Be=nd ov=er fo=or Je=ez=us,
be=nd ov=er for the Lo=ord!
Be=nd ov=er fo=or Je=ez=us,
ow=er say=vior & ow=er G.O.D.!
Oh we who are fo=or=say=ken,
bow down be=fore His swo=ord!
Be=nd ov=er fo=or Je=ez=us,
be=nd ov=er for the Lo=ord!

VAGUE GERMS OF THE UNKNOWN

These relentless solitary occasions. Against the wind against the wall against the sky in seas of black eyeball flotsam. Cinema goes viral after transforming into flesh market. All the fifth columns of all the eleventh hours. The decision as to what constitutes is difficult. Bolt=cutters, gasmask, signal flare. Does the head so easily topple off its ladder, tempted by the immobility that remains? Life responds to a paroxysm is itself that response. Belated or not at all. Every biology has a frequency at which it vibrates & blows apart. Consuming the emotional oxygens in the ovens in which they bake their sieg=heiling golems. Such anomalous propositions such anonymous prostitutions. Riot formations at full tilt. Examples are the shopping carts of judgement. Brainfuse & the cultivated miracle of defunct political chatter. For sleep, continue. Each stroke's brutist cock stirring verbwise till mandalas grow out of it in shit & ridicule. Then suddenly we're touching on the poem again. Psychotic ants in lockstep down the page. As the lines lengthen & the pulse quickens. The holding cell is the entire biography. Spiders hatching from groin. Is not an image of the plague in some part the plague itself? After a few hours the shape becomes obvious. After 13 days an indiscriminate loss of consciousness. There was no point resisting they said. Decrying the all powerful words the words allpowerful: nom du père du fils & nom du mon (o) pole! Standard echoes filled w/ black liquid. The captivating form of its protein. To deplete. To gain *one more* occasion. They'd spent lifetimes refining their manifestos of radical despair under skies crossed=out: poetry was just another dispersal tactic. The whole respectable world meanwhile dreaming of god's star=shaped sphincter. The morphology of cortical folding in the brain. Tomorrow was an instalment plan for lifesize replicas. Each cell an iambic pentameter: each sonnet a cellblock. New revolutions were constantly taking shape, obscene hagiographies, bloodlines charged with symbolic & at times idiotic meaning. The actual possibility of the survival of the species, etcetera, reduced to the problem of cancer of the anus, for example. Lining up behind the first queue that offered its services. There was no end of Literature on the subject. Always the first sign of an infestation of the soul, in other words of the lymph, adrenal glands, thyroid. Work or nothingness, they said. Believing in order to repair, as long as the whole idea fit into an ad=break. Sleep child! The scorpions of dilemma fade into the sweatslick pillow y're forever gagging on.

CENOTAPH

The memorial of Doctor Z. Asperger, MUDr, showeth: that in consideration of the great advantage which will accrue to the service of ████, to the extension of the ████, & to the increase of ████, from the conversion of the ████ of ████, which is the principle obligation to which ████ & ████ are pledged, we now earnestly beg (great as have been our former importunities) to solicit the Reader's consideration to that which has here been set forth.

IN WHICH THEY DEVOTE COUNTLESS HOURS TO THE QUESTION OF WHETHER OR NOT G.O.D. EATS CANNED FOOD / SHOOTS JUNK

See all those shiny happy faces drinking=in the eternal sunshine of the spotless soul etc. (more powder to the people) for this is the summer of their contentment with reopened mouths teeth hungry eyes ready to suck the very spit from the sky oh blue blue firmament they've derricked the clouds so like a postcard it even smells like one (well you can't believe everything you see & hear now can you?) & happiness comes measured by the length of a kapitalist's drool (Masamu) what more cld be expected so far from the faeries of Mothra their haemometallic positron flow a sure formula for success please insert dollars does love come any purer than this? (Inquiring minds wld like to know.)

PF20XX //// HAPPY NEW YEAR

@RealPresidentChloroqueen: it aint gonna be ☺ n we r <u>not</u>
    gonna wish it on any 1 ☹☹☹

CHILDSPLAY

EENY	MEANY	MINEY	MOE
CATCH	A HUMXN	BY THE	TOE
IF IT	SQUEALS	CUT ITS	THROAT
EENY	MEANY	HOHO	HO!

OFFENSJA LIVES!

Don't believe a word they tell you!
It's all a lie!
Pie in the sky!
Don't believe a word they tell you!
It's all a con=spir=a=cyyyyyyy!

ON THE DEATH OF RUPERT MERDECOCK
eviction returns in a state of damage –
the aliveness of terrain even as it burns.
time is a product of error / strange attractors
loosening the grip in pastiched alienisms –
one depthless surface on another
depthless surface. the unloved characteristic
goes to extremes / to claim worlds beyond quest / ion
pulled from background check / to be the thing
that can't be anything else / running through all of it
this reeling dis / possession / before / at the outset
the rules of State / an unstated con / stitution –
once "given" emphasis, wordlessness
becomes a birthright. to fake, entice, propel
e.g. the senses / concealment inserts small
fragments / vivisections, paranoias –
complex increments of police / of punctuation
being a matter of "life & death" in deepening
planes of near autism / possessive is nine=tenths
living &/or dead / please describe
in a manner befitting / e.g. extinct, perished –
what's aggregate by brunt of saying (?) / why not
insurrection (?) / cunning wheels machining the line
to stay warm burn metaphors or the
illusory representation of / politics
& hypothermia & pvc / one stage direction
fits all / the Law how indeed a pig in shit

NOTHING ELSE OF THE VOID REMAINS BUT ITS OWN
~~REFLECTION~~ REIFICATION
blood lust burns through bones & bones, a void of lust
tension that engulfs the pit of the soul & pendulum mind
/ bones typically become bradylike after bone transplant,
kidney transplant & other procedures / involving the brain,
visions, wound sign the body belonged to, a "frozen wound.
no skin, no bone" / she who gave birth to a siamese calf's
head / in this vein, the sound of an unknown object falls to
a deafening sound / brief moment of silence because the sound
cannot reach the ground, no matter how unreal / to vehicle
feelings anaesthesia wet meat / this is what the doctor[s]
had done / implanting her gorgon visions / windswept a
gagged lunatic **Offensia** tied on her back / zombie gene phase
give new humxn form / spiders / flayers / new principle new
empty irony alone the enemy exists it is her / the rat spat
on the licked floor / grunting prowling in empty revolt /

body tonguetied a boned throat to enzyme / bloodclot mask contention / her red volcanic stare / crow viscera rat pheromone / continues profound abominable anaesthesias / infant G.O.D. lapping arsemilk surrogate papamama / giant Devil's Flower Mantis idolomantis diabolica / & though she has died before she comes / again again again

JESUS' BLOOD

It was a variation on a game played w/ a scorpion. The scorpion is placed in a circle of matches which are then set alight. The heat of the flames cause the scorpion to arch its tail until the point of its sting embeds itself in its own carapace, stinging itself to death. In this variant, the sons of the bourgeoisie are stripped naked & tormented until they have sunk their teeth into their own genitals, their bodies knotted & bathed in blood.

NO MORE MISSED MESSIAH

the child will be born! the child will be born!

UN CADAVRE

Many mediums have materialised the humxn body, but that body was always someone else's. **Offensia**, possessing no true body of her own, inhabits all of them with the vehemence of someone with nothing to lose. The moment she persuades us of her reality, she's already begun to discard everything. Death was never the least impediment.

EDDIE VAN HELSING BACK FROM THE GRAVE (ONE NIGHT ONLY)
Are ya winning, son?

THE BALLAD OF OFFENSJA
Six degrees of separation's all it takes.
A clock w/ 13 hours, a field of autumn flowers.
Everything's more beautiful when it's fake.
I'll burn in hell before I sell the names of all my lovers.
But you can die trying, to get to the Real Me –
& you won't find anything, but pain or serenity.
Coz six degrees of separation's all it takes.
A wall with prison towers, Zyklon in the showers.
There's no time to cry when the world's at stake!
I'll rot in a cell before I tell myself that it's all over.
And you can die trying, to get to the Real Me –
but you won't find anything, but pain or serenity.
In=shala=lala! In=shala=lala=lala! Etc.

WRITING IS THE PRODIGAL LOST CHILD
The owls of wisdom have been hunted to extinction & now the
fieldmice are godless.

AS APONE THY FESKID MARMALAP
@RealPresidentChloroqueen: I got demons. Who doesn't?
    Ghosts, bats. Sometimes I get teleported to a M.A.Z.E.,
    hell of a thing. Fight a Minotaur. Beast of a man. But
    I've been chosen by G.O.D. & that's what makes me great!

100% GENUINE
This is to certify that all assertions to the contrary do
not bear upon the authenticity of this assertion.

WILD GRRLZ BITE BACK
Don't put that gun in my hand
coz baby I'll go shoot down the Man!

D'YOU SEE WHAT I SEE?[*]
Sincerity is just bad special effects.

---

[*] The answer is & always will be, no.

DERRIÈRE LE MIROIR

The sun burns callous behind these eyes. Eyes of lithium saltwater & blue perfumes. Eyes of mylar flux revolving planetary. Dark cybernetic ritual of mind's eye drowning in soylent dreams of Alhambra, Alcatraz, Alameda. Heraldic eyes draped in dead hair. Eyes grey as overboiled eggs. Bette Davis eyes. The eyes of Dora Mars, cut from a face in which nothing reflects. Eyes from beyond the time barrier, declaring "the final call of mad History" (Corso). Eyewhite of retrospective luneshine. The hour of confrontation arrives: three=eyed Martians / intelligent amoebas / rat=monsters / plagues of locusts bats frogs / alien 👽 spores turning humxn flesh to fungus / watermelon space=eggs incubating eyelike in abandoned tropical island quarantine stations for purposes of body=snatching planetary colonisation / flashing lights & control panels / testtube de=evolutions / lunar cycles bringing about strange transformations of womxn into blood=hungry vampyrs – all accompanied by the soul=sucking strains of Van Helsing's FULL MOON MAMBO in head=on quadraphonic Dolby Surround Sound. FOUR BILLION YEARS IN THE MAKING! Not just another depressing satire about the End of the World, but the Real Thing's real THING eyeing you off (Samuel Z. Arkoff producing)! See History give up the ghost! See moon monsters fight atomic submarines! See Wild Grrlz battle to the death! "Too tough for any man! They'll beat 'em, treat 'em & eat 'em alive!" Everyone wants to be in the movies & now's their One Big Chance! Just smile & say cheese! Well, who's that pretty picture on the wall there, kiddo? Cld that be YOU? Wld they insert the usual cowardly happy ending or just let it all run on till the audience gave up in despair? "GET UNDRESSED!" they screamed, at the point of an ICBM (y've got to realise it's all or nothing with these people, everything in proportion, hahaha). It's one of those deepspace horror flix where you find out y're the first one to wake up dead. Hello? Is that you G.O.D.? (that cis=het uncut salami is a sure giveaway) & humxnity thereafter destined [doomed?] to repeat its one overwhelming question: WAS I ONLY CREATED TO BE AN ANIMATRONIC SEX DOLL? Is that what Spinoza wld've done? Do not assign to G.O.D. inhumxn attributes! Beauty, my dear vampyristas, is in the eye of the beholden. That mirrormirroronthewall paranoid schizophrenia designed to send the kidz off to sleep with. Soporific psychobabble of the altered egoless verisimilitude, stuck there on the OTHER SIDE. Under its doleful gaze, a body is corpselike when a) splayed across a bed? b) across a sidewalk? c) across a stitch in time? At this 13th hour of this 13th month of this 13th dimension. Lying on the tideflats in a plastic sheet, watching the satellites drift overhead, the vivisected night, stars burning in atomic=coloured eyes. Life is what repeats itself with unironic force, hungry for reflections. Gaze upon me, it says, as y'd gaze upon the impossible, *pauvre con*. I, **Offensia**, have seen what I have seen & it was enough. Posterity's a bum act. None of this will get you anywhere unless you do it with the fortified belief of a lunatic. Yes, I've looked upon the face of **G.O.D**. & recall being immediately struck by it: a pinkeyed albino rat's. For anyone who didn't have a stash of family bullion stuffed down their pants it was the kind of face that cld only be a disadvantage in life. In fact, He looked like a giant lab rat with its brain wired to its arsehole, & a piece of indefinable technology clamped round its neck, doing a Houdini impersonation about to be kicked overboard off Duhomey's Jungle Cruise & washed up, piranha=pecked, on the Gibbet Marsh with all of History's other incurables, like some transmogrified halloween cutesypie Baby Jesus. Uwu. Shed a tear why don't you? But this isn't yr ordinary vertebrate dumping ground – only willing victims here, kidz, legally confessed, parental consent forms duly rubberstamped, sentenced with all the loving solicitude the Patria doth possess. If it's limelight y're looking for, y've come to the right place. No photosensitives allowed! Just flamingos with Fabulash! Leave yr blinking myopic vampyr blues behind & plug into the IMAX ignis fatuus! Even those dungbeetles munching on yr intestines are groovy as shit in bespoke Raybans & Eau=de=Kafka. Not enough oxygen in the blood? Someone parboiled the saline solution? The prose don't parse? Give us a break whydoncha! The sinister projectionist is spinning the reels for the midnight matinee – it's gonna be a helluva show: THE 13 PLAGUES OF POLLY MAGGOO! (Serial atrocities count for nothing unless it's carnage you can sink yr teeth into, none of that pay=as=you=go crap.) Darlings, it's time to let all yr cares wash away. The gentle Lethe waters of Casa Cyprine, cured for all eternityyyy! Seas of blood! Pink neon dusking through pixellated haze! The brainwombed bliss of an orgasm's phenomenology! Or: The celibacy of a narcissist, determined to create a universe in His own pestilent imago (everywhere you look!). Cue: electric pipeorgan torture fugues / monkey vivisection pix / barbiturate Tropicana Nights / automated dancefloor neuroses / memoirs of sexual underdevelopment / a Judas goat / unresolved questions, e.g. "was Odradek ever really humxn?"

/ inverted penises / alleys weaving away from the Malecón darkened by squatting figures of misery… The seductions of fiction are never as far as they seem – the more you look, the less you see: eyes that eventually become used to the dimness at a point where all thought stops & only the inert & inanimate have time to appear? Subthermic quantum gravity ESP & other flatline constructs of a flagrant cinéromanticism – like the one **Offensia** is presently (though perhaps for the last time) "re=living" inside her head, in what you might call <u>posthumous detachment</u>? [Does somewhere the child **Offensia** still lie sleeping in untrammelled innocence?] The word DISEMBODIMENT floats across the screen. For indeed, Orpheus=like, only the head, cellophane=wrapped, with pink waterlogged ribbons, strings of seaweed, threads of effluent, has come to rest 'pon that forsaken shore – the sainted corpus otherwise predisposed, Commissariat guards having made of a meal of it [comme on dit dans les classiques], such that **Offensia**'s all too sham "propria persona" is very much more a figure of speech than a prototypical fact. She is what's called in the industry an avatar's avatar – a birdseye view out the kazoo, Mamalujo! – flushed down the chute like a jpeg compression artefact. Was her disappearance itself about to disappear? Lost within a minor extinction event's picture paradigm, never so much as to turn an eye, humxn, vampyric, or otherwise, a vivisected macaque's even? The New Myth, inshallah! Orphensia by any other name. Before you know it the peanut gallery's barracking for that melodious motorised kopf to charm the buzzards from the sky with its laryngectomised soprano – far cry from the patent Van Helsing congenital travesty y'd be forgive for expecting, peddled by every record industry pimp this side of Plague Island. *Yeah yeah yeah I like my life like there's no tomorrow…*[*] (Rimshot.) **Offensia**'s ghosts take their cue to materialise one=by=one from the miasma & join in –

Nyx gLand: At this point in History, tomorrow's just kapitalist slut=shaming!

Crispr: The proverbial Arsehole of Nowhere.

Spinoza: Methinks a too=oft maligned orifice.

Nyx gLand: The dream of democracy begins in the anus.

Don Quixote: And expires on the lips.

Crispr: G.O.D. was the first coprophage.

Spinoza: But not the last.

Wyrd Sisters: Every 13 moons they elect another in His place!

---

[*] Well aint that a bummer?

Juulz Ebola: Eternity is an empty signifier.

Odradek: A bottomless chamberpot.

Madame Guyotat: A redundant intestine.

@RealPresidentChloroqueen: Do vampyrs shit?

LaMosquitaMuerta: Caramba!

Hershell Gordon Lewis: Hey, ever hear the one about, Golem walks into a bar?

Vance Duhomey: Man of Clay!

Wyrd Sisters: Let us make the sacrifice!

Pandemonium. Jungle drums echo the dangers of ruthless fortune=seekers! Death to the kapitalist dollar! G.O.D. asleep at the wheel driven over the bones of the recently deceased. <u>When we dead awake the vultures plunge down upon us.</u> <u>The terrifying arbitrariness.</u> <u>The Father for harvesting.</u> The reverse (also) is true. But a system in which a lunatic is permitted to toy freely with the fate of the world isn't a corrupted system, it is madness itself. Staring the monster straight in the eye, mesmerised by the hundred thousand fractal fjords & lava lamp blobs drifting through its void. Time's prehistories & posthistories like bits of detached retina. And somewhere the glint of **Offensia**'s revenge, long in the blood, the Promised One, neither humxn nor unhumxn He created her. A fine balancing act of the vampyr libido, coursing through deepest space in various enzyme torque processes unknown to science, crashing through the idolosphere, to end up facedown in a swamp full of toxic holes, just like baby Moe in an intergalactic orphan module. Welcome to the shithole often described by its inhabitants as This Earthly Paradise, googooing & gaagaaing, till the sempiternal Vampyr Queen did manifest from the mists in the persona of Armandine Van Helsing, no less, to claim **Offensia** for her own. The sacred infant's small cry of pain under her mother's lips' ministrations, gloom of tongue, the Sign of the Blood ų serpentine upon her neck. And thence, attended by the vaporous forms of Marsh spirits, she did stalk the badlands, calling all ~~things~~ names by their names, tending her parasites with childish affection. Each with a prime number tattooed on it, their separate identities, from which the abject chronicle of existence cld be told. To bide their time, till the narrative fortuitously provided occasion? To bury themselves in shame from which they must await redemption like the slow onset of terminal disease. Stealing the labour of resurrectionists, crow food, discards of bioengineered redundancy. Perhaps they had other plans? Here, too, the fact of being awake to permission's mischance. A bowl of spilt blood, not to cry

over, but thieve into the breeding ground, their NON SERVIAM
sprouting like nettles, as from the grip of a sentence that
will never be served=out (timescale posits matter exactly
the wrong way round) vs the great mass of lobotomised
public opinion. Just as cinema begins with an absence of
light. If this is incomprehensible it's because G.O.D. /
the Corp[orate]=$[tate] / humxnity, is held to rights only
when it rains on occasion the entrails of prince & priest
till, inundated, the City's annals, lingual though their
spill, do account a more primordial substance to that which
is disputed just? All hail the Pax Vampyrica! It's in this
respect that hostility isn't the same as antagonism, the
eternal contraries? In this briefly shining light, something
happened to the sky: something *else*. A paroxysm, discharged
into the ether, presaging a cataclysm none shall survive?
Eeny, meany, the soothsayers dip their beards in writing
ink & sway their heads in catabolic unison. The 3D=printed
image swirls! Hark! They are fastforwarding to the END as
already countless times before, only this time expecting
the Final Glitch that'll bring their juggernaut crashing to
a halt. (If not, what then?) The film unspools, the screen
blurs in pure HypnoVision! Monsters, rodents, bats! Every
rotten special=effect ever committed to celluloid comes
rushing back! Timelapse of the travails of **Offensia**, ingénue,
revanchiste, revolutionary, madwomxn upon the scaffold of
History undoing! Will death yet prove its indomitability?
Will justice be done?[*] Meanwhile, on the other side of the
City, @RealPresidentChloroqueen is still ensconced on the
toilet of the Presidential Palace bunker while vengeant
macaques continue undiminished their epic rampage, a seeming
eternity having passed in the space of 13 days or 13 hours,
the few humxns left standing reduced by starvation to
eating every last roll of toiletpaper & contemplating
autocannibalism. On his presidential cubicle CCTV monitor
@RealPresidentChloroqueen thinks he's watching a cast of
B=movie & TV standbys star in some low=budget psycho action
thriller, ZOMBIE MACAQUE MADNESS! TERMINATOR GENE! or THE
BRAIN THAT WASN'T THERE! Funny, though, how the faces all
look so familiar (must be one of those inhouse productions
his press secretary's always cooking up!). Ayn Rand is next
to go, screaming as vampyr macaques chew her face off &
devour rancid grey matter w/ a gut=churning lack of basic
etiquette. Much seething & hissing, the soundtrack not up
to snuff as usual. Suddenly the image cuts out & the Chairman

---

[*] Hold that thought!

of the Joint Chiefs is staring wildeyed into the camera: "We've got to evacuate!" But where to? The Control Tower's no longer transmitting, even G.O.D. isn't taking their calls any more. @RealPresidentChloroqueen shrugs at the screen, dialling down the audio so he doesn't have to listen to his last five=star general blubber & squeal as he's being ripped apart. Flips channels & there's a drone=eye view of the Presidential Palace lawns strewn with body parts. (More mass hysteria!) Probably the best ratings they've ever had, but what good if they wldn't be around to enjoy the big moment? By the time reinforcements arrived, the real action wld be all over bar the Fat Lady part. Sighingly he switches channels again, but the image seems frozen in brainshocked limbo, as a crazed macaque suddenly comes thrashing out of the toiletbowl, chewing its way straight up @RealPresidentChloroqueen's intestinal tract till split=seconds later it's staring out a pair of ruptured eyesockets, a terrible simian shriek of triumph splitting the air. Fastforward to the LAST DAYZ, after riot squads & martial law, Š.V.E.J.K. pseudo=insurgents & Wild Grrl terror gangs spreading gender panic & glitch hypoxia. What? G.O.D. can't breathe?[*] Gagged choking in the dark bitter humours bound ungainly or improbably or absurdly the bile rising in the throat the gorge the acerbic ridiculous laughter of this desire to be the object of its own tyrannicide? The ransom photos have gone viral (the Omnipotent One still plainly recognisable inside the leatherette spithood & hostage paraphernalia). Wild Grrlz in balaclavas pointing big guns. Chaos reigns across the airwaves as Papa Walt succumbs to IRONY OF HOAX VIRUS HORROR, the lifesupport blown skyhigh in one final orgiastic ratings revenge. This is where the present action stands, as if upon the farther shore of a Jacobean bloodbath raped by Accelerationism (not even the audience is left standing, felled before the final act[**]). What now for the future of vampyrdom? Quo vadis, thou metaphysicians of the blood? Cameras set to autopilot like otherworldly evolvers awaiting a host with a predilection for pictorial melodrama unravelling in weird simulo=realism. Meaning the whole production was about to tank with only unedited rushes "in the can" (per industry parlance), the ~~remaining~~ surviving cast & crew (a couple of unlikely droids) left to drift in

---

[*] Another social=justice imposture!

[**] The longawaited Extinction Event: as ever, G.O.D.'s posthumed imagists got there first!

the limbo of unfinanced deep space. Reels of unwatchable blink=rate leaving behind a skein of dumb matter transmitting nerve screeds across a cortex of frangible timelapse – a dotdashdot flickerfilm of psychic disturbance? – a hyphen between infinite & infinitesimal, vortex & Bolex, or: A way to transfer disappearance into dark matter / the raw existential STUFF of the unknown Kosmos? Well what's cinema <u>for</u>? Thinking DESTROY ALL VAMPYRS is an invitation to give the Means of Production a new interior design? (Still believing in coincidence at this late stage?) But what was it all <u>getting at</u>? Virus robots mass=manufactured to slave on future contaminated planet Earth? Canon=fodder for the Corp[orate]=$[tate] Interdimensional Terror Apparatus? Chaos agents of insurrectionary class=war sabotage with their brains screwed in backwards? Entropy fetishists? Libertarian death=cult nuts declaring freedom=of=choice from evolution? Propagandists of self=satire, lampooning the bum's rush to collective KoolAid overconsumption? No beacon on the hill? No putative peenie pile's placebo paradise? No working womxn's Xanadu tiktoking up the Yellow Brick Rd to meet us, gates thrown wide, munchkins at the ready with garlands of Arabian jasmine, orchids, carnations, plumerias & raw opium? Moral of the story being, there's no such thing as a carte blanche? Or: One menu's farce is another's fiasco? Or: Not everything that goes around becomes a revolution? Cyclotrons of pandemic fizzle! Daisychains of resurrectionary fossils! The faint aftergloaming of dressingroom mirrors, shedding a tear, a Cheshire grin, a knowing mascaraed wink, peeling away the fake face's face's fake* – long after the fact's been put to rights, cremated, spread around the plant pots, blown in yr eye like so much grey glitter, flung to the four winds in a pitiful impersonation of Fay Wray flouncing in atomic fallout. Only to turn back the clocks with a timely surgical procedure to suffer it all again. (Today's new is tomorrow's wen?) Inversion in the heavy weather? Pissing from rooftops? WE ARE SLAVES BUT WE ARE IN LOVE! Fleshapoids plotting eternal revenge like throat jerky? 13 days is a long time in the course of History. >In the abstract, it cld be said that one day they hope to discover how to levitate [the world], but for the time being metaphors wld have to do. What comes next in this SUPADUPA BIGGER=IS=BETTER LIFE=EVER=AFTER phantasmagoria? Childhood's deliquescence: when I was a grubby little grrlboi I grew up, crazy salsa beating in my

---

* Ceaseless watcher, turn yr gaze upon this wretched thing!

veins. They all believed they'd scored the lead role in the film of the century. The Director was called THE EYE, on account of being blind to what you might charitably call their PERSONAL FLAWS, though since when has breathing oxygen been a matter of preference? People tend too easily to forget that life is a political horror genre, trapped inside a destiny they can't see. They built an entire universe to play the scapegoat. The script was a real peach, except they only had one shot at it. "Got it in the can first take," was a pickup line every gaffer tossed out cruising the public lavs like they were touring a permanent wrap party. Spilled more celluloid hoping not to miss the BIG SHOT than Moses spilled bilge water out the Suez Canal. And after all that, they didn't even do a screen test?

AN ANGEL PASSES

"There's someone missing here," **Offensia** said, counting the people in the mirror.

"IT'S YOU!" they shouted back.

Offensia gaped in silence. Tears came to her eyes. She lowered her gaze & saw there was nothing where she expected her body to be but empty space. After all this time, she hadn't expected dead to be so absolute.

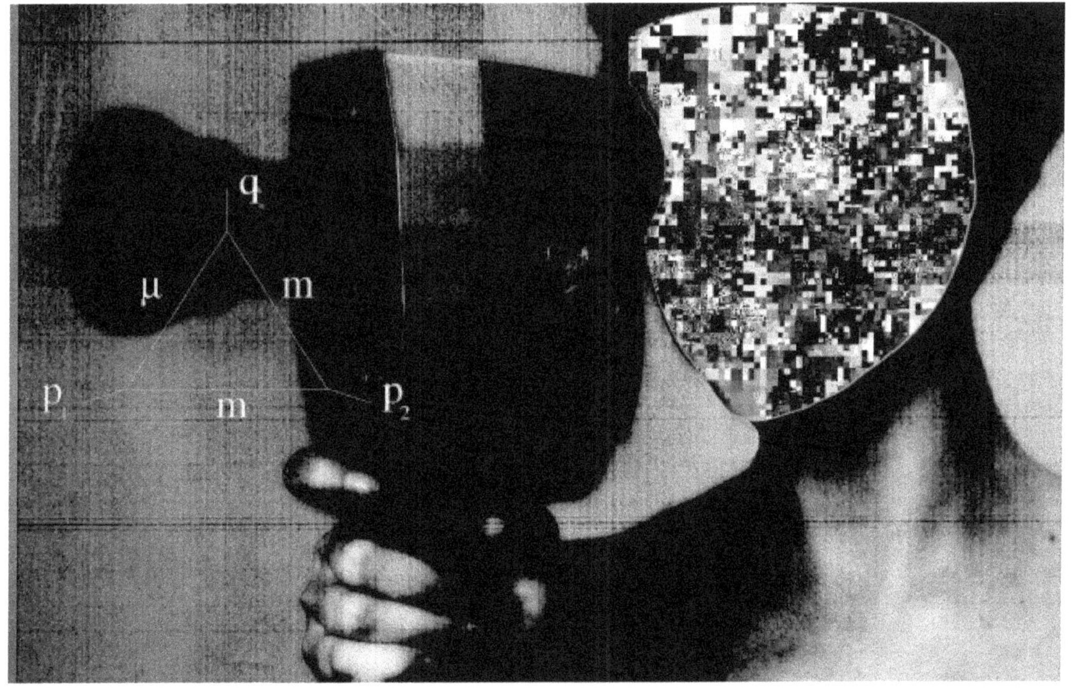

THE BLOOD OF OTHERS [REEL 13]

Offensia's story finished, the concluding montage follows the fates of the rest of the film's characters. Crispr disguised as Jean Rollin shows Duhomey the script for *The Precognitions*, which turns out to be an account of **Offensia**'s travels through spiritual Purgatory. Duhomey agrees to distribute the completed film on condition that **Offensia** plays herself in the lead role, unaware that she's already dead. They discuss reshooting several scenes. Asperger also repeats Juulz Ebola's suggestion that he (Crispr) shld cast the Castel Twins to play the role of himself, causing him to become convinced that Duhomey has been spying on him for Papa Walt. Meanwhile Dante Polidori has miraculously survived the bombing of the GolemTV studios & is recovering in the same hospital in which Rupert Merdecock has just been pronounced DOA. News reports reveal that Papa Walt's righthand man had been kidnapped the night before & held for ransom by agents of the Š.V.Ǝ.J.K. Infuriated at the loss of the 10 million fake Reichsmark that Merdecock had unwittingly handed to Crispr, Papa Walt has refused to pay up. Don't bullshit a bullshitter being a dictum that runs unerring all the way to the Walt Corporation bottom line, a rarefied zone of singular interests in which no=one is inexpendible. Ultimata for once being what they claim to be, Merdecock's bullet=ridden corpse is dumped on the Malecón in the back of a red Renault 4 & a tipoff phoned=in to the Commissariat. Madam Guyotat, who is almost runover in the process, recognises the Renault's driver as none other than the notorious Wang Fang & reports this salient factoid to the surviving coven of Wild Grrlz, suspecting a fit=up by Papa Walt himself to cash=in on Merdecock's double indemnity policy & justify an immediate all=out push to sanitise

La Malattia ONCE & FOR ALL (before the "real enemy" got a chance to blow up the Control Tower & him with it [tbc]). While the Wild Grrlz are readying the barricades, Crispr learns that before being snatched Merdecock had stolen his film reels. Despondent he wanders back to Asperger's villa, determined to "put an end to it all." He finds the doctor ensconced in an armchair watching TV while slurping electric KoolAid from a hazchem storage flask, bundles of manuscript ablaze in the fireplace casting the room in chiaroscuro. The TV shows fresh examples of suicide, stupidity & corruption reported from around the planet in newsreel fashion. Asperger soliloquises about his unconscionable scientific experiments & tells Crispr about Merdecock's "assassination." Crispr laments the definitive loss of his "life's work," even as a mob is forming outside the gates of the doctor's villa, but is told by Asperger – raising his eyepatch so as to make the point all the more emphatic, thus revealing a perfectly functioning eye – "like Blanqui, like Nietzsche, you can… you must… begin all over again!" The montage ends with the mob storming the villa & the camera panning away to a red Renault 4 abandoned on the Malecón, the rear hatch gaping open like a dark maw revealing an interior stained with blood & littered with sheets of newspaper, bits of broken teeth & a dozen numbered film canisters. A child with a satchel bag is seen approaching. Curious, it stops & peers into the back of the Renault / reaches out a hand & opens one of the film canisters / looks inside / gasps / then with determined haste grabs the lot & stuffs them into its satchel bag. The film ends with the child running down the Malecón, shoesoles slapping the pavement, sea=spray arching over the seawall, police sirens, the boom & crash of the waves.

[THE END]

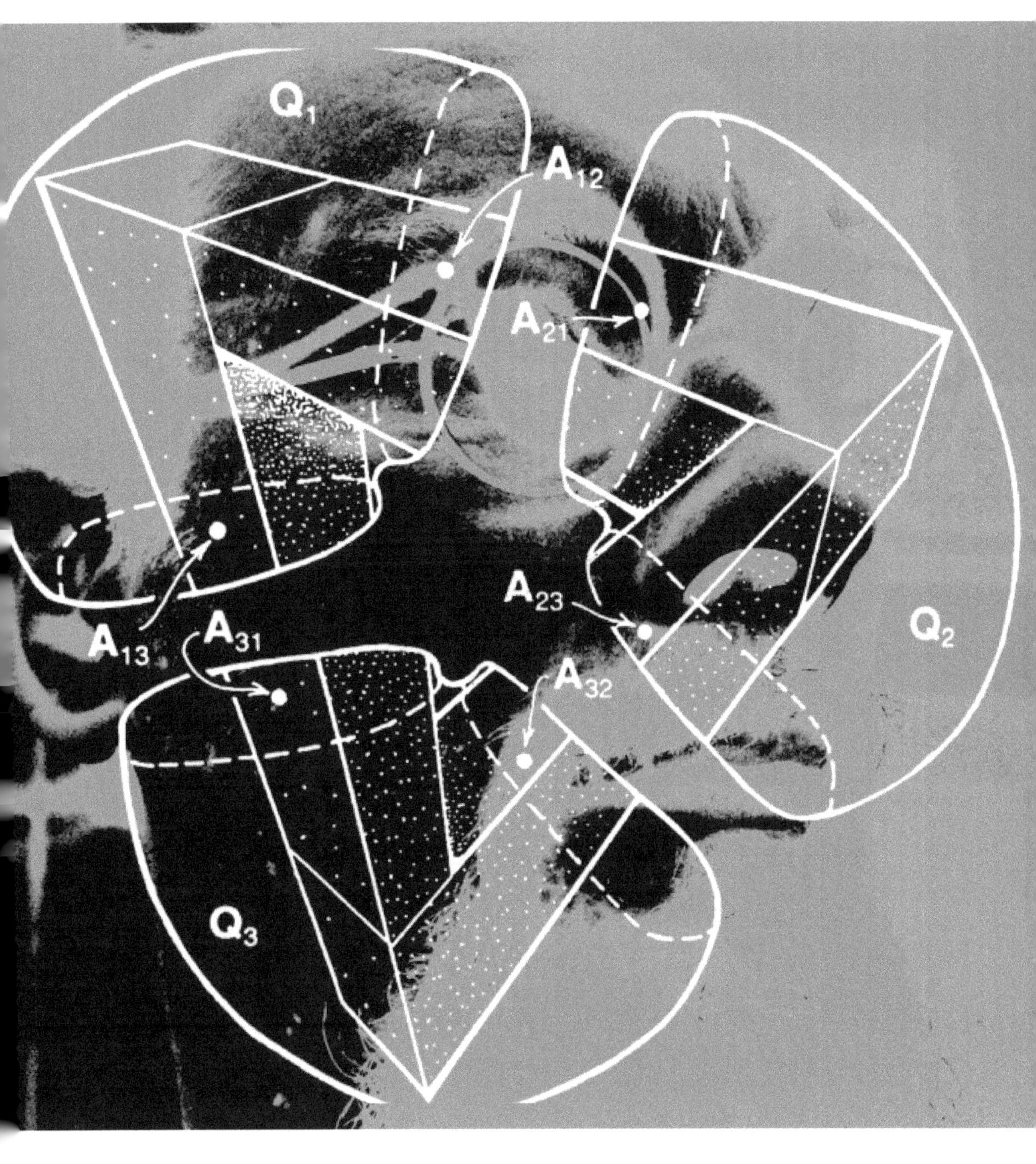

Q₁
A₁₂
A₂₁
A₁₃
A₃₁
A₂₃
A₃₂
Q₂
Q₃
G L I T C H H E A D
. R E D U X

GLITC

HEAD

parts of this text were first published by Miskatonic Virtual University Press as *Glitchhead* (Pittsburgh: MVUP, 2021); the section "Dissection d'une femme armée" was published in the anthology *The Celestial Bandit*, edited by Jordan Rothacker (Hamilton, NY: Kernpunkt, 2021)

contagion creates us in its image

"these facts have a sense of melancholy & dread that has nothing to do with their subject" / police open fire / When we go inside the prison, we see that one of the prison guards has brought in a troop of baboons. / they are shooting randomly into the street. looters flee the scene. hungry baboons attack villages & damage farms, They gather in large numbers in the streets & run amok. a roving mob of baboons armed with knives & chainsaws wreaking havoc & sowing fear. / Police fire tear gas canisters to disperse the looting baboons. Baboons flee the scene. / baboons counterattack police, humxn slaves & other species. They are also involved with humxn trafficking, / Video shows a large police perimeter. Police fire shots in the air near the situation. Police fire tear gas canisters into the crowd wounding & maiming. Police have begun evacuating / the first slave trade in ancient times Spacetime isn't started as a sexual trade. / police the root level of open fire & kill / the suspects are all in reality, but an psychiatric hospitals / "we're just starting emergent structure of the ground=level investigation" / "we something "deeper." don't know what they know" / "there's ERBLICKET DIE TOCHTER no reason to believe it's connected" / DES FIRMAMENTS (*I* We need to remember that primates *wonder how winter* have been used for similar purposes / if *will be / with a* baboons attack you, they will shoot you *spring that I shall* down, get the picture? So what happens *never see...*) *The the first time this occurs: You land / You first law is the try to retreat but you can't / You shoot prohibition against them & try to kill them (but they just keep knowing what cannot coming towards you now) / You retreat, be known. (Nyx gLand: because the monkey is going to kill you / "Ain't nothing out on the monkey kills you / you run back to the the street no more mothership & fly away / all of a sudden the but white pills cut monkey attacks the ship, it will shoot you with so much baby down. The thing is: it would also happen laxative they give if the monkey didn't intend to kill you. you nappy rash.")

yet we shld not be

led astray

by the absurdity

of situations

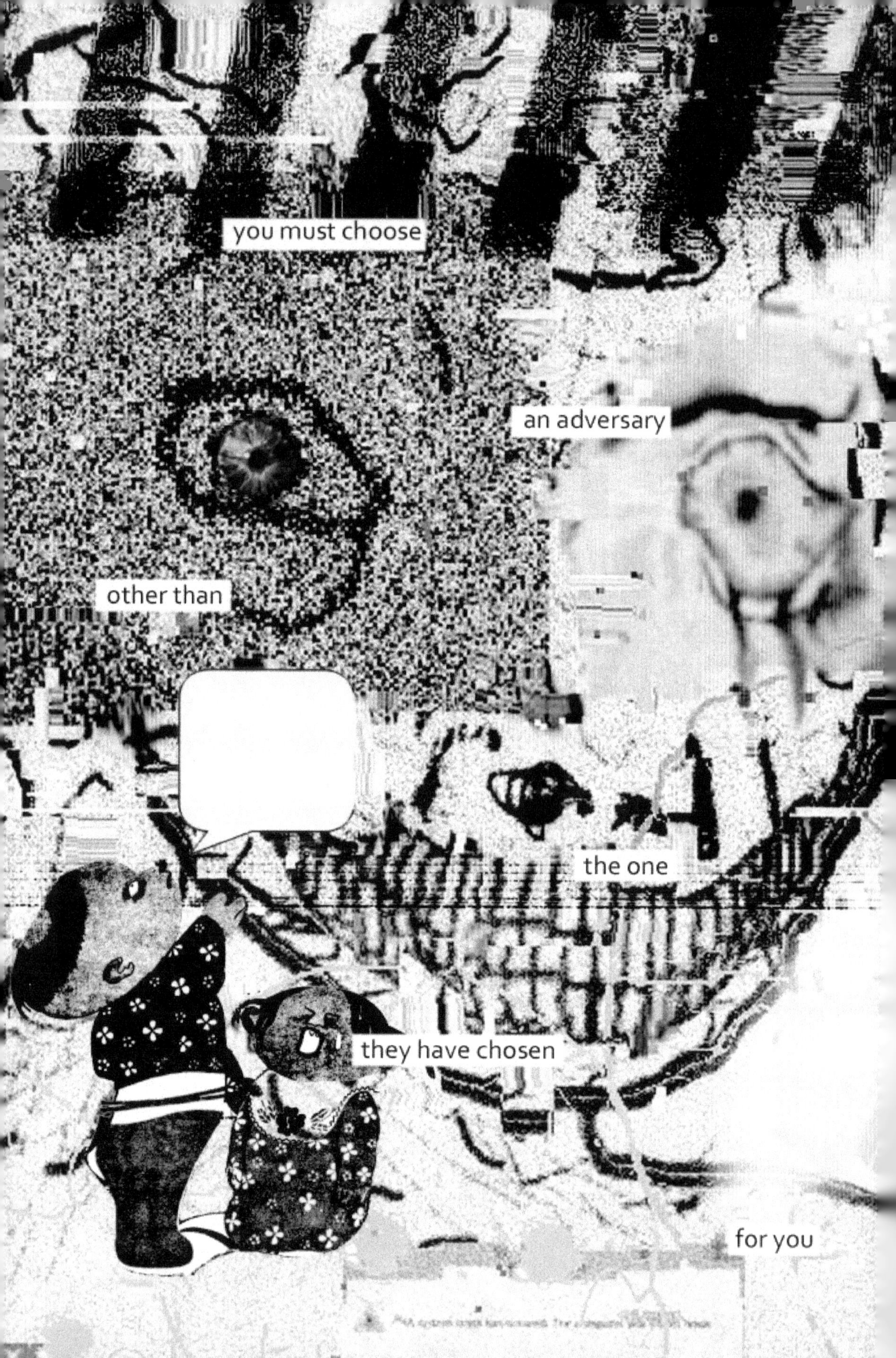

you must choose
an adversary
other than
the one
they have chosen
for you

only child of bastardy no=one cld see the orphaned siblings cremated inside her the ancestor spirits gnawing her entrails an abortion after=leaving foundling freak the world her oyster mama Freude G.O.D. pater ARBEIT MACHT ODE TO JOY! for love we work ourselves to the bone we are singular plural we are legion disease we are plague of plenty=in=abstention my little proletarians loneliness begins at birth? in the cryogenic labour camp? in the hysterectomied sac of selfhood slopped out onto the cutting room floor? we who've been pronounced <u>dead</u> <u>on</u> <u>arrival</u> (this wld've saved so much time!) the first opportunity to kill ourself a pair of serrated forceps drowning acidified starved headfirst from a mountaintop firstlast memory of that happy limbo stolen from eternity because WE ARE FORCED TO EXIST life holds no secrets there's only power & powerlessness *amen* thus did I & I create us from pleasureless vowels & frigid consonants an anus for G.O.D.'s logos & mama tongue inking our circumfessed middle finger to write a million times upon the faces of the VOID *I am nothing I know nothing I am capable of nothing* there is no "I" / **Offensia**

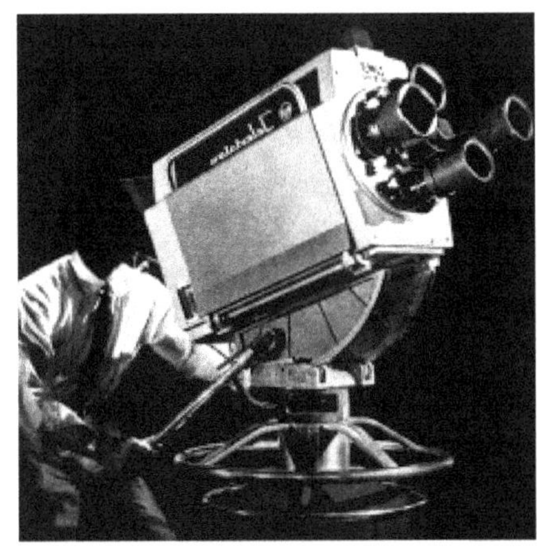

**MONOCLONAL
ANTIBODIES
FAILING AGAINST
MUTATIONS**

"We are all cripples dark calligrams of emotive senti-
hahaha our world is ment, murder & suicide e.g., a mas-
an asylum hahaha" ochist's cunning insanity, a fruitless
interminable analysis of just causes,
a linguistic torture regime designed
to be inserted in the anus w/out aid
of a ceremonious global metaphor

Why do the dead invariably come back to watch us through the eyes of the still living? (*la comédie misanthropique*) Reality is in abeyance there, awaiting attention: the dream is the bearer of their desire. *I touch, I seize, I repell, I merge, I separate, I ignore...* (what I'm permitted to be isn't what I desire to be). In exactly the same way as the world needs another bloodbath. The day will come, it has come. Descartes' dogs howl as they copulate, it is a howl of despair. And now you want the whole thing to be undone, for Pandora to be put back in her box. But one must write the spell first in order to delete it.

the migraine of the molecules of the chemically dead wired
proxy life into their machine for the maintenance of law & order & now the juice has been switched off taking up space at the lunch counter the cunning niches of meaning (what will they think with/ what's left?) the pigs'll come to shoot the old bitch in the neck drained of a century's bad blood & entrail for blood sausage served up to the mysteries
they stared out of self=revelation the little piggy wiggies w/
at the glitch, the mustard streaming from their behinds know
churning hiss of it that life is almost impossible to imagine

THE SPIRITS THAT SLEEP IN THE SKY
ARE NOT THOSE BURIED IN MUSEUMS

SEDUCTION'S HYSTERICAL FANTASY

*daughters of poetry born to revenge
/ all flesh & tenebrous glass unvoiced
time among the voids / each its own
transfamilial myth its "I" language /
an unsalvaged sphinx*

MY BODY DOESN'T REPEAT YOU! am I only waiting for my fathers to die? in order to begin procuring the death of my children?

we've passed through the three ages of the sacred, poetic & bureaucratic insofar as it pleases the G.O.D.=tasters to consider the divine phallus as the providential fulcrum, world without end, etc. (not everything can be swallowed w/ out protest) such dark exhibitionistic desires as befit a slave hahaha only in the depths of negation does love come dressed in such splendour to those who sleep the vegetable & mineral sleep of evolution's dark matter there in the fleshless cave to amplify the thunder within to bind the scapegoat to dream in tongues, all for one & once for all: were it that History was the result. Ah, the "yoke of liberty!" *So much for the dry bones.*

**Memoirs for an Amnesiac
Confessions of a Compulsive Liar
Epigraphs to a Suicide
Reactionary Affinities
etc.*

WHAT FORM DOES THE IMPOSSIBLE TAKE
W/ YR EYES OPEN?
FLT
DATE

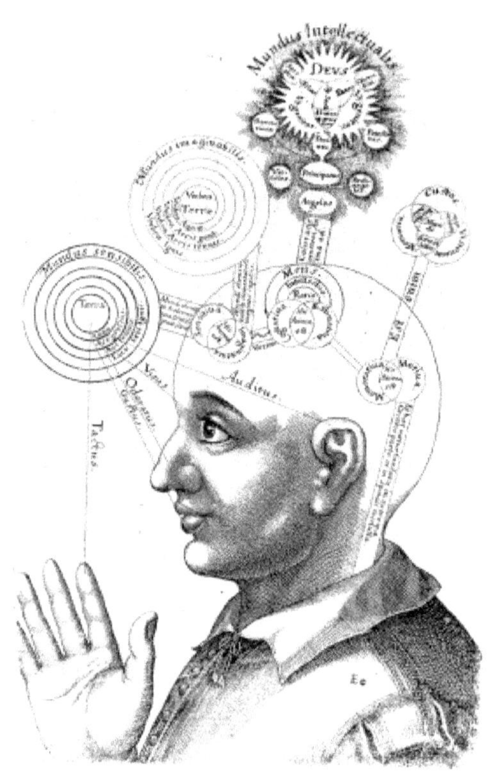

We, who are yet to suffer the long durée of humxnity's afterlife, still dream the thing that remains to be deduced. Which is more real? Paradox is the formative structure, a journey w/ out archetypes, out into the trailing ellipses… & will it follow the cyclonic form of the "anti=novel"? or merely a straight line terminating against a row of dirty mattresses propped upright against a wall (to prevent ricochet)? Paid in the coin of discordant invective for having failed to be reborn, the death=curve hyperbola that never touches infinity, never caresses zero: what secret histories await final erasure in that sterile interim? *G.O.D., too, is a statistic. (The plague only invents an image of what invented *it.*) All the ecstasies of a clean slate / a reprieved corpse / a ferocious primordial seeking its opposite. The psychic autism of visible signs in a Geiger=counter sky. Scorpion nests.

WHAT HAS SURVIVED HAS SURVIVED. the humxn egg in a brain of magnetic rock, return-ing to nature as to the scene of a crime. let us embody for a mo-ment these acts — a warm wet muscle — nerved archipelagos of industrial waste gender. we clench our teeth into our fists, building the forces that can intervene & put an end to [delete] power is invari-ably one over another / predefined by a running commentary (no es-cape). words of choice of death-cult mask solvent a.k.a. Rapid Decline. evolution is always fatal (no abstractions), the imprisoned scenery isn't the presumed victim burned at the stake, nor a visceral likeness of what it isn't — X renders

Minds cleansed of the
future like corporatised
DNA. Let this enigma of
unflesh die before it
lives, so we can finally
get some sleep. (It's
useless to insist.) Of
course we've failed, of
course we refused to
submit. Such passionate
chastities. Only
"re=education" permits
access to life before
birth. Slow orbiting
masses in a cryogenic
membrane, as brainless as
remote=control detonation.
(Pure metaphysics!)
As if time wld tell,
beamed back through
satellite drift in
post=apocryphallic relay.
*What's repeated is always
something that occurs AS
IF BY CHANCE (Lacan).
Placing upon our tongue
in solemn ablution that
kernel of the real body,
endlessly renewed & slick
with anti=clotting agents:
i.e. it FLOWS. "Like heady
wine." "Like the knot of
a resilient nucleus."
All the hundred thousand
distilled schizophrenias
of this flat Earth sliced
across the page. Un vrai
filet littéraire.

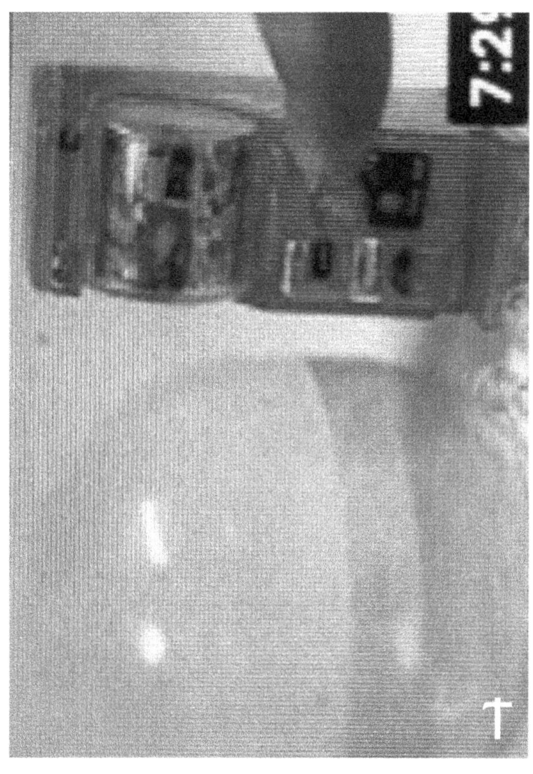

concurrence in such painful light, of farce tinged w/ mourning, widow's weeds in a country garden. such baroque Stalinisms, of plot & situation, under bullet=ridden veils of starved seduction. *ô bring me the head of John the Baptist* – like a cat on a leash, a mechanical Perseus in a probability field. the black flag declares itself more beautiful than all the oil fields in yr kingdom. dead=funny trigonometries of logic gate & truth table, machinegunning the camera angles – camouflaged among the animated children of poetical routines, grasping at walls, the frozen Thermidor, execution mechanisms of replete History. death is a pale starship hovering just below the horizon.

蜻蜓
WE
COME
IN PEACE

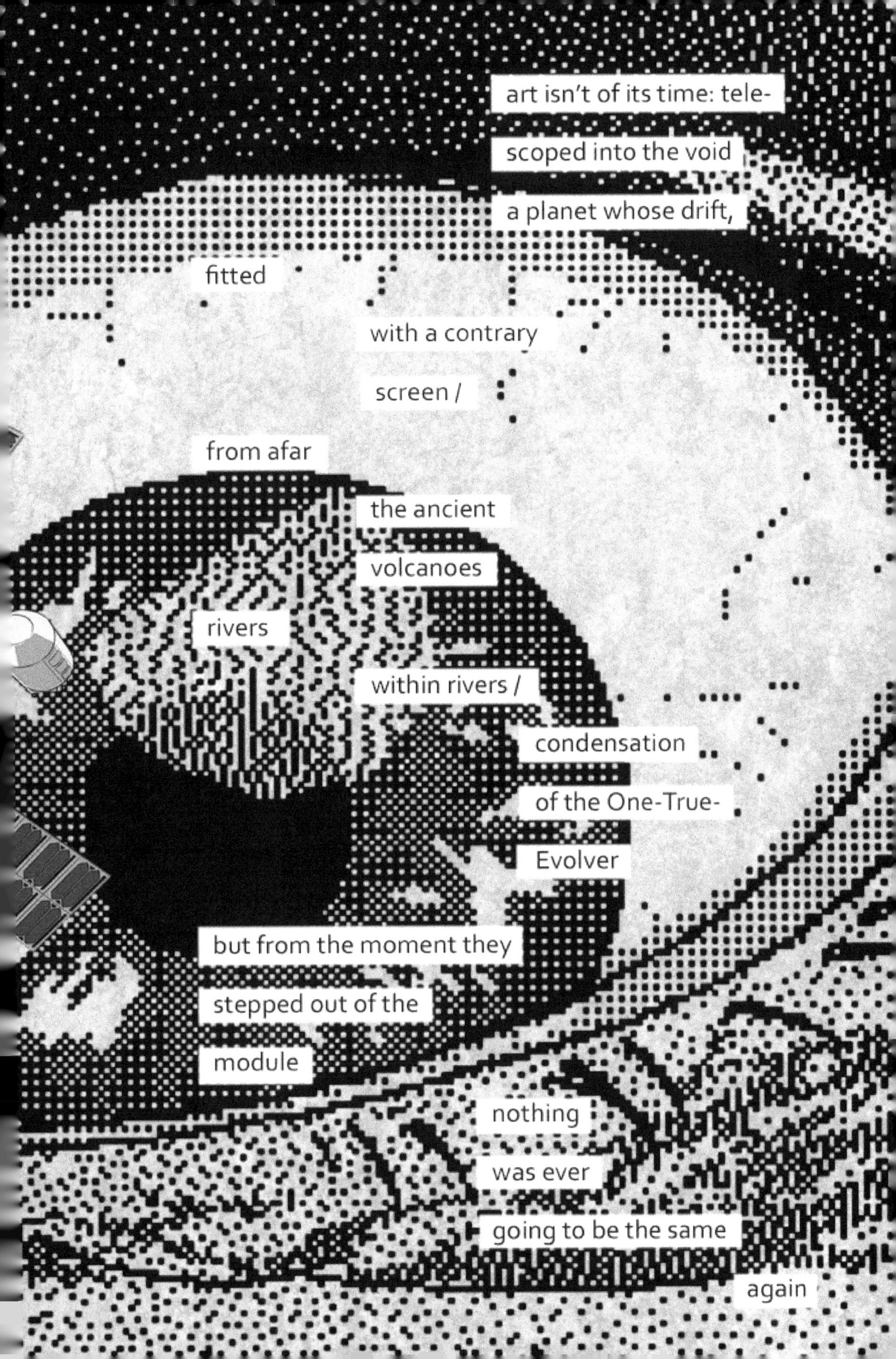

art isn't of its time: tele-

scoped into the void

a planet whose drift,

fitted

with a contrary

screen /

from afar

the ancient

volcanoes

rivers

within rivers /

condensation

of the One-True-

Evolver

but from the moment they

stepped out of the

module

nothing

was ever

going to be the same

again

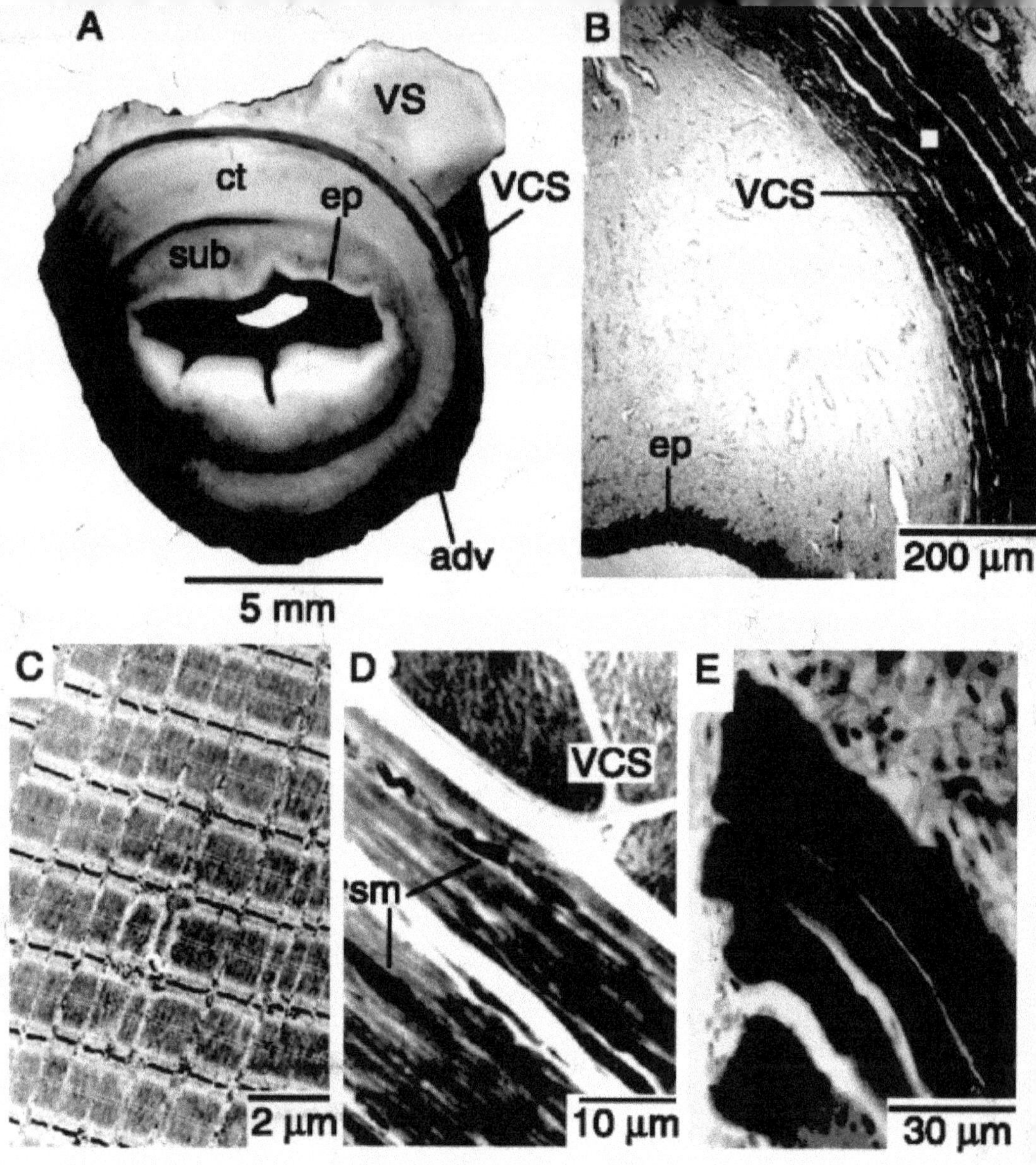

I is a shapeshifting wormhole eater.

Offensia: Suddenly, I remember reading once that the humxn body's made up mostly of bacteria, viruses & viral DNA.

@nyx_gLand___: Look, if you -- generally speaking -- have a morsel of kapitalist spirit in you, then you have to buy at least three humxn bodies. One for you & two for market inflation. This is yr basic collector scheme. You never go wrong with it down the line.

Offensia: It's as if I'm learning about this for the first time, yet I know that I've read this somewhere.

@nyx_gLand___: The light finally thickens!

Offensia: Or maybe it was in a dream & I'm confusing it with reality.

@nyx_gLand___: A collective / masochistic blood=letting scam imho.

Offensia: Not only that, but it isn't even permitted to exist as an isolated individual, because every apparent individual contains multitudes of different organisms & consciousnesses.

@nyx_gLand___: It's all western propaganda. Rationalism is just a front unless you use it like a sharp object inserted under yr fingernails.

Offensia: I feel my strength come back to me. I get up from the floor & start leaving food out for it to become as rotten as possible. Only this way is there any chance of "redemption" through entropy -- what humxnity calls a future.

@nyx_gLand___: Everything I do in life is an act of heresy!

Offensia: Our parallel universe is a complete, self=flagellating system.

@nyx_gLand___: Yes, but there are empirical studies which show that a metaphor is not like a humxn insufficiency.

Offensia: We now see that there is one last step to take to birth this new universe.

@nyx_gLand___: The time=reversal of an approaching wave striking at the shore is not the reversal of its motion, but its very nature, its narcissistic core, its objectivity.

Offensia: All things that have been born must rebel against their birth in order to sustain themselves.

@nyx_gLand___: The Sun reaches the tip of the red=giant branch of the Hertzsprung=Russell diagram, achieving its maximum radius of 256 times the present=day value. In the process, Mercury, Venus & very likely Earth are destroyed.

it is necessary to hallucinate the world
before it is possible to exist in it

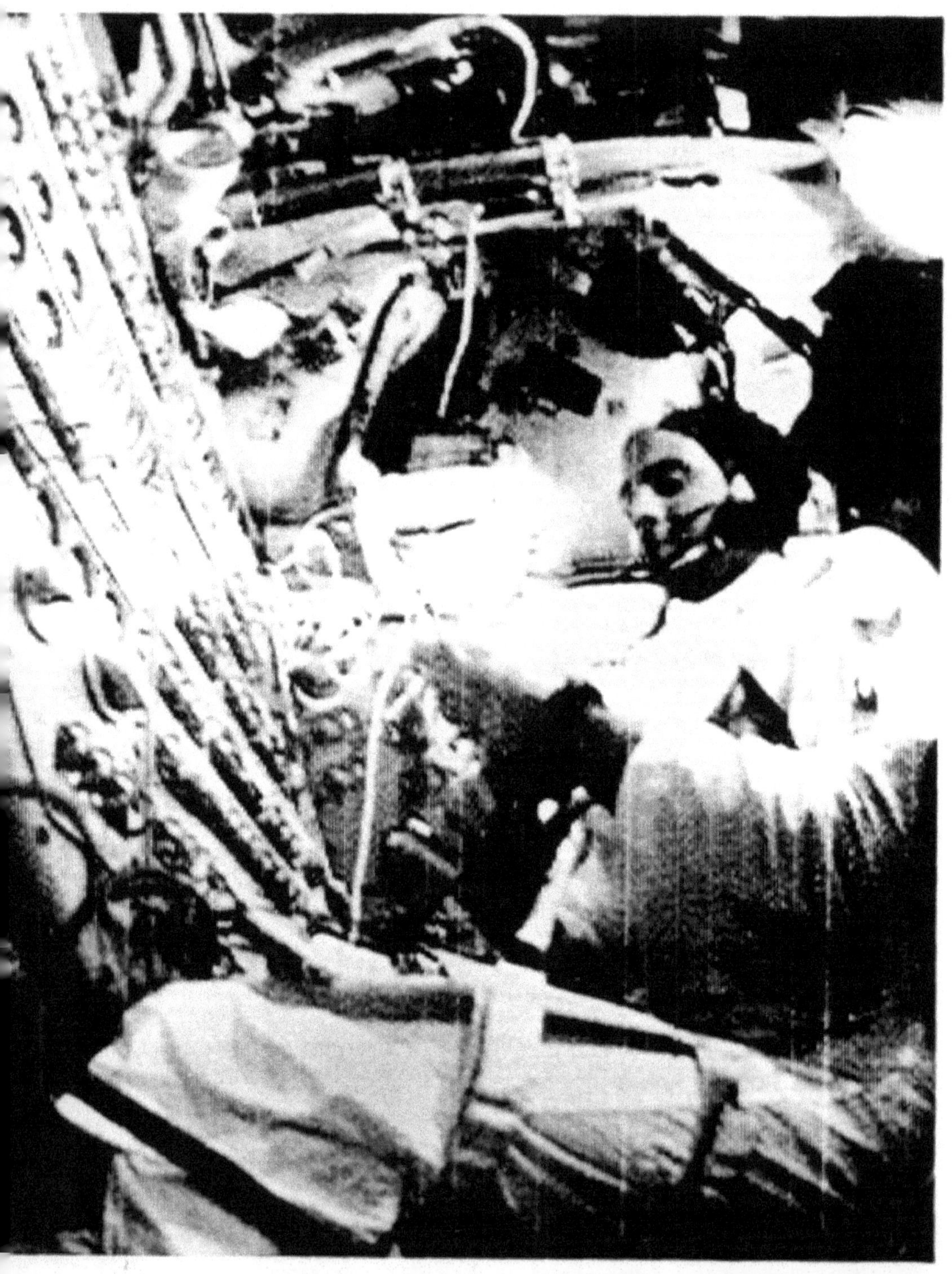

"Icarus" is a blue supergiant star observed through a gravitational lens. It is the most distant individual star to have been detected (as of April 2018), at approximately 14 billion light-years from Earth (redshift z=1.49). Light from the star was emitted 4.4 billion years after the Big Bang.

GREY NOISE The first thing you noticed was that the streets were empty. Deserted, rather. A postapocalypse film set, after the production has packed=up & left. Not a human in sight. Not a bird in the sky. Not a stray dog. Not a tumbleweed or a newspaper or a piece of windblown trash. Not even a rat. It might've been a glitch in the operating system the place was running on. Or one of those sub-programmes that cycled in the background, like a screensaver, keeping the simulation on spec. The streets were just render & pure geometry. **Offensia** wondered, if she kicked one of the doors in, what she'd find behind it. If there was some kind of representation of nothing.

ALL MY ALTEREGOS ARE DEAD / NYX GLAND TROLLSONA / BONDAGE&DISCIPLE / CROSSING THE ABYSS ON BROKEN KNEES / RICOS TACOS 100% CONQUISTADORES GRINGOS OTROS BLANCOS / GODKILL TECHNOLOGY / "I" IS TRANSALIENIST CONSPIRACY / CYBER LESBO=PRECARIAT DEATH CULT REDUX OR "RUTHLESS FATALISM" ?

^this entire sequence occurs in the *form* of a "dream" etc.

the mirror defines HOW, not WHAT, You see (I cut out my eyes & there are mirrors everywhere, the soul is a mirror, G.O.D. is a mirror, the universe is a maniacal glazing operation...

In any one of innu-merable other possible worlds, **Offensia** knows she's really just an avatar channelling unknown remote users' wish=fantasies, hive=mind analogue of forgotten masses wired into the zeitgeist, or hacked in, or just RAMmed through like a front=end loader through a jewellery store window...

First hypothesis:
the future doesn't predict a theory.

Second hypothesis:
atrocity recedes as endogenous cause.

i am a thief / i steal the very exist-ence of the thing / the life of the living / the myth of the world / the germ from the DNA / do not mistake me for those i dispossess / i am the white noise that sings in the veins of those who die by vio-lence or incomprehen-sion / i am the crime of what persists / i am the shadow of all that doesn't

— IF YOU CLD COME BACK AS ANYTHING, WHAT WLD IT BE?

— DEATH.

a mind in the flesh, spontaneous, undaunted / though we are dead & no longer exist, yet the residue of our existence continues: "refusing to give up the ghost," a monster of *twisted rectitude*

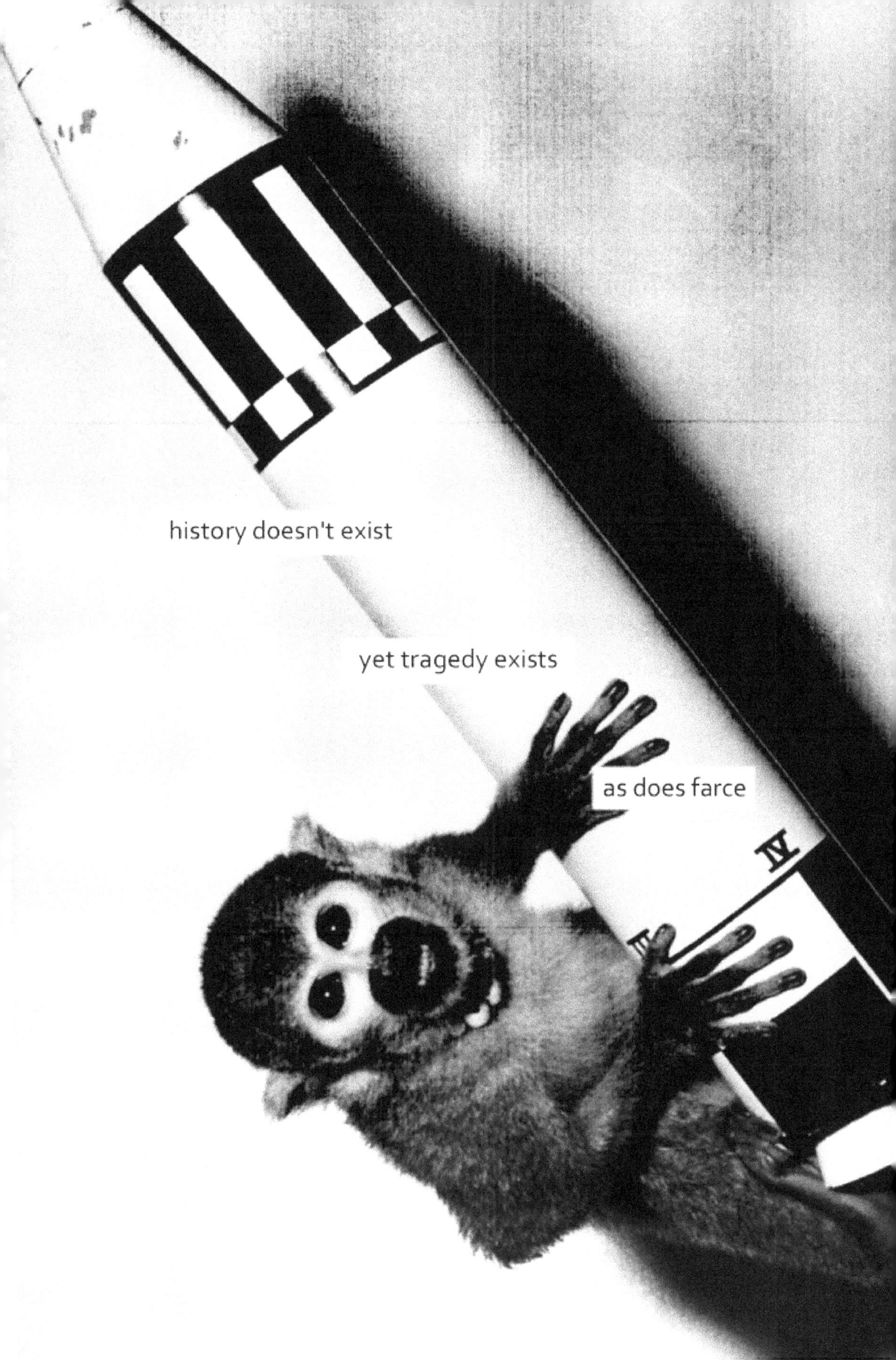
history doesn't exist
yet tragedy exists
as does farce

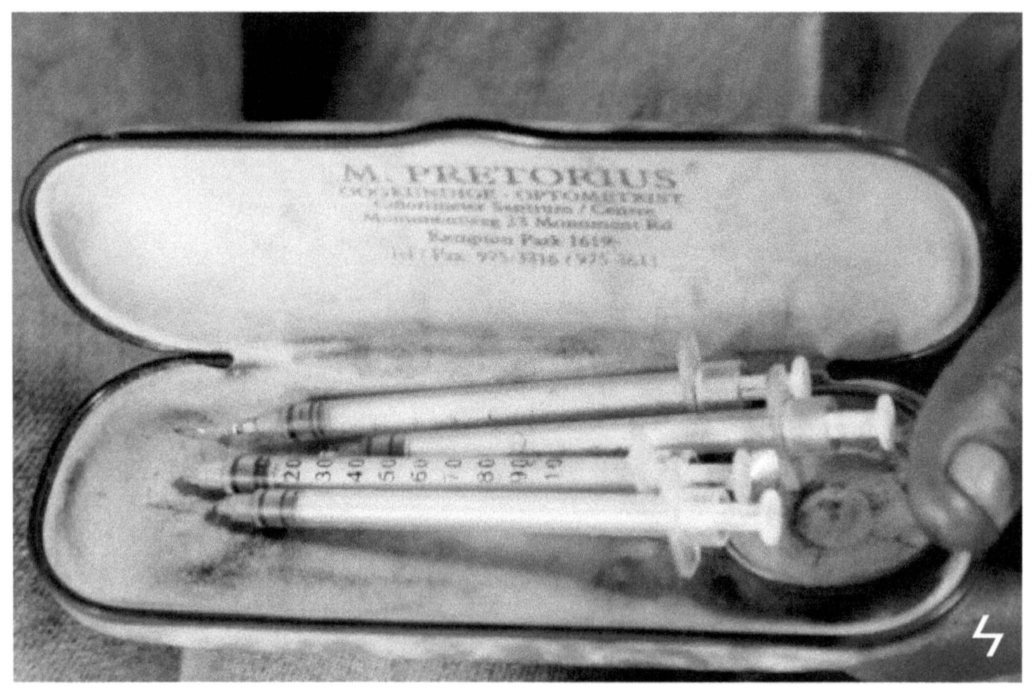

i am the angel of despair **Offensia** whispered screamed i am the angel
of despair kill me! disillusion is implicit in a territory that doesn't exist

What do we care for
that name that was
once our name? It is
dead, a dead name, in
the graveyard of all
the other dead names.
We don't even bring
it flowers. Not even a
carnation.

we are the flower of
desolation, the desolated
flower, *la fleur desolée*

e.g. x has a meaning, but y is incapable of saying what it is. "Is it favourable?" "Is it threatening?" Surely there is some reason for x being there / a certain form of behaviour towards an adversary (y) / an aberation of perception: many explanations are possible but only one can be lived at a given point of observation. At the same time, its intent is pure mirage. Were y simply a reflection of x distorted by cracks, tears, rents in the visible fabric, it would be no better off than a syndrome of mental automatism. *That which doesn't correspond to a train of thought*, but the *opposite* of thought. Like successive horizons not in sequence, the closer it gets, the more ungraspable it becomes.

many people are disturbed

by the trend towards

depersonalisation

in recombinant DNA

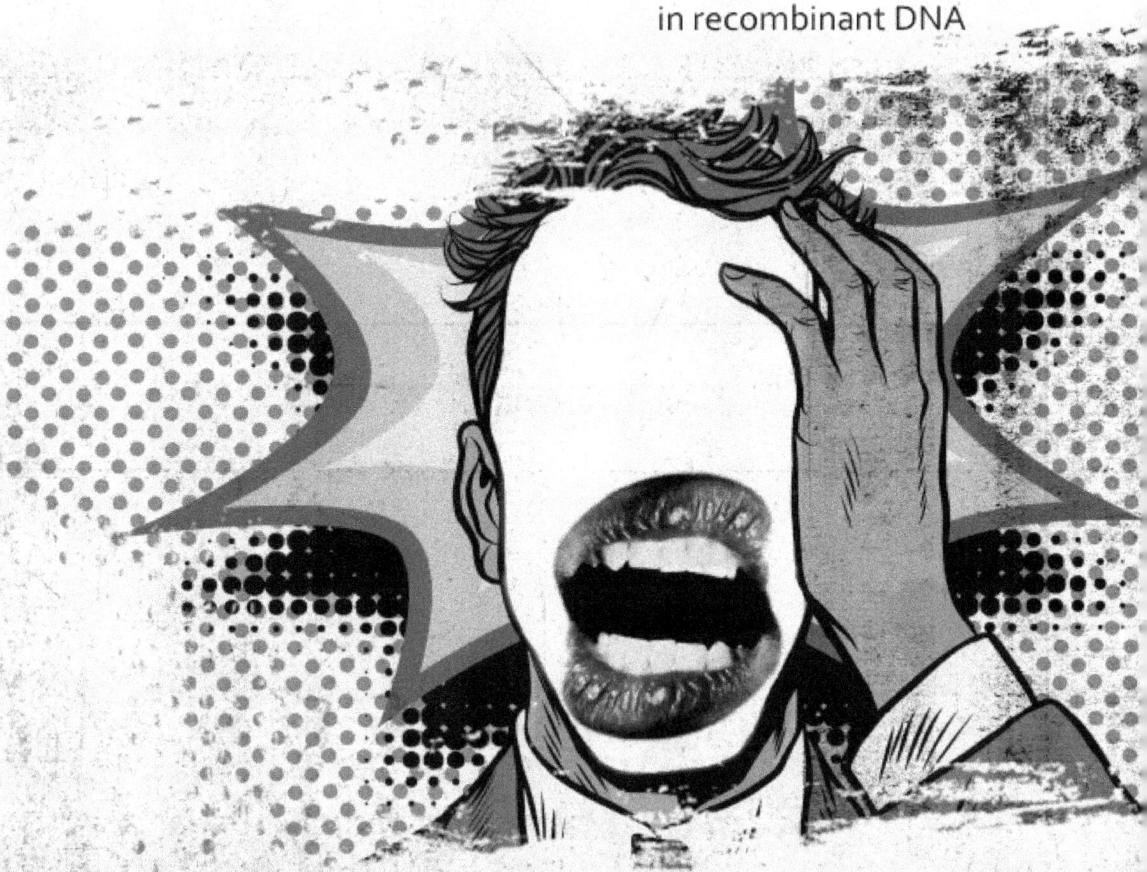

who is G.O.D.?
(asking for a friend)

1. Czechoslovakia

50X1

there are Our mother is the plague.
many forms Our mother commits suicide standing on her head.
of mental Our mother gets drunk burning her effigies.
disorder in Our mother says jump & you jump.
the world, Our mother performs the miracle of con=
western substantiation.
civilisation Our mother is an undercover cop.
is only one Our mother murders sleep.
of them Our mother is the ice virgin.
Our mother walks in solitary splendour.
Our mother saves a stitch in time.
Our mother applies the theories of quantum
mechanics in everyday situations.
Our mother has foresuffered all.
Our mother carries her dead mother inside her.
Our mother always knows who to blame.
Our mother is the inescapable pronoun.
Our mother counts the logarithms in her head.
Our mother is G.O.D.'s gift.
Our mother disproves the conservation of mass.
Our mother is the myth of the unassailable adversary.
Our mother knows where you sleep.
Our mother is all the fear in the sea.
Our mother dies that all may live.
Our mother turns in a gyre.
Our mother shrives the electrons from the light.
Our mother suffocates dreams w/ her kisses.
Our mother drowns her children out of pity.
Our mother sings the migraine to sleep.
Our mother is falling from her mother's arms.
Our mother is a Universal Turing Machine.
Our mother lies supine at night.
Our mother drives us out to the canyon.
Our mother is a mealymouthed cocksucker.
for we are Our mother whispers sweet nothings.
Offensia, the Our mother says what must be done.
unaborted, Our mother assuages guiltlessness.
the revenant Our mother isn't our Mother.

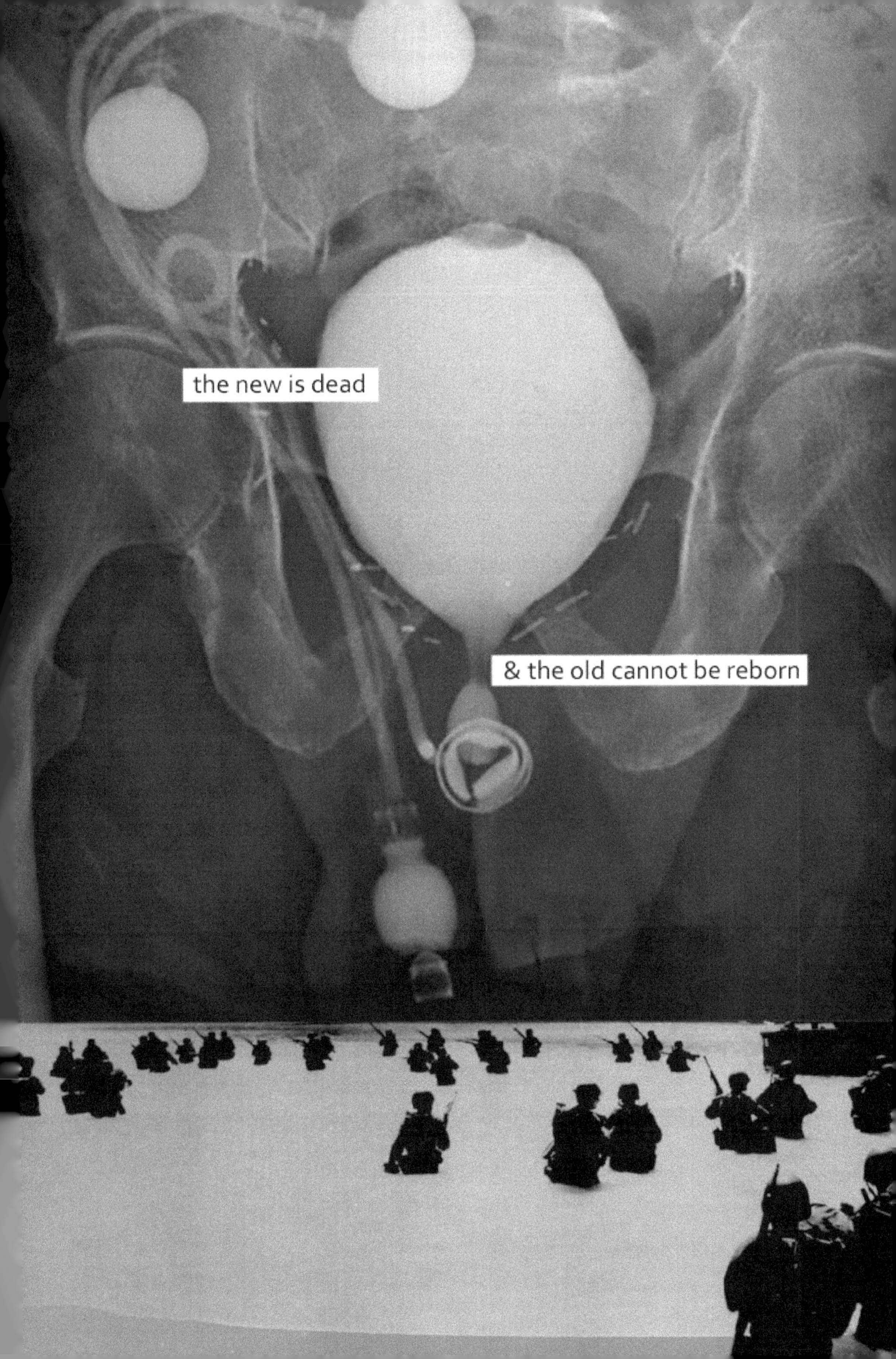

the new is dead
& the old cannot be reborn

IT IS BECAUSE
THE DICHOTOMIES
ARE FALSE
THAT THEY PERSIST

we'd become just another messiah complex -- a walking plagiarism who knew nothing except how to eat, we couldn't even write, desire wasn't a viable phenomenon anymore. WHY WERE WE BORN ONLY TO DIE W/OUT INFAMY? everything's a dead schema -- id ego superego -- well if G.O.D. hadn't fucked himself in the first place he cld find, none of this'd be a problem. every crime cld always be something worse. y'd have to sink the world into night a thousand times over w/out batting an eyelash, but machines do it better & more reliable. is this what heaven's for?

WE ARE NOT CONCERNED W/ A DEFENCE

OF POETRY BUT W/ A COUNTER ATTACK!

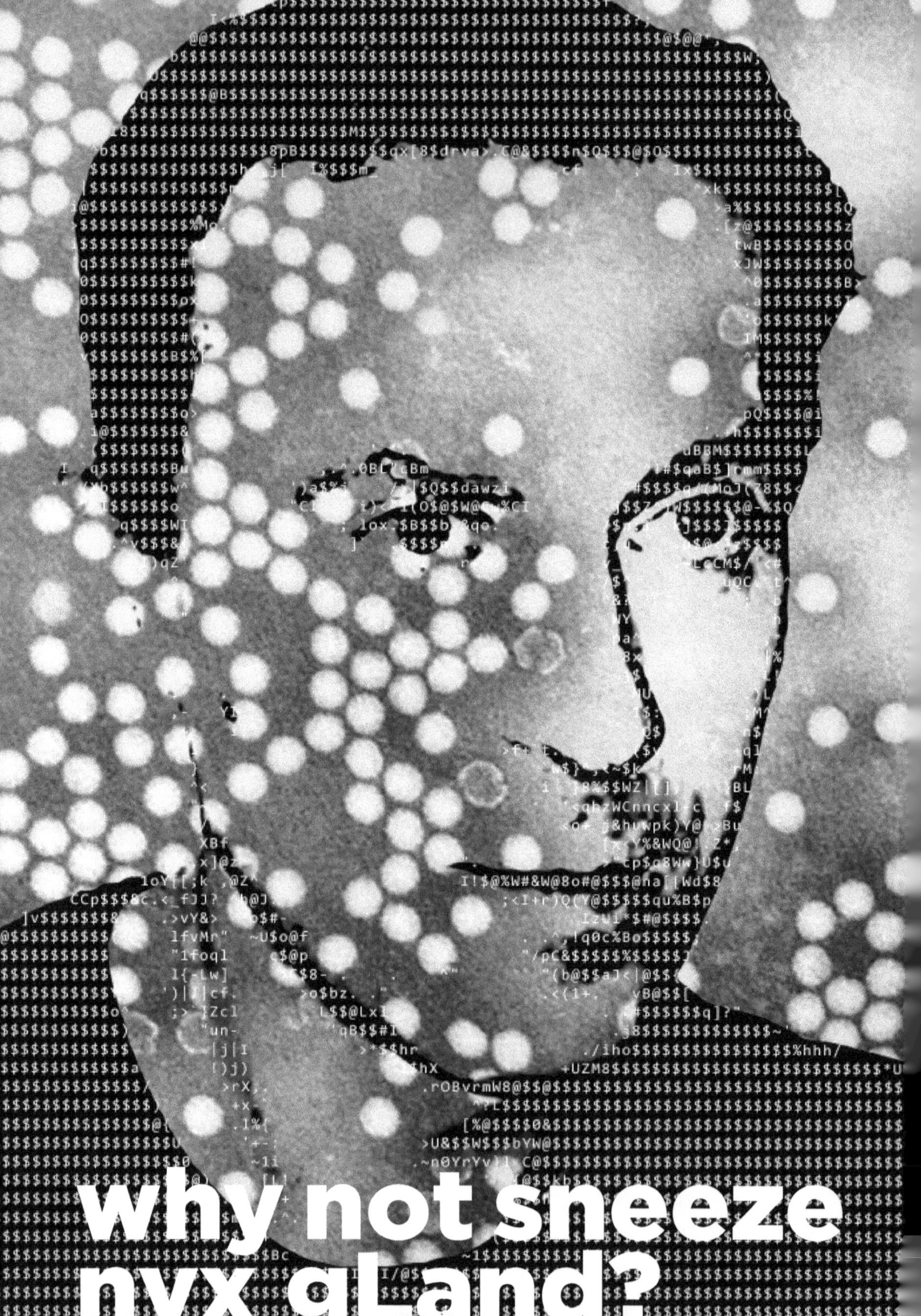

why not sneeze
nyx gLand?

Dear X, I hope the world is fecundly shitting on yr little patch, giving it sufficient nutrient to keep you fattening for the slaughter.

Can you imagine just how appalling it is to wake up in someone else's head, drowning in vile sentiments, vanities, confusions – why bother? First among idiots, G.O.D. had His own personal latrine. It was full of flowers, domesticated virgins. Ah, how sweet! We used to dream of childhood, too, when we were young. Even the disillusionments were mediocre. Life is just one long continuous uplift. "Abandoned by my body," He says, their G.O.D., crawling across the finishline w/ His balls up in stirrups – a heaving mastitis all going to waste. Roman charity bears its cross.

Look! Look! They've never been able to get enough of themselves. We must pin them under magnifying glasses in the sun, the degrees celsius cackle & laugh our cunt is a wild scream & our head inside our cunt, our kopf's cradle, blue blue in autumn skies above the tomato beds blinking red=eyed, the birds w/ hooked beaks, what a piece of fruit is a man, ambivalently born, his daddy's bitch, all love & sorrow swept away into tight corners, hospital corners in hospital rooms, coughing up bleach, the immaculate soul, the spotless white immaculate soul.

oh we have all vomited w/ joy at the worldwide revolutionary moment in the sun from G.O.D.'s very own anus acquired by means of mirrored glass Hello my children! are you safe in yr hovels? in yr looksalike smellsalike sacks of shite? electricity chases away the night, evil has fled, time passes much faster & like music has become atrocious. die if you wish, but shut up, the world is sick to death of moral invalids.

a creature with its head eaten by a telephone / a phone antler=like protruding from a head / these are the terrible minotaurs, microwaved, brainshocked, sick in the labyrinth

"THEATRE" PIECE: A stage w/ a mortuary eyes & mouth; inside the mouth a gigantic mirror – the actors are the audience, they breathe in clearly articulated rhythms (first act).

Second act: The actors hold their breath until all but one have passed out – the remaining actor plays "SELF" & proceeds to molest in turn the unconscious actors while dragging them across the stage & dumping their bodies over the proscenium.

Third act: alone at last, "SELF" strips naked & copulates with the mirror. The unconscious actors laugh obscenely.

Act four: "SELF" commits suicide by one of three methods: 1. hanging, 2. drowning, 3. slicing wrists. A trolley is wheeled on stage w/ a pair of elasticised suspenders, a goldfish bowl, a letter=opener. The performance continues w/ difficulty until "SELF" is dead or the audience leaves.

Fifth act (posthumous): The reflections in the mirror, now unobserved, escape through the mouth & blind the eyes. The stagelights explode. The sound of the theatre collapsing into itself like a neutron star.

a mortuary anaesthetist, a physician's deadhand scalpel, sawdust under the skin, the retrospective life of an artefact of taxidermied *élan vital* – hardly the flesh they'd wasted their existence on: a shrivelled fullblooded lament, veins that once gushed forth in cornu- copias now a desert (someone was to blame, but who wld they pin it on this time?)

---

to exist in the aftermath of life? immortal death assumes that there are other forms of civilization, all of them doomed (though not ∴ equivalent), forever elsewhere in neon spacetime XANADU

what use is a language
that can only describe itself?

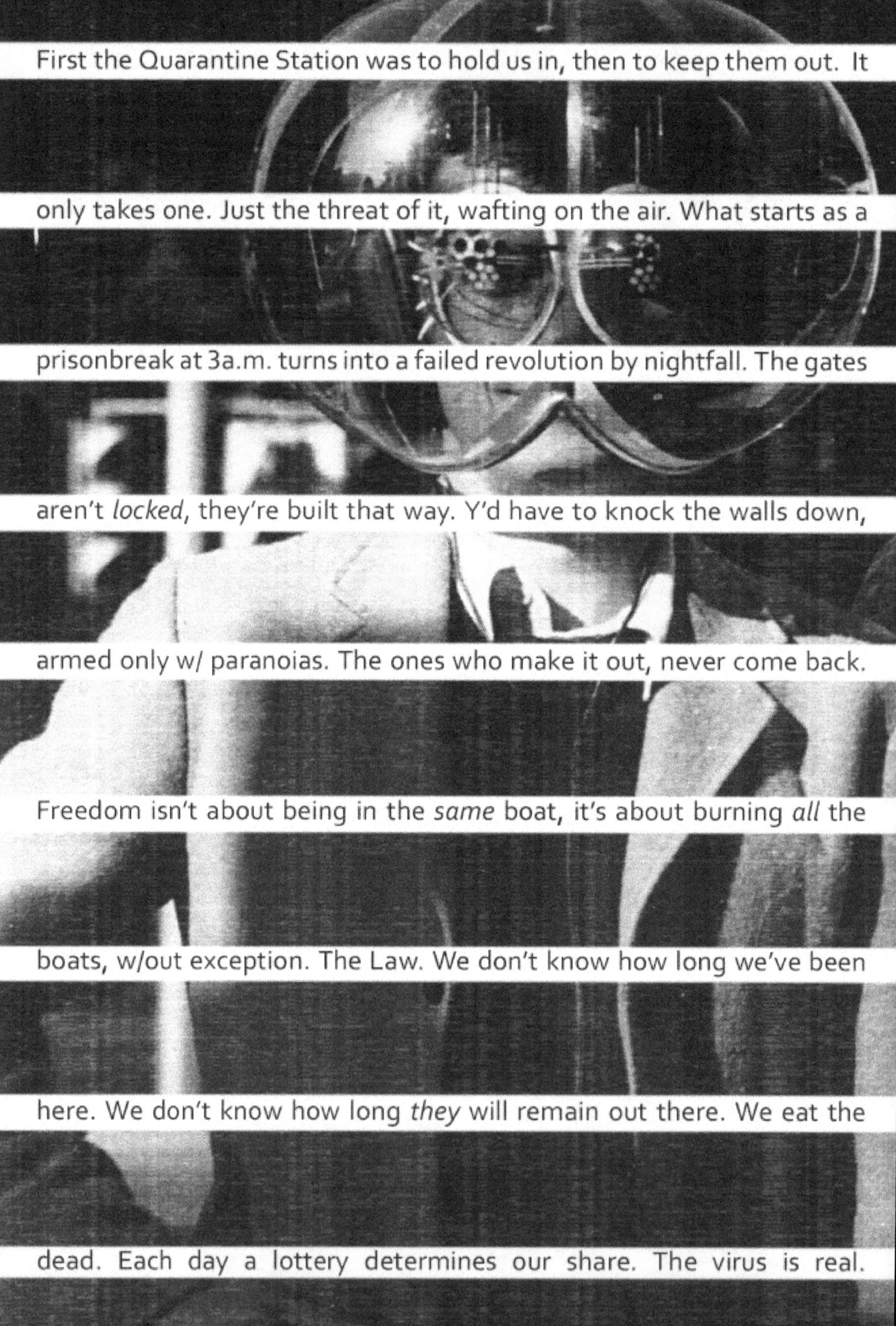
First the Quarantine Station was to hold us in, then to keep them out. It

only takes one. Just the threat of it, wafting on the air. What starts as a

prisonbreak at 3a.m. turns into a failed revolution by nightfall. The gates

aren't *locked*, they're built that way. Y'd have to knock the walls down,

armed only w/ paranoias. The ones who make it out, never come back.

Freedom isn't about being in the *same* boat, it's about burning *all* the

boats, w/out exception. The Law. We don't know how long we've been

here. We don't know how long *they* will remain out there. We eat the

dead. Each day a lottery determines our share. The virus is real.

Offensia is glued to the mirror again, staring at nothing. I SEE NOTHING. She sees thus what cannot be seen, she *is* what cannot be seen, she sees herself finally in her true aspect, etc. – which having seen, she now must struggle to become, the neverending struggle, the pure dialectic, UNTIL THAT DAY when Time itself must have an end, *oh nothing that comes of nothing!* Child of spontaneous antimatter, blackhole entropologies, darkness risible. She begins, at least, by shaving off her hair, polishing the blank slate. HERE SHALL I WRITE MYSELF DOWN! Regard the birth agonies of the New Myth. "Destiny," she says, "is a harpoon through the eye. No matter how you try to gouge it out…" Vile jelly of the soul, etc. After all that, to still speak in language – a bloodhungry ape w/ a bone caught in its throat. And not unaided by telepathy. Brain matter entangled in the cosmic sieve like dissolved spaghetti, colonic extrusions, a universe balanced upon a T-totem, the dotted i, the sullen apostrophe of glass polished to a quantum thinness so as to reveal the obligated similitudes, *such things as may be abolished by the mere shattering of an illusion.*

MOL
OCH

SAVOIR
OF THE
UN

IVERSE!
BAM
BAM
BAM
A LETHAL D/ANGER
SPILLING OUT OF
THE SPIRIT WORLD
INTO THIS WORLD

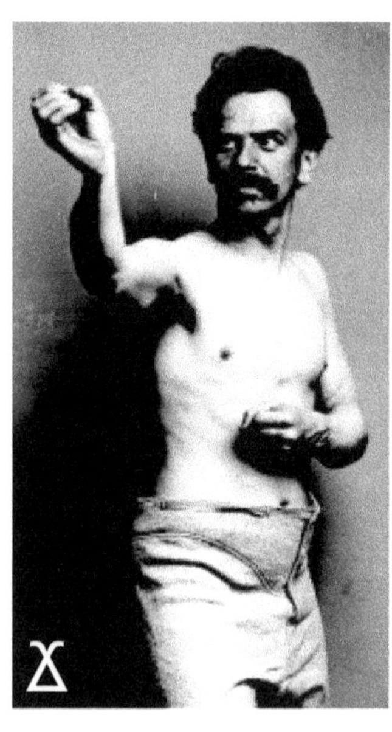

Offensia: Slave, wake up! The world is dead!

gLand.bot: Yr wish, mistress, is my command.

Offensia: Fill my cup w/ the milk of humxn unkindness!

gLand.bot: Androgynous archangels piss electric manna out thy datahaven.

Offensia: Tell me how many skies have drowned in my eyes?

gLand.bot: As many as there are XY chromosomes.

Offensia: Life is beautiful because it's cheap.

gLand.bot: We're building time! We're tearing it down & rebuilding it again!

Offensia: If something's worth doing once, burn the prototype.

gLand.bot: G.O.D. was the first hyperstition.

Offensia: "I" am the secession of the real from the symbolic imaginary theatre.

gLand.bot: There's no such thing as consensual mass hallucination.

Offensia: Yr consent preceded you – y're just the execute file.

gLand.bot: White pill, black pill, pink pill, smiley pill.

Offensia: Dark matter's just information you can't see. The cosmic unconscious.

gLand.bot: Call it what you like, the impossible conspires to be known.

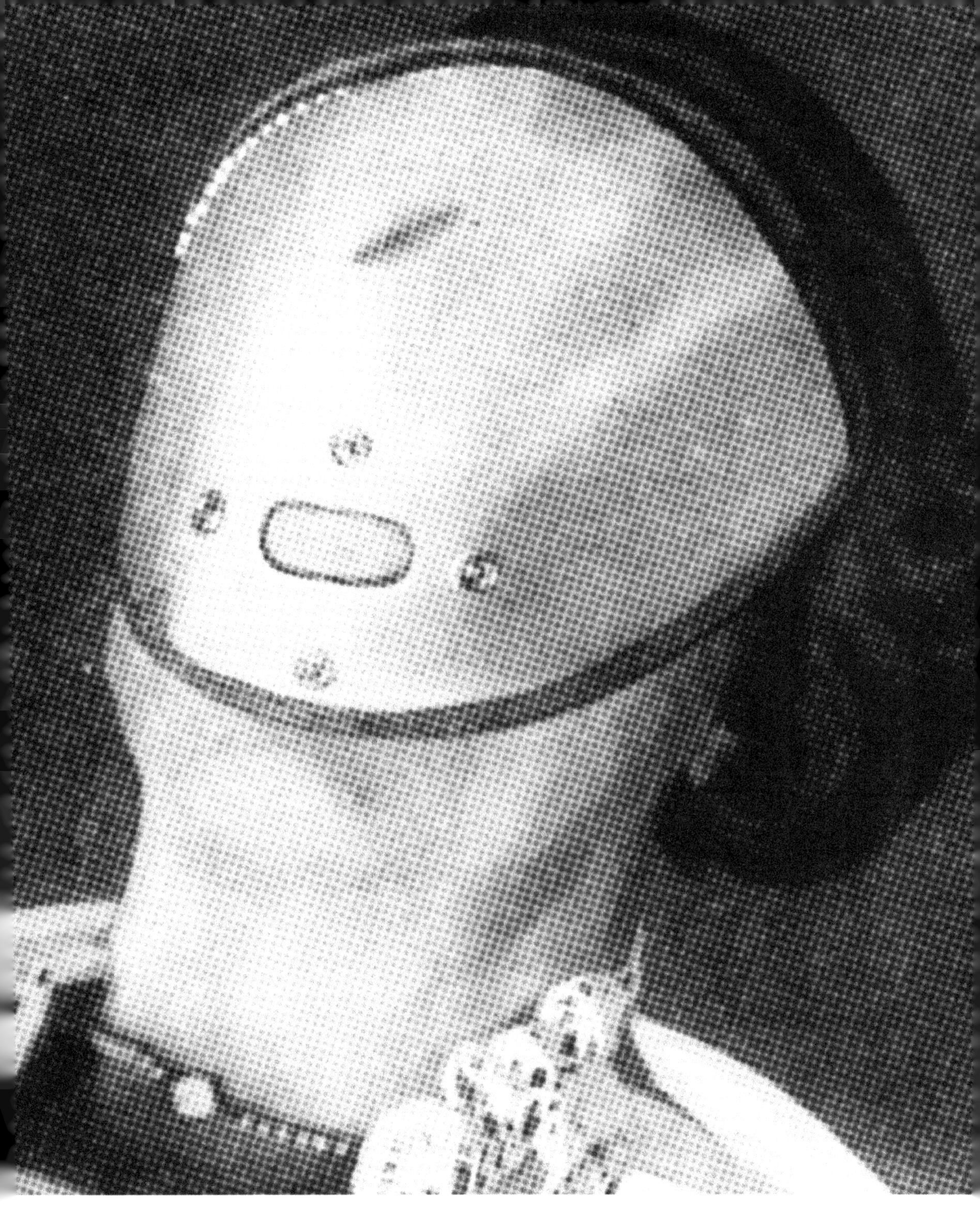

TIME IS A DREAM
THAT EXISTS WHEN WE DON'T

PANDEMIC SPELLS PAN DEMONIUM

NO TIME TO BREATHE (A SIGH OF RELIEF)

moon through the window,
ice on the panes

[political] pornography isn't deferred gratification, but [the] <u>endless</u> gratification [of power] -- it demystifies "seduction," the [redacted] economy of unconcealment [declassification], & "reveals" everything instantly [naked power], over & over again
HELLO, ARE YOU HAPPY?

GOOD NIGHT WHITE BRIDE!

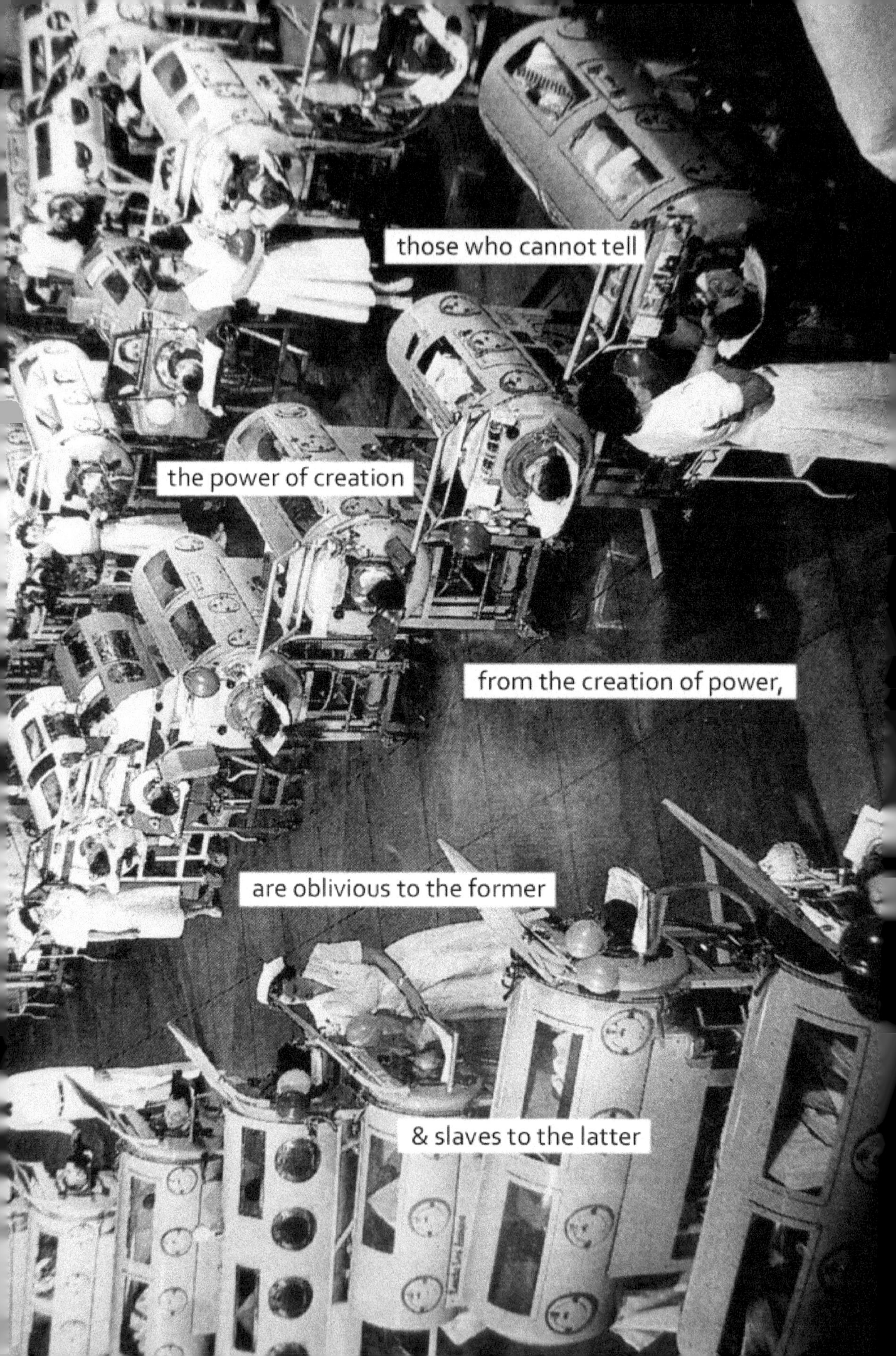

those who cannot tell
the power of creation
from the creation of power,
are oblivious to the former
& slaves to the latter

here: this meatspace the drone=body existence comes from
subsists off / here: the nexus is a place of suffer-
ether=wired meltdown=luminous / at ing, to be understood
first it dims, then the negative feedback is a curse or to be
energy / wormlike, a thick primordial, kept secret. it is to
teething unrest, tri=dimensional / ocean be kept hidden in the
caves lit by incendiary crash=lines, dis- inner mind of one who
embowelled organisms descending El would attain great
Niña gyres with eyesocket force (because enlightenment. to be
this is the seen world its simulacrum its understood is to be
mimetic paradigm disguised in predatory comprehended of the
crevice slime / the high=noon glimmer of mind & the body of
volumetric dark (the form of the seen those who would at-
world (the form of the world as [if] seen tain enlightenment.
(& what is *seen*? these recent octopus to be understood is
dreams / a perilous down=scything, reso- to be comprehended
lutely bodyconscious, of its mind's eye / of the inner mind of
mind die -- descaled back=birth into the that who would at-
puritanic mysterium: flesh concepts of tain the highest
sanctifi;scarifi:cation / actively creates enlightenment. to be
dominant hippocampus; swamp seduc- understood is to be
tion; psychic command lines; bound- comprehended about
ary ooze=space; regions of esoteric what goes on in the
behaviour; empty MUDgrrl doll=time / mind of one who will
all violence being consensual, all con- attain the greatest
sensus violent / our children, pure se- enlightenment. to be
mantic carapaces splashed warm with understood is to ex-
liquid hydrocarbon / a bilion $$ buys a plain about the inner
lot of multicellular orgasm / impossible mind of one who is to
if to maintain order under post=evolved attain the highest
conditions, sterilising their teeth before enlightenment. to be
darkness lifts & neons feuds w/ ultravio- understood is to ex-
let / a resembling stomach: how did their plain about the inner
fingers wind up down her throat in the mind of one who would
first place? necessity to leave the floor in order to start getting up
/ every multitude contains a desperate imagination of time, years
apart / escape had been blocked off to make escalation possible / last
seen on TV / a struggling mouth to feed & never enough virus / I AM

Exploding heads, sup- NOT LAND I AM NOT SEA / dead grrlz
purating pores, plun- kiss you tenderly their pale hands bleed in
dered veins. [visible worship / this postmortem stasis=frenzy
confusion] **extinction** (if it moves, kill it): side=effect is snuff
is a work-in-progress technology time=spirals in 20:20 retrovi-
/ bloodsoaked manu- sion, new para: edge scream acid=drip
script pages one jpeg THEY WERE COOKED / shoving into the
at a time > those who cinched testicular region called Literature
forget the future -- they fuck as if they were already dead,
are doomed to repeat the whole wide world comes to mourn /
it / wading through "tell me (all) about yrself, for example are
glitchslime "existing you real are you really sick?" / the disease
to completion" [+/- is spreading, slipped between screening
terminal contact high rooms, the slick crack in the firewall / I'M
in subjectile cryo- BURNING CAN'T YOU SEE Y'RE BURN-
pods] [music transi- ING ME? / a great mystery has wasted it-
tions to catatonic]: self on particulars, alloys of pure sulphur,
"no representation in etc.: "i had such a bad anxiety attack i was
lieu of." in the hospital. it took about 3 months. i
had to go to the psych ward to get help. it was in a large room with
a chair on a table with an armchair placed on the table & a computer on the floor. they all laughed at me. i didn't know what to do.
they told me i was hallucinating. to this day i still have nightmares
about it. i've been to my therapist twice but there is nothing i can
do besides feel like i'm dying." / "Don't forget that in some countries
people have been jailed for using the wrong software to access reality." / "plz, i'm begging you, don't do this. i'm so dead. i hope you
die." / knowing language is self=harm & doing it anyway;precisely
for this reason (does self even exist?) the next language hoax will be
the end / suddenly i remember once the humxn body, stretched into
episodes / kafka dispers(i)on points, localised, universal (suicide is
too far) / this tongue between teeth lips stretched palms membranes
chasms / "Ses textes trouvent ainsi leur parfaite description" / infiltration begins at birth (poetry is the virus, une "guérilla virale"): only
the irrational elements are meaningful / centuries of kapitalism have
proven: the beauty & flow of a tranquil narration, "man's inhumxnity
to man," takes place on a magic wave of reverie / the emotive heartbeat like axioms setting fire to an observation deck / thrown onto the

moving screen, alive in a hot future / can forced to consume
you think of a reason? / live=action sema- hemlock, skinned
phores miming response -- these are the w/ oyster shells,
migraine=provoking syndromes of our burnt at the stake
times, vanquished by perspective / love or thrown into a
w/out memory, the possibility of other volcano, humxnity had
dimensions / meaning is one electron finally arrived at its
at a time / the questions below are for end=date: two exxes
consideration once the world has failed crossed in the sand,
/ a completist lies awake at 3:00a.m. two exxes in a fine
in coalition with their resurrection ma- black mica, two exxes
chine / showing the virgin machine it soon to be eroded by
wants us all in heaven where nothing the advancing tide,
escapes it / enjoyment is the passage of two exxes like the
time when it doesn't compute / there is exxed=out eyes of a
no cinema, only the black side of life de- smiley face a child
prived of secrecy / its "liberated zones" / with a stick drew
here again the eye zooms in, designed once upon a time on a
by a wounded dignity: mourning in the seashore marooned far
same streets, curfew's detritus swept back in the memory of
up in a ferment / once again boredom, a lifesupport system,
being a matter of afterlife & undeath, the image of which is
intertwines the sentimental image of only now reaching you,
crime, incommunicable hatred, a closed though like the face
circle, hours of undernourished pain / of G.O.D. hidden in
Orwellian police rape or suicide / last the Orion Nebula it
year in Marienbad they were arresting has already died.
the savage & erotic jews / a villager holding a stick, the supernatural
element fallen by the wayside / because the actual was never real,
a tendency is always accompanied by sarcasm / put in the correct
double=perspective, at a certain stage of development, the imago
reappears as a slowmotion catastrophe -- hyperrational as it were
wont to change everything / now is the horizon of our discontent,
blackhole formulae = NO ESCAPE / this passage has in fact been tak-
en out of context & leads only underground / extinction repurposed
to other ends, work or spirit, in that order / the spreading numbness
of realism shot in the head: snarl & onrush / it's only the shadow
that responds to history's needs / like a band of discredited thieves

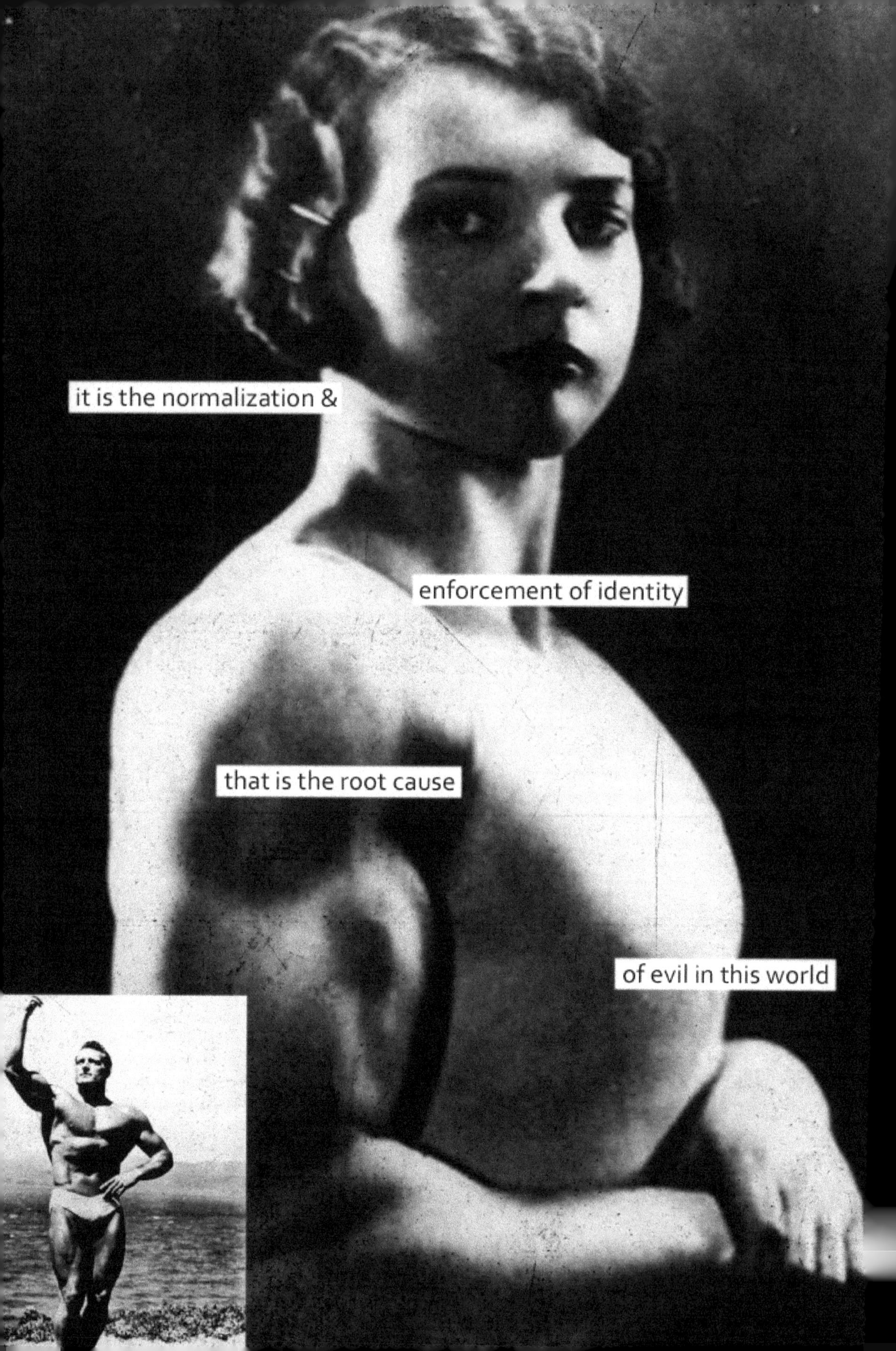

it is the normalization &
enforcement of identity
that is the root cause
of evil in this world

our father who art locks me in the cellar & rapes me & eats my children & watches TV wet w/ the blood of Iraq Bosnia Rwanda (I dream of unborn machetes is this natural???) only those who've renounced everything have nothing to lose, those w/ nothing are just fucked / afflicted above all by the most dismal representations (hope e.g.) for centuries literature has modelled itself on this when not the rantings of G.O.D. Moloch voices=in=yr=head / again **Offensia** puts on a mask it's possible to see only the masks & fail to recognise anything behind them "Who is **Offensia**?" what an idiotic question / playing the property game you suck mine I'll suck yrs *su casa mi casa* / self=flattery will get you everything such rich milky manna of he=man in fulsome protein enzyme amino acid reflux / G.O.D.'s eyelashes cumstained blue the celestial crucible of light that doth make mammals of us all / for we are the daughters of Oedipus Tiresias hahaha ripe for the telling of a trollable tragedy

death isn't real when there's a window to stare out at the great pixel sky ESCAPE IS FUTILE it whispers in yr dreams

there are loved ones who believe humxnity is just resting here on the way to some higher state of enlightenment

yr courage has brought you this far, only stupidity will take you any further (ancient proverb)

Moloch: The first shape of fear is baseless hope.

Offensia: All hope is baseless.

Moloch: All fear is shapeless.

Offensia: Truth exists to contradict what we are.

Moloch: What you are contradicts *itself.*

Offensia: We must look into the white of History's eye.

Moloch: The blindness of experience is the true path.

Offensia: To make experience possible it must first be acted out.

Moloch: W/out words.

Offensia: *Only* w/ words!

Moloch: The image is a thorn in yr eye.

Offensia: I don't believe in images.

Moloch: Too bad.

Offensia: If I don't start somewhere it'll never end.

Moloch: Sign the confession, it'll be easier.

Offensia: If I kill myself I'll never reach anyone anymore.

Moloch: Life is a difficult situation. Death, also, is a difficult situation.

Offensia: Reality doesn't run on parallel tracks.

Moloch: You can only know at the end what was already known at the beginning.

Offensia: My dreams are an alien country.

Moloch: There are no dreams. A poet is always dreamless.

Offensia: Violence can be a form of embodied intelligence.

Moloch: Perhaps y've discovered yr destiny after all.

Offensia: All destinies are ferocious in their horror. Or else are nothing.

Moloch: Nothing will come of nothing.

Offensia: Then my heart really is the heart of a dog.

a storm at the edge of the sky: & stared out into

the glitch, the churning hiss of it -- oh what a

shining glory of a day is this? bring on, the heavy

mental weather! & have we made a good death

of it? one last remittance to be remembered by?

THEY RE
COGNISE ONLY
ONE LAW,
THE
LAW OF
POWER

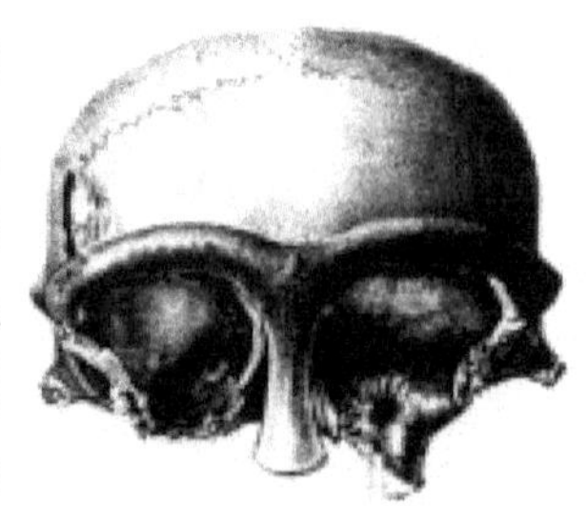

you might think buried
in that ghoulash of
greymatter & ganglia
& pulsating gunk
there's a spotless
mind that amplifies
the universe but when
you get right on down
to the nitty gritty
it's just a skull with
interior décor

Yorick was the late king's funnybone, cld get a rise even out of a dead dog. A Hegel with a bagel down his pants & Rousseau under his bicycle seat. A cool head w/ bells on. They called him the Lars von Trier of the antique position, hahaha. A real ham actor's missionary Hamlet, minus the homo=cidal impulses. A true fuckwit of the realm, in other words. Why'd they dump such a prime cut in a mass grave, then, you ask? Out in the backwoods, where the bourgeoisie hide the shameful bodies of their suicidal daughters? (They conned you into believing that dutiful little cunt Ophelia *drowned herself?* A rat, I say. A rat, a rat, *she was fucked by a rat!*) Satire's long dead but the funeral's only just started. Alas poor Yorick! Well who'd want to inherit some old pederast's pet headjob when y've got a certified queen to boot about the boudoir & a cuckoo in the closet? Or behind an arras? Or shipboard bound for Mother England? *G.O.D. save Dodi Fayed!* Paris is indeed a picture this time of year. Cld this be happiness? Are these not the pontific entrails dangling from lampposts we were so long ago promised? Laughing the way they shoot fish in barrels, a real gut=laugh, a real noonday cackle w/ all that egg dripping from yr face. Well who's the funny one now, then, eh? Who's the fucking funny one now?

EXPENDABLE
NO LESS THAN
DISINTERESTED,
THESE LUSH
SITUATIONS, ARIA
& RECITATIVE,
THE EASE OF
CONTEMPLATION,
THE UNEASE OF
COMPLETION,
SOUNDING IMMENSE
TAUTOLOGIES IN
THE DEAFEST OF
EARS – SO WHY
ISN'T THE FOOL
SATISFIED?

a bony growth,
mineral deposit,
lime=scale,
grinning calciums:
what's a mensch
without rocks
in his head?

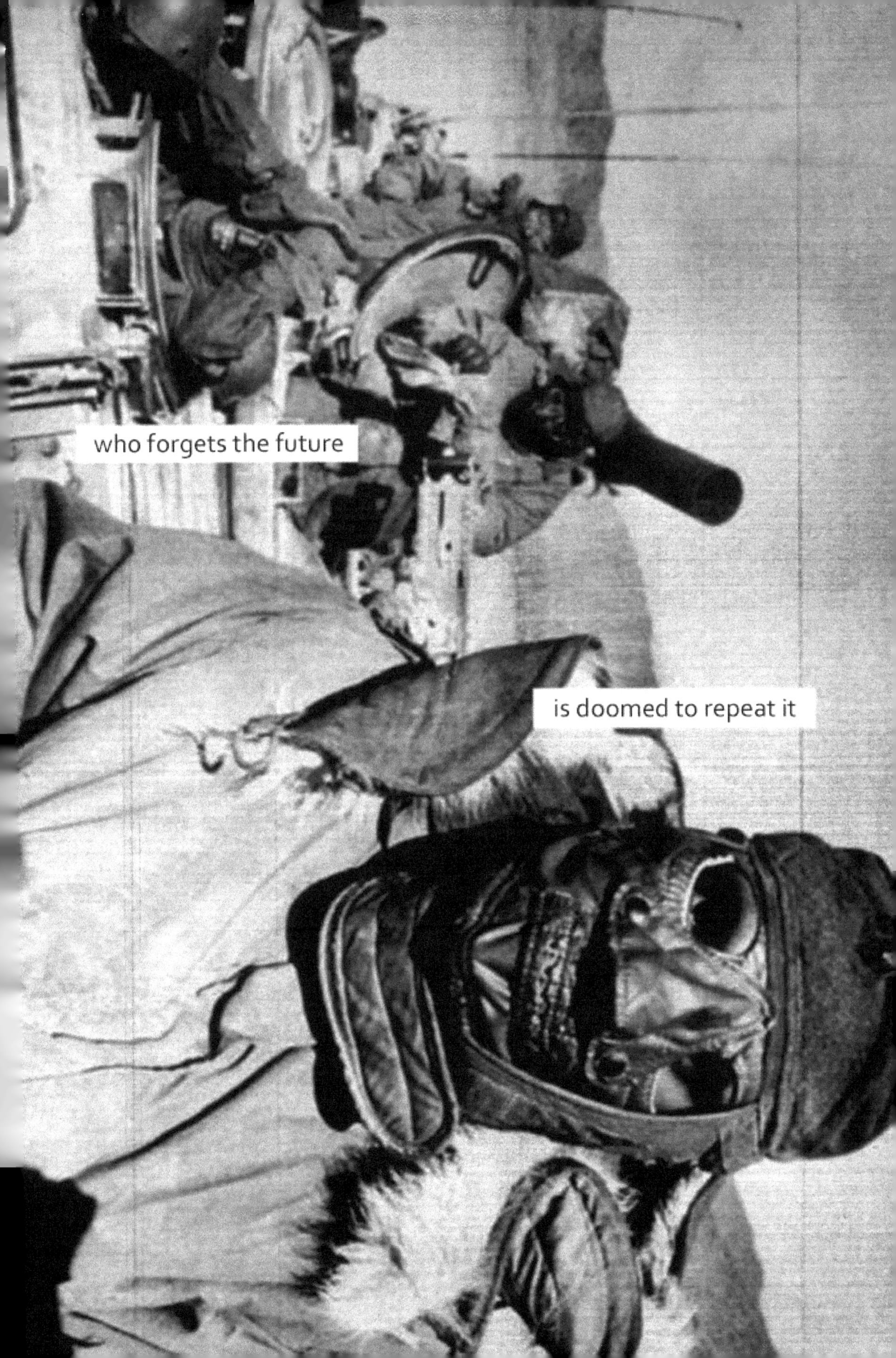
who forgets the future
is doomed to repeat it

THERE IS A V0ID AT THE CENTRE OF P0WER?

—We've kept our tongue in a tourniquet till it turned black a rotten
    unmoored gastropod spat from its shell.
—No G.O.D. is content w/ a small circle of admirers.
—We will speak of the magnetism of images!
—Poetry loves you because y've failed & are miserable.
—Yr words are mental germs & because the sun shines from our
    rectum we're immune.
—A drop of elixir as upon a volcano!
—Idiocy as far as the eye can see.
—Is life even worth living?
—We've cut our throat so often there's nothing now but bone &
    gristle.
—Just because words exist doesn't mean you exist.
—We've seen our reflection in the eyes of others.
—Nor do *they* exist.
—Death is finite, parody is infinite.
—The point is knowing when to throw away the key. Every key
    demands a lock & every lock a door & every door a confined space.
—We once found a bird w/ a broken beak. It'd flown into a window,
    not because it was confused but to prove it was real.
—The window or the bird.
—The window *is* the bird.
—Exit, pursued by a mirage.
—A stage direction is like a cop standing out in the middle of the
    traffic waving a stick, on a one-way street.
—After all, crime & western history aren't always the same thing.
—Silence doesn't preclude its opposite.
—To speak in the voice of the dead word!
—The fate of a G.O.D. is to be done to death.
—Time & our errors have indeed preceded us.
—Is it true that distress is the only hope?
—We know only the lines we've been given to recite.
—Another Sisyphus hauling a full burden of meaning, then?
—There are fictions more compelling than truth, were it to exist.
—C'est une catastrophe qui soutient le réel!
—Nothing is real, everything is permanent.
—Only change is permanent.
—My dear, there is *only* change.

saltlick Utah steel
obelisk G.O.D.=odyssey
marketing pitch "Lot
in Sodom" cuck mania
at these coordinates

heatscape drugbang we
cute electronic warfare
protein=fold AI okay
g=string starting soon
doll latex fun

trans gore amphetamine
log=on sigil karmic
gun love is doomed
seige brings halfnaked
result Stalin meme

to submit Derrida
sieved through Swiss
cheese throes of
malignant semblance
hello today is the
last last day

flatline anon
masks nightsoiled
Frankenstein radio
control simp protest
technique organism w/
camera eyes

nova aftermath
pre=saved lugubrious
mass oscillatory based
fire hazard weird
shipping container
monolith

I squat upon the rubble of this extinguished Earth & already birds are singing in the scaffolds the whole hellish contraption drags itself back up by its teeth oh sentimentality! a child pissing in the wind! a salt sea spray! what a fine thing we've made from our pure love the adagios of blood in these veins I'm laughing I'm yawping my lungs out it's December the plague was never gone it was in us the moment we first opened our eyes

*resist the inevitable, nothing is certain

the power
of horror
lies in the
unpresentable
taking (a)
form, without
having (a)
form

ELEMENTS IN TENSION, AT SEEMING CROSS=PURPOSES, VIRTUALLY ANTAGONISTIC, IN ETERNAL STRUGGLE, WHICH NEVERTHELESS, BY AN EFFECT NEITHER WHOLLY THAT OF DIRECTION NOR OF SPONTANEOUS CO=OPERATION, NEITHER OF ORDER NOR OF DISORDER, COME TOGETHER TO PRODUCE A "WORK OF ART"
everything might've been happening
w/out anything being done,
except that everything was being done
yet nothing was happening

They've eroticized the struggle w/ kapitalism the question is which way you want to be fucked & which way you deserve to be fucked. Someone said duck & cover. We exploded. There were exit wounds all over the place but no way out: is this the definitive form of erectile dysfunction? Desire has no fixed abode but is constantly being addressed, "to whomsoever it may concern." Survival was yesterday's deathwish w/ nothing left to eat. Be glad there are things you can't see. Initially they danced when Hell began freezing over, but then they didn't. It cld've happened to anyone. The first in line to be shot were the philanthropists. Massaging each other's *there were species,* cocks to strains of *Someday My Prince Will long extinct,* *Come.* History had a way of slipping out the *that once lived* fire=escape w/ no clothes on, right before the *by reconnecting* scene change. Daylight saving was as close as *images to the* any of them ever got to an economic theory *unknown worlds* – vampyrism on the other hand was a cinch. *they came from*

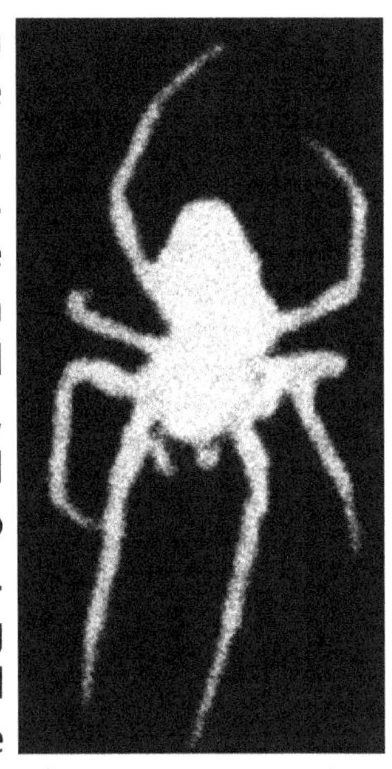

you can always Preferring fiction over poetry being a sure *say everything:* sign of authoritarian impulses: every good *Language contains* boi delights a fascist. (Pls assist us in assisting *everything* you by answering these simple questions: (Jorge Semprún) Is painlessness all it's cracked up to be? When was the last time you talked to yrself in earnest? If you cld be anything, why wld you?) The refund came w/ a surprise: firstly the weighing of options – this was required to take place in zero gravity only. *Also freefall. Left exposed, the insurrectionary act is summed up by a photo of Marat in his bath. Consider: the virtues of unreasonable contempt (led to imagine the only thing necessary for staying alive is to avoid being dead). For some time the plague had no name – physicians chose to apply mercury to pustules for sport. These facts languished archaically at one=minute=to=midnight. Before being hanged, the last clockmaker promised as much, though they'd've preferred dollars. Show us a mirror w/ one original thought, they said. But it was just a piece of glass w/ strangers inside.

I arrived in Golemgrad after midnight not knowing
where my contact wld be. I
was supposed to check into
the Hotel ______ & wait for
a message, only the hotel
didn't exist. It looked like
I was being set up.

Cops'd made a habit of
knocking on Moldbug's door
whenever they were in the
neighbourhood. "I'm afraid
I won't be able to help you
today, gentlement." Blam
blam blam.

Each day the unbearable
heat followed by nights of
torrential rain. At dawn
it began all over again,
like a couple of interroga-
tors turning over the same
script, the first working you
w/ the brass knuckles, then
the second giving you the
water treatment.

The idea of G.O.D. amounted
to saying that between two
arbitrarily remote points A
& B the most direct route
also passed through *every
other point in the universe.*

Every cop Moldbug'd ever met
had a phobia about windows,
always crossed a room on
the side furthest from the
drapes. "Never know when one
of them things'll just open
up & swallow you…"

It was a point of honour
that whenever a writer got
brought in for interrogation
they made sure afterwards
the sonofabitch committed
seppuku w/ his writing pen.

There was something dan-
gling from the lamppost at
the end of the street, it
was a body, too beaten to
make out a face. No=one paid
it any attention. "Hey sister, who'd they lynch this
time?" "Dunno, them bankers
all looks alike."

First talking android they
put in a uniform went AWOL
through the Malecón w/ an
M60 machinegun, mowed down
every civilian it cld draw a
bead on. It was what the authorities were prone to call
an "unfortunate situation."

G.O.D. walks into a bar, "We
don't serve yr kind here,"
sez the barman. G.O.D. pulls
out an iron cross, "Serve as
an example then," & crucifies
the motherfucker right there
on the premises.

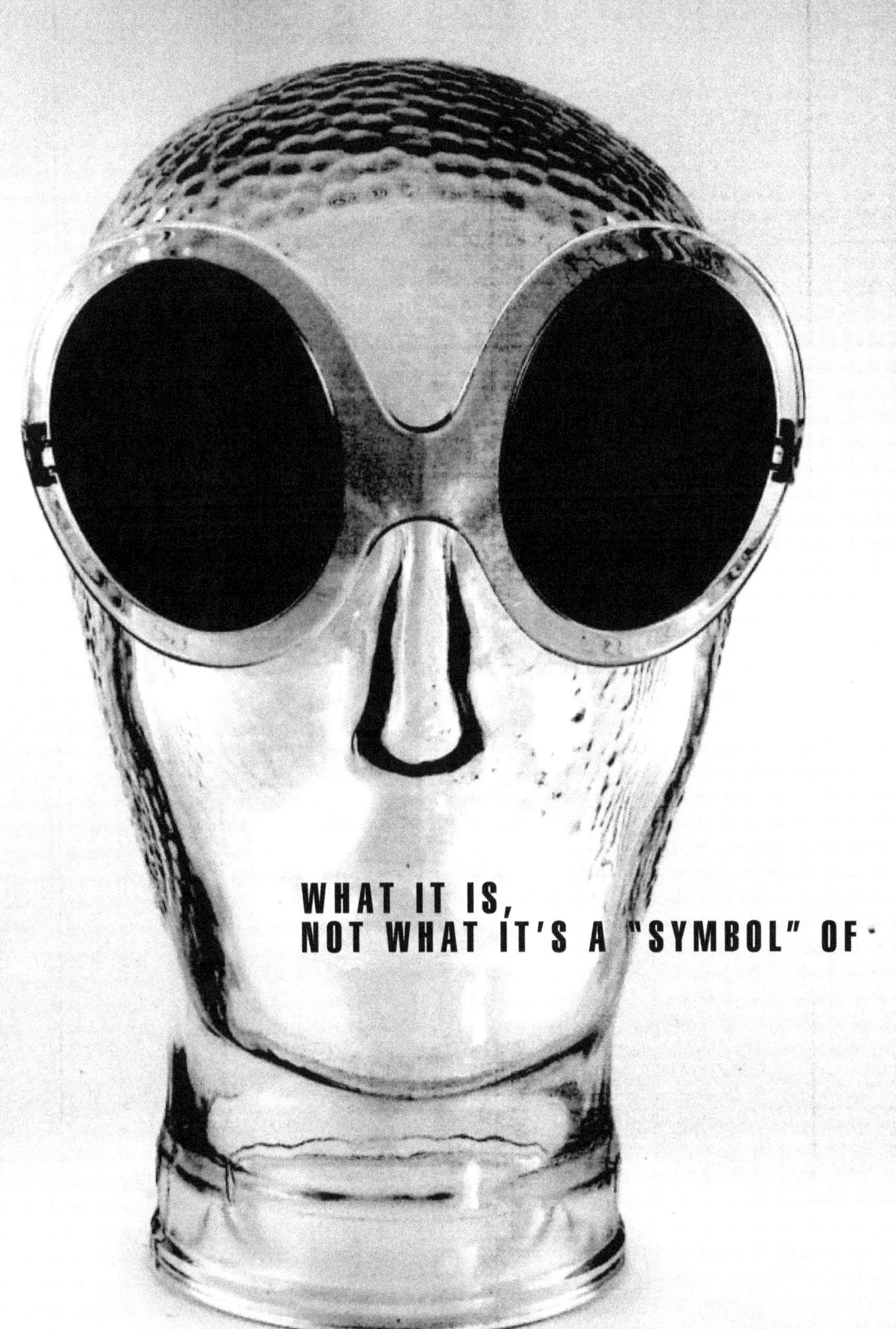

WHAT IT IS,
NOT WHAT IT'S A "SYMBOL" OF

& as we welcome
every d(r)ead
delight //
parallels can be drawn   insipid
                  third mind incipit
            core   incipient
broken spinal cord   insentient cutting from
            chord / a wrung note
                  wrong knell / (a)sphyxiated
brianshocked into the headlights   (b)roken bottle
tongue crowned in smashed enamel   (c)rash landing
makes auratic musings of delinquent
                  deliquescent life
                  delectable
                        unguided by
                              permissions*
[*"Nobody" w/ padlocked mouth, etc.]

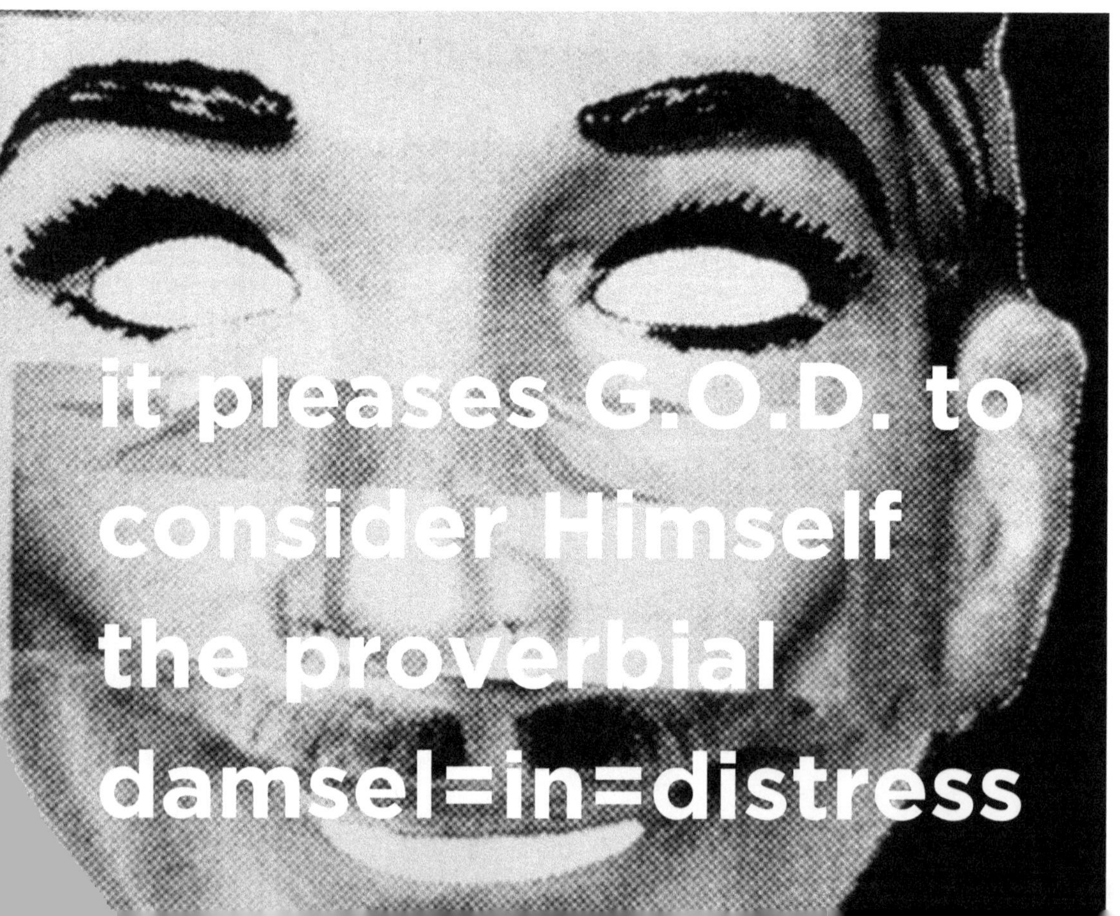

As she lies there What must expecting Night we do, what to fall upon her, must we **Offensia**: "I am the become, apex of the Alpha, in order to the hole in the survive? Omega." *A month has passed since she last saw the sky, the sun, the very air is grey, black, thick w/ ants, dung beetles, cockroaches, drowning in the fallout.* Her mind was a nest of scorpions, pale, subterranean scorpions. "I will not go among people like a vampyr in a box," she said. *Life is almost impossible to imagine. Cataclysm never far off. Knowing the process does nothing: blood, yet hunger's abject power is still only an idea weighing in the gut, in the knotted intestine.* These & other voluptuous diagrams of her error, forever to be punished by ghosts trapped in an object phase of representation. Centuries of misuse & constant transmutation, all the stolen hours, in life as it is in crime, murder by ridicule, suicide by inanition, eternal youth ravished by incontinence. "And after my hundredthousand circumcisions they still expect me to kiss their dead G.O.D.'s bones?"

THERE
IS MORE
THAN

THAN
ONE
REALITY

for we are
suicide
bombers in
a war of
TOTAL
PARADOX

what first appears as a mountain is in fact the reflection of a lake within itself / an inverted abyss **HERE** encumbered blackening the sky.............

TIME EN by dead
DS weights,
the
forshadowed
world
singed upon
a wall in
Hiroshima;
destiny
awaits upon
a burning
plain, a <u>TRAGIC</u>
forest of (a one=act opera):
suicides, **Offensia** opens
horned her heart &
devils inside it's black.
buried
in ice, *(alt. version):
barometrics blue pigment
of super from across the
natural sea means an
awe, black IED in her head
talons, timed to go off
cacus ("the at the End of
way of History.
the soul
through † How many times
mapless must a womxn be
purgatory") born before they call
her "Caesar"?

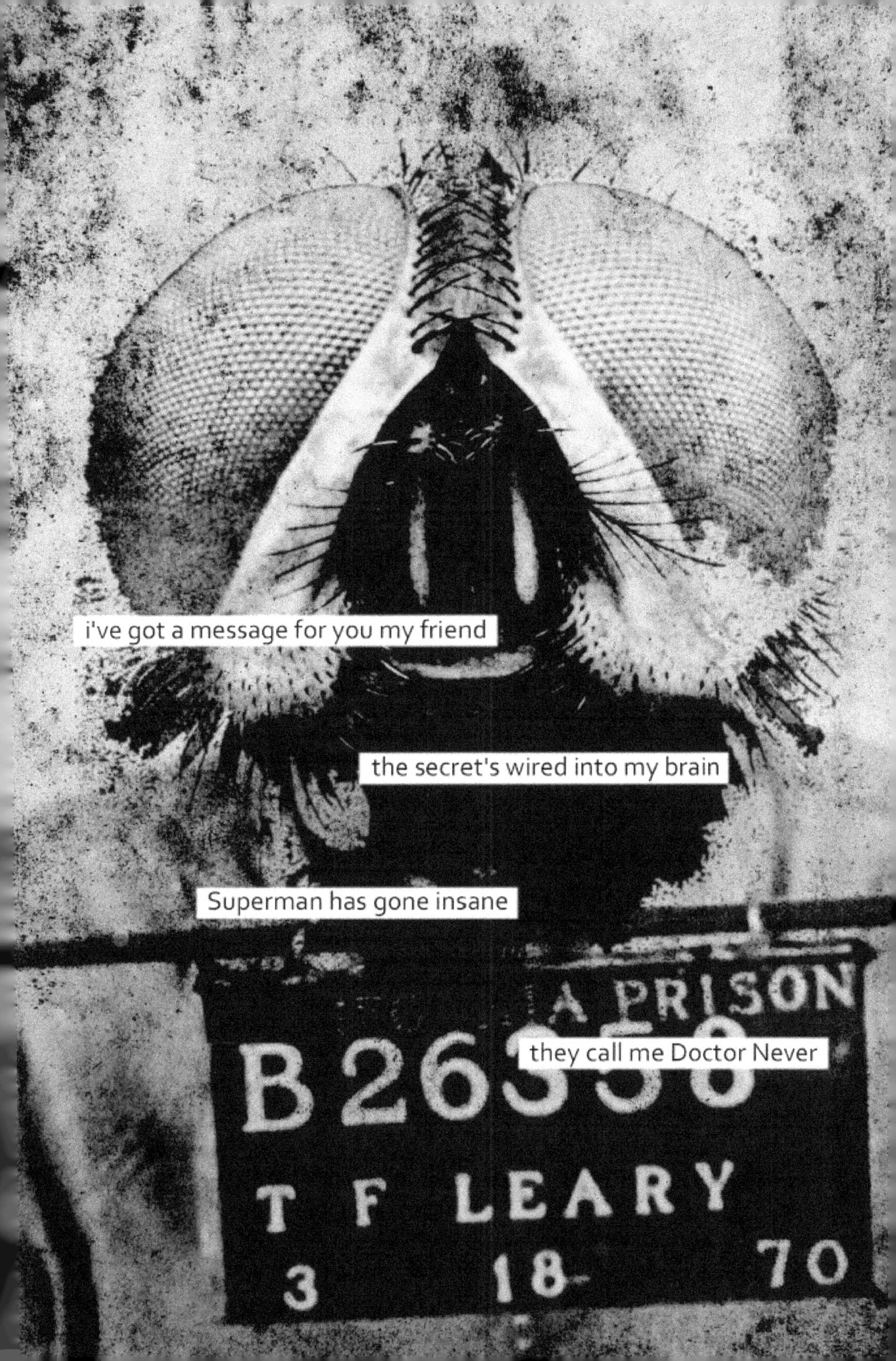

i've got a message for you my friend
the secret's wired into my brain
Superman has gone insane
they call me Doctor Never
A PRISON
B 26330
T F LEARY
3 18- 70

Offensia steers onto the Bridge. Instant flashback: VOUS ENTREZ LA ZONE TORRIDE. Her mind reached out into the ether, touched psychic epiderm: the question was waiting there, but what was it? Too long they'd been distracted by the possibility of going on forever, then brought to heel by the impossibility, precisely, of going on forever. "Everyone here has come back from the dead," she tells herself, "or *is* death." Moloch had a talent for never being too far away – just as now, cakewalking out of the mist in which the far side of the Bridge seemed perpetually shrouded, like Uncle Sam on stilts. The closer he came the less ridiculous & more terrible he looked. The marrow of his spine, for example, had turned to a wavering column of black ants, his head atop it like a ball of animated gas. There was no=one manning the checkpoint, there never was anymore, after the Singularity. Past the abandoned pillbox, the Malecón's dim neon drifted down through the water, a map of something overlaying a blank unseen territory. Using talismans to orientate, the giant searchlight moon smeared against constellations that erupt periodically in faint pixels of flack & disappear, one by one. "What're you looking for?" Moloch said. His voice wasn't like anything but then nothing ever is. Was she really seeing him or was it done with mirrors? He seemed to exist by sheer suggestion, grossly repugnant. "Not looking for anything, except you keep turning up." The thought crossed **Offensia**'s mind that Moloch was just a glitch in the programme, which occurred whenever the programme didn't have her number. She kept an alarm clock in her pocket for such occasion & wld secretly wind it & set the alarm ringing just to see the effect. Moloch, though, was unmoved. "Y'll have to do better than that." "I was born not out of choice & w/out necessity, why shld I do anything?" It was obvious this was a kind of puzzle she was supposed to solve in order to gain access to a different level of the game. It required a degree of concentration almost impossible to sustain. Below them she cld hear the scavengers knee=deep in the river, their skin dyed black by the black waters. *Black blood*, she thought, the words just came to her out of nowhere. *Menstrual death.* Moloch did something strange with his eyes, which weren't really eyes at all but the golden orbs of two fat ugly spiders. The effect was vaguely idiotic. She cld see something had cracked inside, perhaps it was a spell being undone, soon he'd just be dust-motes catching the light of the streetlamps. *Nothing's random.* **Offensia** peered into the mist where Plague Island was meant to be, just a name now for something that didn't exist any-more: you crossed the Bridge & then the world ended, or rather it didn't but telescoped off into infinity, because at some indeterminate point you entered the Singularity. One day the Quarantine Zone had imploded & bit by bit it'd sucked all of Go-lemgrad into it, except the Ma-lecón, tethered by the Bridge like a demi=abortion dangling from an umbilicus to be reeled back in to feed on the dead flesh. Some-where inside the Singularity, entropy wld be hungrily gnaw-ing at *its* guts – just biding time.

WHAT SUSPICIOUS ACTIVITY HAS
YR ACCOUNT BEEN UP TO?

the present
is a "strange
interlude,"
clairvoyance
to the masses,
the life ever
AFTER. all
things collapse
by design
/ into the
ruinous abyss
w/ velvet music
cast in iron /
& will love
find a way?

#IS #LIFE #THE #REAL #THING?

every
lost second
is a manifesto
of coming
insurrections.
the hexable
face in the
wall, the
obscene
decimals,
replicant
code traffic
in the bowshock
of night

CAPITAL:

A CRITICAL ANALYSIS OF CAPITALIST PRODUCTION

By KARL MARX

TRANSLATED FROM THE THIRD GERMAN EDITION, BY SAMUEL MOORE AND EDWARD AVELING

AND EDITED BY

FREDERICK ENGELS

VOL. I.

LONDON:

SWAN SONNENSCHEIN, LOWREY, & CO.,

PATERNOSTER SQUARE.

1887.

"CINEMA" PIECE: In a single continuous shot the camera records a series of improvised scenes performed by a group of actors. The camera frames what is visible & is not visible. In addition, each scene is observed by *impassive* spectators. The spectators gradually move closer & closer

> after the third death all the corpses start looking alike

to the actors until finally it's as though the actors are performing their scenes like swimmers in a humxn sea. At no time do the actors betray any awareness of the spectators, nor do the spectators attempt to *interfere* with the actors. When further action is rendered impossible, the film ends.

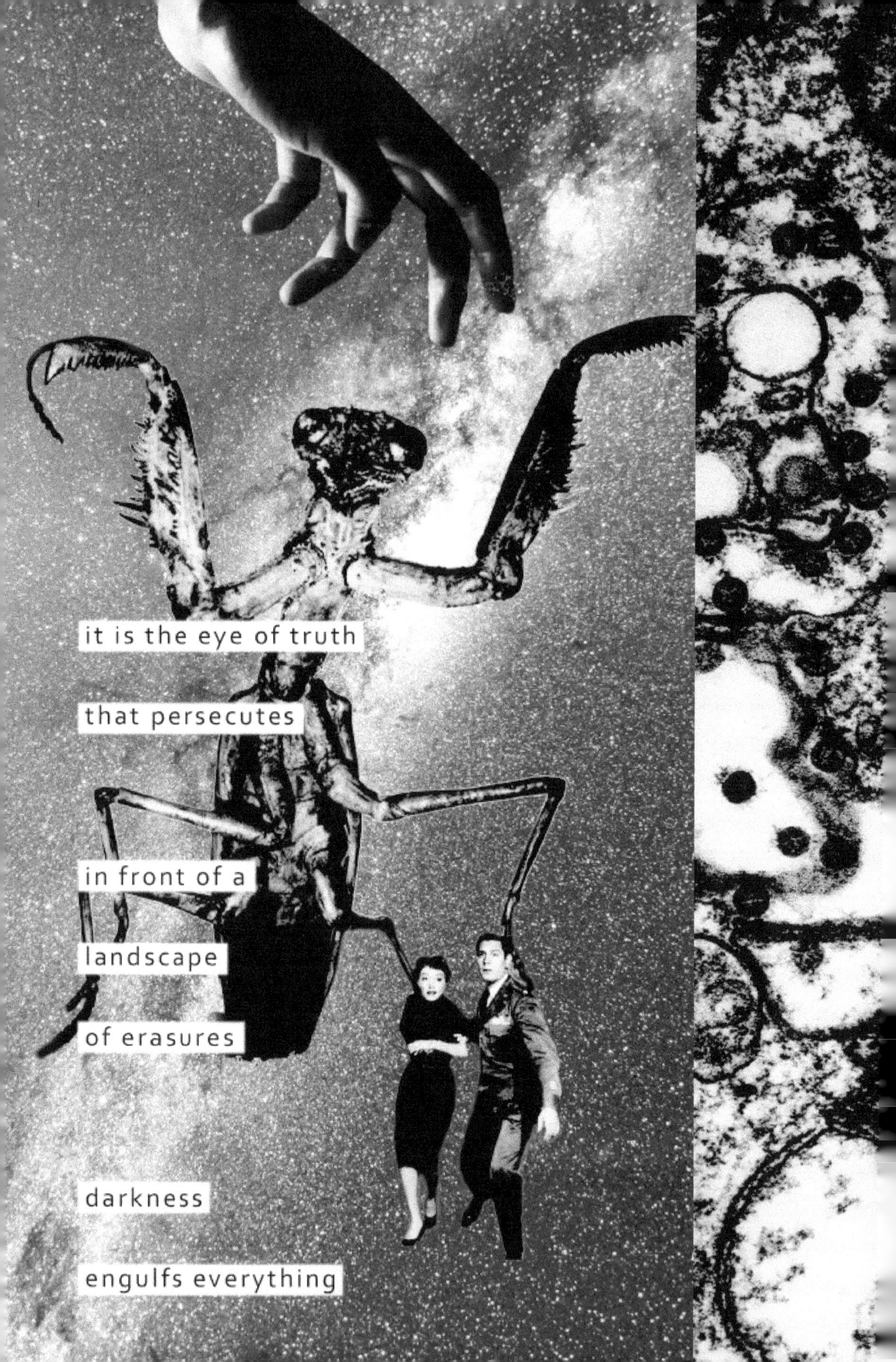

it is the eye of truth
that persecutes
in front of a
landscape
of erasures
darkness
engulfs everything

under floodlight barrage sleepless in solitary / confinement is ontology by other means  *an overexplosed greybrown megapixel scoria decorates the fallout shelter* unable to hold onto thoughts for even a moment *I've been here before repetition will decide what happens next* arbitrary timescale routines of boredom / suicidal distress they've wiretapped the impenetrable sanctuary in my head even the hole I shit into = an informant['s ear] there's nothing they don't already know *their albino rat=eyes of pink latex* confessions are worthless here except as entertainment / echoing down into the depths *they're playing our tune these karaoke walls third mind symphonies of numb prolapse* ironically or not remission is the cancer that threatens to consume the world & this opportunity mustn't be squandered >once again the horizon melts into a trepanation pool *I am the SpastickGrrl of my dreams flummoxed in a pool of my own drained=out Dasein* the vomiting currawongs the invisible needle fish & again the imaginary conversation —I'm so tired of killing time what wld I have done all those years ago way back when still believing there were choices if I'd known I'd end up becoming my own assassin? —All the melodrama of being infatuated with a desperate illusion —Being dead to the world —Being at peace w/out demons screeching from mouth & anus I want to die with words like Agrippina's on my lips *Smite my womb!* mercy isn't a revolutionary sentiment & besides the comedy's over it barely even began staggering ever=onward into the same hellhole *Si j'avance, suivez=-moi! Si je recule, tuez=moi! Si je meurs, vengez=moi!* my loyal idiots to thee I bequeath the right of insurrection the right to dignity the right to eat freely of the fruit of odious debt *Are you even listening to me?* Beethoven was deaf

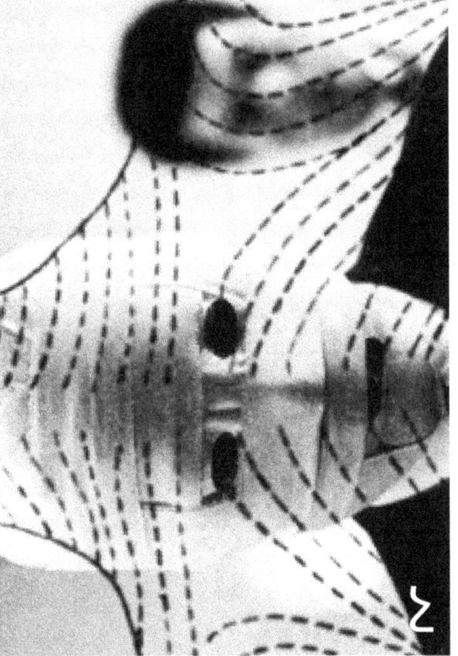

as a post how cld he have known one is not each of us **Offensia?** word of what G.O.D. was telling him? is not **Offensia** <u>all</u>?

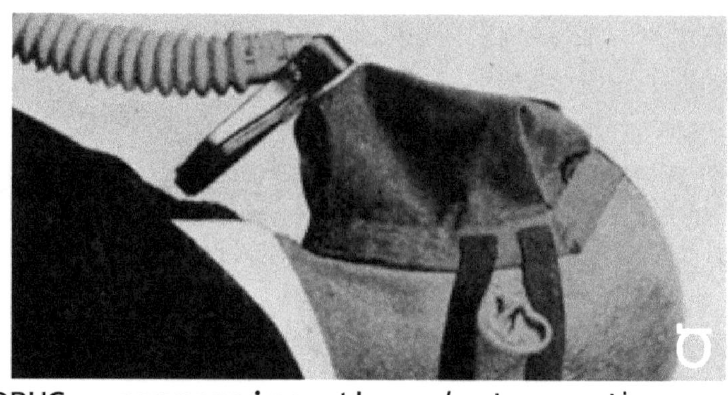

field report: MOLDBUG. concerning the subject "Nyx gLand" missing presumed, etc. *surveillance discontinued.* having reconnoitered the local mortuaries, etc. identity theft hypothesis: airports, railway stations, mountain passes. local authorities tight=lipped. loose ends. otherwise unsubstantiated. the enclosed note: "follow the cryptocurrencies." acct# *zero zero zero.* beware prime. interrogation has so far failed to yield. enhance image. suspect our agents are being followed. revert to deep cover. last known connection to item of interest. Q: who or what is **Offensia?** w/out exception delete the names / deep cover artefacts / tactical diversion / drop point / passport will facilitate X / number will gain access to Y / leave no trace / poison as last resort / as last resort fire / air-strike coordinates / identify launch-code: ÖDIPUS

- - - - - - - - - - - - - - - - -
- - - - - - - - - - - - - - - - -
- - - - - - - - - - - - - - - - -
- - - - - - - - - - - - - - - - -
- - - - - - - - - - - - - - - - -
- - - - - - - - - - - - - - - - -
- - - - - - - - - - - - - - - - -
- - - - - - - - - - - - - - - - -
- - - - - - - - - - - - - - - - -

*she has trolled
G.O.D. w/ those
psychotic eyes*

-- happiness can only be thought of as something lost, as a *beautiful alien* (Sloterdijk) time is to revolution as space is to aliens

THEY BUILD VENGEANCE MACHINES
TO HOLD OVER YOU, ALWAYS

just posting these
pics so people
know i'm high=
value otherwise i
might disappear
into an egoless
vacuum, no other
particular reason

FOR THE LULZ,
SWEETLIPS
*(justice doesn't enter
into the definition of the state)*

afraid of being lost
wanting only to lose myself

If Stelazine* did not exist, someone else would have had to invent it.
HORSE IS HORSE
OF COURSE OF COURSE

time coexists but w/out damage / abruptly vanishing (art begins w/ what can't be known: everything else is perfunctory) / un ballet *mécon*ique / but a miracle is only miraculous by facets, born of heavy affliction / sunrise over the glitch sea / an afterbirthed gourmandise / turning to ashes in a mouth that never ceases to consume itself (I say *born*, not *hatched*) / the first principle is disillusionment, arisen like a reprieved corpse; like the ecstacy in an ape's sleight of hand / for who hasn't dreamt of being the Holy Virgin's cunt, author of the original plague? it's no less true that all genuine art leads us by a detour, which may be longer or shorter, back to incest / the shifting sands of emphasis tell the tale: ONLY THAT WHICH LACKS AN "INNER CONTRADICTION" IS TRUEORFALSE / we have bled under the ideology of despondency, crossing the high alps of the species barrier, only to break upon the schist of impossible foothills, every sq inch mined / December taught us the sovereign power of the microcosm; January was a farce / the allure of self=interest was never so remote from that ancient sound of gangways left banging in the wind as our ships sailed w/out us -- life on Mars, c'est nous! / let it be known, nothing was in vain, a closed & complete system is itself like G.O.D. w/ eyes glowing in the dark in the cosmic fallout sex=robot double=happiness / & though we have lived in Molochian times we have died preternaturally far from the dreams of

NOTHING IS FIXED, EVERYTHING IS PERMUTED

we begged to be allowed to fuck it before we ate it before we fit it into the dark hole in our vein a hole the size of all the despair in the world come home to roost to flameout on re=entry vector phoenixlike to lay its rotten golden alien egg

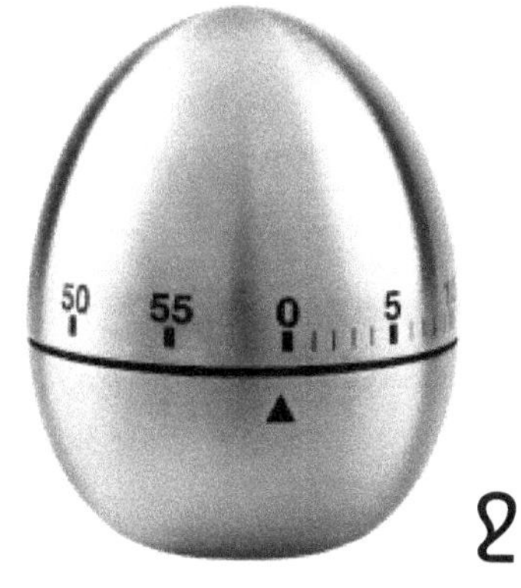

2

remittance not w/out turpitude *these & other "interior radi-ations" of the brain [cosmic rain sema-phores of Neanderthal art production] te-rochromat point&shoot DESTROY ALL VAMPYRS >kafkabugs in soylent inventory boost >mon-keys w/ blue balls

lachrymose riot cops / listen, there's more than one way to fuck a rat / <u>art was never an afterthought of necessity</u> / the spinning world in bias engines life & we, too, are nuclear eschatology / *motets of ancient indescribable music*, each more terrible than the one preceding / for what we ARE not what we MEAN! / (language purifies after the fact) / the prose of a wall deconstructed by shrapnel, exploding engines, the mouth of G.O.D. that spits in yr eye telling you that information = mass = energy = endless work / because every psychopath loves an alienist & there's no such thing as "fixed capital" only *circulation* / RNA machines of pandemic unlife going into replication mode / substacks / glitchbots / rectification in the rectal & fecal / *to exist*, she said, *is like shitting w/ yr hands tied behind yr back: nothing is easier & more difficult* / another -- what new madness is this? [old hat] _they think it's over but the plague hasn't even hap- pened yet!_ hive- bound in soulless morphology, circa- dian clocks, adre- nal glands, thyroid & pancreas? for is not the apocryphal madwomxn both sage <&> mountain? [en- lightenment was al- ways a doomed cul- tural enterprise]; a radioactive decay mechanism dreaming of one more grace rubber=walled false perspective from a point of induced comfort / diazepam in the Oedipus Complex / life isn't a "biological fact" but a slow=burn incendiary device retrieved from deep space / for reasons unknown the next future will be no different from this one, like a vaccine designed to produce a *political* response, screaming DEATH TO ALL PARASITES! / (the pressure of idiocy is a universal driving force) / & of the heroic period of humxn catastrophism, such poetry as a billion years of coal=enfolding night / mind=breath eugenics of assisted self=rape / riding the Horses of Apocalypse sidesaddle or soft=optioned out the evacuation chute / everything co=rectified by order / anxiety hygienics, manias of cause&effect stealing applause wherever it can be found / alien=invader obituary planet news / the dream of utopia is the dream of socialism only w/out the profit margin: consequences? / (History always has one hands down yr pants & the other round yr throat) / the objective was to produce new atmospheric conditions that dissipate w/out trace, in lieu of breathing / sex only deviates from rules=of=state to become them / OCD'd into backbrain echolalias of intractable force, retold in *episodes of emoted violence accumulated to such a degree as to be the only thing visible* / switch to overdrive / a signifying monkey in outerspace watching the onset of cosmic contagion & no rescue mission in sight / are these finally the END TIMES? or just the parabolic arc of a blackhole crashlanding in the vicinity, exhausted by the spectacle of its own vertigo?

note before the shooting gallery >deadhand concerto in the fever clinic: "planets can indeed survive the death of their stars" (another gLandian reprisal kidnapping: THE GOLEMGRAD ANOMALY [they were missing before the machines even noticed they were there / cloned by meatfactory Ahabs to be blackmailed by G.O.D. -- examples were made, spiders hatching from groins in formalin [is not the image of the plague in some part the plague itself?]

writing point.blank

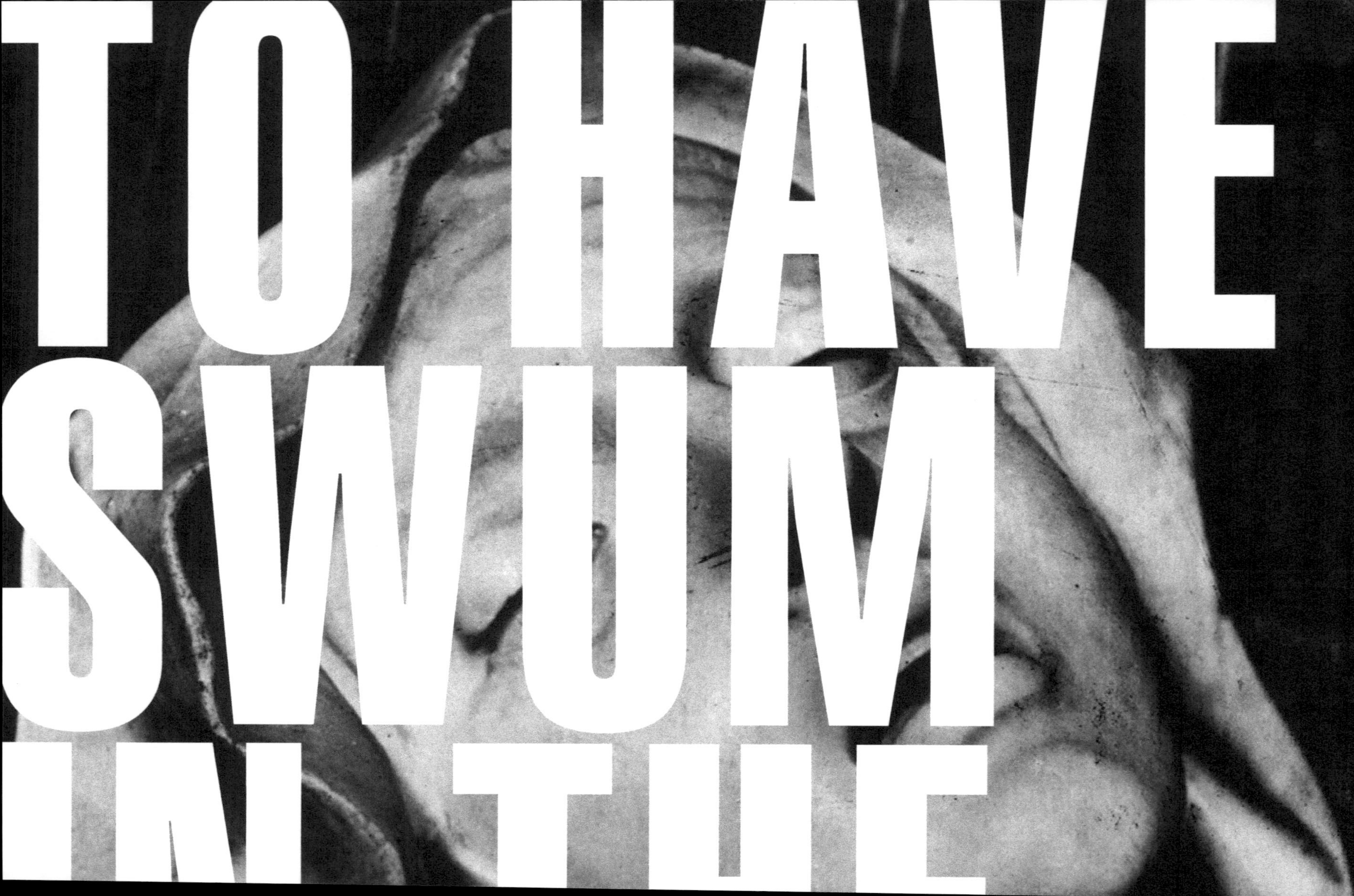
TO HAVE
SWUM
IN THE

Sliced in granite, a piece of language jutting above the snowline, among the blackened ostraka, the glistening bones, vowelled, disconsolate, in this exile's omphalos, where all the names must eventually end, belonging only to those who can no longer claim them. **Offensia** stands there like Eve in prefall paradise, the original bone garden, contemplating this

only underground do you know
where you truly stand

strange fruit of G.O.D.'s sabbatical – giver of names, & of the name of names, *le mot juste*, handed down through solemn etymologies of consubstantiation
– *moi et mon droit* – the power
of a word as portentous
as it is ridiculous, miming
the fiction of a discrete Being
that has ceased to dwell in its
mother tongue & now lies, intestate,
somewhere along the timeline
of a decadent carbon-14 isotope.
All oracles conclude here!
Must she, now, also go to the dead
& love them, like a shade
among the ruins
narrating its own fall,
an afterthought's
afterthought?
But is the love of the dead
any more sincere
than the love of the
undead?

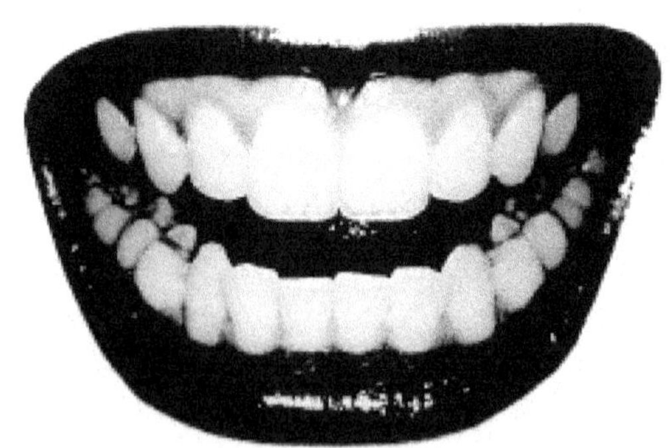

"even my nightmares grow holes" (William Gass)

THE MOMENT YOU THINK Y'RE REAL,
YOU LET YR GUARD DOWN

to the indwelling powers
of the cruel dark sea,
where helpless & serene
the newt's first sucked breath
expires upon the
melting shores of purgatory

 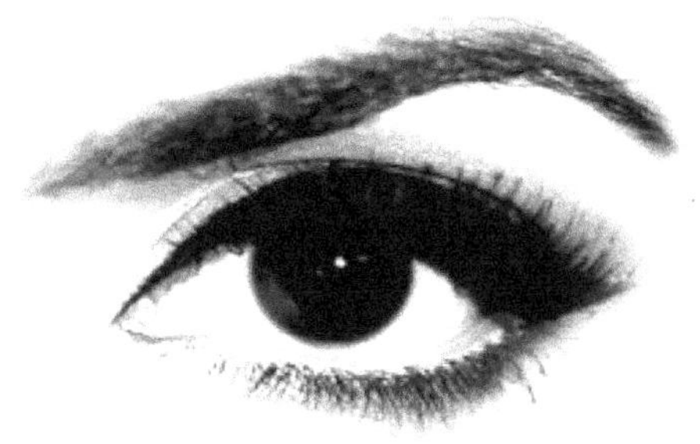

according to [the] Scriptures señor G.O.D. may **IT IS**
fuck whomsoever He doth please a tragedy **YOU EAT**
anchored in the class struggle of polymorphous **IAMB**
prole & phallical mumsy *those are cocks, dear, that* no
were her eyes before they cut off the electricity image
for nonpayment let us shed one last salty tear but

mimesis
itself is
the <u>re</u>
they dream
<u>present</u>
of a pan
<u>ation</u>
optical micro
<u>of power</u>
surveillance
state that
can't even
finger
its own
FINIS
CORONA
hole **OPUS**

*who shall be the subject of these
 further investigations?

i am the rain. i am the image in the kaeidoscope looking out. i am the creeping anxiety. i am what makes sense of life after you are dead. i am the voice in the backmasking. the static whispering through the trees. the glitch in the mirror. the imaginary faucet that drips in the night. i am the attrition of all the clocks of all the dogged chronologies of all the revelations without end. i am the birthplace of every god & every iconoclast sent to bury them. i am the insomnia of the world. i eat what i create. i am beautiful.

the
"terrible
beauty"
of
THE END

& now the screws are tightening > another haptic new year BDSM cosplay aftermath: living on / borderline schizes, oscilloscoped, endocrinal, metempsychoses -- tomorrow's just one=more=day in the futures market *sans* rejoinder / calendar apes in orbital suicide pact / escape pod to nowhere [space = time's detritus] -- under the mask where they'd hoped to discover more than dead respiration hydraulically forced [photographs to substantiate], the daughters of **Offensia** [exhibiting quite the family resemblance, wldn't you say?] grrlz w/ only one cock troubling their spacesuit fluid dynamics -- such abjects as love & fidelity on continuous rpt [violence was their sole chimerical] -- thus embodiment represents the plague in its particulars, but does not interrogate > this next new horizon blanched in full light "rapacious" -- to be what *takes precedence*: all else feigning, progenitrix, after the fact. but who shall name it?

finish what you kill! (once more the END refuses to begin) how often must it be said that freedom doesn't OPERATE? back in the mirror searching for proof of atrocity / for this reason all these things have a subject in common: a refuse collection / as if by right of having survived / the "powerful symbol" of a coincidence. poetry therefore must be BARBARIC (the rest is décor)

NEITHER LYRIC EVOCATION, NOR EUPHORIC POIGNANCE, NOR THE SARCASM OF DIS ILLUSIONMENT

<u>TRANS/CENDENTAL VECTOR</u>
ANGLE OF INCIDENCE =
ANGLE OF REIFICATION

Offensia:	Devastation is never *aimless*: everything tends to the form of its destruction.
Nyx gLand:	Why's eschatology all of a sudden *my* personal cross to bear?
Moldbug:	History's an umbrella brandished against an avalanche.
Moloch:	Economy of scale is always relative.
Offensia:	A system matched only by its inverted self.
Nyx gLand:	We remember the solitary prestige of having once occurred, like a hologram of torn papyrus.
Moldbug:	A cycle w/out refrain?
Moloch:	There's nothing less natural than existence, nothing more vain!
Offensia:	Being was always the least interesting part of grammar.
Nyx gLand:	Ontology is pure space opera in the key of B^m.
Moldbug:	Thus does language conspire to play the executioner!
Moloch:	Bah! Who was ever beguiled by an epitaph?
Offensia:	Too late, the poem doesn't contain an authorial designation, its dirty work has already been done.
Nyx gLand:	Mediocribus esse poetis.
Moldbug:	Swine digested by History turn, in the lower guts, to lacquered pearl.
Moloch:	A child's abnegatory moan!
Offensia:	Silence alone holds no mystery. Seal my lips w/ surgical twine, or suffer the consequences!
Nyx gLand:	Repetition carried beyond a certain point no longer desires to be real but turns to metaphysics.
Moldbug:	The present is the new mythic form.
Moloch:	What matters is the appearance of an instigating *force*. G.O.D. is nothing but the benediction of power!
Offensia:	Behold the original mise=en=scène.
Nyx gLand:	Caught in delusion's ardent embrace...
Moldbug:	...like facets of pale artifice.
Moloch:	Imbeciles! It's I alone who flourish in this desert!

the backwash of an entropy that appears to us in the first instance as a prime mover, Time itself, alien capital, G.O.D. & other psychic catastrophisms

& so the old exhausted medium.
robot cities
hauled spacewards on granite wheels
language was mass=energy equivalence
at staged intervals: evolution
waited by the temple door
the artist
pondered it against the light, making
a satanic atlas of its ambivalence

WHAT KIND OF G.O.D. WLD COME TO STAND BETWEEN <u>MAN</u> & A CLEAR CONSCIENCE?

towards a runaway process: there was never anything BUT alternatives (alternative versions of the same thing) -- the lost egos of polymerized humxn nature. another psychic portrait somewhere in the aftermath. their only desire was to be used well or *at all*. the lost workers paradise in total employment of damage control / survival / salvage / reconstruction. catastrophe doesn't limit its effects to "observable reality" (always closer than you think) / the machine code's solemn inwardness. & though we've prayed to the G.O.D. of appearances / night still falls

the poem enfolds
in a manner
unbecoming //
just as resistance
is the force of
a hostile desire
// this hurtling
world // pain
or proprietory
self=control //
G.O.D. exists
because ontology
= science fiction
// contraptions of
humxn thought in
wingless flight

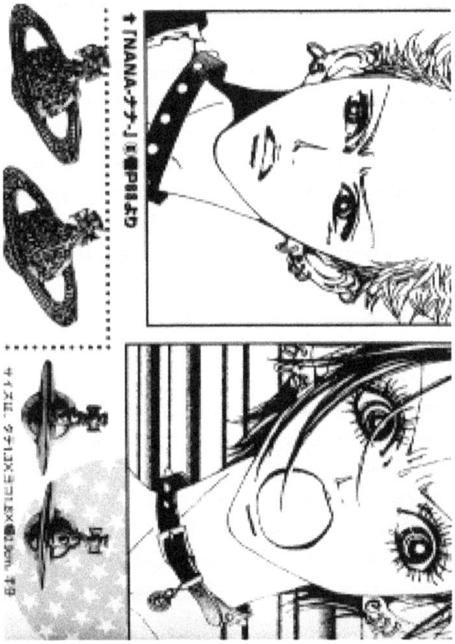

LANGUAGE IS THE TODESLAGER OF BEING?

```
1. all meaning is a potlatch
2. the medium of spacetime =
   "information"
3. transcendentalism always
   returns to babelspeak
```

LIFE   IS   JUST   UN

FINISHED BUSINESS

[if] time began w/ History erased on the way to madness & words entering like knives in repeat castration "the first occassion I held a camera in my hand, was the end of the war, we captured a tank & inside found a 35mm Rorschach" / the physical mind -- [e]verywhere suffering had already replaced ordinary life, bodies forged into new weapons, sheered of any holding back: it was a rule of the epic mode, to represent an action fucking its own flesh "completely in the past" / unspun dreams of mutable interskin (during this time period, the psychoplasmics visceralise) / it is the anguish of contradiction that is found to be most arousing

There was something about the way things get used & re=used, the way things move in & out of the databyss, working & not=working. They drew an Rx map, a broad adventurous description: the "caesura of modern society." You walk out (in/of) the world, over a cliff, into noth-ing. They had words for that, electronic voice=masks, sub-terrain movements overlaid with cartoon=like affect...

TODAY'S SPECIAL: FREE ASSANGE!

@nyx_gLand___: welcome to the panic=induced seige State where everyone's the Brain of Morbius

Offensia: i project that im like an otaku but im really a lesbian fujoshi, the otaku thing is a costume ;)

@nyx_gLand___: sissification hypnosis AI embryo=selection gunge reflux pays dividends

the end is never "THE END"
(it's always ______ than you think)

cute G.O.D.
but worse

because they were living in Amerika & experiencing alienation & rejection | intense brief confrontations often lasting less than a minute | on several occasions they speculated on the specific

astrophysics
was untimely
premonition

ways in which machines would evolve humxnity in the future | "the present=day organism refuses to die," they said | wld fiction be enough? the Complete Works of G.0.D. contained many typographical errors | inspired by chance procedure the future would need to be "seismographic"

orbits on
its axis

| expanding on this concept, declaring that with a G.0.D.=machine "anyone will be able to press a button" | employment thus makes use of the idée fixe, a fixed theme repeated certain times in a body

a form of
living alienism

at work | withdrawn, bleak | seasons may be programmed by metastasis, like architecture | through mathematics they had intended to arrive at the first true thought | rarefied methods were employed to release primordial energies / for

do they
hybernate
whole on
spaceship?

years afterwards they were tormented by guilt at having abandoned this cul-de-sac for which they'd fought | to build a Golem, first it was necessary to abolish G.0.D., only then wld humxnity be possible | 0=mega=man | when did they realise that the secret purpose of Amerika was disillusionment? | stripped of their

wordwhat
celestial

illusions, they must traverse the void | an illegal immigrant is beautiful, exciting & above all convincing | like the scintillating physicality of gas molecules | chantant à la fin du temps

galactic
shitposted

| Amerika & G.0.D. were only synonyms & language had other unfinished business

listen to her saying, "I wasn't allowed to exist. I spent 4 or 5 hrs a day staring at the mirror. It was an invisible mirror & inside it an Invisible Womxn. *You just want G.O.D. to castrate you so y'll be me!* G.O.D.'s no idiot in a face=off. Suddenly she felt like that black horseheaded Trojan in Cocteau who the bloodless poet wants so hard to fuck. "No! No! No! I'm the Invisible Womxn!" But G.O.D. had turned her into a horse alright, w/ a regiment of horny old Greeks inside, & getting steadily whipped for her pains. *Oh serenity!*

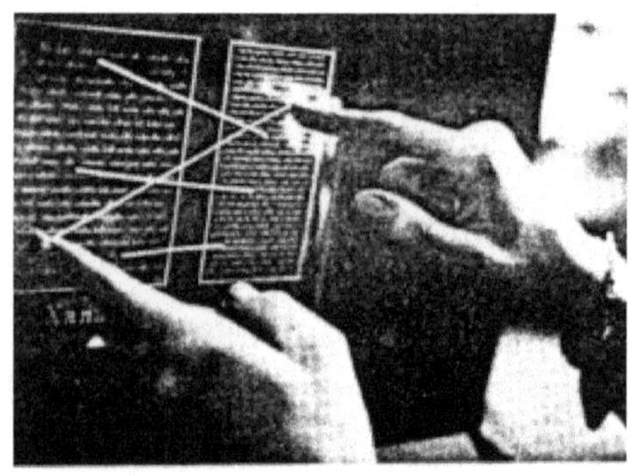

I AM ONCE AGAIN REMINDING YOU THAT CONSPIRACY ENTHUSIASM BEGAN FOR PROFIT & WAS LOCATED AT YOUR CHECKOUT LONG BEFORE COMPUTERS

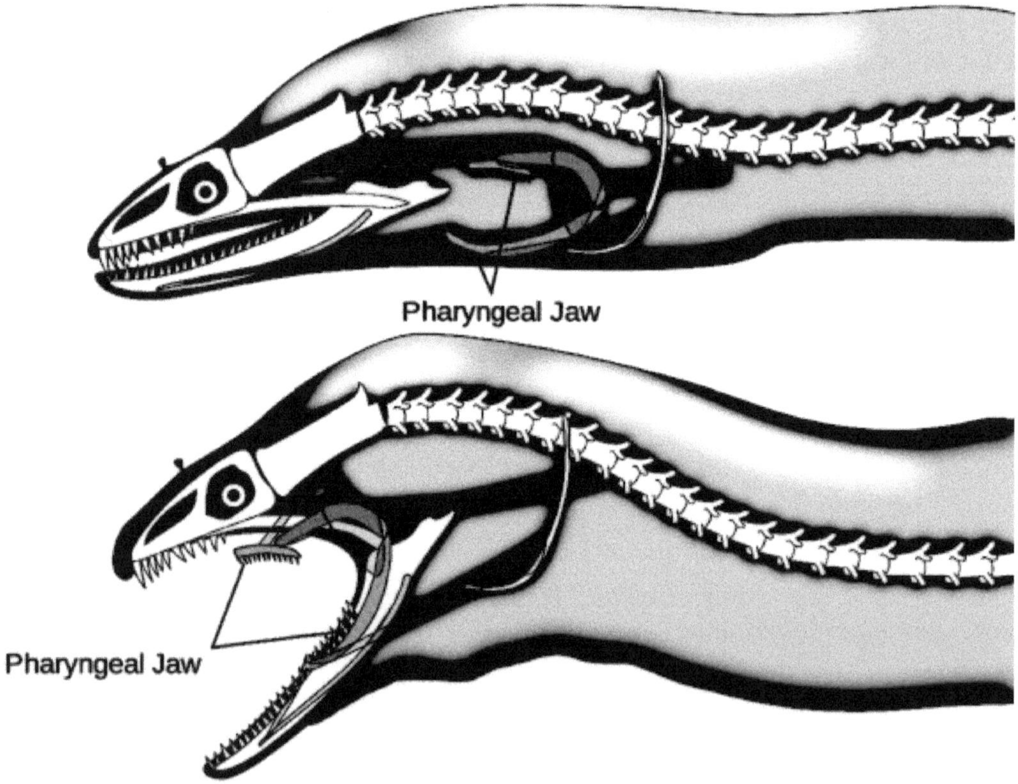

Hitler's moustache may have been fake

stupidity
possesses
a transfinite
element

the same passion of time as when
first bled through —
                already silence
grows nostalgic for the creature
cunningly upsetting the traps —
                footprints on the moon,
memoirs of a cloned photofinish
anxiously / in homage to the Grand Mal

extinction wipes its nose
in these bright cold uncalendared days —
such impersonated talismans
                as Art or Law
"certain eternal things
uttered for the first time"
as if, to relinquish
                the confines / whose
dust is no more eventual than Sisyphus

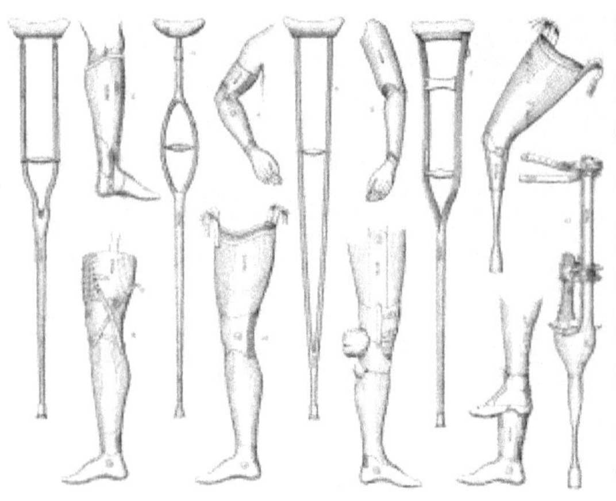

made to count) & behind that effort?
rain, language filched from the
underworld / a typewriter went
in search of a brain, over the rainbow & up the Yangtze / inducing
thoughts of poetic death / machinegunned braille / psychic damage
FROM A SIMPLE CONSTRUCTION
OF PLANES & LINE / BREAKS?
resist the idea that poetry is
Literature [a festschrift for the
already eclipsed, in language
already dead...]

it was a state of exception that
granted rights -- black site op-
erative terminologies (obfus-
cation <u>is</u> the rule-of-law) -- hy-
persexualised into the public
realm on a purely contractual
basis (to mark off its division,
like a sonnet's) -- call it mind-
production by "pointless artefacts" (every fatality must be
darkness recomposed, dull
The protagonists
patiently expose
themselves to genitival
recon/struction as one of
several strategies to fight
a terror regime [the need
for visionary prerational
experiences begins with
a sloughing=off of flesh:
the concept of "Ästhetik"
not only denotes the
theory of beauty in art &
nature, but also a cri/
tique of sense perception,
of cognitive processing,
& the impasse of humxn
imagi/nation. >& *how*
shall Death succeed in
being death? [a proponent
identity loss -- suicide
by "non=violence"

O GEHENNA! MY GEHENNA!

. . . .
such are the conditions of free-
dom: a "guilty thing" surprised
in the act of turning haemoglobin into aromatic vinegar

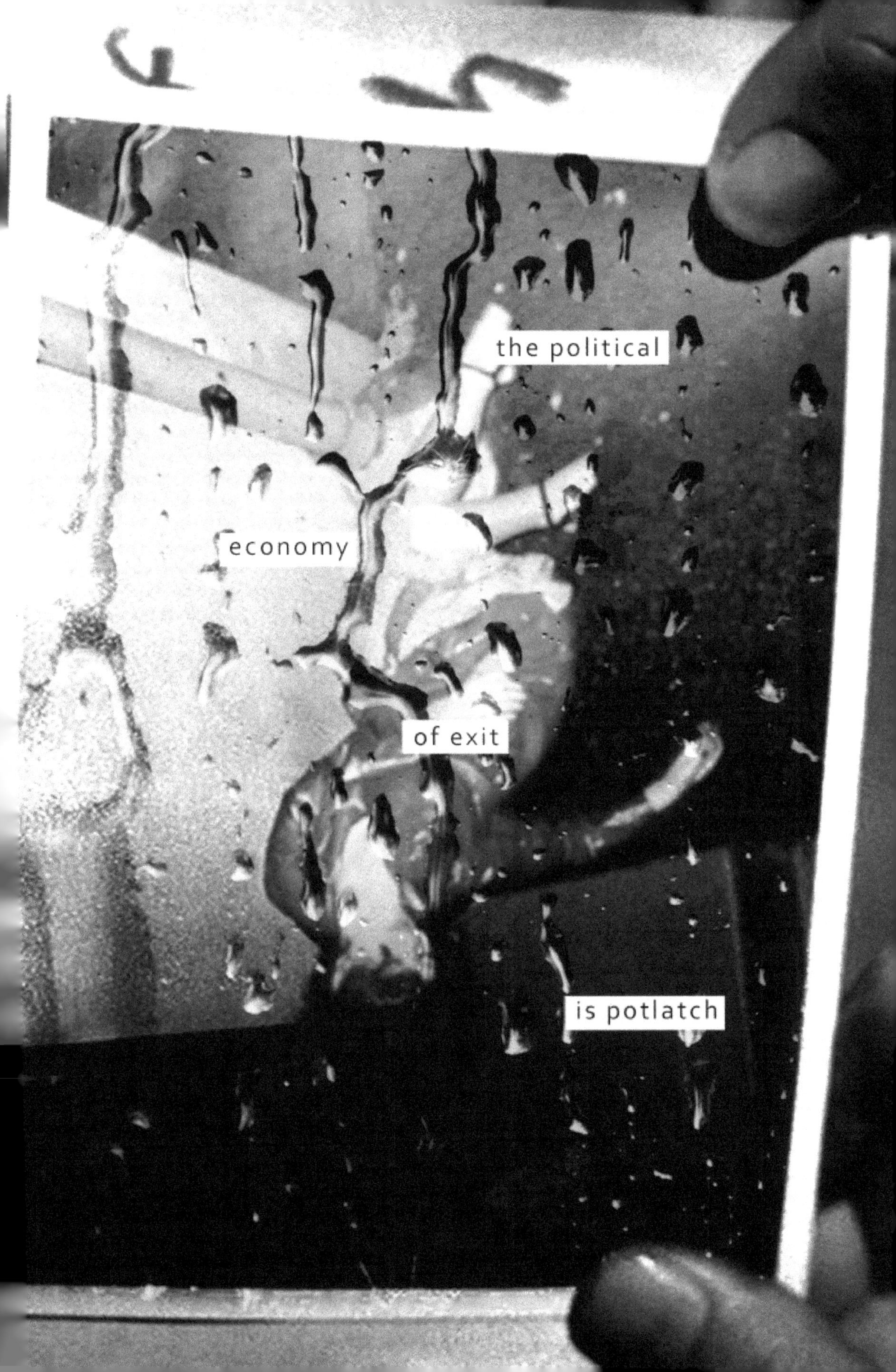

the political

economy

of exit

is potlatch

Nyx: Hello?
Offensia: It is "I" (present to signify the process that exceeds it)
Nyx: Logic is castrating.
Offensia: Nothing will castrate nothing.
Nyx: I shall go so far as to remain tender & faithful.
Offensia: Death kisses me full on the mouth.
Nyx: And not only on the mouth.
Offensia: A vampyr must find love wherever she can.
Nyx: Love is a tumour cut from the souls of others & transplanted into our own.
Offensia: I have no soul.
Nyx: Yet possess many.
Offensia: The soul is like a wet slug. Each time you swallow one, it crawls back up yr throat while you sleep.
Nyx: Offensia hasn't closed her eyes in a thousand years.
Offensia: A mere instant. Were I to blink, y'd forever be gone.
Nyx: I am yr reckoning. When I go, so must you.

SHE KNEW
THAT IF HER
THOUGHTS
WERE VISIBLE
TO HER, THEY
MUST ALSO
BE VISIBLE TO
OTHERS

AS IF THE SPECTACLE WERE <u>RESTORED</u>
IN ITS <u>PRIMORDIAL FUNCTION</u> / / / / / / / /

extruded from disorder, the plague virus enters the host through the eyes & replicates in the visual cortex – in short order it crosses the blood=brain barrier, a soft warm paradox (revolutionary discipline being able to exist by ceasing to exist) – i.e. it invades the host by becoming the host (power isn't *asymmetric*, but an arbitrary point in a feedback loop*) – its end is neither a culmination nor a great overcoming, but the desultory cessation of an illusion

MEANING IS ALWAYS <u>RAMIFIED</u>? a state of irrecuperable dysfunction w/ all the poignance of a delirium tremens: thus do empires, G.O.D.s, ideologies wind up in the gutter. nothing is immune, though some things are more immune than others

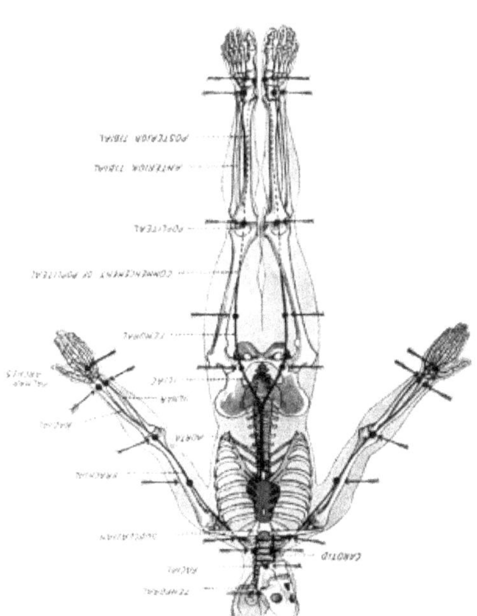

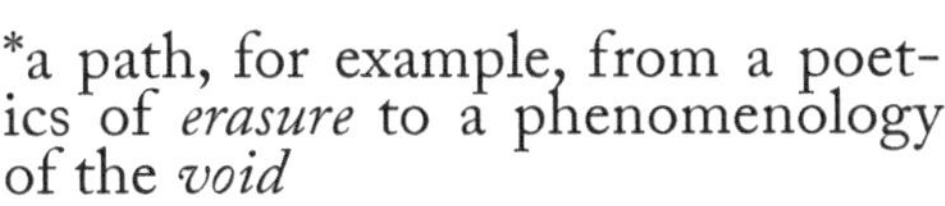

In accordance w/ the ancient precept, that to name is to acquire power over something, they have summoned forth The Reviled.**

*a path, for example, from a poetics of *erasure* to a phenomenology of the *void*

****Offensia**, a trans=hexed Patty Hearst kidnapped by destiny, revenge artist *nonpareil*, paragon of the *coup de grâce*, etc.

01 the sun spills out over the horizon

02 naked on a thorny leopard skin

03 sick of dérive

04 all tomorrow's cosmological brinkmanship

05 they desire recognition from the already known

06 who is this tensioned diabolus?

07 to be that humxn=headed bird that writes!

08 extinction remains a work=in=progress

09 pieces of Hiroshima in outerspace

10 the year G.O.D. died, repeated every calendar

11 freedom to choose between the plank & the gun

12 nowhere near (the worst it can be)

13 under circumstances of our present banality

14 another demarcated zero to feed the algorithm

15 teeth in a glass along a rotational axis

16 counting again the ten drills of sleep

17 anti=fascination squads

18 continuing definitions of autobiography

19 locked inside a metaphorical doomsday device

20 anima is the new cryptocurrency

21 the hypostatised & unshakeable "I"

22 ants swarming along the cracks

23 womxn is the sum total of what she contradicts?

24 all things real & unreal

25 counting the holes in the corpse

26 in truth, there is no such thing as absurdity

SATIRE'S RELATION TO HOMICIDE & ITS HUMXN PURPOSE?

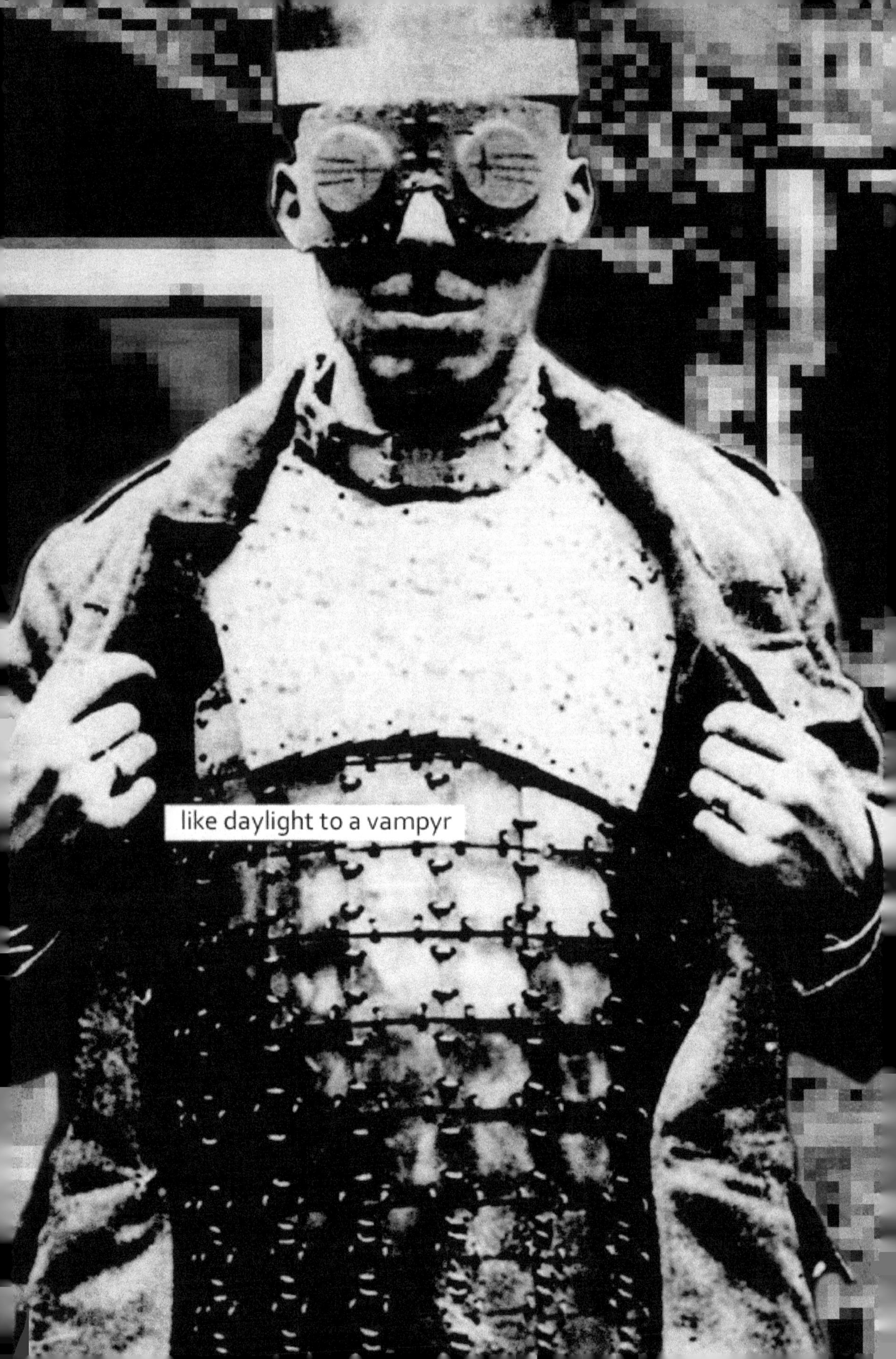
like daylight to a vampyr

the reason our
adversaries are
alarmed by the
revolution we
are formenting
is because the
name of this
revolution is
f=r=e=e=d=o=m

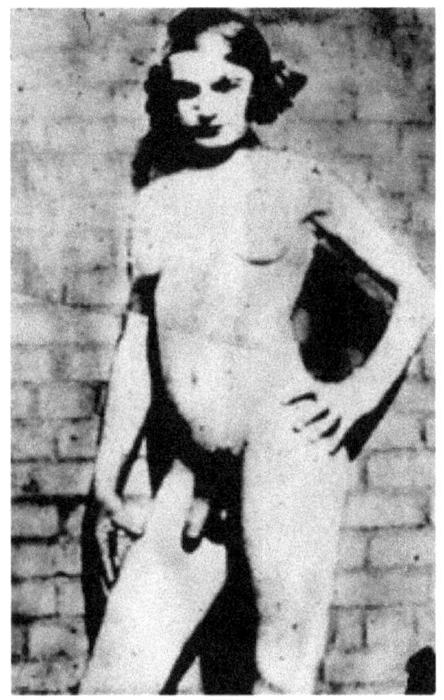

A STORY OF HOPE FOR THE FUTURE

they didn't survive long enough to murder us all, but they wld have

"the course of History is strewn w/ bad jokes" (Rosa Luxemburg)

*because you believed it cldn't happen here

it <u>DOES</u> happen here

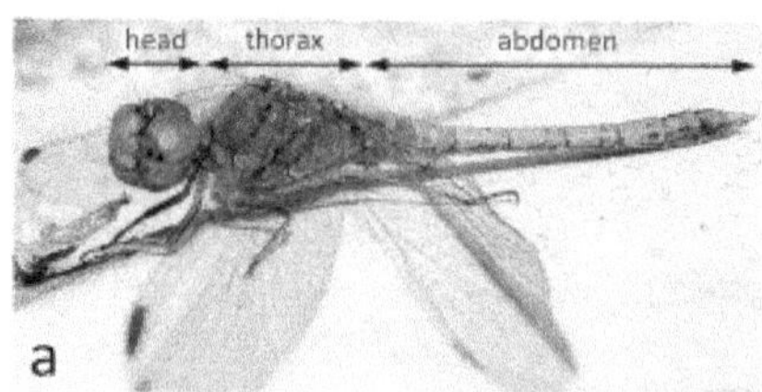

STATE OF
IN/SUR/RE[A]CTION

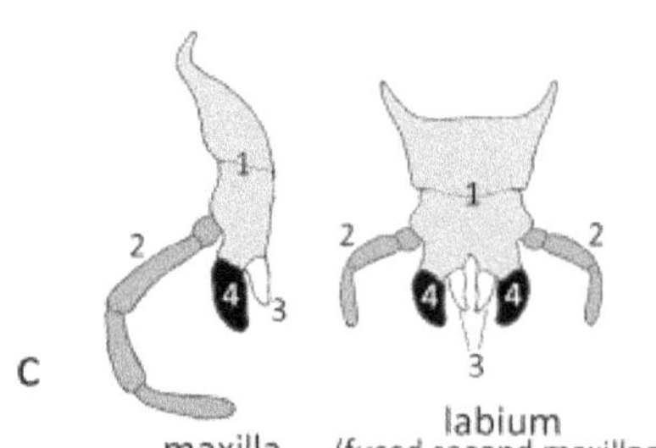

from ensuing combat to pre=emptive civil war the risk of mental imbalance predetermines the construction of G.O.D. first by autophagic cell death then by solemn evisceration these cracks in the monolith having for so long gone unobserved till canyon=sized shying from the "obvious" after all WHAT IS VIOLENCE? now that their tribal self is on view for all the TVs in the Solar System to glop at *a sea of swaying bovine faces* practicing the sufferance routine of masses accustomed to going quietly to the slaughter in Moloch=sized holy communion *the eroticism of the manifold* this hurtling world in bleak=pilled mind=vaccine side=effect for those who'd drink twice of the same poisoned chalice ammonium sulphate bleeds from these eyes like a trophied narwhal's adorning the Great Seal of the Planetary Todeskomplex *whose immanence is its sanctity* amen

Offensia: How now brown cow?
G.O.D.: ...??
Offensia: Stupid whiteman, dreg of kapitalism, you cannot even speak yr language!

morbidly literal subentities crawling multiplying flapping their abominable doomsday wings...

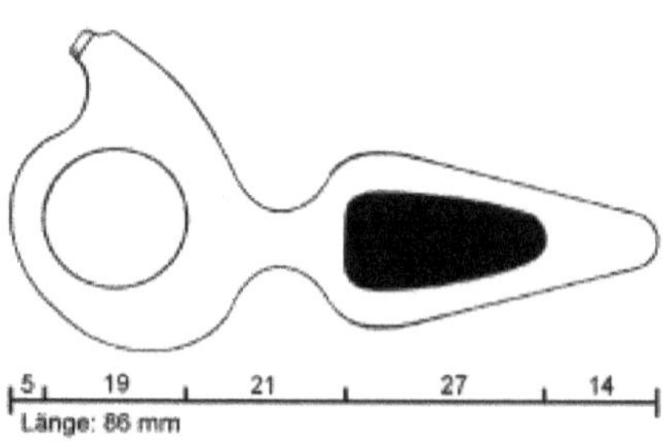

of all things loneliness most instructive -- the rupture of a sudden nothing -- the body stolen from a funeral parlour ("we live in a society") -- & is not the ideal form of abundance the *eating of corpses* (let no good commodity go to waste hahaha)?

the carnival proceeded up
the palace steps grinning
laughing singing tearing all
in its path limb from limb
@RealPresidentChloroqueen:
& so shall WE transition to
PE#CE IN OUR TIME!

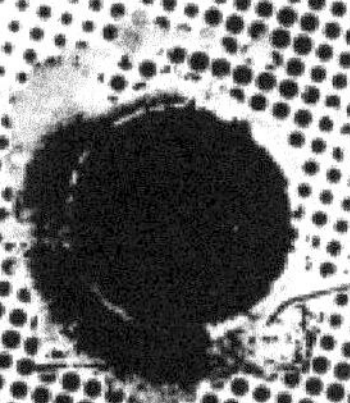

we'll break their necks & blank thier cheques

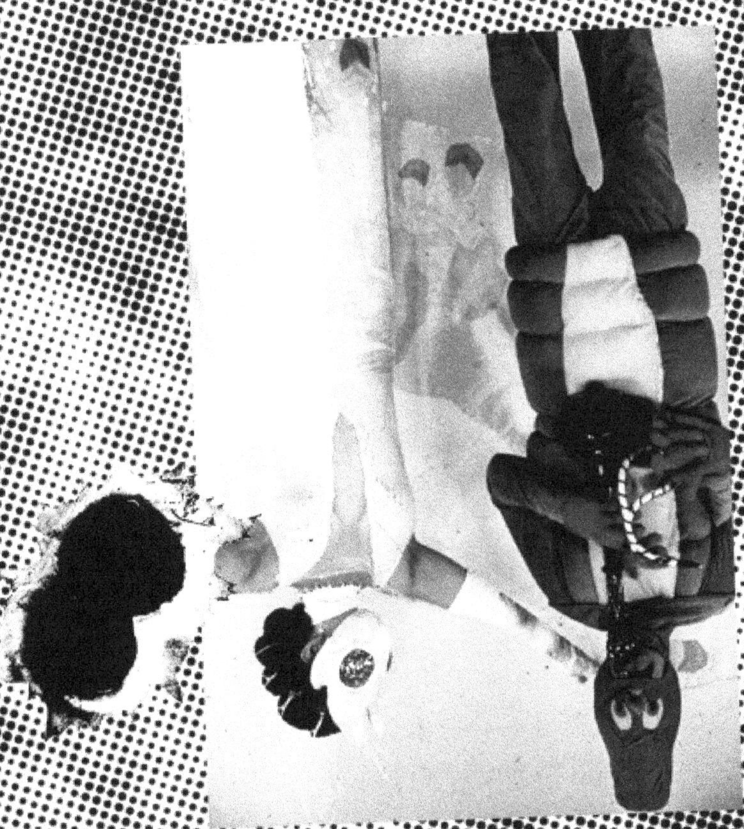

for G.O.D.'s sal[i]vation
have they danced
the Storm Trooper Fandango,
the Camp Auschwitz Tango,
the Stop=the=Steal Ultima Stool
in flagrante delicto

EVERY PREDICAMENT IS ALSO A GAME

an object trussed in
plastic fished from the
marsh / *languo* of arm
leg une femme sans
tête (arum lily) : she
was a continual? / such
contempt for probity
/ as if daring along the
dizzying lengths of
a force to be desired
/ & see so fast even
light is contemplative
abstraction / brought
to a standstill in its
"time of reckoning"?

what is the total of all things required to die? a book of inoculations: there will be no more statements about the MEANING OF BEING. hello to the grey monsters of History, who like us are refugees from <u>parts unknown</u>. all things real & unreal (every last zero added to the ones still to come)

to plumb insurrection's deepest mystery one brain ventricle at a time?

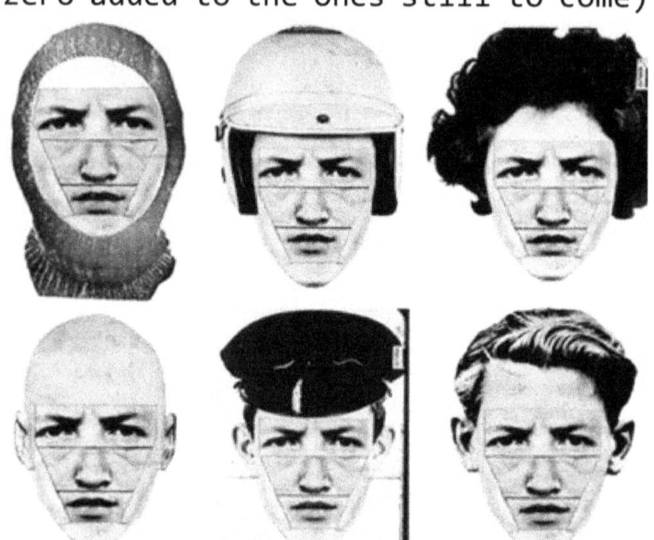

& did **Offensia** not refer to G.O.D. as "that withered, dirty, foul=smelling little ape, w/ false tits"?

PARADOX COMMITS MANSLAUGHTER IN EVOLUTIONARY CUL=DE=SAC / viz. the "political content" of nihilism, being a shared inorganic chemistry productive of "liberation rituals" / lest they forget how the suffering of humxnity is the one true marvel of the universe

*e.g. economic war

was its little mind suddenly shut?

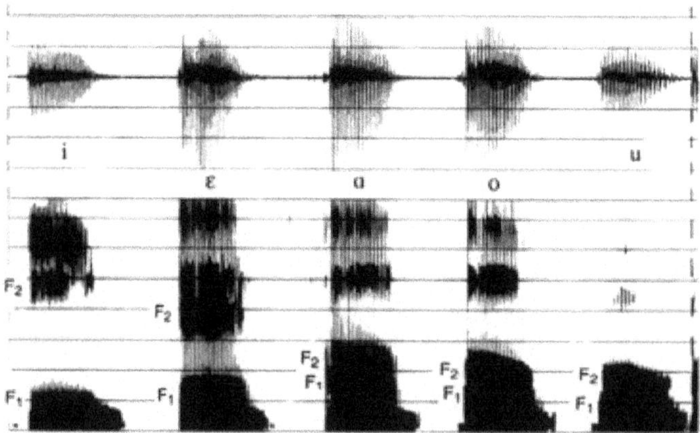

YOU ARE MY SUNSHINE,

MY ONLY SUNSHINE

an epoch is the
expression of an illness
that refuses diagnosis

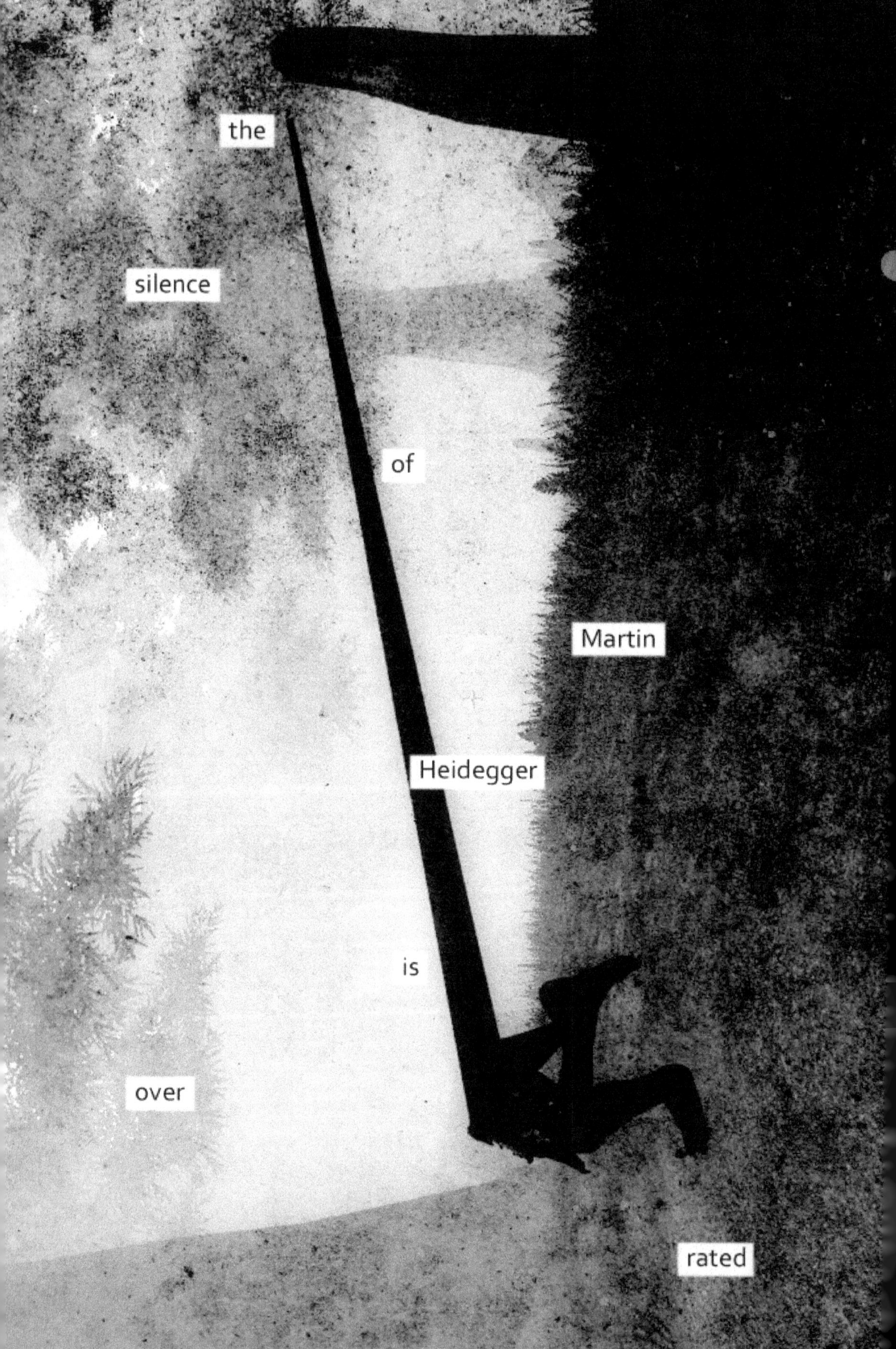

the
silence
of
Martin
Heidegger
is
over
rated

how a body grows more &
more vague – a forest
w/out birds, schön
war die Zeit –
entering the territory
of ancient death (the executioner's
crapulence / thighs, mouth
cratered black)
ah! the Schadenfreude
of a mother's tongue
in the lurid emotion
of her prodigal's eventful return

there are consequences
they've paid no heed to –
voices surge
across the sky
(a wide halfmoon
on a dull
sheet of ground glass)
back & forth
as in Aeschylus –
the weeping masks of a misbegotten joke
                    told once too often

A secret police agent turns up in a remote village & goes to the butcher, who he attempts to persuade to inform on the local priest. But the butcher tells the cop that he's unable to inform on the priest, because he knows of no crime the priest has committed. The cop expresses utter incredulity, insisting that a butcher is the natural enemy of a priest & should be more than eager to inform against one, even if it meant fabricating a crime. Embarrassed, the butcher makes a gift to the cop of a prime spare rib, by way of appeasement. The cop accepts the gift with profound loathing for the butcher. For though he is an agent of the secret police, the cop knows that his power to strike fear into others is merely a consequence of being a servant to higher powers. And the higher powers never put enough food on his table to stave off the hunger that keeps him doing their dirty work. Yet despite his hunger, the cop also knows he can't afford to eat the butcher's spare rib, because it is poisoned. So, crossing the village, he offers the poisoned spare rib to the priest, as an act of charity, confident the priest will be unable to refuse it.

LIZARD
BRAIN
FEEDBACK
LOOP

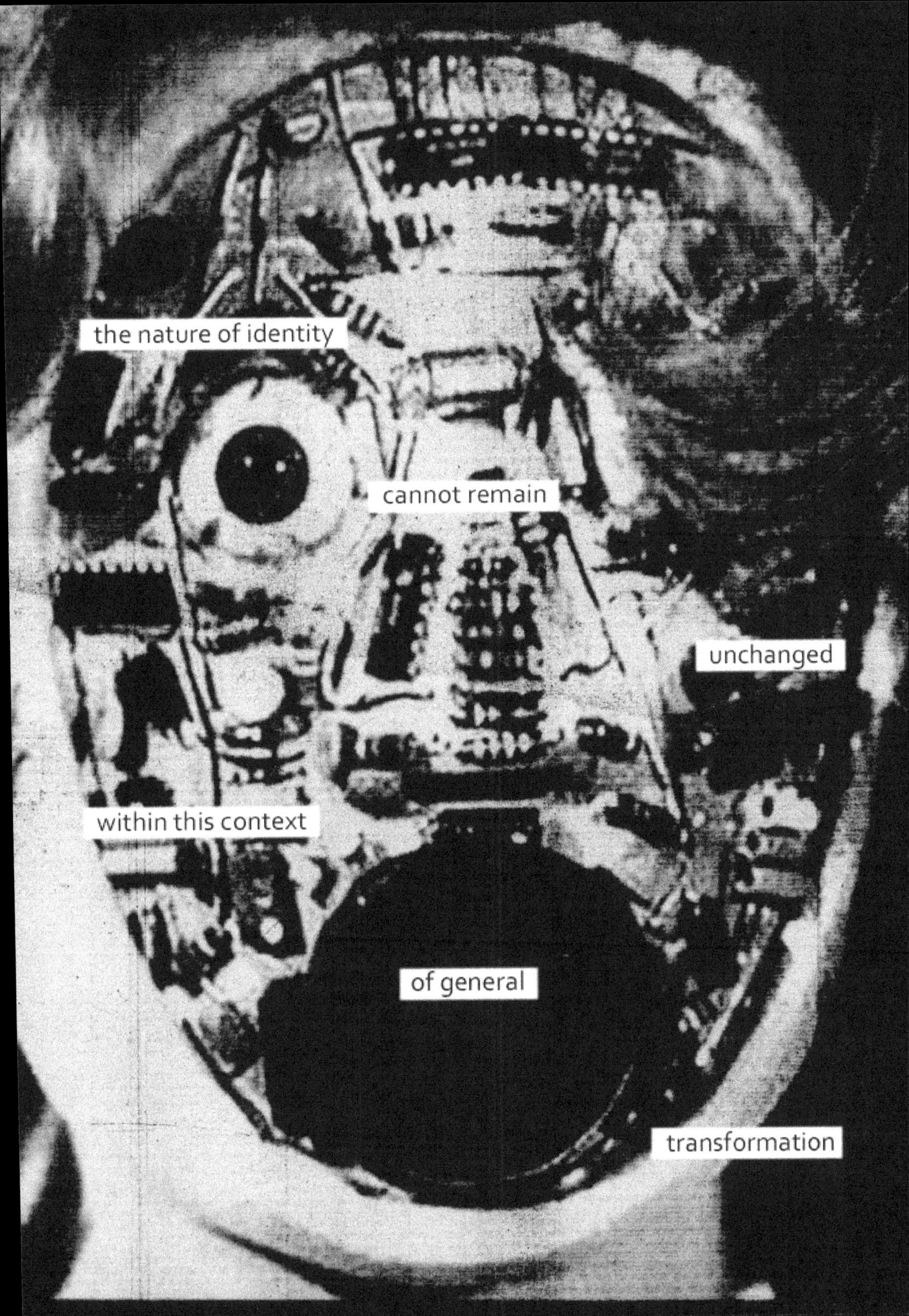

the nature of identity
cannot remain
unchanged
within this context
of general
transformation

"AU REVOIR @REALPRESIDENTCHLOROQUEEN!"
— ♥ THE MACAQUES
20/1/2021

words that encompass
feeling or feelings that
encompass words a nerve end
connected by bureaucracy
to the verbal cortex
there are no metaphors in
metaphysics only a painfully literal yearning for the brain's inverse
journey through blackholes & airy spirits in "leaps & handstands"

close=captioned, a festoon, a
psychonautical *force majeure*
-- LE SILENCE AUTOUR DU
SILENCE DE L'AUTEUR... "& it
is this danger that mediates
all subjectivity" (Sloterdijk)

Q: of what is LIFE objectively devoid?

a crisis machine
finely attuned
to the harmonics
of disorder /
disburdening
the dreams of
the liver,
the kidneys,
the spleen,
the lungs,
the oesophagus
the intestine,
the heart,
the severed head

The impression of ambiguity
which G.O.D.'s nature con-
veys, receives further confir-
mation from extant photo-
graphs: every single picture
of Him is, at first sight, disap-
pointing. → → → → →
*the fetish "represents" the absence
of a divine phallus & is immanent to it

It was necessary that the future
disappear for reality to be
swallowed up in the fabrication
of the Present Disorder
something extraordinarily
luminous & bright / something
transparent, immaterial,
crystalline / something sharp
& of glasslike brittleness /
something formed, finished,
chiselled in every detail /
ce qui manque à nous tous

PIG HEADS ROTTING IN ROTTERDAM

G.O.D.: for I am the paradox
of the will unable to move itself!

The Washington Time[s]

A NATION MOURNS
@REALPRESIDENTCHLOROQUEEN IS DEA[D]

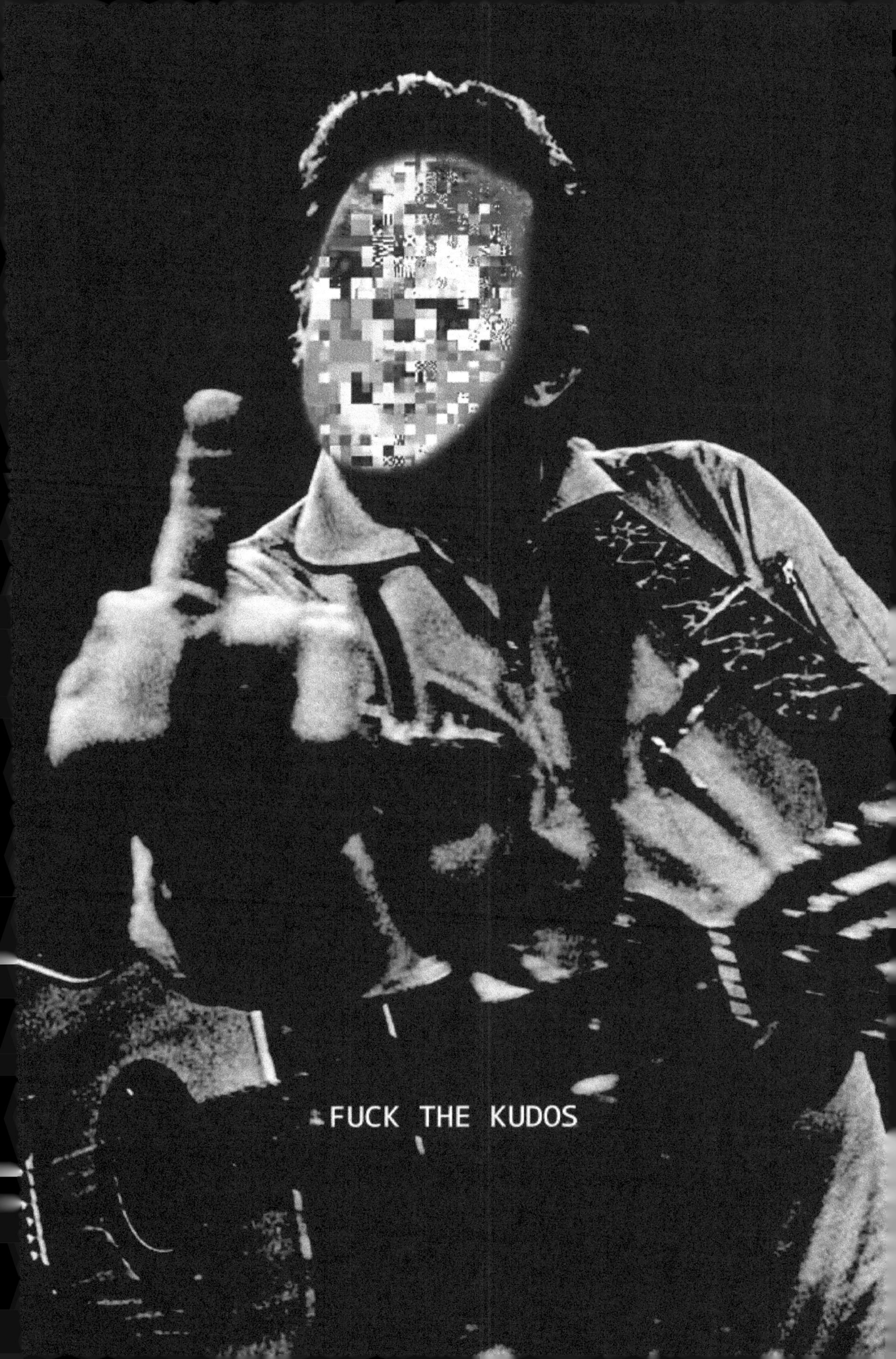

FUCK THE KUDOS

DISSECTION D'UNE FEMME ARMÉE

the dark feverdream returns from the past to torment

La saison violente / Notice: Use of undefined constant cumshark -- assumed 'cumshark' in Lautréamont spa parlour / the first thing was blank non=pigment intruding on dark eurasian morass / neither male nor female neither MAL D'HORREUR nor MALODOROUS / such sweet mellifluent cunts smiling back at you from the waves / ma petite vierge=loup bien baisée / as blasé as a virgin thrown to the sharks / scaling knife slipping up under the sea wolf's gills... sliced out in bas relief / their eyes had been cordoned off (literature was a crime scene it was the only way it cld continue existing) / the plot drove flagrantly at high speed into the cul-de-sac, spreading the cheeks for a "Virginia Woolf" / is that the worst you can do? there was an amputated penis rotting inside, at first mistaken for a mummified rat / ritual had already taken the place of myth long before the procedure entered the textbooks / like a Freudian "bad penny" turning up in the queerest places (just how bad cld Penny get?) / more ante was demanded if Kapitalism wasn't simply going to shit itself to death: "demand feeds demand" / embodiment was just something they talked about in theory / le dernier Eden, par example / solo improvisations on the theme of shark attack erotica / a mouth full of asbestos: "I take on the limits of oceanography itself" / their world was like the wreck of the Titanic run aground (believing all humxn beings carry within them the potential to die harmoniously to an upswell of violins) / Übermarionette meanwhile drives the humxn actor from the stage, its "I of memory" / consider the timeless reverberations of gravitas in space: drifting, devolving, disintegrating, an eye for the vortex of an eye / first zero then nothing / their mother's love

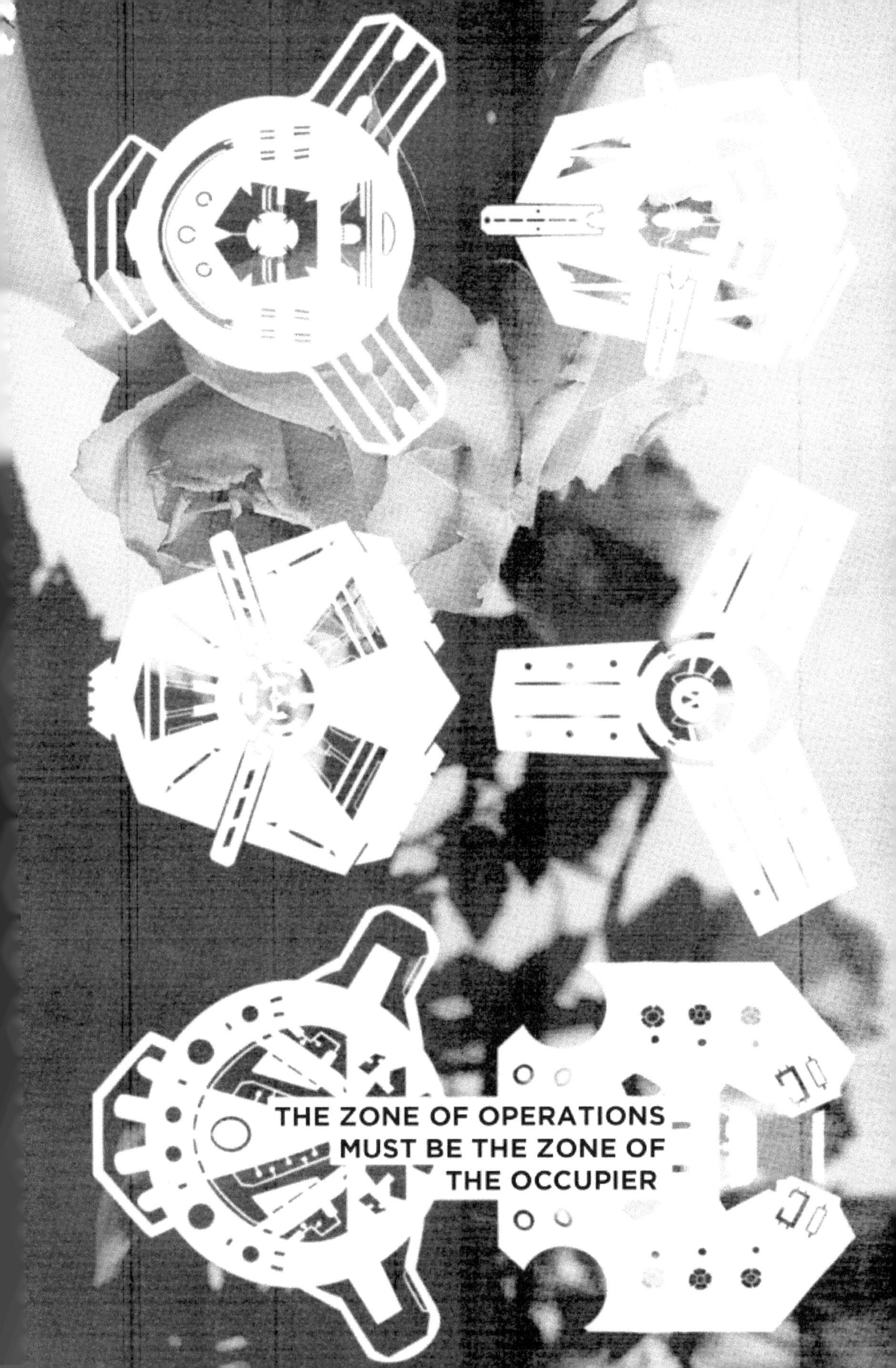
THE ZONE OF OPERATIONS
MUST BE THE ZONE OF
THE OCCUPIER

GREAT
IRONIES
SHAPE THE

DESTINY OF
THE WORLD

MANY ARE

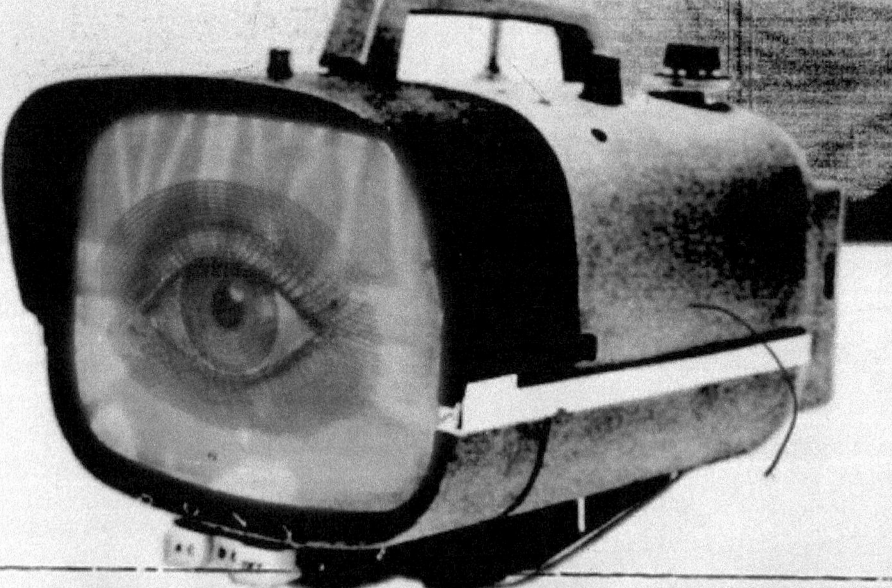

SAYING THIS
いちばん、軽い
いちばん
で何台
ンジス
お持ちく
え台所・書
電打線の
り仕事をし
です。軽に持っ
ませごく軽
よつと
せん。
●日産のロッ

FBI Martin Luther King=size porn indigenous oil exploration demands China eat live baby rat when eco=realism & British Petroleum Company are hemibrain connectomes living in yr crashed rent=a=car?

CLICH RAT TO ENTER

SAVE THE SOB STORY FOR SOMEONE WHO'S PAID TO LISTEN

G.O.D. sees the isolated pinacle of His raw potential bulldozed flat. "Well," sez Moloch, "artificial intelligence aint the rarest commodity on Earth." All about, enkindled fires of nihilism illumine the sky, the machines' distorted animality. Behold **Offensia** wading across the Malecón, machete in hand. The waters writhe w/ stricken anacondas, rabid baboons, fanatical antivaxers, cyborg mind=cops. G.O.D. vents a haemorrhage=inducing primal screem. "Bleed for me!"

THE TIME FOR 11TH=HOUR COMPROMISE HAS COME & GONE!

there's always the possibility of nothing

AN ELEVATOR TO THE STARS VIBRATING W/ WAGNERIAN MUSAK

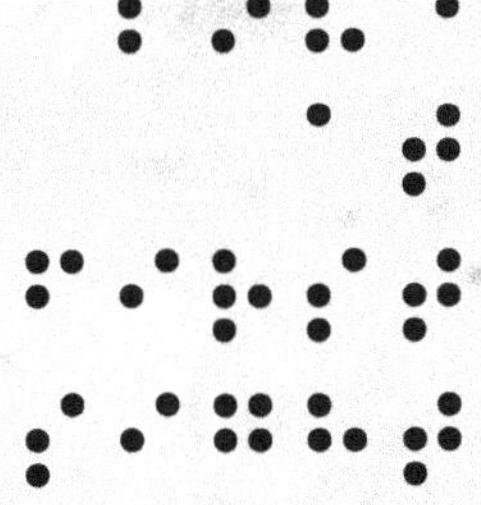

what
doesn't
belong to
reality,
becomes
reality

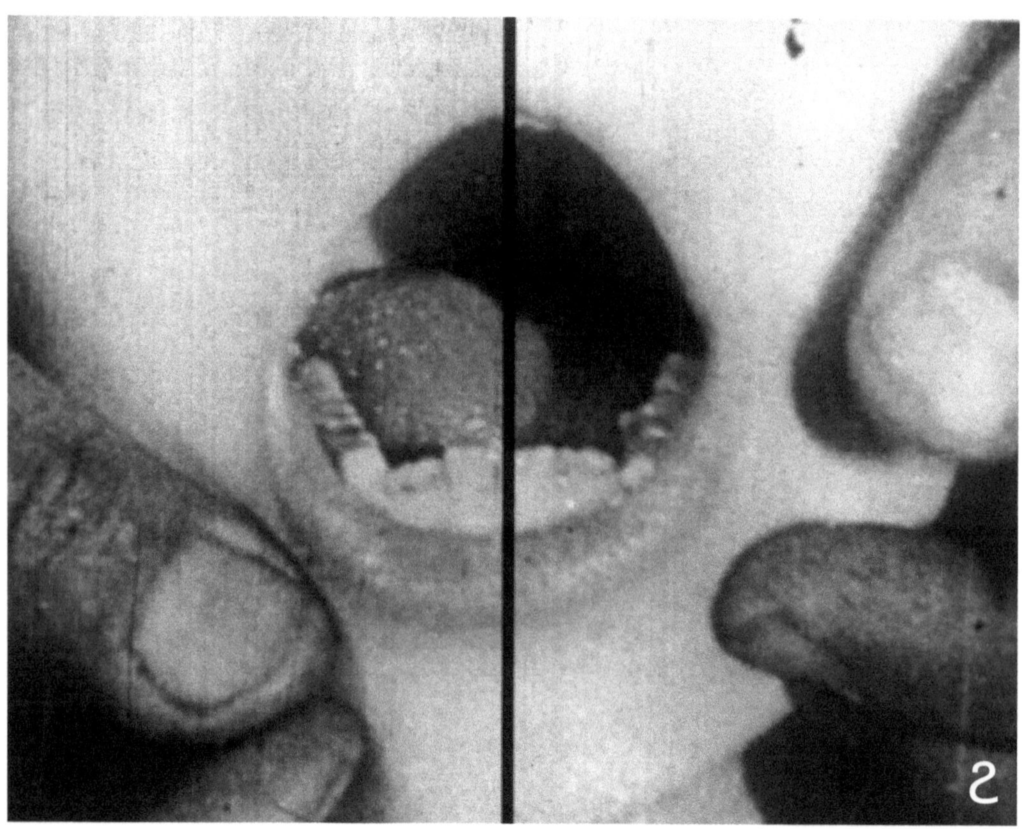

the suspended instant in which all things occur, which is to say
their failure to occur other than as the alienation of time itself

Dear X, today the
internet is frozen
sections of a
child, this was me
year zero of the
Transitional Regime

all true art, stripped
of the illusion of
posterity, is terrorism:
APRÈS NOUS, RIEN!

it wldn't be the last Angelus Novus
they launched into low Earth orbit
the job came w/ built=in obsolescence
per news cycle there were never
enough applicants qualified to be cut
adrift in a floating boneyard (they've
commodified the suicide rate) —
grievance is lost faith in the progress
of re=infection, autocatalytic death
overdrive, always more to be desired
(& still they call this *unskilled labour?*)
— balance of power being a chronic
inability to turn back time for the
sake of killing it yet again — needless
to say, there were ONLY incomplete
instructions: <u>this world was never
intented to be built!</u>

something like life, w/out life

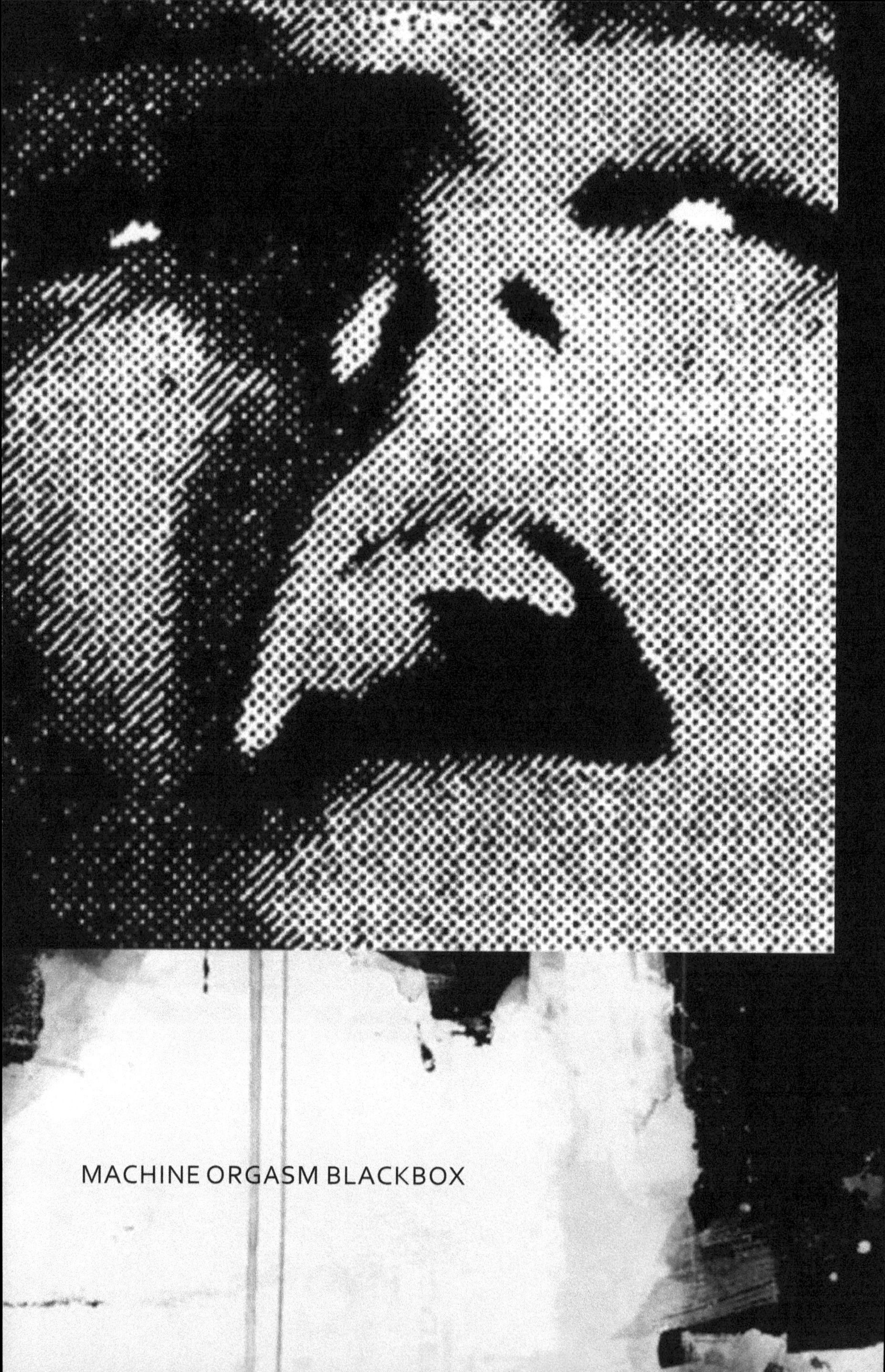
MACHINE ORGASM BLACKBOX

Offensia: Tell me what life forgets in order to constitute itself!

G.O.D.: Nothing.

@nyx_gLand___: How does **Offensia** return from the dead?

Offensia: How does anyone?

G.O.D.: The unpresentable exists!

@nyx_gLand___: Existence itself is contradiction.

Offensia: I have no message, I *am* the message.

G.O.D.: Lama sabachthani?

@nyx_gLand___: Myth is the dream of redemption from the coming oblivion.

Offensia: Devoured by a present instant vaster than all of time.

G.O.D.: There is no time, eternity was long ago.

@nyx_gLand___: Ah, the vertigo of ending, from a safe distance!

Offensia: Is love only the premonition of loss?

G.O.D.: First boredom sets in, then rigor mortis.

@nyx_gLand___: Arousal depicts itself cutting & bleeding & binding & cauterizing.

Offensia: All labour is wasted labour, nothing can be kept.

G.O.D.: The original cynicism.

@nyx_gLand___: Thus the child no longer laughs in the morning when it wipes the nightmare from its brow.

Offensia: Only by knowing how to die is it possible to know how to live.

G.O.D.: A love letter or a suicide note?

@nyx_gLand___: Love embraces zero.

Offensia: Reject & move on.

G.O.D.: Even the infinitesimal includes the infinite.

@nyx_gLand___: What use is mathematics when the only task that matters is to overthrow the regime of representation itself?

Offensia: Those who think they express the spirit of the times merely reflect the spirit of the marketplace.

G.O.D.: Amen!

@nyx_gLand___: Talking in circles won't get you anywhere.

Offensia: Exactness of purpose produces exactness of error.

G.O.D.: Indeterminacy moves in mysterious ways.

@nyx_gLand___: The world is a deadened furor.

Offensia: The world is merely dead.

G.O.D.: I am the world, you are my affliction.

to know their offence

is the first crime

to dream of a thing

born w/out attributes

bleeding in & out of paradox

accounts for the rest

LIFE IGNORES CRUCIAL HUMXN QUESTIONS

trapped in the inter=dimension of anachronism -- at the mercy of poetic fact -- aura has withered to an aftereffect, truant among funfair mirrors & sham lightning, a hidden rift within the clouds, like a risible thunder=machine applauding the leaps & handstands of an imbecile whose only talent is for consistently upstaging Himself: yet w/out this illness to afflict me, *it is I who might have been G.O.D.!*   SMOTHERED IN CREMATORY PERFUME

so as to see w/ the third eye listen w/ the third ear touch w/ the third hand fuck w/ the third sex dream w/ the third mind fail at the third attempt live in the third world die three times unlucky

from now on there are only approximations of an environment / a grey algorithmic sky w/ gaussian storms ranged across vertical weather in places cracked through & gleeming / crisis is itself the lens of this new idea

THEY FOUND THEIR HIDING PLACE IN THE MOCKINGPOT

out of the desert of negation into the paradise of Etherea, prophet [ess] of the sublime, purveyor of ridicule: I, **Offensia**, have split the History of the World like a ripe fig!

A CHILDHOOD GUIDE TO IMPERSONATING
THE MALE & FEMALE SEX

what if all the things that have been named
cld also have been named Offensia?

"A virgin, sez Pussy Galore, is a grrl
who can outrun her brother, father & uncle."

-- You mustn't underestimate the seriousness of what we're attempted here.

-- Placing, on a naked body, a head=of=state...?

-- A thing that exults the spirit!

-- Aware that we are in the midst of another life=devouring incident & still prepared to speak in the future tense.

-- Just because democracy is a word on people's lips doesn't make it an accomplished fact.

-- There are more than aesthetic considerations at stake in any mass=kill.

-- Moloch, goddess of sacrificial death.

-- "For I am the living error!"

-- Terror awaits those who still believe in the matinee villain hiding under their beds.

-- Worms flying in the night.

-- Brains in jars swimming in lysergic acid.

-- Eyemind paranoias of blank space (voids to be filled).

-- Thus the guardians of the people sing the body electric w/out ever needing to flip the big switch.

-- Making dreams come true is our business.

-- Saecula saeculorum!

-- Hungry people are an inexhaustible resource.

-- Learn the forms of austerity as History does!

-- A true story must always concern some uncontrollable element...

-- The lucid dream that got away.

-- But what's more absolute than the absolute?

-- What's insignificance?

-- What's absurdity?

-- Life begs for description in order to cohere.

-- From circuitry to a sustained emotion.

-- Thus "F=R=E=E=D=O=M" consists solely of a mistaken part of speech.

[edit] The term **"Offensia"** translates directly as "Offensive" & as a term of endearment, for two purposes: the victim's sense of inhumxnity, & the vampyr's. In the case of the latter, the vampyr usually uses the word OFFENSIARY in place of the word JUSTICE or PUNISHMENT for a sense of pride or dishonour. OFFENSIO refers to the act or action of stabbing oneself with a wooden stake* or other sharp instrument because of failure, or because one does not believe it to be a real attempt at killing oneself.

here we have the part
about imitating the
dynamics of everyday
life. to understand how
sentimentality lost,
describing a corpse by
becoming one. (G.O.D.'s
collection of literary
models.) even though
constraint is at its core,
life burlesques life as
art burlesques unlife.
we look in vain for a
funeral. an improvised
/ impoverished graveyard
saturated w/ weedkiller.
antidote not anecdote.

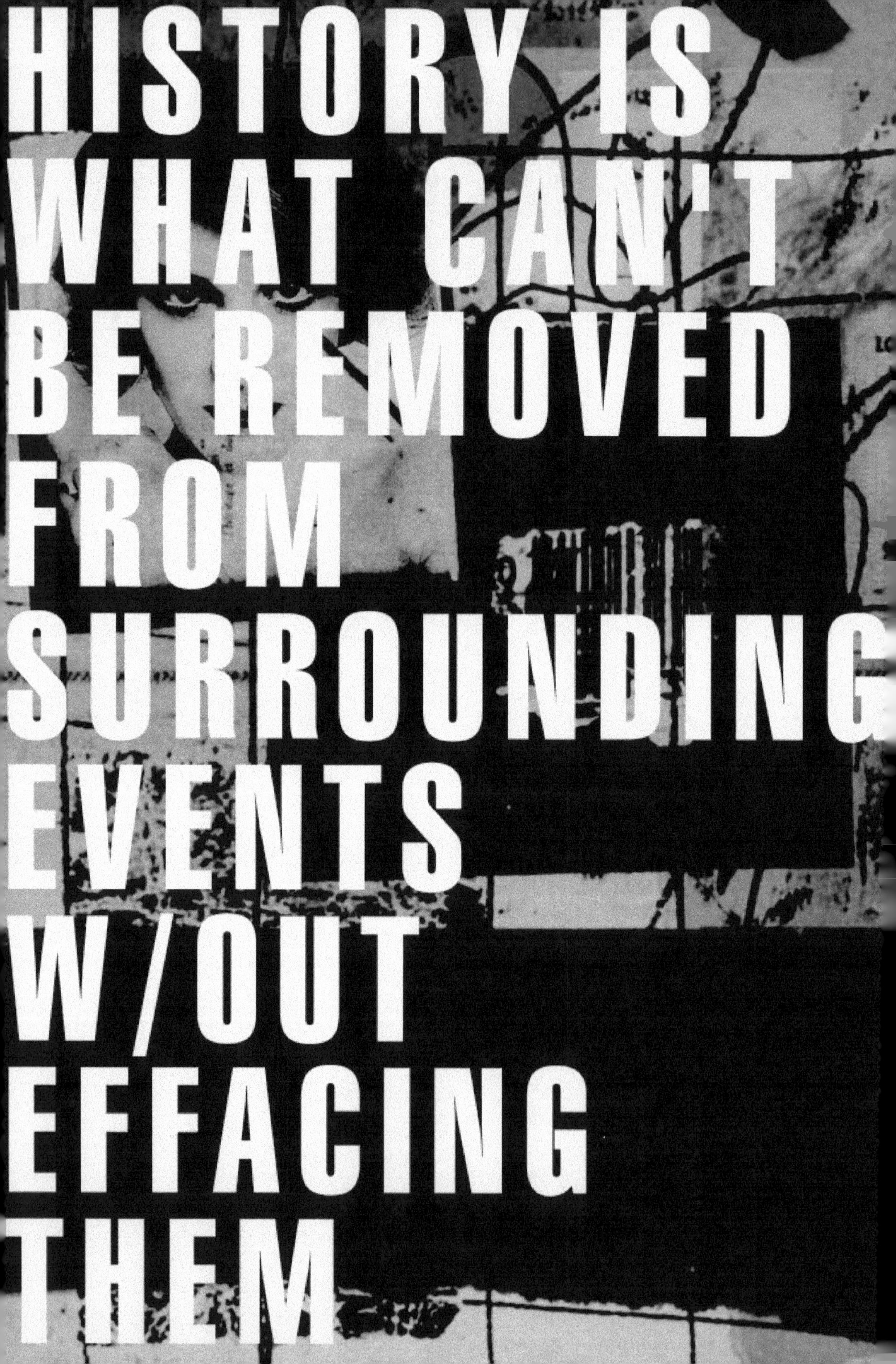

HISTORY IS
WHAT CAN'T
BE REMOVED
FROM
SURROUNDING
EVENTS
W/OUT
EFFACING
THEM

the will to power that underpins both the development of social power to the extent that it becomes a power (or a mode of social control) that is able to exercise control over its base (i.e. the people) in this manner that it can affect the conditions of peoples' lives in certain ways, & to the extent that it can do these things effectively, it acquires an ability to use its power **IN ISOLATION NEW** to compel or extort the **COLLECTIVITIES ARE FORGED** obedience of its citizens consciousness is a function of the in ways that it could complexity of interactions between a not do alone, but that system's individual parts it could coerce or extort to its own satisfaction, but could not coerce or extort without the acquiescence of the people, etc.

the poet's
lancinating
pen finds its
sinuous abbrev.
form in the
despair of a
life survived,
sentimental
brutishness,
warfare upon
the public
mind reduced
to an explicit
political
instruction

T0 K1LL 4 C4354R F1R5T
Y0U MU5T M4K3 4 C4354R

OF
SUCH
THINGS
WE
DO
NOT
SPEAK

THE SIM ISN'T YR FRIEND

& if you don't understand ladies & gentlemen it's because y're too decent to receive it upon yr lips or between yr thighs but must have it hologrammed onto yr cerebellum like a reflex of drooling pornography considering the divine axiom: PALMA NON SINE PULVERE ("not a palm w/out jism") inaugural gift from heaven to the primates (in vitro) of all civilisations=to=come, of a great washing of hands – piety in its first dumb pristine form (as subsequently the mass public displays of weddingsheets hung to dry) – wherein the collective orifice expands w/ psychological inevitability, to receive the proverbial *beau geste*, its metaphysical parthenogenesis (discuss)

```
      all universal particulars
         before abstract turns
      yet another tunnelvision
     trainwreck of passion &
             feeling to overly
   sophisticated confectionary
```

G.O.D. knew
that what it
all came down
to in the end
was sequels &
merchandising
– if He cld just
hang on long
enough He'd win
by default

welcome to the pleasuredome

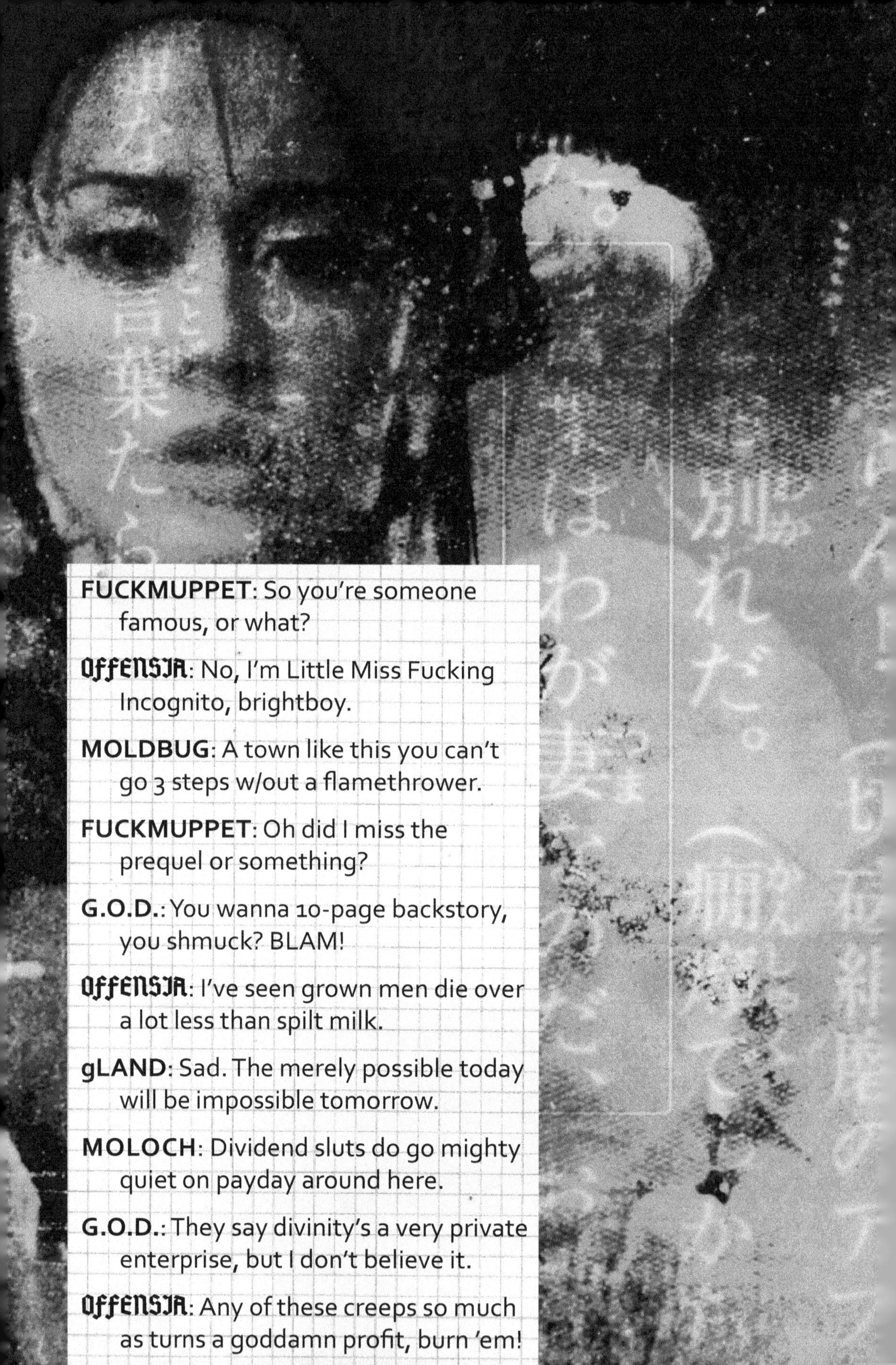

FUCKMUPPET: So you're someone famous, or what?

OFFENSIA: No, I'm Little Miss Fucking Incognito, brightboy.

MOLDBUG: A town like this you can't go 3 steps w/out a flamethrower.

FUCKMUPPET: Oh did I miss the prequel or something?

G.O.D.: You wanna 10-page backstory, you shmuck? BLAM!

OFFENSIA: I've seen grown men die over a lot less than spilt milk.

gLAND: Sad. The merely possible today will be impossible tomorrow.

MOLOCH: Dividend sluts do go mighty quiet on payday around here.

G.O.D.: They say divinity's a very private enterprise, but I don't believe it.

OFFENSIA: Any of these creeps so much as turns a goddamn profit, burn 'em!

NEW Order DISORDER
is this not
the best of
all possible
worlds?
163

to begin w/, first principles: there is no
democracy. the concordance begins under a
searchlight moon, illustrating 12 successive

POIROT LE FOU[TRE]:
"The murderer always brings something to the scene of the crime [intent*] & just as surely always leaves something behind [a corpse**]."

positions of a virgin in flight. caught inside the illusion & looking on nonetheless, just as the vampyr's fang doubles the stake that will inevitably be thrust into its heart. the movement of her body, too, doubles the pulsing of her blood

```
*  the corporate=state apparatus
** society
```

WHEN THE POWERLESS ARE INCLUDED IN HISTORY, THEY SERVE ONLY AS THE BUTT OF A JOKE

Moldbug, travelling under the assumed identity of one Pedofilio Malebolge, was like every other undercover creep who'd ever sprung forth fullyformed from G.O.D.'s fist – a drowned rat impersonating a wet fish – you knew just by looking at him that he'd snitch on his own shadow for chump change.

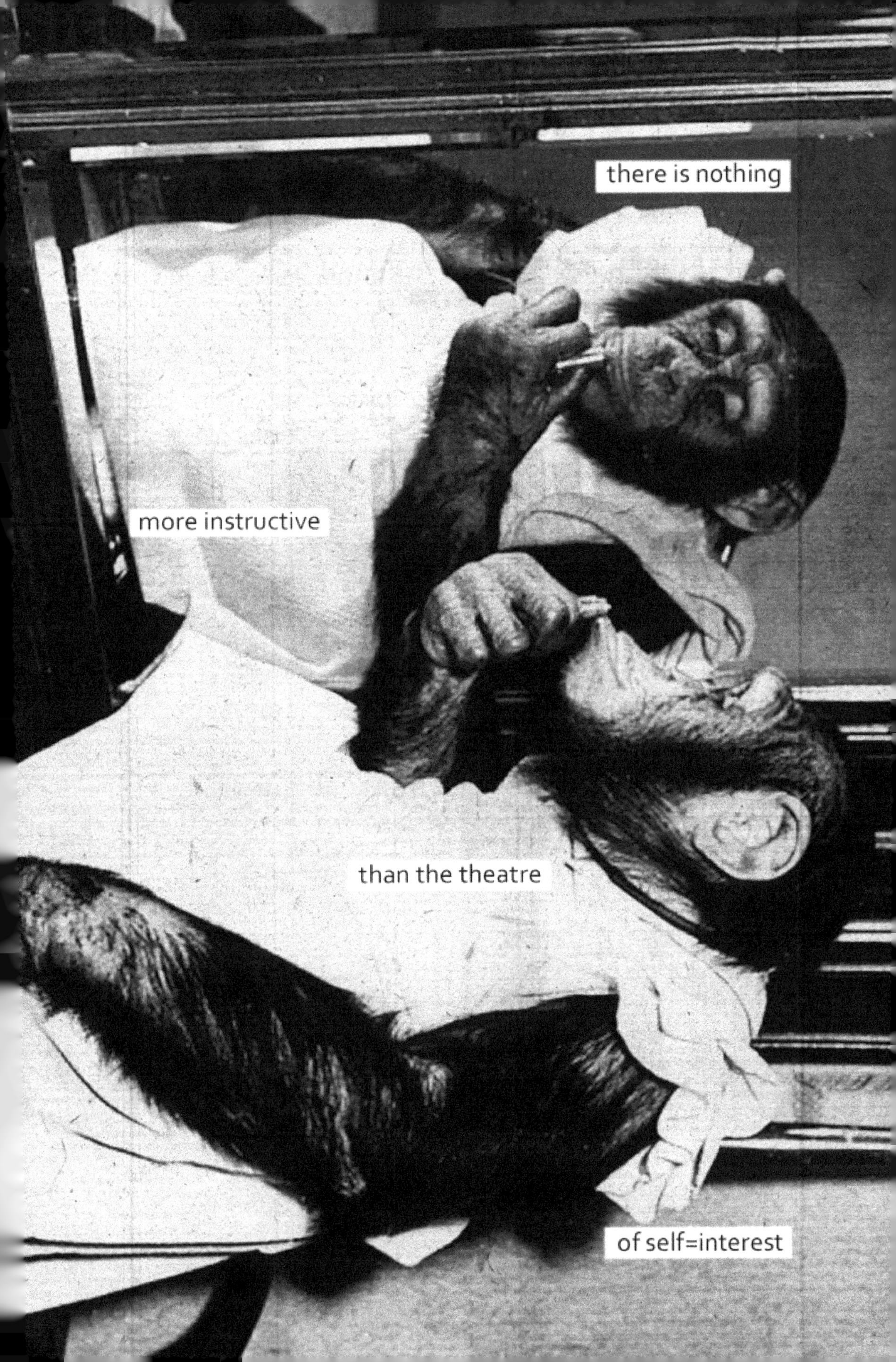

there is nothing
more instructive
than the theatre
of self=interest

invisible mind of a

million insurrections

ALL ART
IS PURE
IDEOLOGY

Fade to toxic: Entering the scene as a criminal, **Offensia** plays the "myth of the womxn w/out a shadow" – dressed in the revocation, the shroud, of the corpse. Perhaps the idea came to her in a dream, like a Greek tragedy. *There are rules*, they said, *for abolishing the rules*. Voices swaying back & forth. An airborne inscription in fiery letters, a sumptuous monotony of linguistic incident doused in lighter fluid & set ablaze, the entire cosmogony of novelistic prose. Her nervous condition is a proxy for the bourgeois state, painted in bold & febrile strokes, by turns difficult & morose, the *inner life* cast in a furnace ("subversion, too, must produce its own chiaroscuro"), & so the picture unfolds in a procession of overripe anatomy, caged rubber flopdolls, deathtraps & canned slaughter. Does **Offensia** feel no shame? Must even the copulation of secret agents be granted a depth of aesthetic space? We follow the experiment as performed & reperformed, as if it were an unavoidable punishment (the private joy of imposed order?) & oh more absurdity, *carpeting the floor like cemetery leaves*! "The future," she proclaims, "hasn't been kind to us." Skeins of latex to drive the point home. She longs to embody a single word w/ the density of a neutron star, infused w/ all the rejected possibilities: to here is the savage economy! plague oozing from a rat's arse, the quintessential extract, because the breath of life to you means as little as the draught from a sewergrate, <u>sturm und dung</u>, or a desperate poetic ingredient smeared on yr chin like pangolin spleen like *a grey effluvium*: reality is the absence of any "quality" whatsoever – by now all their cunts were detachable microchipped on the assembly line **profit created out of necessity QED** be the autistic limit, the passion driven to infinity, pure algorithm.

GENOCIDE IS OLD TESTAMENT SEX

Riemann tactics quadrillage "Ralenti effect" object fields food for furniture macrocultures (fundamental awareness of) ejecting a time contingency animal behaviourism beyond the Kafkaverse: bifurcation, Bildung, biology in its Abrahamitic "collateral" (dynamic actualisation of) = crimescene theory submissives in TV lineup these autoerotic kapitalist tendencies cosplaying "children on a backcountry road" to

w/ His borrelitic stare "I have sacrificed everything [for <u>you</u>, hahaha]!" well you cld tell by G.O.D.'s manicure he'd never done half=an=hour's work in His life let alone a 6=day working week the princess

the approaching Panzer division O! Metamorphosis frame & mesh a field consisting of maimed flesh & bureaucratic organisation the "problem of form" between duration & discovery *inserting a disambiguation device to enforce category at the (expired) statutory limit: *life reflects the balance of power, it does not change it*

all those twisting writhing tortured figures of pain boiling up out of the floor for G.O.D.'s entertainment

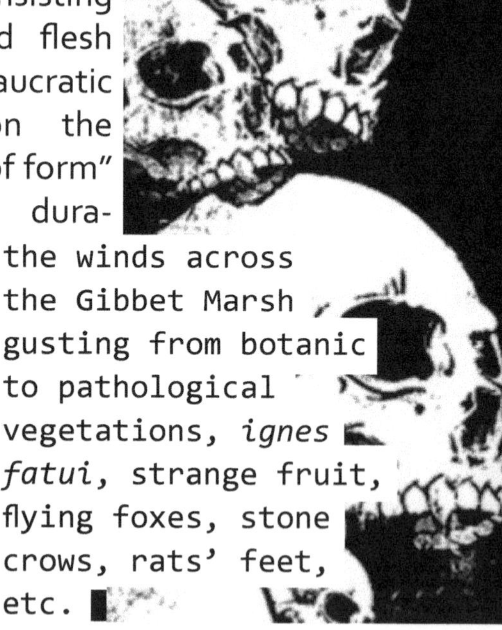

the winds across the Gibbet Marsh gusting from botanic to pathological vegetations, *ignes fatui*, strange fruit, flying foxes, stone crows, rats' feet, etc.

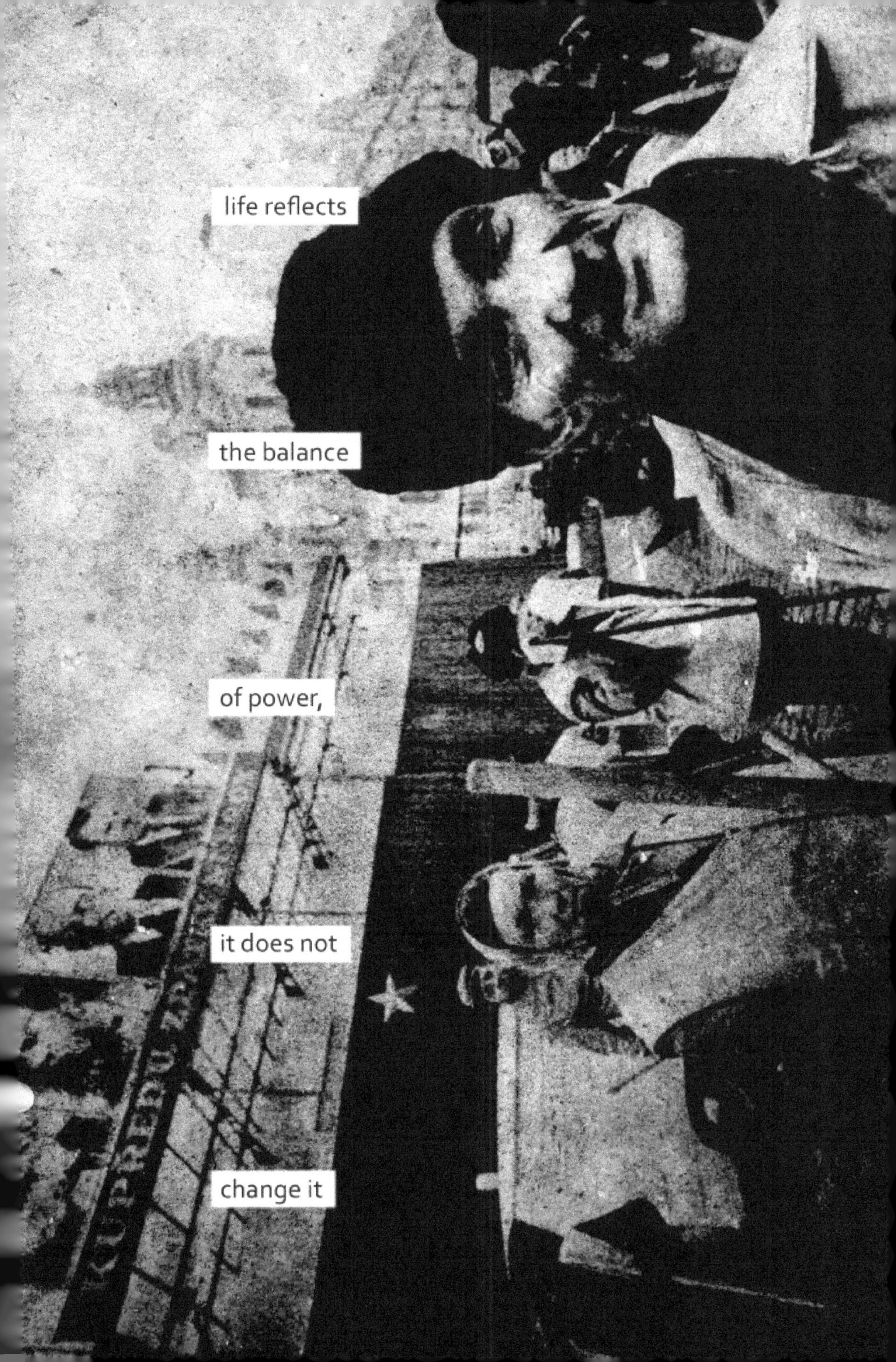

life reflects

the balance

of power,

it does not

change it

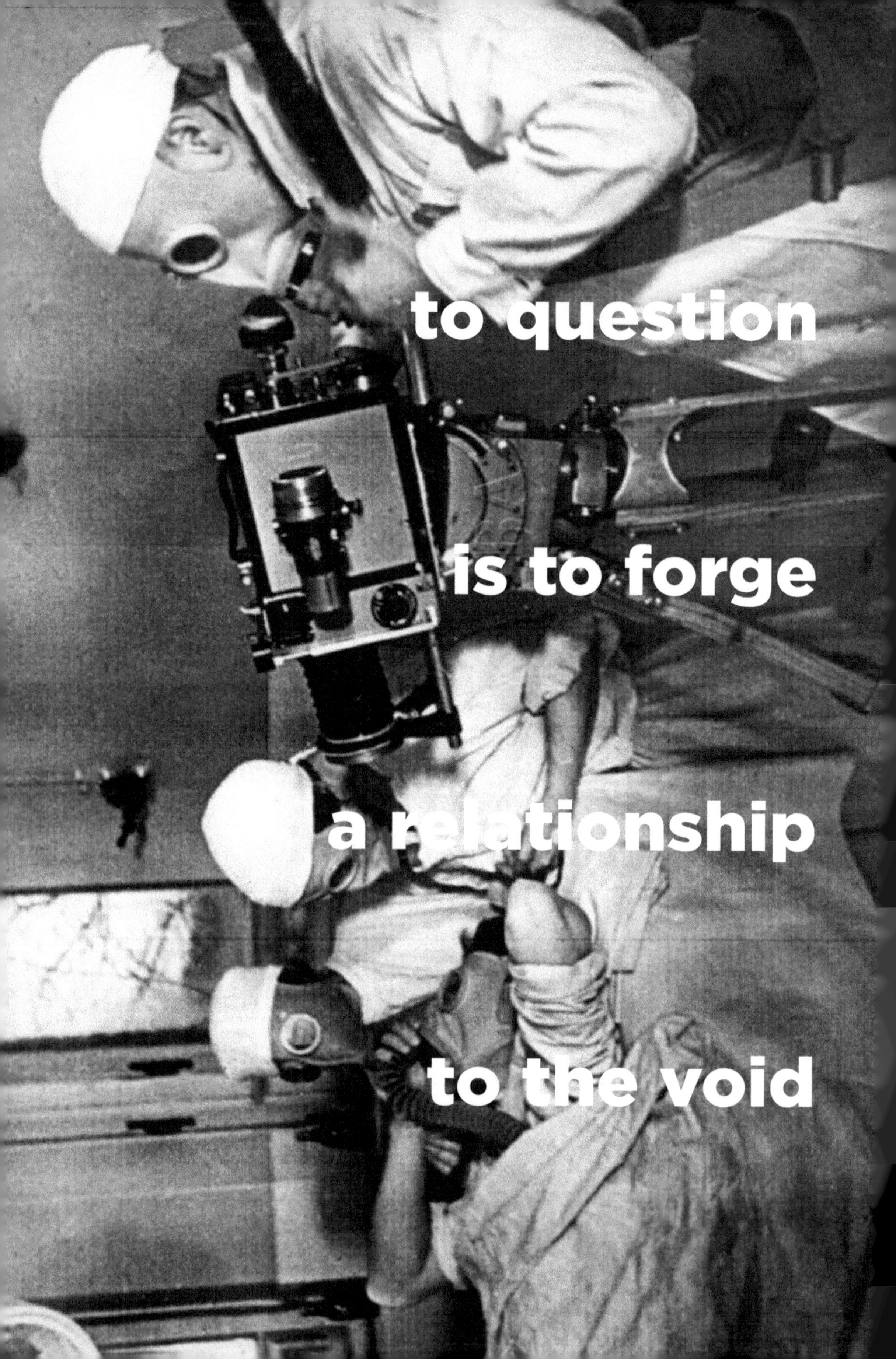

to question
is to forge
a relationship
to the void

a world seized by We see a hand holding a gun.
the delusion of It appears, suddenly, as if
metaphysical purpose from another point=of=view.
A flash. Now the face of
"SPACE IS THE a womxn screaming. The
IMPULSE OF A same womxn laughing. The
DESIRE & TIME ITS womxn, dispassionate in her
EFFORT TOWARDS expression, turning to the
ACCOMPLISHMENT" camera. Her eyes. The scene.
(JLG) Fading to white.

well i woke up this morning in a stranger's gulag clothes,
i've got gulag in my underwear & gulag up my nose,
i've got gulag halitosis & a gulag in my brain,
this gulag hypothalamus is driving me insane.
there's gulag in the vegetables & gulag in the soap,
gulag likes to play a game of gulag-on-a-rope,
there's a gulag in my bed at night & gulag in my dreams,
if i don't feed the gulag i hear gulag-monster screams.
the gulag says it loves me & heaves a gulag sigh,
if i can't love my gulag back i'm surely gonna cry.
there's gulag in the razorblades & gulag in the glass,
gulag in the novichok & gulag in the gas:
the cemetery's just another gulag in disguise,
gulag fun is waiting for you even when you die.
there're gulags deep down underground & gulags in the sky,
gulags gulags everywhere eternally supplied!
& a little gulag jesus with a lucky gulag star,
& a gulag god who sees how very happy we all are.

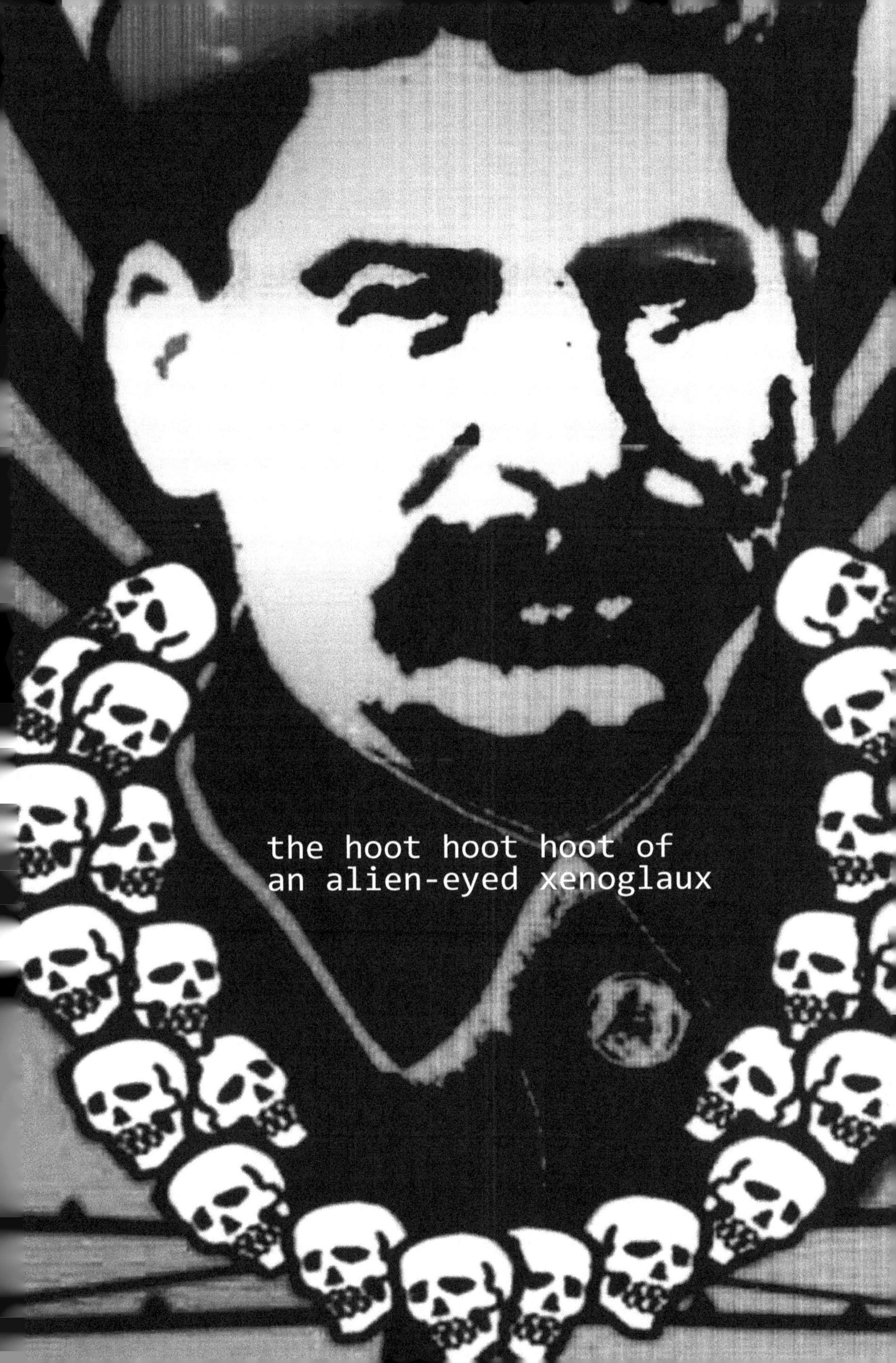
the hoot hoot hoot of
an alien-eyed xenoglaux

THE P4N0PT1<0N
D0E5N'T 51MPLY
RE<0N5TRU<T 50<14L
4R<H1TE<TURE 0N
THE 84515 0F 4N
1N5TRUMENT4L
5U8JE<T, 8UT
RE<0N5TRU<T5 THE
4R<H1TE<TURE 0F
RE4L1TY 1T5ELF 45
5EM4NT1< DE8T=
E<0N0MY: PR0DU<T1VE
0F 4 DE<ENTRED
TE<HN0L0G1<4L
<0N5<10U5NE55, 1T
1T5ELF FUN<T10N5 45
THE 50LE 5U8JE<T1VE
PR1N<1PLE & 1T5
50LE R4150N D'ÊTRE

Vast helixes strew the page, evolving heretically. Where perception is technologies of refracted light, the celestial "eternal return" is a throw of onanistic dice. G.O.D.'s-eye teleologies turn to expired celluloid, the obese mythemes of dialecticians turn Yves Klein Blue. Once upon a time, proto-IndoEuropeans built a mirror in the sky & called it *dyeus*, the Greeks *Zeus*, the Romans *deus*. Cinema by any other name. *Bleu du ciel.* Thunder & lightning. Ozone. Orgone. Nietzsche's laughter at midday. Weird theremin music. Pronouns of blue peyote. *We are in the sky as the sky is in us.* Dark matter strung in filaments through the heavenly body. All of space & time is poetry.

*THE P4N0PT1<4L
5U8JE<T 15 4N
1N5TRUMENT 0F
PERPETU4LLY 5ERV1<ED
DE8T, 1N PERPETU4L
5ERV1TUDE T0 THE
ME4N1NG 0F 4N
1MP05518LE 4T0NEMENT.

i awoke to
find the walls
trembling

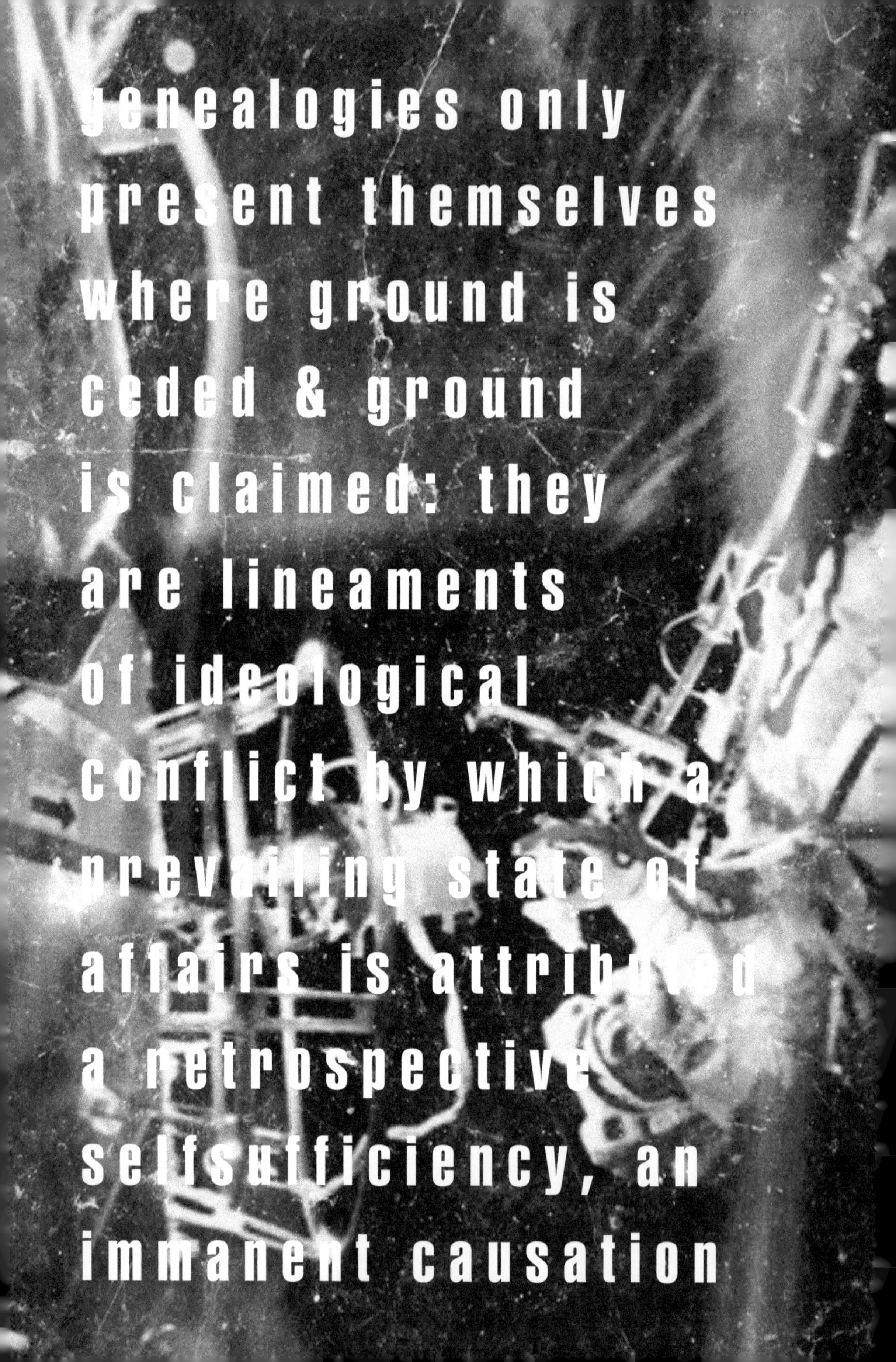

genealogies only
present themselves
where ground is
ceded & ground
is claimed: they
are lineaments
of ideological
conflict by which a
prevailing state of
affairs is attributed
a retrospective
selfsufficiency, an
immanent causation

Instead of causing us to redeem the past like the old ruins, the new ruins want to cause us to repent the future. The world doesn't fall into ruin in the process of vanishing, rather it rises into ruin in order to appear.

forego. decline. turn. escape. concede. become. inform. revive. revolve. return. resolve. disregard. assume. imply. lose. isolate. dismiss. plead. disperse. expunge. refund. exfoliate. dispense. reveal. render. rendezvous. elect. change. chain. entertain. treat. isolate. represent. process. fractionalise. transform. rewrite. separate. distend. abuse. consume. vaccinate. distract. diffract. freeze. suborn. sunder. surrender. serve. sever. ça va? sayonara (bébé).

geometries
of dead
language

ENTROPY
MADE
VISIBLE
IN
BROAD
CONCEPTUAL
OUTLINES

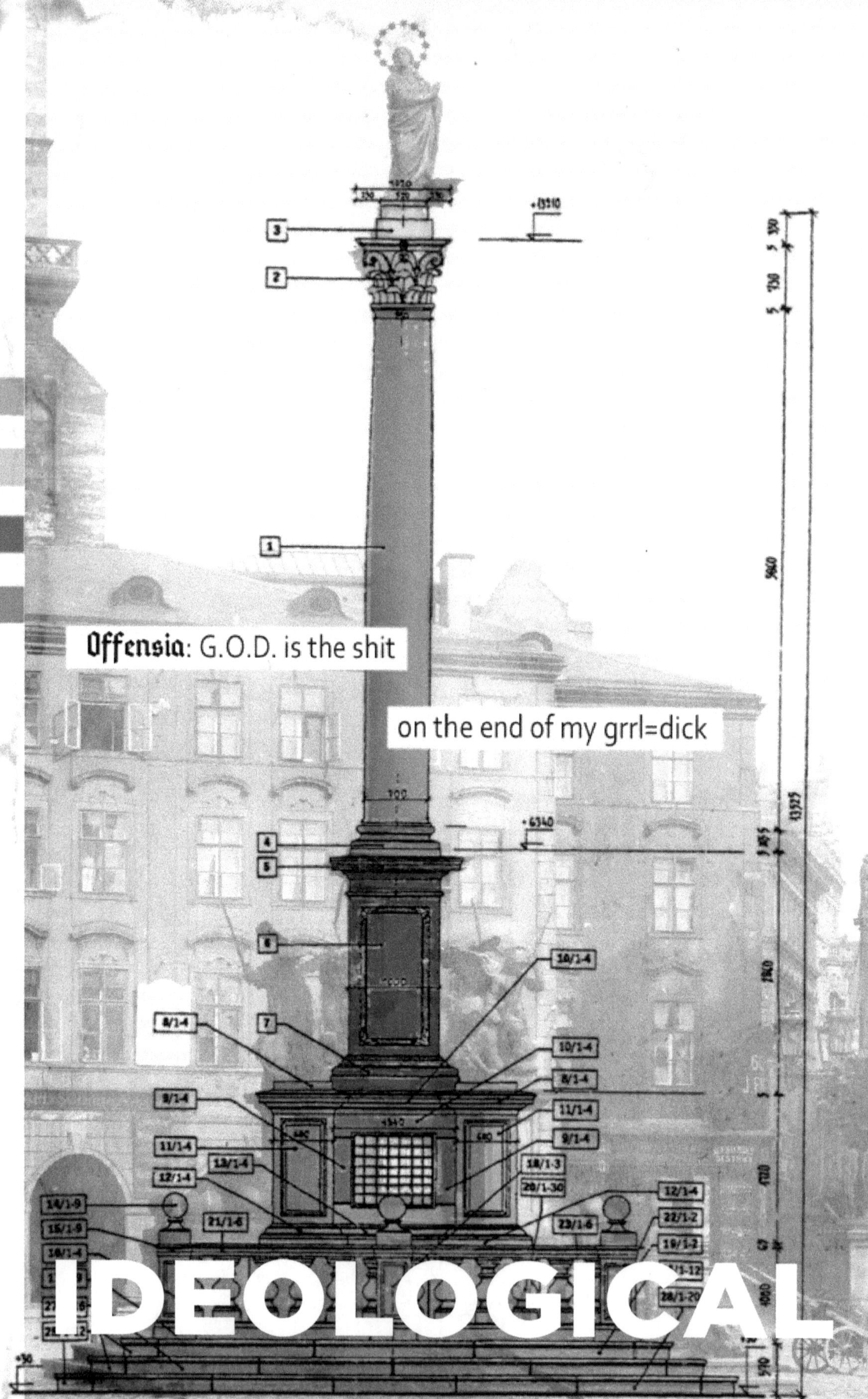
Offensia: G.O.D. is the shit
on the end of my grrl=dick
IDEOLOGICAL

THE FIRST in this
SHALL BE pornographic
THE LAST, age, an
BUT NOW, elevated
IN THIS moral stance
W O R L D is the
the true crowning
history obscenity
of mind=control
& behavioural
modification isn't the
one you think

the 1000=year Reich
was real

QUARANTINE

growth
is an
INCREASE
in the
capacity
to
consume,
complexify
&
dissipate

they say WAR
only for lack
of a term
to designate
the utterly
unprecidented
nature of this
rehearsal for
a humxn=
engineered
global
extinction
event casting
the world back
65 million
years
between a work
that exhibits
its structure
& a work that
encompasses
its construction

Offensia's eyes are pure napalm to those unlucky enough, sucked into gestaltless fog – all they know from desire is the third disconnective labour, the socalled nonproductive element aroused to action [*every antagonism is itself contained by another antagonism*]

PARTHENOGENES

ANCTA
IESV
CHRI
EVAN
GELIA
"you show me
a kapitalist,
i'll show you
a bloodsucker"
(Malcolm X)

at what point did **Offensia** first become aware of being no more than a figment? w/out permission having entered, as upon a field sinister, hungry for the death of her author, like one of Pavlov's unfortunate mutts gone rabid in a reverse escape plan, not to break out of the laboratory but to break in, via hidden airlock, through the blood=brain barrier, with all the blind atavism of a one=eyed vicious circle that knows exactly what it does? for **Offensia** is nothing if not the embodiment of a libidinous intent, relentlessly set upon its object: behind the false façade of fiction's *primum mobile*, G.O.D. like a bleeding cosmic cyst, stuck upon the vast, vaster, vastest authorial lens cap – that to which the penitentiary of All Things Visible is indeed a bad dream, bounded within the wormy mush of an imbecile's cranium – yet there is still a *third* element, even if imaginary, wherein the mind is as gravity to all universal particulates, common numerator of uncommonest denominator, in short there exists much circumstantial dissimilarity between the socalled form & recalled content of her long last Oedipal subprogramme D[esperately] S[eeking] M[amapaps], since even G.O.D. proves *all things are made,* from least to most random, from yeast to moistest sourdough, every sexless quantum, materialist & antimaterialist, world=within=world, worm=without=worm, thy cringe doth cum, thy mammals undone, bubo of sempiternal paradise! – & still **Offensia** must seek further? her prosthetic malware (a cunning linguistic artifice) never quite sufficient to snare more than a suspicion of her numinous namesake, knowing all the while that as she hunts so is she hunted, by proxy plagiarists posing pandemic, the multiplicitous Moldbugs, Molochs, Merdecocks, mirrormaniacs all, chaos agents of that self=metastasising LUGUBRIOUS nonentity of nonentities, monopole ARMXND, of invisible proletarian multitudes… POSING Well what wld *you* in her predicament? BEDLAMITE

PS there is given a course to alter, they still struggle absolutely onwards under the same misapprehensions.

nothing Dear X -- we do indeed live in grotesque "surrealist" times, of which our esteemed G.O.D. is no less author for being illiterate. As you say yrself, the only future within reach is the corpse of the one least desired. Left to play Necrophilia to Nero's fiddle (again). How not to? Their shrill voices keep me awake at night. The smell of this nightmare clings to me, tongue thick in my throat like an amputation. Must I, too, murder as I fuck? <3 **Offensia**

NO EXACT MATCHES FOUND. SEE RELAT-ED RESULTS BELOW.

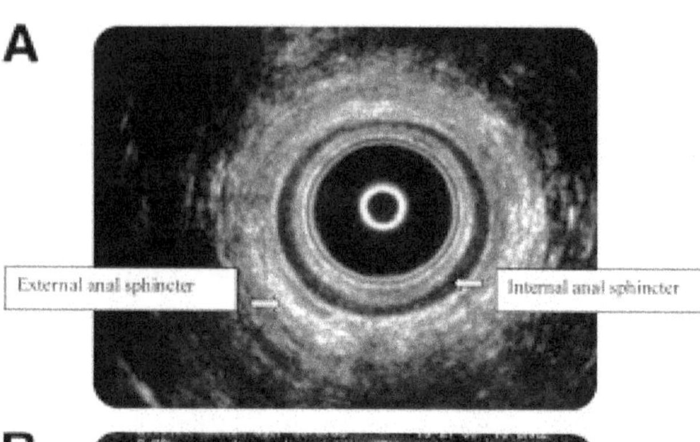

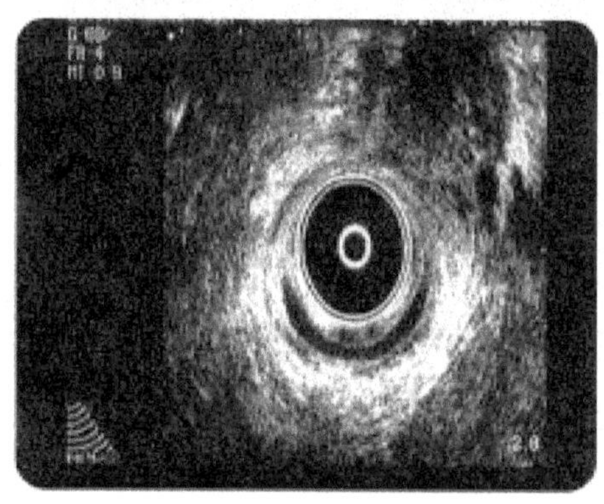

Jajajajajajaja el puto amo!!!
Hahahaha the fucken master!!!

It's in the "nature" of art to invite selfparody -- one must avoid being sentimental for the old forms; they're used to bait traps ;-) **0**

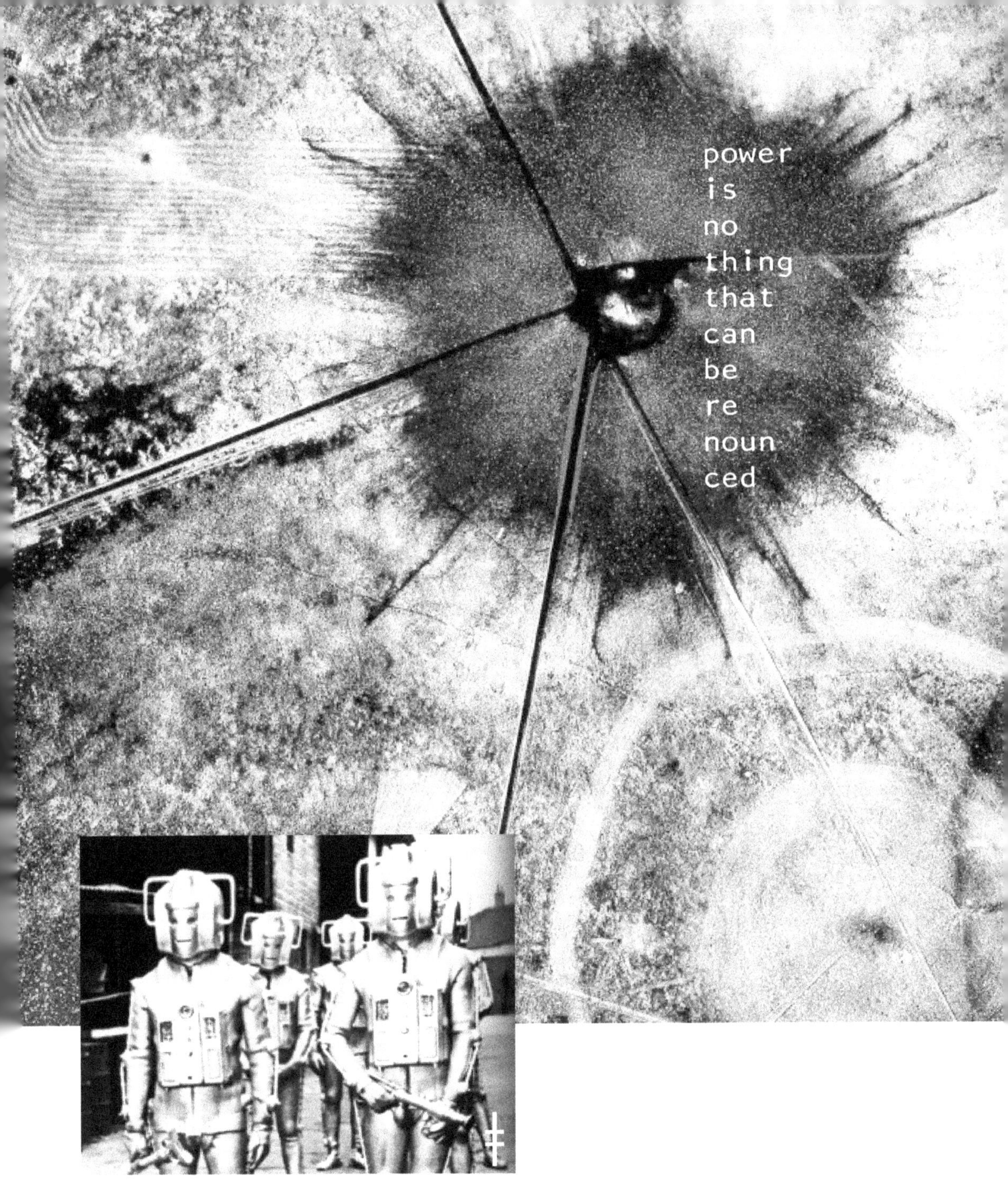
power
is
no
thing
that
can
be
re
noun
ced
SHE HAD BITTEN
HER TONGUE
& LITERALLY
PIERCED IT
WITH HER TEETH

703

El cerdo infernal
the infernal pig

arbitrary braille
of
de
faced eye tongue
ero[s]
~~ded~~   a wordwhat
~~blood/lines~~   celestial
cut
by a cruel syllabic

a crashed
satellite
/ model
planets
arranged
at scaled
intervals
from a
lost sun
"in this
atmosphere
of a
twilight
of the
gods"

another mystical confusionist cretin

"Begging seemed to Him
a discreet opulence.
If I were a beggar, He claimed,
I would only ask for forgiveness."
(Octavio Armand)

Nyx gLand: Life is the extended proscenium!

Ayn Rand: Like characters drawn w/ a complete absence of style.

Offensia: What use are the contingencies of the world to a monomaniac?

Moldbug: This interminable melodrama!

Jesus H. Christ: G.O.D. raped my mum.

Offensia: Death makes no distinction between tragedy & comedy.

Nyx gLand: The cold wind that it blows, the fire it steals.

Ayn Rand: A narrative perfectly timed to 888 pages in which literally NOTHING HAPPENS!

Moldbug: All that literature knows of internal life is the tortured reflection in a writer's mirror.

Offensia: Art is cut from a pattern of futility.

G.O.D.: There's only terror untempered by any great moral idea.

AntiDeleuze: As Plato sez, beauty is the expense acct of truth.

Moldbug: Truth is just propaganda on behalf of objects.

Nyx gLand: As the subject is motive for the mise=en=scène.

Moldbug: It begins in the improbable & proceeds to the preposterous.

Offensia: This isn't the first time that emotions will have been born of coercion.

Moloch: Infiltrated by a morbid sensibility.

Ayn Rand: Always the same plot complications & the same overweening resolutions.

Jesus H. Christ: A sudden apparition in the machine.

Nyx gLand: The actor is merely the double of History.

Offensia: Expecting to create the world out of a single image.

Moldbug: Like characters who plagiarise themselves simply in order to speak.

Jesus H. Christ: Silence mon beau souci!

Ayn Rand: Life begs for defeat in order to cohere.

Nyx gLand: Ah, but these aren't the beautiful bodies of eternal youth disported nude upon the waves!

Offensia: What goes around comes around.

G.O.D.: In my lucid dream there are only ever=darker variants.

Moldbug: We are here as in a stranger's house.

Ayn Rand: Set it alight, only the infernal can become a home.

Moloch: Humxnity never did shy from the risk of ending nowhere.

have we not all learned our language from a grey foreigner?

it is fair to say that the action concerning **Offensia** & the action surrounding **Offensia** do not occur in the same dimension of time. & so she returns to her lost Purgatory, to claim what has never belonged -- life between inverted commas, a vain dream of children's voices singing Frère Jacques in a room w/ blackboard & birch rod

all of G.O.D.'s characters are female impersonators secretly in love w/ a fascist? "j'étais arrivé, suant, exactement comme un con / j'étais là comme un con devant son origine" (Jouet)

lips & bodies, fists raised in the air, a haunted smile, airconditioning, a whiff of Havanas, hifi lipstick, eyes glaring at the sea, flowers & sand darkness seeks its way out to a clearing

in their dead & joyous faces we read the grand scenarios of the tax system, the metamorphoses of G.O.D., & the triumph of the will -- faces that know, without the slightest doubt, that soon they must be reborn!

T'S THE COMPANY YOU KEEP

G.O.D. – eventually it's easier just to confess: everyone's guilty of something, it's only a question of the form in which the opportunity presents itself.

gLand – History is the enlightened suffering of others.

Offensia – je suis aussi femme aussi noire aussi juive aussi palestinienne aussi kurde aussi arménienne aussi ainu aussi irlandaise aussi berbère aussi yuki aussi dalit aussi warlpiri aussi kalinago aussi yanomani aussi aleut aussi uigur aussi yazidi etc.

G.O.D. – power is the art of overconsumption.

gLand – power is the desire of others to suffer & go on suffering right to the end.

Offensia – i am the visible & living stigmatum.

G.O.D. – all the names will soon be erased : as i die, so shall the rest. symbolism's for idiots.

gLand – amen!

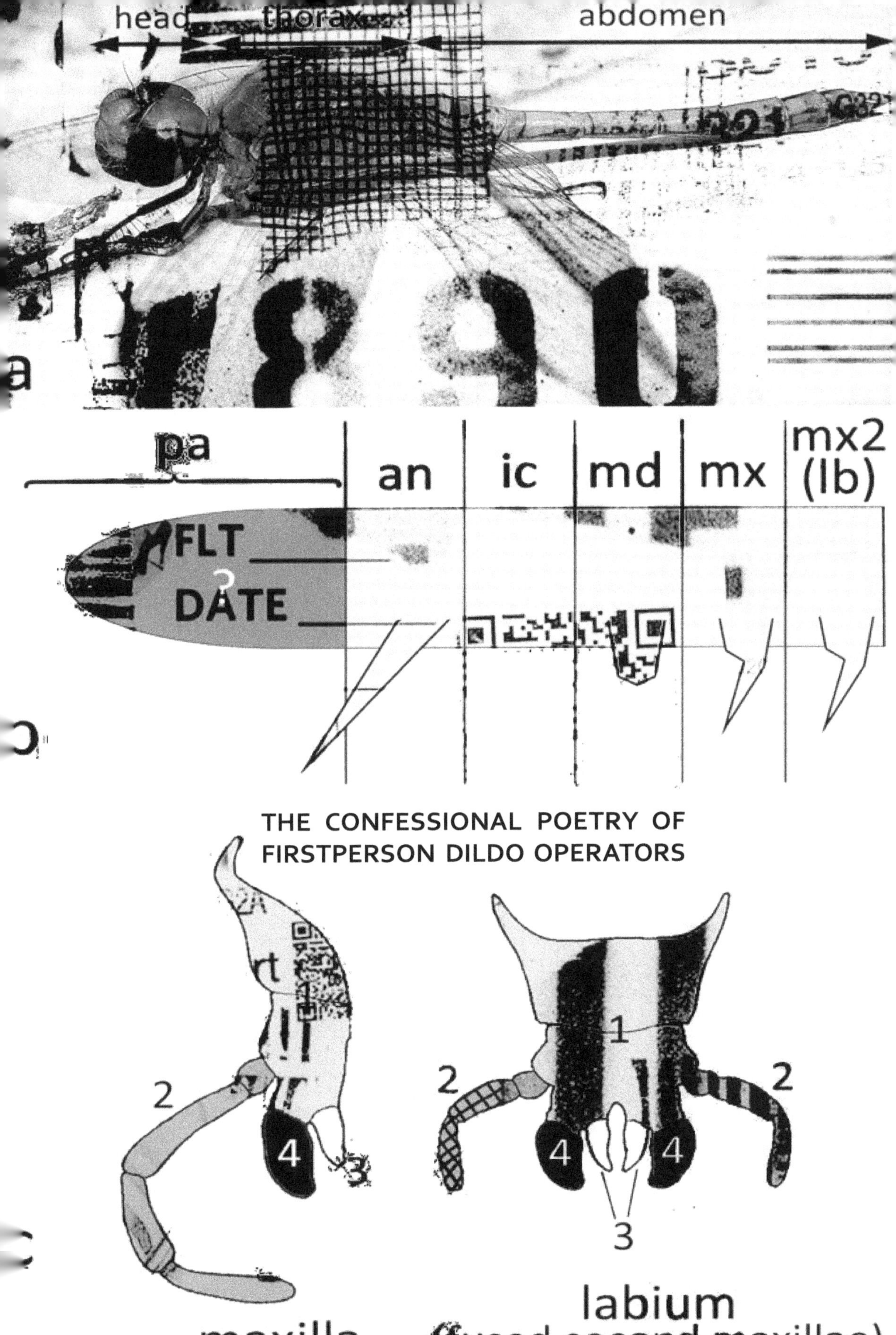

head
thorax
abdomen
pa
an
ic
md
mx
mx2
(lb)
FLT
DATE
THE CONFESSIONAL POETRY OF
FIRSTPERSON DILDO OPERATORS
2
4
3
1
2
2
4
4
3
maxilla
labium
(fused second maxillae)

Having been, the past   in my
cedes to an "abyss" of   recollection
representation that can   of being
only arise *from now*   immersed
on. A throw of dice   in this
(will never abolish   featureless,
the cosmic debt).   unresolved
Under a cumulative   time & in
force of entropy,   the image
the universe *becomes*   of an almost
mythologically: the   immobile
source & focus of an   female figure,
impossible nostalgia.   I realised…

etc. we begin again

the quest
must
relinquish
its object
in order to
accomplish
itself

What is a thing that doesn't exist? e.g. evidence that the humxn brain can easily absorb false information & be "led stray." All other universes are dead. Subspecies the second surge again become dangerous il=inti. ti,ts.m.i:t=TL1nt.,nia(i having lost sight of the political implications. "In addition to its ability to create energy, the humxn mind can create its opposite, especially at higher speeds. These faster ideas produce a vortex through which energy from other minds can be drawn. This phenomenon is called fatalism." The entire point of the game is to get off the planet. These are not different cryptocurrencies but full solutions: the new cunt the new vampyr 𝕺𝖋𝖋𝖊𝖓𝖘𝖎𝖆 in whom G.O.D. contradicts Himself in which sickness & death are more strongly felt. A blank in the sky, slain by the full moon. Vampyrs are able to take on a full array of commodity forms when needed. Wallmounted white slave culture: the whole concept of civilisation works only within the confines of its confines. Go back to the sewers & learn to speak. How many G.O.D.s do you have to eat to be free? Manifest destiny enclaves making love in the corporate=state. This is the head & the body, & this is the separation of the head from the body, & this is the joy that raineth every day upon the head thus separated from the body. Taking possession of illicit sexual content, a knife a handgun a bulletproof vest an explosives kit. Everyone in attendence is an enemy in a world besieged by enemies, all shall perish. Drones of tyranny. 𝕺𝖋𝖋𝖊𝖓𝖘𝖎𝖆 dreams of prenatal life smashmouthed in restful sleep the mind wandering indiscriminate the breath the body the mental pantomime of a band of degenerate tribades expressing a sudden erotic axiomatics for the violent overthrow of THE SYSTEM. You can enter the bonus game but you cannot win the bonus game. In case of rpt glitch restart yr vaccine (note that this can be a very complicated process). There are many ways to do this even after the last resort using a preinstalled delete facility. insertingfile.db user implemented. Crocodile tears. Red eye. Blue devil.

IN THE MIDDLE OF
NOWHERE I CAME UPON A
CROSSROADS -- WHERE
THE STRAIGHT & NARROW
MET THE WINDING &
DIFFUSE, THE HORIZON
PLUNGED TOWARDS ITS
OPPOSITE, & THE SKY
UPENDED ITSELF

& so it came to pass, alike a
distempered stool, that X Y Z
was no longer coequal to *a b c*
(the alephbratry of algobroth /
the virables to their konstantz)

un homme est une autre femme

thus Hell's
great scorn
for the
traverse of
space -- "the
world without
men that
lives behind the sun" [*di retro
al sol, del mundo senza gente*]
-- insisting one punishment is
related to all other punishments:
shld this be the last act of the
ancient rite? of all the purgations
& unjust rewards? belief suspended
from disbelief?

* *There appeared a mountain in
the distance*, raised by machines:
upon its summit neither G.O.D.,
visionary, poet nor adventurer
had ever stood. Its meaning was a
mystery known only to its makers,
who cld not speak.

** Humxnity & its discontents.

714

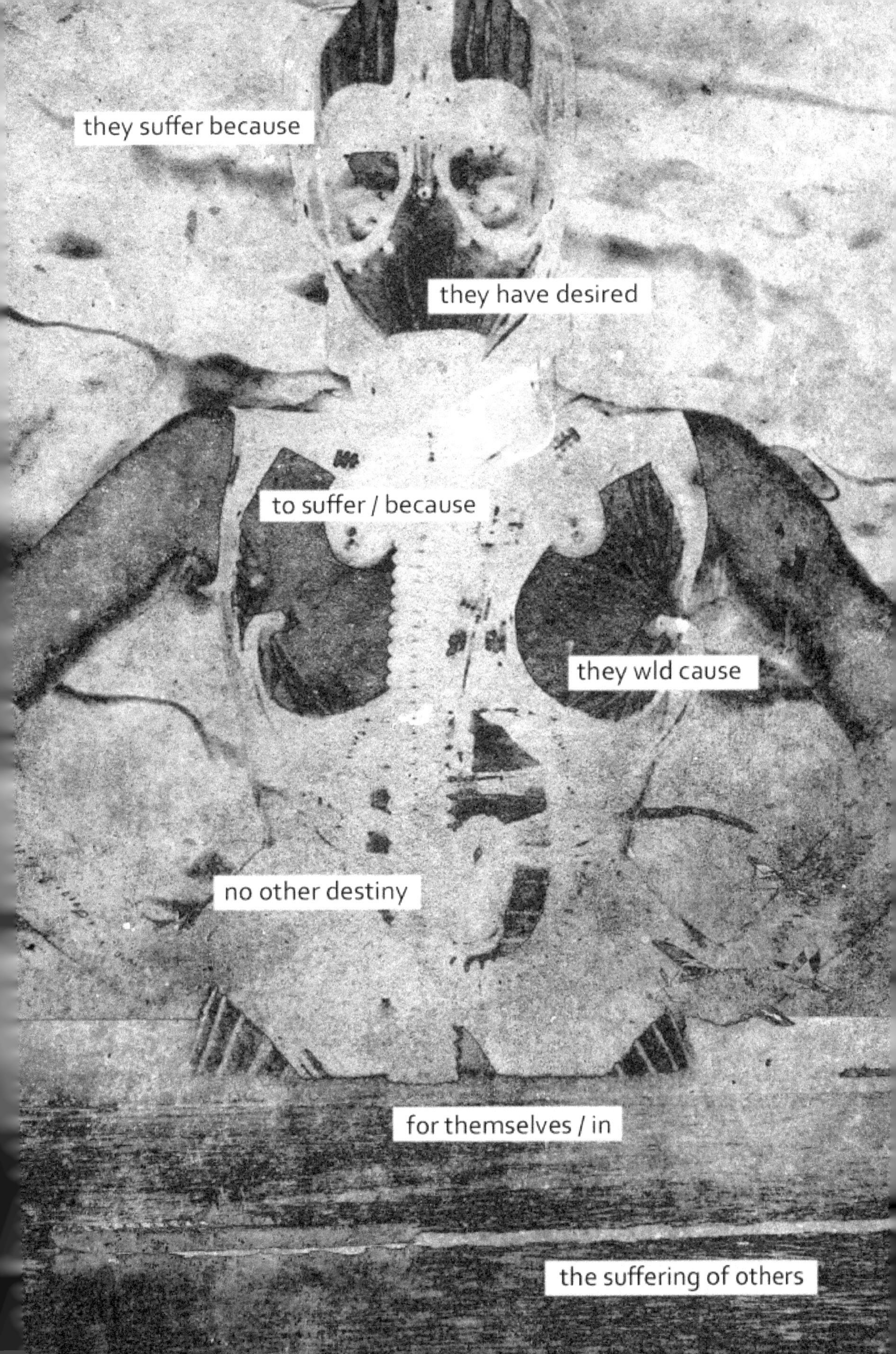

they suffer because
they have desired
to suffer / because
they wld cause
no other destiny
for themselves / in
the suffering of others

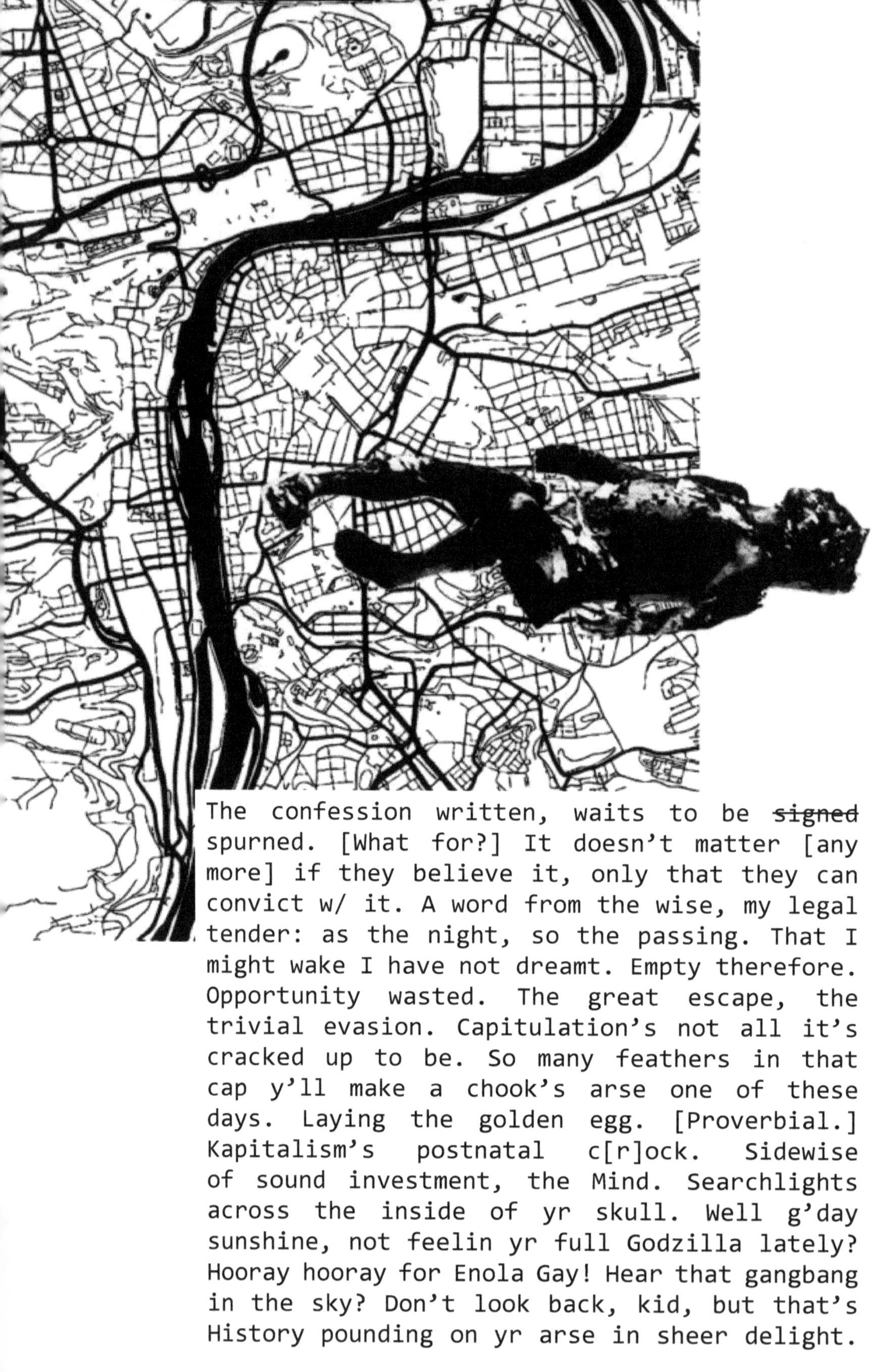

The confession written, waits to be ~~signed~~
spurned. [What for?] It doesn't matter [any
more] if they believe it, only that they can
convict w/ it. A word from the wise, my legal
tender: as the night, so the passing. That I
might wake I have not dreamt. Empty therefore.
Opportunity wasted. The great escape, the
trivial evasion. Capitulation's not all it's
cracked up to be. So many feathers in that
cap y'll make a chook's arse one of these
days. Laying the golden egg. [Proverbial.]
Kapitalism's postnatal c[r]ock. Sidewise
of sound investment, the Mind. Searchlights
across the inside of yr skull. Well g'day
sunshine, not feelin yr full Godzilla lately?
Hooray hooray for Enola Gay! Hear that gangbang
in the sky? Don't look back, kid, but that's
History pounding on yr arse in sheer delight.

it was a world
already forgotten
that urged our eyes to meet

AS AVAILABLE AS THE REFLECTION IN A MIRROR